THE COUNT OF MONTE CRISTO

I BEGAN DIGGING AND ENLARGED THE HOLE

THE COUNT OF MONTE CRISTO

BY

ALEXANDER DUMAS

AUTHOR OF "THE MAN IN THE IRON MASK,"
"THREE GUARDSMEN," ETC.

THE SPENCER PRESS

MANUFACTURED IN THE UNITED STATES OF AMERICA
BY THE CUNEO PRESS, INC.

THE SPENCER PRESS

The avowed purpose of the Spencer Press is to publish classics which have survived the test of time. In the quest for enduring titles more than fifty famous lists of the finest books ever written were consulted. The findings were then tabulated and the list was found to include more than one thousand titles, some of which have been mentioned in the recommendations of as many as thirty-five different authorities. The first hundred titles which were most often mentioned by the critics, were selected on the assumption that any book which had been chosen so often and by so many eminent authorities must be exceptionally fine. Upon considering these titles, thirty books were discarded because they were either too heavy in style or subject matter to find popular favor.

The next problem was to select those twenty books which would form the cornerstone of a fine home library for people of discriminating taste; books with a cultural and educational background that would tend to broaden the vision and develop the inner resources of the reader ... books that were sufficiently thrilling and popular in their appeal to capture the imagination and interest of every member of the family.

It seems significant to mention here that when the final list of twenty volumes was compiled it contained books which had been mentioned on almost every list of worthwhile reading. The titles of this set are submitted with the confidence that each and every volume merits the label "World's Greatest Literature."

The next problem of importance was the designing of a format worthy of the name "Spencer." The services of Mr. Leonard Mounteney, a master craftsman who had served for twenty years as a binder in the studios of Robert Riviere & Sons of London, England, were engaged for this artistic undertaking. Mounteney has in the last ten years won for himself considerable acclaim as one of the world's most eminent binders. He approached the task of designing these books with all the fervor and interest of a skilled artisan who loves his work, applying the same thought to these volumes as is usually accorded the bindings of museum masterpieces, incunabula and priceless first editions. Mounteney was well aware that the name "Spencer" had become identified with handsome illustration, fine printing and exquisite binding and he was most anxious to create books of surpassing beauty.

"The Spencer Press" is named in honor of and as a tribute to the memory of William Augustus Spencer, the son of Lorillard Spencer and Sarah Johnson Griswold. Spencer was born in New York, was educated in Europe and made his home in Paris, frequently visiting the United States. Spencer became an inveterate book collector, specializing in fine French bindings. He soon became a patron of the fine binders of his day and his collection, now on permanent exhibition at the New York Public Library, is rated as one of the finest of modern collections. Unfortunately, Spencer perished in the sinking of the Titanic in 1912 cutting short a career of great promise.

The books collected by Spencer were mostly nineteenth century works. These volumes represent a definite advancement in many spheres of book production. The authors, publishers, printers, engravers and bookbinders are all representative of what is modern in their several arts, for Spencer was a true collector who insisted upon a high state of perfection in every creative phase of the bookmaking art.

This type of publishing depends more than anything else upon patronage for its existence. The history of fine bookmaking is linked with the social history of the countries where it is practised. The wealthy nobility were usually the patrons of this fine art. The Kings of France were notable collectors forming libraries of considerable merit. Jean Grolier, Viscount d'Aguisy (1479-1565), Treasurer-General of the Duchy of Milan, friend of Francis I, and ambassador to Pope Clement VII, friend of

Aldus, the great printer, was perhaps the most lavish patron of the art of binding and collecting books. To Grolier is accorded the first place among all the great names in book collecting history, and to him is owed the dignified standing in which book collecting is esteemed among the gentler arts. To Grolier also goes the honor for creating a most important and fundamental style in the decoration of book covers.

From Grolier to Spencer we find the names of many illustrious notables who have fostered and patronized the advancement of this art. Jean Baptiste Colbert, statesman and minister of finance under Louis XIV, was the founder of the Academy of Inscriptions which concerned itself greatly with book decoration. Then there was Mazarin, Italian and French cardinal and statesman, who founded one of the great libraries of the world which bears his name. During the intervening years there have been thousands of collectors who have patronized the art. In America one thinks of such great names as Weidner, Morgan, Huntington and Hay in this connection.

Such affluent patronage has given aid to many different interpretations of beauty. Books have been handsomely bound in paper, in wood, in parchment, in cloth and fine leathers. They have been inlaid with materials of contrasting colors, hand painted, encrusted with rare and valuable jewels. They have contained gorgeous end papers and fancy doublures. Men have spent years in the binding, tooling and decoration of a single volume.

These bibliophiles collected not only fine titles, bindings and illustrations but fine printing as well. Gutenberg, the father of fine printing, set an early standard which has been difficult if not impossible to excel. The books created by Gutenberg still rank as among the finest examples of book ornamentation ever produced. Then came the handsome volumes of the East with their arabesques, graceful lines and fleurons which found many an eager collector among the gentlemen of Venice. Aldus, the printer, patronized by Grolier, created many examples of fine printing influenced by these same Eastern designs.

The history of fine binding and bookmaking is a long

and interesting one filled with many glorious stories of exquisite books. In the creation of this set of the "World's Greatest Literature," Mounteney has copied the designs of Roger Payne, the one truly great English binder of the nineteenth century. Payne's work was known to have a French influence, a delicate decorative scheme of dots, lines and simple designs. Mounteney has added certain elegant refinements of his own and has endeavored to create a set of books that would be a credit to the memory and name of one of the greatest of all modern collectors . . . a set of books within the reach of the true book-lover so that the appreciation of fine and beautiful books need no longer be a kingly prerogative alone.

The publishers do not claim or even dare to hope that these books are to be compared for richness of binding or makeup with the volumes in the Spencer Library, for some of those books cost thousands of dollars and occupied many years in the lives of master craftsmen. It is true, however, that Mounteney in his careful designing has created books possessing rare beauty of design and exquisite good taste which vie in appearance and handsomeness with the Spencer masterpieces. It should be remembered that the original Spencer volumes were designed by hand, tooled by hand, and often printed by hand, whereas these books were created by one of the world's greatest printers employing every advancement of modern science and efficiency to bring to you books you will treasure over the years . . . books that will add to the richness and fullness of your life.

Reading, Pa. 1936.   LEONARD S. DAVIDOW.

THE COUNT OF MONTE CRISTO

CHAPTER I.

THE ARRIVAL AT MARSEILLES

On the 24th of February, 1815, the Marseilles port lookouts signalled that the three-master Pharaoh was coming up the harbor. She belonged to Morrel and Son, and was homeward bound from Smyrna, Trieste and Naples. The pilot boat ran out to meet her, and the idlers congregated on the waterside to see her come into her mooring-place, with the more interest as she had been built, launched and fitted out from this ancient port.

She came in so slowly that it was easy to guess that she had met some mishap, not to herself, as she was in trim condition, but to some one aboard. By the pilot was seen, standing to transmit his orders, a bright-eyed and active young man.

The vague disquiet of the spectators was peculiarly sharper in one of them who took a boat and man, and was rowed out to meet the vessel.

On seeing him draw near, the ship's officer left the pilot and with his hat off went to lean over the taffrail.

He was a handsome fellow not over twenty, tall but slim, with beautiful black eyes and ebony hair, with all the calmness and resolution of those inured from childhood to wrestle with dangers.

"Ah, is this you, Dantès?" hailed the passenger in the wherry, "what is wrong and why do you all wear such a sad look?"

"A great misfortune befell us, M. Morrel," replied the young man, "and worse for me; off Civita Vecchia, we lost our honest Captain Leclere——"

"But the cargo?" quickly asked the ship-owner.

"That is safe in port, and I believe you will be satisfied on that score; but poor Captain Leclere is dead—not fallen overboard, but carried off by brain fever."

He turned aside to set his crew to work for the letting go the anchor and taking in sail.

"How did all this happen?" asked the ship-master, resuming when the young commander returned to him.

"Most unexpectedly; after a long talk with the harbor-master at Naples, our skipper came aboard in a fret and the fever breaking out in a day, he was done for in three. We gave him the seaman's funeral, and I bring to his widow his sword and cross of the Legion of Honor—it was much good his waging war at sea for ten years against the British to die in his bed like the stay-at-homes at last," sighed the young man.

"Never mind, Edmond, we are all mortal," returned the ship-owner, seeming to be more and more consoled, "and the old must give place to the young or there would be no promotion; and as long as you encourage me about the cargo——"

"I answer for its being in a good state, M. Morrel; I would not advise you to sell without twenty-five thousand profit."

He turned to issue orders, carried out as on a war-ship.

The ship went on so slowly now that the ship-master could step aboard.

"Here is your supercargo coming on deck, to supply you with full information."

Supercargo Danglars was a man of twenty-five, of a moody cast of countenance; obsequious to his superiors he was insolent to his inferiors; besides his being the purser, which is always an object of aversion to seamen, he was as badly viewed by the crew as Dantès was liked.

"Well, M. Morrel," said Danglars, "you have heard of the misfortune?"

"Yes—yes! poor Captain Leclere! He was a brave and honest man!"

"And a first-rate seaman, grown old between sky and sea, as should a man charged with the interests of a house so important as Morrel and Son," replied Danglars.

"But," replied the owner, following with his look Dantès, who was watching the anchoring, "it seems to me that a sailor needs not to be so old as you say, Danglars, to understand his business; for our friend Edmond seems to understand it thoroughly, and not to require instruction from any one."

"Yes," said Danglars, casting towards Edmond a look in which envy was strongly visible. "Yes, he is young, and youth is invariably self-confident. Scarcely was the captain's breath out of his body than he assumed the command without consulting any one, and he caused us to lose a day and a half at the Isle of Elba, instead of making for Marseilles direct."

"As to taking the command of the vessel," replied Morrel, "that was his duty as mate; as to losing a day and a half off the Isle of Elba, he was wrong, unless the ship wanted repairs."

"The ship was as sound as I am, and as, I hope, you are, M. Morrel, and this time was lost from pure whim, for the pleasure of going ashore, and nothing else.

"Dantès!" said the ship-owner, turning towards the young man, "come this way!"

"In a moment, sir," answered Dantès. Then calling to the crew, he said—"Let go!"

The anchor was instantly dropped, and the chain ran rattling through the port-hole. Dantès continued at his post in spite of the presence of the pilot, until this manœuvre was completed, and then he added, "Half-mast the flags and stay the yards ashore."

"You see," said Danglars, "he fancies himself captain already, upon my word."

"And so, in fact, he is," said the owner.

"Except your signature and your partner's, M. Morrel."

"And why should he not have this?" asked the owner; "he is young, it is true, but he seems to me a thorough seaman, and of full experience."

A cloud passed over Danglars' brow. "Your pardon, M. Morrel," said Dantès, approaching, "the ship now rides at anchor, and I am at your service. You hailed me, I think?"

Danglars retreated a step or two. "I wished to inquire why you stopped at the Isle of Elba?"

"I do not know, sir; it was to fulfill a last instruction of Captain Leclere, who, when dying, gave me a packet for Marshal Bertrand."

Morrel looked around him, and then, drawing Dantès on one side, he said suddenly—"And how is the emperor?"

"Very well, as far as I could judge from my eyes. He entered the apartment whilst I was there."

"And you spoke to him?"

"He asked me questions about the ship, the time it left Marseilles, the course she had taken, and what was her cargo. I believe, if she had not been laden, and I had been her master, he would have bought her. But I told him I was only mate, and that she belonged to Morrel and Son. 'Ah! ha!' he said, 'I know them! The Morrels have been ship-owners for generations, though one was a soldier, who served in the same garrison with me, at Valence'."

"By Jove, that is true," exclaimed Morrel delighted, "he means my uncle Policar, who became a captain. Dantès, tell him that the emperor remembered him and you will see the old veteran look moist about the eyes. Come, come," added he, slapping the young officer on the shoulder, "you were quite right to follow Leclere's instructions and stop at Elba, though you might be bothered if known you handed a packet to the marshal and chatted with the exile."

"How could it entangle me?" said Dantès. "I did not know what I carried and the emperor only spoke to me as to any next man. But here come the medical officers and the customs—"

"Attend to them," said Morrel whom Danglars approached, asking him if he were satisfied with the explanations.

"But," said he, "how about the letter of Leclere's which he left at Porto Ferrajo——I was passing the cabin door when I saw that given. But unless he gave you it, I may be mistaken—say nothing to him."

Dantès returned, having settled everything, and the ship-owner asked him to dinner.

"Excuse me," said Edmond, "but I always pay my first visit to my father."

"Right, Dantès, quite right. I always knew you were a good son."

"And," inquired Dantès, with some hesitation, "do you know how my father is?"

"Well, I believe, my dear Edmond, though I have not seen him lately."

"Yes, he likes to keep himself shut up in his little room."

"That proves, at least, that he has wanted for nothing during your absence."

Dantès smiled. "My father is proud, sir; and if he had not a meal left, I doubt if he would have asked anything from any one, except God."

"Well, then, after this first visit has been made we rely on you."

"I must again excuse myself, M. Morrel; for after this first visit has been paid I have another, which I am most anxious to pay."

"True, Dantès, I forgot that there was at the Catalans some one who expects you no less impatiently than your father—the lovely Mercédès."

Dantès blushed.

"Ah! ah!" said the ship-owner, "that does not astonish me, for she has been to me three times, inquiring if there were any news. Edmond, you have a very handsome flame."

"She is not my flame," replied the young sailor, gravely; "she is my betrothed."

"Well, well, my dear Edmond," continued the owner, "do not let me detain you. You have managed my affairs so well that I ought to allow you all the time you require for your own. Do you want any money?"

"No, sir; I have all my pay to take—nearly three months' wages."

"You are a careful fellow, Edmond."

"Say I have a poor father, sir."

"Yes, yes, I know how good a son you are, so now haste away to see your father. I have a son, too, and I should be very wroth with those who detained him from me after a three months' voyage."

"Then I have your leave, sir?"

"Yes, if you have nothing more to say to me."

"Nothing."

"Captain Leclere did not, before he died, give you a letter for me?"

"He was unable to write, sir. But that reminds me that I must ask your leave of absence for some days."

"To get married?"

"Yes, first, and then to go to Paris."

"Very good; have what time you require, Dantès. It will take quite six weeks to unload the cargo, and we can not get you ready for sea until three months after that; only be back again in three months, for the Pharaoh," added the owner, patting the sailor on the back, "cannot sail without her captain."

"Without her captain!" cried Dantès, his eyes sparkling with animation; "pray, mind what you say, for you are touching on the most secret wishes of my heart. Is it really your intention to nominate me captain?"

"If I were sole owner I would appoint you this moment, my dear Dantès, and say it is settled; but I have a partner, and you know the Italian proverb—'He who has a partner has a master.' But the thing is at least half done, as you have one out of two voices. Rely on me to procure you the other, I will do my best."

"Ah! M. Morrel," exclaimed the seaman, with tears in his eyes, and grasping the owner's hand, "I thank you in the name of my father and of Mercédès."

"Stay, Dantès—if you command, would you keep Danglars aboard?"

"I always respect my owners' choice."

"I see you are a good-hearted fellow; but I will not detain you. Good fortune!"

The speaker watched the youth proceed to shore in a row boat, and Danglars did the same, but with hatred.

CHAPTER II.

FATHER AND SON

DANTES passed through the town after landing, to Meillans Alley, where he entered a small house; ascending four flights, he peeped into a little room.

This apartment was occupied by Dantès' father. The news of the arrival had not yet reached the old man, who, mounted on a chair, was amusing himself with staking some nasturtiums which mingled with clematis, formed a trellis at his window. Suddenly, he felt an arm thrown round his body, and a well-known voice behind him exclaimed, "Father! dear father!"

The old man uttered a cry, and turned round; then, seeing his son, he fell into his arms, pale and trembling.

"Come, come, cheer up, my dear father! 'Tis I—really I! They say joy never hurts, and so I come to you without any warning. Come now, look cheerfully at me, instead of gazing as you do with your eyes so wide. Here I am back again, and we will now be happy."

"Yes, yes, my boy, so we will," replied the old man; "but how shall we be happy? Will you never leave me again? Come, tell me all the good fortune that has befallen you."

"God forgive me," said the young man, "for rejoicing at happiness derived from the misery of others; but, Heaven knows, I did not seek this good fortune: it has happened, and I really cannot affect to lament it. Our good Captain Leclere is dead, father, and it is probable that, with the aid of M. Morrel, I shall have his place. Do you understand, father? Only imagine me a captain at twenty, with a hundred louis pay, and a share in the profits! Is this not more than a poor sailor like me could have hoped for?"

"Yes, my dear boy," replied the old man, "and much more than you could have expected."

"Well, then, with the first money I touch, I mean you to have a small house, with a garden. But what ails you, father? Are not you well?"

" 'Tis nothing, nothing; it will soon pass away;" and as he said so the old man's strength failed him, and he fell backwards.

"Come, come," said the young man, "a glass of wine, father, will revive you. Where do you keep your wine?"

"No, no; thank ye. You need not look for it; I do not want it," said the old man.

"Yes, yes, father, tell me where it is," and he opened two or three cupboards.

"It is no use," said the old man, "there is no wine."

"What! no wine?" said Dantès, turning pale, and looking alternately at the hollow cheeks of the old man and the empty cupboards, "What! no wine? Have you wanted money, father?"

"I want nothing since I see you," said the old man.

"Yet," stammered Dantès, wiping the perspiration from his brow,— "yet I gave you two hundred francs when I left, three months ago."

"Yes, yes, Edmond, that is true, but you forgot at that time a little debt to our neighbor, Caderousse. He reminded me of it, telling me if I did not pay for you, he would go to M. Morrel; and so you see, lest he might do you an injury, I paid him."

"But," cried Dantès, "it was a hundred and forty francs I owed Caderousse."

"Ye-es," faltered the old man.

"Then you have only had sixty francs to live on these three months? You rend my heart! But I am home with fine prospects and some cash." He put some coin on the table, which made the old man's eyes glisten.

"Nay, I will use your boon moderately; if seen to be lavish, folks will say I had to wait for your coming to be in funds."

"Do as you like, but hire a servant. I have some coffee and tobacco which I have run past the customs-house sharks. But, hush! here comes Caderousse to congratulate me—lips saying one thing—his heart another!"

Caderousse's black head and bearded face appeared; he was a man about twenty-five; in his hand, as a tailor, was the cloth for a coat-skirt.

He grinned a welcome to Edmond and begged him not to thank him for the kindness to his father.

"Let us only talk of your happy return. I was on the quay to match some cloth when I met friend Danglars who told me you were home again. But you seem to return rich," said he, eyeing the coin greedily.

"No, my father showed me that he had a stock when I asked if he had been short."

"I hear that you were in such a haste to greet your father that you would not dine with the shipper. That is right and yet when one is on the road to be captain he ought to curry favor with the owner! but be captain—nothing will please your friends better! and I know one behind St. Nicholas fort, who will not be sorry to hear it!"

"Mercédès!" exclaimed the old man. "Go! ah, Heaven has blessed you in such a wife as me in such a son."

"Wife!" repeated Caderousse; "how fast you run! Mercédès is a fine slip and has sweethearts by dozens! but go to her!"

He preceded Dantès, and went to join the supercargo at the corner whence they went to a tavern to have wine.

"Why did you stir up his jealousy? asked Danglars.

"Not at all, but she has a strapping fellow with her every time she comes to town."

"Let us go to the Catalans!"

Caderousse was ready to go anywhere as long as another paid the refreshment bills. They stopped at Father Pamphile's Reserve inn, while Dantès kept on his way.

CHAPTER III.

THE BEAUTY OF THE CATALANS

THE Catalans is a small half-Moorish, half-Spanish village, peopled by a race which does not intermix with that at Marseilles. It has but a single street in which a small house contained a beautiful girl, with hair as black as jet, and eyes as velvety as the gazelle's, who was leaning with her back against the wainscot, rubbing, in her slender fingers, a bunch of heath blossoms, the flowers of which she was picking off, and strewing on the floor; her arms bare to the elbow, embrowned, and resembling those of the Venus at Arles, moved with impatience, and she tapped the earth, with her pliant and well-formed foot, so as to display the pure and full shape of her well-turned leg, in its red cotton stocking with grey and blue clocks. At three paces from her, seated in a chair which he balanced on two legs, leaning his elbow on an old worm-eaten table, was a tall man of twenty or two-and-twenty, looking at her with an air in which vexation and uneasiness were mingled. He questioned her with his eyes, but the firm and steady gaze controlled his look.

"You see, Mercédès," said the young man, "here is Easter come round again; tell me, is not this the moment for a wedding? do you forget that it is among the Catalans a sacred law to intermarry?"

"You mistake, Fernand, it is not a law, but merely a custom; and, I pray, do not cite this custom in your favor. You are included in the conscription, Fernand, and are only at liberty on sufferance, liable at any moment to be called upon to take up arms. Once a soldier, what would you do with me, a poor orphan, forlorn, without fortune, with nothing but a hut, half in ruins, containing some ragged nets—a miserable inheritance left by my father to my mother, and by my mother to me? She has been dead a year, and you know, Fernand, I have subsisted almost entirely on public charity. Sometimes you pretend I am useful to you, and that is an excuse to share with me the produce of your fishing, and I accept it, Fernand, because you are the son of my father's brother, because we were brought up together, and still more because it would give you so much pain if I refuse. But I feel very deeply that this fish which I go and sell, and with the produce of which I buy the flax I spin, —this is charity."

"And if it were, Mercédès, poor and lone as you are, you suit me as well as the daughter of the leading ship-owner, or the richest banker of Marseilles! What do such as we desire but a good wife and careful housekeeper, and where can I look for these better than in you?"

"Fernand," answered Mercédès, shaking her head, "a woman becomes a bad manager, and who shall say she will remain an honest wife, when she loves another man better than her husband? I love Edmond Dantès, and none but Edmond shall ever be my husband."

Fernand let fall his head like a defeated man, heaved a sigh which resembled a groan, and then suddenly looking her full in the face, with clenched teeth and expanded nostrils, said,—"But if he is dead——"

"If he is dead, I shall die too."

"If he has forgotten you——"

"Mercédès!" cried a voice, joyously, outside the house.

"Ah!" exclaimed the girl, blushing with delight, and springing up with love, "you see he has not forgotten me, for here he is!" And rushing toward the door, she opened it, saying, "Here, Edmond, here I am!"

Fernand, pale and trembling, receded like a traveler at the sight of a serpent, and fell into a chair. Edmond and Mercédès were clasped in each other's arms. The burning sun, which penetrated by the open door, covered them with a flood of light. At first they saw nothing around them. Their intense happiness isolated them from all the rest of the world, and they only spoke in broken words, which are the tokens of a joy so extreme that they seem rather the expression of sorrow. Suddenly Edmond saw the gloomy countenance of Fernand, as it was defined in the shadow, pale and threatening, and by a movement, for which he could scarcely account, the young Catalan placed his hand on the knife at his belt.

"Ah! your pardon," said Dantès, frowning in his turn; "I did not perceive that there was company." Then, turning to Mercédès, he inquired, "Who is this gentleman?"

"One who will be your best friend, Dantès, for he is my friend, my cousin, my brother; it is Fernand—the man whom, after you, Edmond, I love the best in the world. Do you not remember him?"

"Yes; but I did not know, when I came with such haste to you, that I was to meet an enemy here."

"An enemy!" cried Mercédès, with an angry look at her cousin. "An enemy in my house, do you say, Edmond! If I believed that, I would place my arm under yours and go with you to Marseilles, leaving the house to return to it no more."

Fernand's eye darted lightning. "And should any misfortune occur to you, dear Edmond," she continued, with the calmness which proved to Fernand that the girl had read the very innermost depths of his sinister intention, "if misfortune should occur to you, I would ascend the highest point of Cape Morgion, and cast myself headlong from it."

Fernand became deadly pale. "But you are deceived, Edmond," she continued. "You have no enemy here—there is no one but Fernand, my brother, who will grasp your hand as a devoted friend."

And at these words the girl fixed her imperious look on the Catalan, who, as if fascinated by it, came slowly toward Edmond, and offered him his hand. His hatred, like a powerless though furious wave, was broken by Mercédès' ascendancy. But to touch Dantes' hand was as much as he could constrain himself to do, and he instantly darted out of the house.

He was still running when he was hailed from the tavern, where Danglars had halted with the tailor. The latter had already imbibed heavily but the treater was sober. He saw in the Catalan's eye that fire of revenge and jealousy with which he might burn down his enemy's castle.

While hatching a scheme, he asked the fugitive to sit down and carouse. They were so engaged when the happy couple of Dantès and his beloved strolled along. Mercédès was talking all the time she could as Edmond announced that he had to go to Paris.

Danglars guessed that this singular journey was linked to the letter he had seen confided to the acting captain and as soon as the pair were gone, induced Fernand to write a denunciatory letter to the royal prosecutor which would remove his rival. Caderousse, in his tipsy state, was persuaded that it was only a practical joke.

"Hurrah!" said the supercargo to himself, "the thing is launched and will reach home without any more urging!"

CHAPTER IV.

THE INTERRUPTED WEDDING

It was necessary to have the scheme ready, for Dantès had lost no time on his side. He wished to be married before he started on his mission to the capital. He had a plenteous feast prepared at Reserve Tavern where before noon his crew and friends assembled. Morrel also condescended to participate in the celebration of his mate's happiness. Fernand attended though his features wore a sinister smile.

Neither Mercédès nor Edmond observed the strange expression.

Danglars and Caderousse took their places beside Fernand and old Dantès—the latter of whom attracted universal notice, attired in a suit of black, trimmed with steel buttons, beautifully cut and polished. Beside him crept Caderousse, whose desire to partake of the good things provided for the wedding-party had induced him to become reconciled to the Dantès, father and son, although there still lingered in his mind a faint recollection of events of the preceding night; just as the brain retains on waking the dim and misty outlines of the dream.

As Danglars approached the disappointed lover, he cast on him a look of deep meaning, while Fernand, as he paced behind the happy pair, entirely forgotten by the bride, was pale and abstracted; occasionally, however, a deep flush would overspread his countenance, and a nervous contraction distort his limbs, while he would glance in the direction of Marseilles, like one who either anticipated or foresaw some great event.

Dantès himself was simply clad in the dress peculiar to the merchant navy—a costume somewhat between a military and a civil garb; and his fine countenance was radiant with joy and happiness.

Lovely as the Greeks Mercédès boasted the same bright eyes of jet and coral lips. One of great cities would have hid her glee beneath a veil, or, at least, have cast down her thickly-fringed lashes, but the girl looked around her with a smile that seemed to invite all who saw her to behold, and rejoice with her.

Immediately the bridal pair came in sight of La Réserve, M. Morrel came forth to meet it, followed by the soldiers and sailors there assembled, to whom he had repeated the promise already given, that Dantès should be the successor to the late Captain Leclere. Edmond, at the approach, respectfully placed the arm of his affianced bride within Morrel's, who, forthwith conducting her up the flight of wooden steps leading to the chamber in which the feast was prepared, was followed by the guests, beneath whom they creaked and groaned.

"Father," said Mercédès, stopping when she had reached the centre of the table, "sit, I pray you, on my right hand; on my left I will place him who has ever been a brother to me," pointing with a softness to Fernand; but inflicting torture on him, for his lips became ghastly pale, and even beneath the dark hue of his complexion the blood might be seen retreating to the heart.

During this time, Dantès, at the opposite side of the table, had been occupied in placing his guests. M. Morrel was seated at his right hand, Danglars at his left; while, at a sign from Edmond, the rest of the company ranged themselves as most agreeable.

And now commenced the work of devastation upon the many good things with which the table was loaded.

"A pretty silence truly!" said the old father of the bridegroom, as he carried to his lips a glass of wine of the hue of the roses, just placed before Mercédès herself. "Now, would anybody think that of a party of thirty, who desire nothing better than to laugh?"

"Ah!" sighed Caderousse, "a man cannot always feel happy because he is about to be married."

"The truth is," replied Dantès, "that I am too happy for mirth; that is what you meant by your observation, my worthy friend, you are right; joy takes a strange effect at times, it seems to oppress us almost the same as sorrow."

Danglars looked towards Fernand, whose excitable nature received and betrayed each fresh impression.

"Why, what ails you?" asked he of Edmond. "Do you fear any approaching evil? I should say that you were the happiest man alive at this instant."

"And that is the very thing that alarms me," returned Dantès. "Man does not appear to me to be intended to enjoy felicity so unmixed; happiness is like the enchanted palaces where dragons defend the entrance; and monsters to be overcome. I own that I am lost in wonder to find myself promoted to an honor of which I feel myself unworthy—that of being the husband of Mercédès."

"Nay, nay!" cried Caderousse, smiling, "you have not attained that honor yet. Mercèdés is not yet your wife. Just assume the tone and manner of a husband, and see how she will remind you that your hour is not yet come!"

The bride blushed, and seemed half-inclined to be angry; while Fernand, restless and uneasy, seemed to start at every fresh sound, occasionally applying his handkerchief to his brow to wipe away the large drops of perspiration.

"Well, never mind that, neighbor Caderousse; it is not worth while to contradict me for such a trifle as that. 'Tis true that Mercédès is not actually my wife; but," added he, drawing out his watch, "in an hour and a half from this she will be fast and firm."

A general exclamation of surprise ran round the table, with the exception of the elder Dantès, whose laugh displayed still perfect teeth. Mercédès looked pleased, while Fernand grasped the handle of his knife with a convulsive clutch.

"In an hour?" inquired Danglars, turning pale. "How is that, my friend?"

"Why, thus it is," replied Dantès. "Thanks to the influence of M. Morrel, to whom, next to my father, I owe every blessing I enjoy, every difficulty has been removed. We have purchased permission; and at half-past two o'clock the Mayor of Marseilles will be waiting for us. Now, as a quarter-past one has already struck, I do not consider I have asserted too much in saying, that in another hour and thirty minutes Mercédès will have become Mdme. Dantès."

Fernand closed his eyes, a burning sensation passed across his brow, and he was compelled to support himself by the table to prevent his falling from his chair; but in spite of all his efforts, he could not refrain from uttering a deep groan, which, however, was lost amid the felicitations of the company.

"Upon my word," cried the old man, "you make short work. Arrived here only yesterday morning, and married to-day at three o'clock! Commend me to a sailor for going the quick way to work!"

"So that what was presumed to be merely the betrothal feast turns out to be the actual wedding dinner!" said Danglars.

"No, no!" answered Dantès; "you shall lose nothing by it—rest easy! To-morrow morning, I am off to Paris, so that with my task properly done in a day I can go and return in eight. Back on the first of March, the second shall be the regular wedding feast."

This prospect of additional junketing doubled the jollity so that the elder Dantès, who had at the outset complained of the party being quiet, was making vain efforts amid the babble, to propose his toast to the happiness of the engaged pair. Divining his intention, Edmond rewarded him with a smile of affection, and Mercédès glanced at the cuckoo clock and made a sign to her affianced one.

At this moment Danglars, who had not lost sight of Fernand's look and manner, perceived him stagger and fall back, with an almost convulsive spasm, against a seat placed near one of the open windows. At the same instant the ear caught a sort of indistinct sound on the stairs, followed by the measured tread of soldiery, with the clanking of swords and accoutrements; then came a hum of voices, so as to deaden even the mirth of the bridal party, among whom a vague feeling of curiosity and apprehension quelled every dispositon to talk, and almost instantaneously uneasy stillness prevailed.

Nearer and nearer came those sounds of terror. Three distinct knocks came. Each looked inquiringly in the countenance of his neighbor.

"I demand admittance," said a loud voice outside the room, "in the name of the law!" As no attempt was made to prevent it, the door was opened, and a magistrate, wearing his official scarf, presented himself, followed by four soldiers and a corporal. Uneasiness now yielded to dread.

"May I inquire the reason of this unexpected visit?" said M. Morrel, addressing the magistrate, whom he knew; "there is doubtless some mistake."

"If it be so," replied the magistrate, "rely upon every reparation being made; meanwhile, I am the bearer of an order of arrest, and although I most reluctantly perform the task assigned me, it must, nevertheless, be fulfilled. Who among the persons answers to the name of Edmond Dantès?" Every eye was turned towards the individual so described, who, spite of the agitation he could not but feel, advanced with dignity, and said, in a firm voice, "I am he; what is your pleasure with me?"

"Edmond Dantès," replied the magistrate, "I arrest you in the name of the law!" "Me!" repeated Edmond, slightly changing color, "and wherefore?"

"I cannot inform you, but you will be acquainted at your first examination."

"What is the meaning of all this?" inquired Caderousse, frowningly, of Danglars, who had assumed an air of utter surprise.

"How can I tell you?" replied he; "I am, like yourself, utterly bewildered at all that is going on, not a word of which do I understand." Caderousse then looked around for Fernand, but he had disappeared.

"Where is Fernand?" inquired Caderousse.

"How do I know?" replied Danglars; "gone, as every prudent man ought to do, to look after his own affairs, most likely. Never mind where he is, let you and I go and see what is to be done for our poor friends in affliction."

During this conversation, Dantès, after having exchanged a cheerful shake of the hand with all his sympathizing friends, had surrendered himself, merely saying, "Make yourselves quite easy, there is some little mistake to clear up, and very likely I may not have to go so far as the prison."

"Oh, to be sure!" responded Danglars, who approached, "nothing more."

Dantès descended the staircase, preceded by the magistrate, and followed by the soldiers. A carriage awaited him at the door; he got in, followed by two soldiers and the magistrate, and the vehicle drove off towards Marseilles.

"Adieu! adieu! dearest Edmond!" cried Mercédès, springing out on the balcony.

The prisoner caught the sob of his betrothed, from her heart, as leaning from the coach he cried—"Good-bye, Mercédès!" The vehicle disappeared round one of the turnings of Fort Saint Nicolas.

"Wait for me here!" cried M. Morrell; "I will take the first conveyance I find, and hurry to Marseilles, whence I will bring you word."

"That's right!" exclaimed all voices; "go, and return as quickly as you can!"

This second departure was followed by terrified stupor on the part of those left behind. The old father and Mercédès remained for some time apart, each absorbed in grief; but at length the victims of the same blow raised their eyes, and rushed into each other's arms.

Called upon for an explanation, Danglars suggested that his captain might have been smuggling and this was confirmed by old Dantès confessing that his son had promised him some coffee and tobacco. This had no soothing effect on the girl, who continued sobbing.

After the other's departure, Fernand again became protector to Mercédès, led the girl back to her home, while friends of Dantès conducted the parent to his abode.

The rumor of Edmond's arrest as a Bonapartist agent was not slow in circulating throughout the city.

"Could you ever have credited such a thing, my dear Danglars?" asked M. Morrel, as, on his return to the port for the purpose of gleaning fresh tidings of Dantès, he overtook his supercargo and Caderousse. "Could you have believed such a thing?"

"Why, you know I told you," replied Danglars, "that I considered his having anchored at the Isle of Elba as very suspicious."

"And did you mention these suspicions to any person beside myself?"

"Certainly not!" returned Danglars. Then added in a low whisper,

"You understand that, on account of your uncle, M. Policar Morrel, who served under the other government, and who does not altogether conceal what he thinks on the subject, you are strongly suspected of regretting the abdication of Napoleon. I should injure both Edmond and yourself to a soul. A subordinate, is bound to acquaint the ship-owner with everything that occurs, but many things he ought most carefully to conceal from all else."

" 'Tis well, Danglars—'tis well!" replied M. Morrel. "You are a worthy fellow; and I had already thought of your interests in the event of poor Edmond having become captain of the Pharaoh. I had previously inquired of Dantès what was his opinion of you, and if he should have any reluctance to continue you in your post, for somehow I have perceived coolness between you two that led me to believe that he would rather have another in your place as supercargo."

"He certainly did think he had given you offence in an affair which he merely referred to without entering into particulars, but that whoever possessed the good opinion and confidence of the ship's owners would have his preference also."

"The hypocrite!" murmured Danglars between his teeth. "But now hasten on board, I will join you there ere long." So saying, the worthy ship-owner quitted the two allies, and proceeded.

"You see," said Danglars, addressing Caderousse, "the turn things have taken. Do you still feel any desire to stand up in his defence?"

"Not the slightest, but yet it seems to me a shocking thing a mere joke should lead to such consequences."

"But who perpetrated that joke, let me ask? neither you nor myself, but Fernand: you knew very well that I threw the paper into a corner of the arbor,—indeed, I fancied I had destroyed it."

"Oh, no!" replied Caderousse, "that I can answer for, you did not. I only wish I could see it now as plainly as I saw it lying crumpled in a corner."

"Well, then, if you did, depend upon it, Fernand picked it up, and either copied it or caused it to be copied; perhaps, even, he did not take the trouble of recopying it. And now I think of it, by Heavens! he has sent the letter itself! Fortunately, for me, the handwriting was disguised."

"Then you were aware of Dantès being engaged in a conspiracy?"

"Not I. As I before said, I thought the whole thing was a joke, nothing more. It seems, however, that I have stumbled upon the truth."

"Still," argued Caderousse, "I would give a great deal if nothing of the kind had happened; or, at least, that I had had no hand in it. You will see, Danglars, that it will turn out an unlucky job for both of us."

"Nonsense! If any harm comes of it, it should fall on the guilty person; and that, you know, is Fernand. How can we be implicated in any way? All we have got to do is to keep our own counsel, and remain perfectly quiet, not breathing a word to any living soul; and you will see that the storm will pass away."

"Amen!" responded Caderousse, waving his hand in token of adieu to Danglars, and, moving his head to and fro, and muttering as he went, after the manner of one whose mind was overcharged.

"So far, then," said Danglars, mentally, "all has gone as I would have it. I am, temporarily, commander of the Pharaoh, with the certainty of being permanently so, if that fool Caderousse can be persuaded to hold his tongue. My only fear is the chance of Dantès being released. But bah! he is in the hands of Justice; and," added he, with a smile, "she will keep her prey." So saying, he leaped into a boat, desiring to be rowed on board the Pharaoh, where M. Morrel had appointed to meet him.

CHAPTER V.

THE DEPUTY PROSECUTOR

IN one of the large mansions situated in the Rue du Grand Cours opposite the fountain of Medusas, a second marriage-feast was being celebrated. almost at the same hour with the ill-fated nuptial repast given by Dantès.

The guests were still at table, and the heated and energetic conversation that prevailed betrayed the violent and vindictive passions that then agitated each Southron, where, unhappily, religious strife had long given increased bitterness to the violence of party feeling.

The emperor, now king of the petty Isle of Elba, was looked upon as a ruined man, separated for ever from any fresh connection with France or claim to her throne.

An old man, decorated with the cross of Saint Louis, now rose and proposed the health of King Louis XVIII. This aged individual was the Marquis of Saint-Méran. This toast excited universal enthusiasm; glasses were elevated in the air, and the ladies, snatching their bouquets from their fair bosoms, strewed the table with their floral treasures. In a word, an almost poetical fervor prevailed.

"Ah!" said the Marchioness of Saint-Méran, a woman with a stern, forbidding eye, though still noble and elegant-looking, despite her having reached her fiftieth year—"ah! these revolutionists, who have driven us from those very possessions they afterwards purchased for a mere trifle during the Reign of Terror, would be compelled to own, were they here, that all true devotion was on our side; yes, yes, they could not help admitting that the king, for whom we sacrificed rank, wealth, and station, was truly our 'Louis the Well-beloved,' while their wretched usurper has been, and ever will be, to them their evil genius, their 'Napoleon the accursed.' Am I not right, Villefort?"

"I beg your pardon, madame. I really must pray you to excuse me, but—in truth—I was not attending to the conversation."

"Lady," interposed the same elderly personage who had proposed the toast, "let the young people alone; let me tell you, on one's wedding day there are more agreeable subjects than politics."

"Never mind, dearest mother," said a lovely girl, with a profusion of light brown hair, and eyes that seemed to float in liquid pearl, " 'tis all my fault for seizing upon M. de Villefort, so as to prevent his listening to what you said. But there—now take him—he is your own for as long as you like. M. Villefort, I beg to remind you my mother speaks to you."

"If my lady will deign to repeat the words I but imperfectly caught, I shall be delighted to answer," said M. de Villefort.

"Never mind, Renée," replied the marchioness, with such a look of tenderness as all were astonished to see her harsh dry features capable of expressing; for, however all other feelings may be withered in a woman's nature, there is always one bright smiling spot in the maternal breast, and that is where a dearly-beloved child is concerned,—"I forgive you. What I was saying, Villefort, was, that the Bonapartists had neither our sincerity, enthusiasm, nor devotion."

"They had, however, what supplied the place of those fine qualities," replied the young man, "and that was fanaticism. Napoleon is the Mahomet of the West, and is worshipped by his commonplace but ambitious followers, not only as a leader and lawgiver, but also as the personification of equality. He has still preserved a train of parasitical satellites. Still, it has been so with other usurpers: Cromwell, for instance, who was not half so bad as Napoleon, had his partisans and advocates."

"Do you know, Villefort, that you are talking in a most dreadfully revolutionary strain? But I excuse it; it is impossible to expect the son of a Girondin to be free from the old leaven." A deep crimson suffused the countenance of Villefort.

" 'Tis true," answered he, "that my father was a Girondin, but he was not among the number of those who voted for the king's death. For my own part, I have laid aside even the name of my father, and altogether disown his political principles. He was—nay, probably may still be—a Bonapartist, and is called Noirtier; I, on the contrary, am a stanch royalist, and style myself de Villefort. Let what may remain of revolutionary sap exhaust itself and die away with the old trunk, and condescend only to regard the young shoot which has started up at a distance from the parent tree, without having the power, any more than the wish, to separate entirely from the stock from which it sprung."

"Bravo, Villefort!" cried the marquis; "excellently well said! Come, now, I have hopes of obtaining what I have been for years endeavoring to persuade my lady to promise, namely, perfect amnesty and forgetful· ness of the past."

"With all my heart," replied the marchioness; "let the past be for ever forgotten! I promise you it affords *me* as little pleasure to revive it as it does you. All I ask is, that Villefort will be firm and inflexible for the future in marking his political principles. Remember also, Ville- fort, that we have pledged ourselves to his majesty for your fealty and strict loyalty, and that at our recommendation the king consented to forget the past, as I do" (and here she extended to him her hand)—"at your entreaty. Only, if any conspirator falls under your hand, mark that you will have the more eyes on you from the knowledge that you belong to a line perhaps connected with the plotters."

"Alas, my profession and the times we live in," returned the lawyer, "order me to be severe. I will be so. I have carried some political trials through, and have proven how I stand. We are not at the end, either."

"Do you believe so?" asked the old dame.

"I am afraid so. On the Island of Elba Napoleon is too near to France; almost in sight of our shores, his proximity nourishes his par- tisans' hopes. Marseilles is full of retired officers of his, who daily pick quarrels under flimsy pretexts with the royalists; hence duels among the higher classes and murders among the low."

"I wish you would get up a notable trial," exclaimed Salvieux's daughter, a bright friend of Renée's, "I have never seen a case in court. I am told it is entertaining."

"Very; for instead of a sham drama you have the genuine one, where the villain is led off the stage really to go upon the scaffold. You shall have such a sight, and I wish the chance came early!"

At this moment, and as though the utterance of Villefort's wish had sufficed to effect its accomplishment, a servant entered the room, and whispered a few words. Villefort immediately rose from table and quit- ted the room upon the plea of urgent business: he soon, however, re- turned, his whole face beaming with delight.

"And wherefore were you called away just now?" asked Mdlle. de Saint-Méran, with an air of deep interest.

"For a very serious affair, Bonaparte conspiracy has just been dis- covered."

"Can I believe my ears?" cried the marquise.

"The Royal Prosecutor is informed by a friend to the Throne and

Religion that one Edmond Dantès, first mate of the ship Pharaoh, in this morning from Smyrna, after touching at Naples and Porto Ferrajo, was charged by Murat with a letter for the Usurper, and by the latter with another for the Bonapartist Club at Paris. The proof of his crime will be found on arresting him: for he will have the letter on him, or it will be at his father's, or aboard the ship."

"But," said Renée, "this letter, which, after all, is but an anonymous scrawl, is not even addressed to you, but to the proctor."

"True; but that gentleman being absent, his secretary, by his orders, opened his letters: thinking this one of importance, he sent for me, but not finding me, took upon himself to give the necessary orders for arresting the accused party."

"Oh, Villefort!" cried Renée, clasping her hands, and looking toward her lover with piteous earnestness, "be merciful on this the day of our betrothal."

"Never mind that foolish girl, Villefort," said the marchioness, "she will soon get over these things." So saying, Lady Saint-Méran, extended her dry bony hand to Villefort, who, while imprinting a son-in-law's respectful salute on it, looked at Renée, as much as to say, "I must try and fancy 'tis your dear hand I kiss."

"These are mournful auspices!" sighed poor Renée.

"Upon my word, child!" exclaimed the angry marchioness, "your folly exceeds all bounds. I should be glad to know what connection there can possibly be between your sickly sentimentality and the affairs of the state!"

"Oh, mother!" murmured Renée.

"Nay, madame, I pray you pardon this little traitor; I promise you that to make up for her want of loyalty, I will be most inflexibly severe;" then casting an expressive glance at his betrothed, which seemed to say, "Fear not, for your dear sake my justice shall be tempered with mercy," and receiving a sweet and approving smile in return, Villefort quitted the room.

No sooner had Villefort left, than he assumed the grave air of a man who holds the balance of life and death in his hands. Except the recollection of the line of politics his father had adopted, and which might interfere, unless he acted with the greatest prudence, with his own career, Grand Villefort was as happy as a man could be. Already rich, he held a high official situation, though only twenty-seven. He was about to marry a young and charming woman; and besides her personal attractions, which were very great, Mdlle. Saint-Méran's family possessed considerable political influence, which, they would, of course, exert in his favor.

The prosecutor's deputy found the prisoner guarded in the waiting-room of his residence; he was calm and smiling. Villefort gave him a side glance and taking the charge sheet from a police-officer, entered another room, saying: "Bring in the prisoner!"

Rapid though his glance was, he was inclined toward the captive, but he stifled his compassion and smoothed his features as he sat at his desk. Dantès was brought in, pale but quiet and smiling; saluting his judge with easy politeness, looked round for a seat, as if he had been at M. Morrel's. It was then that he encountered for the first time, Villefort's look,—that look peculiar to justice, which, whilst it seems to read the culprit's thoughts, betrays nought of its own.

"Who and what are you?" demanded Villefort, turning over a pile of papers, containing information relative to the prisoner, that an agent of police had given to him on his entry.

"My name is Edmond Dantès," replied the young man calmly; "I am mate of the Pharaoh, belonging to Messrs. Morrel and Son."

"Your age?" continued Villefort. ——"Nineteen," returned Dantès.

"What were you doing at the moment you were arrested?"

"I was at my wedding feast," said the young man, his voice slightly tremulous, so great was the contrast between that happy moment and the painful ceremony he was now undergoing; so great was the contrast between the sombre aspect of M. de Villefort and the radiant face of Mercédès.

"You were at your marriage feast?" said the deputy, shuddering in spite of himself.

"Yes, sir, I am on the point of marrying a girl I have been attached to for three years." Villefort, impassive as he was, was struck with this coincidence; and the tremulous voice of Dantès, surprised in the midst of his happiness, struck a sympathetic chord in his own bosom;—he also was on the point of being married, and he was summoned from his own happiness to destroy that of another. "This philosophic reflection," thought he, "will make a great sensation at Saint-Méran's;" and he arranged mentally, whilst Dantès awaited further questions, the antithesis by which orators often create a reputation for eloquence. When this speech was arranged, Villefort turned to Dantès.

"It is reported your political opinions are extreme," said Villefort, who had never heard anything of the kind, but was not sorry to make this inquiry, as if it were an accusation.

"My political opinions!" replied Dantès. "Alas! sir, I never had any opinions. I am hardly nineteen. If I obtain the situation I desire, I shall owe it to M. Morrel. Thus all my opinions—I will not say public, but private—are confined to these three sentiments;—I love my father, I respect M. Morrel, and I adore Mercédès. This, sir, is all I can tell you, and you see how uninteresting it is." As Dantès spoke, Villefort gazed at his ingenuous and open countenance, and recollected the words of Renée, who, without knowing who the culprit was, had besought his indulgence for him.

"Faith!" said Villefort, "he is a noble fellow! I hope I shall gain Renée's favor easily by obeying the first command she ever imposed on me. I shall have at least a pressure of the hand in public, and a sweet kiss in private." Full of this idea, Villefort's face became so joyous, that when he turned to Dantès, the latter, who had watched the change on his physiognomy, was smiling also.

"Sir," said Villefort, "have you any enemies, at least that you know?"

"Enemies?" replied Dantès; "my position is not sufficiently elevated for that. As for my temper, that is, perhaps, somewhat too hasty; but I have striven to repress it. I have had ten or twelve sailors under me; and if you question them, they will tell you that they love and respect me, not as a father, for I am too young, but as an elder brother."

"But instead of enemies you may have excited jealousy. You are about to become captain at nineteen—an elevated post; you are about to marry a pretty girl, who loves you; and good fortune may have excited envy."

"You are right; you know men better than I do, and what you say may possibly be the case, I confess; I prefer not knowing them, because then I should be forced to hate them."

"You are wrong; you should always strive to see clearly around you. You seem a worthy young man; I will depart from the strict line of my duty to aid you in discovering the author of this accusation. Here is the paper; do you know the writing?" As he spoke, Villefort drew the letter from his pocket, and presented it to Dantès, who read it. A cloud passed over his brow as he said:

"No, I do not know the writing, and yet it is tolerably plain. Whoever did it writes well. I am very fortunate," added he, looking gratefully at Villefort, "to be examined by such a man as you; for this envious person is a real enemy." And by the rapid glance that the young man's eyes shot forth, Villefort saw how much energy lay hid beneath this mildness.

"Now," said the deputy, "answer me frankly, not as a prisoner to a judge, but as one man to another who takes an interest in him, what truth is there in the accusation contained in this anonymous letter?" And Villefort threw disdainfully on his bureau the letter Dantès had just given back to him.

"None at all. I will tell you the real facts."

And he related the errands entrusted to him by his captain.

"Ah!" said Villefort, "this seems to me the truth. If you have been culpable, it was imprudence, and this was legitimized by the orders of your captain. Give up this letter you have brought from Elba, and pass your word you will appear should you be required, and go and rejoin your friends."

"I am free, then, sir?" cried Dantès, joyfully.——"Yes; but first give me this letter."

"You have it already; for it was taken from me with some others which I see in that packet."

"Stop a moment," said the deputy, as Dantès took his hat and gloves. "To whom is it addressed?"

"To M. Noirtier, Rue Coq-Héron, Paris." Had a thunderbolt fallen into the room, Villefort could not have been more stupefied. He sank into his seat, and hastily turning over the packet, drew forth the fatal letter, at which he glanced with an expression of terror.

"Do you then know him?"

"No," replied Villefort; "a faithful servant of the king does not know conspirators."

"It is a conspiracy, then?" asked Dantès, who, after believing himself free, now began to feel a tenfold alarm.

"Have you shown this letter to any one?" asked Villefort, becoming still more pale.

"To no one, on my honor."

Villefort's brow darkened more and more, his white lips and clenched teeth filled Dantès with apprehension. After reading the letter, Villefort passed his chill hand over his brow and muttered: "If he knew this letter and ever learnt that Noirtier is my father, I should be ruined forever!"

He tossed the paper into the fire where it was consumed.

"You see," said he, "the evidence is destroyed. You and I alone knew of it; and I expect you to deny if questioned."

"I will deny, sir; take it easy," said the captain.

The law officer rang for a policeman who came and who nodded on receiving whispered instructions.

"Go with him," said the vice-prosecutor.

Dantès bowed and withdrew. The moment the door closed the lawyer dropped upon a chair.

"Alas! alas!" murmured he, "if my principal had been at Marseilles I should have been ruined. This accursed letter would have destroyed all my hopes. Oh! my father, must your past career always interfere with my successes?" Suddenly a light passed over his face, a smile played round his mouth, and his lips became unclenched.

"This will do," said he, "and from this letter, which might have ruined me, I will make my fortune." And after having assured himself the prisoner was gone, the deputy hastened to his bride.

CHAPTER VI.

IF CASTLE.

THE commissary of police, as he traversed the antechamber, made a sign to two gendarmes, who placed themselves one on Dantès' right and the other on his left. A door that communicated with the Palace of Justice was opened, and they traversed a long range of gloomy corridors, whose appearance might have made even the boldest shudder. The Palace communicated with the prison,—a sombre edifice. After numberless windings, Dantès saw an iron door. The commissary knocked thrice, every blow seeming to Dantès as if struck on his heart. The door opened, the two gendarmes gently pushed him forward, and the door closed with a loud sound behind him. It was four o'clock when Dantès was placed in this chamber. It was, as we have said, the first of March, and the prisoner was soon buried in darkness. At last, about ten o'clock, and just as Dantès began to despair, steps were heard in the corridor, a key turned in the lock, the bolts creaked, the massy oaken door flew open, and a flood of light from two torches pervaded the apartment. By the torchlight Dantès saw the glittering sabres and carbines of four gendarmes. He had advanced at first, but stopped at the sight of this fresh accession of force.

"Are you come to fetch me?" asked he.——"Yes," replied a gendarme.

"By the orders of the deputy?"——"I believe so." The conviction that they came from Villefort relieved all Dantès' apprehensions; he advanced calmly, and placed himself in the centre of the escort. A carriage waited at the door, the coachman was on the box, and an exempt seated behind him.

Dantès was about to speak; but feeling himself urged forward, and having neither the power nor the intention to resist, he mounted the steps, and was in an instant seated inside between two gendarmes; the two others took their places opposite, and the carriage rolled heavily over the stones.

The prisoner glanced at the windows—they were grated; he had changed his prison for another that was conveying him he knew not whither. Through the grating, however, Dantès saw they were passing to the port.

The carriage stopped, the exempt descended, approached the guardhouse, a dozen soldiers came out and formed themselves in order; Dantès saw the reflection of their muskets by the light of the lamps on the quay.

They all advanced toward a boat, which a customs-house officer held by a chain, near the quay.

The soldiers looked at Dantès with an air of stupid curiosity. In an instant he was placed in the stern-sheets, between the gendarmes, whilst the exempt stationed himself at the bow; a shove sent the boat adrift, and four sturdy oarsmen impelled it rapidly toward the Pilon. At a shout from the boat, the chain that closes the mouth of the port was lowered, and in a second they were outside the harbor.

The most vague and wild thoughts passed through his mind. The boat they were in could not make a long voyage; there was no vessel at anchor outside the harbor; he thought, perhaps, they were going to leave him on some distant point. He was not bound, nor had they made any attempt to handcuff him; this seemed a good augury. Besides, had not the deputy, who had been so kind to him, told him that provided he did not pronounce the dreaded name of Noirtier, he had nothing to apprehend? Had not Villefort in his presence destroyed the fatal letter, the only proof against him? He waited silently, striving to pierce through the darkness.

They had left the lighthouse on the right, and were now opposite Point Catalans. It seemed to the prisoner that he could distinguish a female form on the beach, for it was there Mercédès dwelt. How was it that a presentiment did not warn Mercédès her lover was near her?

One light alone was visible; and Dantès recognized it as coming from the chamber of Mercédès. A loud cry could be heard by her. He did not utter it. What would his guards think if they heard him shout like a madman?

He remained silent, his eyes fixed upon the light; the boat went on, but the prisoner only thought of Mercédès. A rising ground hid the light. Dantès turned and perceived they had got out to sea. Whilst he had been absorbed in thought, they had hoisted the sail.

In spite of his repugnance to address the guards, Dantès turned to the nearest gendarme, and taking his hand:

"Comrade," said he, "I adjure you, as a Christian and a soldier, to tell me where we are going. I am Captain Dantès, a loyal Frenchman, though accused of treason; tell me where you are conducting me, and I promise you on my honor I will submit to my fate."

The gendarme looked irresolutely at his companion, who returned for answer a sigh that said, "I see no great harm in telling him now," and the gendarme replied:

"But my orders."——"Your orders do not forbid your telling me what I must know in ten minutes, in half an hour, or an hour. You see I cannot escape, even if I intended."

"Look round you then." Dantès rose and looked forward, when he saw rise within a hundred yards of him the black and frowning rock on which stands Castle If. This gloomy fortress, which has for more than three hundred years furnished food for so many wild legends, seemed to Dantès like a scaffold to a malefactor.

"The Castle?" cried he. "You think, that I am to be imprisoned there?"

"It is probable; all the formalities have been gone through."

"In spite of M. de Villefort's promises?"——"I do not know what M. de Villefort promised you," said the gendarme, "but I know we are taking you to the Castle."

At this moment a violent shock made the barque tremble. One of the sailors leaped on shore, a cord creaked as it ran through a pulley, and Dantès guessed they were at the end of the voyage.

His guardians, taking hold of his arms, forced him to rise, and dragged him toward the steps that lead to the gate of the fortress, whilst the exempt followed, armed with a bayonet and rifle.

"Where is the prisoner?" said a voice.

"Let him follow me; I am going to conduct him to his cell."

"Go!" said the gendarmes, pushing Dantès.

The prisoner followed his conductor, who led him into a room almost under ground, whose bare and reeking walls seemed as though impregnated with tears; a lamp placed on a stool illumined the apartment faintly, and showed Dantès the features of his conductor, an under-jailer, ill-clothed, and of sullen appearance.

"Here is your chamber for to-night," said he. "It is late, and the governor is asleep. To-morrow, perhaps, he may change you. In the mean time there is bread, water, and fresh straw; and that is all a prisoner can wish for. Good-night." And before Dantès could open his mouth—before he had noticed where the jailer placed his bread or the water—before he had glanced toward the corner where the straw was, the jailer disappeared, taking with him the lamp.

With the first dawn the jailer returned, with orders to leave Dantès where he was. He found the prisoner in the same position, as if fixed there, his eyes swollen with weeping. He passed the night standing, and without sleep. The jailer advanced; Dantès appeared not to perceive him. He touched him on the shoulder, Edmond started.

"Have you not slept?" said the jailer.——"I do not know," replied Dantès.

"Do you wish for anything?"

"I wish to see the governor."

The jailer shrugged his shoulders and left.

Dantès followed him with his eyes, and stretched forth his hands toward the open door; but the door closed. All his emotion then burst forth; he cast himself on the ground, weeping bitterly, and asking himself what crime he had committed that he was thus punished.

The day passed thus; he scarcely tasted food, but walked round and round the cell like a wild beast in its cage.

The next morning the turnkey made his appearance.

"Well," said he, "are you more reasonable to-day?" Dantès made no reply.

"Come, take courage; do you want anything in my power to do for you?"

"I wish to see the governor."

"What you ask is impossible; but if you are very well behaved you will be allowed to walk about, and some day you will meet the governor; and if he chooses to reply, that is his affair."

"But," asked Dantès, "how long shall I have to wait?"

"Ah! a month—six months—a year."

"It is too long a time. I wish to see him at once."

"Ah," said the jailer, "do not always brood over what is impossible, or you will be mad in a fortnight. Yes: we have an instance here: it was by always offering a million of francs to the governor for his liberty that a priest became mad, who was in this chamber before you; he was put in a dungeon."

"Listen!" said Dantès. "I am not a priest or mad; perhaps I shall be, but at present, unfortunately, I am not. I do not offer you a million, because I have it not; but I will give you a hundred crowns if the first time you go to Marseilles, you will seek out a girl named Mercédès, at the Catalans, and give her two lines from me."

"If I took them, and were detected, I should lose my place, which is worth two thousand francs a year; so that I should be a great fool to run such a risk for three hundred."

"Well," said Dantès, "mark this; if you refuse at least to tell Mercédès I am here, I will some day hide myself behind the door, and when you enter, I will dash out your brains with this stool."

"Threats!" cried the jailer, retreating and putting himself on the defensive; "you are certainly going mad. The abbé began like you, and in three days you will want a strait-waistcoat; but, fortunately, there are dungeons here."

The jailer went out, and returned in an instant with a corporal and four soldiers.

"By the governor's orders," said he, "conduct the prisoner to the story beneath."

"To the dungeon?" said the corporal.

"Yes; we must put madmen with madmen." The soldiers seized Dantès, who followed passively.

He descended fifteen steps, and the door of a dungeon was opened, and he was thrust in. The door closed, and Dantès advanced with outstretched hands until he touched the wall; he then sat down in the corner until his eyes became accustomed to the darkness. The jailer was right; Dantès wanted but little of being utterly mad.

When the emperor returned, Noirtier saved his son, but his superior lost his official head. When the Restoration again followed Villefort had but to remind the king that he had traveled post-haste to tell him of the plot he had discovered through Dantès' letter and obtained post; he selected to be proctor at another place.

He was still at Marseilles, its leading legal functionary, when one morning his door opened, and M. Morrel was announced.

He came for advice about the imprisonment of Dantès, and the magistrate suggested a petition. As this was strongly in favor of the mate as a Bonapartist, he did not send it off to headquarters but retained it in case the tables should be turned again.

Dantès remained a prisoner, and heard not the noise of the fall of Louis XVIII.'s throne.

Twice during the Hundred Days had Morrel renewed his demand, and twice had Villefort soothed him with promises. At last there was Waterloo, and Morrel came no more: he had done all that was in his power, and any fresh attempt would only compromise himself uselessly.

Louis XVIII. remounted the throne, Villefort demanded and obtained office at Toulouse, and a fortnight afterwards married Renée.

Danglars comprehended the full extent of the wretched fate that overwhelmed Dantès and like all men of small abilities, he termed this a decree of Providence. But when Napoleon returned to Paris, Danglars' heart failed him, and he feared at every instant to behold Dantès eager for vengeance: he therefore informed M. Morrel of his wish to quit the sea, and obtained a recommendation from him to a Spanish merchant, into whose service he entered at the end of March, that is, ten or twelve days after Napoleon's return. He then left for Madrid, and was no more heard of.

Fernand understood nothing except that Dantès was absent. What had become of him he cared not to inquire. Only, during the respite the absence of his rival afforded him, he reflected, partly on the means of deceiving Mercédès as to the cause of his absence, partly on plans of emigration and abduction, as from time to time he sat sad and motionless on the summit of Cape Pharo, at the spot from whence Marseilles and the village des Catalans are visible, watching for the apparition of a young and handsome man, who was for him also the messenger of vengeance. Fernand's mind was made up: he would shoot Dantès, and then kill himself. But Fernand was mistaken; a man of his disposition never kills himself, for he constantly hopes.

During this time the empire made a last appeal, and every man in France capable of bearing arms rushed to obey the summons of their emperor. Fernand departed with the rest, bearing with him the terrible thought that perhaps his rival was behind him, and would marry Mercédès. Had Fernand really meant to kill himself, he would have done so when he parted from Mercédès. His devotion, and the compassion he showed for her misfortunes, produced the effect they always produce on noble minds—Mercédès had always had a sincere regard for Fernand, and this was now strengthened by gratitude.

"My brother," said she, as she placed his knapsack on his shoulders, "be careful of yourself, for if you are killed, I shall be alone in the world." These words infused a ray of hope into Fernand's heart. Should Dantès not return, Mercédès might one day be his. Mercédès was left alone to gaze on this vast plain that had never seemed so barren, and the sea that had never seemed so vast.

Caderousse was, like Fernand, enrolled in the army, but, being married and eight years older, he was merely sent to the frontier. Old Dantès who was only sustained by hope, lost all hope at Napoleon's downfall. Five months after he had been separated from his son, and almost at the very hour at which he was arrested, he breathed his last in Mercédès' arms. M. Morrel paid the expenses of his funeral and a few small debts the poor old man had contracted.

There was more than benevolence in this action; there was courage; for to assist, even on his death-bed, the father of so dangerous a Bonapartist as Dantès, was stigmatized as a crime.

CHAPTER VII.

ANOTHER PRISONER

A YEAR after Louis XVIII.'s restoration, a visit was made by the inspector general of prisons. Dantès heard from the recesses of his cell the noises made by the preparations for receiving him. He guessed something uncommon was passing among the living; but he had so long ceased to have any intercourse with the world, that he looked upon himself as dead.

The inspector visited the cells and dungeons, one after another.

At last, they descended stairs so foul, so humid, so dark, that the very sight effected the eyes, the smell, and the respiration.

"Oh!" cried the inspector, "who can live here?"

"A most dangerous conspirator, a man we are ordered to keep the most strict watch over, as he is daring and resolute. He attempted to kill the turnkey; the very one who is lighting us. Is it not true, Antoine?" asked the governor.

"True enough; he wanted to kill me!" replied the turnkey.

"He must be mad," said the inspector.

"He is worse than that,—he is a devil!" returned the turnkey.

"Shall I complain of him?" demanded the inspector.

"Oh, no; it is useless. Besides he is almost mad now, and in another year he will be quite so."

"So much the better for him,—he will suffer less," said the inspector. He was, as this remark shows, a man full of philanthropy, and in every way fit for his office.

"You are right, sir," replied the governor; "and this remark proves that you have deeply considered the subject. Now we have in a dungeon about twenty feet distant, and to which you descend by another stair, an abbé, ancient leader of a party in Italy, who has been here since 1811, and in 1813 he went mad, and the change is astonishing. He used to weep, he now laughs; he grew thin, he now grows fat. You had better see him, for his madness is amusing."

"I will see them both," returned the inspector; "I must conscientiously perform my duty." This was the inspector's first visit: he wished to display his authority.

At the sound of the key turning in the lock, and the creaking of the hinges, Dantès, who was crouched in a corner of the dungeon, raised his head. At the sight of a stranger, lighted by two turnkeys, accompanied by two soldiers, and to whom the governor spoke bareheaded, Dantès, who guessed the truth, and that the moment to address himself to the superior authorities was come, sprang forward with clasped hands.

The soldiers presented their bayonets, for they thought he was about to attack the inspector, and the latter recoiled two or three steps. Dantès saw he was represented as a dangerous prisoner. Then infusing all the humility he possessed into his eyes and voice, he addressed the inspector, and sought to inspire him with pity.

The inspector listened attentively; then, turning to the governor, observed, "He will become religious—he is already more gentle; he is afraid, and retreated before the bayonets—madmen are not afraid of anything; I made some curious observation on this at Charenton madhouse." Then, turning to the prisoner, he asked, "What do you demand?"

"What crime I have committed—to be tried; and if I am guilty, may be shot; if innocent, I may be set at liberty."

"Are you well fed?" said the inspector.

"I believe so—I know not, but that matters little; what matters really, not only to me, but to everyone, is, that an innocent man should languish in prison, the victim of an infamous denunciation."

"We shall see," said the inspector; then turning to the governor, "On my word, the poor devil touches me. You must show me the proofs against him."

"Certainly; but you will find terrible notes against him."

"Monsieur," continued Dantès, "I know it is not in your power to release me; but you can plead for me—you can have me tried—and that is all I ask. Tell me at least to hope."

"I cannot tell you that," replied the inspector; "I can only promise to examine into your case. Who arrested you?"

"M. Villefort. See him, and hear what he says."

"M. Villefort is no longer at Marseilles; he is now at Toulouse."

"I am no longer surprised at my detention," murmured Dantès, "since my only protector is removed."

"Had M. de Villefort any cause of personal dislike to you?"

"None; on the contrary, he was very kind to me."

"I can, then, rely on the notes he has left concerning you?"—"Entirely."

"That is well; wait patiently, then." Dantès fell on his knees, and prayed earnestly. The door closed; but this time a fresh inmate was left with Dantès—Hope.

"Will you see the register at once," asked the governor, "or proceed to the other cell?"

"What is his craze?"

"He fancies he possesses an immense treasure. The first year he offered government a million of francs for his release; the second, two; the third, three; and so on progressively. He is now in his fifth year of captivity; he will ask to speak to you in private, and offer you five millions."

"How curious!—what is his name?"——"Abbé Faria."

"No. 27," said the inspector.

"It is here; unlock the door, Antoïne." The turnkey obeyed, and the inspector gazed curiously into the cell of the Mad Priest.

In the centre of the cell, in a circle traced with a fragment of plaster detached from the wall, sat a man whose tattered garments scarcely covered him. He was drawing in this circle geometrical lines, and seemed absorbed in his problem.

He did not move at the sound of the door, and continued his problem until the flash of the torches lighted up with an unwonted glare the sombre walls of his cell; then, raising his head, he perceived with astonishment the number of persons in his cell. He hastily seized the coverlid of his bed, and wrapped it round him.

"What do you demand?" said the inspector.

"I!" replied the abbé, with an air of surprise—"I demand nothing."

"You do not understand," continued the inspector; "I am sent here by government to visit, and hear the requests of the prisoners."

"Oh, that is different," cried the abbé; "and we shall understand each other, I hope."

"There now," whispered the governor, "it is just as I told you."

"Sir," continued the prisoner, "I am the Abbé Faria, born at Rome. I was for twenty years Cardinal Spada's secretary; I was arrested, why I know not, in 1811; since then I have demanded my liberty from the Italian and French government."

"Why from the French government?"

"Because I was arrested at Piombino; and I presume that, like Milan and Florence, Piombino has become the capital of some French department.

"Ah!" said the inspector, "you have not the latest intelligence from Italy."

"They date from the day on which I was arrested," returned Faria; "and as the emperor had created the kingdom of Rome for his infant son, I presume that he has realized the dream of Machiavel and Caesar Borgia, which was to make Italy one vast kingdom."

"Sir," returned the inspector, "Providence has changed this gigantic plan you advocate so warmly."

"It is the only means of rendering Italy happy and independent."

"Very possibly; only I am not come to discuss politics, but to inquire if you have anything to ask or to complain of."

"The food is the same as in other prisons,—that is, very bad; the lodging is very unwholesome, but, on the whole, passable for a dungeon; but it is not that which I speak of, but a secret I have to reveal of the greatest importance."

"We are coming to the point," whispered the governor.

"It is for that reason I am delighted to see you," continued the priest, "although you have disturbed me in a most important calculation, which, if it succeeded, would possibly change Newton's system. Could you allow me a few words in private? I would speak to you of a large sum, amounting to five millions."

"The very sum you named," whispered, in his turn, the inspector.

"However," continued Faria, perceiving the inspector was about to depart, "it is not absolutely necessary we should be alone; the governor can be present."

"Unfortunately," said the governor, "I know beforehand what you are about to say; it concerns your treasures, does it not?" Faria fixed his eyes on him with an expression that would have convinced any one else of his sanity.

"The government does not want your treasures," replied the inspector;

"keep them until you are liberated." The Abbé's eyes glistened; he seized the inspector's hand.

"But what if I am not liberated," cried he, "and am detained here until my death? Had not government better profit by it? I will offer six millions, and I will content myself with the rest."

"On my word," said the inspector, in a low tone, "had I not been told beforehand this man was mad, I should believe what he says."

"I am not mad!" replied Faria, with that acuteness of hearing peculiar to prisoners. "The treasure I speak of really exists; and I offer to sign a treaty with you, in which I promise to lead you to the spot you shall dig; and if I deceive you, bring me here again,—I ask no more."

The governor laughed. "Is the spot far from here?"——"A hundred leagues."

"It is not a bad idea," said the governor.

"If every prisoner took it into his head to travel a hundred leagues, and their guardians consented to accompany them, they would have a capital chance of escaping."

"The scheme is well known," said the governor; "and the reverend has not even the merit of its invention. I inquired if you are well fed?"

"Monsieur, you run no risk, for, I will stay here; so there is no chance of my escaping."

"You do not reply to my question," replied the inspector, impatiently.

"Nor you to mine," cried the abbé. "You will not accept my gold; I will keep it for myself. You refuse me my liberty; God will give it me." And, casting away his coverlid, the priest resumed his place, and continued his calculations.

"What is he doing there?" said the inspector.

"Counting up his treasures," replied the governor.

Fara replied to this sarcasm by a glance of profound contempt.

Thus finished the adventure of the Abbé Faria. He remained in his cell, and this visit only increased the belief of his insanity.

The inspector kept his word with Dantès; he examined the register, and found the following note concerning him:—

EDMOND DANTES. { Violent Bonapartist; took an active part in the Return from Alba.
The greatest watchfulness and care to be exercised.

This note was in a different hand from the rest, which proved it had been added since his confinement. The inspector could not contend against this accusation; he simply wrote,—"Nothing to be done."

This visit had infused new vigor into Dantès; he had, till then, forgotten the date; but now, with a fragment of plaster, he wrote the date, 30th July, 1816; and made a mark every day, in order not to lose his reckoning again. Days and weeks passed away, then months,—Dantès still waited; he at first expected to be freed in a fortnight. This fortnight expired; he reflected the inspector would do nothing until his return to Paris; and that he would not reach there until his circuit was finished; he therefore fixed three months: three months passed away, then six more. During these ten months no favorable change had taken place; and Dantès began to fancy the inspector's visit was but a dream, an illusion of the brain.

At the expiration of a year the governor was changed; he had obtained the government of Ham. He took with him several of his subordinates, and amongst them Dantès' jailer. A fresh governor arrived: it would have been too tedious to acquire the names of the prisoners, he learned their numbers instead. This horrible place consisted of fifty chambers; their inhabitants were designated by the number of their chamber; and the unhappy young man was no longer called Edmond Dantès,—he was now number 34.

He commenced with pride, a natural consequence of hope and a consciousness of innocence; then he began to doubt his own innocence, which justified in some measure the governor's belief in his mental alienation. Having exhausted all human resources, he turned to God.

Spite of his earnest prayers, Dantès remained a prisoner.

Then a gloomy feeling took possession of him.

Rage succeeded to this. Dantès uttered blasphemies that made his jailer recoil with horror, dashed himself furiously against the walls of his prison, attacked everything, and chiefly himself, and the least thing —a grain of sand, a straw, or a breath of air that annoyed him. Then the letter he had seen that Villefort had showed to him recurred to his mind, and every line seemed visible in fiery letters on the wall. He said that it was the vengeance of man, and not of Heaven, that had thus plunged him into the deepest misery. He devoted these unknown persecutors to the most horrible tortures he could imagine, and found them all insufficient, because after torture came death, and after death, if not repose, at least that insensibility that resembles it.

By dint of constantly dwelling on the idea that repose was death, and, in order to punish, other tortures than death must be invented, he began to reflect on suicide.

He chose starvation and persisted in this course till he had barely strength enough to throw his food out of window, to resist temptation. He was lying on the borderland of that shrouded country known as Death when, at nine o'clock, he heard a noise in the wall. It lasted nearly three hours; he then heard a noise of something falling, and all was silent.

Some hours afterward, it began nearer and more distinct; Edmond became already interested in that labor, when the jailer entered.

For a week that he had resolved to die, and for four days that he put this resolution into execution, Edmond had not spoken to this man, had not answered him when he inquired what was the matter with him, and turned his face to the wall when he looked too curiously at him; but now the jailer might hear this noise and put an end to it, thus destroying a ray of something like hope that soothed his last moments.

The jailer brought him his breakfast. Dantès raised himself up, and began to speak on everything: on the bad quality of his food, on the coldness of his dungeon, grumbling and complaining, in order to have an excuse for speaking louder, and wearying the patience of his jailer, who had solicited broth and white bread for his prisoner, and who had brought it.

Fortunately he fancied Dantès was delirious; and placing his food on the rickety table, he withdrew. Edmond listened, and the sound became more and more distinct.

He turned his eyes toward the soup his jailer had brought him, rose, staggered towards it, raised the vessel to his lips and drank off the contents with a feeling of indescribable pleasure. He had often heard that shipwrecked persons had died through having eagerly devoured too much food; Edmond replaced on the table the bread he was about to devour, and returned to his couch—he did not wish to die. He soon felt that his ideas became again collected—he could think, and strengthen his thoughts by reasoning. Then he said to himself, "I must put this to the test, but without compromising anybody. If it is a workman, I need but knock against the wall, and he will cease to work, in order to find out who is knocking, and why he does so; but as his occupation is sanctioned by the governor, he will soon resume it. If, on the contrary, it is a prisoner, the noise I make will alarm him, he will cease, and not recommence until he thinks every one is asleep."

Dantès rose again, but this time his legs did not tremble, and his eyes were free from mists; he advanced to a corner of his dungeon, detached a stone, and with it knocked against the wall where the sound came. He struck thrice. At the first blow the sound ceased, as if by magic.

Edmond listened intently; an hour passed, two hours passed, and no sound was heard from the wall—all was silent there.

Full of hope, Dantès swallowed a few mouthfuls of bread and water, and, thanks to the excellence of his constitution, found himself wellnigh recovered.

The day passed away in utter silence—night came without the noise having recommenced.

"It is a prisoner," said Edmond joyfully. The night passed in perfect silence. He did not close his eyes.

In the morning the jailer brought him fresh provisions—he had already devoured those of the previous day; he ate these, listening anxiously for the sound, walking round and round his cell, shaking the iron bars of the loophole, restoring by exercise vigor and agility to his limbs, and preparing himself thus for his future destiny. At intervals he listened if the noise had not begun again, and grew impatient at the prudence of the prisoner, who did not guess he had been disturbed by a captive as anxious for liberty as himself.

Three days passed—seventy-two long tedious hours!

At length one evening, as the jailer was visiting him for the last time that night, Dantès fancied he heard an almost imperceptible movement among the stones. Edmond recoiled from the wall, walked up and down his cell to collect his thoughts, and replaced his ear against the wall.

There could be no doubt something was passing on the other side; the prisoner had discovered the danger, and had substituted the lever for the chisel.

Encouraged by this discovery, Dantès determined to assist the indefatigable laborer. He began by moving his bed, and sought with his eyes anything with which he could pierce the wall, penetrate the cement, and displace a stone.

He saw nothing, he had no knife or sharp instrument, the grating of his window alone was of iron, and he had too often assured himself of its solidity. All his furniture consisted of a bed, a chair, a table, a pail, and a jug. The bed had iron clamps, but they were screwed to the wood, and it would have required a screwdriver to take them off. The table and chair had nothing, the pail had had a handle removed.

Dantès had but one resource, which was to break the jug, and with one of the sharp fragments attack the wall. He let the jug fall on the floor, and it broke in pieces.

Dantès concealed two or three of the sharpest fragments in his bed, leaving the rest on the floor. The breaking of his jug was too natural an accident to excite suspicion. Edmond had all the night to work in, but in the darkness he could not do much, and he soon felt his instrument was blunted against something hard; he pushed back his bed, and awaited the day.

All night he heard the subterranean workman, who continued to mine his way. The day came, the warden entered. Dantès told him the jug had fallen from his hands in drinking, and the jailer went grumblingly to fetch another, without giving himself the trouble to remove the fragments of the broken one. He returned speedily, recommended the prisoner to be more careful, and departed.

Edmond heard joyfully the key grate in the lock, he listened until the sound of steps died away, and then, hastily displacing his bed, saw by the faint light that penetrated into his cell, that he had labored uselessly the previous evening in attacking the stone instead of removing the plaster that surrounded it.

The damp had rendered it friable, and Dantès saw joyfully the plaster detach itself; in small morsels, it is true; but at the end of half an hour he had scraped off a handful: a mathematician might have calculated that in two years, supposing that the rock was not encountered, a passage, twenty feet long and two feet broad, might be formed.

The prisoner reproached himself with not having thus employed the hours he had passed in prayers and despair. In six years (the space he had been confined) what might he not have accomplished?

In three days he had succeeded, with the utmost precaution, in removing the cement, and exposing the stone; the wall was formed of rough stones, to give solidity to which were embedded, at intervals, blocks of hewn stone. It was one of these he had uncovered, and which he must remove from its sockets.

Dantès strove to do so with his nails, but they were too weak. The fragments of the jug broke, and after an hour of useless toil, he paused.

Was he to be thus stopped at the beginning, and was he to wait inactive until his fellow-workman had completed his toils? Suddenly an idea occurred to him,—he smiled, and the perspiration dried on his forehead.

The turnkey always brought Dantès' soup in an iron saucepan: this saucepan contained the soup of a second prisoner; for Dantès had remarked that it was either quite full, or half empty, according as the turnkey gave it to himself or his companion first.

The handle of this saucepan was of iron; Dantès would have given ten years of his life in exchange for it.

The jailer poured the contents of this saucepan into Dantès' plate, who after eating his soup with a wooden spoon, washed the plate, which thus served for every day. In the evening Dantès placed his plate on the ground near the door; the jailer as he entered, stepped on it and broke it.

This time he could not blame Dantès. He was wrong to leave it there, but the man was wrong not to have looked before him.

The warden, therefore, contented himself with grumbling. Then he looked about him for something to pour the soup into; Dantès' whole furniture consisted of one plate—there was no alternative.

"Leave the saucepan," said Dantès; "you can take it away when you bring me my breakfast." This advice was to the man's taste, as it spared him the necessity of ascending, descending, and ascending again. He left the saucepan.

Dantès was beside himself with joy. He rapidly devoured his food, and after waiting an hour, lest the jailer should change his mind and return, he removed his bed, took the handle of the saucepan, inserted the point between the hewn stone and rough stones of the wall, and employed it as a lever. A slight oscillation showed Dantès all went well.

At the end of an hour the stone was extricated from the wall, leaving a cavity of a foot and a half in diameter.

Dantès carefully collected the plaster, carried it into the corners of his cell, and covered it with earth. Then, wishing to make the best use of this night, in which chance, or rather his own strategem, had placed so precious an instrument in his hands, he continued to work without ceasing. At the dawn of day he replaced the stone, pushed his bed against the wall and lay down. The breakfast consisted of a piece of bread: the jailer entered and placed the bread on the table.

"Well, you do not bring me another plate," said Dantès.

"No," replied the turnkey, "you destroy everything. First you break your jug, then you make me break your plate; if all the prisoners followed your example, the government would be ruined. I shall leave you the saucepan, and pour your soup into that. So for the future I hope you will not be so destructive to your furniture."

Dantès raised his eyes to heaven, clasped his hands beneath the coverlid, and prayed. He felt more gratitude for the possession of this piece of iron than he had ever felt for anything. He had, however, remarked that the prisoner on the other side had ceased to labor; no matter, this was a greater reason for proceeding—if his neighbor would not come to him, he would go to him. All day he toiled on untiringly, and by the evening he had succeeded in extracting ten handfuls of plaster and fragments of stone. When the hour for his jailer's visit arrived, Dantès straightened the handle of the saucepan as well as he could, and placed it in its accustomed place. The man poured his ration of soup into it, together with the fish, for thrice a week the prisoners were made to abstain from meat: this would have been a method of reckoning time, had not Dantès long ceased to do so. Having poured out the soup, the warden retired. Dantès wished to ascertain whether his neighbor had really ceased to work. He listened—all was silent, as it had been for the last three days. Dantès sighed; it was evident that his neighbor distrusted him. However, he toiled on all the night without being discouraged; but after two or three hours he encountered an obstacle. The iron made no impression, but met with a smooth surface, Dantès touched it, and found it was a beam. This beam crossed, or rather blocked up, the hole Dantès had made; it was necessary, therefore, to dig above or under it. The unhappy young man had not thought of this. "Oh, my God!" murmured he, "I have so earnestly prayed to you, that I hoped my prayers had been heard. After having deprived me of my liberty, after having deprived me of death, after having recalled me to existence, my God! have pity on me, and do not let me die in despair."

"Who talks of God and despair at the same time?" said a voice that seemed to come from beneath the earth, and, deadened by the distance, sounded hollow and sepulchral in the young man's ears. Edmond's hair stood on end, and he rose on his knees.

"Ah!" said he, "I hear a human voice." Edmond had not heard any one speak save his jailer for four or five years; and a jailer is a man to a prisoner—he is a living door added to his door of oak, a barrier of flesh and blood added to his barriers of iron.

CHAPTER VIII.

THE CRAZY PRIEST.

"In the name of heaven," cried Dantès, "speak again, though the sound of your voice terrifies me."

"Who are you?" said the voice.

"An unhappy prisoner," replied Dantès, who made no hesitation in answering. Edmond Dantès, a French seaman."

"How long have you been here?"——"Since the 28th of February, 1815."

"Your crime?"——"I am innocent."

"But of what are you accused?"

"Of having conspired to aid the emperor's return."

"How, for the emperor's return?—is the emperor no longer on the throne?"

"He abdicated at Fontainebleau in 1814, and was sent to the island of Elba. But how long have you been here that you are ignorant of all this?"

"Since 1811."

Dantès shuddered: this man had been four years longer than himself in prison.

"Do not dig any more," said the voice; "only tell me how high up is your excavation?"——"On a level with the floor, behind my bed."

"What does your chamber open on?"——"A corridor and that on a yard."

"Alas!" murmured the voice.

"Oh, what is the matter?" cried Dantès.

"I am deceived, and the imperfection of my plans has ruined all. An error of a line in the plan has been equivalent to fifteen feet in reality, and I took the wall you are mining for the wall of the fortress."

"But then you were close to the sea?"——"That is what I hoped. I should have thrown myself into the sea, gained one of the islands near here—Daume or Tiboulen—and then I was safe."

"Could you have swum so far?"——"Heaven would have given me strength; but now all is lost."

"All?"——"Yes; stop up your excavation carefully: do not work any more, and wait until you hear from me."

"Tell me, at least, who you are!"——"I am—I am No. 27."

"You mistrust me, then," said Dantès. Edmond fancied he heard a bitter laugh proceed from the unknown.

"Oh, I am a Christian," cried Dantès, guessing instinctively that this man meant to abandon him. "I swear to you by Him who died for us that nought shall induce me to breathe one syllable to my jailer; but I conjure you do not abandon me. If you do, I swear to you that I will dash my brains out against the wall, and you will have my death to reproach yourself with."

"How old are you? Your voice is of a young man's."

"I do not know my age, for I have not counted the years I have been here. All I do know is, that I was just nineteen when I was arrested, the 28th of February, 1815."

"Not quite twenty-six!" murmured the voice; "at that age he cannot be a traitor."

"Oh! no, no!" cried Dantès. "I swear to you again, rather than betray you they shall hew me to pieces!"

"You have done well to speak to me, and entreat me, for I was about to form another plan, and leave you; but your age reassures me. I will not forget you. Expect me, I will give you the signal."

"But you will not leave me; you will come to me, or you will let me come to you. We will escape, and if we cannot escape we will talk; you of those whom you love, and I of those whom I love. You must love somebody?"

"No, I am alone in the world."

"Then you will love me. If you are young, I will be your comrade; if you are old, I will be your son. I have a father who is seventy if he yet lives; I only love him and a girl called Mercédès. My father has not yet forgotten me, I am sure; but God alone knows if she loves me still; I shall love you as I loved my father."

"It is well," returned the voice; "to-morrow."

These few words were uttered with an accent that left no doubt of his sincerity; Dantès rose, dispersed the fragments with the same precaution as before, and pushed back his bed against the wall. He then gave himself up to his happiness; he would no longer be alone. He was, perhaps, about to regain his liberty; at the worst, he would have a companion; and captivity shared is but half captivity.

All day Dantès walked up and down his cell.

The jailer came in the evening: Dantès was on his bed. It seemed to him that thus he better guarded the unfinished opening. Doubtless there was a strange expression in his eyes, for the man said, "Come, are you going mad again?"

Dantès did not answer: he feared that the emotion in his voice would betray him. The jailer retired, shaking his head. The night came; Dantès hoped that his neighbor would profit by the silence to address him, but he was mistaken. The next morning, however, just as he removed his bed from the wall, he heard three knocks; he threw himself on his knees.

"Is it you?" said he, "I am here."

"Is your jailer gone?"

"Yes," said Dantès; "he will not return until the evening; so that we have twelve hours before us."

"I can work, then," said the voice.

"Oh yes, yes, without delay, I entreat you."

In an instant the portion of the floor on which Dantès (half buried in the opening) was leaning his hands, gave way; he cast himself back, whilst a mass of stones and earth disappeared in a hole that opened beneath the aperture he himself had formed. Then from the bottom of this passage, the depth of which it was impossible to measure, he saw appear, first the head, then the shoulders, and lastly the body of a man, who sprang lightly into his cell.

CHAPTER IX

A LEARNED ITALIAN.

Rushing toward the friend so long and ardently desired, Dantès almost carried him toward the window, in order to obtain a better view of his features by the aid of the imperfect light that struggled through the grating of the prison.

He was a man of small stature, with hair blanched rather by suffering and sorrow than years. A deep-set, penetrating eye, almost buried beneath the thick grey eyebrow, and a long (and still black) beard reaching down to his breast.

The stranger might have numbered sixty, or sixty-five years; but briskness and vigor in his movements made it probable that he was aged more from captivity than the course of time. He received the enthusiastic greeting of his young acquaintance with evident pleasure, as though his chilled affections seemed rekindled and invigorated by his contact with one so warm and ardent. He thanked him with grateful cordiality for his kindly welcome, although he must at that moment have been suffering bitterly to find another dungeon where he had fondly reckoned on discovering a means of regaining his liberty.

"Let us first see," said he, "whether it is possible to remove the traces of my entrance here—our future comforts depend upon our keepers being entirely ignorant of it." Advancing to the opening, he stooped and raised the stone as easily as though it had not weighed an ounce; then, fitting it into its place, he said:

"You removed this stone very carelessly; but I suppose you had no tools to aid you."

"Why," exclaimed Dantès, with astonishment, "do you possess any?"

"I made myself some; and with the exception of a file, I have all that are necessary—a chisel, pincers, and lever."

"Oh, how I should like to see these products of your industry and patience."

"Well, in the first place, here is my chisel." So saying, he displayed a sharp strong blade, with a handle made of beechwood.

"And with what did you contrive to make that?" inquired Dantès.

"With one of the clamps of my bedstead; and this very tool has sufficed me to hollow out the road by which I came hither, a distance of at least fifty feet. My labor is all in vain, for I find that the corridor looks into a courtyard filled with soldiers."

"That's true," said Dantès; "but the corridor you speak of only bounds *one* side of my cell; there are three others—do you know anything of their situation?"

"This one is built against the solid rock, and it would take ten experienced miners, duly furnished with the requisite tools, as many years to perforate it. This adjoins the lower part of the governor's apartments, and were we to work our way through, we should only get into some lock-up cellars, where we must necessarily be recaptured. The fourth and last side of your cell looks out—looks out—stop a minute, now where does it open to?"

The side which thus excited curiosity was the one in which was fixed the loophole by which the light was admitted into the chamber. This loophole, which gradually diminished as it approached the outside, until only an opening through which a child could not have passed, was, for better security, furnished with three iron bars, so as to quiet all apprehensions even in the mind of the most suspicious jailer as to the possibility of a prisoner's escape. As the stranger finished his self-put question, he dragged the table beneath the window.

"Climb up," said he to Dantès. The young man obeyed, mounted on the table, and, divining the intentions of his companion, placed his back securely against the wall and held out both hands. The stranger, whom as yet Dantès knew only by his assumed title of the number of his cell, sprang up with an agility by no means to be expected in a person of his years, and, light and steady as the bound of a cat or a lizard, climbed from the table to the outstretched hands of Dantès, and from them to his shoulders; then, almost doubling himself in two, for the ceiling of the dungeon prevented his holding himself erect, he managed to slip his head through the top bar of the window, so as to be able to command a perfect view from top to bottom.

An instant afterwards he hastily drew back his head, saying, "I thought so!" and sliding from the shoulders of Dantès as dexterously as he had ascended, he nimbly leapt from the table to the ground.

"This side of your chamber looks out upon a kind of open gallery, where patrols are continually passing, and sentries keep watch day and night. I saw the soldier's shako and the top of his musket; that made me draw in my head so quickly; for I was fearful he might also see me. You perceive the utter impossibility of escaping through your dungeon? the will of God be done!" and as the old man slowly pronounced those words, an air of profound resignation spread itself over his care-worn countenance. Dantès gazed on the individual who could thus philo-sophically resign hopes so long and ardently nourished with an astonishment mingled with admiration.

"Tell me, I entreat of you, who and what you are?" said he at length; "never have I met with so remarkable a person as yourself."

The stranger smiled a melancholy smile. "Then listen," said he. "I am the Abbé Faria, and have been imprisoned in this castle since the year 1811; previously to which I had been confined for three years in the fortress of Fenestrelle. In the year 1811 I was transferred to Piedmont in France. It was at this period I learned that the destiny which seemed subservient to every wish formed by Napoleon, had bestowed on him a son, named king of Rome even in his cradle. I was very far then from expecting the change you have just informed me of; namely, that four years afterwards, this colossus of power would be overthrown. Then who reigns in France at this moment—Napoleon II.?"

"No, Louis XVIII.!"

"The brother of Louis XVI.! How inscrutable are the ways of Providence—for what great and mysterious purpose has it pleased Heaven to abase the man once so elevated, and raise up the individual so beaten down and depressed?"

Dantès' whole attention was riveted on a man who could thus forget his own misfortunes while occupying himself with the destinies of others.

"But so it was," continued he, "in England. After Charles I. came Cromwell; to Cromwell succeeded Charles II., and then James II., who was succeeded by some son-in-law or relation. Ah, my friend!" said the abbé, turning towards Dantès, and surveying him with the kindling gaze of a prophet, "these are the changes and vicissitudes that give liberty to a nation. Mark what I say! You are young, and may see my words come to pass, that such will be the case with France—you will see it. I say."

"Probably, if ever I get out of prison!"

"True," replied Faria, "we are prisoners; but I forget this sometimes, and there are even moments when my mental vision transports me beyond these walls, and I fancy myself at liberty."

"But wherefore are you here?"

"Because in 1807 I meditated the very scheme Napoleon wished to realize in 1811. Italy seems fated to be unlucky." The old man uttered these last words in a tone of deep dejection, and his head fell listlessly on his breast.

To Dantès all this was perfectly incomprehensible.

"Pray excuse my question," said he, beginning to partake of the jailer's opinion touching the state of the priest's brain, "but are you not the priest who is considered throughout the castle—to—be—queer?"

"Mad, you mean, don't you?"

"I did not like to say so," answered Dantès smiling.

"Well, then," resumed Faria, with a bitter smile, "let me answer your question in full, by acknowledging that I am the poor mad prisoner for many years permitted to amuse the different visitants to the prison with what is said to be my insanity; and, in all probability, I should be promoted to the honor of making sport for the children, if such innocent beings could be found in an abode devoted like this to suffering and despair."

Dantès remained for a short time mute and motionless; at length he said,—"Then you abandon all hope of flight?"

"I perceive its utter impossibility; and I consider it impious to attempt that which the Almighty evidently does not approve."

Dantès held down his head, that his companion might not perceive how little of real regret at the failure of the scheme was expressed on his countenance; but in truth, the young man could entertain no other feeling than delight at finding his prison would be no longer solitary or uncheered by human participation.

The abbé sunk upon Edmond's bed, while Edmond himself remained standing, lost in a train of deep meditation.

After some time, the young man suddenly exclaimed, "I have found what you were in search of! I will tell you what we must do. We must pierce through the corridor by forming a side opening about the middle, as it were the top part of a cross. This time you will lay your plans more accurately; we shall get out into the gallery you have described; kill the sentinel who guards it, and make our escape. All we require to insure success is courage, and that you possess, and strength, which I am not deficient in; as for patience, you have abundantly proved yours—you shall now see me prove mine."

"One instant, my dear friend," replied the abbé; "I have thought it no sin to bore through a wall, or destroy a staircase; but I cannot so easily persuade myself to pierce a heart or take away a life." A slight start of surprise escaped Dantès.

"Is it possible," said he, "that where your liberty is at stake you can allow any such scruple to deter you from obtaining it?"

"Tell me," replied Faria, "what has hindered you from knocking down your jailer with a piece of wood torn from your bedstead, dressing yourself in his clothes, and endeavoring to escape?"

"Simply that I never thought of such a scheme," answered Dantès.

"Because," said the old man, "the natural repugnance to the commission of such a crime prevented its bare idea from occurring to you; and so it ever is with all simple and allowable things. Our natural instincts keep us from deviating from the strict line of duty."

Dantès remained confused and silent by this explanation of the thoughts which had unconsciously been working in his mind, or rather soul; for there are two distinct sorts of ideas, those that proceed from the head and those from the heart.

"Since my imprisonment," said Faria, "I have thought over all the most celebrated cases of escape recorded. Among the many that have failed in obtaining the ultimate release of the prisoner, I consider there has been a precipitation—a haste wholly incompatible with such undertakings. I have come to the conclusion, that chance frequently affords opportunities we should never ourselves have thought of. Let us, therefore, wait patiently for some favorable moment; rely upon it, you will not find me more backward than yourself in seizing it."

"Ah!" said Dantès, "you might well endure the tedious delay; you were constantly employed in the task you set yourself, and when weary with toil, you had your hopes to refresh and encourage you."

"I assure you," replied the old man, "I did not turn to that source for recreation or support."

"What did you do then?"——"I wrote or studied."

"Were you then permitted the use of pens, ink, and paper?"

"Oh, no!" answered the abbé; "I had none but what I made for myself."

Dantès gazed with kindling eyes and rapidly increasing admiration on the wonderful being whose hand seemed a magician's wand; some doubt, however, still lingered in his mind, which was quickly perceived by the penetrating eye.

"When you pay me a visit in my cell, my young friend," said he, "I will show you an entire work, the fruits of the thoughts and reflections of my whole life. The work I speak of is called 'On the Practicability of forming Italy into one General Monarchy,' and will make one large quarto volume."

"And on what have you written all this?"

"On two of my shirts. I invented a preparation that makes linen as smooth and as easy to write on as parchment."

"But for such a work you must have needed books—had you any?"

"I possessed nearly 5,000 volumes in my library at Rome; but after reading them over many times, I found out that with 150 well-chosen books a man possesses a complete analysis of all human knowledge, or at least all that is either useful or desirable to be acquainted with. I devoted three years of my life to reading and studying these 150 volumes, till I knew them nearly by heart; so that since I have been in prison, a very slight effort of memory has enabled me to recall their contents as readily as though the pages were open before me."

"You are, doubtless, acquainted with a variety of languages, so as to have been able to read all these?"

"Yes, I speak five of the modern tongues—, German, French, Italian, English, and Spanish; by the aid of ancient Greek I learned modern Greek—I don't speak it so well as I could wish, but I am still trying to improve myself."

"Improve yourself!" repeated Dantès; "why, how can you manage to do so?"

"Why, I made a vocabulary of the words I knew; turned, returned and arranged them, so as to enable me to express my thoughts through their medium. I know nearly one thousand words, which is all that is absolutely necessary, although I believe there are nearly one hundred thousand in the dictionaries. I cannot hope to be very fluent, but I certainly should have no difficulty in explaining my wants and wishes; and that would be quite as much as I should ever require."

Stronger grew the wonder of Dantès, who almost fancied he had to do with one gifted with supernatural powers; still hoping to find some imperfection which might bring him down to a level with human beings, he added, "Then if you were not furnished with pens, how did you manage to write the work you speak of?"

"I made myself some excellent ones, which would be universally preferred to all others if once known. You are aware what huge whitings are served to us on fast days. Well, I selected the cartilages of the heads, and you can scarcely imagine the delight with which I welcomed the arrival of each day, affording me the means of increasing my stock of pens; for I will freely confess that my historical labors have been my greatest solace and relief. While retracing the past, I forget the present; and while following the free and independent course of historical record, I cease to remember that I am myself immured within the gloomy walls of a dungeon."

"But the ink requisite for copying down your ideas," said Dantès, "how have you procured that?"

"I will tell you," replied Faria. "There was formerly a fireplace in my dungeon, but closed up long ere I became an occupant of this prison. Still, it must have been many years in use, for it was thickly covered with a coating of soot: this soot I dissolved in a portion of the wine brought to me every Sunday, and I assure you a better ink cannot be desired. For very important notes, for which closer attention is required, I have pricked one of my fingers, and written the facts claiming notice in blood."

"And when," asked Dantès, "will you show me all this?"

"Whenever you please," replied the abbé.

"Oh, then let it be directly!" exclaimed the young man.

"Follow me, then," said the priest, as he re-entered the subterraneous passage, in which he soon disappeared, followed by Dantès.

After having passed with tolerable ease through the subterranean passage, which, however, did not admit of their holding themselves erect, the two friends reached the further end of the corridor, into which the cell of the abbé opened; from that point the opening became much narrower, barely permitting an individual to creep through on his hands and knees. The floor of the cell was paved, and it had been by raising one of the stones in the most obscure corner that Faria had been able to commence the laborious task of which Dantès had witnessed the completion.

As he entered the chamber of his friend, Dantès cast around one eager and searching glance in quest of the expected marvels, but nothing more than common met his view.

"It is well," said the abbé; "we have some hours before us—it is now just a quarter past twelve o'clock." Instinctively Dantès turned round to observe by what watch or clock the abbé had been able so accurately to specify the hour.

"Look at this ray of light which enters by my window," said the abbe, "and then observe the lines traced on the wall. Well, by means of these lines, I am enabled to ascertain the precise hour with more minuteness than if I possessed a watch."

This last explanation was wholly lost upon Dantès, who had always imagined, from seeing the sun rise from behind the mountains and set in the Mediterranean, that it moved, and not the earth.

"Come," said he, "show me the wonderful inventions you told me of —I am all impatience to behold them."

The priest smiled, and, proceeding to the disused fireplace, raised, by the help of his chisel, a long stone, which had doubtless been the hearth, beneath which was a cavity of considerable depth, serving as a safe depository of the articles mentioned to Dantès.

"What do you wish to see first?" asked the abbé.

"Oh! your great work on the monarchy of Italy!"

Faria then drew forth from his hiding-place three or four rolls of linen, laid one over the other, like the folds of papyrus found in mummy-cases. These rolls consisted of slips of cloth about four inches wide and eighteen long; they were all carefully numbered and closely covered with writing, so legible that Dantès could easily read it, as well as make out the sense—it being in Italian, a language he, as a Provençal, perfectly understood.

"There!" said he, "there is the work complete—I wrote the word *finis* at the end of the last page about a week ago. I have torn up two of my shirts, and as many handkerchiefs as I was master of, to complete the precious pages. Should I ever get out of prison, and find a printer courageous enough to publish what I have composed, my literary reputation is for ever secured."

"I see," answered Dantès. "Now let me behold the curious pens with which you have written your work."

"Look!" said Faria, showing to the young man a slender stick about six inches long, and much resembling the size of the handle of a fine painting-brush, to the end of which was tied, by a piece of thread, one of those cartilages of which the abbé had before spoken to Dantès; it was pointed, and split at the nib like an ordinary pen. Dantès examined it with intense admiration, then looked around to see the instrument with which it had been shaped so correctly into form.

"Ah, I see," said Faria, "you are wondering where I found my penknife, are not you?" Well, I must confess that I look upon that article of my ingenuity as the very perfection of all my handiworks. I made it, as well as this knife, out of an old iron candlestick." The penknife was sharp and keen as a razor; as for the other knife, it possessed the double advantage of being capable of serving either as a dagger or a knife.

Dantès examined the various articles shown to him with the same attention he had bestowed on the curiosities and strange tools exhibited in the shops at Marseilles as the works of the savages in the South Seas from whence they had been brought by the different trading vessels.

"As for the ink," said Faria, "I told you how I managed to obtain that—and I only just make it from time to time, as I require it."

"There is one thing puzzles me still," observed Dantès, "and that is how you managed to do all this by daylight?"

"I worked at night also," replied Faria. "I separated the fat from the meat served to me, melted it, and made a most capital oil—here is my lamp." So saying, he exhibited a sort of floating wick lamp.

"But how do you procure a light?"

"Oh, here are two flints and a morsel of burnt linen."

"And your matches?"

"Were easily prepared. I feigned a disorder of the skin, and asked for a little sulphur, which was readily supplied. Dantès laid the different things he had been looking at gently on the table, and stood with his head drooping on his breast, as though overwhelmed by the persevering spirit and strength of character developed in each fresh trait of his new-found friend's conduct.

"You have not seen all yet," continued Faria, "for I did not think it wise to trust all my treasures in the same hiding-place. Let us shut this one up, and then you shall see what else I have to display." Dantès helped him to replace the stone as they first found it; the abbé sprinkled a little dust over it to conceal the traces of its having been removed, rubbed his foot well on it to make it assume the same appearance as the other, and then, going toward his bed, he removed it from the spot it stood in. Behind the head of the bed, and concealed by a stone fitting in so closely as to defy all suspicion, was a hollow space, and in this space a ladder of cords, between twenty-five and thirty feet in length. Dantès closely and eagerly examined it: he found it firm, solid, and compact enough to bear any weight.

"Who supplied you with the materials for making this wonderful work?" asked Dantès.

"No one but myself. I tore up several of my shirts, and unravelled the sheets of my bed, during my three years' imprisonment at Fenestrelle; and when I was removed to the Château d'If, I managed to bring the ravellings with me, so that I have been able to finish my work here."

"And was it not discovered that your sheets were unhemmed?"

"Oh, no! for when I had taken out the thread I required, I hemmed the edges over again."

"With what?"

"With this needle!" said the abbé, as, opening his ragged vestments, he showed Dantès a long, sharp fish-bone, with a small perforated eye for the thread, a small portion of which still remained in it. "I once thought," continued Faria, "of removing these iron bars, and letting myself down from the window, which, as you see, is somewhat wider than yours, although I should have enlarged it still more preparatory to my flight; however, I discovered that I should merely have dropped into a sort of inner court, and I therefore renounced the project altogether as too full of risk and danger. Nevertheless, I carefully preserved my ladder against one of those unforeseen opportunities of which I spoke just now, and which sudden chance frequently brings about." While affecting to be deeply engaged in examining the ladder, the mind of

Dantès was, in fact, busily occupied by the idea that a person so intelligent, ingenious, and clear-sighted, might probably be enabled to dive into the dark recesses of his own misfortunes, and cause that light to shine upon the mystery connected with them he had in vain sought to elicit.

"What are you thinking of?" asked the abbé smilingly, imputing the deep abstraction in which his visitor was plunged to the excess of his awe and wonder.

"I was reflecting, in the first place," replied Dantès, "upon the enormous degree of intelligence and ability you must have employed to reach the high perfection to which you have attained. If you thus surpass all mankind while but a prisoner, what would you not have accomplished free?"

"Possibly nothing at all; the overflow of my brain would probably, in a state of freedom, have evaporated in a thousand follies; it needs trouble and difficulty and danger to hollow out various mysterious and hidden mines of human intelligence. Pressure is required, you know, to ignite powder: captivity has collected into one single focus all the floating faculties of my mind; they have come into close contact in the narrow space in which they have been wedged; and you are well aware that from the collision of clouds electricity is produced—from electricity comes the lightning, from whose flash we have light amid our greatest darkness."

"Alas, no!" replied Dantès. "I know not that these things follow in such natural order. Oh, I am very ignorant! and you must be blessed indeed to possess the knowledge you have."

The abbé smiled. "Well," said he, "but you had another subject for your thoughts besides admiration for me; did you not say so just now?"——"I did!"

"You have told me as yet but one of them,—let me hear the other."

"It was this:—that while you had related to me all the particulars of your past life, you were perfectly unacquainted with mine."

"Your life, my young friend, has not been of sufficient length to admit of your having passed through any very important events."

"It has been long enough to inflict on me a misfortune so great, so crushingly overwhelming, that, unconscious as I am of having in any way deserved it, I would fain know who, of all mankind, has been the accursed author of it, that I may no longer accuse Heaven, as I have done in my fury and despair, of wilful injustice toward an innocent and injured man."

"Then you profess ignorance of the crime with which you are charged?"

"I do, indeed; and this I swear by the two beings most dear to me upon earth—my father and Mercédès."

"Come," said the abbé, closing his hiding-place, and pushing the bed back to its original situation, "let me hear your story."

Dantès obeyed.

His recital finished, the abbé reflected long and earnestly.

"There is," said he at the end of his meditations, "a clever maxim:— that if you wish to discover the guilty, seek him to whom the perpetration is advantageous. Now, to apply it in your case:—to whom could your disappearance have been serviceable?"

"To no breathing soul. Why, who could have cared about the removal of so insignificant a person as myself?"

"Do not speak thus, for your reply evinces neither logic nor philosophy; but let us return to your world. You say you were on the point of being appointed captain of the Pharaoh?"

"And about to become the husband of a young and lovely girl?"——"True."

"Now, could any one have had any interest in preventing the accomplishment of these two circumstances? But let us first settle the question as to its being the interest of anyone to hinder you from being captain of the Pharaoh. What say you?"

"I cannot believe such was the case. I was generally liked on board; and had the sailors possessed the right of selecting a captain themselves, I feel convinced their choice would have fallen on me. There was only one person among the crew who had any feeling of ill-will towards me. I had quarrelled with him some time previously, and had even challenged him to fight me; but he refused."

"Now we are getting on. And what was this man's name?"——"Danglars, the supercargo."

"And had you been captain, should you have retained him in his employment?"

"Not if the choice had remained with me, for I had frequently observed inaccuracies in his accounts."

"Good again! Now then, tell me, was any person present during your last conversation with Captain Leclere?"——"'No, stay! now I recollect,—Danglars himself passed by just as Captain Leclere was giving me the packet for the grand marshal."

"That will do," cried the abbé; "now we are on the right scent. Did you take anybody with you when you put into the port of Elba?"——"Nobody."

"Somebody there received your packet, and gave you a letter in place of it, I think?"——"Yes: the grand marshal did."

"And what did you do with that letter?"——"Put it into my pocketbook on my return to the ship."

"And what did you do with this same letter while returning from Porto Ferrajo to your vessel?"——"I carried it in my hand."

"So that when you went on board everybody could perceive you held a letter in your hand? Danglars as well as the rest?"——"Yes; he as well as others."

"Now, listen to me, and try to recall every circumstance attending your arrest. Do you recollect the words in which the information against you was couched?"

Dantès paused a few instants, as though collecting his ideas, then said, "This is it, word for word:— 'The Royal Persecutor is informed by a friend to the Throne and Religion that one Edmond Dantès, first mate of the ship *Pharaoh,* in this morning from Smyrna, after touching at Naples and Porto Ferrajo, was charged by Murat with a letter for the Usurper, and by the latter with another for the Bonapartist Club at Paris. The proof of his crime will be found on arresting him; for he will have the letter on him, or it will be at his father's, or aboard the ship.' "

The abbé shrugged up his shoulders. "The thing is clear as day," said he; "and you must have had a very unsuspecting nature, as well as a good heart, not to have suspected the origin of the whole affair."

"Do you really think so? Ah, that would indeed be the treachery of a villain!"

"How did Danglars usually write?"——"Oh! extremely well."

"And how was the anonymous letter written?"

"All the wrong way—backwards, you know." Again the abbé smiled. "In fact it was a disguised hand?"——"I don't know; it was very boldly written, if disguised."

"Stop a bit," said the abbé, taking up what he called his pen, and, after dipping it into the ink, he wrote on a morsel of prepared linen, with his left hand, the first two or three words of the accusation. Dantès drew back, and gazed on the abbé with a sensation almost amounting to terror.

"How very astonishing!" cried he, at length. "Why your writing exactly resembles that of the accusation!"

"Simply because that accusation had been written with the left hand; and I have always remarked one thing——"

"What is that?"——"That whereas all writing with the right hand varies, that performed with the left hand is invariably similar."

"Now as regards the second question. Was there any person whose interest it was to prevent your marriage with Mercédès?"

"Yes, a young man who loved her, Fernand, a Catalan."

"You imagine him capable of writing the letter?"

"Oh, no! he would more likely have got rid of me by sticking a knife into me."

"That is in strict accordance with the Spanish character; an assassination they will unhesitatingly commit, but an act of cowardice, never."

"Besides," said Dantès, "the various circumstances mentioned in the letter were wholly unknown to him."

"You had never spoken of them yourself to any one?"

"No, not even to my betrothed bride."

"Then it is Danglars, beyond a doubt."

"Pray was Danglars acquainted with Fernand?"

"No——yes, he was. Now I recollect them both sitting at table together beneath an inn arbour the evening before the day fixed for my wedding. They were in earnest conversation. Danglars was joking in a friendly way, but Fernand looked pale and agitated."

"Were they alone?"——"There was a third person with them whom I knew perfectly well, and who had, in all probability, made their acquaintance; a tailor named Caderousse, but he was quite intoxicated. Stay!—stay!—How strange that it should not have occurred to me before! Now I remember quite well, that on the table round which they were sitting were pens, ink, and paper. Oh! the heartless treacherous scoundrels!" exclaimed Dantès, pressing his hand to his throbbing brows.

"Is there anything else I can assist you in discovering, besides the villainy of your friends?" inquired the abbé.

"Yes, yes," replied Dantès, eagerly; "I would beg of you, who see so completely to the depths of things, and to whom the greatest mystery seems but an easy riddle, to explain to me how it was that I underwent no second examination, was never brought to trial, and above all, my being condemned without ever having had sentence passed on me?"

"That is altogether a different and more serious matter," responded the abbé. "The ways of justice are frequently too dark and mysterious to be easily penetrated. All we have hitherto done in the matter has been child's play. If you wish me to enter upon the more difficult part of the business, you must assist me by the most minute information on every point."

"That I will gladly. So pray begin, my dear abbé, and ask me whatever questions you please; for, in good truth, you seem to turn over the pages of my past life far better than I could do myself."

"In the first place, then, who examined you,—the prosecutor, his deputy, or a magistrate?"

"The deputy."

"Was he young or old?"——"About six or seven-and-twenty years of age, I should say."

"To be sure," answered the abbé. "Old enough to be ambitious, but not sufficiently so to have hardened his heart. And how did he treat you?"

"With more of mildness than severity. He seemed quite overcome at the thoughts of the danger I was in."

"*You* were in?"——"Yes: for whom else could he have felt any apprehensions!"

"Then you feel quite convinced he sincerely pitied your misfortune?"

"Why, he gave me one great proof of his sympathy, at least. He burnt the sole proof that could at all have criminated me, the letter I was entrusted to convey to Paris."

"Ay, indeed! that alters the case, and leads to the conclusion that this man might, after all, be a greater scoundrel than I at first believed."

"Upon my word," said Dantès, "you make me shudder. If I listen much longer to you, I shall believe the world is filled with tigers and crocodiles."

"Only remember that two-legged tigers and crocodiles are more dangerous than those that walk on four. You tell me he burnt the letter in your presence?"

"He did; saying at the same time, 'You see I thus destroy the only proof existing against you'."

"This action is somewhat too sublime to be natural. To whom was this letter addressed?"

"To M. Noirtier. No. 13, Rue Coq-Héron, Paris."

"Noirtier," repeated the abbé; "Noirtier!—I knew a person of that name at the court of the Queen of Etruria,—a Noirtier, a Girondin during the Revolution! What was your deputy named?"

"De Villefort!" The abbé burst into a fit of laughter; while Dantès gazed on him in utter astonishment.

"What ails you?" said he, at length.

"Do you see this ray of light?"——"I do."

"Well! I see my way into the full meaning of all the proceedings against you more clearly than you even discern that sunbeam. Poor fellow! poor young man! And you tell me this magistrate expressed great sympathy and commiseration for you, and destroyed your compromising letter?"

"He burnt it before me!"

"Why, you poor short-sighted simpleton, can you not guess who this Noirtier was, whose very name he was so careful to keep concealed?"

"Indeed I cannot!"

"No other than the father of your sympathetic deputy-prosecutor."

Had a thunderbolt fallen at the feet of Dantès, or hell opened its yawning gulf before him, he could not have been more completely transfixed with horror than at the sound of words so wholly unexpected, revealing as they did the fiendish perfidy which had consigned him to wear out his days in the dark cell of a prison that was to him as a living grave. Starting up, he clasped his hands around his head as though to prevent his very brain from bursting, as in a choked and almost inarticulate voice he exclaimed, "His father! oh, no! not his father, surely!"

"His own father, I assure you," replied the abbé; "his right name was Noirtier de Villefort!" At this instant a bright light shot through the mind of Dantès, and cleared up all that had been dark and obscure before. He hurried to the opening conducting from the cell to his own, and said,—"I must be alone to think over all this."

When he regained his dungeon, he threw himself on his bed, where the turnkey found him at his evening visit, sitting, with fixed gaze and contracted features, still and motionless as a statue; but during hours of deep meditation, which to him had seemed but as minutes, he had formed a fearful resolution, and bound himself to its fulfilment by a solemn oath. Dantès was at length roused from his reverie by the voice of Faria who, having also been visited by his jailer had come to invite his fellow sufferer to share his supper. The reputation of being out of his mind, though harmlessly and even amusingly so, had procured for the abbé greater privileges than allowed in general. He was supplied with bread of a finer, whiter description than the usual prison fare, and even regaled each Sunday with wine: the present day chanced to be Sunday, and the priest came, delighted at having such luxuries to offer his new friend. Dantès followed him with a firm and assured step; his features had lost their almost spasmodic contraction, and now wore their usual expression; but there was that in his whole appearance that bespoke one who had come to a fixed and desperate resolve. Faria bent on him his penetrating eye: "I regret now," said he, "having helped you in your late inquiries, or having given you the information I did, because it has instilled a new passion in your heart— that of vengeance."

A bitter smile played over the features of the young man: "Let us talk of something else," said he.

Again the abbé looked at him, then mournfully shook his head; but in accordance with Dantès request he began to speak of other matters.

"You must teach me a small part of what you know," said Dantès, "if only to prevent your growing weary of me. I can well believe that so learned a person as yourself would prefer absolute solitude to being tormented with the company of one as ignorant and uninformed as myself. If you will only agree to my request, I promise you never to mention another word about escaping." The abbé smiled. "Alas! my child," said he, "human knowledge is confined within very narrow limits; and when I have taught you mathematics, physics, history, and the three or four modern languages with which I am acquainted, you will know as much as I do myself. Now, it will scarcely require two years for me to communicate to you the stock of learning I possess."

"Two years!" exclaimed Dantès; "do you really believe I can acquire all these things in so short a time?"——"Not their application, certainly, but their principles you may; to learn is not to know; there are the learners and the learned. Memory makes the one, philosophy the other.

"But can I not learn philosophy as well as other things?"

"My son, philosophy, as I understand it, is reducible to no rules by which it can be learned; it is the amalgamation of all the sciences, the golden cloud which bears the soul to heaven."

"Well, then," said Dantès, "leaving philosophy out of the question, tell me what you shall teach me first? I feel my great need of scientific knowledge, and long to begin the work of improvement; say, when shall we commence?"

"Directly, if you will," said the abbé. And that very evening the prisoners sketched a plan of education, to be entered upon the following day. Dantès possessed a prodigious memory, combined with an astonishing quickness and readiness of conception; absorbed in the acquisition of knowledge, days, even months, passed by unheeded in one rapid and instructive course; time flew on, and at the end of a year Dantès was a new man.

They began a fresh tunnel. In fifteen months, it was made, the excavation completed beneath the gallery, and the two workmen could distinctly hear the measured tread of the sentinel as he paced to and fro over their heads.

Compelled, as they were, to await a night sufficiently dark to favor their flight, they were obliged to defer their final attempt till that auspicious moment should arrive; their greatest dread now was lest the stone through which the sentry was doomed to fall should give way before its right time, and this they had in some measure provided against by placing under it, a prop, discovered among the foundations. Dantès was occupied in arranging this piece of wood when he heard Faria, who had remained in Edmond's cell for the purpose of cutting a peg to secure their rope-ladder, call to him in suffering. Dantès hastened to his dungeon, where he found him standing in the middle pale as death, his forehead streaming with perspiration, and his hands clenched.

"Heavens!" exclaimed Dantès, "what is the matter? what ails you?"

"Quick! quick!" returned the abbé, "listen. I am seized with a terrible, perhaps mortal illness; I can feel that the paroxysm is fast approaching. I had a similar attack the year previous to my imprisonment. This malady admits but of one remedy; I will tell you what that is. Go into my cell as quickly as you can; draw out one of the feet that support the bed; you will find it has been hollowed out for the purpose of containing a small phial you will see there half-filled with a red-looking fluid. Bring it to me—or rather, no, no! I may be found here; therefore help me back to my room while I have any strength to drag myself along. Who knows what may happen, or how long the fit may last?"

Spite of the misfortune which thus suddenly frustrated his hopes, Dantès lost not his presence of mind, but descended into the corridor, dragging his unfortunate companion with him; then, half carrying, half supporting him, he managed to reach the abbé's chamber, when he immediately laid the sufferer on his bed.

"Thanks!" said the poor priest, shivering as though his veins were filled with ice. "Now that I am safely here, let me explain to you the nature of my attack, and the appearance it will present. I am seized with a fit of catalepsy; when it comes to its height, I may, probably, lie still and motionless as though dead, uttering neither sigh nor groan. On the other hand, the symptoms may be much more violent, and cause me to fall into fearful convulsions, cover my lips with foaming, and force from me the most piercing shrieks. This last evil you must carefully guard against, for, were my cries to be heard, it is more than probable I should be removed to another part of the prison, and we be separated for ever. When I become quite motionless, cold, and rigid as a corpse, then, and not before, you understand, force open my teeth with a chisel, pour from eight to ten drops of the liquor contained in the phial down my throat, and I may perhaps revive."

"Perhaps?" exclaimed Dantès, in grief-stricken tones.

"Help! help!" cried the abbé, "I—I—die—I——"

So sudden and violent was the fit, that the unfortunate prisoner was unable to complete the sentence begun. The fit lasted two hours; then, more helpless than an infant, and colder and paler than marble, more crushed and broken than a reed trampled under foot, he stretched himself out as though in the agonies of death, and became of the ghastly hue of the tomb.

Edmond waited till life seemed extinct in the body of his friend, then, taking up the chisel, he with difficulty forced open the closely-fixed jaws, carefully poured the appointed number of drops down the rigid throat, and anxiously awaited the result. An hour passed away without the old man's giving the least sign of returning animation. At length a slight color tinged the livid cheeks, consciousness returned to the dull, open eyeballs, a faint sigh issued from the lips, and the sufferer made a feeble effort to move.

"He is saved! saved!" cried Dantès, in a paroxysm of delight.

The sick man was not yet able to speak, but he pointed with evident anxiety toward the door. Dantès listened, and plainly distinguished the approaching steps of the jailer. It was therefore near seven o'clock; but Edmond's anxiety had put all thoughts of time out of his head. The young man sprang to the entrance, darted through it, carefully drawing the stone over the opening, and hurried to his cell. He had scarcely done so before the door opened, and disclosed to the jailer's inquisitorial gaze the prisoner seated as usual on the side of his bed. Almost before the key had turned in the lock, and before the departing steps of the jailer had died away in the long corridor he had to traverse, Dantès, whose restless anxiety concerning his friend left him no desire to touch the food brought him, hurried back to the abbé's chamber, and raising the stone by pressing his head against it, was soon beside the sick man's couch. Faria had now fully regained his consciousness, but he till lay helpless and exhausted on his miserable bed.

"I did not expect to see you again," said he, feebly, to Dantès.

"And why not?" asked the young man. "Did you fancy yourself dying?"

"No, I had no such idea; but, knowing that all was ready for your flight, I considered you had availed yourself of it, and were gone." The deep glow of indignation suffused the cheeks of Dantès.

"And did you really think so meanly of me," cried he, "as to believe I would depart without you?"——"At least," said the abbé, "I now see how wrong such an opinion would have been. Alas, alas! The attack which has just passed away, condemns me for ever to the walls of a prison. None can fly from their dungeon but those who can walk. Here, remain till the hour of my deliverance arrives; and that, in all human probability, will be the hour of my death. As for you, who are young and active, delay not on my account, but fly—go—I give you back your promise."

"It is well," said Dantès. "And now hear my determination also." Then, rising and extending his hand with an air of solemnity over the old man's head, he slowly added, "Here I swear to remain with you so long as life is spared to you, and that death only shall divide us."

Faria gazed fondly on his noble-minded but single-hearted young friend, and read in his honest, open countenance ample confirmation of truthfulness, as well as sincere, affectionate, and faithful devotion.

"Thanks, my child," murmured the invalid, extending the one hand of which he still retained the use. "Thanks for your generous offer, which I accept as frankly as it was made." Then, after a short pause, he added, "You may one of these days reap the reward of your disinterested devotion. But as I cannot, and you will not, quit this place, it becomes necessary to fill up the excavation beneath the soldier's gallery; he might, by chance, find out the hollow sound produced by his footsteps over the excavated ground, and call the attention of his officer to the circumstance. That would bring about a discovery which would inevitably lead to our being separated. Go, then, and set about this work, in which, unhappily, I can offer you no assistance; keep it all night, if necessary, and do not return here to-morrow till after the jailer has visited me. I shall have something of the greatest importance to communicate to you."

Dantès took the hand of the abbé who smiled encouragingly, and retired with the respect and obedience pledged to his aged friend.

CHAPTER X.

THE CARDINAL'S TREASURE.

WHEN Dantès returned next morning to the chamber of his companion in captivity, he found Faria calmly seated. In the ray of light which entered by the narrow window, he held open in his left hand, of which alone, he retained the use, a morsel of paper, which, from being constantly rolled into a small compass, had the form of a cylinder, and was not easily kept open. He did not speak, but showed the paper to Dantès.

"Look at it," said the abbé, with a smile.

"I have looked at it with all possible attention," said Dantès, "and I only see a half-burnt paper, on which are traces of Gothic characters, traced with a peculiar kind of ink."

"This paper, my friend," said Faria. "I may now avow to you, since I have proved you—this paper is my treasure, of which, from this day forth, one half belongs to you."

A cold damp started to Dantès' brow.

"Alas!" murmured he, "this is a terrible relapse! There was only this blow wanting." Then he said aloud, "My dear friend, your attack has, perhaps, fatigued you; had you not better repose awhile? Tomorrow, if you will, I will hear your narrative; but to-day I wish to nurse you carefully. Besides," he said, "a treasure is not a thing we need hurry."

"On the contrary, it must be hurried, Edmond!" replied the old man. "Who knows if to-morrow, or the next day after, the third attack may not come on? and then must not all be finished? Yes, indeed, I have often thought with a bitter joy that these riches, which would make the wealth of a dozen families, will be for ever lost to those men who persecute me. This idea was one of vengeance to me, and I tasted it slowly in the night of my dungeon and the despair of my captivity. But now I have forgiven the world for the love of you;

now I see you young and full of hope and prospect—now that I think of all that may result to you in the good fortune of such a disclosure, I shudder at any delay, and tremble lest I should not assure to one as worthy as yourself the possession of so vast an amount of hidden treasure." Edmond turned away his head with a sigh.

"You persist in your incredulity, Edmond," continued Faria. "My words have not convinced you. I see you require proofs. Well, then, read this paper, which I have never shown to any one."

"To-morrow, my dear friend," said Edmond, desirous of not yielding to the old man's madness. "I thought it was understood that we should not talk of that until to-morrow."——"Then we will not talk of it until to-morrow; but read this paper to-day."

"Let us not irritate him," thought Edmond, and taking the paper, of which part was wanting, having been burnt, no doubt by some accident, he read—

this treasure's existence, amount
millions of Roman crowns; it wi
eth rock starting in a straight li
caves are two openings; the tre
inmost—which treasure I leave a
25th April, 1498.

"Why," said Dantès, "I see nothing but broken lines and unconnected words, illegible by fire."

"Yes, to you, my friend, who read them for the first time; but not for me, who have grown pale over them by many nights' study, and have reconstructed every phrase, completed every thought."

"And do you believe you have discovered the concealed sense?"

"I am sure I have, and you shall judge for yourself; but first listen to the history of this paper."

"Silence!" exclaimed Dantès. "Steps approach—I go—adieu."

And Dantès, happy to escape the story and explanation which could not fail to confirm to him his friend's malady, glided like a snake along the narrow passage; whilst Faria, restored by his alarm to activity, pushed with his foot the stone into its place, and covered it with a mat in order the more effectually to avoid discovery.

It was the governor, who, hearing of Faria's accident from the jailer, had come in person to see him.

During this time, Edmond, seated on his bed with his head in his hands, tried to collect his scattered thoughts. All was so rational, grand, and logical, with Faria, since he had known him, that he could not understand how so much wisdom on all points could be allied to madness in any one. Was Faria deceived as to his treasure, or was all the world deceived as to Faria?

Dantès remained in his cell all day, not daring to return to his friend, thinking thus to defer the moment when he should acquire the certainty that the priest was mad—such a conviction would be so terrible!

But, toward the evening after the usual visitation, Faria, not seeing the young man appear, tried to move, and get over the distance which separated them. Edmond shuddered when he heard the painful efforts which the old man made to drag himself along; his leg was inert, and he could no longer make use of one arm. Edmond was compelled to draw him toward himself, for otherwise he could not enter by the small aperture which led to Dantès' chamber.

"Here I am, pursuing you remorselessly," he said, with a benignant smile. "You thought to escape my munificence, but it is in vain. Listen to me."

Edmond saw there was no escape, and placing the old man on his bed, he seated himself on the stool beside him.

"You know," said the abbé, "that I was the secretary and intimate friend of Cardinal Spada, the last of the princes of that name. I owe to this worthy lord all the happiness I ever knew. He was not rich, although the wealth of his family had passed into a proverb, and I heard the phrase very often, 'Rich as a Spada.' But he, like public rumor, lived on this reputation for wealth. His palace was my paradise. I instructed his nephews, who are dead; and when he was alone in the world, I returned to him, by an absolute devotion to his will, all he had done for me during ten years. The house of the cardinal had no secrets for me. I had often seen my noble patron annotating ancient volumes, and eagerly searching amongst dusty family manuscripts. One day when I was reproaching him for his unavailing searches, and the prostration that followed them, he looked at me, and, smiling bitterly, opened a volume of the History of the City of Rome. There, in the twentieth chapter of the Life of Pope Alexander VI., were the following lines, which I can never forget:—

"'The great wars of la Romagna had ended; Cæsar Borgia, who had completed his conquest, had need of money to purchase all Italy. The pope had also need of money to conclude with Louis, the twelfth king of France, formidable still in spite of his recent reverses; and it was necessary, therefore, to have recourse to some profitable speculation, which was a matter of great difficulty in the impoverished condition of poor exhausted Italy. His holiness had an idea. He determined to make two cardinals.'

"The pope and Cæsar Borgia first found the two future cardinals; they were Rospigliosi, who held four of the highest dignities of the holy seat; and Spada, one of the noblest and richest of the Roman nobility; both felt the high honor of such a favor from the pope. They were ambitious; and, Cæsar Borgia soon found purchasers for their appointments. The result was, that Rospigliosi and Spada paid for being cardinals, and eight other persons paid for the offices the cardinals held before their elevation, and thus eight hundred thousand crowns entered into the coffers of the speculators.

"It is time now to proceed to the last part of the speculation. The pope having almost smothered Rospigliosi and Spada with caresses, having bestowed upon them the insignia of cardinal, and induced them to realize their fortunes, and settle at Rome, he and Cæsar invited the two cardinals to dinner.

"The table was laid in a vineyard belonging to the pope, near San Pietro, outside the limits, a charming retreat which the cardinals knew very well by report. Rospigliosi, quite giddy with his dignity, prepared his appetite and assumed his best looks. Spada, a prudent man, and greatly attached to his only nephew, a young captain of highest promise, took paper and pen and made his will. He then sent to his nephew to await him in the vicinity of the vineyard: but it appeared the servant did not find him.

"Spada set out about two o'clock to Saint-Peter's. The pope awaited him. The first figure that struck the eyes of Spada was his nephew, in full costume, and Cæsar Borgia paying him most marked attentions. Spada turned pale, as Cæsar looked at him with an ironical air, which proved that he had anticipated all, and that the snare was well spread. They began dinner, and Spada was only able to inquire of his nephew if he had received his message. The nephew replied no; perfectly comprehending the meaning of the question. It was too late, for he had already drunk a glass of excellent wine, placed for him expressly by the papal butler. Spada at the same moment saw another bottle approach him, which he was pressed to taste. An hour afterwards a physician declared they were both poisoned through eating mushrooms. Spada died on the threshold of the vineyard; the nephew expired at his own door, making signs which his wife could not comprehend.

"Then Cæsar and the pope hastened to lay hands on the property, under pretense of seeking for the papers of the dead man. But the inheritance consisted in this only, a scrap of paper on which Spada had written:—'I bequeath to my beloved nephew my coffers, my books, amongst other, my breviary with the gold clasps, which I beg he will preserve in remembrance of his affectionate uncle.'

"The heirs sought everywhere, admired the breviary, laid hands on the furniture, and were greatly astonished that Spada, the rich man, was really the most miserable of uncles—no treasures—unless of science, composed in the library and laboratories. This was all: Cæsar and his father searched, examined, scrutinized, but found nothing, or at least very little; not exceeding a few thousand crowns in plate, and about the same in ready money, but the nephew had time to say to his wife before he had expired:—'Look well among my uncle's papers; there is a will.'

"They sought even more thoroughly than the august heirs had done, but it was fruitless. Months and years rolled on. Alexander VI. died poisoned. Cæsar, poisoned at the same time, escaped after sloughing off his skin like a snake, and assumed a new cuticle, on which the poison left spots, like those we see on a tiger; then, compelled to quit Rome, he went and was killed himself in a night skirmish, scarcely noticed in history. After the pope's death and his son's exile, it was supposed the Spada family would again make the splendid figure they had before the cardinal's time; but this was not the case. The Spadas remained in doubtful ease, a mystery hung over this dark affair, and the public rumor was, that Cæsar, a better politician than his father, had carried off from the pope the fortune of the two cardinals. I say the two, because Cardinal Rospigliosi, who had not taken any precaution, was completely despoiled.

"Up to this time," said Faria, interrupting the thread of his narrative, "this seems to you very ridiculous, no doubt, eh?"

"Oh, my friend," cried Dantès, "on the contrary, it seems as if I were reading a most interesting narrative; go on, I pray of you."

"The family began to feel accustomed to this obscurity. Years rolled on, and amongst the descendants some were soldiers, others diplomatists; churchmen, bankers; some grew rich, and some were ruined. I come now to the last of the family, whose secretary I was —Count Spada. I had often heard him complain of the disproportion of his rank with his fortune; and I advised him to sink all he had in an annuity. He did so, and thus doubled his income. The celebrated breviary remained in the family, and was in his possession. It had been handed down from father to son; for the singular clause of the only will that had been found, had rendered it a relic, preserved in the family with superstitious veneration. It was an illuminated book, with beautiful Gothic characters, and so weighty with gold ornaments, that a servant always carried it before the cardinal on days of great solemnity.

"At the sight of papers of all sorts,—titles, contracts, parchments, which were kept in the archives of the family, all descending from the poisoned cardinal, I, like twenty servitors, stewards, secretaries before me, in my turn examined the immense bundles of documents; but in spite of the most accurate researches, I found—nothing. Yet I had read, I had even written a history of the Borgia family, for the sole purpose of assuring myself whether any increase of fortune had occurred to them on the death of the Cardinal Cæsar Spada; but could only trace the acquisition of the property of the Cardinal Rospigliosi, his companion in misfortune.

"I was then almost assured that the inheritance had neither profited the Borgias nor the family, but had remained unpossessed like the treasures of the Arabian Nights, which slept in the bosom of the earth under the eyes of a genie. I searched, ransacked, counted, calculated a thousand and a thousand times the income and expenditure of the family for three hundred years. It was useless. I remained in my ignorance, and Spada in his poverty. My patron died. He had reserved from his annuity his family papers, his library, composed of five thousand volumes, and his famous breviary. All these he bequeathed to me, with a thousand Roman crowns, which he had in ready money, on condition that I would have said anniversary masses for the repose of his soul, and that I would draw up a geneological tree and history of his house. All this I did scrupulously.

"In 1807, a month before I was arrested, and fifteen days after the death of Spada, on the 25th of December (you will see presently how the date became fixed in my memory), I was reading, for the thousandth time, the papers I was arranging, for the palace was sold to a stranger, and I was going to leave Rome and settle at Florence, intending to take with me twelve thousand francs I possessed, my library, and famous breviary, when, tired with my constant labor at the same thing, and overcome by a heavy dinner I had eaten, my head dropped on my hands, and I fell asleep about three o'clock in the afternoon. I awoke as the clock was striking six. I raised my head; all was in darkness. I rang for a light, but as no one came, I determined to find one for myself. It was indeed the habit of a philosopher which I should soon be under the necessity of adopting. I took a wax-candle in one hand, and with the other groped about for a piece of paper (my matchbox being empty), with which I proposed to produce a light from the small flame still playing on the embers. Fearing, however, to make use of any valuable piece of paper, I hesitated for a moment, then recollected that I had seen in the famous breviary, which was on the table beside me, a slip of old paper quite yellow with age, which had served as a marker for centuries, kept there by the request of the heirs. I felt for it, found it, twisted it up together, and putting it into the expiring flame, set light to it.

"But beneath my fingers, as if by magic, in proportion as the fire ascended, I saw yellowish characters appear on the paper. I grasped it in my hand, put out the flame as quickly as I could, lighted my taper in the fire itself, and opened the crumpled paper with inexpressible emotion, recognizing, when I had done so, that these characters had been traced in mysterious and sympathetic ink, only appearing when exposed to the fire: nearly one-third of the paper had been consumed by the flame. It was that paper you read this morning; read it again, Dantès, and then I will complete for you the incomplete words and unconnected sense."

Faria, with an air of triumph, offered the paper to Dantès, who this time read the following words, traced with an ink of color, which most nearly resembled rust:

"This day, the 25th April, 1498, invit
Pope Alessandro VI., and fearing tha
paid for the cardinal's hat, he wi
me the fate of Cardinals Caprara an
I declare to my exclusive heir, m
buried in a spot which he knows fr
er words, in the caves of Mont
bullion and coin and jewels, pre
this treasure's existence, amount
millions of Roman crowns; it wi
eth rock starting in a straight li
caves are two openings; the tre
inmost—which treasure I leave a
    25th April, 1498.

"And now," said the abbé, "read this other paper;" and he presented to Dantès a second leaf with fragments of lines on it, which Edmond read as follows:

ed to dinner by his Holiness the
t, not satisfied with my having
shes to be my heir and intends for
d Bentivoglio, who died of poison,
y nephew Guido Spada, that I have
om having visited it with me, in oth-
e Cristo Islet, all my property in gold
cious stones, and gems; I alone know of
ing to the value of upwards of two
ll be found on overturning the twenti-
ne from the East Creek. In these
asure is in the farthest corner of the
nd give unto him as my sole heir.
    CESARO † SPADA."

"And now," he said, when he saw Dantès had read the last line, "put the two fragments together, and judge for yourself." Dantès obeyed, and the joined pieces gave the following:

"This day, the 25th April, 1498, invited to dinner by his Holiness the Pope Alessandro VI., and fearing that, not satisfied with my having paid for the cardinal's hat, he wishes to be my heir and intends for me the fate of Cardinals Caprara and Bentivoglio, who died of poison, I declare to my exclusive heir, my nephew Guido Spada, that I have buried in a spot which he knows from having visited it with me, in other words, in the caves of Monte Cristo Islet, all my property in, gold bullion and coin and jewels, precious stones, and gems; I alone know of this treasure's existence, amounting to the value of upwards of two millions of Roman crowns; it will be found on overturning the twentieth rock starting in a straight line from the East Creek. In these caves are two openings: the treasure is in the farthest corner of the inmost—which treasure I leave and give unto him as my sole heir.

25th April, 1498.   CESARO † SPADA."

"Well, do you comprehend now?" inquired Faria.

"It is the declaration of Cardinal Spada, and the will so long sought for," replied Edmond, still incredulous.

"Of course; what else could it be?"——"And who completed it as it now is?"

"I did. Aided by the remaining fragment, I guessed the rest; measuring the length of the lines by those of the paper, and divining the hidden meaning by means of what was in part revealed, as we are guided in a cavern by the small ray of light above us."

"And what did you do when you arrived at this conclusion?"

"I resolved to set out, and did set out that very instant, carrying with me the beginning of my great work of forming Italy into one kingdom; but for some time the infernal police (who at this period, quite contrary to what Napoleon desired so soon as he had a son born to him, wished for a petition of provinces) had their eyes on me; and my hasty departure, the cause of which they were unable to guess, having aroused their suspicions, I was arrested at the very moment I was leaving Piombino.

"Now," continued Faria, addressing Dantès with an almost paternal expression, "now, my dear fellow, you know as much as I do myself. If we ever escape together, half this treasure is yours; if I die here, and you escape alone, the whole belongs to you."

"But," inquired Dantès, hesitating, "has this treasure no more legitimate possessor in this world than ourselves?"

"No, no, be easy on that score; the family is extinct."

"This treasure belongs to you, my dear friend," replied Dantès, "and to you only. I have no right to it. I am no relation of yours."

"You are my son, Dantès," exclaimed the old man. "You are the child of my captivity. My profession condemns me to celibacy. God has sent you to me to console, at one and the same time, the man who could not be a father and the prisoner who could not get free." And Faria extended the arm of which alone the use remained to him to the young man, who threw himself on his neck and wept bitterly.

CHAPTER XI.

THE FATAL ATTACK.

Now that this treasure, which had so long been the object of the abbé's meditations, could insure the future happiness of him whom Faria really loved as a son, it had doubled its value in his eyes, and every day he expatiated on the amount, explaining to Dantès all the good which, with fifteen millions of francs, a man could do in these days to his friends; and then Dantès' countenance became gloomy, for the oath of vengeance he had taken recurred to his memory, and he reflected how much ill, in these times, a man with millions could do to his enemies.

The abbé did not know the isle of Monte-Cristo; but Dantès knew it, and had often passed it, situated twenty-five miles from Pianosa, between Corsica and Elba, and had once touched at it. This island was, always had been, and still is, completely deserted. It is a rock of almost conical form, which seems as though produced by some volcanic effort from the depth to the surface of the ocean. Dantès traced a chart of the island to Faria, and Faria gave Dantès advice as to the means he should employ to recover the treasure. But Dantès was far from being as enthusiastic and confident as the old man. It was past a question now that Faria was not a lunatic, and the way in which he had achieved the discovery, which had given rise to the suspicion of his madness, increased his admiration of him; but at the same time he could not believe that that deposit, supposing it had ever existed, still existed; and though he considered the treasure as by no means chimerical, he yet believed it was no longer there.

Thus, if not actually happy, yet the days these two unfortunates passed together went quickly. Faria, who for so long a time had kept silence as to the treasure, now perpetually talked of it.

Whole hours sometimes passed whilst Faria was giving instructions to Dantès—instructions which were to serve him when he was at liberty. Then, once free, from the day and hour and moment when he was so, he could have but one only thought, which was, to gain Monte-Cristo by some means, and remain there alone under some pretext which would give no suspicions; and once there, to endeavor to find the wonderful caverns, and search in the appointed spot.

All went on as if in existences in which misfortune has deranged nothing, and which glide on mechanically and tranquilly beneath the eye of Providence.

One night Edmond awoke suddenly, believing he heard some one calling him.

He moved his bed, drew up the stone, rushed into the passage, and reached the opposite extremity; the secret entrance was open. By the light of the wretched and wavering lamp, of which we have spoken, Dantès saw the old man, pale, but yet erect, clinging to the bedstead. His features were writhing with those horrible symptoms which he already knew, and which had so seriously alarmed him when he saw them for the first time.

"Alas! my dear friend," said Faria in a resigned tone, "you understand, do you not; and I need not attempt to explain to you?"

"There is not a hope, but no matter, God wills it that man whom he has created, and in whose heart He has so profoundly rooted the love of life, should do all in his power to preserve that existence, which, however painful it may be, is yet always so dear."

"Oh! yes, yes!" exclaimed Dantès, "and I tell you you shall yet be saved!"

"Do as you did before, only do not wait so long. All the springs of life are now exhausted in me, and death," he continued, looking at his paralyzed arm and leg, "has but half its work to do. If, after having made me swallow twelve drops instead of ten, you see that I do not recover, then pour the rest down my throat. Now lift me on my bed, for I can no longer support myself."

Edmond took the old man in his arms, and laid him on the bed.

"And now my dear old friend," said Faria, "sole consolation of my wretched existence,—I bless thee!" The young man cast himself on his knees, leaning his head against the old man's bed.

"Listen, now, to what I say in this my dying moment. The treasure of the Spadas exists. God grants me that I see it in the depths of the inner cavern. My eyes pierce the inmost recesses of the earth, and are dazzled at the sight of so much riches. If you do escape, remember that the poor priest, whom all the world called mad, was not so. Hasten to Monte-Cristo—avail yourself of the fortune—for you have indeed suffered long enough. Your hand, Dantès! Adieu!—adieu!" And raising himself by a final effort, in which he summoned all his faculties, he said—"Monte-Cristo! forget not Monte-Cristo!" And he fell back in his bed. The crisis was terrible, his writhing limbs, his swollen eyelids, a foam of blood and froth in his lips; a frame quite rigid, was soon extended on this bed of agony, in place of the intellectual being there but so lately.

Dantès took the lamp, placed it on a projecting stone above the bed, whence its tremulous light fell with strange and fantastic ray on this discomposed countenance and this inert and stiffened body. With fixed eyes he awaited boldly the moment for administering the hoped-for restorative.

When he believed the instant had arrived, he took the knife, unclosed the teeth, which offered less resistance than before, counted one after the other twelve drops, and watched, the phial contained, perhaps, twice as much more. He waited ten minutes, a quarter of an hour, half an hour, nothing moved. Trembling, his hair erect, his brow bathed with perspiration he counted the seconds by the beatings of his heart. Then he thought it was time to make the last trial, and he put the phial to the violet lips of Faria, and without having occasion to force open his jaws, which had remained extended, he poured the whole of the liquid down his throat.

The draught produced a galvanic effect, a violent trembling pervaded the old man's limbs, his eyes opened until it was fearful to gaze upon them, he heaved a sigh which resembled a shriek, and then all this vibrating frame returned gradually to its state of immobility, only the eyes remained open.

Half an hour, an hour, an hour and a half elapsed, and during this time of anguish, Dantès still doubted; but as soon as the daylight gained, he saw that he was alone with a corpse.

It was time, for the jailer was coming. On this occasion he began his rounds at Dantès' cell, and on leaving him he went on to Faria's dungeon, where he was taking breakfast and some linen. Nothing betokened that the man knew anything of what had occurred. He went on his way.

Dantès was then seized with an indescribable desire to know what was going on in the dungeon of his unfortunate friend. He therefore returned by the subterraneous gallery, and arrived in time to hear the exclamations of the turnkey, who called out for help. Others came, and then was heard the regular tramp of soldiers even when not on duty—behind them came the governor.

Edmond heard the noise of the bed in which they were moving the corpse, heard the voice of the governor, who desired them to throw water on the face; and seeing that, in spite of this application, the prisoner did not recover, sent for the doctor. The governor then went out, and some words of pity fell on Dantès listening ears, mingled with brutal laughter.

Edmond did not lose a word, but comprehended very little of what was said. The voices soon ceased, and it seemed to him as if the persons had all left the cell. Still he dared not to enter, as they might have left some keeper to watch the dead. He remained, therefore, mute and motionless, restraining even his respiration. At the end of an hour, he heard a faint noise, which increased. It was the governor who returned, followed by the doctor and other attendants. There was a moment's silence,—it was evident that the doctor was examining the dead body. The inquiries soon commenced.

The doctor analyzed the symptoms of the malady under which the prisoner had sunk, and declared he was dead. "He is really dead," said the doctor; "this burn in the heel is decisive. The poor fool is cured of his folly, and delivered from his captivity."

"Wasn't his name Faria?" inquired one of the officers who accompanied the governor.

"Yes, sir; and, as he said, it was an ancient name. He was too, very learned, and rational enough on all points which did not relate to his treasure; but on that, indeed, he was obstinate."

"It is the malady we call monomania," said the doctor.

"You had never anything to complain of?" said the governor to the jailer who had charge of the abbé.

"Never, sir," replied the jailer, "never; on the contrary, he sometimes amused me very much by telling me stories. One day, too, when my wife was ill, he gave me a prescription which cured her."

"Ah, ah!" said the doctor, "I was ignorant that I had a competitor; but I hope, M. Governor, that you will show him all proper respect in, consequence."

"Yes, yes, make your mind easy; he shall be decently interred in the newest sack we can find. Will that satisfy you?"

"Must we do this last formality in your presence, sir?" inquired a turnkey.

"Certainly. But make haste—I cannot stay here all day."

"This evening," said the governor, when the task was ended.

"At what o'clock?" inquired a turnkey.——"Why, about ten or eleven o'clock."

"Shall we watch by the corpse?"——"Of what use would it be? Lock the dungeon as if he were alive—that is all." Then the steps retreated, and the voices died away in the distance; the noise of the door, with its creaking hinges and bolts, ceased, and a silence duller than any solitude ensued—the silence of death, which pervaded all, and struck its icy chill through the young man's whole frame. Then he raised the flag-stone cautiously with his head, and looked carefully round the chamber. It was empty; and Dantès, quitting the passage, entered it.

CHAPTER XII.

THE PRISON CEMETERY.

ON the bed, at full length, and faintly lighted by the pale ray that penetrated the window, was visible a sack of coarse cloth, under the large folds of which were stretched a long and stiffened form; it was Faria's last winding-sheet—a winding-sheet which, as the turnkey said, cost so little. All, then, was completed. The idea of suicide, driven away by his friend, and forgotten in his presence whilst living, arose like a phantom before him in presence of his dead body.

"If I could die," he said, "I should go where he goes, and should assuredly find him again. No, I desire to live; I desire to struggle to the very last; I wish to reconquer the happiness of which I have been deprived. Before I die I must not forget that I have my executioners to punish, and perhaps too, who knows, some friends to reward. Yet they will forget me here, and I shall die in my dungeon like Faria." As he said this, he remained motionless, his eyes fixed like a man struck with a sudden idea, but whom this idea fills with amazement. Suddenly he rose, lifted his hand to his brow as if his brain were giddy, paced twice or thrice round his chamber, and then paused abruptly at the bed.

"Ah!" he muttered, "who inspires me with this thought? Is that thou, gracious God? Since none but the dead pass freely from this dungeon, let me assume the place of the dead!" Without giving himself time to re-consider his decision, and, indeed, that he might not allow his thoughts to be distracted from his desperate resolution, he bent over the appalling sack, opened it with the knife which Faria had made, drew the corpse from the sack, and transported it along the gallery to his own chamber, laid it on his couch, passed round its head the rag he wore at night round his own, covered it with his counterpane, once again kissed the ice-cold brow, and tried vainly to close the resisting eyes, which glared horribly; turned the head toward the wall, so that the jailer might, when he brought his evening meal, believe that he was asleep, as was his frequent custom; returned along the gallery, threw the bed against the wall, returned to the other cell, took from the hiding-place the needle and thread, flung off his rags, that they might feel naked flesh only beneath the coarse sackcloth, and getting inside the sack, placed himself in the posture in which the dead body had been laid, and sewed up the mouth of the sack withinside.

The beating of his heart might have been heard, if by any mischance the keepers had entered at that moment. Dantès might have waited until the evening visit was over, but he was afraid the governor might change his resolution, and order the dead body to be removed earlier. In that case his last hope would have been destroyed. Now his project was settled under any circumstances, and he hoped thus to carry it into effect. If during the time he was being conveyed the grave-diggers should discover that they were conveying a live instead of a dead body, Dantès did not intend to give them time to recognize him, but with a sudden cut of the knife, he meant to open the sack from top to bottom, and, profiting by their alarm, escape; if they tried to catch him, he would use his knife.

If they conducted him to the cemetery and laid him in the grave, he would allow himself to be covered with earth, and then, as it was night, the grave-diggers could scarcely have turned their backs, ere he would have worked his way through the soft soil and escape, hoping that the weight would not be too heavy for him to support. If he was deceived in this, and the earth proved too heavy, he would be stifled, and then, so much the better, all would be over. Dantès had not eaten since the previous evening, but he had not thought of hunger or thirst, nor did he now think of it. His position was too precarious to allow him even time to reflect on any thought but one.

The first risk that Dantès ran was, that the warden, when he brought him his supper at seven o'clock, might perceive the substitution he had effected; fortunately, twenty times at least, from misanthropy or fatigue, Dantès had received his jailer in bed, and then the man placed his bread and soup on the table, and went away without saying a word. This time the jailer might not be silent as usual, but speak to Dantès, and seeing that he received no reply, go to the bed, and thus discover all.

When seven o'clock came, Dantès agony really commenced. His hand placed upon his heart was unable to press its throbbings, whilst, with the other, he wiped the perspiration from his temples. From time to time shudderings ran through his whole frame, and collapsed his heart as if it were frozen. Then he thought he was going to die. Yet the hours passed on without any stir, and Dantès felt he had escaped this first danger: it was a good augury. At length, about the hour the governor had appointed, footsteps were heard on the stairs. Edmond felt that the moment had arrived, and summoning all his courage, held his breath, happy if at the same time he could have repressed in like manner the hasty pulsation of his arteries. They stopped at the door—there were two steps, and Dantès guessed it was the two grave-diggers who came to seek him—this idea was soon converted into certainty, when he heard the noise they made in putting down the hand-bier. The door opened, and a dim light reached Dantès' eyes through the coarse sack that covered him; he saw two shadows approach his bed, a third remaining at the door with a torch in his hand. Each of these two men, approaching the ends of the bed, took the sack by its extremities.

"He's heavy though for a thin old man," said one, as he raised the head

"**They** say every year adds half a pound to the weight of the bones," said another, lifting the feet.

"Have you tied the knot?" inquired the first speaker.

"What would be the use of carrying so much more weight?" was the reply; "I can do that when we get there."

"Yes, you're right," replied the companion.

"What's the knot for?" thought Dantès.

They deposited the supposed corpse on the bier. Edmond stiffened himself in order to play his part of a dead man, and then the party, lighted by the man with the torch, who went first, ascended the stairs. Suddenly he felt the fresh and sharp night air, and Dantès recognized the *Mistral*. It was a sudden sensation, at the same time replete with delight and agony. The bearers advanced twenty paces, then stopped, putting their litter down on the ground. One of them went away, and Dantès heard his shoes on the pavement.

"Where am I then?" he asked himself.

"Really, he is by no means a light load!" said the other bearer, sitting on the edge of the hand-barrow. Dantès first impulse was to escape, but fortunately he did not attempt it.

"Light me, you sir," said the other bearer, "or I shall not find what I am looking for." The man with the torch complied, although not asked in the most polite terms.

"What can he be looking for?" thought Edmond. "The spade, perhaps." An exclamation of satisfaction indicated that the grave-digger had found the object of his search. "Here it is at last," he said, "not without some trouble though."

"Yes," was the answer, "but it has lost nothing by waiting."

As he said this, the man came towards Edmond, who heard a heavy and sounding substance laid down beside him, and at the same moment a cord was fastened round his feet with sudden and painful violence.

"Well, have you tied the knot?" inquired the grave-digger, who was looking on. "Yes, and pretty tight too, I can tell you," was the answer.

"Move on, then." And the bier was lifted once more, and they proceeded.

They advanced fifty paces farther, and then stopped to open a door, then went forward again. The noise of the waves dashing against the rocks on which the castle is built, reached Dantès' ear distinctly as they progressed.

"Bad weather!" observed one of the bearers; "not a pleasant night for a dip in the sea."

"Why, yes, the priest runs a chance of being baptised," said the other; and then there was a burst of brutal laughter. Dantès did not comprehend the jest, but his hair stood erect on his head.

"Well, here we are at last," said one of them; "a little farther—a little farther," said the other. "You know very well that the last was stopped on his way, dashed on the rocks, and the governor told us next day that we were careless fellows."

They ascended five or six more steps, and then Dantès felt that they took him one by the head and the other by the heels, and swung him to and fro. "One!" said the grave-diggers, "two! three, and away!" And at the same instant Dantès felt himself flung into the air like a wounded bird falling, falling with a rapidity that made his blood curdle. Although drawn downwards by the same heavy weight which hastened his rapid descent, it seemed to him as if the time were a century. At last, with a terrific dash, he entered the ice-cold water, and as he did so he uttered a shrill cry, stifled in a moment by his immersion beneath the waves.

Dantès had been flung into the sea, into whose depths he was dragged by a thirty-six pound ball tied to his feet. The sea is the cemetery of If Castle.

CHAPTER XIII.

RESCUED.

DANTÈS, although giddy and almost suffocated, had yet sufficient presence of mind to hold his breath; and as his right hand (prepared as he was for every chance) held his knife open, he rapidly ripped up the sack, extricated his arm, and then his body; but in spite of all his efforts to free himself from the bullet, he felt it dragging him down still lower. He then bent his body, and by a desperate effort severed the cord that bound his legs, at the moment he was suffocating. With a vigorous spring he rose to the surface of the sea, whilst the bullet bore to its depths the sack that had so nearly become his shroud.

Dantès merely paused to breathe, and then dived again, in order to avoid being seen. When he arose a second time, he was fifty paces from where he had first sunk. Behind him, blacker than the sea, blacker than the sky, rose, like a phantom, the giant of granite, whose projecting crags seemed like arms extended to seize their prey; and on the highest rock was a torch that lighted two figures. He fancied these two forms were looking at the sea; doubtless these strange undertakers had heard his cry. Dantès dived again, and remained a long time beneath the water. When he reappeared the light had disappeared.

It was necessary to strike out to sea.

Suddenly the sky seemed to him to become still darker and more dense, and compact clouds lowered towards him; at the same time he felt a violent pain in his knee. His imagination told him a ball had struck him, and that in a moment he would hear the report; but he heard nothing, Dantès put out his hand, and felt resistance; he then extended his leg, and felt the land, and in an instant guessed the nature of the object he had taken for a cloud.

Before him rose a mass of strangely-formed rocks, that resembled nothing so much as a vast fire petrified at the moment of its most fervent combustion. It was the isle of Tiboulen.

An overhanging rock offered him a temporary shelter, and scarcely had he availed himself of it when the tempest burst forth in all its fury.

A flash of lightning, as if the whole of the heavens were opened, illumined the darkness. By its light, between the isle of Lemaire and Cape Croiselle, a half mile distant, Dantès saw, like a spectre, a fishing-boat driven rapidly on by the force of the winds and waves. A second after, he saw it again, approaching nearer. Dantès cried at the top of his voice to warn them of their danger, but the crew saw it themselves. At the same moment a violent crash was heard, and cries of distress. Perched on the summit of the rock, Dantès saw, by the lightning, the vessel in pieces; and amongst the fragments were visible the agonized features of the unhappy sailors. Then all became dark again.

Dantès ran down the rocks at the risk of being himself dashed to pieces; he listened, he strove to examine, but he heard and saw nothing —all human cries had ceased, and the tempest alone continued to rage. By degrees the wind abated, vast grey clouds rolled toward the west, and the blue firmament appeared studded with bright stars. Soon a red streak became visible in the horizon, the waves whitened, a light played over them, and gilded their foaming crests with gold. It was day.

Dantès stood silent and motionless before this vast spectacle, for since his captivity he had forgotten it. He turned towards the fortress, and looked both at the sea and the land. The gloomy building rose from the bosom of the ocean with that imposing majesty of inanimate objects which seems to watch and to command. It was about five o'clock. The sea continued to grow calmer.

He saw appear, at the extremity of the isle of Ponègue, like a bird skimming over the sea, a small bark, that the eye of a sailor alone could recognize as a Genoese tartane. She was coming out of Marseilles harbor, and was standing out to sea rapidly, her sharp prow cleaving through the waves. "Oh!" cried Edmond, "to think that in half an hour I could join her, did I not fear being questioned, detected, and conveyed back to Marseilles! What can I do? What story can I invent? Under pretext of trading along the coast, these men, who are in reality smugglers, will prefer selling me to doing a good action. I must wait. But I cannot—I am starving. In a few hours my strength will be utterly exhausted: besides, perhaps I have not been missed at the fortress. I can pass as one of the sailors wrecked last night. This story will pass current, for there is no one left to contradict me."

As he spoke, Dantès looked toward the spot where the fishing-vessel had been wrecked, and started. The red cap of one of the sailors hung to a point of the rock, and some beams that had formed part of the vessel's keel, floated at the foot of the crags. In an instant Dantès' plan was formed. He swam to the cap, placed it on his head, seized one of the beams, and struck out so as to cross the line the vessel was taking.

"I am saved!" murmured he. And this conviction restored his strength.

He soon perceived the vessel, which, having the wind right ahead, was tacking between If Castle and the tower of Planier. For an instant he feared lest the bark, instead of keeping in shore, should stand out to sea; but he soon saw by her manœuvres that she wished to pass, like most vessels bound for Italy, between the islands of Jaros and Calaseraigne. However, the vessel and the swimmer insensibly neared one another, and in one of its tacks the bark approached within a quarter of a mile of him. He rose on the waves, making signs of distress; but no one on board perceived him, and the vessel stood on another tack. Dantès would have cried out, but he reflected that the wind would drown his voice.

It was then he rejoiced at his precaution in taking the beam, for without it he would have been unable, perhaps, to reach the vessel—certainly to return to shore, should he be unsuccessful in attracting attention.

Dantès, although almost sure as to what course the bark would take, had yet watched it anxiously until it tacked and stood toward him. Then he advanced; but before they had met, the vessel again changed her direction. By a violent effort he rose half out of the water, waving his cap and uttering a loud hail. This time he was both seen and heard, and the tartane instantly steered toward him. At the same time, he saw they were about to lower the boat.

An instant after, the boat, rowed by two men, advanced rapidly toward him. Dantès abandoned the beam, which he thought now useless, and swam vigorously to meet them. But he had reckoned too much upon his strength, and then he felt how serviceable the beam had been to him. His arms grew stiff, his legs had lost their flexibility, and he was almost breathless.

He uttered a second cry. The two sailors redoubled their efforts, and one of them cried in Italian, "Courage!"

The word reached his ear as a wave which he no longer had the strength to surmount passed over his head. He rose again to the surface, supporting himself by one of those desperate efforts a drowning man makes, uttered a third cry, and felt himself sink again, as if the fatal bullet were again tied to his feet. The water passed over his head, and the sky seemed livid. A violent effort again brought him to the surface. He felt as if something seized him by the hair, but he saw and heard nothing. He had fainted.

When he opened his eyes, Dantès found himself on the deck of the tartane.

"Who are you?" said the pilot, in bad French.

"I am," replied Dantès, in bad Italian, "a Maltese sailor. We were coming from Syracuse laden with grain. The storm of last night overtook us at Cape Morgion, and we were wrecked on these rocks, to which I had the good luck to cling while our captain and the rest were all lost. I saw your craft, and fearful of being left to perish on the desolate island, I swam off on a fragment of the vessel in order to try and gain your bark. You have saved my life, and I thank you," continued Dantès. "I was lost when one of your sailors caught hold of my hair."

"It was I," said a sailor of a frank appearance; "and it was time, for you were sinking."

"Yes," returned Dantès, holding out his hand, "I thank you again."

"I almost hesitated though," replied the sailor; "you looked more like a brigand than an honest man, with your beard six inches and your hair a foot long." Dantès recollected that his hair and beard had not been cut all the time he was in jail.

"Yes," said he, "I made a vow to our Lady of the Grotto, in a moment of danger, not to cut my hair or beard for ten years; but to-day the vow expires."

"Now what are we to do with you?" said the captain.

"Alas! anything you please. My captain is dead; I have barely escaped; but I am a good sailor."

"I say, captain," said the sailor who had cried "Courage!" to Dantès, "if what he says is true, what hinders his staying with us?"

"If he says true," said the captain, "we can agree very well, if you are reasonable."

"Give me what you give the others, and all will be arranged," returned Dantès.

Jacopo dived into the hold and returned with what Edmond wanted.

"Now, then, do you wish for anything else?" said the patron.

"A piece of bread and another glass of the capital rum I tasted, for I have not eaten or drunk for a long time." He had not tasted food for forty hours. A piece of bread was brought, and Jacopo offered him the gourd.

"Larboard your helm," cried the captain to the steersman. Dantès glanced to the same side as he lifted the gourd to his mouth; but his hand stopped.

"Halloa! what's the matter at If Castle?" said the captain.

A small white cloud which had attracted Dantès attention, crowned the summit of the bastion. At the same moment the faint report of a gun was heard. The sailors looked at one another.

"What is this?" asked the captain.

"A prisoner has escaped from the Castle If; and they are firing the alarm gun," replied Dantès. The captain glanced at him; but he had lifted the rum to his lips, and was drinking with so much composure, that his suspicions, if he had any, died away.

"At any rate," murmured he, "if it be, so much the better, for I have made a rare acquisition." Under pretense of being fatigued, Dantès asked to take the helm; the steersman, enchanted to be relieved, looked at the captain, and the latter by a sign indicated that he might abandon it to his new messmate. Dantès could thus keep his eyes on Marseilles.

"What is the day of the month?" asked he of Jacopo, who sat down beside him.

"The 28th of February!"

"In what year?"

"You have forgotten?"

"I have been so frightened last night," replied Dantès, smiling, "that I have almost lost my memory. I ask you what year is it?"

"The year 1829," returned Jacopo.

It was fourteen years day for day since Dantès' arrest. He was nineteen when he entered If; thirty-three when he escaped. A sorrowful smile passed over his face; he asked himself what had become of Mercédès, who must believe him dead. Then his eyes lighted up with hatred as he thought of the three men who had caused him so long and wretched a captivity. He renewed against Danglars, Fernand, and Villefort the oath of implacable vengeance he had made in his dungeon. This oath was no longer a vain menace; for the fastest sailor in the Mediterranean would have been unable to overtake the little tartane, with every stitch of canvas set, flying before the wind to Leghorn.

CHAPTER XIV.

THE SMUGGLERS.

DANTÈS had not been a day on board before he had an insight into the persons with whom he sailed. Dantès was on board a smuggling lugger.

In the first instance the master had received Dantès on board with a certain degree of mistrust. When he saw the light smoke floating like a plume above the Castle and heard the distant explosion, he was instantly struck with the idea that he had on board his vessel one for whom, like the goings in and comings out of kings, they accord salutes of cannons.

This made him less uneasy, it must be owned, than if the new-comer had proved a custom-house officer; but this latter supposition also disappeared like the first, when he beheld the perfect tranquillity of his recruit.

Edmond thus had the advantage of knowing what the owner was, without the owner knowing who he was; and however the old sailor and his crew tried to "pump" him, they extracted nothing more from him.

It was thus, in this reciprocal position, that they reached Leghorn. Here Edmond was to undergo another trial; it was to see if he should recognize himself, never having beheld his own features for fourteen years. He had preserved a tolerably good remembrance of what the youth had been, and was now to find what the man had become. His comrades believed that his vow was fulfilled, as he had twenty times touched at Leghorn before he remembered a barber in the Rue Saint-Ferdinand; he went there to have his beard and hair cut.

When the operation was concluded, when Edmond felt his chin was completely smooth, and his hair reduced to its usual length, he requested a looking-glass in which he might see himself. He was now, as we have said, three-and-thirty years of age, and his fourteen years' imprisonment had produced a great moral change in his appearance.

To the elegance of a nervous and slight form had succeeded the solidity of a rounded and muscular figure. As to his voice, prayers, sobs, and imprecations had changed it now into a soft and singularly touching tone, and now into a sound rude and almost hoarse. Moreover, being perpetually in twilight or darkness, his eyes had acquired that singular faculty of distinguishing objects in the night common to the hyena and the wolf. Edmond smiled when he beheld himself: it was impossible that his best friend—if, indeed, he had any friend left—could recognize him; he could not recognize himself.

The master of *La Jeune Amélie,* who was very desirous of retaining amongst his crew a man of Edmond's value, had offered an engagement to Dantès; but Dantès, who had his own projects, would not agree for a longer time than three months.

La Jeune Amélie had a very active crew, very obedient to their captain, who lost as little time as possible. He had scarcely been a week at Leghorn before the hold of his vessel was filled with goods on which the Crown had forgotten to put its mark. The master was to get all this out of Leghorn free of duties, and land it on the shores of Corsica, where speculators undertook to forward the cargo to France.

When the profits were shared out, each man had a hundred Tuscan livres. But the voyage was not ended. They turned the bowsprit towards Sardinia, where they intended to take in a cargo, which was to replace what had been discharged. The second operation was as successful as the first, *La Jeune Amélie* was in luck. This new cargo was destined for the coast of the Duchy of Lucca, and consisted almost entirely of Havannah cigars, sherry, and Malaga wines.

Two months and a half elapsed in these trips, and Edmond had become as skilful a coaster as he had been a hardy seaman; he had formed an acquaintance with all the smugglers on the coast, and learned all the masonic signs by which these half pirates recognize each other. He had passed and re-passed his isle of Monte-Cristo twenty times, but not once had he found an opportunity of landing there. In vain did he rack his imagination; fertile as it was, he could not devise any plan for reaching the wished-for isle without being accompanied thither.

Dantès was tossed about on these doubts and wishes, when the patron, who had great confidence in him, and was very desirous of retaining him in his service, took him by the arm one evening and led him to a tavern, where the leading smugglers of Leghorn used to congregate. It was here they discussed coast business. Already Dantès had visited this maritime Bourse two or three times, and seeing all these hardy free-traders, who supplied the whole coast for nearly two hundred leagues in extent, he had asked himself what power might not that man attain who should give the impulse of his will to all these contrary and diverging links. This time it was a greater matter that was under discussion, connected with a vessel laden with Turkey carpets, stuffs of the Levant, and cashmeres. It was requisite to find some neutral ground on which an exchange could be made, and then to try and land these goods on the coast of France. If successful the profit would be enormous, there would be fifty or sixty piastres each for the crew.

The master of *La Jeune Amélie* proposed as a place of landing the isle of Monte-Cristo, which being completely deserted, and having neither soldiers nor revenue officers, seem to have been placed in the midst of the ocean by Mercury, the god of merchants and robbers, classes which we in modern times have separated if not made distinct, but which antiquity appears to have included in the same category. At the mention of Monte-Cristo Dantès started with joy; he rose to conceal his emotion, and took a turn round the smoky tavern, where all the languages of the known world were jumbled in a *lingua franca*. When he again joined the two persons who had been discussing, it had been decided that they should touch at Monte-Cristo, and set out on the following night. Edmond, being consulted, was of opinion that the island offered every possible security, and that great enterprises to be well done should be done quickly. Nothing then was altered in the plan arranged, and orders were given to get under way next night, and wind and weather permitting, to gain, the day after, the waters of the neutral isle.

CHAPTER XV.

MONTE-CRISTO ISLAND

THUS, at length, by one of those pieces of unlooked-for good fortune which sometimes occur to those on whom misfortune has for a long time spent itself, Dantès was about to arrive at his wished-for opportunity by simple and natural means, and land in the island without incurring any suspicion. One night only separated him from his departure so ardently wished for.

The night was one of the most feverish that Dantès had ever passed, and during its progress all the charms good and evil passed through his brain. The day came at length, and was almost as feverish as the night had been, but it brought reason to aid his imagination, and Dantès was then enabled to arrange a plan which had hitherto been vague and unsettled in his brain. Night came, and with it the preparation for departure, and these preparations served to conceal Dantès' agitations. He had by degrees assumed such authority over his companions that he was almost like a commander on board; and as his orders were always clear, distinct, and easy of execution, his comrades obeyed him with celerity and pleasure.

The old Skipper did not interfere, for he too had recognized the superiority of Dantès over the crew and himself. He saw in the young man his natural successor, and regretted that he had not a daughter, that he might have bound Edmond to him by a distinguished alliance. At seven o'clock in the evening all was ready, and at ten minutes past seven they doubled the lighthouse just as the beacon was kindled. The sea was calm, and, with a fresh breeze from the south-east, they sailed beneath a bright blue sky, in which God also lighted up in turn His beacon-lights, each of which is a world. Dantès told them that all hands might turn in, and he would take the helm. When the Maltese (for so they called Dantès) had said this, it was sufficient, and all went to their cots contentedly. This frequently happened. Dantès, rejected by all the world, frequently experienced a desire for solitude; and what solitude is at the same time more complete, more poetical, than that of a bark floating isolated on the sea during the obscurity of the night, in the silence of immensity, and under the eye of Heaven?

Now this solitude was peopled with his thoughts, the night lighted up by his illusions, and the silence animated by his anticipations. When the master awoke, the vessel was hurrying on with every sail set, and every sail full with the breeze. They were making nearly ten knots an hour. The isle of Monte-Cristo loomed large in the horizon. Edmond resigned the bark to the master's care, and went and lay down in his hammock; but in spite of a sleepless night, he could not close his eyes for a moment. Two hours afterwards he came on deck, as the boat was about to double the isle of Elba. They were just abreast of Mareciana, and beyond the flat but verdant isle of La Pianosa. The peak of Monte-Cristo, reddened by the burning sun, was seen against the azure sky. Dantès desired the helmsman to put down his helm, in order to leave La Pianosa on the right hand as he knew that he should thus decrease the distance by two or three knots. About five o'clock in the evening the island was quite distinct, and everything on it was plainly perceptible, owing to that clearness of the atmosphere which is peculiar to the light which the rays of the sun cast at its setting.

Night came, and at ten o'clock p. m. they anchored. The *Amélie* was the first at the rendezvous. In spite of his usual command over himself, Dantès could not restrain his impetuosity. He was the first who jumped on shore. It was dark; but at eleven o'clock the moon rose in the midst of the ocean, whose every wave she silvered, and then played in floods of pale light on the rocky hills of this second Pelion.

The island was familiar to the crew of *La Jeune Amélie*—it was one of her halting-places. As to Dantès, he had passed it on his voyages to and from the Levant, but never touched at it. He questioned Jacopo. "Where shall we pass the night?" he inquired.

"Why, on board the tartane," replied the sailor.

"Should we not be better in the caves of the island?"

"I do not know of any," replied Jacopo.

For a moment Dantès was speechless; then he remembered that these caves might have been filled up by some accident, or even stopped up, for the sake of greater security, by Cardinal Spada. The point was, then, to discover the last opening. It was useless to search at night, and Dantès therefore delayed all investigation until the morning. Besides, a signal made half a league out at sea, and to which *La Jeune Amélie* also replied by a similar signal, indicated that the moment was arrived for business. The boat that now arrived, assured by the answering signal that all was right, soon came in sight, white and silent as a phantom, and cast anchor within a cable's length of shore.

Then the landing began.

No one had the slightest suspicion; and when next day, taking a fowling-piece, powder, and shot, Dantès testified a desire to go and kill some of the wild goats that were seen springing from rock to rock, his wish was construed into a love of sport, or a desire for solitude. However, Jacopo insisted on following him; and Dantès did not oppose this, fearing if he did so that he might incur distrust. Scarcely, however, had he gone a quarter of a league than, having killed a kid, he begged Jacopo to take it to his comrades, and request them to cook it, and when ready to let him know by firing a gun.

When all was ready, they fired the signal and saw him hurrying down the crags; but his foot slipped and he had a fall. He vowed that he was internally injured so that they had to leave him there, alone—though Jacopo wanted to stay by him—with the intention of calling for him in a little time.

Needless to say, next morning he was up with the sun and began his search solitarily on the lines which Faria had laid down. The hoard was cunningly concealed but he was too sagely directed to fail. The Spadas' treasure was contained in a chest, which was opened by his pick.

Three compartments divided the coffer. In the first, blazed piles of golden coin; in the second, ingots, which possessed nothing attractive save their value, were ranged; in the third, Dantès grasped handfuls of diamonds, pearls, and rubies, which, as they fell on one another, sounded like hail against glass. After having touched, felt, examined these treasures, Edmond rushed through the caverns like a man seized with frenzy; he leapt on a rock, from whence he could behold the sea. He was alone. Alone with these countless, these unheard-of treasures! Was he awake, or was it but a dream?

He soon felt himself calmer and more happy, for now only he began to credit his felicity. He then set himself to count his fortune. There were a thousand bricks of gold, each weighing from two to three pounds; then he piled up twenty-five thousand crowns, each worth about twenty dollars of our money, and bearing the effigies of Alexander VI. and his predecessors; and he saw that the compartment was not half empty. And he measured ten double handfuls of precious stones, many of which, mounted by the most famous workmen, were valuable for their execution. Dantès saw the light gradually disappear; and fearing to be surprised in the cavern, left it, his gun in his hand. A piece of biscuit and a small quantity of rum formed his supper, and he snatched a few hours' sleep, lying over the mouth of the cave.

On the sixth day the smugglers returned. They had merely come to Monte-Cristo to fetch him away, so he embarked that same evening, and proceeded with the captain to Leghorn. Arrived, he repaired to the house of a Jew dealer in precious stones, to whom he disposed of four of his smallest diamonds, for five thousand francs each. Dantès half feared that such valuable jewels in the hands of a poor sailor like himself might excite suspicion; but the cunning purchaser asked no troublesome questions concerning a bargain by which he gained at least four thousand francs.

The following day Dantès presented Jacopo with an entirely new vessel, accompanying the gift by a donation of one hundred piastres, that he might provide himself with a suitable crew and other requisites for his outfit, upon conditions of his going direct to Marseilles for the purpose of inquiring after an old man named Louis Dantès, residing in

Meillan Alley, and also a young female called Mercédès, an inhabitant of the Catalan village. Jacopo could scarcely believe his senses at receiving this munificent present, which Dantès hastened to account for by saying that he had merely been a sailor from whim and a desire to spite his friends who did not allow him as much money as he liked to spend; but that on his arrival at Leghorn he had come into possession of a large fortune, left him by an uncle, whose sole heir he was. The superior education of Dantès gave an air of such extreme probability to this statement that it never once occurred to Jacopo to doubt its accuracy. The term for which Edmond had engaged to serve on board *La Jeune Amélie* having expired, Dantès took leave of the captain, who at first tried all his powers of persuasion to induce him to remain one of the crew, but having been told the history of the legacy, he ceased to importune him further. The succeeding morning Jacopo set sail for Marseilles, with directions from Dantès to join him at the island of Monte-Cristo.

Having seen Jacopo fairly out of the harbor, Dantès proceeded to make his final adieus on board *La Jeune Amélie,* distributing so liberal a gratuity among her crew as procured him the unanimous good wishes and expressions of cordial interest in all that concerned him; to the captain he promised to write when he had made up his mind as to his future plans; this leave-taking over, Dantès departed for Genoa. At the moment of his arrival a small yacht was being tried in the bay; this yacht had been built by order of an Englishman, who, having heard that the Genoese excelled all other builders along the shores of the Mediterranean in the construction of fast-sailing vessels, was desirous of possessing a specimen of their skill; the price agreed upon between the Englishman and the Genoese builder was forty thousand francs. Dantès, struck with the beauty and capability of the little vessel, applied to its owner to transfer it to him, offering sixty thousand francs, upon condition of being allowed to take immediate possession of it.

The following day Dantès sailed with his yacht from the port of Genoa, amid the gaze of an immense crowd drawn together by curiosity to see the rich Spanish nobleman who preferred managing his vessel himself. But their wonder was soon exchanged to admiration at the perfect skill with which Dantès handled the helm, and, without quitting it, making his little vessel perform every movement he chose to direct: his bark seemed, indeed, replete with all but human intelligence, so promptly did it obey the slightest impulse given; and Dantès required but a short trial of his beautiful craft to acknowledge that it was not without truth the Genoese had attained their high reputation in the art of ship-building. The spectators followed the little vessel with their eyes so long as it remained visible; they then turned their conjectures upon her probable destination. Some insisted she was making for Corsica, others the isle of Elba; bets were offered to any amount that she was bound for Spain;

while Africa was positively reported by many persons as her intended course; but no one thought of Monte-Cristo. Yet thither it was that Dantès guided his vessel, and at Monte-Cristo he arrived at the close of the second day. Early on the following morning he commenced the removal of his riches, and ere nightfall the whole of his immense wealth was safely deposited in the secret compartments of his hidden closet.

Upon the eighth day of his being on the island he discerned a small vessel crowding all sail towards Monte-Cristo. As it neared, he recognized it as the bark given to Jacopo. He immediately signalled it. His signal was returned, and in two hours afterwards the bark lay at anchor beside the yacht. A mournful answer awaited each of Edmond's eager inquiries as to the information Jacopo had obtained. Old Dantès was dead, and Mercédès had disappeared. Dantès listened to these melancholy tidings with outward calmness; but, leaping lightly ashore, he signified his desire to be quite alone. In a couple of hours he returned. Two of the men from Jacopo's bark came on board the yacht to assist in navigating it, and he commanded she should be steered direct to Marseilles. For his father's death he was in some manner prepared; but how to account for the mysterious disappearance of Mercédès he knew not.

Without divulging his secret, Dantès could not give sufficiently clear instructions to an agent. There were, besides, other particulars he was desirous of ascertaining, and those were of a nature he alone could investigate in a manner satisfactory to himself. His looking-glass had assured him, during his stay at Leghorn, that he ran no risk of recognition; added to which, he had now the means of adopting any disguise he thought proper. One fine morning, then, his yacht, followed by the little bark, boldly entered the port of Marseilles, and anchored exactly opposite the memorable spot from whence, on the never-to-be-forgotten night of his departure for the Castle If, he had been put on board the vessel destined to convey him thither. Still Dantès could not view without a shudder the approach of a gendarme who accompanied the officers deputed to demand his bill of health ere the yacht was permitted to hold communication with the shore; but with that perfect self-possession he had acquired during his acquaintance with Faria, Dantès coolly presented an English passport he had obtained from Leghorn, and, with that prompt attention which all such documents receive, he was informed there existed no obstacle to his immediate debarkation.

The first object that attracted the attention of Dantès, as he landed on the Canerbière, was one of the crew belonging to the *Pharaoh*. Edmond hailed the appearance of this man, who had served under himself, as a sure test of the safe and perfect change time had worked in his own appearance. Going straight toward him, he commenced a variety of questions on different subjects, carefully watching the man's countenance as he did so; but not a word or look implied his having the slightest idea of ever having seen before the individual with whom he was then conversing. Giving the sailor a piece of money in return for his civility, Dantès proceeded onwards; but ere he had gone many steps he heard the man loudly calling him to stop. Dantès instantly turned to meet him. "I beg your pardon, sir," said the honest fellow, in almost breathless haste, "but I believe you have made a mistake: you intended to give me a two-franc piece, and see, you gave me a double Napoleon."——"Thank you, my good friend. I see that I have made a trifling mistake, as you say; but by way of rewarding your honest spirit I give you another double Napoleon, that you may drink to my health, and be able to ask your messmates to join you."

So extreme was the surprise of the sailor, that he was unable even to thank Edmond, whose receding figure he continued to gaze after in speechless astonishment. At length, when Dantès had wholly disappeared, he drew a deep breath, and, with another look at his gold, he returned to the quay, saying to himself, "Ah, that's a nabob from India."

Dantès, meanwhile, continued his route. Each step he trod oppressed his heart with fresh emotion: his first and most indelible recollections were there; not a tree, not a street that he passed but seemed filled with dear and cherished reminiscences. And thus he proceeded onward till he found himself at the door of the house in which his father had lived. Dantès succeeded in inducing the janitor to go up to the present possessors of the fifth flat, and ask permission for a gentleman to be allowed to look at them. The tenants of the humble lodging, once the scene of all Dantès' early joys, consisted of a young couple who had been scarcely married a week; and the sight of a wedded happiness he was doomed never to experience drove a bitter pang through his heart.

The young couple gazed with astonishment at the sight of their visitor's emotion, and wondered to see the large tears silently chase each other down his otherwise stern and immovable features; but they felt the sacredness of his grief, and kindly refrained from questioning him as to its cause, while, with instinctive delicacy, they left him to indulge his sorrow alone. When he withdrew from the scene of his painful recollections, they both accompanied him down-stairs, reiterating their hope that he would come again whenever he pleased, and assuring him their poor dwelling should ever be open to him. As Edmond passed the door of similar rooms on the fourth floor, he paused to inquire whether Caderousse the tailor still dwelt there, but he received for reply, that the individual in question had got into difficulties, and at the present time kept a small inn on the Bellegarde-Beaucaire road.

Having obtained the address of the person to whom the house in Meillan Alley belonged, Dantès next proceeded thither, and, under the name of Lord Wilmore (the same as that in his passport), purchased the small dwelling for the sum of 25,000 francs, at least 10,000 more than it was worth; but had its owner asked ten times the sum he did, it would unhesitatingly have been given. The very same day the occupants of the apartments on the fifth floor of the house, now become the property of Dantès, were duly informed by the notary who had arranged the necessary transfer of deeds, &c., that the new landlord gave them their choice of any of the rooms in the house, without the least augmentation of rent, upon condition of their giving instant possession of the two small chambers they at present inhabited.

This strange event served to find food for wonder and curiosity in the neighborhood, and a multitude of various conjectures were afloat as to the probable cause of the house being so suddenly and mysteriously disposed of; but each surmise seemed to wander farther and farther from the truth. But that which raised public astonishment to a climax, and set all speculations at defiance, was the circumstance of the same stranger who had in the morning visited Meillan Alley being seen in the evening walking in the little village of the Catalans, and afterwards observed to enter a poor fisherman's hut, and to pass more than an hour in inquiring after persons who had either been dead or gone away for more than fifteen or sixteen years. But on the following day the family from whom all these particulars had been asked received a handsome present, consisting of an entirely new fishing-boat, with a full supply of excellent nets. The delighted recipients of these munificent gifts would gladly have poured out their thanks to their generous benefactor; but they had seen him, upon quitting the hut, merely give some orders to a sailor, and then, springing lightly on horseback, quit Marseilles.

CHAPTER XVI.

THE ROADHOUSE.

MIDWAY between the town of Beaucaire and the village of Bellegarde, stood a small roadside inn, from the front of which hung, creaking and flapping in the wind, a sheet of tin covered with a caricature resemblance of the Pont du Gard.

For nearly the last eight years the small inn we have just been describing had been kept by a man and his wife, with two servants. But, alas! the occupation of each domestic was but nominal, for a canal recently made had proved a most successful speculation, and had transferred the mode of sending merchandize and luggage from the heavy wagons to the towed barge, while travelers forsook the diligence to glide over the smooth waters by the more agreeable aid of the steamboat. And, as though to add to the daily misery which the prosperous canal inflicted on the unfortunate man, whose utter ruin it was fast accomplishing, it was situated not a hundred steps from the forsaken inn, of which we have given so faithful a description.

The host himself was a man of from forty to fifty-five years of age, tall, strong, and bony, a perfect specimen of the natives of those southern latitudes; he had the dark, sparkling, and deep-set eye, curved nose, and teeth white as a carnivorous animal; his hair, which, spite of the light touch time had as yet left on it, seemed as though it refused to assume any other color than its own, was like his beard, which he wore under his chin, thick and curly, and but slightly mingled with a few silvery threads. His naturally muddy complexion had assumed a still further shade of brown from the habit the unfortunate man had acquired of stationing himself from early morning till latest eve at the threshold of his door, in eager hope that some traveler, either equestrian or pedestrian, might give him the delight of once more seeing a guest enter his doors; but his patience and his expectations were alike useless; yet there he stood, day after day, exposed to the beams of a burning sun, with no other protection for his head than a red handkerchief twisted around it, after the manner of Spanish muleteers. This anxious, careworn host was no other than our acquaintance Caderousse.

His wife, Madeleine, was pale, meagre, and sickly-looking. She remained nearly always in her chamber, situated on the first floor; sitting shivering in her chair, or extended languid and feeble on her bed, while her husband kept his daily watch at the door—a duty he performed with so much the greater willingness, as it saved him the necessity of listening to the endless plaints and murmurs of his helpmate, who never saw him without breaking out into bitter invectives against fate and the unmerited hardships she was called upon to endure; to all of which her husband would calmly return an unvarying reply, couched in these philosophic words:

"Cease to grieve about it, La Carconte. It is God's pleasure that you should suffer, and whether you like it or not, you must bear it."

The sobriquet of La Carconte had been bestowed on Madeleine Radelle from the circumstance of her having been born in a village so called, and her husband had bestowed on her the name in place of her sweet and euphonious name of Madeleine, which, in all probability, his rude guttural language would not have enabled him to pronounce. Still, let it not be supposed that amid this affected resignation to the will of Providence, the unfortunate host did not writhe under the double misery of seeing the hateful canal carry off alike his customers and profits, and the daily implication of his peevish partner's lamentations.

Like others of the south, he was of sober habits and moderate desires, but vain, and addicted to display. During the days of his prosperity, no festivity, or ceremonial took place without himself and wife being among the spectators. He dressed in the picturesque costume worn in the south, while La Carconte displayed the charming fashion prevalent among the females of Arles, a mode of attire borrowed equally from Greece and Arabia. But, by degrees, Gaspard Caderousse, unable to appear abroad in splendor, had given up any further participation in these pomps, both for himself or wife, although a bitter feeling of envious discontent filled his mind as merry sounds reached even the miserable hostelry to which he still clung, more for shelter than profit.

Caderousse was, as usual, at his place of observation before the door, his eyes sadly glancing from a piece of closely-shaven grass—on which some fowls were picking—to the deserted road, north and south, when he was roused by the shrill voice of his wife. Murmuring, he proceeded to the chamber of his better half—taking care to set the entrance-door wide open.

At the moment Caderousse quitted the door, the road on which strained his sight was void and lonely as a desert at mid-day. There it lay stretched out, bordered by tall, meagre trees; no one could imagine that any traveler would expose himself to such a formidable Sahara. Nevertheless, had Caderousse but retained his post, he might have caught sight from the direction of Bellegarde, a man and horse, between whom the kindest and most amiable understanding appeared to exist. His rider was a priest, dressed in black, and wearing a three-cornered hat; spite of the ardent rays the pair came on at a tolerably smart trot.

Having arrived, the horse stopped, but whether for his own pleasure or his rider's would be difficult to say. However, the priest, dismounting, led his steed to a handle that projected from a shutter, he tied the animal, and, having drawn a red cotton handkerchief from his pocket, wiped away the perspiration that streamed from his brow. He struck thrice with his iron-shod stick. At this unusual sound a huge black dog came, snarling and displaying his sharp white teeth, with hostility that proved how little he was accustomed to society. A heavy footstep was heard descending the wooden staircase from the upper floor, and, with many bows, mine host welcomed the priest.

Said the astonished Caderousse. "Now, then, Margontin," cried he, "will you be quiet? Pray don't heed him, sir!—he only barks, he never bites! a glass of good wine would be acceptable this measly hot day!" Then perceiving for the first time the description of traveler he had to entertain, Caderousse exclaimed: "A thousand pardons, your reverence! I did not observe whom I had the honor to receive. What would you please to have, father? I am at your service."

The priest gazed on the individual with a long and searching gaze—

even seemed to court a similar scrutiny on the landlord's part; then, remarking in the countenance no other expression than extreme surprise at his own want of attention to an inquiry, he deemed it as well to terminate this emotion, and said, speaking with a strong Italian accent: "You are, I presume, M. Caderousse?"

"Your reverence is quite correct," answered the host, even more surprised at the question than by the silence; "I am Gaspard Caderousse, at your service."

"Gaspard Caderousse! Yes, that agrees both with the baptismal appellation and surname. You formerly lived, I believe, in Meillan Alley, on the fourth floor; where you followed the business of a tailor?"

"True, till the trade fell off. Then, it is so very hot at Marseilles, that the inhabitants will be obliged to leave off clothes. But talking of heat, can't I offer you refreshment?"

"Yes; let me have a bottle of your best, and then, with your permission, we will resume our conversation from where we left off."

"As you please," said Caderousse, who, anxious not to lose the present customer for one of the few bottles of Cahors still remaining, hastily raised a trap-door in the floor of the parlor and kitchen. Upon his issuing in five minutes, he found the abbé seated on a stool, leaning his elbow on a table, while Margontin, appeased by the traveler having pronounced the unusual command for refreshments, had his long, skinny neck resting on his lap, while his dim eye was fixed on the traveler.

"Are you quite alone?" inquired the guest, as Caderousse placed before him the bottle and a glass.

"Quite, quite alone, or, all but so, for my poor wife is laid up with illness, and unable to render me the least assistance, poor Carconte!"

"You are married, then?" said the priest, with interest, glancing round as he spoke at the humble fittings-up.

"Ah, father," said Caderousse, with a sigh, "in this world a man does not thrive the better for being honest." The abbé fixed on him a piercing glance.

"I can certainly say that much for myself," replied the publican, sustaining the scrutiny; "I can boast with truth of being an honest man; and," continued he, shaking his head, "that is more than every one can say now-a-days."

"So much the better, if what you assert be true," said the abbé; "for I am firmly persuaded that, sooner or later, the good will be rewarded, and the wicked punished."

"Such words belong to your profession," answered Caderousse, with a bitter expression, "you cannot make people believe them."

"You are wrong to speak thus," said the abbè; "and perhaps I may, in my own person, be able to prove it."

"What mean you?" inquired Caderousse, with surprise.

"In the first place, it is requisite I should be satisfied you are the person I am in search of."

"What proofs do you require?"

"Did you, in the year 1814 or 1815, know of a sailor named Dantès?"

"Did I? I should think I did. Poor dear Edmond! Why, Edmond! Why, Edmond Dantès and myself were intimate friends!" exclaimed Caderousse, whose countenance assumed an almost purple hue, as he caught the penetrating gaze of the abbé fixed on him, while the clear, calm eye of the questioner seemed to cover him with confusion.

"You remind me," said the priest, "that the young man concerning whom I asked you was said to bear the name of Edmond."

"Said to bear the name!" repeated Caderousse, becoming excited and eager. "Why, he was so called as truly as I myself bore the appellation of Gaspard Caderousse; but, M. l'Abbé, tell me, I pray, what has become of poor Edmond. Did you know him? Is he alive and at liberty? Is he prosperous and happy?"

"He died a more wretched, hopeless, heart-broken prisoner than the felons who pay the penalty of their crimes at the galleys of Toulon."

A deadly paleness succeeded the deep suffusion which had before spread over the countenance of Caderousse, who turned away, but not so much so as to prevent the priest's observing him wiping away the tears from his eyes with the corner of the red handkerchief twisted round his head.

"Poor fellow! poor fellow!" murmured Caderousse. "Well, there, M. l'Abbé, is another proof that good people are never rewarded on this earth, and that none but the wicked prosper. Ah," continued Caderousse, speaking in the highly-colored language of the South, "the world grows worse and worse. Why does not God, if He really hates the wicked, as He is said to do, send down brimstone and fire, and consume them altogether?"

"You speak as though you had loved this young Dantès," observed the abbé, without taking any notice of his companion's vehemence.——

"And so I did," replied Caderousse; "though once, I confess, I envied him his good fortune. But I swear to you, M. l'Abbé, I swear to you, by everything a man holds dear, I have, since then, deeply and sincerely lamented his unhappy fate." There was a brief silence, during which the fixed, searching eye of the abbé was employed in scrutinizing the agitated features of the aubergiste.

"You knew the poor lad, then?" continued Caderousse.

"Nay, I was merely called to see him when on his dying bed, that *I* might administer to him the consolations of religion."

"And of what did he die?" asked Caderousse in a choking voice.

"Of what, think you, do young and strong men die in prison? Edmond Dantès died in prison of sorrow and a broken heart." Caderousse wiped away the perspiration gathered on his brow.

"But the strangest part of the story is," resumed the abbé, "that Dantès, even in his dying moments, swore by his crucified Redeemer, that he was utterly ignorant of the cause of his imprisonment."

"And so he was," murmured Caderousse. "How should he have been otherwise? Ah, the poor fellow told you the truth."

"And for that reason, he besought me to try and clear up a mystery he had never been able to penetrate, and to clear his memory should any foul spot or stain have fallen on it." And here the look of the abbé, becoming more and more fixed, seemed to rest with ill-concealed satisfaction on the gloomy depression which seemed rapidly spreading over the countenance of Caderousse.

"A rich Englishman," continued the abbé, "who had been his companion in misfortune, but had been released from prison during the second restoration, was possessed of a diamond of immense value: this precious jewel he bestowed on Dantès upon himself quitting the prison, as a mark of his gratitude for the kindness and brotherly care with which Dantès had nursed him in a severe illness he underwent during his confinement. Instead of employing this diamond in attempting to bribe his jailers, who might only have taken it and then betrayed him to the governor, Dantès carefully preserved it, that in the event of his getting out of prison he might have wherewithal to live, for the produce of such a diamond would have quite sufficed to make his fortune."

Calmly drawing from his pocket a small box covered with black shagreen, the abbé opened it, and displayed to the delighted eyes of Caderousse the sparkling jewel it contained, set in a ring of admirable workmanship. "And that diamond," cried Caderousse, almost breathless with eager admiration, "you say, is worth 50,000 francs?"

"It is, without the setting, which is also valuable," replied the priest as he closed the box, and returned it to his pocket, while its brilliant hues seemed still to dance before the eyes of the fascinated.

"But how comes this diamond in your possession? Did Edmond make you his heir?"

"No, merely his testamentary executor. When dying, the unfortunate youth said to me, 'I once possessed four dear and faithful friends, besides the maiden to whom I was betrothed: and I feel convinced they have all unfeignedly grieved over my loss. The name of one of the four friends I allude to is Caderousse.'" He shivered as though he felt the dead cold hand of the betrayed Edmond grasping his own.

"'Another of the number,'" continued the abbé, without seeming to notice the emotion, "'is called Danglars; and the third, spite of being my rival, entertained a very sincere affection for me.'" A fiendish smile played over the features of Caderousse, who was about to break in upon the abbé's speech, when the latter, waving his hand, said: "Allow me to finish first, and then if you have any observations to make, you can do

so afterwards. 'The third of my friends, although my rival, was much attached to me,—his name was Fernand: that of my betrothed was——'
"Mercédès," cried Caderousse eagerly.

"To be sure. 'Well, then,' said Dantès,—for you understand, I repeat his words just as he uttered them—'you will go to Marseilles. For the purpose of selling this diamond; the produce of which you will divide into five equal parts, and give an equal portion to the only persons who have loved me upon earth.' "——"But why into five parts?" asked Caderousse; "you only mentioned four persons."

"Because the fifth is dead, as I hear. The fifth sharer in Edmond's bequest was his own father."——"Too true, too true!" ejaculated Caderousse, almost suffocated by the contending passions which assailed him, "the poor old man did die."

"I learned so much at Marseilles," replied the abbé, making a strong effort to appear indifferent; "but from the length of time that has elapsed since the death of the elder Dantès, I was unable to obtain any particulars of his end. You possibly may be capable of furnishing me with such minute circumstances as may serve to substantiate the decease of the elder Dantès."

"I do not know who could if I could not," said Caderousse. "Why I lived almost on the same floor with the poor old man. Ah, yes! about a year after the disappearance of his son the old man died. The doctors called his complaint an internal inflammation, I believe; his acquaintances say he died of grief; but I, who saw him in his dying moments, I say he died of downright starvation."

"Starvation!" exclaimed the abbé, springing from his seat, "Oh, it is impossible—utterly impossible?"

"What I have said, I have said," answered Caderousse.

"And you are a fool for having said anything about it," said a voice from the top of the stairs. "Why should you meddle with what does not concern you?"

The two male speakers turned round quickly, and perceived the sickly countenance of La Carconte leaning over the rail of the staircase; attracted by the sound of voices, she had feebly dragged herself down the stairs, and, seated on the lower step, she had listened to the foregoing conversation.

"I pledge you my sacred word, madame," said the abbé, "that my intentions are free from all sorts of harm or injury to you or yours; and that whatever evils may befall you, they will not be occasioned by my instrumentality, that I solemnly promise you."

Some inarticulate sounds escaped La Carconte, then letting her head, which she had raised during the excitement of conversation, again droop on to her lap, she commenced her usual anguish trembling, the result of her feverish attack, leaving the two speakers to resume the conversation, but still remaining herself so placed as to be able to hear every word they uttered. The abbé had been obliged to swallow a draught of water to calm the emotions that threatened to overpower him. When he had sufficiently recovered himself, he said:—"It appears, then, that the miserable old man you were telling me of, was forsaken by every one. Surely, had not such been the case, he would not have perished by so dreadful a death as you described."

"Why, he was not altogether forsaken," continued Caderousse; "for Mercédès the Catalan and M. Morrel were very kind to him; but somehow the poor old man had contracted a profound hatred of Fernand— the very person," added Caderousse, with a bitter smile, "that you named just now as being one of Dantès' faithful and attached friends. Can a man be faithful to another whose wife he covets and desires for himself? But Dantès was so honorable and true in his own nature, that he believed everybody's professions of friendship. Poor Edmond! he was cruelly deceived; but it was a happy thing he never knew it, or he might have found it more difficult, when on his deathbed, to pardon his enemies. And, whatever people may say," continued Caderousse, in his native language, which was not altogether devoid of rude poetry, "I cannot help being more frightened at the idea of the malediction of the dead than the hatred of the living."——"Weak-minded coward!" exclaimed La Carconte.

"Do you, then, know in what manner Fernand injured Dantès?" inquired the abbé of Caderousse.

"Why, what good would it do?" asked Caderousse. "If the poor lad were living, and came to me to beg I would candidly tell which were his true and which his false friends, why, perhaps, I should not hesitate. But you tell me he is no more, and therefore can have nothing to do with hatred or revenge; so let all such feelings be buried with him."

"You prefer, then," said the abbé, "allowing me to bestow on men you say are false and treacherous, the reward intended for faithful friendship?"

"That is true enough," returned Caderousse. "You say truly, the diamond of poor Edmond was not meant for such traitors as Fernand and Danglars; besides, what would it be to them? no more than a drop of water in the ocean."

"Diamond!" exclaimed La Carconte, rising and descending to the chamber with a tolerably firm step; "what diamond are you talking about?"

"Why, did you not hear all we said?" inquired Caderousse. "It is a beautiful diamond left by poor Edmond Dantès, to be sold, and the money divided among his father, Mercédès, his betrothed bride, Fernand, Danglars, and myself. The jewel is worth at least 50,000 francs and might all be ours—a holy man would not deceive."

But Carconte retired to her room, reluctant, while her husband said, shaking his head: "The tale is a sad one—perhaps you know the beginning?"

"Yes," answered the abbé: "Edmond related to me everything until the moment he was arrested in a small tavern close to Marseilles."

"At La Réserve! Oh, yes!"

"His betrothal feast that began so gaily had a very sorrowful ending: a commissary of police, followed by four soldiers, entered, and Dantès was arrested.

"Well, when Dantès was arrested, M. Morrel hastened to obtain the particulars, and they were very sad. The old man returned alone to his home, would not go to bed at all, for I was underneath him heard him walking the whole night. The next day Mercédès went nplore the protection of Attorney Villefort; she did not obtain it, how r, and went to visit the old man; when she saw him so miserable a leartbroken, she wished him to go with her that she might take care him; but the old man would not consent. He seemed to dislike se me. One night, however, I heard his sobs, and I could not resist m esire to go up to him, but when I reached his door he was no longer ping but praying.

"From day to day he lived on alone, and more and more s ary. M. Morrel and Mercédès came to see him, but his door was closed nd, although I was certain he was at home he would not make any a er. Dantès was left all to himself, and I only saw strangers go up t im and come down again with some bundle they tried to hide; but I gu ed what these bundles were, and he sold by degrees what he had to pa r his subsistence. At length, the poor old fellow reached the end of a e had; he owed three quarters' rent, and they threatened to turn him ; he begged for another week, which was granted to him. I went l told M. Morrel, and then ran on to Mercédès. They both came imm ately, M. Morrel bringing a doctor, and the doctor said it was an af tion of the stomach, and ordered him a limited diet. I was there too, a I never shall forget the old man's smile at this prescription. From th time he opened his door, he had an excuse for not eating any more, as t doctor had put him on a diet. M. Morrel's wish also, who would fai have conveyed the old man against his consent; but the old man resistec and cried so, that they were actually frightened. Mercédès remained therefore, by his bedside, and M. Morrel went away, making a sign tc the Catalane that he had left his purse on the chimney-piece. But availing himself of the nine days' despair and fasting, the old man died, cursing those who had caused his misery, and saying to Mercédès,—'If you ever see my Edmond again, tell him I die blessing him.' "

"This was, indeed, a horrid event," said the priest, in a hoarse voice.

"The more so, sir, as it was men's and not God's doing."

"Tell me of those men," said the abbé, "and remember too," he added, in a voice that was nearly menacing in its tone, "you have promised to tell me everything. Tell me, therefore, who are these men who have killed the son with despair, and the father with famine?"——"Two men jealous of him, sir; one from love, and the other ambition,—Fernand and Danglars. They denounced Edmond as a Bonapartist agent. Danglars wrote the denunciation with his left hand, that his writing might not be recognized, and Fernand put it in the post. They had made me drink to such an excess that I nearly lost all perception. I said all that a man in such a state could say; but they both assured me that it was a jest they were carrying on, and perfectly harmless."

"Next day—next day, sir, you must have seen plain enough what they had been doing, yet you said nothing, though you were present when Dantès was arrested."——"Yes, sir, I was there, and very anxious to speak! but Danglars restrained me. 'If he should really be guilty,' said he, 'and did really put in at Elba; if he is really charged with a letter for the Bonapartist committee at Paris, and if they find this letter upon him, those who have supported him will pass for his accomplices.' I confess I had my fears, in the state in which politics then were, and I held my tongue. It was cowardly, I confess, but it was not criminal."

There was a brief silence; the abbé rose and paced up and down pensively, and then resumed his seat. "You have two or three times mentioned a M. Morrel," he said; "who was he?"——"The owner of the Pharaoh and employer of Dantès."

"And what part did he play in this sad drama?" inquired the abbé.

"The part of an honest man, full of courage and real regard. Twenty times he interceded for Edmond. When the emperor returned, he wrote, implored, threatened, and so energetically, that on the second restoration he was persecuted as a Bonapartist. Ten times, as I told you, he came to see Dantès' father, and offered to receive him in his own house; and the night or two before his death, as I have already said, he left his purse on the mantelpiece, with which they paid the old man's debts, and buried him decently; and then Edmond's father died, as he had lived, without doing harm to any one. I have the purse still by me—a large one, made of red silk."

"And," asked the abbé, "is M. Morrel still alive?"——"Yes," replied Caderousse.

"In this case," replied the abbé, "he should be rich and happy." Caderousse smiled bitterly. "Yes, happy as myself," said he. "After five-and-twenty years of labor, after a most honorable name in the trade of Marseilles, M. Morrel is utterly ruined. He has lost five ships in two years, has suffered by the bankruptcy of three large houses, and his only hope now is in that very Pharaoh which poor Dantès commanded, and expected from the Indies with a cargo of cochineal and indigo. If this ship founders, like the others, he is a ruined man."——"And has the unfortunate man wife or children?" inquired the abbé.

"Yes, he has a wife, who in all this behaved like an angel; he has a daughter, who was about to marry the man she loved, but whose family will not allow him to wed the daughter of a ruined man; he has, besides, a son, a lieutenant in the army; and, as you may suppose, all this, instead of soothing, doubles his grief. If he were alone in the world he would blow out his brains, and there would be an end."

"Horrible!" ejaculated the priest.

"And it is thus Heaven recompenses virtue, sir," added Caderousse. "You see, I, who never did a bad action but that I have told you of—am in destitution, seeing my poor wife die of a fever, unable to do anything in the world for her; I shall die of hunger, as old Dantès did, whilst Fernand and Danglars are rolling in wealth."

"How is that?"

"Because all their malpractices have turned to luck, while honest men have been reduced to misery."

"What has become of Danglars, the instigator, and therefore the most guilty?"

"Why, he left Marseilles, and was taken, on the recommendation of M. Morrel, who did not know his crime, as cashier into a Spanish bank. During the war with Spain he was employed in the commissariat of the French army, and made a fortune; then with that money he speculated in the funds, and trebled or quadrupled his capital; and, having first married his banker's daughter, who left him a widower, he has married a second time, a widow, a Mdme. de Nargonne, daughter of Servieux, the king's chamberlain, in high favor at court. He is a millionaire, and Baron Danglars, with mansion, horses in his stables, footmen in his ante-chamber, and I know not how many hundreds of thousands in his strong-box."

"Ah!" said the abbé, with a peculiar tone, "he is happy. And Fernand?"——"Fernand! He has both fortune and position—both."

"Some days before the return of the emperor, Fernand was drawn in the conscription. The Bourbons left him quietly enough at the Catalans, but Napoleon returned, an extraordinary muster was determined on, and Fernand was compelled to join. Fernand was enrolled in the active forces, went to the frontier with his regiment, and was at the battle of Ligny. The night after that battle he was sentry at the door of a general who carried on a secret correspondence with the enemy. That same night the general was to go over to the English. He proposed to Fernand to accompany him, Fernand agreed, deserted, and followed the general. That which would have brought Fernand to a court-martial if Napoleon remained on the throne, served for his recommendation to the Bourbons. He returned to France with the epaulette of sub-lieutenant, and as the protection of the general, who is in the highest favor, was accorded to him, he was a captain in 1823, during the Spanish war—that is to say, at the time when Danglars made his early speculations. Fernand was a Spaniard, and being sent to Spain to ascertain the feeling of his fellow-countrymen, found Danglars there, became on very intimate terms with him, and rendered such services in this brief campaign that, after the taking of Trocadero, he was made colonel, and received the title of count and officer of the Legion of Honor. The war with Spain being ended, Fernand's career was checked by the long peace which seemed likely to endure throughout Europe. Greece only had risen against Turkey, and had begun her war of independence; Fernand obtained leave to go and serve in Greece, still having his name kept on the rolls. Some time after, it was stated that the Count of Morcerf (the name he bore) had entered the service of Ali Pacha with the rank of instructor-general. Ali Pacha was killed, as you know; but before he died he recompensed the services of Fernand by leaving him a considerable sum, with which he returned to France, when his rank of lieutenant-general was confirmed. He possesses a magnificent house—No. 27, Rue du Helder, Paris."

The abbé hesitated, then, making an effort over himself, he said, "And Mercédès—they tell me that she has disappeared?"

"Disappeared," said Caderousse, "yes, as the sun disappears, to rise the next day with still more splendor. Mercédès is at this moment one of the greatest ladies in Paris," replied Caderousse. "In the midst of her despair, a fresh trouble overtook her. This was the departure of Fernand—whose crime she did not know, and whom she regarded as her brother. Fernand went, and Mercédès remained alone.

"Fernand, when he learned the old man's death, returned. He was now a lieutenant. At his coming he had not said a word of love to Mercédès; at the second he reminded her that he loved her. Mercédès begged for six months more to expect and bewail Edmond. Then the marriage took place in the church of Accoules. A week after the wedding they left Marseilles."——"Did you ever see Mercédès again?" inquired the priest.

"Yes, during the war of Spain, at Perpignan, when Fernand had left her; she was attending to the education of her son, little Albert. She is rich, a countess, and yet she is not happy," said Caderousse. "When I found myself very wretched, I thought my old friends would, perhaps, assist me. So I went to Danglars, who would not even receive me. I called on Fernand, who sent me a hundred francs by his valet-de-chambre."

"Then you did not see either of them?"

"No, but Mdme. de Morcerf saw me. As I went away a purse fell at my feet—it contained five-and-twenty louis; I raised my head quickly, and saw Mercédès, who shut the blinds directly."

"And M. de Villefort?" asked the abbé.——"Oh, he never was a friend of mine. I only know that some time after having arrested him, he married Mdlle. Saint-Méran, and soon after left Marseilles; no doubt but he has been as lucky as the rest; no doubt he is as rich as Danglars, as high in station as Fernand. I only, as you see, have remained poor, wretched, and forgotten."

"You are mistaken, my friend," replied the abbé: "God may seem sometimes to forget for a while, whilst His justice reposes, but there always comes a moment when He remembers—and behold! a proof." As he spoke, the abbé took the diamond from his pocket, and giving it to Caderousse, said,—"Here, my friend, take this diamond, it is yours."

"What! for me only?" cried Caderousse; "ah! sir, do not jest with me!"

"In exchange," he continued, "give me the red silk purse that M. Morrel left on old Dantès' chimney-piece, and which you tell me is still in your hands. May this money profit you! Adieu! I go far from men who thus so bitterly injure each other." The abbé with difficulty got away from the enthusiastic thanks of Caderousse, opened the door himself, got out and mounted his horse, once more saluted the innkeeper, who kept uttering his loud farewells, and then returned by the road he had traveled in coming. When Caderousse turned round, he saw behind him La Carconte, paler and trembling more than ever.

"Fifty thousand francs?" muttered she; "it is a large sum of money, but it is not a fortune."

CHAPTER XVII.

THE PRISON REGISTER.

THE day after, a man of about thirty, dressed in a bright blue frock-coat, nankeen trousers, and a white waistcoat, having the appearance and accent of an Englishman, presented himself before the mayor of Marseilles.

"Sir," said he, "I am chief clerk of Messrs. Thomson and French, of Rome. We are, and have been these ten years, connected with the house of Morrel and Son, of Marseilles. We have a hundred thousand francs or thereabouts engaged in speculation with them, and we are a little uneasy at reports that have reached us that the firm is on the eve of ruin. I have come, therefore, express from Rome, to ask you for information as to this house."

"Sir," replied the mayor, "I know very well that during the last four or five years, misfortune seems to pursue M. Morrel. He has lost four or five vessels, and suffered by three or four bankruptcies; but it is not for me, although I am a creditor myself to the amount of ten thousand francs to give any information as to the state of his finances. Ask of me, as mayor, what is my opinion of M. Morrel, I shall say he is a man honorable to the last degree, and who has up to this time fulfilled every engagement with scrupulous punctuality. This is all I can say, sir: if you wish to learn more, address yourself to Boville, the inspector of prisons, No. 15, Rue de Nouailles; he has, I believe, two hundred thousand francs in the hands of Morrel and if there be any grounds for apprehension, as this is a greater amount than mine, you will most probably find him better informed than myself."

The Englishman seemed to appreciate this extreme delicacy, made his bow, and went away towards the street mentioned. Boville was in his private room, and the Englishman, on perceiving him, made a gesture of surprise, which seemed to indicate that it was not the first time he had been in his presence. As to M. de Boville, he was in such a state of despair, that it was evident all the faculties of his mind, absorbed in the thought which occupied him at the moment, did not allow either his memory or his imagination to stray to the past. The Englishman, with the coolness of his nation, addressed him in terms nearly similar to those with which he had accosted the mayor of Marseilles. "Oh, sir," exclaimed Boville, "your fears are unfortunately but too well founded, and you see before you a man in despair. I had informed M. Morrel of my desire to have payments punctually, and he has been here within the last half-hour to tell me that if his ship, the Pharaoh, did not come into port on the 15th, he would be wholly unable to make his payment. I consider it lost."

"Well, then, I will buy it of you!"

"But at a tremendous discount, of course?"

"No, for two hundred thousand francs. Our house," added the Englishman, with a laugh, "does not do things in that way."

The Englishman drew from his pocket a bundle of bank-notes, twice the sum M. de Boville feared to lose. A ray of joy passed across M. de Boville's countenance, yet he made an effort over himself, and said,— "Sir, I ought to tell you that, in all probability, you will not have six per cent. of this sum."

"Sir," replied the Englishman, laughing, "I am like my house, and do not do such things—no, the commission I ask is quite different."

"Name it, sir, I beg."——"You are the inspector of prisons, keeping registers and notes relative to the prisoners?"

"There are special reports on every prisoner."

"Well, sir, I was educated at Rome by a poor priest, who disappeared suddenly. I have since learned that he was confined in Castle If, and I should like to learn some particulars of his death."

"What was his name?"

"The Abbé Faria."

"Oh, I recollect him perfectly," cried M. de Boville; "he was crazy. He pretended to know of an immense treasure, and offered vast sums to the government if they would liberate him."

"Poor devil! is he dead?"

"Yes, sir; five or six months ago, last February."

"You have a good memory, sir, to recollect dates so well!"

"I recollect this, because the poor devil's death was accompanied by a singular circumstance."

"May I ask what that was?" said the Englishman, with an expression of curiosity in his phlegmatic countenance.

"Oh dear, yes, sir; the abbé's dungeon was forty or fifty feet distant from that of an old agent of Bonaparte's—a very resolute and very dangerous man. It appears, sir, that this Edmond Dantès had procured tools, or made them, for they found a passage by which the prisoners communicated, formed, no doubt, with an intention of escape; but unfortunately for the prisoners, the Abbé Faria had an attack of catalepsy, and died."

"That must have cut short the projects of escape."

"For the dead man, yes," replied M. de Boville, "but not for the survivor, on the contrary, this Dantès saw a means of accelerating his escape. He, no doubt, thought that prisoners who died in the Château d'If were interred in a burial-ground as usual, and he conveyed the dead man into his own cell, assumed his place in the sack in which they had sewn up the defunct, and awaited the moment of interment."——"It was a bold step, and one that indicated some courage," remarked the Englishman.

"As I have already told you, sir, he was a very dangerous man; and, fortunately, by his own act disembarrassed the government of the fears it had on his account."

"The castle has no cemetery, and they simply throw the dead into the sea, after having fastened a thirty-six pound ball to their feet. You may imagine the amazement of the fugitive when he found himself flung headlong beneath the rocks! I should like to have seen his face at that moment."

"And so," continued the Englishman, who first gained his composure, "he was drowned?"

"Unquestionably."

"But to return to these registers."

"So, sir, you wish to see all relating to the poor abbé, who really was gentleness itself."

And they both entered M. de Boville's study. All was arranged in order. The inspector begged the Englishman to seat himself in an armchair, and placed before him the register and documents relative to Castle If, giving him all the time he desired to examine it, whilst De Boville seated himself in a corner, to read his newspaper. The Englishman easily found the entries relative to the Abbé Faria; but it seemed that the story which the inspector had related interested him greatly, for after having perused the first documents he turned over the leaves until he reached the deposition respecting Edmond Dantès. There he found everything arranged in due order—the denunciation, examination, Morrel's petition, Villefort's marginal notes. He folded up the denunciation quietly and put it as quietly in his pocket; read the examination, and saw that Noirtier was not mentioned in it; perused, too, the application, dated 10th April, 1815, in which Morrel by the deputy's advice, exaggerated with the best intentions (for Napoleon was then on the throne) the services Dantès had rendered to the imperial cause—services which Villefort's certificates rendered indispensable. Then he saw through all. This petition to Napoleon kept back by Villefort, had become, under the second restoration, a terrible weapon against him in the lawyer's hands. He was no longer astonished when he searched on to find in the register this note, placed in a bracket against his name:

EDMOND DANTÈS, { An inveterate Bonapartist; took an active part in the return from the Isle of Elba.
To be kept in complete solitary confinement, and to be strictly watched and guarded.

Beneath these lines was written, in another hand: "See Note above—nothing can be done." He compared the writing in the bracket with the writing of the certificate placed beneath Morrel's petition, and discovered that the note in the bracket was the same writing as the certificate—that is to say, was in Villefort's handwriting. As to the note which accompanied this, the Englishman understood that it might have been added by some inspector, who had taken a momentary interest in Dantès' situation, but who had, from the remarks we have quoted, found it impossible to give any effect to the interest he experienced.

As we have said, the inspector, from discretion, and that he might not disturb the Abbé Faria's pupil in his researches, had seated himself in a corner, and was reading. He did not see the Englishman fold up and place in his pocket the denunciation written by Danglars which had the post-mark of Marseiiies, 2nd March, delivery 6 o'clock P. M. But it must be said that if he had seen it, he attached so small importance to this scrap of paper, and so great importance to his 200,000 francs, that he would not have opposed what the Englishman did, how incorrect it might be.

"Thanks!" said the latter, closing the register with a noise, "I have

all I want; now it is for me to perform my promise. Give me a simple
assignment of your debt; acknowledge therein the receipt of the cash,
and I will hand you over the money." He rose, gave his seat to M. de
Boville, who took it without ceremony, quickly drew out the required
assignment, whilst the Englishman was counting out the bank-notes on
the other side of the desk.

———

CHAPTER XVIII.

THE FIRM OF MORREL AND SON.

Any one who had quitted Marseilles a few years previously, well acquainted with the interior of Morrel's house, and had returned at this
date, would have found a great change. In the deserted corridor and
the empty office, out of all the numerous clerks that used to fill the office,
but two remained. One was a young man of three- or four-and-twenty,
who was in love with M. Morrel's daughter, and had remained with him,
in spite of the efforts of his friends to induce him to withdraw; the
other was an old one-eyed cashier, named Coclès.

In the midst of the distress of the house, Coclès was the only one
unmoved. But this did not arise from a want of affection, but, on the
contrary, from a firm conviction. It seemed as impossible to him that
the house should stop payment, as it would to a miller that the river
that had so long turned his mill should cease to flow.

Nothing had as yet occurred to shake Coclès belief; the last month's
payment had been made with the most scrupulous exactitude; Coclès
had detected an error of fourteen sous to the prejudice of Morrel, and
the same evening he had brought them to M. Morrel, who, with a melancholy smile, threw them into an almost empty drawer, saying:

"Thanks, Coclès; you are the pearl of cashiers."

Coclès retired perfectly happy, for this eulogium of M. Morrel, himself the pearl of the honest men of Marseilles. flattered him more than a
present. But since the end of the month, M. Morrel had passed many an
anxious hour. His resources were now exhausted. Credit, owing to the
reports afloat, was no longer to be had; and to meet the sum due on the
15th of the present month to Boville, and that due on the 15th of the
next month, Morrel had, in reality, no hope but the return of the Pharaoh,
whose departure he had learnt from a vessel which had weighed anchor

at the same time, and which had already arrived in harbor. But this vessel, which, like the Pharaoh, came from Calcutta, had arrived a fortnight ago, whilst no intelligence had been received of the Pharaoh.

Such was the state of things when, the day after his interview with M. de Boville, the confidential clerk of the house of Thomson and French, presented himself at M. Morrel's. Emmanuel received him; the young man whom every fresh visage alarmed, for each fresh visage announced a fresh creditor, who, in his alarm, came to question the head of the house. The young man, wishing to spare his employer the pain of this interview, questioned the newcomer; but the stranger declared he had nothing to say to M. Emmanuel, and that his business was with M. Morrel in person. Emmanuel sighed, and summoned Coclès. Coclès appeared, and the young man bade him conduct the stranger to M. Morrel's apartment. Coclès went first, and the stranger followed him. On the staircase they met a beautiful girl of sixteen or seventeen, who looked with anxiety at the stranger.

"Is M. Morrel in his room, mademoiselle?" said the cashier.

"Yes; I think so, at least," said the girl, hesitatingly. "Go and see, Coclès and if my father is there, announce this gentleman."

"It will be useless to announce me, miss," returned the Englishman. "M. Morrel does not know my name; this worthy gentleman has only to announce the confidential clerk of the house of Thomson and French, of Rome, with whom your father does business."

The girl turned pale, and continued to descend, while the stranger and Coclès continued to mount the staircase. She entered the office where Emmanuel was, whilst Coclès, by the aid of a key, opened a door on the second staircase, conducted the stranger into an antechamber, opened a second door, which he closed behind him, and after having left the clerk alone, returned and signed to him that he could enter. The Englishman entered, and found Morrel seated at a table, turning over the formidable columns of his ledger, which contained the list of his liabilities. At the sight of the stranger, M. Morrel closed the ledger, rose, and offered a seat to the stranger; and when he had seen him seated, resumed his own chair. Fourteen years had changed the worthy merchant, who, in his thirty-sixth year at the opening of this story, was now in his fiftieth; his hair had turned white, time and sorrow had ploughed deep furrows on his brow, and his look, once so firm and penetrating, was now irresolute and wandering as if he feared being forced to fix his attention on an idea or a man. The Englishman looked at him with an air of curiosity, evidently mingled with interest. "Sir," said Morrel, whose uneasiness was increased by this examination, "you wish to speak to me."

"Yes, sir; you are aware from whom I come?"

"The house of Thomson and French; at least, so my cashier tells me."

"He has told you rightly. The house of Thomson and French had 300,000 or 400,000 francs to pay this month in France; and, knowing your strict punctuality, have collected all the bills bearing your signature, and charged me as they became due to present them and to employ the money otherwise."

"Here is," said the Englishman, taking a quantity of papers from his pocket, "an assignment of 200,000 francs to our house by M. de Boville, the inspector of prisons, to whom they are due. You acknowledge, of course you owe this sum to him?"

"I do," said Morrel, whose face was suffused as he thought that, for the first time in his life, he would be unable to honor his own signature. "Is this all?"

"No, I have for the end of the month these bills which have been assigned to us by Pascal, and the Wild and Turner, of Marseilles, amounting to nearly 55,000 francs; in all, 287,500 francs." It is impossible to describe what Morrel suffered during this enumeration. "I will not," continued the other, after a moment's silence, "conceal from you that whilst your probity and exactitude up to this moment are universally acknowledged, yet the report is current in Marseilles that you are not able to meet your engagements."

At this almost brutal speech Morrel turned deathly pale.

"Sir," said he, "up to this time—and it is now more than four-and-twenty years since I received the direction of this house from my father, who had himself conducted it for five-and-thirty years—never has anything bearing the signature of Morrel and Son been dishonored."

"I know that," replied the Englishman. "But as a man of honor should answer another, tell me fairly, shall you pay these with the same punctuality?" Morrel shuddered, and looked at the man, who spoke with more assurance that he had hitherto shown. "To questions frankly put," said he, "a straightforward answer should be given. Yes, I shall pay, if, as I hope, my vessel arrives safely; for its arrival will again procure me the credit of which the numerous accidents, of which I have been the victim, have deprived me; but if the Pharaoh should be lost, and this last resource be gone——" The poor man's eyes filled with tears.——"Well," said the other, "if this last resource fail you?"——"Well," returned Morrel, "it is a cruel thing to be forced to say, but, already used to misfortune, I must habituate myself to shame. I fear I shall be forced to suspend my payments."

"What is that?" said the Englishman. "What is the meaning of this noise?"

"Oh! Oh!" cried Morrel, turning pale, "what?" A loud noise was heard on the stairs, of people moving hastily, and half-stifled sobs. Morrel rose and advanced to the door; but his strength failed him and he sank into a chair. The two men remained opposite one another. At this instant the second door opened, and the girl, her eyes bathed with tears, appeared. Morrel rose tremblingly, supporting himself by the arm of the chair. He would have spoken, but his voice failed him. "Oh, father!" said she, clasping her hands, "forgive your child for being the messenger of ill."

"The Pharaoh has then perished?" said Morrel in a hoarse voice. The girl did not speak; but she nodded as she lay on her father's breast.

"And the crew?" asked Morrel.

"Saved," said the girl; "saved by the crew of the vessel that has just entered the harbor." Morrel raised his two hands to heaven with an expression of resignation and sublime gratitude. "Thanks, my God," said he, "at least Thou strikest but me alone." Spite of his phlegm a tear moistened the eye of the Englishman, as all went out, leaving him again with the merchant.

"Well, sir," said Morrel, sinking into a chair, "you have heard all, and I have nothing further to tell you."

"I see," returned the Englishman, "that you wish for time to pay?"

"A delay would save my honor, and consequently my life."

"How long a delay do you wish for?" Morrel reflected. "Two months," said he.

"I will give you three," replied the stranger. "Well, renew these bills up to the 5th of September; and on the 5th of September, at eleven o'clock (the hand of the clock pointed to eleven), I shall come to receive the money."——"I shall expect you," returned Morrel; "and I will pay you—or I shall be dead." These last words were uttered in so low a tone, that the stranger could not hear them. The bills were renewed, the old ones destroyed, and the poor shipowner found himself with three months before him to collect his resources. The Englishman received his thanks with the phlegm peculiar to his nation; and Morrel, overwhelming him with grateful blessings, conducted him to the staircase. The stranger met Julie on the stairs: she affected to be descending, but in reality she was waiting for him. "Oh, sir——" said she, clasping his hand.

"Mademoiselle," said the stranger, "one day you will receive a letter signed 'Sinbad the Sailor.' Do exactly what the letter bids you, however strange it may appear."

"Yes, sir," returned Julie.

"It is well. Adieu! Remain as pure and virtuous as you are at present, and I have great hopes that Heaven will reward you by giving you Emmanuel for a husband."

Julie uttered a faint cry, blushed like a rose, and leaned again the baluster, while the stranger waved his hand and went on down-stairs.

In the yard he spied Penelon, boatswain of the Pharaoh, to whom he beckoned and said:

"Come with me, my man—I have business with you."

Penelon disappeared after this interview, and with him all the crew of the wreck.

Thanks to the grace, Morrel kept his head above water until August. Then he went up to Paris to beg a loan of Danglars, who was worth millions and had unlimited credit. He would not help his old master to any extent, though even his word would have saved him.

The ship-owner returned shamed by the repulse.

The ladies guessed that they were in peril: they wrote to Nismes where Julie's brother was in the garrison to ask him over. Besides, Maximilian Morrel, though hardly two-and-twenty, had great influence over his father. He was a strong-minded, upright young man. At the time when he decided on his profession his father had no desire to choose for him, but had consulted young Maximilian's taste. They had not mistaken the gravity of this event, for the moment after Morrel had entered his cabinet with Coclès, Julie saw the latter leave it pale, trembling, and his features betraying the utmost consternation. She would have questioned him as he passed by her, but the worthy creature hastened down the staircase with unusual precipitation, and only raised his hands to Heaven and exclaimed, "Oh, what a dreadful misfortune! Who could ever have believed it!" A moment afterwards Julie saw him go up-stairs carrying two or three heavy ledgers, a pocket-book, and a bag of money.

Morrel examined the ledgers, opened the pocket-book, and counted the money. All his funds amounted to 6000 or 8000 francs, his expectancies up to the 5th to 4000 or 5000, which, making the best of everything, gave him 14,000 francs to meet bills amounting to 287,500 francs. He could not make such a proposal.

During the night, between the 4th and 5th of September, Mdme. Morrel remained listening for every sound, and, until three o'clock in the morning, she heard her husband pacing the room in great agitation. It was three o'clock when he threw himself on the bed. The mother and daughter passed the night together. They had expected Maximilian since the previous evening. At eight o'clock in the morning Morrel entered their chamber. He was calm; but the agitation of the night was legible in his pale and careworn visage. They did not dare to ask him how he had slept. Morrel was kinder to his wife, more affectionate to his daughter, than he had ever been. He could not cease gazing at and kissing the sweet girl. Julie, mindful of Emmanuel's request, was following her father when he quitted the room, but he said to her sharply,—"Remain with your mother, dearest."

This was the first time Morrel had ever so spoken, but he said it in a tone of paternal kindness, and Julie did not dare refuse compliance. She remained at the same spot standing, mute and motionless. An instant afterwards, the door opened, she felt arms encircle her, and a mouth pressed her forehead. She looked up, and uttered an exclamation of joy.

"Maximilian! my dearest brother!" she cried. At these words Mdme. Morrel rose, and threw herself into her son's arms. "Mother!" said the young man, looking alternately at Mdme. Morrel and her daughter, "what has occurred—what has happened? your letter has frightened me, and I have come hither with all speed."

"Julie," said Mdme. Morrel, making a sign to the young man, "go and tell your father that Maximilian has just arrived." The young lady rushed out of the apartment, but on the first step of the staircase she found a man holding a letter in his hand.

"Are you not Mdlle. Julie Morrel?" inquired the man, with a strong Italian accent. "Read this letter," he said, handing it to her. "It concerns the best interests of your father."

The girl hastily took the letter from him. She opened it quickly and read:

"Go this moment to Meillan Alley, enter the house No. 15, ask the porter for the key of the room on the fifth floor, enter it, take from the mantelpiece a purse netted in red silk, and give it to your father. It is important that he should receive it before eleven o'clock. You promised to obey me implicitly. Remember your oath. Sinbad the Sailor."

Julie hesitated, and resolved to take counsel. Yet, by a singular feeling, it was neither to her mother nor her brother that she applied, but to Emmanuel. She hastened down and told him what had occurred on the day when the agent of Thomson and French had come to her father's, related the scene on the staircase, repeated the promise she had made, and showed him the letter. "You must go, then, mademoiselle. I will wait you at the corner and if you are so long absent as to make me uneasy, I will hasten and rejoin you, and woe to him of whom you shall have cause to complain to me!"

"Then, Emmanuel," said the young girl, with hesitation, "it is your opinion that I should obey this invitation?"——"Yes. Did not the messenger say your father's safety was in it?"

"But what danger threatens him, then, Emmanuel?" she asked.

"Why, if to-day before eleven o'clock your father has not found some one who will come to his aid, he will be compelled at twelve o'clock to declare himself a bankrupt."

"Oh, come, then, come!" cried she, hastening away with the young man. During this time Madame Morrel had told her son everything. He was thunderstruck. Then, rushing hastily out of the apartment, he ran up-stairs, expecting to find his father in his cabinet, but he rapped there in vain. Whilst he was yet at the door of the cabinet he heard the bedroom door open, turned, and saw his father. Instead of going direct to his cabinet, M. Morrel had returned to his bedchamber, which he was only this moment quitting. Morrel uttered a cry of surprise at the sight of his son, of whose arrival he was ignorant. He remained motionless on the spot, pressing with his left hand something he had concealed under his coat. Maximilian sprang down the staircase, and thew his arms around his father's neck; but suddenly he recoiled, and placed his right hand on Morrel's breast. "Father!" he exclaimed, turning pale as death, "what are you going to do with the brace of pistols under your coat?"

"Maximilian," replied Morrel, looking fixedly at his son, "you are a man, and a man of honor. Come, and I will explain to you."

And with a firm step Morrel went up to his cabinet, whilst Maximilian followed him, trembling as he went. Morrel opened the door, and closed it behind his son; then, crossing the ante-room, went to his desk, on which he placed the pistols, and pointed with his finger to an open ledger. In this ledger was made out an exact balance-sheet of affairs. Morrel had to pay, within half-an-hour, 287,500 francs. All he possessed was 15,257 francs. "Read!" said Morrel. "Blood washes out dishonor," said Morrel.

"You are right, father; I understand you." Then extending his hand toward one of the pistols, he said, "There is one for you and one for me —thanks!" Morrel checked his hand. "Your mother—your sister! Who will support them?" A shudder ran through the young man's frame. "Father," he said, "do you reflect that you are bidding me to live?"——"Yes, I do bid you," answered Morrel; "it is your duty. You have a calm, strong mind, Maximilian. Maximilian, you are no ordinary man. I desire nothing—I command nothing; I only say to you, examine my position as if it were your own, and then judge for yourself."

The young man reflected an instant, then an expression of sublime resignation appeared in his eyes, and with a slow and sad gesture he took off his two epaulettes, the marks of his rank. "Be it so, then, my father," he said, extending his hand to Morrel, "die in peace, my father; I will live." Morrel was about to cast himself on his knees before his son, but Maximilian caught him in his arms, and those two noble hearts were pressed against each other for a moment. "You know it is not my fault," said Morrel. Maximilian smiled. "I know, father, you are the most honorable man I have ever known."——"Good, my son. And now all is said; go now and rejoin your mother and sister."

"My father," said the young man, bending his knee, "bless me!" Morrel took his head between his hands, drew him toward him, and kissing his forehead several times, said, "Oh, yes, yes, I bless you in my own name, and in the name of three generations of irreproachable men, who say by my voice, 'The edifice which misfortune has destroyed, Providence may be build up again.' On seeing me die such a death, the most inexorable will have pity on you. Living, my best friends would avoid my house; dead, all Marseilles will follow me in tears to my last home. Living, you would feel shame at my name; dead, you may raise your head and say, 'I am the son of him you killed, because, for the first time, he has been compelled to fail in his word.' "

The young man uttered a groan, but appeared resigned.

"Have you no particular commands to leave with me, my father?" inquired Maximilian, in a faltering voice.

"The house of Thomson and French is the only one who, from humanity, or, it may be, selfishness—it is not for me to read men's hearts—have had any pity for me. His agent, who will in ten minutes present himself to receive the amount of a bill of 287,500 francs, I will not say granted, but offered me three months. Let this house be the first repaid, my son, and respect this man,"——"Father, I will," said Maximilian.

And he rushed out of the cabinet. When his son had left him, Morrel fell back in his chair, his eyes fixed on the clock: there were seven minutes left, that was all.

At this moment of mortal agony, a damp passed over his brow, an agony stronger than death clutched at his heart-strings. He heard the door of the staircase creak on its hinges—the clock gave its warning to strike eleven—the door of his cabinet opened; Morrel did not turn round —he expected these words of Coclès, "The agent of Thomson and French."

He placed the muzzle of the pistol between his teeth. Suddenly he heard a cry—it was his daughter's voice. He turned and saw Julie. The pistol fell from his hands. "My father!" cried the girl, out of breath, and half dead with joy—"saved! you are saved!" And she threw herself into his arms, holding in her extended hand a red netted silk purse.

"Saved! my child!" said Morrel; "what do you mean?"

"Yes, saved—saved! see, see!" said she.

Morrel took the purse, and started as he did so, for a vague remembrance reminded him that it once belonged to himself. At one end was the bill for the 287,500 francs *receipted,* and at the other end was a diamond as large as a hazel-nut, with these words on a small slip of parchment:

"JULIE'S DOWRY."

Morrel passed his hand over his brow; it seemed to him a dream. At this moment the clock struck eleven. The sound vibrated as if each stroke of the hammer struck on Morrel's heart. "Explain, my child," he said, "explain—where did you find this purse?"

"In a house in Meillan Alley, on the corner of a mantelpiece in a small room on the fifth floor."

"But," cried Morrel, "this purse is not yours!" Julie handed to her father the letter she had received in the morning.

"And did you go alone?" asked Morrel, after he had read it.

"Emmanuel accompanied me, father. He was to have waited for me at the corner of the Rue de Musée, but, strange to say, he was not there when I returned."——"M. Morrel!" exclaimed a voice on the stairs—

"It is his voice!" said Julie. At this moment Emmanuel entered, his countenance full of animation and joy. "The Pharaoh!" he cried, "they signal the Pharaoh! The Pharaoh is coming up the harbor!" Morrel fell back in his chair, his strength was failing him; his understanding, weakened by such events, refused to comprehend such incredible, unheard, fabulous facts. But his son came in. "Father!" cried Maximilian, "how could you say the Pharaoh was lost? The watch-tower has signalled her, and they say she is now coming into port."

"My dear friends!" said Morrel, "if this were so, it must be a miracle of Heaven! Impossible! impossible!"

But what was real and not less incredible was the purse he held in his hand, the acceptance receipted—the splendid diamond.

"Ah! sir," exclaimed Coclès, "what can it mean?—the Pharaoh?"

"Come, my dear," said Morrel, rising from his seat, "let us go and see, and heaven have pity upon us if it be false intelligence!" They all went out, and on the stairs met Mdme. Morrel, who had been afraid to go up into the cabinet. In an instant they were at the pier. All the crowd gave way before Morrel. "The Pharaoh! the Pharaoh!" said every voice.

And, wonderful to say, in front of the tower of Saint-Jean, was a ship bearing on her stern these words, painted in white letters, "The Pharaoh, Morrel and Son, of Marseilles." It was precisely resembling the other Pharaoh, and loaded, as that had been, with cochineal and indigo. It cast anchor, brailed all sails, and on the deck was Captain Gaumard giving orders, and Boatswain Penelon making signals to M. Morrel. To doubt any longer was impossible; there was the evidence of the senses, and ten thousand persons who came to corroborate the testimony. As Morrel and his son embraced on the pier-head, in the presence and applause of the whole city witnessing this prodigy, a man with his face half-covered by a black beard, and who, concealed behind a sentry-box, watched the scene with delight, uttered these words in a low tone, "Be happy, noble heart, be blessed for all the good thou hast done and wilt do hereafter, and let my gratitude rest in the shade with your kindness."

And with smile in which joy and happiness were revealed, he left his hiding-place, and without being observed, descended one of those flights of steps which serve for debarkation, and shouted "Jacopo!" Then a gig came to shore, took him on board, and conveyed him to a yacht splendidly fitted up, on whose deck he sprung with the activity of a sailor; thence he once again looked toward Morrel, who, weeping with joy, was shaking hands most cordially with all the crowd around him, and thanking with a look the unknown benefactor whom he seemed to be seeking in the skies. "And now," said the unknown, "farewell kindness, humanity, and gratitude! Farewell to all the feelings that expand the heart! I have been heaven's substitute to recompense the good—now the god of vengeance yields to me his power to punish the wicked!" At these words he gave a signal, and, as if only awaiting this signal, the yacht instantly put out to sea.

CHAPTER XIX.

SINBAD THE SAILOR.

TOWARDS the commencement of the year 1838, two young gentlemen belonging to the first society of Paris, Viscount Albert de Morcerf and Baron Franz d'Epinay, were at Florence. They had agreed to see the Carnival at Rome that year, and that Franz, who for the last three or four years had inhabited Italy, should act as *cicerone* to Albert. They wrote to Pastrini, the proprietor of the Hôtel de Londres, to reserve comfortable apartments for them. Pastrini replied that he had only two rooms and a cabinet, which he offered at the low charge of a louis per diem. They accepted his offer; but wishing to make the best use of the time that was left, Albert started for Naples. As for Franz, he remained at Florence. After having passed several days here, he took a fancy into his head, after having already visited Corsica, the cradle of Bonaparte, to visit Elba, the halting-place of Napoleon.

One evening he cast off a barque from the iron ring that secured it to the port of Leghorn, laid himself down, wrapped in his cloak, at the bottom, and said to the crew,—"To the Isle of Elba!" The barque shot out of the harbor like a bird, and the next morning Franz disembarked at Porto Ferrajo. He traversed the island, after having followed the traces which the footsteps of the giant have left, and re-embarked for Marciana. Two hours after he again landed at Pianosa, where he was assured red partridges abounded. The sport was bad; Franz only succeeded in killing a few partridges, and, like every unsuccessful sportsman, he returned to the boat very much out of temper. "Ah, if your excellency chose," said the captain, "you might have capital sport on the island of Monte-Cristo."

"But I have no permission to shoot over this island."

"Your excellency does not require a permission, for the island is un-inhabited. It is a mass of rocks, and does not contain an acre of land capable of cultivation."

"What game shall I find there?"———"Thousands of wild goats."

"Where can I sleep?"

"On shore, in the caves, or on board in your cloak: besides, if your excellency pleases, we can leave as soon as the chase is finished—we can sail as well by night as by day, and if the wind drops we can use our oars."

As Franz had sufficient time, and besides had no longer his apartments at Rome to seek after, he accepted the proposition.

The captain gave his orders, the helm was put up, and the barque was soon sailing in the direction of the island.

The wind blew strongly, the barque sailed six or seven knots an hour and they were within fifteen miles of Monte-Cristo when the sun began to set; half an hour after, and the night was quite dark.

Suddenly, a great light appeared on the strand; land might resemble a cloud, but the fire was not a meteor. "What is this light?" asked he.

"Silence!" said the captain; "it is a fire."

"But you told me the isle was uninhabited?"

"I said there was no fixed habitations on it, but I said also that it served sometimes as a harbor for smugglers."

"And for pirates?"———"And for pirates," returned Gaetano, repeating Franz's words.

"You think, then, that this fire announces unwelcome neighbors?"

"That is what we must ascertain," returned Gaetano.

Gaetano consulted with his companions, and after five minutes' discussion a manœuvre was executed which caused the vessel to rapidly approach the isle, and was soon within fifty paces of it. Gaetano lowered the sail, and the barque remained stationary.

The captain had thrown off his vest and shirt, and secured his trousers round his waist; his feet were naked, so he had no shoes and stockings to take off; after these preparations he placed his finger on his lips, and lowering himself noiselessly into the sea, swam towards the shore with such precaution that it was impossible to hear the slightest sound; he could only be traced by the phosphorescent line in his wake. This track soon disappeared; it was evident that he had touched the shore. Every one on board remained motionless during half an hour, when the same luminous track was again observed, and in two strokes he had regained the barque.

"Well!" exclaimed Franz and the sailors altogether.

"They are Spanish smugglers," said he; "they have with them two Corsican bandits."——"And what are these Corsican bandits doing here with Spanish smugglers?"

"Alas!" returned the captain, with an accent of the most profound pity, "we ought always to help one another. Very often the bandits are hard pressed by gendarmes or carbineers; well, they see a barque, and good fellows like us on board, they come and demand hospitality of us; you can't refuse help to a poor hunted devil; we receive them, and for greater security we stand out to sea. This costs us nothing, and saves the life, or at least the liberty, of a fellow-creature, who on the first occasion returns the service by pointing out some safe spot where we can land our goods without interruption."

"Ah!" said Franz, "then you are a smuggler occasionally, Gaetano?" ——"Your excellency, we must live somehow," returned the other, smiling in a way impossible to describe."

"Then you know the men who are now on Monte-Cristo?"——"Oh, yes, we sailors are like freemasons, and recognize each other by signs."

"And do you think we have nothing to fear if we land?"

"Nothing at all!"

"Then, for the last time, steer to Monte-Cristo."

Through the darkness Franz, whose eyes were now accustomed to it, distinguished the granite giant by which the barque was sailing, and then, turning an angle of the rock, he saw the fire more brilliant than ever, round which five or six persons were seated. The blaze illumined the sea for a hundred paces round. Gaetano skirted the light, carefully keeping the barque out of its rays; then, when they were opposite the fire, he entered into the center of the circle, singing a fishing song, of which his companions sung the chorus. At the first words of the song, the men seated round the fire rose and approached the landing-place, their eyes fixed on the barque, of which they evidently sought to judge the force and divine the intention. They soon appeared satisfied and returned (with the exception of one, who remained on the shore) to their fire, at which a whole goat was roasting. When the barque was within twenty paces of the shore, the man on the beach made with his carbine the movement of a sentinel who sees a patrol, and cried, "Who goes there!" in Sardinian. Franz coolly cocked both barrels. Gaetano then exchanged a few words with this man, which the traveler did not understand, but which evidently concerned him. "Will your excellency give your name, or remain *incognito?*" asked the captain.

"My name must rest unknown,—merely say I am a Frenchman traveling for pleasure." As soon as Gaetano had transmitted this answer, the sentinel gave an order to one of the men seated round the fire, who rose and disappeared among the rocks. Not a word was spoken, every one seemed occupied, Franz with his disembarkment, the sailors with their sails, the smugglers with their goat; but in the midst of all this carelessness it was evident that they mutually observed each other. The man who had disappeared returned suddenly, on the opposite side to that by which he had left; he made a sign with his head to the sentinel, who, turning to the barque, uttered these words, *"S' accomodi."* The sailors did not wait for a second invitation; four strokes of the oar brought them to the land; Gaetano sprang to shore, exchanged a few words with the sentinel, then his comrades descended, and lastly came Franz's turn. One of his guns was swung over his shoulder, Gaetano had the other, and a sailor held his rifle; his dress, half artist, half dandy, did not excite any suspicion, and, consequently, no disquietude. The barque was moored to the shore, and they advanced a few paces to find a comfortable bivouac; but, doubtless, the spot they chose did not suit the smuggler who filled the post of sentinel, for he cried out, "Not that way, if you please."

Gaetano faltered an excuse, and advanced to the opposite side, whilst two sailors kindled torches at the fire to light them on their way. They advanced about thirty paces, and then stopped at a small esplanade, surrounded with rocks, in which seats had been cut, not unlike sentry-boxes. Around in the crevices of the rocks grew a few dwarf oaks and thick bushes of myrtles. Franz lowered a torch, and saw, by the light of a mass of cinders, that he was not the first to discover this retreat, which was, doubtless, one of the halting-places of the wandering visitors of Monte-Cristo. As for his anticipation of events, once on *terra firma,* once that he had seen the indifferent, if not friendly, appearance of his hosts, his pre-occupation had disappeared, or rather, at sight of the goat, had turned to appetite. He mentioned this to Gaetano, who replied that nothing could be more easy than to prepare a supper when they had in their boat bread, wine, half-a-dozen partridges, and a good fire to roast them by. "Besides," added he, "if the smell of their roast meat tempts you, I will go and offer them two of our birds for a slice."

"You seem born for negotiation," returned Franz; "go and try."

During this time the sailors had collected dried sticks and branches, with which they made a fire. Franz waited impatiently, smelling the odor of the goat, when the captain returned with a mysterious air.——"Well," said Franz, "anything new?—do they refuse?"——"On the contrary," returned Gaetano, "the chief was told you were a Frenchman, and invites you to sup with him."

"Well," observed Franz, "this chief is very polite, and I see no objection—the more so as I bring my share of the supper."

"Oh, it is not that—he has plenty, and to spare, for supper; but he attaches a singular condition to your presentation at his house."

"His house! has he built one here, then?"

"No, but he has a very comfortable one, all the same, so they say."

"You know this chief, then?"——"I have heard talk of him."

"Ill or well?"

"Both."

"The devil!—and what is this condition?"

"That you are blindfolded, and do not take off the bandage until he himself bids you." Franz looked at Gaetano, to see, if possible, what he thought of this proposal.

"What should you do in my place?"

"I, who have nothing to lose, I should go."

"You would accept?"

"Yes, were it only out of curiosity."

"There is something very curious about this chief, then?"

"Listen," said Gaetano, lowering his voice, "I do not know if what they say is true—" He stopped to look if any one was near.

"What do they say?"

"That this chief inhabits a cavern to which the Pitti Palace is nothing."

"What nonsense!" said Franz, reseating himself.

"It is no nonsense; it is quite true. I know their yacht."

"And if this person be not a smuggler, who is he?"

"A wealthy signor, who travels for his pleasure."

"What is his name?"

"If you ask him he says Sinbad the Sailor; but I doubt its being his real name."

"Have you ever seen him?"——"Sometimes."

"What sort of a man is he?"——"Your excellency will judge for yourself."

"Where will he receive me?"

"No doubt in the subterranean palace Gaetano told you of."

"His excellency waits for you," said a voice, which he recognized as the sentinel's. He was accompanied by two of the yacht's crew. Franz drew his handkerchief from his pocket, and presented it to the man who had spoken to him. Without uttering a word, they bandaged his eyes with a care that showed their apprehensions of his committing some indiscretion. Afterwards he was made to promise he would not make the least attempt to raise the bandage. He promised. Then his two guides took his arms, and he advanced, guided by them, and preceded by the sentinel. Presently, by a change in the atmosphere, he comprehended that they were entering a cave; after going on for a few seconds more he heard a crackling, and it seemed to him as though the atmosphere again changed, and became balmy and perfumed. At length his feet touched on a thick and soft carpet, and his guides let go their hold of him. There was a moment's silence, and then a voice, in excellent French, although with a foreign accent, said: "Welcome, sir. I beg you will remove your bandage." It may be supposed, then, Franz did not wait for a repetition of this permission, but took off the handkerchief, and found himself in the presence of a man, from thirty-eight to forty years of age, dressed in Tunisian costume. Although of a paleness almost livid, this man had a remarkably handsome face.

This pallor was so peculiar, that it seemed as though it were that which would be exhibited by a man enclosed for a long time in a tomb, and unable to resume the healthy glow and hue of the living. He was not particularly tall, but extremely well made, and, like the men of the South, had small hands and feet. But what astonished Franz, who treated Gaetano's description as a fable, was the splendor of the apartment. The host gave Franz time for his surprise, and, moreover, rendered him look for look, not even taking his eyes off him. "Sir," he said after some pause, "a thousand excuses for the precaution taken in your introduction hither; but as, during the greater portion of the year, this island is deserted, if the secret of this abode were discovered, I should, doubtless, find on my return my temporary retirement in a state of great disorder, which would be exceedingly annoying, not for the loss it occasioned me, but because I should not have the certainty I now possess of separating myself from all the rest of mankind at pleasure. Let me now endeavor to make you forget this temporary unpleasantness, and offer you what no doubt you did not expect to find here—that is to say, a tolerable supper and pretty comfortable beds. But such as is my hermitage, it is at your disposal; such as is my supper, it is yours to share, if you will. Ali, is the supper ready?" At this moment the tapestry moved aside, and a Nubian, black as ebony, and dressed in a plain white tunic, made a sign to his master that all was prepared. "Now," said the unknown to Franz, "I do not know if you are of my opinion, but I think nothing is more annoying than to remain two or three hours without knowing by name how to address one another. Pray observe, that I too much respect the laws of hospitality to ask your name or title. I only request you to give me one by which I may have the pleasure of addressing you. As for myself, that I may put you at your ease, I tell you that I am generally called 'Sinbad the Sailor.'"

"And I," replied Franz, "will tell you, as I only require his wonderful lamp to make me precisely like Aladdin, that I see no reason why at this moment I should not be called Aladdin. That will keep us from going away from the East, whither I am tempted to think I have been conveyed by some good genius."——"Well, then, Signor Aladdin," replied the singular Amphitryon, "you heard our repast announced; will you now take the trouble to enter the dining-room, your humble servant going first to show the way?" At these words, moving aside the tapestry, Sinbad preceded his guest. Franz proceeded from one enchantment to another; the table was splendidly covered, and once convinced of this important point, he cast his eyes around him. The hall was scarcely less striking than the boudoir he had just left; it was entirely of marble. The supper consisted of a roast pheasant, garnished with Corsican blackbirds; a boar's ham, a quarter of a kid, a glorious turbot, and a gigantic lobster. Between these large dishes were smaller ones containing various dainties. The dishes were of silver, and the plates of Japanese china.

Franz rubbed his eyes in order to assure himself that this was not a dream. Ali alone was present to wait at table, and acquitted himself so admirably, that the guest complimented his host thereupon. "Yes," replied he, whilst he did the honors of the supper with much ease and grace—"yes, he is a poor devil who is much devoted to me, and does all he can to prove it. He remembers I saved his life, and as he has a regard for his head, he feels some gratitude towards me for having kept it on his shoulders." Ali approached his master, took his hand, and kissed it.

"And like the celebrated sailor whose name you have assumed," he said, by way of changing the conversation, "you pass your life in traveling?"——"Yes. I made a vow at a time when I little thought I should ever be able to accomplish it," said the unknown, with a singular smile; "and I made some others also, which I hope I may fulfil in due season." Although Sinbad pronounced these words with much calmness, his eyes darted gleams of singular ferocity.

"You have suffered a great deal, sir?" said Franz, inquiringly.

Sinbad started and looked fixedly at him, as he replied, "What makes you suppose so?"——"Everything!" answered Franz,—"your voice, your look, your pallid complexion, and even the life you lead, you seem to me like a man who, persecuted by society, has a fearful account to settle with it."——"Ah!" responded Sinbad, laughing with his singular laugh, which displayed his sharp teeth. "You have not guessed rightly! Such as you see me I am, a sort of philosopher, and one day perhaps I shall go to Paris to rival your philanthropists."

"And will that be the first time you ever took that journey?"

"Yes, it will! I must seem to you by no means curious, but I assure you that it is not my fault I have delayed it so long—it will happen one day or the other."

"I should like to be there at the time you come, and I will endeavor to repay you, as far as lies in my power, for your liberal hospitality displayed to me at Monte-Cristo."

"I should avail myself of your offer with pleasure," replied the host, "but, unfortunately, if I go there, it will be, in all probability, incognito."

The supper appeared to have been supplied solely for Franz, for the unknown scarcely touched one or two dishes of the splendid banquet to which his guest did ample justice. Then Ali brought on the dessert, or rather took the baskets from the hands of statues and placed them on the table. Between the two baskets he placed a small silver cup, closed with a lid of the same. The care with which Ali placed this cup on the table roused Franz's curiosity. He raised the lid and saw a kind of greenish paste, something like preserved angelica, but which was perfectly unknown to him. He replaced the lid, as ignorant of what the cup contained as he was before he had looked at it, and then casting his eyes towards his host he saw him smile at his disappointment. "You cannot guess," said he, "what there is in that small vase, can you?"

"No, I really cannot."

"Well, then, that kind of green preserve is nothing less than the ambrosia which Hebe served at the table of Jupiter. Are you a man for the substantials, and is gold your god? taste this, and the mines of Peru, Guzerat, and Golconda are open to you. Are you a man of imagination—a poet? taste this, and the boundaries of possibility disappear; the fields of infinite space open to you, you advance free in heart, free in mind, into the boundless realms of unfettered reverie. Is it not tempting what I offer you, and is it not an easy thing, since it is only to do thus? look!" At these words he uncovered the small cup, took a tea-spoonful of the magic marmalade, raised it to his lips, and swallowed it slowly, with his eyes half shut and his head bent backwards. Franz did not disturb him whilst he absorbed his favorite, but when he had finished, he inquired,—"What, then, is this precious stuff?"

"Did you ever hear," he replied, "of the Old Man of the Mountain, who attempted to assassinate Philip Augustus? He reigned over a rich valley which was overhung by the mountain whence he derived his picturesque name. In this valley were magnificent gardens planted by Hassen-ben-Sabah, and in these gardens isolated pavilions. Into these pavilions he admitted the elect; and there, says Marco Polo, gave them to eat a certain herb, which transported them to Paradise, in the midst of ever-blooming shrubs, ever-ripe fruit, and ever-lovely virgins."

"Then," cried Franz, "it is hasheesh! I know that—by name at least."

"That is it precisely, Signor Aladdin; it is—the purest and most unadulterated of Alexandria,—the *fhang* of Abou-Gor, the celebrated maker, the only man, the man to whom there should be built a palace, inscribed with these words, '*A grateful world to the dealer in happiness.*'"

"Do you know," said Franz, "I have a very great inclination to judge for myself of the truth or exaggeration of your eulogies."

"Judge for yourself, Signor Aladdin—taste, guest of mine—taste the hasheesh!"

Franz's only reply was to take a tea-spoonful of the marvellous preparation, about as much in quantity as his host had eaten, and lift it to his mouth.

"I do not know if the result will be as agreeable as you describe, but the thing does not appear to me as succulent as you say."

"Because your palate has not yet attained the sublimity of the substances it flavors. Only eat for a week, and nothing in the world will seem to you to equal the delicacy of its flavor, which now appears to you sleepy and distasteful. Let us now go into the chamber beside you, which is your apartment, and Ali will bring us coffee and pipes." They both arose, and whilst he who called himself Sinbad,—gave some orders to the servant, Franz entered the adjoining apartment. It was simply yet richly furnished. It was round, and a large divan completely encircled it. Skins were strewn in profusion one on the other, so that it seemed like walking over the most mossy turf, or reclining on the most luxurious bed. Both laid themselves down on the divan; chibooques with jasmine tubes and amber mouthpieces were within reach, and all prepared so that there was no need to smoke the same pipe twice. Each of them took one, which Ali lighted, and then retired to prepare the coffee. There was a moment's silence. Ali brought in the coffee. "How do you take it?" inquired the unknown; strong or weak, sugar or none, with milk, cool or boiling? As you please; it is ready in all ways."——"I will take it *à la Turque*," replied Franz.

"And you are right," said his host; "it shows you have a tendency for an Oriental life. Ah! those Orientals; they are the only men who know how to live. As for me," he added, with one of those singular smiles which did not escape the young man, "when I have completed my affairs in Paris, I shall go and die in the East; and should you wish to see me again, you must seek me at Cairo, Bagdad, or Ispahan."

"Faith!" said Franz, "it would be the easiest thing in the world; for I feel eagle's wings springing out at my shoulders, and with these wings I could make a tour of the world in four-and-twenty hours."

"Ah! ah! it is the *fhang* operating. Well, unfurl your wings, and fly into superhuman regions; fear nothing, there is a watch over you; and if your wings, like those of Icarus, melt before the sun, we are here to receive you." He then said some Arabian words to Ali, who made a sign of obedience and withdrew, but not to any distance. As to Franz, a strange transformation had taken place in him. All the bodily fatigue of the day, all the pre-occupation of mind which the events of the evening had brought on, disappeared. With his eyes closed upon all nature his senses awoke to impassable impressions, and he was under the painful yet delicious enthralment produced by the hasheesh, whose enchantment had brought up marvelous and thrilling visions.

When Franz returned to himself, exterior objects seemed a second portion of his dream. He found that he was in a grotto, went towards the opening, and through a kind of fanlight saw a blue sea and an azure sky. The air and water were shining in the beams of the morning sun; on the shore sailors were sitting, chatting and laughing; and at ten yards from them the barque was at anchor, dancing gracefully on the water.

Remembrance became busy again in his memory. He recalled his arrival on the island, his presentation to a smuggler chief, a subterranean palace full of splendor, an excellent supper, and a spoonful of hasheesh. It seemed, however, even in the very face of open day, that at least a year had elapsed since all these things had passed, so deep was the impression made in his mind by the dream, and so strong a hold had it taken of his imagination. Thus every now and then his fancy placed amidst the sailors, seated on a rock, or saw undulating in the vessel, one of those shadows which had shared his dreams with their looks and their kisses. Otherwise, his head was perfectly clear, and his limbs entirely reposed; he was free from the slightest headache; on the contrary, he felt a certain degree of lightness, a faculty of absorbing the pure air, and enjoying the bright sunshine more vividly than ever.

He went gaily up to the sailors, who rose as soon as they perceived him; and the patron, accosting him, said, "Signor Sinbad has left his compliments for your excellency, and desires us to express the regret he feels at not being able to take his leave in person; but he trusts you will excuse him, as very important business calls him to Malaga."

Gaetano pointed in a direction in which a small vessel was making sail towards the southern point of Corsica. Franz adjusted his telescope, and directed it toward the barque. Gaetano was not mistaken. At the stern the mysterious stranger was standing up, looking toward the shore, and holding a spy-glass in his hand. He was attired as he had been on the previous evening, and waved his pocket-handkerchief to his guest in token of adieu. Franz returned the salute by shaking his handkerchief as an exchange of signals. After a second, a slight cloud of smoke was seen at the stern of the vessel, which rose gracefully as it expanded in the air, and then Franz heard a slight report. "There, do you hear?" observed Gaetano; "he is bidding you adieu." The young man took his carbine and fired it in the air, but without any idea that the noise could be heard at the distance which separated the yacht from the shore.

Then he lost two hours in his attempts to find the cave, which were utterly useless. At the end of this time he gave up his research, and Gaetano smiled.

When Franz appeared again on the shore, the yacht only seemed like a small white speck on the horizon. He looked again through his glass, but even then he could not distinguish anything. Gaetano reminded him that he had come for the purpose of shooting goats, which he had utterly forgotten. He took his fowling-piece, and began to hunt over the isle with the air of a man who is fulfilling a duty, rather than enjoying a pleasure; and at the end of a quarter of an hour he had killed a goat and two kids. These animals, though wild and agile as chamois, were too much like domestic goats, and Franz could not consider them as game. Moreover, other ideas, much more powerful, occupied his mind. Sitting on the spot where he was on the previous evening when his mysterious host had invited him to supper, he saw the little yacht, row like a sea-gull on the wave, continuing her flight towards Corsica. "Why," he remarked to Gaetano, "you told me that Signor Sinbad was going to Malaga, whilst it seems he is in the direction of Porto-Vecchio."

"Don't you remember," said the patron, "among the crew there were two Corsican brigands; he is going to land them. Ah! he is an individual who fears neither God nor devil, they say, and would at any time run fifty leagues out of his course to do a poor devil a service."

"But such services as these might involve him with the authorities of the country in which he practises this kind of philanthropy," said Franz.

"And what cares he for that," replied Gaetano with a laugh, "or any authorities? He smiles at them. Let them try to pursue him! why, in the first place, his yacht is not a ship, but a bird, and he would beat any frigate three knots in every nine; and if he were to throw himself on the coast, why, ain't he certain of finding friends everywhere?"

It was perfectly clear that the Signor Sinbad, Franz's host, had the honor of being on excellent terms with the smugglers and bandits along the whole coast of the Mediterranean, which placed him in a position singular enough. As to Franz, he had no longer any inducement to remain at Monte-Cristo. He had lost all hope of detecting the secret of the grotto; he consequently despatched his breakfast, and, his barque being ready, he hastened on board, and they were soon under way. Next morning, when the sun rose, they had lost sight of Monte-Cristo. When Franz had once again set foot on shore, he forgot, for the moment at least, the events which had just passed, whilst he finished his affairs of pleasure at Florence, and then thought of nothing but to rejoin his companion, awaiting him at Rome.

CHAPTER XX.

ROMAN BANDITTI.

AN apartment, as we have said had been retained beforehand, and thus he had but to go to the hotel. But this was not so easy a matter, for the streets were thronged with people, and Rome was already a prey to that low and feverish murmur which precedes all great events; and at Rome there are four great events in every year—the Carnival,

the Holy Week, the Fête Dieu, and St. Peter's. The apartment consisted of two small rooms and a closet. The two rooms looked on to
the street—a fact which Pastrini commented upon as an inappreciable
advantage. The remainder of the story was hired by a very rich
gentleman, who was supposed to be a Sicilian or Maltese; but the host
was unable to decide to which of the two nations the traveler belonged.
"Very good, Maître Pastrini," said Franz; "but we must have some
supper instantly, and a carriage for to-morrow and the following
days."——

"Be easy, my dear boy; they will come in due season; it is only
a question of how much be charged for them." Morcerf then, with
that delighted philosophy which believes that nothing is impossible
to a full purse and well-lined pocket-book, supped, went to bed, slept
soundly, and dreamed he was racing all over Rome at Carnival time
in a coach with six horses.

The next morning Franz woke first, and instantly rang the bell. The
sound had not yet died away when Pastrini himself entered.

"Well, excellency," said the landlord, triumphantly, and without
waiting for Franz to question him, "I feared yesterday, when I would
not promise you anything, that you were too late—there is not a
single carriage to be had—that is, from Sunday to Tuesday evening,
but from now till Sunday you can have fifty if you please."

"Ah! that is something," said Albert; "to-day is Thursday, and who
knows what may arrive between this and Sunday?"

"Ten or twelve thousand travelers will arrive," replied Franz,
"which will make it still more difficult."

"My friend," said Morcerf, "let us enjoy the present without gloomy
forebodings for the future."——"At least we can have a window?"

"Ah, a window!" exclaimed Pastrini,—"utterly impossible, there
was only one left on the fifth floor of the Doria Palace, and that has
been let to a Russian prince for twenty sequins a day."

The two young men looked at each other with an air of stupefaction.

"Well," said Franz to Albert, "do you know what is the best thing
we can do? It is to pass the Carnival at Venice; there we are sure
of obtaining gondolas if we cannot have carriages."

"Ah! the devil! no," cried Albert; "I came to Rome to see the
Carnival, and I will, though I see it on stilts."

"Bravo! an excellent idea! We will disguise ourselves as monster
clowns and we shall have complete success."

"Do your excellencies still wish for a carriage from now to Sunday
morning? I will do all I can, and I hope you will be satisfied."

"And now we understand each other."

"When do you wish the carriage to be here?"——"In an hour."

"In an hour it will be at the door."

An hour after the vehicle was at the door; it was a hack conveyance which was elevated to the rank of a private carriage in honor of the occasion; but, in spite of its humble exterior, the young men would have thought themselves happy to have secured it for the last three days of the Carnival.

Franz and Albert descended; the carriage approached the palace; their excellencies stretched their legs along the seats: the cicerone sprang into the seat behind. But Albert did not know that it takes a day to see Saint Peter's, and a month to study it. The day was passed at Saint Peter's alone. Suddenly the daylight began to fade away; Franz took out his watch—it was half-past four. They returned to the hotel; at the door Franz ordered the coachman to be ready at eight. He wished to show Albert the Colosseum by moonlight, as he had shown him St. Peter's by daylight. When we show a friend a city one has already visited, we feel the same pride as when we point out a woman whose lover we have been. He was to leave the city by the Porta del Popolo, skirt the outer wall, and re-enter by the Porta San Giovanni; thus they would behold the Colosseum without being in some measure prepared by the sight of the Capitol, the Forum, the Arch of Septimus Severus, the Temple of Antonius and Faustina, and the Via Sacra. They sat down to dinner. Maître Pastrini had promised them a banquet; he gave them a tolerable repast. At the end of the dinner he entered in person. Franz concluded he came to hear his dinner praised, and began accordingly, but at the first words he interrupted him. "Excellency," said he, "I am delighted to have your approbation, but it was not for that I came."——"Did you come to tell us you have procured a carriage?" asked Albert, lighting his cigar.

"No; and your excellencies will do well not to think of that any longer: at Rome things can or cannot be done; when you are told anything cannot be done, there is an end of it. You intend visiting *Il Colosseo.*"

"You mean the Colosseum?"

"It is the same thing. You have told your coachman to leave the city by the Porta del Popolo, to drive round the walls, and re-enter by the Porta San Giovanni? Well, this route is very dangerous, to say the least."

"Dangerous! and why?"

"On account of the famous Luigi Vampa."

"Pray, who may this famous Luigi Vampa be?" inquired Albert.

"He was a shepherd-boy attached to the farm of Count San-Felice, between Palestrina and the lake of Gabri, he was born at Pampinara, and entered the count's service when five years old; his father was also a shepherd, who owned a small flock, and lived by the wool and the milk, which he sold at Rome. When quite a child, the little Vampa was of a most extraordinary tendency. He learnt almost of himself and by himself to read and write and to carve wood excellently.

"A girl of six or seven—that is, a little younger than Vampa—tended sheep on a farm near Palestrina; she was an orphan, born at Valmontone, and was named Teresa. The two children met, sat down near each other, let their flocks mingle together, played, laughed and conversed together; in the evening they separated the flocks and returned to their respective farms, promising to meet the next morning. The next day they kept their word, and thus grew up. Vampa was twelve, and Teresa eleven. The two children grew up together, passing all their time with each other, and giving themselves up to the wild ideas of their different characters. Thus, in all their dreams, their wishes, and their conversations, Vampa saw himself the captain of a vessel, general of an army, or governor of a province. Teresa saw herself rich, superbly attired, and attended by a train of liveried domestics. Then, when they had thus passed the day in building castles in the air, they separated their flocks, and descended from the elevation of their dreams to the reality of their humble position.

"One day the young shepherd told the count's steward he had seen a wolf come out of the Sabine mountains, and prowl around his flock. The steward gave him a gun; this was what Vampa longed for. This gun had an excellent barrel, made at Brechia, and carrying a ball with the precision of an English rifle; but one day the count broke the stock, and had then cast the gun aside. This, however, was nothing to a sculptor like Vampa; he examined the ancient stock, calculated what change it would require to adapt the gun to his shoulder, and made a fresh stock, so beautifully carved that it would have fetched fifteen or twenty piastres, had he chosen to sell it. From this moment Vampa devoted all his leisure time to perfecting himself in the use of this precious weapon.

"One evening a wolf emerged from a pine-wood near which they were usually stationed, but the wolf had scarcely advanced ten yards ere he was dead. All these circumstances had gained Luigi considerable reputation. The man of superior abilities always finds admirers, go where he will. He was spoken of as the most adroit, the strongest, and the most courageous *contadino* for ten leagues round; and although Teresa was universally allowed to be the most beautiful girl of the Sabines, no one had ever spoken to her of love, because it was known that she was beloved by Vampa. When Teresa was seventeen and Vampa eighteen, a band of brigands established in the Lepini mountains began to be much spoken of. The brigands have never been really extirpated from the neighborhood of Rome. Sometimes a chief is wanted, but when a chief presents himself he rarely wants a band.

"The celebrated Cucumetto, pursued in the Abruzzo, driven out of the kingdom of Naples, where he had carried on a regular war, had come to take refuge on the banks of the Amasine. He strove to re-organize a band, and followed the footsteps of Decesaris and Gasperone, whom he hoped to surpass. Many young men joined the band of Cucumetto. After some time Cucumetto became the object of universal attention; the most extraordinary traits of ferocious daring and brutality were related of him. From Fondi to Percuse, every one trembled at the name of Cucumetto. These narratives were frequently the themes of conversation between Luigi and Teresa. The girl trembled very much at all these tales; but Vampa reassured her with a smile, tapping the butt of his good fowling-piece, which threw its ball so well; and if that did not restore her courage, he pointed to a crow, perched on some dead branch, took an aim, touched the trigger, and the bird fell dead at the foot of the tree. Time passed on, and the two young people had settled to be married when Vampa should be twenty and Teresa nineteen years of age. They were both orphans, and had only their employers' leave to ask, which had been already sought and obtained. One day when they were talking over their plans for the future, they heard two or three reports of firearms, and then suddenly a man came out of the wood, near which the two young persons used to graze their flocks, and hurried towards them. When he came within hearing, he exclaimed, 'I am pursued; can you conceal me?' They knew full well that this fugitive must be a bandit: but there is an innate sympathy between the Roman brigand and the Roman peasant, and the latter is always ready to aid the former. Vampa, without saying a word, hastened to the stone that closed up the entrance to their grotto, drew it away, made a sign to the fugitive to take refuge there, in a retreat unknown to every one, closed the stone upon him, and then went and resumed his seat by Teresa. Instantly afterwards four carbineers, on horseback, appeared on the edge of the wood; three of them appeared to be looking for the fugitive, whilst the fourth dragged a brigand prisoner by the neck. The three carbineers scrutinized on all sides, saw the young peasants, and, galloping up, interrogated them. They had seen no one. 'That is very annoying,' said the brigadier; 'for the man we are looking for is the chief.'——
'Cucumetto?' cried Luigi and Teresa at the same moment.

"'Yes,' replied the brigadier; 'and as his head is valued at a thousand Roman crowns, there would have been five hundred for you, if you had helped us to catch him.' The two young persons exchanged looks. The brigadier had a moment's hope. Five hundred Roman crowns are three thousand francs, and three thousand francs are a fortune for two poor orphans who are going to be married.

"'Yes, it is very annoying,' said Vampa; 'but we have not seen him.'

"Then the carbineers scoured the country in different directions, but in vain; then, after a time, they disappeared. Vampa then removed the stone, and Cucumetto came out. He had seen, through the crevices in the granite, the two young peasants talking with the carbineers, and guessed the subject of their parley. He had read in the countenances of Luigi and Teresa their steadfast resolution not to surrender him, and he drew from his pocket a purse full of gold, which he offered to them. But Vampa raised his head proudly; as to Teresa, her eyes sparkled when she thought of all the fine gowns and gay jewelry she could buy with this purse of gold.

"Cucumetto was a cunning fiend, and had assumed the form of a brigand instead of a serpent, and this look of Teresa revealed to him that she was a worthy daughter of Eve, and he returned to the forest, pausing several times on his way, under the pretext of saluting his protectors. Several days elapsed, and they neither saw nor heard of Cucumetto. The time of the Carnival was at hand. The Count San-Felice announced a grand masque ball, to which all that were distinguished in Rome were invited. Teresa had a great desire to see this ball. Luigi asked permission of his protector, the steward, that she and he might be present amongst the servants of the house. This was granted. The ball was given by the count for the particular pleasure of his daughter Carmela, whom he adored. Carmela was precisely the age and figure of Teresa, and Teresa was as handsome as Carmela. On the evening of the ball Teresa was attired in her best, her most brilliant hair ornaments, and gayest glass beads,—she was in the costume of the women of Frascati. Luigi wore the very picturesque garb of the Roman peasants at holiday time.

"Carmela was attired like a woman of Sonnino.

"Two of her companions were dressed, the one as a woman of Nettuno, and the other as a woman of La Riccia. Four young men of the richest and noblest families of Rome accompanied them with that Italian freedom which has not its parallel in any other country in the world. They were attired as peasants. We need hardly add that these peasant costumes, like those of the females, were brilliant with gold and jewels.

"Carmela wished to make a uniform quadrille, but there was one lady waiting. Carmela looked all around her, but not one of the guests had a costume similar to her own, or those of her companions. The Comte de San-Felice pointed out to her, in the group of peasants, Teresa, who was hanging on Luigi's arm. 'Will you allow me, father?' said Carmela.——'Certainly,' replied the comte, 'are we not in Carnival time?'——Carmela turned towards the young man who was talking with her, and saying a few words to him, pointed with her finger to Teresa. The young man followed with his eyes the lovely hand which made this indication, bowed in obedience, and then went to Teresa, and invited her to dance in a quadrille directed by the count's daughter. Teresa felt something like a flame pass over her face; she looked at Luigi, who could not refuse his assent. Luigi slowly relinquished Teresa's arm, which he had held beneath his own, and Teresa, accompanied by her elegant cavalier, took her appointed place with much agitation in the aristocratic quadrille. Luigi was jealous! He felt that, influenced by her ambition and coquettish disposition, Teresa might escape him.

"When the chill of the night had driven away the guests from the gardens, and the gates of the villa were closed on them for the fête indoors, Luigi took Teresa quite away, and as he left her at her home, he said,—

" 'Teresa, what were you thinking of as you danced opposite the young Comtesse de San-Felice?'——'I thought,' replied the young girl, with all the frankness of her nature, 'that I would give half my life for a costume such as she wore.'

" 'Well, then, you shall have it!'

"The girl, much astonished, raised her head to look at him, but his face was so gloomy and terrible that her words froze to her lips. As Luigi spoke thus, he left her. Teresa followed him with her eyes into the darkness as long as she could, and when he had quite disappeared, she entered her apartment with a sigh.

"That night a great accident happened, no doubt from the imprudence of some servant who had neglected to extinguish the lights. The Ville de San-Felice took fire in the rooms adjoining the very apartment of the lovely Carmela. Awoke in the night by the light of the flames, she had sprung out of bed, wrapped herself in a dressing-gown, and attempted to escape by the door, but the corridor by which she hoped to fly was already a prey to the flames. She had then returned to her room, calling for help as loudly as she could, when suddenly her window, which was twenty feet from the ground, was opened, a young peasant jumped into the chamber, seized her in his arms, and with superhuman skill and strength conveyed her out safe and uninjured. Her preserver was everywhere sought for, but did not appear; no one had seen him.

"The next day, at the usual hour, the two young peasants were on the borders of the forest. Luigi arrived first. He came towards Teresa in high spirits, and seemed to have completely forgotten the events of the previous evening. The girl was very pensive, but seeing Luigi so cheerful, she on her part assumed a smiling air, which was natural to her when no excitement of passion came to disturb her. Luigi took her arm beneath his own and led her to the door of the grotto. Then he paused. The girl, perceiving that there was something extraordinary, looked at him steadfastly. 'Teresa,' said Luigi, 'yesterday evening you told me you would give all the world to have a costume similar to that of the count's daughter.'——'Yes,' replied the girl, whose astonishment increased at every word uttered by Luigi, 'but of course your reply was only to please me.'

"'I have promised no more than I have given you, Teresa,' said Luigi, proudly. 'Go into the grotto and dress yourself.' At these words he drew away the stone, and showed Teresa the grotto, lighted up by two wax lights, which burnt on each side of a splendid mirror; on a rustic table, made by Luigi, were spread out the pearl necklace and the diamond pins, and on a chair at the side was laid the rest of the costume.

"Teresa uttered a cry of joy, and, without inquiring whence this attire came, or even thanking Luigi, darted into the grotto transformed into a dressing-room. Luigi pushed the stone behind her, for he saw on the crest of a small adjacent hill which prevented him from seeing Palestrina from where he was, a traveler on horseback. The traveler, had mistaken his way; he begged Luigi to be his guide. In ten minutes Luigi and the traveler reached the cross-roads alluded to by the young shepherd. On arriving there, with an air as majestic as that of an emperor, he stretched his hand toward that one of the roads which the traveler was to follow.—'That is your road, excellency, and now you cannot again mistake.'——'And here is your recompense,' said the traveler, offering the young herdsman some pieces of small money.

"'Thank you,' said Luigi, drawing back his hand; 'I render a service, I do not sell it.'——'Well,' replied the traveler, who seemed used to this difference between the servility of a man of the cities and the pride of the mountaineer, 'if you refuse pay, you will, perhaps, accept of a present. Take these two Venitian sequins and give them to your bride, to make herself a pair of earrings.'

"'And then do you take this poniard,' said the young herdsman: 'you will not find one better carved between Albana and Civita-Cas-tellana.'

"'I accept it,' answered the traveler. 'What is your name?' inquired the traveler.

"'Luigi Vampa,' replied the shepherd, with the same air as would have replied Alexander, King of Macedon. 'And yours?'

"'I,' said the traveler, 'am called Sinbad the Sailor.'

"Yes," replied the narrator; "that was the name which the traveler gave to Vampa as his own."

"Well, and what may you have to say against this name?" inquired Albert; "it is a very pretty name, and the adventures of the gentle-man of that name amused me very much in my youth, I must confess."

—Franz said no more. The name of Sinbad the Sailor, as may well be supposed, awakened in him a world of recollections, as had the name of the Count of Monte-Cristo on the previous evening.

"Vampa put the two sequins haughtily into his pocket, and slowly returned by the way he had gone. As he came within two or three hundred paces of the grotto, he thought he heard a scream. He cast his eyes around him, and saw a man carrying off Teresa, as did the Centaur Nessus Dejanira. This man, who was hastening toward the wood, was already three-quarters of the way on the road from the grotto to the forest. Vampa measured the distance: the man was at least two hundred paces in advance of him, and there was not a chance of overtaking him. The young shepherd stopped, as if his feet had been rooted to the ground; then he put the butt of his carbine to his shoulder, took aim at the ravisher, followed him for a second in his track, and then fired. The ravisher stopped suddenly, his knees bent under him, and he fell with Teresa in his arms. The girl rose instantly, but the man lay on the earth struggling in the agonies of death. The ball, had pierced his heart. Vampa gazed on him for a moment without betraying the slightest emotion; whilst, on the contrary, Teresa, shuddering in every limb, dared not approach the slain ruffian but by degrees, and threw a hesitating glance at the dead body over the shoulder of her lover. Suddenly Vampa turned towards his mistress:— 'Ah! ah!' said he—'good, good! you are attired; it is now my turn to dress myself.'

"Teresa was clothed from head to foot in the garb of San-Felice's daughter. Vampa took Cucumetto's body in his arms and conveyed it to the grotto, whilst in her turn Teresa remained outside. If a second traveler had passed, he would have seen a strange thing; a shepherdess watching her flock, clad in a cachemire gown, with earrings and necklace of pearls, diamond pins, and buttons of sapphires, emeralds, and rubies. At the end of a quarter hour Vampa quitted the grotto; his costume was no less elegant than Teresa's. He had assumed the entire costume of Cucumetto. The young man saw the effect produced on his betrothed, and a smile of pride over his lips.—'Now,' he said to Teresa, 'are you ready to share my fortune, whatever it may be?'——Oh, yes!' exclaimed the girl enthusiastically.——'And follow me wherever I go?'——'To the world's end.'——'Then take my arm, and let us on, we have no time to loose.'—The girl did so without questioning her lover as to where he was conducting her, for he appeared to her at this moment, as handsome, proud, and powerful as a god. They went towards the forest, and soon entered it. We need scarcely say that all the paths of the mountain were known to Vampa; he therefore went forward without a moment's hesitation, although there was no beaten track; but he knew his path by looking at the trees and bushes; and thus they kept on advancing for nearly an hour and a half. At the end of this time they had reached the thickest of the forest. Suddenly, about ten paces from them, a man advanced from behind a tree and aimed at Vampa.—'Not another step,' he said, 'or you are a dead man.'——'What then!' said Vampa, raising his hand with a gesture of disdain, whilst Teresa, no longer able to restrain her alarm, clung closely to him: 'do wolves rend each other?'——'Who are you?' inquired the sentinel.——'I am Luigi Vampa, shepherd of the farm of San-Felice. I would speak with your companions in the recess at Rocca Bianca'——'Follow me, then,' said the sentinel; 'or, as you know your way, go first.'—Vampa smiled disdainfully at this precaution of the bandit, went before Teresa, and continued to advance with the same firm and easy step as before. At the end of ten minutes the bandit made them a sign to stop. The two young persons obeyed. Then the bandit thrice imitated the caw of a crow; a croak answered this signal. —'Good!' said the sentry: 'you may now advance.'—Luigi and Teresa again set forward; as they advanced, Teresa clung tremblingly to her lover, as she saw through the trees arms appear and the barrels of carbines shine. The retreat of Rocca Bianca was at the top of a small mountain, which no doubt in former days had been a volcano. Teresa and Luigi reached the summit, and all at once found themselves in the presence of twenty bandits. 'Here is a young man who seeks and wishes to speak to you,' said the sentinel.——'What has he to say?' inquired the young man who was in command in the chief's absence.——'I wish to say that I am tired of a shepherd's life,' was Vampa's reply.——'I come to ask to be your captain,' said the young man. The bandits shouted with laughter. 'And what have you done to aspire to this honor?' demanded the lieutenant.—'I have killed your chief, Cucumetto, whose dress I now wear; and I set fire to the Villa San-Felice to procure a wedding-dress for my betrothed.' An hour afterwards Luigi Vampa was chosen captain, *vice* Cucumetto deceased."

"Well, my dear Albert," said Franz, turning towards his friend, "what think you of citizen Luigi Vampa?"

"I say he is a myth," replied Albert, "and never had an existence."

"And you say that Vampa exercises his profession at this moment in the environs of Rome? Then the police have vainly tried to lay hands on him?"——"Why, you see, he has a good understanding with the shepherds on the plains, the fishermen of the Tiber, and the smugglers of the coast. They seek for him in the mountains, and he is on the water; they follow him on the waters, and he is on the open sea; then they pursue him, and he has suddenly taken refuge on the isle Monte-Cristo; and when they hunt for him there, he reappears suddenly at Albano, Tivoli, or La Riccia."

"And how does he behave towards travelers?"

"Alas! his plan is very simple. It depends on the distance he may be from the city, whether he gives eight hours, twelve hours, or a day wherein to pay their ransom; and when that time has elapsed he allows another hour's grace. At the sixtieth minute of this hour, if the money is not forthcoming, he blows out the prisoner's brains with a pistol-shot, or plants his dagger in his heart, and that settles the account."

The two young men went down the staircase, and got into the carriage.

CHAPTER XXI.

THE COLOSSEUM.

FRANZ had so managed his route, that during the ride to the Colosseum they passed not a single ancient ruin, so that no gradual preparation was made on the mind for the colossal proportions of the gigantic building they came to admire. This itinerary possessed the advantage of leaving Franz at full liberty to indulge his deep reverie upon the subject of the story recounted by Pastrini, in which his mysterious host of the isle of Monte-Cristo was so strangely mixed up.

But however the mind of the young man might be absorbed in these reflections, they were at once dispersed at the sight of the dark frowning ruins of the stupendous Colosseum, through the various openings of which the pale moonlight played and flickered like the unearthly gleam from the eyes of the wandering dead. The carriage stopped near the Meta Sundans, the door was opened, and the young men, eagerly alighting, found themselves opposite a cicerone, who appeared to have sprung up from the ground, so unexpected was his appearance.

As for Albert and Franz, they essayed not to escape from their ciceronian tyrants; and, indeed, it would have been so much the more difficult to break their bondage, as the guides alone are permitted to visit these monuments with torches in their hands. Thus, then, the young men made no attempt at resistance, but blindly and confidingly surrendered themselves into the care and custody of their conductors. Scarcely had the reflective Franz walked a hundred steps beneath the interior porticoes of the ruin, then, abandoning Albert to the guides, ascended a half-dilapidated staircase, and, leaving them to follow their monotonous round, seated himself at the foot of a column, and immediately opposite a large chasm, which permitted him to enjoy a full and undisturbed view of the gigantic dimensions of this majestic ruin.

Franz had remained for nearly a quarter of an hour perfectly hidden by the shadow of the vast column, when all at once his ear caught a sound resembling a stone rolling down the staircase opposite the one by which he had himself ascended. Some one was approaching the spot where he sat. Conjecture soon became certainty, for a man was distinctly visible to Franz, gradually emerging from the staircase opposite, upon which the moon was at that moment pouring a full tide of silvery brightness.

The stranger thus presenting himself was probably a person who, like Franz, preferred the enjoyment of solitude and his own thoughts to the frivolous gabble of the guides. And his appearance had nothing extraordinary in it; but the hesitation with which he proceeded onwards, stopping and listening with anxious attention at every step he took, convinced Franz he expected the arrival of some person.

From the imperfect means Franz had of judging, he could only come to one conclusion—that the individual whom he was thus watching certainly belonged to no inferior station of life. Some few minutes had elapsed, and the stranger began to show manifest signs of impatience, when a slight noise was heard outside the aperture in the roof, and almost immediately a dark shadow seemed to obstruct the flood of light that had entered it, and the figure of a man was clearly seen gazing with eager scrutiny on the immense space beneath him; then, as his eye caught sight of the individual in the mantle, he grasped a floating mass of thickly-matted boughs, and glided down by their help to within three or four feet of the ground, and then leaped lightly on his feet. The man who had performed this daring act with so much indifference wore the costume of Transtevere. "I beg your excellency's pardon for keeping you waiting," said the man, in the Roman dialect, "but I don't think I'm many minutes after my time; ten o'clock has just struck by the clock of Saint-Jean-de-Latran."

"Say not a word about being late," replied the stranger, in purest Tuscan; "'tis I who am too soon. But even if you had caused me to wait a little while, I should have felt quite sure that the delay was not occasioned by any fault of yours."

"Your excellency is perfectly right in so thinking," said the man; "I came here direct from the Castle San Angelo, and I had an immense deal of trouble before I could get to speak to Beppo. He is employed in the prison, and I give him so much a year to let me know what is going on within his holiness's Castle."

"Indeed! You are a provident person, I see."

"Why, you see, no one knows what may happen. Perhaps some of these days I may be entrapped, like poor Peppino, and may be very glad to have some little nibbling mouse to gnaw the meshes of my net, and so help me out of prison."

"Briefly, what did you glean?"

"That two executions of considerable interest will take place the day after to-morrow at two o'clock, as is customary at Rome at the commencement of all great festivals. One of the culprits will be *mazzolato;* he is an atrocious villain, who murdered the priest who brought him up, and deserves not the smallest pity. The other sufferer is to be beheaded; and he, is poor Peppino."

"The fact is, that you have inspired not only the pontifical government, but also the neighboring states, with such extreme fear, that they are glad of an opportunity of making an example."——"But Peppino did not even belong to my band; he was merely a poor shepherd, whose only crime consisted in furnishing us with provisions.

"One thing I have resolved on, and that is, to stop at nothing to restore a poor devil to liberty, who has got into this scrape solely from having served me. I should hate and despise myself as a coward, did I desert the brave fellow in his present extremity."

"And what do you mean to do?"——"To surround the scaffold with twenty of my best men, who, at a signal from me, will rush forward directly Peppino is brought for execution, and, by the assistance of their stilettos, drive back the guard, and carry off the prisoner."

"That seems to me as hazardous as uncertain, and convinces me my scheme is far better than yours."

"And what is your excellency's project?"

"Take what precautions you please, if it is any satisfaction to you to do so; but rely upon my obtaining the reprieve I seek."

"And how shall I know whether your excellency has succeeded or not?"

"Oh! that is very easily arranged; I have engaged the three lower windows at the Palace Rospoli; should I have obtained the requisite pardon for Peppino, the two windows will be hung with yellow damasks and the centre with white, having a large cross in red marked on it."

"And whom will you employ to carry the reprieve to the officer directing the execution?"—"Send one of your men disguised as a penitent friar, and I will give it to him: his dress will procure him the means of approaching the scaffold itself, and will deliver the official order to the officer, who, in his turn, will hand it to the executioner; in the meantime, it will be as well to acquaint Peppino with what we have determined on, if it be only to prevent his dying of fear or losing his senses, because in either case a very useless expense will have been incurred."

"Only fulfill your promise of rescuing Peppino, and henceforward you shall receive not only devotedness, but the most absolute obedience from myself and those under me that one human being can render to another."

"Hush!" interrupted the stranger; "I hear a noise."

" 'Tis some travelers, who are visiting the Colosseum by torchlight."

" 'Twere better we should not be seen together; those guides are nothing but spies, and might possibly recognize you; and, however I may be honored by your friendship, my worthy friend, if once the extent of our intimacy were known, I am sadly afraid both my reputation and credit would suffer thereby."

"All is then understood between us. Adieu, your excellency, depend upon me as firmly as I do upon you."

Saying these words, the Transtevere disappeared down the staircase, while his companion, muffling his features more closely than before in the folds of his mantle, passed almost close to Franz, and descended to the arena by an outward flight of steps. The next minute Franz heard himself called by Albert, who made the lofty building re-echo with the sound of his friend's name. Franz, however, did not obey the summons till he had satisfied himself the two individuals, whose conversation he had thus surprised, were at a sufficient distance to prevent his encountering them in his descent, not wishing that they should suspect having had a witness to their discourse, who, if unable to recognize their faces, had at least heard every word that passed. In ten minutes from the parting of the strangers, Franz was on the road to the Hôtel d'Espagne, listening with mortified indifference to the learned dissertation delivered by Albert. Franz longed to be alone, and able, undisturbedly, to ponder over all that had occurred. One of the two men, whose mysterious rendezvous in the Colosseum he had so unintentionally witnessed, was an entire stranger to him, but not so the other; and though Franz had been unable to distinguish his features, from his being either wrapped in his mantle or obscured by the shadow, the tones of his voice had made too powerful an impression on him the first time he heard them for him ever again to forget them, hear them when or where he might. It was more especially when speaking in a manner half-jesting, half-bitter, that Franz's ear recalled most vividly the deep, sonorous, yet well-pitched voice, that had spoken to him in the grotto of Monte-Cristo, and which he heard for the second time amid the darkness and ruined grandeur of the Colosseum! And the more he thought, the more entire was his conviction, that the individual in the mantle was no other than his former host and entertainer, "Sinbad the Sailor."

CHAPTER XXII.

THE EXECUTION.

THE Carnival was to commence on the morrow: therefore Albert had not an instant to lose in setting forth the programme of his hopes, expectations, and claims to notice. With this design he had engaged a box in the most conspicuous part of the Argentino theatre, and exerted himself to set off his personal attractions by the most elaborate toilet. The box taken by Albert was in the first circle, who knew but that, thus advantageously placed, he could not fail to attract the notice of some fair Roman; and an introduction might ensue that would procure him the offer of a seat in a carriage, or a place in a princely balcony, from which he might behold the gaieties of the Carnival?

The truth was, that the anticipated pleasures of the Carnival, with the "Holy Week" that was to succeed it, so filled every fair breast, as to prevent the least attention being bestowed even on the business of the stage. Toward the close of the first act, the door of a box which had been hitherto vacant was opened; a lady entered to whom Franz had been introduced in Paris, where, indeed, he had imagined she still was. The quick eye of Albert caught the involuntary start with which his friend beheld the new arrival, and turning to him, he said hastily—"Do you know the female who has just entered the box?——"Countess Guiccioli——"

"Ah! I know her by name," exclaimed Albert; "she is said to possess as much wit and cleverness as beauty! I was to have been presented to her when I met her at Mdme. Villefort's ball."

"Shall I assist you in repairing your negligence?" asked Franz.

"My dear fellow, are you really on such good terms with her as to venture to take me to her box?"——"Why, I have only had the honor of being in her society and conversing with her three or four times in my life; but you know that even such an acquaintance as that might warrant my doing what you ask." At this instant, the countess perceived Franz, and graciously waved her hand to him, to which he replied by a respectful inclination of the head.

The curtain at length fell on the performances, to the infinite satisfaction of Viscount Morcerf, who seized his hat, rapidly passed his fingers through his hair, arranged his cravat and wristbands, and signified to Franz that he was waiting for him to lead the way.

Franz presented Albert as one of the most distinguished young men of the day, both as regarded his position in society and extraordinary talents: nor did he say more than the truth, for in Paris and the circle in which the viscount moved, he was looked upon and cited as a model of perfection.

The countess, in reply, bowed gracefully to Albert, and extended her hand with cordial kindness to Franz; then, inviting Albert to take the vacant seat beside her, she recommended Franz to take the next best, if he wished to view the ballet, and pointed to the one behind her own chair. Albert was soon deeply engrossed in discoursing upon Paris and Paris matters, speaking to the countess of the various persons they both knew there. Franz perceived how completely he was in his element; and, unwilling to interfere with the pleasure he so evidently felt, took up Albert's glasses, and began in his turn to survey the audience. Sitting alone, in the front of a box immediately opposite, but situated on the third row, was a female of exquisite beauty, dressed in a Greek costume, which it was evident, from the ease and grace with which she wore it, was her national attire. Behind her, but in deep shadow, was the outline of a male figure; but the features of this latter personage it was not possible to distinguish. Franz could not forbear breaking in upon the apparently interesting conversation passing between the countess and Albert, to inquire of the former if she knew who was the fair Albanaise opposite, since beauty such as hers was well worthy of being remarked by either sex. "All I can tell you about her," replied the countess, "is, that she has been at Rome since the beginning of the season; for I saw her where she now sits the very first night of the theatre's opening, and since then she has never missed a performance. Sometimes accompanied by the individual who is with her, and at others merely attended by a black servant."

"And what do you think of her personal appearance?"——"Oh, I consider her perfectly lovely—she is just my idea of what Medora must have been."

Franz and the countess exchanged a smile, and then the latter resumed her conversation with Albert, while Franz returned to his previous survey of the house and company. The curtain rose on the ballet. However much it might have claimed his attention, Franz was too deeply occupied with the beautiful Greek to take any note of it, while she seemed to experience an almost child-like delight in watching it; her eager, animated looks, contrasting strongly with the utter indifference of her companion, who, during the whole time the piece lasted, never even moved.

The overture to the second act began; and at the first sound of the violin, Franz observed the sleeper slowly arise and approach the Greek girl, who turned round to say a few words to him, and then, leaning forward again on her box, she became as absorbed as before in what was going on. The countenance of the person who had addressed her remained so completely in the shade, that, though Franz tried his utmost, he could not distinguish a single feature. The curtain drew up, and the attention of Franz was attracted by the actors; and his eyes quitted their gaze at the box containing the Greek girl and her strange companion to watch the business of the stage.

Most of my readers are aware that the second act of "Parisina" opens with the celebrated and effective duet in which Parisina, while sleeping, betrays to Azzo the secret of her love for Ugo. Excited beyond his usual calm demeanor, Franz rose with the audience, and was about to join the loud enthusiastic applause that followed; but suddenly his purpose was arrested, his hands fell by his sides, and the half-uttered "bravos" expired on his lips. The occupant of the box in which the Greek girl sat appeared to share the universal admiration that prevailed, for he left his seat to stand up in the front, so that, his countenance being fully revealed, Franz had no difficulty in recognizing him as the mysterious inhabitant of Monte-Cristo, and the very same individual he had encountered the preceding evening in the ruins of the Colosseum, and whose voice and figure had seemed so familiar to him. All doubt of his identity was now at an end: his singular host evidently resided at Rome. The surprise and agitation occasioned by this full confirmation of Franz's former suspicion had no doubt imparted a corresponding expression to his features; for the countess, after gazing with a puzzled look on his speaking countenance, burst into a fit of laughter, and begged to know what happened. "Madame," returned Franz, totally unheeding her raillery, "I asked you a short time since if you knew any particulars respecting the Albanian lady opposite; I must now beseech you to inform me who and what is her husband?"

"All I can say," continued the countess, taking up the glasses, and directing it to the box in question, "is, that the gentleman, whose story I am unable to furnish, seems to me as though he had just been dug up; he looks more like a corpse permitted by some friendly grave-digger to quit his tomb for a while, and revisit this earth of ours, than anything human. How ghastly pale he is!"

"Oh, he is always as colorless as you now see him," said Franz.

"Then you know him?" almost screamed the countess. "Oh! pray do, for Heaven's sake, tell us all about——is he a vampire, or a resuscitated corpse, or what?"

"I fancy I have seen him before; and I even think he recognizes me."

"He is no other than Lord Ruthven himself in a living form." This fresh allusion to Byron drew a smile to Franz's countenance; although he could but allow that if anything was likely to induce belief in the existence of vampires, it would be the presence of such a man as the mysterious personage before him.

"I'll tell you," answered the countess. "Byron had the most perfect belief in the existence of vampires, and even assured me he had seen some. The description he gave me perfectly corresponds with the features and character of the man before us. Oh! it is the exact personification of what I have been led to expect. The coal black hair, large bright glittering eyes, in which a wild, unearthly fire seems burning,—the same ghastly paleness. Then observe, too, that the very female he has with him is altogether unlike all others of her sex. She is a foreigner—a stranger. Nobody knows who she is, or where she comes from. No doubt she belongs to the same horrible race he does, and is, like himself, a dealer in magical arts. I entreat of you not to go near him—at least to-night; and if to-morrow your curiosity still continues as great, pursue your researches if you will; but to-night you neither can nor shall. For that purpose I mean to keep you all to myself."

On his return from the countess's to his own hotel, Franz found Albert glad to see him.

"My friend," cried he, "a bright idea has flashed across my brain. You agree, do you not, that obtaining a carriage is out of the question?"

"True; we have offered any sums, but have failed."

"Well, now, what do you say to a cart? With a cart and a couple of oxen our business can be managed. The cart must be tastefully ornamented; and if you and I dress ourselves as Neapolitan reapers, we may get up a striking tableau, after the manner of that splendid picture by Leopold Robert. It would add greatly to the effect if the countess would join us in the costume of a peasant. Our group would then be quite complete, more especially as the countess is quite beautiful."

"Well," said Franz, "this time, Albert, I am bound to give you credit for having hit upon a most capital idea."

"And quite a national one, too," replied Albert with gratified pride. "A mere masque borrowed from our own festivities. Ha! ha! you Romans, thought to make us, unhappy strangers, trot at the heels of your processions, like so many lazzaroni, because no carriages or horses are to be had in your beggarly city. But you don't know us; when we can't have one thing we invent another."

"And have you communicated your triumphant idea to any person?"

"Only to our host. Gone in search of our equipage: I expect him every minute." At this instant the door opened, and Pastrini appeared.

"Now, then," asked Albert, eagerly; "have you found the desired cart and oxen?"

"Better than that!" replied Pastrini, with the air of a man perfectly well satisfied with himself.

"Take care, my worthy host," said Albert, "*better* is a sure enemy to *well*."

"Your excellencies are aware," responded the landlord, swelling with importance, "that the Count of Monte-Cristo is living on the same floor with yourselves!"

"I should think we did know it," exclaimed Albert, "since it is owing to that circumstance that we are packed into these small rooms, like two poor students in the back streets of Paris."

"Well, then, the Count of Monte-Cristo, hearing of the dilemma in which you are placed, has sent to offer you seats in his carriage and two places at his windows in the Palace Rospoli." The friends looked at each other with unutterable surprise.

At this instant some one knocked at the door. "Come in!" said Franz. A servant, wearing a livery of considerable style and richness, appeared at the threshold, and placing two cards in the landlord's hands, who forthwith presented them to the two young men, he said, "Please to deliver these, from Count of Monte-Cristo, to Viscount Albert Morcerf and M. Franz Epinay. The Count of Monte-Cristo," continued the servant, "begs these gentlemen's permission to wait upon them as their neighbor, and he will be honored by an intimation of what time they will please to receive him."

"Faith, Franz," whispered Albert, "there is not much to find fault with here."——"Tell the count," replied Franz, "that we will do ourselves the pleasure of calling on him." The servant bowed and retired.

"That is what I call an elegant mode of attack," said Albert. "Still, I must own I am sorry to be obliged to give up the cart and the group of reapers—it would have produced such an effect! And were it not for the windows at the Palace Rospoli, by way of recompense for the loss of our beautiful scheme, I don't know but what I should have held on by my original plan. What say you, Franz?"

"Oh, I agree with you; the windows in the Palace Rospoli alone decided me." The truth was, that the mention of two places in the Palace Rospoli had recalled to Franz's mind the conversation he had overheard in the Colosseum. The next day must clear up every doubt, and, unless his near neighbor and would-be friend, the Count of Monte-Cristo, possessed the ring of Gyges, and by its power were able to render himself invisible, it was very certain he could not escape this time. Eight o'clock found Franz up and dressed, while Albert, who had not the same motives for early rising, was still profoundly asleep. The first act of Franz was to summon his landlord, who presented himself with his accustomed obsequiousness.

"Pray, Pastrini," asked Franz, "is not some execution appointed to take place to-day?"——"Yes, your excellency; but if your reason for inquiry is that you may procure a window to view it from, you are much too late."

"Oh, no!" answered Franz, "I had no such intention; but in case I feel disposed, give me some particulars of to-day's executions."

"That happens just lucky, your excellence! Only a few minutes ago they brought me the *tavolettas,* wooden tablets hung up at the corners the evening before an execution, on which is pasted up a paper containing the names of the condemned persons, their crimes, and mode of punishment. The reason for so publicly announcing all this is, that all good and faithful Catholics may offer up their prayers for the unfortunate culprits, and, above all, beseech of Heaven to grant them a sincere repentance."

"Oblige me by a sight of one of these *tavolettas.*"

"Nothing can be easier than to comply with your excellency's wish," said the landlord, opening the door of the chamber; "I have caused one to be placed on the landing, close by your apartment." Then, taking the tablet from the wall, he handed it to Franz, who read as follows:—

" 'The public is informed that on Wednesday, February 23rd, being the first day of the Carnival, two executions will take place in the Place del Popolo, by order of the Tribunal de la Rota, of two individuals, named Andrea Rondola, and Peppino, otherwise called Rocca Priori; the former found guilty of the murder of a venerable and exemplary priest, named Don César Torlini, canon of the church of Saint-Jean-de-Latran; and the latter convicted of being an accomplice of the atrocious and sanguinary bandit, Luigi Vampa, and his troupe. The first-named malefactor will be *mazzolato,* the second culprit, *decapitato.* The prayers of all good Christians are entreated for these unfortunate men, that it may please God to awaken them to a sense of their guilt, and to grant them a hearty and sincere repentance for their crimes.' "

This was precisely what Franz had heard the evening before in the ruins of the Colosseum. In all probability, therefore, the Transtevere was no other than the bandit Luigi Vampa himself, and the man shrouded in the mantle the same he had known as "Sinbad the Sailor," but who, no doubt, was still pursuing his philanthropic expedition in Rome as he had already done at Porto-Vecchio and Tunis. Time was getting on, however, and Albert entered in perfect costume for the day. The anticipated delights of the Carnival had so run in his head as to make him leave his pillow long before his usual hour. "Now, my excellent Pastrini," said Franz, addressing his landlord, "since we are both ready, do you think we may proceed at once to visit the Count of Monte-Cristo?"
——"Most assuredly," replied he.

The landlord preceded the friends across the landing, which was all that separated them from the apartments of the count, rang at the bell, and the door being opened, a servant bowed respectfully, and invited them to enter. They passed through two rooms, furnished with a style and luxury they had not calculated on finding under the roof, and were shown into an elegantly fitted-up room, "If your excellencies will please to be seated," said the man, "I will let M. le Comte know you are here."

And with these words he disappeared behind one of the *portières*. As the door opened, the sound of a *guzla* reached the ears of the young men, but was almost immediately lost, for the rapid closing of the door merely allowed one rich swell of harmony to enter the saloon. Franz and Albert looked inquiringly at each other, then at the gorgeous fittings-up of the apartment. All seemed even more splendid at a second view than it had done at their first rapid survey.

"Well," said Franz to his friend, "what think you of all this?"

"Why, upon my soul, my dear fellow, it strikes me our elegant and attentive neighbor must either be some successful stock-jobber who has speculated in the fall of the Spanish funds or some prince traveling *incog.*"

"Hush! hush!" replied Franz. Almost immediately the tapestry was drawn aside, and the owner of all these riches stood before the two young men. Albert instantly rose to meet him, but Franz remained, in a manner, spell-bound on his chair, for in the person of him who had just entered he recognized not only the mysterious visitant to the Colosseum, and the occupant of the Argentino box, but also his singular host at Monte-Cristo Island.

"Gentlemen," said the Count of Monte-Cristo as he entered, "I pray you excuse me for suffering my visit to be anticipated; but I feared to disturb you by presenting myself earlier at your apartments; besides, you sent me word you would come to me, and I have held myself at your disposal."

"Franz and I have to thank you a thousand times, M. le Comte," returned Albert; "you extricated us from a great dilemma, and we were on the point of inventing some very fantastic vehicle when your friendly invitation reached us."——"Indeed!" returned the count, motioning the two young men to sit down. "It was the fault of that blockhead Pastrini, that I did not sooner assist you in your distress. He did not mention a syllable of your embarrassment to me, when he knows that, alone and isolated as I am, I seek every opportunity of making the acquaintance of my neighbors. As soon as I learned I could in any way assist you, I most eagerly seized the opportunity of offering my services." The two young men bowed. Franz had, as yet, found nothing to say; he had adopted no determination; and as nothing in the count's manner manifested the wish that he should recognize him, he did not know whether to make any illusion to the past, or wait until he had more proof; besides, although sure it was he who had been in the box the previous evening, he could not be equally positive that he was the man he had seen at the Colosseum. He resolved, therefore, to let things take their course without making any direct overture to the count. Besides, he had this advantage over him, he was master of his secret, whilst he had no hold on Franz, who had nothing to conceal. However, he resolved to lead the conversation to a subject which might possibly clear up his doubts.

"Count," said he, "you have offered us places in your carriage, and at your windows of the Rospoli Palace. Can you tell us where we can obtain a sight of the Place del Popolo?"——"Ah!" said the count, negligently, looking attentively at Morcerf, "is there not something like an execution upon the Place del Popolo?"

"Yes," returned Franz, finding that the count was coming to the point he wished.——"Stay, I think I told my steward yesterday to attend to this; perhaps I can render you this slight service also." He extended his hand, and rang the bell thrice. "Did you ever occupy yourself," said he to Franz, "with the employment of time and the means of simplifying the summoning your servants? I have: when I ring once, it is for my valet; twice, for my steward; thrice, for my steward: thus I do not waste a minute or a word. Here he is!" A man of about five-and-forty to fifty entered, exactly resembling the smuggler who had introduced Franz into the cavern; but he did not appear to recognize him. It was evident he had his orders. "M. Bertuccio," said the count, "have you procured me windows looking on the Place del Popolo, as I ordered you yesterday?"

"Yes, excellency," returned the steward; "it was let to Prince Lobanieff; but I was obliged to pay a hundred——"

"That will do—that will do, M. Bertuccio; spare these gentlemen all such domestic arrangements. You have the windows, that is sufficient. Give orders to the coachman; and be in readiness on the stairs to conduct us to it." The steward bowed, and was about to quit the room. "Ah!" continued the count, "be good enough to ask Pastrini if he has received the *tavoletta,* and if he can send us an account of the execution."

"There is no need to do that," said Franz, taking out his tablets; "for I saw the account, and copied it down."

"Very well, you can retire, Bertuccio; let us know when breakfast is ready. These gentlemen," added he, turning to the two friends, "will, I trust, do me the honor to breakfast?"

"But," said Albert, "we shall abuse your kindness."

"Not at all; on the contrary, you will give me great pleasure. You will, one or other of you, perhaps both, return it to me at Paris. Maître Bertuccio, lay covers for three." He took Franz's tablets out of his hand. " 'We announce,' he read, in the same tone with which he would have read a newspaper, 'that to-day, the 23rd of February, will be executed Andrea Rondolo, etc., convicted of complicity with the detestable bandit Luigi Vampa, and the men of his troop.' Hum! 'The first will be broken on the wheel, the second beheaded.' Yes," continued the count, "it was first arranged in this way; but I think since yesterday some change has taken place in the order of the ceremony."

"Really!" said Franz.

"Yes, I passed the evening at Cardinal Rospigliosi's, and there mention was made of something like a pardon for one of the two men."

"For Andrea Rondolo?" asked Franz.

"No," replied the count, carelessly; "for the other (he glanced at the tablets as if to recall the name), for Peppino, *alias* Rocca Priori. You are thus deprived of seeing a man guillotined; but the *mazzolato* still remains, which is a very curious punishment when seen for the first time, and even the second, whilst the other, as you must know, is very simple. The *mandaïa* never fails, never trembles, never strikes ineffectually. Ah!" added the count, in a contemptuous tone, "do not tell me of European punishments, they are in the infancy, or rather the old age, of cruelty."

"Really," replied Franz, "one would think that you had studied the different tortures of all the nations of the world."

"There are, at least, few that I have nct seen," said the count coldly.

"And you took pleasure in beholding these dreadful spectacles?"

"My first sentiment was horror, the second indifference, the third curiosity."——"Curiosity! that is a terrible word."

"Why so? in my opinion, death may be a torture, but it is not an expiation."

"I do not quite understand you," replied Franz; "pray explain your meaning, for you excite my curiosity to the highest pitch."

"Listen," said the count, and deep hatred mounted to his face, as the blood would to the face of any other. "If a man had by unheard-of and excruciating tortures destroyed your father, mother, or mistress; in a word, one of those beings who, when they are torn from you, leave desolation, a wound that never closes in your breast, do you think the reparation that society gives you sufficient by causing the knife of the guillotine to pass between the base of the occiput and the trapezal muscles of the murderer, because he who has caused us years of moral sufferings undergoes a few moments of physical pain?"

"Yes, I know," said Franz, "that human justice is insufficient to console us; she can give blood in return for blood, that is all; but you must demand from her only what it is in her power to grant."

"I will put another case to you," continued the count; "that where society, attacked by the death of a person, avenges death by death. But are there not a thousand tortures by which a man may be made to suffer without society taking the least cognizance of them, or offering him even the insufficient means of vengeance, of which we have just spoken? Are there not crimes for which the impalement, the stake and the brand, are inadequate tortures, and which are unpunished by society? Answer me, do not these crimes exist?"

"Yes," answered Franz; "and it is to punish them that duelling is tolerated."

"Ah, duelling!" cried the count; " a pleasant manner, upon my soul, of arriving at your end when that end is vengeance! A man has carried off your mistress, seduced your wife, dishonored your daughter; rendered the whole life of one who had the right to expect from Heaven that portion of happiness God has promised to every one, an existence of misery and infamy; and you think you are avenged because you send a bullet through the head, or pass a sword through the breast, of that man who has planted madness in your brain, and despair in your heart. Without recollecting that it is often he who comes off victorious from the strife, absolved of all crime in the eyes of the world! No, no," continued the count; "had I to avenge myself, it is not thus I would take revenge."

"Then you disapprove of duelling! you would not fight a duel?" asked Albert in his turn, astonished at this strange theory.

"Oh, yes," replied the count; "understand me, I would fight a duel for a trifle, for an insult, for a blow; but the less so that, thanks to my skill in all bodily exercises, and the indifference to danger I have gradually acquired, I should be almost certain to kill my man. Oh! I would fight for such a cause; but in return for a slow, profound, eternal torture, I would give back the same, were it possible: an eye for an eye, a tooth for a tooth."

"But," said Franz to the count, "with this theory, which renders you at once judge and executioner of your own cause, it would be difficult to adopt a course that would for ever prevent your falling under the power of the law. Hatred is blind; rage carries you away; and he who pours out vengeance, runs the risk of tasting a bitter draught."

"Yes, if he be poor and inexperienced; not if he be rich and skilful; beside the worst that could happen to him would be the punishment of which we have already spoken, and which the philanthropic French Revolution has substituted for being torn to pieces by horses or broken on the wheel. What matters this punishment, as long as he is avenged? On my word, I almost regret that in all probability this miserable Peppino will not be *decapitato,* as you might have had an opportunity then of seeing how short a time the punishment lasts, and whether it is worth even mentioning; but, really, this is a most singular conversation for the Carnival gentlemen; how did it arise? Ah! I recollect, you asked for a place at my window; you shall have it; but let us first sit down to table, for here comes the servant to inform us breakfast is ready." As he spoke, a servant opened one of the four doors of the salon, saying— "*Al suo commodo!*" The two young men rose and entered the breakfast-room.

During the meal, which was excellent, and admirably served, Franz looked repeatedly at Albert, who ate like a man who for the last four or five months had been condemned to partake of Italian cookery—that is, the worst in the world. As for the count, he just touched the dishes; he seemed as if he fulfilled the duties of an entertainer by sitting down with his guests, and awaited their departure to be served with some strange or more delicate food. This brought back to Franz, in spite of himself, the recollection of the terror with which the count had inspired the countess and her firm conviction that the man in the opposite box was a vampire. At the end of the breakfast Franz took out his watch. "Well," said the count, "what are you doing?"——"You must excuse us," returned Franz, "but we have still much to do. We have no disguises, and it is absolutely necessary to procure them."

"Do not concern yourself about that; we have, I think, a private room in the Place del Popolo; I will have whatever costumes you choose brought to us, and you can dress there."

"After the execution?" cried Franz.——"The scaffold forms part of the fête."

"I have reflected on the matter," said Franz, "I thank you for your courtesy, but I shall content myself with accepting a place in your carriage and at your window at the Rospoli Palace, and I leave you at liberty to dispose of my place at the Place del Popolo."

"But I warn you, you will lose a very curious sight," returned the count.

"You will relate it to me," replied Franz, "and the recital from your lips will make as great an impression on me as if I had witnessed it. I have more than once intended witnessing an execution, but I have never been able to make up my mind: and you, Albert?"

"I," replied the viscount—"I saw Castaing executed, but I think I was rather intoxicated that day, for I had quitted college the same morning, and we had passed the previous night at a tavern."

"Besides it is no reason because you have not seen an execution at Paris, that you should not see one anywhere else; when you travel, it is to see everything. If you went to Spain, would you not see the bullfights? Well, suppose it is a bull-fight you are going to see? Recollect the ancient Romans of the Circus, and the sports where they killed three hundred lions and a hundred men. Think of the eighty thousand applauding spectators, the sage matrons who took their daughters, and the charming Vestals who made with the thumb of their white hands the fatal sign that said, 'Come, despatch this man, already nearly dead.'"

"Shall you go, then, Albert?" asked Franz.

"Yes; like you, I hesitated, but the count's eloquence decides me!"

——"Let us go, then," said Franz, "since you wish it; but on our way to the Piazza del Popolo, I wish to pass through the Corso. Is this possible?"

"On foot, yes! in a carriage, no!"

"I will go on foot, then!"

"Is it important that you should pass through this street?"

"Yes, there is something I wish to see!"

"Well, we will pass by the Corso. We will send the carriage to wait for us on the Piazza del Popolo, by the Strada del Babuino, for I shall be glad to pass, myself, through the Corso, to see if some orders I have given have been executed."

"Excellency," said a servant, opening the door, "a man in the dress of a penitent wishes to speak to you."

"Ah! yes!" returned the count, "I know who he is, gentlemen; will you return to the salon? you will find on the centre table some excellent cigars. I will be with you directly." The young men rose and returned into the salon, whilst the count, again apologizing, left by another door.

"Well," asked Franz, "what think you of the Count of Monte-Cristo?"

——"What do I think?" said Albert, evidently surprised at such a question; "I think that he is a delightful fellow, who does the honors of his table admirably; who has traveled much, read much, is, like Brutus, of the Stoic school, and moreover," added he, sending a volume of smoke up towards the ceiling, "that he has excellent cigars." Such was Albert's opinion of the count, and as Franz well knew that. "But," said he, "did you remark one very singular thing. How attentively he looked at you."

"Ah!" replied he, sighing, "that is not very surprising; I have been more than a year absent from Paris, and my clothes are of a most antiquated cut; the count takes me for a rustic. The first opportunity you have, undeceive him, I beg, and tell him I am nothing of the kind."

Franz smiled: an instant after, the count entered.

"I am now quite at your service, gentlemen," said he. "The carriage is going one way to the Place del Popolo, and we will go another; and if you please, by the Corso. Take some more of these cigars, M. de Morcerf."

"With all my heart," returned Albert; "these Italian cigars are horrible. When you come to Paris, I will return all this."

"I will not refuse; I intend going there soon, and since you allow me, I will pay you a visit. Come! we have not any time to lose, it is half-past twelve—let us set off!" All three descended: the coachman received his master's orders, and drove down the Via del Babuino. Whilst the three gentlemen walked towards the Place d'Espagne and the Via Frattina, which led directly between the Fiano and Rospoli Palaces, all Franz's attention was directed towards the windows of that last palace, for he had not forgotten the signal agreed upon between the man in the mantle and the Transtevere peasant. "Which are your windows?" asked he of the count, with as much indifference as he could assume. "The three last," returned he, with a negligence evidently unaffected, for he could not imagine with what intention the question was put. Franz glanced rapidly toward the three windows. The side windows were hung with yellow damask, and the centre one with white damask and a red cross. The man in the mantle had kept his promise to the Transtevere, and there could now be no doubt that he was the count. The three windows were still untenanted. Preparations were making on every side; chairs were placed, scaffolds were raised, and windows were hung with flags. The masks could not appear; the carriages could not move about; but the masks were visible behind the windows, the carriages, and the doors.

Franz, Albert and the count continued to descend the street: as they approached the Place del Popolo, the crowd became more dense, and above the heads of the multitude two objects were visible; the obelisk, surmounted by a cross, which marks the centre of the place, and before the obelisk, at the point where the three streets meet, the two upright of the scaffold, between which glittered the curved knife of the *mandaïa.* At the corner of the street they met the count's steward, who was awaiting his master. The window, let at an exorbitant price, which the count had doubtless wished to conceal from his guests, was on the second floor of the great palace, situated between the Rue del Babuino and the Monte Pincio. It consisted, as we have said, of a small dressing-room, opening into a bedroom, and when the door of communication was shut, the inmates were quite alone. On two chairs were laid as many elegant clown costumes in blue and white satin. "As you left the choice of your costumes to me," said the count to the two friends, "I have had these brought, as they will be the most worn this year; and they are most suitable, on account of the *confetti* (sugarplums), as they do not show the flour."

Franz heard the words but imperfectly, and he perhaps did not fully appreciate this new attention to their wishes; for he was wholly absorbed by the spectacle that the Piazza presented, and by the terrible instrument that was in the centre. It was the first time Franz had ever seen a guillotine,—because the Roman *mandaïa* is formed on almost the same model as the French instrument: the knife, which is shaped like a crescent, that cuts with the convex side, falls from a less height, and that is all the difference. Two men, seated on the movable plank on which the culprit is laid, were eating their breakfasts, whilst waiting for the criminal. Their repast consisted, apparently, of bread and sausages. One of them lifted the plank, took thence a flask of wine, drank some, and then passed it to his companion. These two men were the executioner's assistants. At this sight Franz felt the perspiration start forth upon his brow. The prisoners, transported the previous evening from the Carcere Nuovo to the little church of Santa Maria del Popolo, had passed the night, each accompanied by two priests, in a chapel closed by a grating, before which were two sentinels, relieved at intervals. A double line of carbineers, placed on each side of the door of the church, reached to the scaffold, and formed a circle round it, leaving a path about ten feet wide, and around the guillotine a space of nearly a hundred feet. What the count said was true—the most curious spectacle in life is that of death. And yet, instead of the silence and solemnity demanded by the occasion, a noise of laughter and jest rose from the crowd: it was evident that this execution was, in the eyes of the people, only the commencement of the Carnival. Suddenly the tumult ceased, as if by magic; the doors of the church opened. A brotherhood of penitents, clothed from head to foot in robes of grey sackcloth, with holes for the eyes alone, and holding in their hand a lighted taper, appeared first; the chief marched at the head. Behind the penitents came a man of vast stature and proportions. He was naked, with the exception of cloth drawers, at the left side of which hung a large knife in a sheath, and he bore on his right shoulder a heavy mace. This man was the executioner. He had, moreover, sandals bound on his feet by cords. Behind the executioner came, in the order in which they were to die, first Peppino and then Andrea. Each was accompanied by two priests. Neither had their eyes bandaged. Peppino walked with a firm step, doubtless aware of what awaited him. Andrea was supported by two priests. Each of them kissed, from time to time, the crucifix a confessor held out to them. At this sight alone Franz felt his legs tremble under him. He looked at Albert—he was white as his shirt, and mechanically cast away his cigar, although he had not half smoked it. The count alone seemed unmoved—nay, more, a slight color seemed striving to rise in his pale cheeks. His nostril dilated like a wild beast that scents its prey, and his lips, half opened, disclosed his white teeth, small and sharp like a jackal's. And yet his features wore an expression of smiling tenderness, such as Franz had never before witnessed in them; his black eyes especially were full of kindness and pity. However, the two culprits advanced, and as they approached their faces became visible. Peppino was a handsome young man of four- or five-and-twenty, bronzed by the sun; he carried his head erect, and seemed to look on which side his liberator would appear. Andrea was short and fat; his visage marked with brutal cruelty, did not indicate age; he might be thirty. In prison he had suffered his beard to grow; his head fell on his shoulder, his legs bent beneath him, and he seemed to obey a mechanical movement of which he was unconscious.

"I thought," said Franz, to the count, "that you told me there would be but one execution!"

"I told you true," replied he, coldly.

"However, here are two culprits."

"Yes; but only one of these two is about to die; the other has long years to live!"

"If the pardon is to come there is no time to lose."

"And, see, here it is," said the count. At the moment when Peppino arrived at the foot of the *mandaïa,* a penitent, who seemed to arrive late, forced his way through the soldiers, and, advancing to the chief of the brotherhood, gave him a folded paper. The piercing eye of Peppino had noticed all. The chief took the paper, unfolded it, and, raising his hand,

"Heaven be praised! and his Holiness also!" said he, in a loud voice; "here is a pardon for Peppino, called Rocca Priori." And he passed the paper to the officer commanding the carbineers, who read and returned it to him.

"For Peppino!" cried Andrea, who seemed aroused from the torpor in which he had been plunged. "Why for him and not for me? We ought to die together. I was promised he should die with me. You have no right to put me to death alone. I will not die alone—I will not!" And he broke from the priests, struggling and raving like a wild beast, and striving desperately to break the cords that bound his hands. The executioner made a sign, and his assistant leaped from the scaffold and seized him.

"What is passing?" asked Franz of the count: for, as all this occurred in the Roman dialect, he had not perfectly comprehended it.

"Do you not see," returned the count, "that this human creature who is about to die is furious that his fellow-sufferer does not perish with him? Here is a man who had resigned himself to his fate, who was going to the scaffold to die—like a coward, it is true, but he was about to die without resistance. Do you know what gave him strength?—do you know what consoled him! It was, that another partook of his punishment—his anguish—and was to die before him! Lead two sheep to the butcher's, two oxen to the slaughterhouse, and make one of them understand his companion will not die; the sheep will bleat for pleasure, the ox will bellow with joy. But man—man, whom God created in his own image—man, upon whom God has laid his first, his sole commandment, to love his neighbor—man, to whom God has given a voice to express his thoughts—what is his first cry when he hears his fellow-man is saved? A blasphemy! Honor to man, this master-piece of nature, this king of the creation!" And the count burst into a laugh; but a terrible laugh, that showed he must have suffered horribly to be able thus to laugh. However, the struggle still continued, and it was dreadful to witness. The people all took part against Andrea, and twenty thousand voices cried, "Put him to death! put him to death!" Franz sprang back, but the count seized his arm, and held him before the window. "What are you doing?" said he. "Do you pity him? If you heard the cry of 'Mad dog!' you would take your gun—you would unhesitatingly shoot the poor beast, who, after all, was only guilty of having been bitten by another dog. And yet you pity a man who, without being bitten by one of his race, has yet murdered his benefactor; and who, now unable to kill any one, because his hands are bound, wishes to see his companion in captivity perish. No, no—look, look!"

This recommendation was needless. Franz was fascinated by the horrible spectacle. The two assistants had borne Andrea to the scaffold, and there, spite of his struggles, his bites, and his cries, had forced him to his knees. During this time the executioner had raised his mace, and signed to them to get out of the way; the criminal strove to rise, but, ere he had time, the mace fell on his left temple. A dull and heavy sound was heard, and the man dropped like an ox on his face, and then turned over on his back. The executioner let fall his mace, drew his knife, and with one stroke, opened his throat, and mounting on his stomach, stamped violently on it with his feet. At every stroke a jet of blood sprang from the wound.

This time Franz could sustain himself no longer, but sank, half fainting, into a seat. Albert, with his eyes closed, was standing grasping the window-curtains. The count was erect and triumphant, like the Avenging Angel.

CHAPTER XXIII.

THE CARNIVAL AT ROME.

When Franz recovered his senses, he saw Albert drinking a glass of water, of which his paleness showed he stood in great need, and the count, who was assuming his costume. He glanced mechanically toward the place: all had disappeared—scaffold, executioners, victims; nought remained but the people, full of noise and excitement. The bell of Monte Citorio, which only sounds on the pope's decease and the opening of the Carnival, was ringing a joyous peal.

"Well," asked he of the count, "what has, then, happened?"

"Nothing," replied the count; "only, as you see, the Carnival has commenced. Make haste and dress yourself."——"In reality," said Franz, "this horrible scene has passed away like a dream."

"It is but a dream—the nightmare that has disturbed you."

"Yes, that I have suffered; but the culprit?"

"That is a dream also; only he has remained asleep, whilst you are awake; and who knows which of you is the most fortunate?"

"But Peppino—what has become of him?"——"Peppino is a lad of sense, who, unlike most men, who are furious if they pass unnoticed, was delighted to see that the general attention was directed toward his companion. He profited by this distraction to slip away amongst the crowd, without even thanking the worthy priests who accompanied him. Decidedly man is an ungrateful and egotistical animal. But dress yourself; see, M. de Morcerf sets you the example." Albert was drawing on the satin pantaloon over his black pants and varnished boots.

"Well, Albert," said Franz, "do you feel much inclined to join the revels? Come, answer frankly."

"No," returned Albert. "But I am really glad to have seen such a sight; and I understand what the count said—that when you have once habituated yourself to a similar spectacle, it is the only one that causes you any emotion."

"Without reflecting, that this is the only moment in which you can study characters," said the count; "on the steps of the scaffold death tears off the mask that has been worn through life, and the real visage is disclosed. It must be allowed Andrea was not very handsome, the hideous scoundrel! Come, dress yourselves, gentlemen, dress yourselves." Franz felt it would be ridiculous not to follow his two companions' example. He assumed his costume, and fastened on his mask, that scarcely equaled the pallor of his own face. Their toilette finished, they descended; the carriage awaited them at the door, filled with sweetmeats and bouquets. They fell into the line of carriages. It is difficult to form an idea of the perfect change that had taken place. Instead of the spectacle of gloomy and silent death, the Place del Popolo presented a spectacle of gay and noisy mirth and revelry. Franz and Albert were like men who, to drive away a violent sorrow, have recourse to wine, and who, as they drink and become intoxicated, feel a thick veil drawn between the past and the present. They saw, or rather continued to see, the image of what they had witnessed; but little by little the general vertigo seized them, and they felt themselves obliged to take part in the noise and confusion.

The strife had fairly commenced, and the recollection of what they had seen half an hour before was gradually effaced from the young men's minds, so much were they occupied by the gay and glittering procession they now beheld. As for the Count of Monte-Cristo, he had never for an instant shown any appearance of having been moved. At the second turn the count stopped the carriage, and requested permission to quit them, leaving the vehicle at their disposal. Franz looked up—they were opposite the Rospoli Palace. At the centre window, the one hung with white damask with a red cross, was a blue domino, beneath which Franz's imagination easily pictured the beautiful Greek of the Argentina. "Gentlemen," said the count, springing out, "when you are tired of being actors, and wish to become spectators of this scene, you know you have places at my windows. In the meantime, dispose of my coachman, my carriage, and my servants." We have forgotten to mention, that the count's coachman was attired in a bearskin, and the two footmen behind were dressed up as green monkeys, with spring masks, which grimaced at every one who passed. Franz thanked the count for his attention. As for Albert, he was busily occupied throwing bouquets at a carriage full of Roman peasants passing near him. At one of these encounters, accidentally or purposely, Albert's mask fell off. He instantly rose and cast the remainder of the bouquets into the carriage. Doubtless one of the charming females Albert had divined beneath their coquettish disguise was touched by his gallantry; for, in her turn, as the carriage of the two friends passed her, she threw a bunch of violets into it. Albert seized it, and as Franz had no reason to suppose it was addressed to him, he suffered Albert to retain it. Albert placed it in his button-hole, and the carriage went triumphantly on.

"Well," said Franz to him; "here is the commencement of an adventure."

The jest, soon appeared to become earnest; for when Albert and Franz again encountered the carriage, the one who had thrown the violets to Albert, clapped her hands when she beheld them in his button-hole.

"Bravo! bravo!" said Franz; "things go wonderfully. Shall I leave you? Perhaps you would prefer being alone?"——"No;" replied he; "I will not be caught like a fool at a first demonstration by a rendezvous beneath the clock, as they say at the opera-balls. If the fair peasant wishes to carry matters any further, we shall find her, or rather, she will find us to-morrow: then she will give me some sign or other, and I shall know what I have to do."

"On my word," said Franz, "you are wise as Nestor and prudent as Ulysses, and your fair Circe must be very skilful or very powerful if she succeed in changing you into a beast of any kind." Albert was right; the fair unknown had resolved, doubtless, to carry the intrigue no farther; for although the young men made several more turns, they did not again see the calèche, which had turned up one of the neighboring streets. Then they returned to the Rospoli Palace; but the count and the blue domino had also disappeared; the two windows, hung with yellow damask, were still occupied by the persons whom the count had invited. At this moment the same bell that had proclaimed the commencement of the mascherata sounded the retreat. The file on the Corso broke the line, and in a second all the carriages had disappeared. Franz and Albert's coachman, without saying a word, drove up and stopped at the door of the hotel. Pastrini came to the door to receive his guests. Franz's first care was to inquire after the count, and to express his regret that he had not returned in sufficient time to take him; but Pastrini reassured him by saying, that the Count of Monte-Cristo had ordered a second carriage for himself, and that it had gone at four o'clock to fetch him from the Rospoli Palace. The count had, moreover, charged him to offer the two friends the key of his box at the Argentina. Franz questioned Albert as to his intentions; but Albert had great projects to put into execution before going to the theatre; and instead of making any answer, he inquired if M. Pastrini could procure him a tailor to "make us between now and to-morrow two costumes of Roman peasants," returned Albert.

"We have them ready-made. Leave all to me; and to-morrow, when you wake, you shall find a collection of costumes with which you will be satisfied."——"My dear Albert," said Franz, "leave all to our host; he has already proved himself full of resources; let us dine quietly, and afterwards go and see the Opera."

"Agreed," returned Albert; "but recollect, Pastrini, that both my friend and myself attach the greatest importance to having to-morrow the costumes we have asked for." The host again assured them they might rely on him, and that their wishes should be attended to; upon which Franz and Albert mounted to their apartments, and proceeded to disencumber themselves of their costume. Albert, as he took off his dress, carefully preserved the bunch of violets; it was his sign of recognition for the morrow. The two friends sat down to table; but they could not refrain from remarking the difference between the table of the Monte-Cristo and Pastrini. Truth compelled Franz, spite of the dislike he seemed to have taken to the count, to confess that the advantage was not on Pastrini's side. During dessert, the servant said: "His excellency the Count of Monte-Cristo had given positive orders that the carriage was to remain at their lordships' orders all the day, and they could therefore dispose of it without fear of indiscretion."

They resolved to profit by the count's courtesy, and ordered the horses to be harnessed, whilst they substituted an evening costume for that which they had on, and which was somewhat the worse for the numerous combats they had sustained. This precaution taken, they went to the theatre, and installed themselves in the count's box. During the first act, the Countess Guiccioli entered hers. Her first look was at the *loge* where she had seen the count the previous evening, so that she perceived Franz and Albert in the box of the very person concerning whom she had expressed so strange an opinion to Franz. Her opera-glass was so fixedly directed toward them, that Franz saw it would be cruel not to satisfy her curiosity; and, availing himself of one of the privileges of the spectators of the Italian theatres, which consists in using their boxes as their drawing-room, the two friends quitted their box to pay their respects to the countess. Scarcely had they entered, when she motioned to Franz to assume the seat of honor. Albert, in his turn, sat behind.

"Well," said she, hardly giving Franz time to sit down, "it seems you have nothing better to do than to make the acquaintance of this new Lord Ruthven, and you are the best friends in the world."

"Without being so far advanced as that, Countess," returned Franz, "I cannot deny we have abused his good nature all day."

"All day? You know him, then? Very well. Did any one introduce you to him?"

"No; it was he who introduced himself to us, last night, after we left you."

"Through what medium?"

"The very prosaic one of our landlord."

"He is staying, then, at the Hotel de Londres with you?"

"Not only in the same hotel, but on the same floor."

"What is his name: for, of course, you know?"

"The Count of Monte-Cristo, the name of the isle he has purchased."

"And he is a count?"

"A Tuscan count."

"Well, we must put up with that," said the countess, herself of one of the oldest families of Venice. "What sort of a man is he?"

"Ask the Viscount de Morcerf."

"You hear, M. de Morcerf, I am referred to you," said the countess.

"We should be very hard to please, madam," returned Albert, "did we not think him delightful: a friend of ten years' standing could not have done more for us, or with a more perfect courtesy."

"Come," observed the countess, smiling, "I see my vampire is only some millionaire, who has taken the appearance of Lara in order to avoid being confounded with Rothschild; and you have seen the beautiful Greek of yesterday."

"No; we heard, I think, the sound of her *guzla,* but she remained perfectly invisible."——"When you say invisible," interrupted Albert, "it is only to keep up the mystery; for whom do you take the blue domino at the window with the white curtains at the Rospoli Palace."

"The count had three windows at the Rospoli Palace?"

"Yes. Did you pass through the Corso?"

"Yes."

"Well, did you remark two windows hung with yellow damask, and one with white damask with a red cross? Those were the count's windows."

"Why, he must be a nabob! Do you know what those three windows were worth?"

"Two or three hundred Roman crowns?"

"Two or three thousand!"

"The devil!"

"Does his isle produce him such a revenue?"

"It does not bring him a bajocco."

"Then why did he purchase it?"

"For a whim."

"He is an eccentric, then?"

"In reality," observed Albert, "he seemed to me somewhat eccentric; were he at Paris, and a frequenter of the theatres, I should say he was a poor devil literally mad. This morning he made two or three exits worthy of an actor." At this moment a fresh visitor entered, and, according to custom, Franz gave up his seat to him. This circumstance had, moreover, the effect of changing the conversation; an hour afterward the two friends returned to their hotel. Pastrini had already set about procuring their disguises for the morrow; and he assured them they would be perfectly satisfied. The next morning, at nine o'clock, he entered Franz's room, followed by a tailor, who had eight or ten costumes of Roman peasants on his arm; they selected two exactly alike, and charged the tailor to sew on each of their hats about twenty yards of riband, and to procure them two of those long silken sashes of different colors with which the lower orders decorate themselves on holidays. Franz complimented Albert, who looked at himself in the glass with an unequivocal smile of satisfaction. They were thus engaged when the Count of Monte-Cristo entered.

"Gentlemen," said he, "although a companion is agreeable, perfect freedom is sometimes still more agreeable. I come to say that to-day, and the remainder of the Carnival, I leave the carriage entirely at your disposal. The host will tell you I have three or four more, so that you do not deprive me in any way of it. Employ it, I pray you, for your pleasure or your business."

The young men wished to decline, but they could find no good reason for refusing an offer so agreeable to them. The Count of Monte-Cristo remained a quarter of an hour with them, conversing on all subjects with the greatest ease. He was, as we have already said, perfectly well acquainted with the literature of all countries. A glance at the walls of his salon proved to Franz and Albert that he was an amateur of pictures. A few words he let fall showed them he was no stranger to the sciences, and he seemed much occupied with chemistry. The two friends did not venture to return the count the breakfast he had given them: it would have been too absurd to offer him in exchange for his excellent table the very inferior one of Pastrini. They told him so frankly, and he received their excuses with the air of a man who appreciated their delicacy. Albert was charmed with the count's manners, and he was only prevented from recognizing him for a veritable gentleman by his science. The permission to do what he liked with the carriage pleased him above all, for the fair peasants had appeared in a most elegant carriage the preceding evening, and Albert was not sorry to be upon an equal footing with them. At half-past one they descended; the coachman and footman had put on their livery over their disguises, which gave them a more ridiculous appearance than ever, and which gained them the applause of Franz and Albert. Albert had fastened the faded bunch of violets to his button-hole. At the first sound of the bell they hastened into the Corso by the Via Vittoria. At the second turn, a bunch of fresh violets, thrown from a carriage filled with female clowns, indicated to Albert that, like himself and his friend, the peasants had changed their costume also; and whether it was the result of chance, or whether a similar feeling had possessed them both, whilst he had changed his costume they had assumed his.

It is almost needless to say that the flirtation between Albert and the fair peasant continued all day. In the evening, on his return, Franz found a letter from the embassy, to inform him he would have the honor of being received by his holiness the next day. On his return from the Vatican, Franz brought away with him a treasure of pious thoughts, to which the mad gaiety would have been profanation. At ten minutes past five Albert entered overjoyed. The clown had resumed her peasant's costume, and as she passed she raised her mask. She was charming. Franz congratulated Albert, who received his congratulations with the air of a man conscious they are merited. He had recognized, by certain unmistakable signs, that his fair *incognita* belonged to the aristocracy. He had made up his mind to write to her the next day.

The next morning he saw Albert pass and repass. He held an enormous bouquet, which he doubtless meant to make the bearer of his amorous epistle. This belief was changed into certainty when Franz saw the bouquet (remarkable by a circle of white camellias) in the hand of a charming clown dressed in rose-colored satin. The evening was no longer joy, but delirium. Albert nothing doubted but that the fair unknown would reply in the same manner. Franz anticipated his wishes by telling him the noise fatigued him, and that he should pass the next day in writing and looking over his journal. Albert was not deceived, for the next evening Franz saw him enter shaking triumphantly a folded paper he held by one corner. "Well," said he, "was I mistaken?"—— "She has answered you!" cried Franz.

"Read!" This word was pronounced in a manner impossible to describe. Franz took the letter, and read:

"Tuesday evening, at seven o'clock, descend from your carriage opposite the Via dei Pontefici, and follow the Roman peasant who snatches your *moccoletto* from you. When you arrive at the first step of the church of San Giacomo, be sure to fasten a knot of rose-colored ribands to the shoulder of your costume, in order that you may be recognized. Until then you will not see me.—CONSTANCY AND DISCRETION."

"Well," asked he, when Franz had finished, "what do you think of that."

"I think the adventure is assuming a very agreeable appearance."

"I think so also," replied Albert; "and I very much fear you will go alone to the Duke of Bracciano's ball." Franz and Albert had received that morning an invitation from the celebrated Roman banker. "Take care, Albert," said Franz. "All the nobility of Rome will be present; and if your fair *incognita* belong to the higher class of society, she must go there."

"Whether she goes there or not, my opinion is still the same," returned Albert.

"If my unknown be as amiable as she is beautiful," said Albert, "I shall fix myself at Rome for six weeks, at least. I adore Rome, and I have always had a great taste for archæology."

"Come, two or three more such adventures, and I do not despair of seeing you a member of the academy." Doubtless Albert was about to discuss seriously his right to the academic chair when they were informed dinner was ready. After dinner, the Count of Monte-Cristo was announced. They had not seen him for two days. Pastrini informed them that business had called him to Civita Vecchia. He had started the previous evening, and had only returned an hour since. The count had learned the two friends had sent to secure a box at the Argentina Theatre, and were told they were all let. In consequence, he brought them the key of his own—at least such was the apparent motive of his visit. Franz and Albert made some difficulty, alleging their fear of depriving him of it; but the count replied that, as he was going to the Palli Theatre, the box at the Argentina would be lost if they did not profit by it. This assurance determined the two friends to accept it.

Franz had become by degree accustomed to the count's paleness, which had so forcibly struck him the first time he saw him. He could not refrain from admiring the severe beauty of his features, the only defect, or rather the principal quality of which was the pallor. Veritable hero of Byron! The count was no longer young. He was at least forty; and yet it was easy to understand he was formed to rule the young men with whom he associated at present. In reality, to complete his resemblance with the fantastic heroes of the English poet, the count seemed to have the power of fascination. Albert was constantly expatiating on their good fortune in meeting such a man. Franz was less enthusiastic; but the count exercised over him also the ascendency a strong mind always acquires.

At length arrived Tuesday, the last and most tumultuous day of the Carnival. Tuesday, the theatres open at ten o'clock in the morning, as Lent begins after eight at night. On Tuesday, all those who through want of money, time or enthusiasm, have not been to see the Carnival before, mingle in the gaiety, and contribute to the noise and excitement. From two o'clock till five Franz and Albert followed in the fête, exchanging handfuls of confetti with the other carriages and the pedestrians, who crowded amongst the horses' feet and the carriage wheels without a single accident, a single dispute, or a single fight. The fêtes are veritable days of pleasure to the Italians. The author of this history, who has resided five or six years in Italy, does not recollect to have ever seen a ceremony interrupted by one of those events so common in other countries. Albert was triumphant in his costume. A knot of rose-colored ribands fell from his shoulder almost to the ground. In order that there might be no confusion, Franz wore his peasant's costume.

As the day advanced, the tumult became greater. There was not on the pavement, in the carriages, at the windows, a single tongue that was silent, a single arm that did not move. It was a human storm, composed of a thunder of cries, and a hail of sweetmeats, flowers, eggs, oranges, and nosegays. At three o'clock the sound of fireworks, (heard with difficulty amid the din and confusion) announced that the races were about to begin. The races, like the *moccoli,* are one of the episodes peculiar to the last days of the Carnival. At the sound of the fireworks the carriages instantly broke the ranks, and retired by the adjacent streets. All these evolutions are executed with an inconceivable address and marvellous rapidity, without the police interfering in the matter. The pedestrians ranged themselves against the walls; then the trampling of horses and the clashing of steel were heard. A detachment of carbineers, fifteen abreast, galloped up the Corso in order to clear it for the *barberi.* When the detachment arrived at the Place de Venise, a second volley of fireworks was discharged, to announce that the street was clear. Almost instantly, in the midst of a tremendous and general outcry, seven or eight horses, excited by the shouts of three hundred thousand spectators, passed by like lightning. Then the Castle of Saint Angelo fired three cannons to indicate that number three had won. Immediately, without any other signal, the carriages moved on, flowing on toward the Corso, down all the streets, like torrents pent up for a while, which again flow into the parent river; and the immense stream again continued its course between its two banks of granite.

A new scource of noise and movement was added to the crowd. The sellers of *moccoletti* entered on the scene. The *moccoli,* or *moccoletti,* are candles which vary in size from the pascal taper to the rushlight, and which cause the actors on the great scene which terminates the Carnival two different sources of thought:—1st. How to preserve their *moccoletto* alight. 2nd. How to extinguish the *moccoletti* of others. The *moccoletto* is like life: man has found but one means of transmitting it. But he has discovered a thousand means of taking it away, although the devil has somewhat aided him. The *moccoletto* is kindled by approaching it to a light. But who can describe the thousand means of extinguishing the *moccoletto?*—the gigantic bellows, the monstrous extinguishers, the superhuman fans. Every one hastened to purchase *moccoletti*—Franz and Albert among the rest.

The night was rapidly approaching; and already, at the cry of *"Moccoletto!"* repeated by the shrill voices of a thousand vendors, two or three stars began to burn among the crowd. It was a signal. At the end of ten minutes fifty thousand lights glittered, descending from the Vénice Palace to the Popolo, and mounting from the Popolo to the Vénice. It seemed the fête of Jack-o-lanterns. It is impossible to form any idea of it without having seen it. Suppose all the stars had descended from the sky and mingled in a wild dance on the face of the earth; the whole accompanied by cries that were never heard in any other part of the world. The *facchino* follows the prince, the Transtevere the citizen, every one blowing, extinguishing, relighting. Had old *Æolus* appeared at this moment, he would have been proclaimed king of the *moccoli,* and Aquilo, the heir-presumptive to the throne. This flaming race continued for two hours; the Corso was light as day; the features of the spectators on the third and fourth stories were visible. Every five minutes Albert took out his watch; at length it pointed to seven. The two friends were in the Via dei Pontefici. Albert sprang out, bearing his *moccoletto* in his hand. Two or three masks strove to knock his *moccoletto* out of his hand: but Albert, a first-rate pugilist, sent them rolling in the street, one after the other, and continued his course towards the Church of San Giacomo. The steps were crowded with masks, who strove to snatch each other's flambeau. Franz followed Albert with his eyes, and saw him mount the first step. Instantly a mask, wearing the well-known costume of a female peasant, snatched his *moccoletto* from him without his offering any resistance. Franz was too far off to hear what they said, but, without doubt, nothing hostile passed, for he saw Albert disappear arm-in-arm with the peasant girl. He watched them pass through the crowd some time, but at length he lost sight of them in the Via Macello. Suddenly the bell that gives the signal for the end of the Carnival sounded, and at the same instant all the *moccoletti* were extinguished as if by enchantment. It seemed as though one immense blast of the wind had extinguished every one. Franz found himself in utter darkness. The Carnival was finished.

CHAPTER XXIV.

THE CATACOMBS.

In his whole life, perhaps, Franz had never before experienced so sudden an impression, so rapid a transition from gaiety to sadness, as in this moment. It seemed as though Rome, under the magic breath of some demon of the night, had suddenly changed into a vast tomb. By a chance, which added yet more to the intensity of the darkness, the moon, which was on the wane, did not rise until eleven o'clock, and the streets which the young man traversed were plunged in the deepest obscurity. The distance was short: and at the end of ten minutes his carriage, or rather the count's, stopped before the Hôtel de Londres. Dinner was waiting; but as Albert had told him that he should not return so soon, Franz sat down without him.

Franz resolved to wait for Albert as late as possible. He ordered the carriage, therefore, for eleven o'clock, desiring Pastrini to inform him the moment Albert returned to the Hôtel. At eleven o'clock Albert had not come back. Franz dressed himself, and went out, telling his host that he was going to pass the night at the Duke of Bracciano's. The house of the Bracciano is one of the most delightful in Rome; his lady, one of the last Colonnas, does its honors with the most consummate grace, and thus their *fêtes* have a European celebrity. Franz and Albert had brought to Rome letters of introduction to them; and the first question on Franz's arrival was to ask him where was his traveling companion. Franz replied that he had left him at the moment they were about to extinguish the *moccoli,* and that he had lost sight of him in the Via Macello. "Then he has not returned?" said the duke.

"I waited for him until this hour," replied Franz.

"And do you know whither he went?"——"No, not precisely; however, I think it was something very like a love assignation."

"You should not have allowed him to go," said the duke to Franz; "you, who know Rome better than he does."

"You might as well have tried to stop number three of the steeds, who gained the prize in the race to-day," replied Franz; "and then, moreover, what could happen to him?"

"Who can tell? The night is gloomy, and the Tiber is very near the Via Macello." Franz felt a shudder run through his veins at observing the feeling of the duke and the countess so much in unison with his own personal disquietude. "I informed them at the hotel that I had the honor of passing the night here, Duke," said Franz, "and desired them to come and inform me of his return."

"Ah!" replied the duke, "here, I think, is one of my servants who is seeking you."

The duke was not mistaken; when he saw Franz, the servant came up to him. "Your excellency," he said, "the master of the Hôtel has sent to let you know that a man is waiting for you with a letter from the Viscount de Morcerf."——"A letter from the viscount!" exclaimed Franz.

"And where is the messenger!"

"He went away directly he saw me enter the ball-room to find you."

"Oh!" said the countess to Franz, "go with all speed—poor young man? Perhaps some accident has happened to him."

Franz took his hat and went away in haste. He had sent away his carriage with orders for it to fetch him at two o'clock: fortunately the

Palazzo Bracciano, which is on one side in the Corso and on the other in the Place des Saints Apôtres, is hardly ten minutes' walk from the Hôtel de Londres. As he came near the hotel, Franz saw a man in the centre of the street. He had no doubt that it was the messenger from Albert. The man was wrapped up in a large cloak. He went up to him, but, to his extreme ashonishment, this individual first addressed him. "What wants your excellency of me?" inquired the man, retreating a step or two, as if to keep on his guard.

"Are not you the person who brought me a letter," inquired Franz, "from the Viscount Morcerf?"

"Your excellency's name—"

"Is Baron Franz d'Epinay."

"Then it is to your excellency that this letter is addressed."

"Is there any answer?" inquired Franz, taking the letter from him.

"Yes—your friend at least hopes so."——"Come up-stairs with me, and I will give it to you."——"I prefer waiting here," said the messenger, with a smile.

"And why?"

"Your excellency will know when you have read the letter."

Franz entered the hotel. On the staircase he met Pastrini.

"You have seen the man who desired to speak with you from your friend?" he asked of Franz.

"Yes, I have seen him," he replied, "and he has handed this letter to me. Light the candle in my apartment, if you please." The innkeeper gave orders to a servant to go before Franz with a candle. The young man had found Pastrini looking very much alarmed, and this had only made him the more anxious to read Albert's letter; and thus he went instantly towards the waxlight, and unfolded the letter.

"MY DEAR FELLOW,—The moment you have received this, have the kindness to take from my pocket-book, which you will find in the square drawer of the secretary, the letter of credit; add your own to it, if it be not sufficient. Run to Torlonia, draw from him instantly four thousand piastres, and give them to the bearer. It is urgent that I should have this money without delay. I do not say more, relying on you as you may rely on me.

"Your friend,   ALBERT DE MORCERF.

"P.S.—I now believe in Italian banditti."

Below these lines were written, in a strange hand, in Italian; what reads in English thus:

"If by six in the morning the four thousand piastres are not in my hands, by seven o'clock the Viscount Albert de Morcerf will have ceased to live."   "Luigi Vampa."

This second signature explained all to Franz, who now understood the objection of the messenger to coming up into the apartment; the street was safer for him. Albert, then, had fallen into the hands of the famous chief of banditti in whose existence he had for so long refused to believe. There was no time to lose. He hastened to open the secretary, and found the pocket-book in the drawer, and in it the letter of credit. There were in all six thousand piastres, but of these six thousand Albert had already expended three thousand. As to Franz, he had no letter of credit, as he lived at Florence, and had only come to Rome to pass seven or eight days; he had brought but a hundred louis, and of these he had no more than fifty left. Thus seven or eight hundred piastres were wanting to them both to make up the sum that Albert required. True, he might in such a case rely on the kindness of M. Torlonia. He was, therefore, about to return to the Palazza Bracciano without loss of time, when suddenly a luminous idea crossed his mind. He remembered the count of Monte-Cristo. Franz was about to ring for Pastrini, when that worthy presented himself. Franz went along the corridor, and a servant introduced him to the count. He was in a small cabinet which Franz had not yet seen, and which was surrounded with sofas. The count came towards him. "Well, what good wind blows you hither at this hour?" said he; "have you come to sup with me? It would be very kind of you."

"No; I have come to speak to you of a very serious matter."

Franz gave him Albert's letter. "Read that," he said. The count read it.

"Ah! ah!" said he.

"Did you see the postscript? What think you of that!" inquired Franz.

"Have you the money he demands?"

"Yes, all but eight hundred piastres." The count went to his secretary, opened it, and pulling out a drawer filled with gold, said to Franz,—"I hope you will not offend me by applying to any one but myself."

"You see, on the contrary, I come to you first and instantly," replied Franz.——"And I thank you; have what you will;" and he made a sign to Franz to take what he pleased.

"Is it absolutely necessary, then, to send the money to Luigi Vampa?" asked the young man, looking fixedly in his turn at the count.

"I think that if you would take the trouble of reflecting, you could find a way of simplifying the negotiation," said Franz.

"How so?" returned the count, with surprise.

"If we were to go together to Luigi Vampa, I am sure he would not refuse you Albert's freedom."

"What influence can I possibly have over a bandit?"

"Have you not saved Peppino's life?"

"Ah! ah!" said the count, "who told you that?"

"No matter, I know it." The count knit his brows, and remained silent an instant. "And if I went to seek Vampa, would you accompany me?"

"If my society would not be disagreeable."——"Be it so. It is a lovely night, and a walk without Rome will do us both good. Where is the man who brought the letter?"

"In the street."

"I must learn where we are going. I will summon him hither."

"It is useless: he would not come up."

"To your apartments perhaps; but he will not make any difficulty in entering mine." The count went to the window that looked on to the street, and whistled in a peculiar manner. The man in the mantle quitted the wall, and advanced into the centre of the street. *"Salite!"* said the count, in the same tone in which he would have given an order to his servant. The messenger obeyed without the least hesitation, but rather with alacrity, and, mounting the steps of the passage at a bound, entered the hotel; five seconds afterwards he was at the door of the cabinet. "Ah, it is you, Peppino," said the count. But Peppino, instead of answering, threw himself on his knees, seized the count's hand, and covered it with kisses. "Ah," said the count, "you have, then, not forgotten that I saved your life; that is strange, for it is a week ago!"

"No, excellency; and never shall I forget it," returned Peppino, with an accent of profound gratitude.

"Never! That is a long time; but it is something that you believe so. Rise and answer." Peppino glanced anxiously at Franz. "Oh, you may speak before his excellency," said he: "he is one of my friends. You allow me to give you this title?" continued the count in French; "it is necessary to excite this man's confidence."

"You can speak before me," said Franz; "I am a friend of the count's."

"Good!" returned Peppino, "I am ready to answer any question your excellency may address to me."

"How did the Viscount Albert fall into Luigi's hands?"

"Excellency, the Frenchman's carriage passed several times the one in which was Teresa."——"The chief's mistress?"

"Yes. The Frenchman threw her a bouquet; Teresa returned it; all this with the consent of the chief, who drove, as the coachman," replied Peppino. "Well, then, the Frenchman took off his mask; Teresa, with the chief's consent, did the same. The Frenchman asked for a rendezvous; Teresa gave him one—only, instead of Teresa, it was Beppo who was on the steps of the Church of San Giacomo."

"What!" exclaimed Franz, "the peasant girl who snatched his *moccoletto* from him——"

"Was a lad of fifteen," replied Peppino. "But it was no disgrace to your friend to have been deceived; Beppo has taken in plenty of others."

"And Beppo led him outside the walls?" said the count.

"Exactly so; a carriage was waiting at the end of Via Macello. Beppo got in, inviting the Frenchman to follow him, and he did not wait to be asked twice. He gallantly offered the right-hand seat to Beppo, and sat by him. Beppo told him he was going to take him to a villa a league from Rome; the Frenchman assured him he would follow him to the end of the world. The coachman went up the Rue di Ripetta and the Porte San Paolo; and when they were two hundred yards outside, as the Frenchman became somewhat too forward, Beppo put a brace of pistols to his head, the coachman pulled up, and did the same. At the same time, four of the band, who were concealed on the banks of the Almo, surrounded the carriage. The Frenchman made some resistance, and nearly strangled Beppo; but he could not resist five armed men, and was forced to yield. They made him get out, walk along the banks of the river, and then brought him to Teresa and Luigi, who were waiting for him in the Catacombs of St. Sebastian."

"Well," said the count, turning towards Franz, "it seems to me that this is a very likely story. He is in a very picturesque place—do you know the Catacombs of St. Sebastian?"

"I was never in them, but I have often resolved to visit them."

"Well, here is an opportunity. Have you a carriage?"——"No."

"That is of no consequence; I always have one ready, day and night, I am a very capricious being, and I should tell you that sometimes when I rise, or after my dinner, or in the middle of the night, I resolve on starting for some particular point, and away I go." The count rang, and a footman appeared. "Order out the carriage," he said, "and remove the pistols which are in the holsters. You need not awaken the coachman; Ali will drive." In a very short time the noise of wheels was heard, and the carriage stopped at the door. The count took out his watch. "Half-past twelve," he said. "We might start at five o'clock and be in time, but the delay may cause your friend to pass an uneasy night, and therefore we had better go with all speed to extricate him from the hands of the infidels."

Franz and the count went down-stairs, accompanied by Peppino. At the door they found the carriage. Ali was on the box, in whom Franz recognized the dumb slave of the grotto of Monte-Cristo. Franz and the count got into the carriage. Peppino placed himself beside Ali, and they set off at a rapid pace. Ali had received his instructions, and reached the gates of St. Sebastian. There the porter raised some difficulties, but the Count of Monte-Cristo produced an authority from the governor of Rome to quit or enter the city at any and all hours of the day or night; the portcullis was therefore raised, the porter had a louis for his trouble, and they went on their way. The road which the carriage now traversed was the ancient Appian Way, and bordered with tombs. From time to time, by the light of the moon, which began to rise, Franz imagined that he saw something like a sentinel appear from various points of the ruin, and suddenly retreat into the darkness on a signal from Peppino. A short time before they reached the circus of Caracalla the carriage stopped, Peppino opened the door, and the count and Franz alighted.

"In ten minutes," said the count to his companion, "we shall arrive there."

He then took Peppino aside, gave him some order in a low voice, and Peppino went away, taking with him a torch, brought with them in the carriage. Five minutes elapsed, during which Franz saw the shepherd advance along a narrow path in the midst of the irregular ground which forms the convulsed soil of the plain of Rome, and disappear in the midst of the high red herbage, which seemed like the bristling mane of some enormous lion. "Now," said the count, "let us follow him." Franz and the count in their turn then advanced along the same path, which led them by various ways, to a burial-ground. Five roads diverged like the rays of a star, and the walls, dug into niches, placed one above the other in the shape of coffins, showed that they were at last in the catacombs. In one of the cavities, whose extent it was impossible to determine, some rays of light were visible. The count laid his hand on Franz's shoulder. "Would you like to see a camp of bandits in repose?" he inquired. "Come with me, then. Peppino, extinguish the torch." Peppino obeyed, and Franz and the count were suddenly in utter darkness, only fifty paces in advance of them there played along the wall some reddish beams of light, more visible since Peppino had put out his torch. They advanced silently, the count guiding Franz as if he had the singular faculty of seeing in the dark. Franz, himself, however, distinguished his way more plainly in proportion as he advanced towards the rays of light, which served them for guides: three arcades, of which the middle served as the door, offered themselves. These arcades opened on one side to the corridor, in which were the count and Franz, and on the other to a large square chamber, entirely surrounded by niches similar to those of which we have spoken. In the midst of this chamber were four stones, which had formerly served as an altar, as was evident from the cross which still surmounted them. A lamp, placed at the base of a pillar, lighted up with its pale and flickering flame the singular scene which presented itself to the eyes of the two visitors concealed in the shadow. A man was seated with his elbow leaning on the column, and was reading with his back turned to the arcades, through the openings of which the new-comers contemplated him. This was the chief of the band, Luigi Vampa. Around him, and in groups, according to their fancy, lying in their mantles, or with their backs against a kind of stone bench, which went all around the Columbarium, were to be seen twenty brigands or more, each having his carbine within reach. At the bottom, silent, scarcely visible, and like a shadow, was a sentinel, who was walking up and down before a kind of opening, which was only distinguishable because in that spot the darkness seemed thicker. When the count thought Franz had gazed sufficiently on this picturesque tableau, he raised his finger to his lips, to warn him to be silent, and, ascending the three steps which led to the corridor of the Columbarium, entered the chamber by the centre arcade, and advanced towards Vampa who was so intent on the book before him that he did not hear the noise of his footsteps.

"Who goes there?" cried the sentinel, less occupied, and who saw by the lamp's light a shadow which approached his chief. At this sound, Vampa rose quickly, drawing at the same moment a pistol from his girdle. In a moment all the bandits were on their feet, and twenty carbines were levelled at the count. "Well," said he, in a voice perfectly calm, and no muscle of his countenance disturbed, "well, my dear Vampa, it appears to me that you receive a friend with a great deal of ceremony!"——"Ground arms!" exclaimed the chief, with an imperative sign of the hand, whilst with the other he took off his hat respectfully; then, turning to the singular personage who had caused this scene, he said, "Your pardon my lord, but I was so far from expecting the honor of a visit, that I did not really recognize you."

"Was it not agreed," asked the count, "that not only my person, but also that of my friends, should be respected by you?"

"And how have I broken that treaty, your excellency?"——"You have this evening carried off and conveyed hither Viscount Morcerf. Well," continued the count in a tone that made Franz shudder, "this young gentleman is one of *my friends*—lodges in the same hotel as myself—has been up and down the Corso for eight hours in my private carriage, and yet, I repeat to you, you have carried him off, and conveyed him hither, and," added the count, taking the letter from his pocket, "you have set a ransom on him, as if he were an indifferent person."

"Why did you not tell me all this—you?" inquired the brigand chief, turning towards his men, who all retreated before his look. "Why have you exposed me thus to fail in my word towards a gentleman like the count, who has all our lives in his hands? By heavens! if I thought one of you knew that the young gentleman was the friend of his excellency, I would blow his brains out with my own hand!"

"Well," said the count, turning towards Franz, "I told you there was some mistake in this."

"Are you not alone?" asked Vampa, with uneasiness.

"I am with the person to whom this letter was addressed, and to whom I desire to prove that Luigi Vampa was a man of his word.— Come, your excellency, here is Luigi Vampa, who will himself express to you his deep regret at the mistake he has committed."

Franz approached, the chief advancing several steps to meet him.

"Welcome amongst us, your excellency," he said to him: "you heard what the count just said, and also my reply; let me add that I would not for the four thousand piastres at which I had fixed your friend's ransom, that this had happened."——"But," said Franz, looking round him uneasily, "where is the viscount?—I do not see him."

"Nothing has happened to him, I hope?" said the count, frowningly.

"The prisoner is there," replied Vampa, pointing to the hollow space in front of which the bandit was on guard, "and I will go myself and tell him he is free. The chief went toward the place he had pointed out as Albert's prison, and Franz and the count followed him. "What is the prisoner doing?" inquired Vampa of the sentinel.

"Captain," replied the sentry, "I do not know, for the last hour I have not heard him stir."

"Come in, your excellency," said Vampa. The count and Franz ascended seven or eight steps after the chief, who drew back a bolt, and opened a door. Then, by the gleam of a lamp, similar to that which lighted the Columbarium, Albert was to be seen wrapped up in a cloak which one of the bandits had lent him, lying in a corner in profound slumber. "Come!" said the count, smiling with his own peculiar smile, "not so bad for a man who is to be shot at seven o'clock to-morrow morning!" Vampa looked at Albert with a kind admiration; he was not insensible to such a proof of courage.

"You are right," he said; "this must be one of your friends." Then, going to Albert, he touched him on the shoulder, saying—"Will your excellency please to awaken?" Albert stretched out his arms, rubbed his eyelids, and opened his eyes. "Ah! ah!" said he, "is it you, captain? You should have allowed me to have slept. I had such a delightful dream: I was dancing at Torlonia's with the countess." Then he drew from his pocket his watch, which he had preserved, that he might see how time sped.

"Half-past one only," said he. "Why the devil do you rouse me at this hour?"

"To tell you that you are free, your excellency."

"My dear fellow," replied Albert, with perfect ease of mind, "remember, for the future, Napoleon's maxim, 'Never awaken me but for bad news;' if you had let me sleep on, I should have finished my galop, and have been grateful to you all my life. So, then, they have paid my ransom?"

"No, your excellency! A person to whom I can refuse nothing has come to demand you."

"Really! then that person is a most amiable person." Albert looked round, and perceived Franz. "What!" said he, "is it you, my dear Franz, whose devotion and friendship are thus displayed?"

"No, not I," replied Franz, "but our neighbor, the Count of Monte-Cristo."

"Ah! the count," said Albert gaily, and arranging his cravat and wristbands, "you are really most kind, and I hope you will consider me as your eternally obliged, in the first place for the carriage, and in the next for this!" and he put out his hand to the count, who shuddered as he gave his own, but who nevertheless did give it. The bandit gazed on this scene with amazement; he was evidently accustomed to see his prisoners tremble before him, and yet here was one whose gay temperament was not for a moment altered; as for Franz, he was enchanted at the way in which Albert had sustained the national honor in the presence of the bandit. "My dear Albert," he said, "if you will make haste, we shall yet have time to finish the night at Torlonia's. You may conclude your interrupted galop, so that you will owe no ill-will to Signor Luigi, who has, indeed, throughout this whole affair acted like a gentleman."——"You are decidedly right, and we may reach the Palazzo by two o'clock. Signor Luigi," continued Albert, "is there any formality to fulfil before I take leave of your excellency?"

"None, sir," replied the bandit, "you are as free as air."

"Well, then, a happy and merry life to you. Come, gentlemen, come."

And Albert, followed by Franz and the count, descended the staircase, crossed the square chamber, where stood all the bandits, hat in hand. "Peppino," said the brigand chief, "give me the torch."

"What are you going to do then?" inquired the count.

"I will show you the way back myself," said the captain.

They advanced to the plain. "Ah! your pardon!" said Albert, turning round; "will you allow me, captain?" And he lighted his cigar at Vampa's torch. "Now, Count," he said, "let us on with all the speed we may. I am enormously anxious to finish my night at the Duke of Bracciano's." They found the carriage where they had left it. The count said a word in Arabic to Ali, and the horses went off at great speed. It was just two o'clock by Albert's watch when the two friends entered into the dancing-room. Their return was quite an event, but as they entered together, all uneasiness on Albert's account ceased instantly. "Madame," said the Viscount Morcerf, advancing towards the countess, "yesterday you were so condescending to promise me a galop; I am rather late in claiming this gracious promise, but here is my friend, whose character for veracity you well know, and he will assure you the delay arose from no fault of mine." And as at this moment the music gave the warning for the waltz, Albert put his arm round the waist of the countess, and disappeared with her in the whirl of dancers. In the meanwhile Franz was considering the singular shudder that had pervaded the count of Monte-Cristo's frame at the moment when he had been, in some sort, forced to give his hand to Albert.

Albert's first words to his friend, on the following morning, contained a request that he would accompany him to visit the count; true, he had warmly and energetically thanked him the previous evening; but services such as he had rendered could never be too often acknowledged. Franz, who seemed attracted by some invisible influence towards the count, in which terror was strangely mingled, felt an extreme reluctance to permit his friend to be exposed alone to the singular fascination the mysterious count seemed to exercise over him, and therefore made no objection to Albert's request, but at once accompanied him to the desired spot, and after a short delay, the count joined them in the saloon. "M. le Comte," said Albert, advancing to meet him, "permit me to repeat the poor thanks I offered last night, and to ask you whether, in my own person, my family, or connections, I can in any way serve you? My father, the Comte de Morcerf, although of Spanish origin, possesses considerable influence, both at the court of France and Madrid, and I unhesitatingly place the best services of myself, and all to whom my life is dear, at your disposal."——"M. de Morcerf," replied the count, "your offer, far from surprising me, is precisely what I expected from you, and I accept it in the same spirit of hearty sincerity with which it is made;— nay, I will go still further, and say that I had previously made up my mind to ask a great favor at your hands."—"Oh, pray name it."

"I am wholly a stranger to Paris—it is a city I have never yet seen; but I have to ask you, my dear M. de Morcerf" (these words were accompanied by a most peculiar smile), "whether you undertake, upon my arrival in France, to open to me the doors of that fashionable world of which I know no more than a Huron or native of Cochin-China?"

"Oh, that I do, and with infinite pleasure!" answered Albert; "and so much the more readily as a letter received this morning from my father summons me to Paris, in consequence of a treaty of marriage (my dear Franz, do not smile, I beg of you) with a family of high standing, and connected with the very élite of Parisian society."

"Connected by marriage, you mean," said Franz, laughingly.

"Well, never mind how it is," answered Albert, "it comes to the same thing in the end. Perhaps by the time you return to Paris, I shall be quite a sober, staid father of a family! When do you propose going thither?"

"Have you made up your mind when you shall be there yourself?"

"Certainly I have; in a fortnight or three weeks' time: that is to say, as fast as I can get there!"

"Nay," said the count; "I will give you three months ere I join you; you see I make an ample allowance for all delays and difficulties."

"And in three months' time," said Albert, "you will be at my house?"

"Shall we make a positive appointment for a particular day and hour?" inquired the count; "only let me warn you that I am proverbial for my punctilious exactitude in keeping my engagements."

"The very thing!" exclaimed Albert; "yes, by all means, let us have this rendezvous duly drawn up and attested."

"So be it, then," replied the count, and extending his hand towards an almanac, suspended near the chimney-piece, he said, "To-day is the 21st of February;" and drawing out his watch, added, "it is exactly half-past ten o'clock. Now promise me to remember this, and expect me the 21st of May at the same hour in the forenoon."

"Capital!" exclaimed Albert: "and you shall find everything and everybody ready to receive you."

"Well, since we must part," said the count, holding out a hand to each of the young men, "allow me to wish you both a safe and pleasant journey." It was the first time the hand of Franz had come in contact with that of the mysterious individual before him, and unconsciously he shuddered at its touch, for it felt cold and icy as that of a corpse.

The young men then rose, and, courteously bowing to their singular acquaintance, quitted the room. "What is the matter?" asked Albert of Franz, when they had returned to their own apartments; "you seem more than commonly thoughtful."—"I will confess to you, Albert," replied Franz, "that I am deeply puzzled to unravel the real career of this strange count; and the appointment you have made to meet him in Paris fills me with a thousand apprehensions."

"Then, listen to me." Franz then related to his friend the story of Monte-Cristo. Albert listened with the most profound attention. "Well," said he, when Franz had concluded, "what do you find to object to in all you have related? The count is fond of travelling, and, being rich, possesses a vessel of his own. Now, by way of having a resting-place during his excursions, avoiding the wretched cookery which has been trying its best to poison me during the last four months, while you have manfully resisted its effects for as many years, and obtaining a bed on which it is impossible to slumber, Monte-Cristo has furnished for himself a temporary abode where you first found him; but, to prevent the possibility of the Tuscan government taking a fancy to his enchanted palace, and thereby depriving him of the advantages naturally expected from so large an outlay of capital, he has wisely enough purchased the island, and assumed the title of its count." "Well," said Franz, with a sigh, "do as you please, my dear Viscount, for your arguments are beyond my powers of refutation. Still, in spite of all, you must admit that this Count of Monte-Cristo is a most singular personage."—"He is a philanthropist," answered the other; "and no doubt his motive in visiting Paris is to compete for the Monthyon prize, given in the interests of virtue and humanity. If my vote and interest can obtain it for him, I will readily give him the one and promise the other. And now, my dear Franz, let us talk of something else. Come, shall we take our luncheon, and then pay a last visit to St. Peter's?" Franz silently assented; and the following afternoon, at half-past five o'clock, the young men parted, Albert de Morcerf to return to Paris, and Franz d'Epinay to pass a fortnight at Venice.

CHAPTER XXV.

THE GUESTS.

In the house in Helder street, where Albert had invited the Count of Monte-Cristo, everything was being prepared on the morning of the 21st of May to fulfil the engagement. Morcerf inhabited a summer house situated at the corner of a large court, and directly opposite another building, the servants' apartments. Two windows only of the pavilion faced the street; three other windows looked into the court, and two at the back into the garden. Between the court and the garden, built in the heavy style of the imperial architecture, was the large and fashionable dwelling of the Count and Countess Morcerf. A high wall surrounded the whole of the hotel, surmounted at intervals by vases filled with flowers, and broken in the centre by a large gate of gilt iron, which served as the carriage entrance. A small door, close to the lodge of the concierge, gave ingress and egress to the servants and masters when they were on foot.

It was easy to discover that the delicate care of a mother, unwilling to part from her son, and yet aware he required the full exercise of his liberty, had chosen this habitation for Albert. On the other hand was visible the intelligent independence of youth, enchanted with the free and idle life of a young man. On the first floor were the same rooms, with the addition of a third, formed out of the ante-chamber: these three rooms were a salon, a boudoir, and a bedroom. The salon down-stairs was only an Algerian divan, for the use of smokers. The boudoir up-stairs communicated with the bedchamber by an invisible door on the staircase; it was evident every precaution had been taken. Above this floor was a large study, which had been increased in size by pulling down the partitions; a pandemonium, in which the artist and the dandy strove for pre-eminence. On the walls, over the doors on the ceiling, were swords, daggers, Malay creeses, maces, battle-axes, suits of armour, gilded, damasked, and inlaid, dried plants, minerals, and stuffed birds, opening their flame-colored wings as if for flight, and their beaks that never close. This was the favorite sitting-room of Albert.

However; the morning of the appointment, the young man had estab-lished himself in the small parlor down-stairs. There, on a table, sur-rounded at some distance by a large and luxurious divan, every species of tobacco known, was exposed in those pots of crackled earthenware of which the Dutch are so fond; beside them, in boxes of fragrant wood, were ranged, according to their size and quality, pueros, regalias, hav-annas, and manillas; and, in an open cabinet, a collection of German pipes, of chibooques, with their amber mouth-pieces ornamented with coral, and of narguillahs, with their long tubes of morocco, awaited the caprice or the sympathy of the smokers. Albert had himself presided at the arrangement, or, rather, the symmetrical derangement which, after coffee, the guests at a breakfast of modern days love to contemplate through the vapor that escapes from their mouth, and ascends in long and fanciful wreaths to the ceiling. At a quarter to ten, a valet entered; he composed with a little groom named John, and who only spoke English, all Albert's establishment, although the cook of the hotel was always at his service, and on great occasions the count's chasseur also. This valet, whose name was Germain, and who enjoyed the entire con-fidence of his young master, held in one hand a number of papers, and in the other a packet of letters, which he gave to Albert. Albert glanced carelessly at the different missives, selected two written in a small and delicate hand, and inclosed in scented envelopes, opened them, and perused their contents with some attention.

Albert threw himself on the divan, tore off the cover of two or three of the papers, looked at the playbills, made a face at perceiving they played an opera, and not a ballet; hunted vainly amongst the advertise-ments for a new tooth-powder of which he had heard, and threw down, one after the other, the three leading papers of Paris, muttering, "These papers become more and more stupid every day." A moment after, a carriage stopped before the door, and the servant announced M. Lucien Debray. A tall young man, with light hair, clear gray eyes, and thin and compressed lips, dressed in a blue coat with buttons of gold, beautifully carved, a white neckcloth, and a tortoiseshell eye-glass, suspended by a silken thread, and which, by an effort of the nerves, he fixed in his eye, entered, with a half-official air, without smiling or speaking. "Good-morning, Lucien! good-morning!" said Albert; "your punctuality really alarms me. What do I say? punctuality! You, whom I expected last, you arrive at five minutes to ten, when the time fixed was half-past? Have ministers resigned?"——"No, my dear fellow," returned the young man, seating himself on the divan; "reassure yourself; we are tottering always, but we never fall; and I begin to believe that we shall pass into a state of innobility, and then the affairs of the Peninsula will completely consolidate us."

"Ah, true! you drive Don Carlos out of Spain."—"No, no, my dear fellow, do not confound our plans. We take him to the other side of French frontier, and offer him hospitality at Bourges. All Paris knew it yesterday, and the day before it had already transpired on the Bourse, and M. Danglars (I do not know by what means that man contrives to obtain intelligence as soon as we do) made a million."

"I passed the night writing five-and-twenty despatches. I returned home at daybreak, and strove to sleep; but my head ached, and I got up to have a ride for an hour. Dullness and hunger attacked me at once,—two enemies who rarely accompany each other, and who are yet leagued against me. I then recollected you gave a breakfast this morning, and here I am. I am hungry, feed me; I am bored, amuse me."

"It is my duty as your host," returned Albert, ringing the bell, whilst Lucien turned over, with his gold-mounted cane, the papers that lay on the table. "Germain, a glass of sherry and a biscuit. In the meantime, my dear Lucien, here are cigars—contraband, of course—try them, and persuade the minister to sell us such instead of poisoning us with cabbage-leaves."

"Really, my dear Count," replied Lucien, lighting a manilla at a rose-colored taper that burnt in a stand beautifully enamelled—"how happy you are to have nothing to do: you do not know your own good fortune!"

"And what would you do, my dear diplomatist," replied Morcerf, with a slight degree of irony in his voice, "if you did nothing? What! can you not amuse yourself? Well, I will amuse you."——"How?"—— "By introducing to you a new acquaintance."

"A man or a woman?"

"A man."

"I know so many already."

"But you do not know this man."

"Where does he come from—the end of the world?"

"Farther still, perhaps."

"The devil! I hope he does not bring our breakfast with him."

"Oh, no; our breakfast comes from my father's kitchen. Are you hungry?"

"Humiliating as such a confession is, I am. But I dined at Villefort's, and lawyers always give you very bad dinners. You would think they felt some remorse; did you ever remark that?"

"Ah! depreciate other persons' dinners; you ministers give such splendid ones."

"Yes; but we do not invite people of fashion. If we were not forced to entertain a parcel of country boobies because they think and vote with us, we should never dream of dining at home, I assure you."

"But I hear Beauchamp in the next room; you can dispute together, and that will pass away the time."

"M. Beauchamp," announced the servant. "Enter, enter," said Albert, rising and advancing to meet the young man. "Here is Debray, who detests you without reading you, so he says."

"He is quite right," returned Beauchamp; "for I criticize him without knowing what he does."

"Come, come! that is not bad!" said Lucien. "Why do you not join our party, my dear Beauchamp? With your talents you would make your fortune in three or four years."

"I only await one thing before following your advice; that is, a minister who will hold office for six months. My dear Albert, one word; for I must get poor Lucien a respite. Do we breakfast or dine? I must go to the Chamber, for our life is not an idle one."

"You only breakfast: I await two persons: and the instant they arrive we shall sit down to table."

"Be it so; I will stay; I must do something to distract my thoughts."

"You are like Debray; and yet it seems to me that when the minister is out of spirits, the opposition ought to be joyous."

"Ah, you do not know with what I am threatened. I shall hear this morning M. Danglars make a speech at the Chamber of Deputies; and at his wife's this evening I shall hear the tragedy of a peer of France. The devil take the constitutional government! and since we had our choice, as they say, at least, how could we choose that?"

"I understand; you must lay in a stock of hilarity."

"Do not run down M. Danglars' speeches," said Debray; "he votes for you, for he belongs to the opposition."

"That is the worst of all: I am waiting until you send him to speak at the Luxembourg, to laugh at my ease."

"My dear friend," said Albert to Beauchamp, "it is plain the affairs of Spain are settled, for you are most desperately out of humor this morning. Recollect that Parisian gossip has spoken of a marriage between myself and Mlle. Eugénie Danglars; I cannot in conscience, therefore, let you run down the speeches of a man who will one day say to me, 'You know I give my daughter two millions.'"

"Ah, this marriage will never take place," said Beauchamp. "The king has made him a baron, and can make him a peer, but he cannot make him a gentleman; and the Count de Morcerf is too aristocratic to consent, for the paltry sum of eighty thousand pounds, to a *mésalliance*. The Viscount de Morcerf can only wed a marchioness."

"But two millions is a nice little sum," replied Morcerf.

"It is the capital of a theatre, or a local railroad."

"Never mind what he says, Morcerf," said Debray, "do you marry her. You marry a ticket of a money-bag, it is true; well, but what does that matter? It is better to have a blazon less and a figure more on it."

"M. de Château-Renaud! M. Maximilian Morrel!" said the servant, announcing two fresh guests.

"Now, then, to breakfast," said Beauchamp; "for, if I remember, you told me you only expected two persons, Albert."

"Morrel! Morrel! who is he?" But before Albert had finished, Château-Renaud, a handsome young man of thirty, a thorough gentleman, took Albert's hand.

"My dear Albert," said he, "let me introduce to you M. Maximilian Morrel, captain of Spahis, my friend; and what is more—however the man speaks for himself—my preserver. Salute my hero, Viscount." And he stepped on one side, exhibiting the large and open brow, the piercing eyes, and black moustache of the fine and noble young man whom our readers have already seen at Marseilles, under circumstances sufficiently dramatic not to be forgotten. A rich uniform, half French, half Oriental, set off his broad chest, decorated with the order of the Legion of Honor, and his graceful and stalwart figure. The young officer bowed with easy and elegant politeness. "Monsieur," said Albert, with affectionate courtesy, "Count Château-Renaud knew how much pleasure this introduction would give me; you are his friend, be ours also."

"Well said!" interrupted Château-Renaud; "and pray that, if you should ever be in a similar predicament, he may do as much for you as he did for me."——"What has he done?" asked Albert.

"You all know that I had the fancy of going to Africa."

"It is a road your ancestors have traced for you," said Albert gallantly.

"Yes, but I doubt that your object was like theirs—to rescue the Holy Sepulchre."

"You are quite right, Beauchamp," observed the young aristocrat. "It was only to fight as an amateur. I cannot bear duelling ever since two seconds, whom I had chosen to accommodate a quarrel, forced me to break the arm of one of my best friends, one whom you all know —poor Franz d'Epinay."

"Ah, true!" said Debray, "you did fight some time ago;—about what?"

"The devil take me, if I remember!" returned Château-Renaud. "But I recollect perfectly one thing: that, being unwilling to let such talents as mine sleep, I wished to try upon the Arabs new pistols given to me. In consequence I embarked for Oran, and went from thence to Constantine, where I arrived just in time to witness the raising of the seige. I retreated with the rest, during eight-and-forty hours. I supported the rain during the day and the cold during the night tolerably well, but the third morning my horse died of cold. I was retreating on foot, for my horse was dead. Six Arabs came up, full gallop, to cut off my head. I shot two with my double-barrelled gun, and two more with my pistols, but I was then disarmed, and two were still left; one seized me by the hair (that is why I now wear it so short, for no one knows what may happen), the other encircled my neck with the yataghan, when this gentleman whom you see here charged them, shot the one who held me by the hair, with a pistol, and cleft the skull of the other with his sabre. He had assigned himself the task of saving the life of a man that day; chance caused that man to be myself."

"Yes," said Morrel, smiling, "it was the 5th of September, the anniversary of the day on which my father was miraculously preserved; therefore, as far as it lies in my power, I endeavor to celebrate it by some——"

"Heroic action," interrupted Château-Renaud. "I was chosen. But this is not all: after rescuing me from the sword, he rescued me from the cold, not by sharing his cloak with me, like St. Martin, but by giving it me all; then from hunger by sharing with me—guess what?"

"A Strasbourg pie?" asked Beauchamp.

"No, his horse; of which we each of us ate a slice with a hearty appetite. It was very hard."

"The horse!" said Morcerf, laughing.

"No, the sacrifice," returned Château-Renaud. "What time do you breakfast, Albert?"

"At half-past ten."

"Precisely?" asked Debray, taking out his watch.

"Oh! you will give me five minutes' grace," replied Morcerf, "for I also expect a preserver."

"Of whom?"

"Of myself," cried Morcerf; "do you think I cannot be saved as well as any one else, and that only Arabs cut off heads? Our breakfast is a philanthropic one, and we shall have at table—at least, I hope so—two benefactors of humanity."

"And where does he come from?" asked Debray. "You have already answered the question once, but so vaguely, that I venture to put it a second time."

"Really," said Albert, "I do not know; when I invited him three months ago, he was then at Rome, but since that time, who knows where he may have gone?"

"And you think him capable of being exact?" demanded Debray.

"I think him capable of everything."

"Well, with the five minutes' grace, we have only ten left."

"I will profit by them to tell you something about my guest. I was at Rome the last Carnival."

"We know that," said Beauchamp.

"Yes, but what you do not know is that I was carried off by bandits, who conducted me to a most gloomy spot, called the Catacombs of Saint Sebastian."

"I know it," said Château-Renaud; "I narrowly escaped catching a fever there."

"And I did more than that," replied Morcerf, "for I caught one. I was informed I was a prisoner until I paid the sum of 4,000 Roman crowns—about 24,000 francs. Unfortunately, I had not above 1,500. I was at the end of my journey and of my credit. I wrote to Franz— and were he here he would confirm every word—that if he did not come with the four thousands crowns before six, at ten minutes past I should have gone to join the blessed saints and glorious martyrs, in whose company I had the honor of being; and Signor Luigi Vampa, such was the name of the chief of these bandits, would have scrupulously kept his word."

"But Franz did come with the four thousand crowns," said Château-Renaud. "A d'Epinay or Morcerf has not much difficulty in procuring them."

"No, he arrived accompanied simply by the guest I am going to present to you."

"Ah! this gentleman is a Hercules killing Cacus, a Perseus freeing Andromeda!"

"No, he is a man about my own size."

"Armed to the teeth?"

"He had not even a knitting-needle."

"But he paid your ransom?"

"He said two words to the chief, and I was free."

"Why, he is a second Ariosto."

"No, his name is the Count of Monte-Cristo."

"There is no Count of Monte-Cristo," said Debray.

"I do not think so," added Château-Renaud, with the air of a man who knows the whole of the European nobility perfectly.

"Does any one know anything of a Count of Monte-Cristo?"

"He comes possibly from the Holy Land, and one of his ancestors possessed Calvary, as the Montemarts did the Dead Sea."

"I think I can assist your researches," said Maximilian. "Monte-Cristo is a little island I have often heard spoken of by the old sailors my father employed—a grain of sand in the centre of the Mediterranean, an atom in the infinite."

"Precisely!" cried Albert. "Well, he of whom I speak is the lord and master of this grain of sand; he has purchased the title of count somewhere in Tuscany."

"He is rich, then?"

"Have you read the 'Arabian Nights'?"

"What a question!"

"Well, do you know if the persons you see there are rich or poor, if their sacks of wheat are not rubies or diamonds? They seem like poor fishermen, and suddenly they open some mysterious cavern filled with the wealth of the Indies."

"Go on!"

"My Count of Monte-Cristo is one of those fishermen. He has even a name taken from the book, since he calls himself Sinbad the Sailor, and has a cave filled with gold."

"And you have seen this cavern, Morcerf?" asked Beauchamp.

"No, but Franz has: for Heaven's sake, not a word of this before him. Franz went in with his eyes blindfolded, and was served by mutes and women to whom Cleopatra was nothing. Only he is not quite sure about the women, for they did not come in until after he had taken some drug, so that what he took for women might have been simply a row of statues."

The two young men looked at Morcerf as if to say,—

"Are you mad, or are you laughing at us?"——"And I also," said Morrel, thoughtfully, "have heard something like this from an old sailor named Penelon."

"Ah!" cried Albert, "it is very lucky that M. Morrel comes to aid me; you are vexed, are you not, that he thus gives a clue to the labyrinth?"

"My dear Albert," said Debray, "what you tell us is so extraordinary. Every one has not black slaves, superb galleys, Arabian horses, and Greek mistresses."

"Have you seen his Greek?"

"I have both seen and heard her. I saw her at the theatre, and heard her one morning when I breakfasted with the count."

"He eats, then?"

"Yes; but so little, it can hardly be called eating."

"He must be a vampire."

"Laugh, if you will; the Countess Guiccioli, who had known Lord Ruthven, declared the count was a vampire."

"Ah, Capital!" said Beauchamp. "For a man not connected with newspapers, here is the pendant to the famous sea-serpent."

"Wild eyes, the iris of which contracts or dilates at pleasure," said Debray; "facial angle strongly developed, magnificent forehead, livid complexion, black beard, sharp and white teeth, politeness unexceptionable."

"Just so, Lucien," returned Morcerf; "you have described him feature for feature. Yes, keen and cutting politeness. This man has often made me shudder! and one day that we were viewing an execution, I thought I should faint, more from hearing the cold and calm manner in which he spoke of every description of torture than from the sight of the executioner and the culprit."

"Did he not conduct you to the ruins of the Colosseum and suck your blood?" asked Beauchamp.

"Or, after having delivered you, make you sign a blood-colored parchment surrendering your soul to him?"——"Rail on, rail on at your ease, gentlemen," said Morcerf, somewhat piqued.

"Confess you have dreamed this, and let us sit down to breakfast," continued Beauchamp. But the sound of the clock had not died away when Germain announced, "His Excellency the Count of Monte-Cristo." The involuntary start every one gave proved how much Morcerf's narrative had impressed them, and Albert himself could not prevent sudden emotion. He had not heard a carriage stop in the street, or steps in the ante-chamber; the door had itself opened noiselessly. The count appeared, dressed with the greatest simplicity; but the most fastidious dandy could have found nothing to cavil at in his toilette: every article of dress—hat, coat, gloves, and boots—were from the first makers. He seemed scarcely five-and-thirty. But what struck everybody was his extreme resemblance to the portrait Debray had drawn. The count advanced, smiling, into the centre of the room, and approached Albert, who hastened toward him, holding out his hand.

"Punctuality," said Monte-Cristo, "is the politeness of kings, according to one of your sovereigns, I think; but it is not the same with travelers. However, I hope you will excuse the two or three seconds I am behindhand; five hundred leagues are not to be accomplished without some trouble, and especially in France, where, it seems, it is forbidden to beat the postilions."

"Count," replied Albert, "I was announcing your visit to some of my friends, whom I had invited in consequence of the promise you did me the honor to make, and whom I now present to you. They are Count Château-Renaud, whose nobility goes back to the twelve peers, and whose ancestors had a place at the Round Table; M. Lucien Debray, private secretary to the Internal Department; M. Beauchamp, an editor of a paper, and the terror of the French Government, but of whom, in spite of his celebrity, you have not heard in Italy, since his paper is prohibited there; and M. Maximilian Morrel, captain of Spahis."

At this name the count, who had hitherto saluted every one with courtesy, but at the same time with coldness and formality, stepped a pace forward, and a slight tinge of red colored his pale cheeks. "You wear the uniform of the new French conquerors, sir," said he; "it is a handsome uniform." No one could have said what caused the count's voice to vibrate so deeply, and what made his eye flash, in general so clear, lustrous, and limpid when he pleased. "You have never seen our African Legion, Count?" said Albert. "Never," replied the count, who was by this time perfectly master of himself again.

"Well, beneath this uniform beats one of the bravest and noblest hearts in the whole army."

"Oh, M. de Morcerf!" interrupted Morrel.

"Let me go on, captain! And we have just heard," continued Albert, "of a fresh action, and so heroic that, although I have seen him to-day for the first time, I request you to allow me to introduce him as my friend." At these words it was still possible to remark in Monte-Cristo that fixed gaze, that passing color, and that slight trembling of the eyelid, that showed his emotion. "Ah! you have a noble heart," said the count; "so much the better." This exclamation, which corresponded to the count's own thought rather than to what Albert was saying, surprised everybody, and especially Morrel, who looked at Monte-Cristo with surprise. But, at the same time, the intonation was so soft that, however strange the exclamation might seem, it was impossible to be offended at it.

"Gentlemen," said Albert, "Germain informs me breakfast is ready. My dear Count, allow me to show you the way." They passed silently into the breakfast-room; every one took his place. "Gentlemen," said the count, seating himself, "permit me to make a confession which must form my excuse for any blunder I may commit. I am a stranger, and to such a degree, that this is the first time I have ever been at Paris. The French way of living is utterly unknown to me, and up to the present time I have followed the Eastern customs, entirely in contrast to the Parisian. I beg you, therefore, to excuse if you find anything in me too Turkish, too Italian, or too Arabian. Now, then, let us breakfast."

"With what an air he says all this!" muttered Beauchamp; "decidedly he is a great man."

"A great man in his country," added Debray.

"A great man in every country, M. Debray," said Château-Renaud. The count was, it may be remembered, a most temperate guest. Albert remarked this, expressing his fears lest, at the outset, the Parisian mode of life should displease the traveler in the most essential point. "My dear Count," said he, "I fear one thing, and that is, that the fare of the Rue du Helder is not so much to your taste as that of the Place d'Espagne. I ought to have consulted you on the point, and have had some dishes prepared expressly."——"Did you know me better," returned the count, smiling, "you would not give one thought of such a thing for a traveler like myself. I eat everywhere, and of everything, only I eat but little; and to-day, that you reproach me with my want of appetite, is my day of appetite, for I have not eaten since yesterday morning."

"What!" cried all the guests, "you have not eaten for four-and-twenty hours?"——"No," replied the count; "I was forced to go out of my road to obtain some information near Nimes, so that I was somewhat late, and therefore I did not choose to stop."

"And you ate in your carriage?" asked Morcerf.——"No, I slept, as I generally do when I am weary without having the courage to amuse myself, or when I am hungry without feeling inclined to eat."

"But you can sleep when you please, monsieur?" said Morrel.

"Yes."

"You have a receipt for it?"

"An infallible one of which I make no secret of it. It is a mixture of excellent opium, which I fetched myself from Canton in order to have it pure, and the best hasheesh which grows in the east,—formed into pills. Ten minutes after one is taken, the effect is produced. Ask Baron Franz d'Epinay; I think he tasted them one day."

"Yes," replied Morcerf, "he said something about it to me."

"But," said Beauchamp, who, in his capacity of journalist, was very incredulous, "you always carry this drug about you?"——"Always."

"Would it be an indiscretion to ask to see those precious pills?" continued Beauchamp, hoping to take him at a disadvantage.——"No, monsieur," returned the count; and he drew from his pocket a marvellous *bonbonnière,* formed out of a single emerald, and closed by a golden lid, which unscrewed and gave passage to a small ball of a greenish color, and about the size of a pea. This ball had an acrid and penetrating odor. There were four or five more in the emerald, which would contain about a dozen. The *bonbonnière* passed round the table, but it was more to examine the admirable emerald than to see the pills that it passed from hand to hand. "And is it your cook who prepares these pills?" asked Beauchamp.

"Oh, no, monsieur," replied Monte-Cristo; "I do not thus betray my enjoyments to the vulgar. I am a tolerable chemist, and prepare my pills myself."

"This is a magnificent emerald, and the largest I have ever seen," said Château-Renaud, "although my mother has some remarkable family jewels."

"I had three similar ones," returned Monte-Cristo. "I gave one to the Grand, who mounted it in his sabre; another to our holy father the Pope, who had it set in his tiara, opposite to nearly as large, though not so fine a one, given by the Emperor Napoleon to his predecessor, Pius VII. I kept the third for myself, and I had it hollowed out, which reduced its value, but rendered it more commodious for the purpose I intended it for." Every one looked at Monte-Cristo with astonishment; he spoke with so much simplicity that it was evident he spoke the truth, or that he was mad. However, the sight of the emerald made them naturally incline to the former belief. "And what did these two sovereigns give you in exchange for these magnificent presents?" asked Debray.——"The Grand Seignior, the liberty of a woman," replied the count; "the Pope, the life of a man; so that once in my life I have been as powerful as if heaven had made me come into the world on the steps of a throne."

And it was Peppino you saved, was it not?" cried Morcerf; "it was for him that you obtained pardon?"

"Perhaps," returned the count, smiling.

"Count, you have no idea what pleasure it gives me to hear you speak thus," said Morcerf. "I had announced you beforehand to my friends as an enchanter of the 'Arabian Nights,' or wizard of the Middle Ages; but the Parisians are so subtle in paradoxes, that they mistake for caprices of the imagination the most incontestable truths, when these truths do not form a part of their daily existence. For example, here is Debray who reads and Beauchamp who prints, every day, 'A member of the Jockey Club has been stopped and robbed on the Boulevard; that four persons have been assassinated at St. Germain; that ten, fifteen, or twenty thieves, have been arrested, and who yet contest the existence of the bandits of the Pontine Marshes. Tell them yourself that I was taken by bandits, and that without your generous intercession I should now have been sleeping in the Catacombs of St. Sebastian, instead of receiving them in my humble abode in Helder Street."

"Ah," said Monte-Cristo, "you promised me never to mention that circumstance."——"It was not I who made that promise," cried Morcerf; "it must have been some one else whom you have rescued in the same manner, and whom you have forgotten. Pray speak of it, for I know not, how you contrived to inspire with such respect the bandits of Rome, who have so little respect for anything; I assure you, Franz and I were lost in admiration."

"Nothing more simple," returned the count. "I had known the famous Vampa for more than ten years. When he was quite a child, and only a shepherd, I gave him, for having shown me the way to a place, some pieces of gold; he, in order to repay me, gave me a poniard, the hilt of which he had carved with his own hand, and which you may have seen in my collection of arms. In after years whether he had forgotten this interchange of presents, which ought to have cemented our friendship, or whether he did not recollect me, he sought to take me, but, on the contrary, it was I who captured him and a dozen of his band. I might have handed him over to Roman justice, which is somewhat expeditious, and which would have been still more so with him; but I did nothing of the sort—I suffered him and his band to depart."

"With the condition that they should sin no more," said Beauchamp, laughing. "I see they kept their promise."

"No," returned Monte-Cristo, "upon the simple condition that they should respect myself and my friends. Perhaps what I am about to say may seem strange to you, who vaunt humanity and your duty to your neighbor, but I never seek to protect society who does not protect me, and whom I will even say, in general, occupies itself about me only to injure me; and thus giving them a low place in my esteem, and preserving a neutrality towards them, it is society and my neighbor who are indebted to me."——"Bravo!" cried Château-Renaud; "you are the first man I ever met sufficiently courageous to preach egotism. Bravo!"

"It is frank, at least," said Morrel. "But I am sure that the count does not regret having once deviated from the principles he has so boldly avowed."

"How have I deviated from those principles, monsieur?" asked Monte-Cristo, who could not help looking at Morrel with so much intensity, that two or three times the young man had been unable to sustain the clear and piercing eye of the count.

"Why, it seems to me," replied Morrel, "that in delivering M. de Morcerf, whom you did not know, you did good to your neighbor and to society."——"Of which he is the brightest ornament," said Beauchamp, drinking off a glass of champagne.

"Count," cried Morcerf, "you are at fault; you, one of the most formidable logicians I know—and you must see it clearly proved, that instead of being an egotist, you are a philanthropist. The first day you set foot in Paris you instinctively possess the greatest virtue, or rather the chief defect, of us eccentric Parisians,—that is, you assume the vices you have not, and conceal the virtues you possess."——"My dear sir," returned Monte-Cristo, "I do not see, in all I have done, anything that merits, either from you or these gentlemen, the pretended eulogies I have received. I will appeal to any of these gentlemen, could I leave my guest in the hands of a hideous bandit, as you term him? Besides, you know, I had the idea that you could introduce me into some of the Paris *salons* when I came to France. You might some time ago have looked upon this resolution as a vague project, but to-day you see it was a reality, and you must submit to it under penalty of breaking your word."

"I will keep it," returned Morcerf; "but I fear that you will be much disappointed, accustomed as you are to picturesque events and fantastic horizons. France is so prosaic, and Paris so civilized a city, that you will not find in it a single hill on which there is not a telegraph, or a grotto in which the commissary of police has not put up a gas-lamp. There is but one service I can render you, and for that I place myself entirely at your orders: that is, to present, or make my friends present, you everywhere; besides, you have no need of any one to introduce you—with your name, and your fortune, and your talent" (Monte-Cristo bowed with a somewhat ironical smile) "you can present yourself everywhere, and be well received; I can be useful in one way only—if knowledge of Parisian habits, of the means of rendering yourself comfortable, or of the bazaars, can assist, you may dispose of me to find you a fitting dwelling here. I dare offer to share my apartments with you, as I shared yours at Rome—for, except myself, these rooms would not contain a shadow, unless it were the shadow of a female."

"Ah," said the count, "that is a most conjugal reservation; I recollect that at Rome you said something of a projected marriage. May I congratulate you?"

"The affair is still in projection. My father is most anxious about it; and I hope, ere long, to introduce you, if not to my wife, at least to my intended—Mdlle. Eugénie Danglars."——"Danglers!" said Monte-Cristo; "tell me, is not her father Baron Danglers?"

"Yes," returned Morcerf; "a baron of a new creation."

"I do not know him," returned Monte-Cristo: "but I shall probably soon make his acquaintance, for I have a credit opened with him by the house of Richard and Blount, of London, Arstein and Eskeles of Vienna, and Thomson and French at Rome." As he pronounced the two last names, the count glanced at Maximilian Morrel. If the stranger expected to produce an effect he was not mistaken—Maximilian started as if he had been electrified. "Thomson and French!" said he; "do you know this house, sir?"

"They are my bankers in the capital of the Christian world," returned the count quietly. "Can my influence with them be of any service to you?"

"Oh, my lord, you could assist me perhaps in researches which have been, up to the present, fruitless. This house, in past years, did ours a great service, and has, I know not for what reason, always denied having rendered us this service."

"I shall be at your orders," said Monte-Cristo, inclining himself.

"But," continued Morcerf, "we have strangely wandered from the subject. We were speaking of a suitable habitation for the Count of

Monte-Cristo. Come, gentlemen, let us all propose some place: where shall we lodge this new guest in our great capital?"

Various fashionable quarters were suggested.

"You have no idea, then, Morrel?" asked Château-Renaud: "you do not propose anything."

"Oh, yes," returned the young man, smiling; "on the contrary, I have one; but I expected the count would be tempted by one of the brilliant proposals made him; yet as he has not replied to any of them, I will venture to offer him a suite of apartments in a charming house in the Pompadour style, that my sister has inhabited for a year, in Meslay street."

"You have a sister?" asked the count.——"Yes, sir, who married the man she loved, who remained faithful to us in our fallen fortunes —Emmanuel Herbaut." Monte-Cristo smiled imperceptibly. "I live there during my leave of absence," continued Maximilian; "and I shall be, together with my brother-in-law Emmanuel, at the disposition of the count, whenever he thinks fit to honor us."

"Thanks, captain," said Monte-Cristo; "I shall content myself with being presented to your sister and her husband, if you will do me the honor to introduce me; but I cannot accept the offer of any one of these gentlemen, since my habitation is already prepared. As I determined to have a house to myself, I sent on my valet, and he ought by this time to have bought the house and furnished it."

"Have you, then, a man who knows Paris?" said Beauchamp.

"It is the first time he has ever been in Paris. He is black, and cannot speak," returned Monte-Cristo.

"It is Ali!" cried Albert, in the midst of the general surprise.

"Yes, Ali himself, my Nubian mute, whom you saw, I think, at Rome."

"Certainly," said Morcerf; "I recollect him perfectly. But how could you charge a Nubian to purchase a house, and a mute, to furnish it?—he will do everything wrong."

"Undeceive yourself, monsieur," replied Monte-Cristo; "I am quite sure, that, on the contrary, he will choose everything as I wish. He knows my tastes, my caprices, my wants; he has been here a week, with the instinct of a hound, hunting by himself; he will organize everything for me. He knew I should arrive to-day at ten o'clock; since nine he awaited me at Fontainebleau. He gave me this paper; it contains the number of my new abode; read it yourself," and Monte-Cristo passed a paper to Albert. "Ah, that is really original," said Beauchamp.

"And very princely," added Château-Renaud.

"What! do you not know your house?" asked Debray.

"No," said Monte-Cristo; "I told you I did not wish to be behind my time; I dressed myself in the carriage and descended at the viscount's door." The men looked at each other; they did not know if it was a comedy Monte-Cristo was playing; but every word he uttered had such an air of simplicity, that it was impossible to suppose what he said was false: besides, why should he tell a falsehood? "We must content ourselves, then," said Beauchamp, "with rendering M. le Comte all the little services in our power. I, as a journalist, open all the theatres to him."

"Thanks," returned Monte-Cristo, "my steward has orders to take a box at each theatre."

"Is your steward also a Nubian?" asked Debray.

"No, he is a countryman of yours, if a Corsican is a countryman of anyone's. But you know him, M. de Morcerf."

"Is it that excellent M. Bertuccio, who understands hiring windows so well?"——"Yes, you saw him the day I had the honor of receiving you; he has been a soldier, a smuggler—in fact, everything. I would not be quite sure that he has not been mixed up with the police for some trifle—a stab with a knife, for instance."

"And you have chosen this honest citizen for your steward," said Debray. "Of how much does he rob you every year?"

"On my word," replied the count, "not more than another. I am sure he answers my purpose, knows no impossibility, and so I keep him."——"Then," continued Château-Renaud, "since you have an establishment, a steward, and a mansion in the Champs Elysées, you only want a housekeeper."

Albert smiled. He thought of the fair Greek he had seen in the count's box at the theatres.

"I have something better than that," said Monte-Cristo; "I have a slave. You procure yours from the Opera, the Vaudeville, or the Variétés; I purchased mine at Constantinople: it cost me more, but I have nothing to fear."

"But you forget," replied Debray, laughing, "that we are Frank by name and frank by nature, as King Charles said; and that the moment she put her foot in France your slave becomes free."

"Who will tell her?"

"The first person who sees her."

"She only speaks Romanic."

"That is different."

"But at least we shall see her," said Beauchamp, "or do you keep eunuchs as well as mutes?"

"Oh, no," replied Monte-Cristo; "I do not carry brutalism so far. Everyone who surrounds me is free to quit me, and when they leave me will no longer have any need of me or any one else; it is for that reason, perhaps, that they do not quit me."

They had long since passed to dessert and cigars.

"My dear Albert," said Debray, rising, "I must return to the minister's. I will tell him of the count, and we shall soon know who he is."

"Take care," returned Albert; "no one has been able to accomplish that."

"Oh, we have three millions for our police."

"And when you know, will you tell me?"

"I promise you. Gentlemen, good morning."

"Bravo!" said Beauchamp to Albert; "I shall not go to the house, but I have something better to offer my readers than a speech of M. Danglars."

"For heaven's sake, Beauchamp," returned Morcerf, "do not deprive me of the merit of introducing him everywhere. Is he not peculiar?"

"He is more than that," replied Château-Renaud; "he is one of the most extraordinary men I ever saw." Morrel left the room with Château-Renaud, leaving Monte-Cristo alone with Morcerf.

CHAPTER XXVI.

THE PRESENTATION.

WHEN Albert found himself alone with Monte-Cristo, he said: Allow me to commence my ciceroneship by showing you a specimen of a bachelor's apartment." Monte-Cristo was a worthy appreciator of all that Albert had collected.

Albert expected to have something new this time to show to the traveler, but, to his great surprise, the latter, without seeking for the signatures, many of which, indeed, were only initials, named instantly the author of every picture in such a manner that it was easy to see that each name was not only known to him, but that each of their styles had been appreciated and studied by him. They passed into the bed-chamber; a model of taste and simple elegance. A single portrait, signed Leopold Robert, shone in its carved and gilded frame. This portrait attracted the Count of Monte-Cristo's attention, for he made three rapid steps in the chamber, and stopped suddenly before it. It was the portrait of a woman of five and twenty, with a dark complexion, and light and lustrous eyes, veiled beneath long lashes. She wore the picturesque costume of the Catalian fisherwomen, a red and black bodice, and golden pins in her hair. She was looking at the sea, and her outline was defined on the blue ocean and sky. The light was so faint in the room that Albert did not perceive the paleness that spread itself over the count's visage, or the nervous heaving of his chest and shoulders. Silence prevailed for an instant, during which Monte-Cristo gazed intently on the picture.

"You have there a most charming idol, Vicount," said the count in a perfectly calm tone; "and this costume—a fancy one, doubtless—becomes her admirably."

"Ah!" returned Albert, "I would never forgive you this mistake if you had seen another picture beside this. You do not know my mother; she it is whom you see here: she had her portrait painted thus six or eight years ago. This costume is a fancy one, it appears, and the resemblance is so great that I think I still see my mother the same as she was in 1830. The countess had this portrait painted during the count's absence. She doubtless intended giving him an agreeable surprise; but, strange to say, this portrait seemed to displease my father, and the value of the picture, which is, as you see, one of the best works of Leopold Robert, could not overcome his dislike to it. It is true, between ourselves, that Morcerf is one of the most assiduous peers at the Luxembourg, a general renowned for theory, but a most mediocre amateur of art. It is different with my mother, who paints exceedingly well, and who, unwilling to part with so valuable a picture, gave it to me to put here, where it would be less likely to displease Morcerf, whose portrait, by Gros, I will also show you. Excuse my talking of family matters; but as I shall have the honor of introducing you to the count, I tell you this to prevent you making any illusions to this picture. The picture seems to have a malign influence, for my mother rarely comes here without looking at it, and still more rarely does she look at it without weeping. This disagreement is the only one that has ever taken place between the count and countess, who are still as much united, although married more than twenty years, as the first day of their wedding."

Monte-Cristo glanced rapidly at Albert, as if to seek a hidden meaning in his words; but it was evident the young man uttered them in the simplicity of his heart. "Now," said Albert, "that you have seen all my treasures, allow me to offer them to you, unworthy as they are. You are somewhat used up, I know, and family scenes have not much effect on Sinbad the Sailor, who has seen so many others. However, accept what I propose to you as an initiation into Parisian life—a life of politeness, visiting, and introductions." Monte-Cristo bowed without making any answer; he accepted the offer without enthusiasm and without regret, as one of those conventions of society which every gentleman looks upon as a duty. Albert summoned his servant, and ordered him to acquaint M. and Mdme. de Morcerf of the arrival of the

Count of Monte-Cristo. Albert followed him with the count. When they arrived at the drawing-room the most conspicuous object was another portrait of a man, from five to eight-and-thirty, in the uniform of a general officer; the riband of the Legion of Honor round his neck, showed he was a commander; and on the breast, on the right, the star of a grand officer of the Order of the Saviour, and on the left that of the grand cross of Charles III., which proved that the person represented by the picture had served in the wars of Greece and Spain; or, the same thing as regarded decorations, had fulfilled some diplomatic mission.

Monte-Cristo was engaged in examing this portrait with no less care than he had bestowed upon the other, when another door opened, and he found himself opposite to Count Morcerf himself. He was a man of forty-five years, but he seemed at least fifty, and his black moustache and eyebrows contrasted strangely with his almost white hair, which was cut short, in military fashion. He was dressed in plain clothes, and wore at his button-hole the ribands of the different orders to which he belonged. This man entered with a tolerably dignified step, and with haste. Monte-Cristo saw him advance toward him without making a single step. It seemed as if his feet were rooted to the ground, and his eyes on Morcerf.

"Father," said the young man, "I have the honor of presenting to you the Count de Monte-Cristo, the generous friend whom I had the good fortune to meet in the critical juncture of which I have told you."

"You are most welcome, sir," said Morcerf, saluting Monte-Cristo with a smile; "and you have rendered our house, in preserving its only heir, a service which insures our eternal gratitude." As he said these words, Morcerf pointed to a chair, whilst he seated himself in another opposite the window.

Monte-Cristo, whilst he took the seat Morcerf offered him, placed himself in such a manner as to remain concealed in the shadow of the large velvet curtains, and read on the care-worn and livid features of the count a whole history of secret griefs written in each wrinkle time had planted there. "The lady," said Morcerf, "was at her toilette when she was informed of the visit she was about to receive. She would, however, be down in ten minutes."

"It is a great honor for me," returned Monte-Cristo, "to be thus, on the first day of my arrival in Paris, brought in contact with a man whose merit equals his reputation, and to whom fortune has for once been equitable; but has she not still on the plains of Mitidja, or in the mountains of Atlas, a marshal's staff to offer you?"

"Oh," replied Morcerf, reddening slightly, "I have left the service. Made a peer at the Restoration, I served through the first campaign under the orders of Marshal Bourmont. I could, therefore, expect a higher rank, and who knows what might have happened had the elder branch remained on the throne? But the Revolution of July was, it seems, sufficiently glorious to allow itself to be ungrateful; and it was so for all services that did not date from the imperial period. I tendered my resignation; for when you have gained your epaulets on the battle-field, you do not know how to manœuvre on the slippery floor. I have hung up my sword, and cast myself into politics. I have devoted myself to industry; I study the useful arts. During the twenty years I served, I often wished to do so, but I had not the time."

"These are the ideas that render your nation superior to any other," returned Monte-Cristo. "A gentleman of high birth, possessor of an ample fortune, you have consented to gain your promotion as an obscure soldier, step by step—this is uncommon; then become general, peer of France, commander of the Legion of Honor, you consent to again commence a second apprenticeship, without any other hope or any other desire than that of one day becoming useful to your fellow-creatures; this, indeed, is praiseworthy,—nay, more, it is sublime." Albert looked on and listened with astonishment; he was not used to see Monte-Cristo give vent to such bursts of enthusiasm. "Alas!" continued the stranger, doubtless to dispel the slight cloud that covered Morcerf's brow, "we do not act thus in Italy; we grow according to our race and our species, and we pursue the same lines, and often the same uselessness, all our lives."

"But," said Morcerf, "you have been free to choose your career, and you have chosen the path strewed with flowers."

"Precisely," replied Monte-Cristo, with one of those smiles that a painter could never represent or a physiologist analyze.

Ah! here is my mother," cried the viscount. Monte-Cristo turned round hastily, and saw Lady Morcerf at the door opposite to that by which her husband had entered, pale and motionless; when Monte-Cristo turned round, she let fall her arm, which for some unknown reason had been resting on the gilded door-post. She had been there some moments, and had overheard the last words of the visitor. The latter rose and bowed to the countess, who inclined herself without speaking. "Ah! good heavens, madame!" said the count, "are you unwell, or is it the heat of the room that affects you!"

"Are you ill, mother?" cried the viscount, springing towards her.

She thanked them both with a smile. "No," returned she, "but I feel some emotion on seeing, for the first time, the man without whose intervention we should have been in tears and desolation. Sir," continued the countess, advancing with the majesty of a queen, "I owe to you the life of my son, and for this I bless you. Now I thank you for the pleasure you give me in thus affording me the opportunity of thanking you as I have blessed you, from the bottom of my heart." The count bowed again, but lower than before; he was even paler than Mercédès. "My lady," said he, "the count and yourself recompense too generously a simple action. To save a man, to spare a father's feelings, or a mother's sensibility, is not to do a good action, but a simple deed of humanity." At these words uttered with the most exquisite sweetness and politeness, Lady Morcerf replied,—"It is very fortunate for my son, that he found such a friend, and I thank God that things are thus." And Mercédès raised her fine eyes to heaven with so fervent an expression of gratitude, that the count fancied he saw tears in them. Morcerf approached her. "Madame," said he, "I have already made my excuses to the count for quitting him, and I pray you to do so also. The sitting commences at two; it is now three, and I am to speak."

"Go, then, and we will strive our best to forget your absence!" replied the countess, with the same tone of deep feeling. "Count," continued she, turning to Monte-Cristo, "will you do us the honor of passing the rest of the day with us?"

"Believe me, madame, I feel most grateful for your kindness, but I got out of my traveling carriage at your door this morning, and I am ignorant how I am installed in Paris, which I scarcely know; this is but a trifling inquietude, I know, but one that may be appreciated."

"We shall have this pleasure another time!" said the countess; "you promise that?" Monte-Cristo inclined himself without answering; but the gesture might pass for assent. "I will not detain you," continued the countess; "I would not have our gratitude become indiscreet or importunate."

"My dear Count," said Albert, "I will endeavor to return your politeness at Rome, and place my coupé at your disposal until your own be ready."

"A thousand thanks for your kindness, Viscount," returned the Count of Monte-Cristo; "but I suppose that Bertuccio has suitably employed the four hours and a half I have given him, and that I shall find a carriage of some sort ready at the door." Albert was used at the count's manner of proceeding: he knew that, like Nero, he was in search of the impossible, and nothing astonished him; only wishing to judge with his own eyes how far the count's orders had been executed, he accompanied him to the door of the hotel. Monte-Cristo was not deceived. As soon as he appeared in Morcerf's ante-chamber, a footman, the same who at Rome had brought the count's card to the two young men, and announced his visit, sprang into the vestibule, and when he arrived at the door the illustrious traveler found his carriage awaiting him. It was a first class coupé, and with horses and harness for which Drake had, to the knowledge of all the lions of Paris, refused on the previous day seven hundred guineas.

"Sir," said the count to Albert, "I do not ask you to accompany me to my house, as I can only show you a habitation fitted up in a hurry, and I have, as you know, a reputation to keep up as regards not being taken by surprise. Give me, therefore, one more day before I invite you; I shall then be certain not to fail in my hospitality."

"If you ask me for a day, Count, I know what to anticipate; it will not be a house I shall see, but a palace. You have decidedly some genius at your control."

"Spread that idea," replied Monte-Cristo, putting his foot on the velvet-lined steps of his splendid carriage, "and that will be worth something to me among the ladies." As he spoke, he sprang into the vehicle, the door was closed, but not so rapidly that Monte-Cristo perceived the almost imperceptible movement which stirred the curtains of the apartment in which he had left Lady Morcerf. When Albert returned to his mother, he found her in the boudoir reclining in a large velvet arm-chair; the whole room so obscure that only the shining spangle, fastened here and there to the drapery, and the angles of the gilded frames of the pictures, gave a kind of light to the room. The young man, standing up before her, gazed upon her with that filial affection which is more tender and endearing with children whose mothers are still young and handsome. Then, seeing her eyes closed, but hearing her breathe gently, he believed she had dropped asleep, and left the apartment on tiptoe, closing the door after him with the utmost precaution. "This devil of a fellow," he muttered, shaking his head; "I said at the time he would create a sensation here, and I measure his effect by an infallible thermometer. My mother has noticed him, and he must therefore, perforce, be remarkable." He went down to the stables, not without some slight annoyance, when he remembered that the Count of Monte-Cristo had laid his hands on a "turnout" which sent his bays down to number 2 in the opinion of connoisseurs. "Most decidedly," said he, "men are not equal, and I must beg my father to develop this theorem in the Chamber of Peers."

CHAPTER XXVII.

A SINGULAR STEWARD.

DURING this time the count had arrived at his house; it had taken him six minutes to perform the distance; but these six minutes were sufficient to induce twenty young men who knew the price of the equipage they had been unable to purchase themselves, to put their horses in a gallop in order to see the rich foreigner who could afford to give 20,000 francs apiece for his horses. The house Ali had chosen, and which was to serve as a town residence to Monte-Cristo, was situated on the right hand as you ascended the Champs Elysées. A thick clump of trees and shrubs rose in the centre, and masked a portion of the front; around this shrubbery two alleys, like two arms, extended right and left, and formed a carriage-drive from the iron gates to a double portico, on every step of which stood a porcelain vase, filled with flowers. This house, isolated from the rest, had, besides the main entrance, another in the Rue Ponthieu. Even before the coachman had hailed the janitor, the massy gates rolled on their hinges:—he had seen the count coming, and at Paris, as everywhere else, he was served with the rapidity of lightning. The coachman entered, and descending the half-circle without slackening his speed, the gates were closed ere the wheels had ceased to sound on the gravel. The carriage stopped at the left side of the portico, two men presented themselves at the carriage-window; the one was Ali, who, smiling with an expression of the most sincere joy, seemed amply repaid by a mere look from Monte-Cristo. The other bowed respectfully, and offered him arm to assist the count in descending. "Thanks, M. Bertuccio," said the count, springing lightly up the three steps of the portico; "and the notary?"

"He brought the transfer deeds of the property your excellency has purchased out of town."

No sooner was the master alone than he referred to a notebook with a lock-clasp. The key was hung on a chain round his neck. The item he looked at was "Auteuil, No. 28, Fontaine Street."

"It is the house just bought," he muttered, "and now, am I to rely upon an avowal extorted by religious or physical terror? However, in an hour I shall know all. Bertuccio!" cried he, striking a light hammer with a pliant handle on a small gong. "Bertuccio!" The steward appeared at the door. "Monsieur Bertuccio," said the count, "did you never tell me that you had traveled in France?"

"In some parts of France—yes, excellency."

"You know the environs of Paris, then?"

"No, excellency, no," returned the steward, with a sort of nervous trembling, which Monte-Cristo, a judge in all emotions, rightly attributed to great disquietude.

"It is unfortunate," returned he, "that you have never visited the environs, for I wish to see my new property this evening, and had you gone with me, you could have given me some useful information."

"To Auteuil!" cried Bertuccio, whose copper complexion became livid—"I go to Auteuil?"

"Well, what is there surprising in that? When I live at Auteuil, you must come there, as you belong to my service." It was unexampled for a servant of the count's to dare to dispute an order of his; so the steward, without saying a word, followed his master, who got into the carriage, and signed him to follow, which he did, seating himself respectfully on the front seat.

CHAPTER XXVIII.

THE HOUSE OF AUTEUIL.

MONTE-CRISTO had remarked that, as they descended the staircase, Bertuccio crossed himself in the Corsican manner, that is, had formed the sign of the cross in the air with his thumb, and as he seated himself in the carriage, muttered a short prayer. Any one but a curious man would have had pity on seeing the steward's extraordinary repugnance for the count's projected ride; but it seemed the count was too curious to excuse Bertuccio this little journey. In twenty minutes they were at Auteuil. No. 28 was situated at the extremity of the village; during the ride night had set in, or rather a black cloud, charged with electricity, gave to these vapors the appearance and solemnity of a dramatic episode. The carriage stopped, the footman sprang off the box, and opened the door. "Well," said the count, "you do not get out, M. Bertuccio—you are going to stay in the carriage, then? What are you thinking of this evening?" Bertuccio sprang out, and offered his shoulder to the count, who, this time, leaned upon it as he descended the three steps of the carriage. "Knock," said the count, "and announce me." Bertuccio knocked, the door opened, and the porter appeared. "What is it?" asked he.

"It is your new master, my good fellow," said the footman. And he held out the notary's order.

"The house is sold, then?" demanded he; "and this gentleman is coming to live here?"

"Yes, my friend," returned the count; "and I will endeavor to give you no cause to regret your old master."——"Oh," said the man, "I shall not have much cause to regret him, for he came here but seldom; it is five years since he was here last; and he did well to sell the house, for it did not bring him in anything at all."

"What was the name of your old master?" said Monte-Cristo.

"The Marquis of Saint-Méran. Oh, I am sure he has not sold the house for what he gave for it."

"Saint-Méran!" returned the count. "The name is not unknown to me."

"An old nobleman," continued the concierge, "a staunch follower of the Bourbons; he had an only daughter, who married M. de Villefort, who had been the Nîmes proctor and afterwards at Versailles." Monte-Cristo glanced at Bertuccio, who became whiter than the wall against which he leaned to prevent himself from falling. "And is not this daughter dead?" demanded Monte-Cristo; "I fancy I have heard so."

"Yes, sir, one-and-twenty years ago; and since then we have not seen the poor marquis three times."

"Thanks, thanks," said Monte-Cristo, judging from the steward's utter prostration that he could not stretch the cord further without danger of breaking it.

"Bertuccio, take one of the carriage-lamps, and show me the apartments." The steward obeyed in silence.

"Ah! here is a private staircase," said the count; "that is convenient. Light me, M. Bertuccio, and go first; we will see where it leads to."

"Sir," replied Bertuccio, "it leads to the garden."

"And, pray, how do you know that?"

"It ought to do so, at least."

"Well, let us be sure of that." Bertuccio sighed, and went on first: the stairs led, in reality, to the garden. At the outer door the steward paused. "Go on, Bertuccio," said the count. But he to whom he spoke was stupified, bewildered, stunned; his haggard eyes glanced round, as if in search of the traces of some terrible event, and with his clenched hands he seemed striving to shut out some horrible recollections. "Well!" insisted the count. "No, no," cried Bertuccio, setting down the lantern at the angle of the interior wall. "No, it is impossible; I can go no further."

"What does this mean?" demanded the irresistible voice of Monte-Cristo.

"Why, you must see," cried the steward, "that this is not natural;

that, having a house to purchase, you purchase it exactly at Auteuil; and that, purchasing it at Auteuil, this house should be No. 28, Rue de la Fontaine. Oh! why did I not tell you all? I am sure you would not have forced me to come. I hoped your house would have been some other one than this; as if there was not another house at Auteuil than that of the assassination!"——"Ah! ah!" cried Monte-Cristo, stopping suddenly, "what words did you utter? Devil of a man, Corsican that you are—always mysteries or superstitions. Come, take the lantern, and let us visit the garden; you are not afraid of ghosts with me, I hope?" Bertuccio raised the lantern, and obeyed. The door, as it opened, disclosed a gloomy sky, in which the moon strove vainly to struggle through a sea of clouds that covered her with their sombre wave, that she illumined for an instant, and was then lost in the darkness. The steward wished to turn to the left. "No, no, monsieur," said Monte-Cristo. "What is the use of following the alleys? Here is a beautiful lawn; let us go on straight forwards."

Bertuccio wiped the perspiration from his brow, but obeyed; however, he continued to take the left hand. Monte-Cristo, on the contrary, took the right hand; arrived near a clump of trees, he stopped. The steward could not restrain himself. "Move, monsieur—move away, I entreat you; you are exactly in the spot!"

"What spot?"——"Where he fell."

"My dear Bertuccio," said Monte-Cristo, laughing, "recover yourself; we are no longer at Sartène or at Corte. This is not a marsh but a garden; badly kept, I own, but still you must not calumniate it for that."

"I implore you, do not stay there!"

"I think you are going mad, Bertuccio," said the count coldly. "If that is the case, I warn you, I shall have you put in a lunatic asylum."

"But, my lord," replied Bertuccio, hesitatingly, "did not Father Busoni, who heard my confession in the prison at Nîmes, tell you I had a heavy reproach to make against myself?"——"Yes; but as he said you would make an excellent steward, I concluded you had stolen—that was all. Or, as you are a Corsican, that you had been unable to resist the desire of making a *peau,* as you call it."

"Yes, my good master," cried Bertuccio, casting himself at the count's feet, "it was simply a vengeance—nothing else."

"I understand that, but I do not understand what it is that galvanizes you in this manner."——"But, sir, it is very natural," returned Bertuccio, "since it was in this house that my vengeance was accomplished." ——"What! my house?"——"Oh, it was not yours, then."——"Whose, then? The Marquis de Saint-Méran's, I think, the porter said. What had you to revenge on Saint-Méran?"——"Oh, it was not on him, monsieur; it was on another."

"Well, come, collect yourself, and tell me all." And the count, humming an air from *Lucia,* went to sit down on a bench, whilst Bertuccio followed him, collecting his thoughts. Bertuccio remained standing before him.

"The story begins in 1815."

"Ah," said Monte-Cristo, "1815 is not yesterday."

"No; and yet I recollect all things as clearly as if they had happened but then. I had a brother, an elder brother, who was in the service of the emperor; he had become lieutenant in a regiment composed entirely of Corsicans. This brother was my only friend; we became orphans—I at five, he at eighteen. He brought me up as if I had been his son, and in 1814 he married. When the emperor returned from the island of Elba, my brother instantly joined the army, was slightly wounded at Waterloo, and retired with the army behind the Loire.

"One day we received a letter. I should tell you that we lived in the little village of Rogliano, at the extremity of Cape Corse. This letter was from my brother. He told us that the army was disbanded, and that he should return; and, if I had any money, he prayed me to leave it for him at Nîmes, with an innkeeper with whom I had dealings."

"In the smuggling line?" said Monte-Cristo.

"Every one must live."

"Certainly; continue."

"I loved my brother tenderly, as I told your excellency, and I resolved not to send the money but to take it to him myself. I possessed a thousand francs. I left five hundred with Assunta, my sister-in-law, and with the other five hundred I set off for Nîmes.

"Just at this time the famous massacres of the south of France took place. Two or three brigands, called Trestaillon, Truphemy, and Graffan, publicly assassinated everybody whom they suspected of Bonapartism. As I entered Nîmes, I literally waded in blood; at every step you encountered dead bodies and bands of the murderers, who killed, plundered, and burned. I hastened to the inn. My presages had been but too true: my brother had arrived the previous evening at Nîmes, and, at the very door of the house where he was about to demand hospitality, he had been assassinated. I did all in my power to discover the murderers, but no one durst tell me their names, so much were they dreaded. I then thought of that French justice of which I had heard so much, and which feared nothing and I went to the proctor, named Villefort; he came from Marseilles, where he had been deputy. His zeal had procured him advancement, and he was said to be one of the first who had informed the government of the departure from the island of Elba.

"I said, 'My brother was assassinated yesterday in the streets of Nîmes, I know not by whom, but it is your duty to find out. You are the head of justice here, and it is for justice to avenge those she has been unable to protect.'

" 'Who was your brother?' asked he.——'A lieutenant in the Corsican battalion.'——'A soldier of the usurper then?'——'A soldier of the French army.'——'Well,' replied he, 'he has smitten with the sword, and has perished by the sword.'——'You are mistaken, monsieur,' I replied; 'he has perished by the dagger.'——'What do you want me to do?' asked the magistrate.——'I have already told you—avenge him.'——'On whom?'——'On his murderers.'——'How should I know who they are?'——'Order them to be sought for.'——'Why, your brother has been involved in a quarrel, and killed in a duel. All these old soldiers commit excesses which were tolerated in the time of the emperor, but which are not suffered now; for the people here do not like soldiers of such disorderly conduct.'——'Sir,' I replied, 'it is not for myself that I entreat your interference—I should grieve for him or avenge him; but my poor brother had a wife, and, were anything to happen to me, the poor creature would perish from want; for my brother's pay alone kept her. Pray, try and obtain a small government pension for her.'

" 'Every revolution has its catastrophes,' returned M. de Villefort; 'your brother has been the victim of this. It is a misfortune, and government owes nothing to his family. If we are to judge by all the vengeance that the followers of the usurper exercised on the partisans of the king, when, in their turn, they were in power, your brother would be to-day, in all probability, condemned to death. What has happened is quite natural, and is only the law of reprisals.'

" 'What!' cried I, 'do you, a magistrate, speak thus to me?'

" 'All you Corsicans are mad, on my honor,' replied M. de Villefort; 'they fancy that their countryman is still emperor. You have mistaken the time; you should have told me this two months ago; it is too late now. Depart instantly, or I will compel you to do so.'

"I looked at him an instant to see if, by renewed entreaties, there was anything to hope. But this man was of stone. I approached him, and said in a low voice, 'Well, since you know the Corsicans so well, you know that they always keep their word. You think that it was a good deed to kill my brother, who was a Bonapartist, because you are a royalist! Well, I, who am a Bonapartist also, declare one thing to you, which is, that I will kill you! From this moment I declare the vendetta against you; so protect yourself as well as you can, for the next time we meet your last hour has come!' And before he had recovered from his surprise, I opened the door and left the room.

"During three months I watched M. de Villefort; for three months he took not a step out of doors without my following him. At length I discovered that he went mysteriously to Auteuil. I followed him thither, and I saw him enter the house where we now are; only, instead of entering by the great door that looks into the street, he came on horse-back, or in his carriage, left the one or the other at the little inn, and entered by the gate you see there!"

Monte-Cristo made a sign with his head that he could discern amid the darkness the door to which Bertuccio alluded.

"As I had nothing more to do at Versailles, I went to Auteuil, and gained all the information I could. If I wished to surprise him, it was evident this was the spot to lie in wait for him. The house belonged to Saint-Méran, Villefort's father-in-law. Saint-Méran lived at Marseilles so that this country house was useless to him, and it was reported to be let to a young widow, known only by the name of 'the Baroness.'

"One evening, as I was looking over the wall, I saw a young and handsome woman who was walking alone in that garden, which was not overlooked by any windows, and I guessed that she was awaiting M. de Villefort. When she was sufficiently near to distinguish her features, I saw she was from eighteen to nineteen, tall and very fair. As she had a loose muslin dress on, and as nothing concealed her figure, I saw she would ere long become a mother. A few moments after, the little door was opened and a man entered; the young female hastened to meet him; they threw themselves into each other's arms, embraced tenderly, and returned together to the house. This man was M. de Villefort; I fully believed that when he went out in the night he would be forced to traverse the whole of the garden alone.

"That evening, I could have killed him; but as I was not sufficiently master of the localities, I was fearful of not killing him on the spot, and that, should his cries give the alarm, I could not escape, I put it off until the next occasion, and in order that nothing should escape me, I took a chamber looking into the street along which ran the wall of the garden. Three days after, about seven o'clock in the evening, I saw a servant on horseback leave the house at full gallop, and take the road that led to Sèvres. I conjectured he was going to Versailles, and I was not deceived. Three hours after, the man returned covered with dust, his errand was performed: and ten minutes after, another man on foot, muffled in a mantle, opened the little door of the garden, which he closed after him. I descended rapidly; although I had not seen Villefort's face, I recognized him by the beating of my heart. I crossed the street, and stopped at a post placed at the angle of the wall, and by means of which I had once before looked into the garden. This time I did not content myself with looking, but I took my knife out of my pocket, felt that the point was sharp, and sprang over the wall. My first care was to run to the door; he had left the key in it, taking the simple precaution of turning it twice in the lock. Nothing, then, preventing my escape by this means, I examined the localities. The garden formed a long square; a terrace of smooth turf extended in the middle, and at the corners were islands of trees with thick and massy foliage, that mingled with the shrubs and flowers. In order to go from the door to the house, or from the house to the door, M. de Villefort was compelled to pass by one of these clumps.

"It was the end of September; the wind blew violently. The faint glimpses of the pale moon, hidden at every instant by the masses of dark clouds that were sweeping across the sky, whitened the gravel walks that led to the house, but were unable to pierce the obscurity of the thick shrubberies, in which a man could conceal himself without any fear of discovery. I hid myself in the one nearest to the path Villefort must take; and scarcely was I there when, amidst the gusts of wind, I fancied I heard groans; he who is about to commit an assassination fancies he hears low cries perpetually ringing in his ears. Two hours passed thus, during which I imagined I heard these moans repeated. Midnight struck. As the last stroke died away, I saw a faint light shine through the windows of the private staircase by which we have just descended. The door opened, and the man in the mantle re-appeared. The terrible moment had come! but I had so long been prepared for it that my heart did not fail in the least; I drew my knife from my pocket again, opened it, and prepared myself to strike. The man in the mantle advanced toward me, but as he drew near I saw he had a weapon in his hand. I was afraid, not of a struggle, but of a failure. When he was only a few paces from me, I saw that what I had taken for a weapon was only a spade. I was still unable to divine for what reason M. de Villefort had this spade in his hands, when he stopped close to the clump, glanced around, and began to dig a hole in the earth. I then perceived that he hid something beneath his mantle, which he laid on the grass in order to dig more freely. Then, I confess, curiosity became mixed with my hatred; I wished to see what Villefort was going to do there, and I remained motionless and holding my breath. Then an idea crossed my mind, which was confirmed when I saw the procureur du roi lift from under his mantle a box, two feet long, and six or eight inches deep. I let him place the box in the hole he had made; then, whilst he stamped with his feet to remove all traces of his occupation, I rushed on him and plunged my knife into his breast, exclaiming,—'I am Giovanni Bertuccio; thy death for my brother's; thy treasure for his widow; thou seest that my vengeance is more complete than I had hoped.' I know not if he heard these words; I think he did not, for he fell without a cry, I felt his blood gush over my face, but I was intoxicated, I was delirious, and the blood refreshed, instead of burning me. In a second I had disinterred the box; then, that it might not be known I had done so, I filled up the hole, threw the spade over the wall, and rushed through the door, which I doubled-locked, carrying off the key.

I hastened to the river, sat down on the bank, and with my knife forced open the lock of the box. In a fine linen cloth was wrapped a new-born child. As I had been assistant at the hospital at Bastia, I did what a doctor would have done—I inflated the lungs by blowing air into them, and at the expiration of a quarter of an hour, I saw the breathing commence, and a feeble cry was heard. In my turn I uttered a cry, but of joy. 'God has not cursed me then,' I cried, 'since he permits me to save the life of a human creature, in exchange for the life I have taken away.' "

"And what did you do with the child?" asked Monte-Cristo. "It was an embarrassing load for a man seeking to escape."——"I had not for a moment the idea of keeping it, but I knew that at Paris there was an hospital where they receive these poor creatures. I wrapped half the linen round the child, whilst the other remained in my possession, I rang the bell, and fled with all speed. A fortnight after I was at Rogliano, and I said to Assunta,—'Console thyself, sister; Israel is dead, but he is avenged. She demanded what I meant, and when I had recounted all to her, 'Giovanni,' said she, 'you should have brought this child with you; we would have replaced the parents it has lost, have called it Benedetto, and then, in consequence of this good action, God would have blessed us.' In reply I gave her the half of the linen I had kept in order to reclaim him if we became rich."

"What letters were marked on the linen?" said Monte-Cristo.

"And H and an N, surmounted by a baron's coronet."

"Partly to drown the recollections of the past that haunted me, partly to supply the wants of the poor widow, I eagerly returned to my trade of smuggler, which had become more easy since that relaxation of the laws which always follows a revolution.

"My journeys became more and more extensive and more productive. Assunta took care of all, and our little fortune increased. One day that I was setting off on an expedition, said she: 'on your return I will give you a surprise.' I questioned her but in vain; she would tell me nothing, and I departed. When I entered the house, the first thing I beheld in the centre of Assunta's chamber was a cradle that might be called sumptuous compared with the rest of the furniture, and in it a baby of seven or eight months old. Poor Assunta had guessed all. She had profited by my absence, and furnished with the half of the linen, and having written down the day and hour at which I had deposited the child at the hospital, had set off for Paris, and had reclaimed it. No objection was raised, and the infant was given up to her.

"God made this infant the instrument of our punishment. Never did a perverse nature declare it self more prematurely; and yet it was not owing to any fault in his bringing up. He was a most lovely child. It is true that the indulgence of his mother encouraged him. One day when Benedetto was about five or six, our neighbor Wasilio, who, according to the custom of the country, never locked up his purse or his valuables—for, as your excellency knows, there are no thieves in Corsica—complained that he had lost a louis out of his purse; we thought he must have made a mistake in counting his money, but he persisted in the accuracy of his statement. One day, Benedetto, who had quitted the house since the morning, to our great anxiety, did not return until late in the evening, dragging a monkey after him, which he said he had found chained to the foot of a tree. For more than a month past, the mischievous child, who knew not what to wish for, had taken it into his head to have a monkey. A boatman, who had passed by Rogliano, and who had several of these animals, whose tricks had greatly diverted him, had, doubtless, suggested this idea to him. 'Monkeys are not found in our woods chained to trees,' said I; 'confess how you obtained this animal.' Benedetto maintained the truth of what he had said, and accompanied it with details that did more honor to his imagination than to his veracity. I became angry; he began to laugh; I threatened to strike him, and he made two steps backwards. 'You cannot beat me,' said he; 'you have no right, for you are not my father.'

"We never knew who had revealed this fatal secret, which we had so carefully concealed from him; however, it was this answer, in which the child's whole character revealed itself, that almost terrified me, and my arm fell without touching him. The boy triumphed, and this victory rendered him so audacious, that all the money of Assunta, whose affection for him seemed to increase as he became more unworthy of it, was spent in caprices she knew not how to contend against, and follies she had not the courage to prevent. When he was only eleven, he chose his companions from among the young men of eighteen or twenty, the worst characters in Bastia, or, indeed, in Corsica: and they had already, for some pieces of mischief, been several times threatened with a prosecution. I became alarmed, as any prosecution might be attended with serious consequences. I was compelled, at this period, to leave Corsica on an important expedition.

"Our expedition commenced favorably. We anchored our bark, which had a double hold, where our goods were concealed, amidst a number of other vessels that bordered the banks of the Rhône from Beaucaire to Arles. On our arrival there we began to discharge our cargo in the night, and to convey it into the town, by the help of those with whom we were connected. Whether success rendered us imprudent, or whether we were betrayed, I know not; but one evening, our vessel was surrounded, and amongst the custom-house officers I observed several gendarmes; and, as terrified at the sight of their uniforms as I was brave at the sight of any other, I sprang into the hole, opened a port, and dropped into the river, dived, and only rose at intervals to breathe, until I reached a cutting that lead from the Rhône to the canal that runs from Beaucaire to Aigues Mortes. I was now safe, for I could swim along the cutting without being seen, and I reached the canal in safety. I had designedly taken this direction. I have already told your excellency of an innkeeper of Nîmes who had set up a little inn on the road from Bellegarde to Beaucaire.

"He had, seven or eight years before this period, sold his establishment to a tailor of Marseilles, who, having almost ruined himself in his old trade, wished to make his fortune in another. Of course, we made the same arrangements with the new landlord that we had with the old; and it was of this man that I intended to ask shelter.

"This Gaspard Caderousse; he had married a woman from the village of Carconte, and whom we did not know by any other name than that of her village. She was suffering from the marsh-fever, and seemed dying by inches. As for her husband, he was a strapping fellow of forty, or five-and-forty, who had more than once, in time of danger, given ample proof of his presence of mind and courage.

"It was from Caderousse that I intended demanding shelter; and, as we never entered by the door that opened on to the road, I resolved not to break through the rule, and, climbing over the garden-hedge, I crept amongst the olive and wild fig trees; and, fearing that Caderousse might have some one there, I entered a kind of shed in which I had often passed the night, and which was only separated from the inn by a partition, in which holes had been made in order to enable us to watch an opportunity of announcing our presence. If Caderousse were alone, I would tell him the news and go back under cover of the brewing storm to see how our ship and men got on. I went into the inn hanger which was lucky, for the host had a guest.

"This guest was a jeweller to whom Caderousse had a gem to offer. He was higgling over the price, 50,000 francs, for which valuable he accounted by saying that it had been sent him by a friend of his youth, a sailor named Edmond Dantès, dead in prison. Dantès had it from a rich Englishman imprisoned with him and whose life the seaman had saved by nursing him through sickness.

"Caderousse sold the stone, and as the tempest impended persuaded the merchant to stop overnight. For my part, I was overpowered and I went to sleep where I was. The thunder lulled me and even its peals did not disturb me. But in the night I heard screams and a pistol shot.

"I climbed through a window and entered the house. In a chamber up-stairs I found Caderousse's wife dying of the gunshot and in a bed-room the jewel-peddler dead of knife-wounds. Caderousse had fled and I easily guessed that he had committed the double crime to possess himself of the jewel. Unfortunately he was luckier than I, for the shot and shrieks had been heard on the road and a force of revenue officers and the mounted police surrounded the inn and captured me, as it seemed, red handed from the deeds.

"The magistrates at Nismes committed me for trial, and in three months or so the assizes would have dealt with me. Luckily, the good priest Busoni, whose name I had caught in the talk of Caderousse and his wife as transmitter of the diamond to them, came in answer to my general appeal for a witness in my favor. It also pleased Providence to let Caderousse be caught. He was given a life-sentence on the ground of his wife having incited him, which I had related though he did not raise the pleas himself.

"I was set at liberty and thanks to Abbé Busoni interesting himself in me, I procured this situation with your lordship. I trust you are content?"

"Bertuccio, I have ever found you faithful, honest, and deserving. One fault I find with you, and that is, your not having placed sufficient confidence in me. How comes it, that having both a sister and an adopted son, you have never spoken to me of either?"——"Alas! I have still to recount the most distressing period of my life. Anxious as you may suppose I was to behold and comfort my dear sister, I lost no time in hastening to Corsica, but when I arrived at Rogliano I found a house of mourning and of desolation, the consequences of a scene so horrible that the neighbors remember and speak of it to this day. Acting by my advice, my poor sister had refused to comply with the unreasonable demands of Benedetto.

"With a gang of his fellows, he came in and to extort money from her, roasted the soles of her feet; her clothes caught fire and the ruffians fled, leaving her to her dreadful doom in the fired cottage. They took away all portable articles, and I have heard no more of the villain."

"And in what light did you view the tragical occurrence?" inquired Monte-Cristo.

"As a punishment for the crime I had committed," answered Bertuccio.

"Oh, those Villeforts are an accursed race!"——"Truly they are," murmured the count, with a most singular expression.

CHAPTER XXIX.

AN UNLIMITED ACCOUNT.

THAT same evening, upon reaching his abode in the Champs Elysées, the Count of Monte-Cristo went over the whole building with the air of one long acquainted with each nook or corner. Nor, although preceding the party, did he once mistake one door for another, or commit the smallest error when choosing any particular corridor or staircase to conduct him to a place or suite of rooms he desired to visit. Ali was his principal attendant during the somewhat late hour of his survey. Having given various orders to Bertuccio relative to the improvements and alterations he desired to make in the house, the count, drawing out his watch, said to the attentive Nubian, "It is half-past eleven o'clock; Haydée will not be long ere she arrives. Have the French attendants been summoned to await her coming?" Ali extended his hands towards the apartments destined for the fair Greek, which were at a distance from the habitable part of the dwelling, and so effectually concealed, by means of a tapestried entrance, that it would have puzzled the most curious to have divined that beyond that spot lay hid a suite of rooms fitted up with a rich magnificence worthy of the lovely being who was to tenant them.

Just at that moment voices were heard hailing the concierge. The gate opened, a carriage rolled down the avenue, and stopped at the flight of steps leading to the house. The count hastily descended, and presented himself at the already opened carriage-door to assist a young female, completely enveloped in a mantle of green and gold, to alight. The female raised the hand extended toward her to her lips, and kissed it with a mixture of love and respect. Some few words passed between them in that sonorous language in which Homer makes his gods converse. The female spoke with an expression of deep tenderness, while the count replied with an air of gentle gravity. Preceded by Ali, who carried a rose-colored light in his hand, the female, who was no other than the lovely Greek who had been Monte-Cristo's companion in Italy, was conducted to her apartments, while the count retired to the pavilion reserved for himself. In another hour every light in the house was extinguished, and it might have been thought that all its inmates slept.

CHAPTER XXX.

UNLIMITED CREDIT.

ABOUT two o'clock the following day a carriage, drawn by a pair of magnificent English horses, stopped at the door of Monte-Cristo, and a person dressed in a blue coat, with buttons of a similar color, a white waistcoat, over which was displayed a massive gold chain, brown pants, and a quantity of black hair descending so low over his eyebrows as to leave it doubtful whether it were not artificial, so little did its jetty glossiness assimilate with the deep wrinkles stamped on his features—a person, in a word, who, although evidently past fifty, desired to be taken for not more than forty, bent forwards from the carriage-door, on the panels of which were emblazoned the armorial bearings of a baron, and directed his groom to inquire at the porter's lodge whether the Count of Monte-Cristo resided there, and if he were within. While waiting, the occupant of the carriage surveyed the house, the garden so far as he could distinguish it, and the livery of the servants who passed to and fro, with an attention so close as to be somewhat impertinent. The glance of this individual was keen, but evincing rather cunning than intelligence; his lips were straight, and so thin that, as they closed, they were compressed within the mouth; his cheek-bones were broad and projecting, a never-failing proof of audacity and craftiness; while the flatness of his forehead, and the enlargement of the back of his skull, which rose much higher than his large and vulgarly-shaped ears, combined to form a physiognomy anything but prepossessing, save in the eyes of such as considered that the owner of so splendid an equipage must needs be all that was admirable and enviable, more especially when they gazed on the enormous diamond that glittered in his shirt, and the red riband that depended from his button-hole.

The groom, in obedience to his orders, tapped at the window of the janitor's lodge, saying, "Pray, does the Count of Monte-Cristo live here?"——"His excellency does reside here," replied the concierge; "but——" added he, glancing an inquiring look at Ali. Ali returned a sign in the negative. "But what?" asked the groom.

"His excellency does not receive visitors to-day."——"Then take my master's card. You'll see who master is—Baron Danglars! Be sure to give the card to the count, and say that, although in haste to attend the Chamber, my master came out of his way to have the honor of calling upon him."

"I never speak to his excellency," replied the porter; "the footman will carry your message." The groom returned to the carriage. "Well?" asked Danglars. The man, somewhat crestfallen by the rebuke he had received, detailed to his master all that had passed. "Bless me!" murmured Baron Danglars, "this must surely be a prince instead of a count by their styling him 'excellency,' and only venturing to address him by the medium of his valet-de-chambre. However, it does not signify; he has a letter of credit on me, so I must see him when he requires his money."

Then, throwing himself back in his carriage, Danglars called out to his coachman, in a voice that might be heard across the road, "To the House!"

Apprised in time of the visit paid him, Monte-Cristo had, from behind the blinds of his pavilion, as minutely observed the baron by means of an excellent spy-glass as Danglars himself had scrutinized the house, garden, and servants. "That fellow has a decidedly bad countenance," said the count, in a tone of disgust, as he shut up his glass into its ivory case. "How comes it that all do not retreat in aversion at sight of that flat, receding, serpent-like forehead, round, vulture-shaped head, and sharp-hooked nose, like the beak of a buzzard? Ali!" cried he, striking at the same time on the brazen gong. Ali appeared. "Summon Bertuccio!" said the count. Almost immediately Bertuccio entered the apartment. "Did your excellency desire to see me?" inquired he. "I did," replied the count. "You no doubt observed the horses standing a few minutes since at the door?"——"Certainly, your excellency: I noticed them for their remarkable beauty."

"Then how comes it," said Monte-Cristo, with a frown, "that, when I desired you to purchase for me the finest pair of horses to be found in Paris, you permitted so splendid a couple as those I allude to to be in the possession of any one but myself?"——"Permit me to assure your excellency," said Bertuccio, "that the horses you speak of were not to be sold when I purchased yours." Monte-Cristo shrugged up his shoulders. "It seems," said he, "that you have yet to learn that all things are to be sold to such as care to pay the price."

"My lord is not, perhaps, aware that M. Danglars gave 16,000 francs for his horses?"

"Very well! then offer him double that sum: a banker never loses an opportunity of doubling his capital."

"Is your excellency really in earnest?" inquired the steward. Monte-Cristo regarded the person who durst presume to doubt his words with the look of one equally surprised and displeased. "I have to pay a visit this evening," replied he. "I desire that these horses, with completely new harness, may be at the door with my carriage." Bertuccio bowed, and was about to retire; but when he reached the door, he paused, and then said, "At what o'clock does your excellency wish the carriage and horses ready?"

"At five o'clock," replied the count.

At the stroke of five, the steward entered.

"My horses!" said Monte-Cristo.

"They are at the door harnessed to the carriage as your excellency desired. Does my lord wish me to accompany him?"

"No, the coachman, Ali, and Baptistin will be sufficient without you." The count descended to the door of his mansion, and beheld his carriage drawn by the very pair of horses he had so much admired in the morning as the property of Danglars. As he passed them he said,—"They are extremely handsome certainly, and you have done well to purchase them, although you were somewhat remiss not to have procured them sooner."

"Indeed, your excellency, I had very considerable difficulty in obtaining them, and, as it is, they have cost an enormous price."

"Does the sum you gave for them make the animals less beautiful?" inquired the count, shrugging his shoulders.

"Nay, if your excellency is satisfied, all is as I could wish it. Whither does my lord desire to be driven?"

"To the residence of Baron Danglars."

The count descended the terrace steps, and sprang into his carriage, which, drawn by the beautiful animals so expensively purchased, was whirled along with incredible swiftness, and stopped only before the hotel of the banker. Danglars was engaged at that moment, presiding over a railway committee. But the meeting was nearly concluded when the name of his visitor was announced. As the count's title sounded on his ear he rose, and addressing his colleagues, many of whom were members of either chamber, he said,—"Gentlemen, I must pray you to excuse my quitting you thus; but a most ridiculous circumstance has occurred, which is this,—Thomson and French, the bankers at Rome, have sent to me a certain individual calling himself the Count of Monte-Cristo, who is desirous of opening an account with me to any amount he pleases. I confess this is the drollest thing I have ever met with in the course of my extensive foreign transactions, and you may readily suppose it has greatly roused my curiosity; indeed, so much did I long to see the bearer of so unprecedented an order for an unlimited credit, that I took the trouble this morning to call on the pretended count, for his title is a mere fiction—of that I am persuaded. We all know counts nowadays are not famous for their riches. But, would you believe, upon arriving at the residence of the Count of Monte-Cristo, I was very coolly informed 'He did not receive visitors that day!' Upon my word such airs are ridiculous, and befitting only some great millionaire or a capricious beauty. I made inquiries, and found that the house where the said count resides in the Champs Elysées is his own property, and certainly it was very decently kept up and arranged, as far as I could judge from the gardens and exterior of the hotel. But," pursued Danglars, with one of his sinister smiles, "an order for unlimited credit calls for something like caution on the part of the banker to whom that order is given. These facts stated, I will freely confess I am very anxious to see the individual just now announced. I suspect a hoax is intended, but the good folks who thought fit to pay it off on me knew but little whom they had to deal with. Well! well! we shall see. 'They laugh best who laugh last!' "

Having delivered himself of this pompous speech, uttered with a degree of energy that left the baron almost out of breath, he bowed to the assembled party and withdrew to his drawing-room, whose sumptuous fittings-up of white and gold had caused a great and admiring sensation. It was to this apartment he had desired his guest to be shown, fully reckoning upon the overwhelming effect so dazzling a *coup d' œil* would produce. He found the count standing before some copies that had been passed off to the banker as originals; but which, copies of the paintings of those great masters as they were, seemed to feel their degradation in being brought into juxtaposition with the gaudy gilding that covered the ceiling. The count turned round as he heard the entrance of Danglars into the room. With a slight inclination of the head, Danglars signed to the count to be seated, pointing significantly to a gilded arm-chair, covered with white satin embroidered with gold. The count obeyed. "I have the honor, I presume, of addressing M. de Monte-Cristo."

The count bowed. "And I of speaking to the Baron Danglars, Chevalier of the Légion d'Honneur, and Member of the Chamber of Deputies?"

With an air of extreme gravity, Monte-Cristo slowly enumerated the various titles engraved on the card left at his hotel by the baron.

Danglars felt all the irony contained in the address of his visitor. For a minute or two he compressed his lips as though seeking to conquer his rage ere he trusted himself to speak. Then, turning to his visitor, he said,—"You will, I trust, excuse my not having called you by your title when I first addressed you, but you are aware we are living under a popular form of government, and that I am myself a representative of the liberties of the people."

"So much so," replied Monte-Cristo, "that while preserving the habit of styling yourself baron, you have deemed it advisable to lay aside that of calling others by their titles."

"Upon my word," said Danglars, with affected carelessness, "I attach no sort of value to such empty distinctions; but the fact is, I was made baron, and also Chevalier of the Légion d'Honneur in consequence of some services I had rendered government, but——"

"You have abdicated your titles after the example set you by Montmorency and Lafayette? Well, you cannot possibly choose more noble models for your conduct."

"Why," replied Danglars, "I do not mean to say I have altogether laid aside my titles; with the servants, for instance—there I think it right to preserve my rank with all its outward forms."

"I see: by your domestics you are 'my lord,' 'the Baron!' the journalists of the day style you 'monsieur!' while your constituents term you 'citizen.'" Again Danglars bit his lips with baffled spite; he saw well enough that he was no match for Monte-Cristo in an argument of this sort, and he therefore hastened to turn to subjects more familiar to him, and calculated on having all the advantages on his side.

"Permit me to inform you, Count," said he, bowing, "that I have received a letter of advice from Thomson and French, of Rome."

"I am glad to hear it, Baron, for I must claim the privilege of so addressing you as well as your servants; I have acquired the bad habit of calling persons by their style and title from living in a country where barons are still met with, simply because persons are never suddenly elevated to a rank which is possessed only in right of ancestry. But as regards the letter of advice, I am charmed to find it has reached you; that will spare me the troublesome and disagreeable task of coming to you for money myself. You have received a regular letter of advice, therefore my cheques will be duly honored, and we shall neither of us have to go out of our way in the transaction."

"There is one slight difficulty," said Danglars, "and that consists in my not precisely comprehending the letter itself. Well, this letter gives the Count of Monte-Cristo unlimited credit on our house."

"And what is there that requires explaining in that simple fact, may I ask, Baron?"

"Merely the term *unlimited*—nothing else, certainly."——"Is not that word known in France? Is it possible that Thomson and French are not looked upon as safe and solvent bankers? Pray tell me what you think, Baron, for I feel uneasy, I can assure you, having some considerable property in their hands."

"Thomson and French are bankers of the highest repute," replied Danglars, with an almost mocking smile; "and it was not of their solvency or capability I spoke, but of the word *unlimited,* which, in financial affairs, is so extremely vague a term—that—that——"

"In fact," said Monte-Cristo, "that its sense is also without limitation."

"Precisely what I was about to say," cried Danglars. "Now what is vague is doubtful; and, says the wise man, 'where there is doubt there is danger!'"

"Meaning to say," rejoined Monte-Cristo, "that however Thomson and French may be inclined to commit acts of imprudence and folly, Baron Danglars is not disposed to follow their example."

"How so?"

"Simply thus: the banking-house of Thomson and Co. set no bounds to their engagements, while M. Danglars' has its limits; truly he is wise as the sage whose prudent apophthegm he quoted but just now."

"Sir!" replied the banker, drawing himself up with a haughty air, "the amount of my capital, or the extent and solvency of my engagements, has never yet been questioned."

"It seems, then, reserved for me," said Monte-Cristo, coldly, "to be the first to do so."

"By what right, sir?"

"By right of the objections you have raised, and the explanations you have demanded, which certainly imply considerable distrust on your part, either of yourself or me—the former most probably." Again did Danglars, by a forcible effort, restrain himself from betraying the vindictive passions which possessed his mind at this second defeat by an adversary who calmly fought him with his own weapons: his forced politeness sat awkwardly upon him, while his splenetic rage, although essaying to veil itself under a playful, jesting manner, approached at times almost to impertinence. Monte-Cristo, on the contrary, preserved a graceful suavity of demeanor, aided by a certain degree of simplicity he could assume at pleasure, and thus, calm and wholly at his ease, possessed an infinite advantage over his irascible companion.

"Well, sir," resumed Danglars, after a brief silence, "I will endeavor to make myself understood, by requesting you to inform me for what sum you propose to draw upon me?"

"Why, truly," replied Monte-Cristo, determined not to lose an inch of the ground he had gained, "my reason for desiring an 'unlimited' credit was precisely because I did not know what money I might expend."

The banker now thought it his turn to show off, and make a display of wealth and consequence. Flinging himself back therefore in his arm-chair, he said, with an arrogant and purse-proud air,—"Let me beg of you not to hesitate in naming your wishes; should you be hard pressed, the concern, of which I am the head, would not scruple to accommodate you to the amount of a million."

"A million!" retorted the count; "and what use can you possibly suppose so pitiful a sum would be to me? My dear sir, if a trifle like that could suffice me, I should never have given myself the trouble of opening an account for so contemptible an amount. A million! Excuse my smiling when you speak of a sum I am in the habit of carrying in my pocket-book or dressing-case." And with these words Monte-Cristo took from his pocket a small case containing his visiting-cards, and drew forth two orders on the treasury for 500,000 francs each, payable at sight to the bearer. A man like Danglars was wholly inaccessible to any gentler method of correction; his upstart arrogance, his ostentatious vulgarity, were only assailable by blows dealt with the force and vigor of the present shock; its effect on the banker was perfectly stunning; and as though scarcely venturing to credit his senses, he continued gazing from the paper to the count with a confused and mystified air.

"Come, come," said Monte-Cristo, "confess honestly that you have not perfect confidence in the responsibility of the house of Thomson and French—there is nothing very strange in your exercising what seems to you a necessary caution; however, foreseeing that such might be the case, I determined, spite of my ignorance in such matters, to be provided with the means of banishing all scruples from your mind, and at the same time leaving you quite at liberty to act as you please in the affair. See, here are two similar letters to that you have yourself received; the one from the house of Arstein and Eskeles, of Vienna, to Baron de Rothschild; the other drawn from Baring, of London, to M. Laffitte. Now, sir, you have but to say the word, and I will spare you all uneasiness and alarm on the subject, by presenting my letter of credit at one or other of the establishments I have named." The blow had struck home, and Danglars was entirely vanquished; with a trembling hand he took the two letters from Vienna and London from the count, who held them carelessly between his finger and thumb, as though to him they were mere every-day matters, to which he attached but very little interest. Having carefully perused the documents in question, the banker proceeded to ascertain the genuineness of the signatures, and this he did with a scrutiny so severe as might have appeared insulting to the count, had it not suited his present purpose to mislead the banker in every respect. "Well, sir," said Danglars, rising, after he had well convinced himself of the authenticity of the documents he held, and bowing, as though in adoration of a man, the thrice happy possessor of as many orders for unlimited credit on the three principal banks of Paris, "you have three signatures worth untold wealth; although your conversation and vouchers put an end to all mistrust in the affair, you must pardon me, Count, for confessing the most extreme astonishment."

"Nay, nay," answered Monte-Cristo, with the easiest and most gentlemanly air imaginable, "'tis not for such trifling sums as these to startle or astonish the banking-house of Baron Danglars. Then, as all is settled as to forms between us, I will thank you to send a supply of money to me to-morrow."

"By all means. What sum do you want?"

"Why," replied Monte-Cristo, "now that we have come to so clear an understanding, and that all distrust and suspicion are laid at rest, we may as well fix a sum as the probable expenditure of the first year:— suppose we say six millions to——"

"Six millions!" gasped out Danglars—"certainly, whatever you please."

"Then, if I should require more," continued Monte-Cristo, in a care-less, indifferent manner, "why, of course, I should draw upon you; but my present intention is not to remain in France more than a year, and during that period I scarcely think I shall exceed the sum I mentioned. However, we shall see."

"The money you desire shall be at your house by ten o'clock to-morrow morning, my lord," replied Danglars. "How would you like to have it? in gold, silver, or notes?"——"Half in gold, and the other half in bank-notes, if you please," said the count, rising from his seat.

"I must confess to you," said Danglars, "that I have hitherto imag-ined myself acquainted with the degree of fortune possessed by all the rich individuals of Europe, and still wealth such as yours has been wholly unknown to me. May I presume to ask whether you have long possessed it?"

"It has been in the family a very long while," returned Monte-Cristo, "a treasure expressly forbidden to be touched for a period, during which the compound interest has doubled the capital. The period appointed by the testator for the disposal of these riches occurred only a short time ago; and they have only been employed by me within the last few years. Your ignorance on the subject, therefore, is easily accounted for. How-ever, you will be better informed as to me and my possessions ere long." And the count, while pronouncing these latter words, accompanied them with one of those ghastly smiles that used to strike terror into poor d'Epinay.

"With your tastes, and means of gratifying them," continued Dang-lars, "you will exhibit a splendor that must effectually put us poor miserable millionaires quite in the background. If I mistake not, you are an admirer of paintings, at least I judged so from the attention you appeared to be bestowing on mine when I entered the room. But per-haps you will prefer putting off your inspection of my poor pictures, until another opportunity, when we shall be better known to each other. For the present, I will confine myself (if perfectly agreeable to you) to introducing you to Lady Danglars—excuse my impatience, but a person of your wealth and influence cannot receive too much attention." Monte-Cristo bowed, in sign that he accepted the proferred honor, and the financier immediately rang a small bell, which was answered by a servant in a showy livery. "Is Lady Danglars at home?" inquired Danglars.——"Yes, my lord," answered the man.

"And alone?"——"No, my lord, her ladyship has visitors."

"And who is with madame?—M. Debray?" inquired Danglars, with an air of indulgence and good-nature that made Monte-Cristo smile, acquainted as he was with the secrets of the banker's domestic life.

"Yes, my lord," replied the servant, "M. Debray is with madame." Danglars nodded his head; then, turning to Monte-Cristo, said, "M.

Lucien Debray is an old friend of ours, and private secretary to the Home Department. As for my wife, I must tell you, she lowered herself by marrying me, for she belongs to one of the most ancient husband in France. Her maiden name was De Servières, and her first families was Colonel the Marquis de Nargonne."

"I have not the honor of knowing Lady Danglars; but I have already met M. Lucien Debray, at the house of M. de Morcerf."

"My lady is waiting to receive you, gentlemen," said the servant, who had gone to inquire the pleasure of his mistress. "With your permission," said Danglars, bowing, "I will precede you, to show you the way."

"By all means," replied Monte-Cristo; "I follow you."

CHAPTER XXXI.

THE GREYS.

THE baron, followed by the count, traversed a long suite of apartments, in which the prevailing characteristics were heavy magnificence and the gaudiness of ostentatious wealth, until he reached the boudoir, the only one throughout the vast hotel in which any distinctive taste prevailed. The ornamental part of the fittings-up of Mdme. Danglars' boudoir had then been left entirely to herself and Lucien Debray. M. Danglars, however, while possessing a great admiration for the antique, as it was understood during the time of the Directory, entertained the most sovereign contempt for the simple elegance of his wife's favorite sitting-room, where, by the way, he was never permitted to intrude, unless, indeed, he excused his own appearance by ushering in some more agreeable visitor than himself; and even then he had rather the air and manner of a person who was himself introduced, than as being the presenter of another, his reception being either cordial or frigid, in proportion as the individual who accompanied him chanced to please or displease his lady wife.

As Danglars now entered he found the lady (who, although past the first bloom of youth, was still strikingly handsome) seated at the piano, while Lucien Debray, standing before a small work-table was turning over an album. Lucien had found time, preparatory to the count's arrival, to relate many particulars respecting him to Lady Danglars. It will be remembered that Monte-Cristo had made a lively impression on the minds of all the party at the breakfast given by

Morcerf; consequently the description given by Lucien to the baroness bore the highly-colored tinge of his own heated imagination. A most gracious welcome and unusual smile were bestowed on M. Danglars; the count, in return for his gentlemanly bow, received a formal though graceful courtesy, while Lucien exchanged with the count a sort of distant recognition, and with Danglars a free and easy nod.

"Baroness," said Danglars, give me leave to present to you the Count of Monte-Cristo, most warmly recommended to me by my correspondents at Rome. I need but mention one fact to make all the ladies in Paris court his notice, and that is, that the noble individual before you has come to take up his abode in our fine capital for one year, during which brief period he proposes to spend six millions of money—think of that! It sounds very much like an announcement of balls, fêtes, dinners, and picnic parties, in all of which I trust the count will remember us, as he may depend upon it we shall him, in all the entertainments we may give, be they great or small." Spite of the gross flattery and coarseness of this address, Lady Danglars could not forbear gazing with considerable interest on a man who had selected Paris for the scene of his princely extravagance.

"You have selected a most unfavorable moment for your first visit to our city. Paris is a horrid place in summer! Balls, parties, and fêtes are over; the Italian opera is in London; the French opera everywhere except in Paris. As for the Théâtre Français you know, of course, that it is nowhere. The only amusements left us are the indifferent races held in the Champ de Mars and Satory. Do you propose entering any horses at either of these races?"

"I assure you," replied Monte-Cristo, "my present intentions are to do whatever will tend to render my sojourn in Paris most agreeable to myself and others. I only pray I may find some kind, pitying friend who will commiserate my lamentable ignorance of such matters, and instruct me rightly to understand the habits and etiquette of this polished city."

"Are you fond of horses?"

"I have passed a considerable part of my life in the East, madam, and you are doubtless aware that the inhabitants of those climes value only two things—the fine breeding of their horses and the beauty of their females."——"Nay," said the baroness, "it would have been somewhat more gallant to have placed the ladies before the animals."

"You see, madame, how rightly I spoke when I said I required a preceptor to guide me in all my sayings and doings here." At this instant the favorite attendant of Danglars entered the boudoir; approaching her mistress, she spoke some words in an undertone. Danglars turned very pale, then exclaimed—"I cannot believe it; the thing is impossible."

"I assure you, madame," replied the woman, "it is even as I have said." Turning impatiently toward her husband, Danglers demanded, "Is this true? That when my coachman was about to prepare my carriage, he discovered that the horses had been removed from the stables without his knowledge. I desire to know what is the meaning of this?"

"Be kind enough, madame, to listen to me," said Danglars.

"Fear not my listening—ay, and attentively, too; for in truth, I am most curious to hear what explanation you propose offering for conduct so unparalleled. These two gentlemen shall decide between us; but, first I will state the case to them. Gentlemen," continued the baroness, "among the ten horses in the stables of Baron Danglars, are two that belong exclusively to me—a pair of the handsomest and most spirited creatures to be found in Paris. But at least, M. Debray, I need not give a further description, because to you my beautiful pair of dappled greys were well known. Well! I had promised Mdme. de Villefort the loan of my carriage to drive to-morrow to the Bois de Boulogne; but when my coachman goes to fetch the greys from the stables they are gone—positively gone. No doubt, M. Danglars has sacrificed them to the selfish consideration of gaining some thousands of paltry francs. Oh, how I hate and detest that money-grasping nature! Heaven defend me from all the race of mercenary speculators!"

"Madame," replied Danglars, "the horses were not sufficiently quiet for you; they were scarcely four years old, and they made me extremely uneasy on your account."

"Nonsense!" retorted the baroness; "you could not have entertained any alarm on the subject, because you are perfectly well aware that I have recently engaged a coachman who is said to be the best in Paris. But, perhaps, you have disposed of the coachman as well as the horses?"

"My dear love! pray, do not say any more about them, and I promise you another pair exactly like them in appearance, only more quiet and steady." The baroness shrugged up her shoulders with an air of ineffable contempt, while her husband, affecting not to observe it, turned towards Monte-Cristo, and said—"Upon my word, my lord, I am quite sorry I was not sooner aware of your establishing yourself in Paris."——"And wherefore?" asked the count.

"Because I should have liked to have made you the offer of these horses. I have almost given them away, as it is; but as I before said, I was anxious to get rid of them upon any terms. They were only fit for a young man; not at all calculated for a person at my time of life."

"I am much obliged by your kind intentions towards me," said Monte-Cristo: "but this morning I purchased a very excellent pair of carriage-horses, and I do not think they were dear. There they are. Come, M. Debray, you are a connoisseur, I believe, let me have your opinion upon them." As Debray walked towards the window, Danglars approached his wife. "I could not tell you before others," said he, in a low tone, "the reason of my parting with the horses; but a most enormous price was offered me this morning for them. Some madman or fool, bent upon ruining himself as fast as he can, actually sent his steward to me to purchase them at any cost; and the fact is, I have gained 16,000 francs by the sale of them. Come, don't look so angry, and you shall have 4,000 francs of the money to do what you like with, and Eugénie shall have 2,000. There, what do you think now of the affair? Wasn't I right to part with the horses?" Lady Danglars surveyed her husband with a look of withering contempt.

"What do I see?" suddenly exclaimed Debray. "Here are your horses! The very animals we were speaking of, harnessed to the count's carriage!"——"My dear, beautiful dappled greys?" demanded the baroness, springing to the window. "'Tis indeed they!" said she. Danglars looked absolutely stupified. "How very singular!" cried Monte-Cristo, with well-feigned astonishment. Lady Danglars whispered a few words in the ear of Debray, who approached Monte-Cristo, saying, "The baroness wishes to know what you paid her husband for the horses."

"I scarcely know," replied the count; "it was a little surprise prepared for me by my steward; he knew how desirous I was of meeting with precisely such a pair of horses—and—so he bought them. I think, if I remember rightly, he hinted that he had given somewhere about 30,000 francs." Debray conveyed the count's reply to the baroness. Poor Danglars looked crestfallen and discomfited; he was occupied in anticipations of the coming scene between himself and the baroness, whose threatening looks and frowning brow, like that of Olympian Jove, predicted a fearful storm. Debray, who perceived the gathering clouds, and felt no desire to witness the explosion of Mdme. Danglars' rage, suddenly recollected an appointment, which compelled him to take his leave; while Monte-Cristo, unwilling by prolonging his stay to destroy the advantages he hoped to obtain, made a farewell bow and departed, leaving Danglars to endure the angry reproaches of his wife.

Two hours afterwards, Baroness Danglars received a most flattering epistle from the count, in which he entreated her to receive back her favorite "dappled greys," protesting that he could not endure the idea of making his *début* in the Parisian world with the knowledge that his splendid equipage had been obtained at the price of a lovely woman's regrets. The horses were sent back wearing the same harness they had done in the morning; the only difference consisted in the rosettes worn on the heads of the animals being adorned with a large diamond placed in the centre of each, by order of the count.

To Danglars, Monte-Cristo also wrote, requesting him to excuse the whimsical gift of a capricious millionaire, and to beg pardon for the Eastern fashion adopted in the return of the horses.

During the evening, Monte-Cristo quitted Paris for Auteuil, accompanied by Ali. The following day, about three o'clock, a single blow struck on the gong summoned Ali to the presence of the count. "Ali," observed his master, as the Nubian entered the chamber, "you have frequently explained to me how more than commonly skilful you are in throwing the lasso, have you not?" Ali drew himself up proudly, and then returned a nod.

"It is well," said Monte-Cristo. "Then listen to me. Ere long a carriage will dash past here, drawn by the pair of dappled grey horses you saw me with yesterday; now, at the risk of your own life, you must manage to stop those horses before my door."

Ali descended to the street, and marked a straight line on the pavement immediately at the entrance of the house, and then pointed out the line he had traced to the count, who was watching him. The count patted him gently on the back, his usual mode of praising Ali, who, pleased and gratified with the commission assigned him, walked calmly towards a projecting stone forming the angle of the street and house, and, seating himself thereon, began to smoke his chibooque, while Monte-Cristo re-entered his dwelling, perfectly assured of the success of his plan. Suddenly a distant sound of rapidly-advancing wheels was heard, and almost immediately a carriage appeared, drawn by a pair of wild, ungovernable horses, who rushed forward as though urged by the fiend himself, while the terrified coachman strove in vain to restrain their furious speed.

In the vehicle was a female, apparently young, and a child of about seven or eight years of age. Terror seemed to have deprived them even of the power of uttering a cry, and both were clasped in each other's arms, as though determined not to be parted by death itself.

Then Ali knew the right moment was come, and, throwing down his chibooque, he drew the lasso from his pocket, threw it so skilfully as to catch the forelegs of the near horse in its triple fold, suffered himself to be dragged on for a few steps, by which time the tightening of the well-cast lasso had so completely hampered the furious animal as to bring it to the ground, and falling on the pole, it snapped, and therefore prevented the other animal from pursuing its headlong way. Gladly availing himself of this opportunity, the coachman leaped from his box; but Ali had promptly seized the nostrils of the second horse, and held them in his iron grasp, till the maddened beast, snorting with pain, sunk beside his companion. All this was achieved in much less time than is occupied in the recital. The brief space had, however, been sufficient for an individual, followed by a number of servants, to rush from the house before which the accident had occurred, and, as the coachman opened the door of the carriage, to take from it a lady who was convulsively grasping the cushions with one hand, while with the other she pressed to her bosom her young companion, who had lost all consciousness of what was passing.

Monte-Cristo carried them both to the salon, and deposited them on a sofa.

With a calm smile and gentle wave of the hand, Monte-Cristo signed to the distracted mother to lay aside her apprehensions; then opening a casket that stood near, he drew forth a phial composed of Bohemian glass, containing a liquid of the color of blood, of which he let fall a single drop on the child's lips. Scarcely had it reached them, ere the boy, though still pale as marble, opened his eyes, and eagerly gazed around him. At this unhoped-for sight, the wild delight of the mother equalled her former despair. "Where am I?" exclaimed she, when her first raptures at her son's recovery were past; "and to whom am I indebted for so happy a termination to my late dreadful alarm?"——— "Madame," answered the count, "you are under the roof of one who esteems himself most fortunate in having been able to save you from a further continuance of your sufferings."

"My wretched curiosity has brought all this about," pursued the lady. "All Paris rung with the praises of Mdme. Danglars' beautiful horses, and I had the folly to desire to know whether they really merited the high character given of them."

"Is it possible," exclaimed the count, with well-feigned astonishment, "that these horses belong to that lady?"

"They do, indeed. May I inquire if you are acquainted with Madame Danglars?"

"I have that honor; and my happiness at your escape from the danger that threatened you is redoubled by the consciousness that I have been the unwilling and unintentional cause of all the peril you have incurred. I yesterday purchased these horses of the baron; but as the baroness evidently regretted parting with them, I ventured to send them back to her, with a request that she would gratify me by accepting them from my hands."

"You are, then, doubtless, the Count of Monte-Cristo, of whom Hermine has talked to me so much?"

"You have rightly guessed, madame," replied the count.

"And I am Madame Héloise de Villefort." The count bowed with the air of a person who hears a name for the first time. "How grateful will M. de Villefort be for all your goodness; how thankfully will he acknowledge that to you alone it is owing that his wife and child exist! Most certainly, but for the prompt assistance of your intrepid servant, this dear child and myself must both have perished."———"Indeed, I still shudder at the recollection of the fearful danger you were placed in, as well as your interesting child."

"I trust you will not object to my offering a recompense to your noble-hearted servant, proportionate to the service he has rendered me and mine."

"I beseech you, madame," replied Monte-Cristo, "not to spoil Ali, either by too great praise or rewards. I cannot allow him to acquire the habit of expecting to be recompensed for every trifling service he may render. Ali is my slave, and in saving your life he was but discharging his duty to me."

Mdme. de Villefort made no further reply: her mind was utterly absorbed in the contemplation of the singular individual, who, from the first instant of her beholding him, had made so powerful an impression on her. During the evident preoccupation of Mdme. de Villefort, Monte-Cristo scrutinized the features and appearance of the boy she kept folded in her arms, lavishing on him the most tender endearments. The child was small for his age, and unnaturally pale. A mass of straight black hair, defying all attempts to train or curl it, fell over his projecting forehead, and hung down to his shoulders, giving increased vivacity to eyes already sparkling with a youthful love of mischief and fondness for every forbidden enjoyment. His mouth was large, and the lips, which had not yet regained their color, were particularly thin; in fact, the deep and crafty look, forming the principal character of the child's face, belonged rather to a boy of twelve or fourteen years of age than to one so young. His first movement was to free himself by a violent push from the encircling arms of his mother, and to rush forward to the casket from whence the count had taken the phial of elixir, then, without asking permission of any one, he proceeded, in all the wilfulness of a spoiled child unaccustomed to restrain either whims or caprices, to pull the corks out of all the bottles in the casket.

"Touch nothing, my little friend," cried the count, eagerly; "some of those liquids are not only dangerous to taste, but even to smell."

Mdme. de Villefort became very pale, and, seizing her son's arm, drew him anxiously toward her; but, once satisfied of his safety, she also cast a brief but expressive glance on the casket, which was not lost upon the count.

"Will you permit me to inquire," said Mdme. de Villefort, "whether you usually reside here?"

"No, I do not," replied Monte-Cristo; "it is a small place I have purchased quite lately. My place of abode is No. 30, Avenue des Champs Elysées; but I am delighted to see your countenance seems expressive of a perfect return to tranquillity. You have quite recovered from your fright, and are, no doubt, desirous of returning home. Anticipating your wishes, I have desired the same horses you came with to be put to one of my carriages, and Ali, he whom you think ugly," continued he, addressing the boy with a smiling air, "will have the honor of driving you home, while your coachman remains here to attend to the necessary repairs of your calèche. Directly that important business is concluded, I will have a couple of my own horses harnessed to convey it direct to Mdme. Danglars."

"I dare not return with those dreadful horses," said Mdme. de Villefort.

"You will see," replied Monte-Cristo, "that they will be as different as possible in the hands of Ali. With him they will be gentle and docile as lambs." Ali had, indeed, given proof of this; for, approaching the animals, he quietly harnessed the pacified animals to the count's chariot, took the reins in his hands, and mounted the box, when to the utter astonishment of those witnessing the ungovernable spirit and maddened velocity of the same horses, he was actually compelled to apply his whip in no very gentle manner ere he could induce them to start; and even then all that could be obtained from the celebrated "dappled greys," now changed into a couple of dull, sluggish, stupid brutes, was a slow, pottering pace, kept up with so much difficulty that Mdme. de Villefort was more than a couple of hours returning to her residence in the Faubourg St. Honoré.

Scarcely had the first congratulations upon her marvellous escape been gone through, than she retired to her room, ostensibly for the purpose of seeking a little repose, but in reality to write to Mdme. Danglars her account of it.

Nothing was talked of throughout the evening but the adventure. Albert related it to his mother, Château-Renaud recounted it at the Jockey Club, and Debray detailed it at length in the salons of the minister; even Beauchamp accorded twenty lines in his journal to the relation of the count's courage and gallantry, thereby placing him as the greatest hero of the day before the eyes of all the fair members of the aristocracy of France. Vast was the crowd of visitors and inquiring friends who left their names at the hôtel of Mdme. de Villefort, with the design of renewing their visit at the right moment, of hearing from her lips all the interesting circumstances of this most romantic adventure. M. de Villefort donned his best black suit, drew on a pair of new white kid gloves, ordered the servants to attend the carriage dressed in their full livery, and forthwith drove to the count's residence.

CHAPTER XXXII.

IDEOLOGY.

HATED by many, but warmly protected by others, without being really liked by anybody, M. de Villefort held a high position in the magistracy, and maintained his eminence. His drawing-room regenerated by a young wife and a daughter by his first marriage scarcely eighteen, was still one of those well-regulated Paris drawing-rooms where the worship of traditional customs and the observance of rigid etiquette were carefully maintained. A freezing politeness, a strict fidelity to government principles, a profound contempt for theories and theorists, a deep-seated hatred of ideality,—these were the elements of private and public life displayed by M. de Villefort.

M. de Villefort was not only a magistrate, he was almost a diplomatist. He had the reputation of being the least inquisitive and the least wearisome man in France. He gave a ball every year, at which he appeared for a quarter of an hour only,—that is to say, five-and-forty minutes less than a king is visible at his balls. He was never seen in any place of public resort. Occasionally, but seldom, he played at whist, and then care was taken to select partners worthy of him. Such was the man whose carriage had just now stopped before the Count of Monte-Cristo's door. The valet-de-chambre announces M. de Villefort at the moment when the count, leaning over a large table, was tracing on a map the route from St. Petersburg to China.

The Attorney General entered with the same grave and measured step employed in entering a court of justice. He was the same man, or rather the completion of the same man, whom we have heretofore seen as deputy of Marseilles. From slender he had become meagre; from pale, yellow; his deep-set eyes were now hollow, and gold spectacles, as they shielded his eyes, seemed to make a portion of his face. All his costume was black, with the exception of his white cravat, and this funeral appearance was only broken in upon by the slight line of red riband which passed almost imperceptibly through his button-hole, and which appeared like a streak of blood traced with a pencil. Although master of himself, Monte-Cristo scrutinized with irrepressible curiosity the magistrate, whose salute he returned, and who, distrustful by habit, and especially incredulous as to social marvels, was much more disposed to see in the noble stranger, as Monte-Cristo was already called, a *chevalier d'industrie,* who had come to try new ground, or some malefactor who had broken his prescribed limits, than a prince of the Holy See, or a sultan of the "Arabian Nights."

"Sir," said Villefort, in the tone assumed by magistrates in their oratorical periods, and of which they cannot, or will not, divest themselves in society,—"sir, the signal service which you yesterday rendered to my wife and son has made it a duty in me to offer you my thanks. Allow me, therefore, to discharge this duty, and to express to you all my gratitude." And as he said this, the magistrate had lost nothing of his habitual arrogance. These words he articulated in the voice of a lawyer, with the rigid inflexibility of neck and shoulders which caused his flatterers to say that he was the living statue of the law.

"Sir," replied the count, with a chilling air, "I am very happy to have been the means of preserving a son to his mother, for they say that the sentiment of maternity is the most holy of all; and the good fortune which occurred to me, monsieur, might have enabled you to dispense with a duty which, in its discharge, confers an undoubtedly great honor; for I am aware that M. de Villefort is not lavish of the favor he bestows on me, but which, however estimable, is unequal to the satisfaction which I internally experience." Villefort, astonished at this reply, which he by no means expected, started like a soldier who feels the blow levelled at him over the armour he wears, and a curl of his disdainful lip indicated that from that moment he noted in the tablets of his brain that the Count of Monte-Cristo was by no means a highly-bred gentleman. He glanced around, in order to seize on something on which the conversation might turn, and seem to fall easily. He saw the map which Monte-Cristo had been examining when he entered, and said,—"You seem geographically engaged, sir? It is a rich study for you, who, as I learn, have seen as many lands as are delineated on this map."

"Yes, sir," replied the count; "I have sought to make on the human race, taken as a mass, what you practice every day on individuals—a physiological study. I have believed it was much easier to descend from the whole to a part than to ascend from a part to the whole. It is an algebraic axiom, which makes us proceed from a known to an unknown quantity, and not from an unknown to a known; but sit down, sir, I beg of you."

Monte-Cristo pointed to a chair, which the caller was obliged to take the trouble to move forward himself, whilst the count merely fell back into his own, on which he had been kneeling when M. Villefort entered. Thus the count was half-way turned toward his visitor, having his back toward the window, his elbow resting on the geographical chart which afforded the conversation for the moment,—a conversation which assumed, as had done those with Danglars and Morcerf, a turn analogous to the persons, if not the situation. "Ah, you philosophize," replied Villefort, after a moment's silence, during which, like a wrestler who encounters a powerful opponent, he took breath; "well, sir, really, if, like you, I had nothing else to do, I should seek a more amusing occupation."

"Why, in truth, sir," was Monte-Cristo's reply, "man is but an ugly caterpillar for him who studies him through a solar microscope; but you said, I think, that I had nothing else to do. Now, really, let me ask, sir, have you?—do you believe you have anything to do? or to speak in plain terms, do you really think that what you do deserves being called anything?"

Villefort's astonishment redoubled at this second thrust so forcibly made by his strange adversary. It was a long time since the magistrate had heard a paradox so strong, or rather, to say the truth more exactly, it was the first time he had ever heard of it. He exerted himself to reply. "Sir," he responded, "you are a foreigner, and I believe you say yourself that a portion of your life has been spent in Oriental countries: thus, then, you are not aware how human justice, so expeditious in barbarous countries, takes with us a prudent and well-studied course."——"Oh, yes—yes, I do, sir, it is the *pede claudo* of the ancients. I know all that, for it is with the justice of all countries especially that I have occupied myself—it is with the criminal procedure of all nations that I have compared natural justice, and I must say, sir, that it is the law of primitive nations, that is, the law of retaliation, that I have most frequently found to be according to the law of God."

"But with what motive have you studied all this?" inquired Villefort, astonished. Monte-Cristo smiled.

"Really, sir," he observed, "I see that in spite of the reputation which you have acquired as a superior man, you contemplate everything in the material and vulgar view of society, beginning with man, and ending with man—with eyes fixed on the social organizations of nations, you see only the springs of the machine, and lose sight of the sublime workman who makes them act; I say that you do not recognize before you and around you any but those placemen whose brevets have been signed by the minister or the king; and that the men whom God has put above those titulars, ministers, and kings, by giving them a mission to follow out, instead of a post to fill—I say that they escape your narrow, limited ken. It is thus that human weakness fails, from its debilitated and imperfect organs."

"Then," said Villefort, more and more amazed, and really supposing he was speaking to a mystic or a madman, "you consider yourself as one of extraordinary beings?"

"And why not?" said Monte-Cristo, coldly.

"Your pardon, sir," replied Villefort, quite astounded, "upon my word, you overcome me. I really never heard a person speak as you do."

"Because you remain eternally encircled in a round of general conditions, and have never dared to raise your wing into those upper spheres which God has peopled with invisible or marked beings."

"Ah!" said Villefort, smiling, "I confess I should like to be warned when one of these beings is in contact with me."

"You have been served as you desire, monsieur, for you have been warned just now, and I now again warn you."

"Then you yourself are one of these marked beings?"

"Yes, monsieur, I believe so; for until now, no man has found himself in a position similar to mine. The dominions of kings are limited either by mountains or rivers, or a change of manners, or an alteration of language. My kingdom is bounded only by the world, for I am neither an Italian, nor a Frenchman, nor a Hindoo, nor an American, nor a Spaniard—I am a cosmopolitan. No country can say it saw my birth. God alone knows what country will see me die. I adopt all customs, speak all languages. You believe me to be a Frenchman, for I speak French with the same facility and purity as yourself. Well, Ali, my Nubian, believes me to be an Arab; Bertuccio, my steward, takes me for a Roman; Haydée, my slave, thinks me a Greek. You may, therefore, comprehend, that being of no country, asking no protection from any government, acknowledging no man as my brother, not one of the scruples that arrest the powerful, or the obstacles which paralyze the weak, paralyze or arrest me. I have only two adversaries—I will not say two conquerors, for with perseverance I subdue even them, though they are time and distance. There is a third, and the most terrible—that is my condition as a mortal being. This alone can stop me in my onward career, and before I have attained the goal at which I aim, for all the rest I have calculated. What men call the chances of fate—namely, ruin, change, circumstances—I have anticipated them all; and if any of these should overtake me, yet they will not overwhelm me. Unless I die, I shall always be what I am, and therefore it is that I utter the things you have never heard, even from the mouths of kings—for kings have need, and other persons have fear of you. For who is there who does not say to himself, in society as incongruously organized as ours, 'Perhaps some day I shall have to do with the Public Prosecutor!'"

"But can you not say that, sir? For the moment you become an inhabitant of France, you are naturally subjected to the French law."

"I know it, sir," replied Monte-Cristo; "but when I visit a country I begin to study, by all the means which are available, the men from whom I may have anything to hope or to fear, until I know them as well, perhaps better, than they know themselves. It follows from this, that the Attorney General be he who he may, with whom I should have to deal, would assuredly be more embarrassed than I should."

"That is to say," replied Villefort, with hesitation, "that human nature being weak, every man, according to your creed, has committed faults."——"Faults or crimes," responded Monte-Cristo, with a negligent air.

"And that you alone, amongst the men whom you do not recognize as your brothers—for you have said so," observed Villefort, in a tone that faltered somewhat—"you alone are perfect."

"No, not perfect," was the count's reply, "only impenetrable, that's all. But let us leave off this strain, sir, if the tone of it is displeasing to you; I am no more disturbed by your justice than are you by my second-sight."

"No! no!—by no means," said Villefort, who was afraid of seeming to abandon his ground. "No; by your brilliant and almost sublime conversation you have elevated me above the ordinary level; we no longer talk, we rise to dissertation. But I will say to you, rude as it may seem, 'My brother, you sacrifice greatly to pride, you may be above others, but above you there is God.'"

"Above us all, sir," was Monte-Cristo's response, in a tone and with an emphasis so deep, that Villefort involuntarily shuddered. "I have my pride for men—serpents always ready to erect themselves against every one who may pass without crushing them. But I lay aside that pride before God, who has taken me from nothing to make me what I am."

"Then, my lord, I admire you," said Villefort, who for the first time in this strange conversation, used the aristocratical title to the unknown personage. "Yes, and I say to you, if you are really strong, really superior, really pious, or impenetrable, which you were right in saying amounts to the same thing—yet be proud, sir, that is the characteristic of predominance—yet you have unquestionably some ambition."

"I too, as happens to every man once in his life, have been taken by Satan into the highest mountain in the earth, and when there he showed me all the kingdoms of the earth, and as he said before, so said he to me, 'Child of earth, what wouldst thou have to make thee adore me?' I reflected long, for a gnawing ambition had long preyed upon me, and then I replied, 'Listen,—I have always heard tell of Providence, and yet I have never seen Him, nor anything that resembles Him, or which can make me believe that He exists. I wish to be Providence myself, for I feel that the most beautiful, noblest, most sublime thing in the world, is to recompense and punish.' Satan bowed his head, and groaned. 'You mistake,' he said; 'Providence does exist, only you have never seen Him, because the child of God is as invisible as the parent. You have seen nothing that resembles Him, because He works by secret springs, and moves by hidden ways. All I can do for you is to make you one of the agents of that Providence.' The bargain was concluded. I may sacrifice my soul, but what matters it?" added Monte-Cristo. "If the thing were to do again, I would again do it."

Villefort looked at Monte-Cristo with extreme amazement. "My lord," he inquired, "have you any relatives?"

"No sir, I am alone in the world."

"So much the worse."——"Why?" asked Monte-Cristo.

"Because then you might witness a spectacle calculated to break down your pride. There is something to fear besides death, old age, and madness. For instance, there is apoplexy—that lightning-stroke which strikes but does not destroy you, and yet after which all is ended. Come, if so you will, and continue this conversation at my house, any day you may be willing to see an adversary capable of understanding and anxious to refute you, and I will show you my father, M. Noirtier de Villefort, one of the most fiery Jacobins of the French Revolution; most remarkable audacity, seconded by a most powerful organization—a man who, perhaps, has not, like yourself, seen all the kingdoms of the earth, but who has helped to overturn one of the most powerful; in fact, a man who, like you, believed himself one of the envoys—not of God—but of a Supreme Being; not of Providence, but of Fate. Well, sir, the rupture of a blood-vessel on the lobe of the brain has destroyed all this—not in a day, not in an hour—but in a second. Noirtier, so redoubted, was the next morning *poor old Noirtier,* the helpless old man, at the tender mercies of the weakest creature in the household, that is, his grandchild, Valentine; a dumb and frozen carcass, in fact, who only lives without suffering, that time may be given to his frame to decompose without his consciousness of his decay."

"Alas, sir!" said Monte-Cristo, "this spectacle is neither strange to my eye nor my thought. I am something of a physician, and have, like my fellows, sought more than once for the soul in living and in dead matter; yet, like Providence, it has remained invisible to my eyes, although present to my heart. A hundred writers have made the comparison, and yet I can well understand that a father's sufferings may effect great changes in a son. I will call on you, sir, since you bid me contemplate, for the advantage of my pride, this terrible spectacle, which must spread so much sorrow throughout your house."

"It would have done so unquestionably, had not God given me so large a compensation. In presence of the old man, who is dragging his way to the tomb, are two children just entering into life—Valentine, the daughter by my first wife, Mdlle. Renée de Saint-Méran, and Edward, the boy whose life you have this day saved."

"And what do you argue from this compensation, sir?" inquired Monte-Cristo.

"My reasoning is," replied Villefort, "that my father, led away by his passions, has committed some fault unknown to human justice, but marked by the justice of God. That God, desirous in His mercy to punish but one person, has visited this justice on him alone." Monte-Cristo, with a smile on his lips, had yet a groan at his heart, which would have made Villefort flee had he but heard it. "Adieu, sir," said the magistrate, who had risen from his seat; "I leave you, bearing a remembrance of you—a remembrance of esteem, which I hope will not be disagreeable to you when you know me better; for I am not a man to bore my friends, as you will learn. Besides, you have made an eternal friend of Mdme. de Villefort." The count bowed, and contented himself with seeing Villefort to the door of his cabinet, the proctor being escorted to his carriage by two footmen, who, on a signal from their master, followed him with every mark of attention. When he had gone, Monte-Cristo drew a hard breath from his oppressed bosom, and said,— "Enough of this poison, let me now seek the antidote."

CHAPTER XXXIII.

THE MORREL FAMILY.

In a short time the count reached No. 7 in the Rue Meslay. The house was of white stone, and in a small court before it were two small beds full of beautiful flowers. In the janitor that opened the gate the count recognized Coclès; but as he had but one eye, and that eye had considerably weakened in the course of nine years, Coclès did not so readily recognize the count. The house, raised above the kitchens and cellars, had, besides the ground-floor, two stories and attics. The whole of the property, consisting of an immense workshop, two pavilions at the bottom of the garden, and the garden itself, had been purchased by Emmanuel, who had seen at a glance that he could make a profitable speculation of it. He had reserved the house and half the garden, and building a wall between the garden and the workshops, had let them upon lease with the pavilions at the bottom of the garden. So that for a trifling sum he was as well lodged, and as perfectly shut out from observation, as the inhabitants of the finest mansion. The whole of the second story was set apart for Maximilian; it was precisely the same as his sister's apartments, except that the breakfast-parlor was changed into a billiard-room, where he received his friends. He was superintending the dressing down of his horse, and smoking his cigar at the entrance of the garden, when the count's carriage stopped at the door.

"The Count of Monte-Cristo?" cried Morrel, throwing away his cigar and hastening to the carriage; "I should think we would see him. Ah! a thousands thanks, for not having forgotten your promise." And the young officer shook the count's hand so warmly, that the latter could not be mistaken as to the sincerity of his joy, and he saw that he had been expected with impatience, and was received with pleasure. "Come, come!" said Maximilian, "I will serve as your guide: such a man as you ought not to be introduced by a servant. My sister is in the garden plucking the dead roses; my brother reading his two papers, within five steps of her, or wherever you see Mdme. Herbault, you have only to look within a circle of four yards and you will find M. Emmanuel, and 'reciprocally,' as they say at the Polytechnic School."

At the sound of their steps a young woman of twenty, dressed in a silk wrap, and busily engaged in plucking the dead leaves off the splendid rose-tree, raised her head. This female was Julie, who had become, as the clerk of the house of Thomson and French had predicted, Mdme. Emmanuel Herbault. She uttered a cry of surprise at the sight of a stranger, and Maximilian began to laugh. "Don't disturb yourself, Julie," said he. "The count has only been two or three days in Paris, but he already knows what a woman of fashion of the Swampward is, and if he does not, you will show him."

"Ah!" returned Julie, "it is unfair in my brother to bring you thus, but he never has any regard for his poor sister. Penelon!" An old man, who was digging busily at one of the beds of roses, stuck his spade in the earth, and approached, cap in hand, and striving to conceal a quid of tobacco thrust into his cheek. A few locks of grey mingled with his hair, which was still thick and matted, whilst his bronzed features and determined glance announced the old sailor who had braved the heat of the equator and the storms of the tropics. "I think you hailed me, Mdlle. Julie?" said he. "Penelon," replied Julie, "go and inform M. Emmanuel of this gentleman's visit, and Maximilian will conduct him to the parlor." Then, turning to Monte-Cristo, continued she, "I hope you will permit me to leave you for a few minutes," and without awaiting any reply, disappeared behind a clump of trees, and entered the house by a lateral alley.

"I am sorry to see," observed Monte-Cristo to Morrel, "that I cause no small disturbance in your house."

"Look there," said Maximilian, laughing; "there is her husband changing his jacket for a coat. I assure you, you are well known in the Rue Meslay."

"Your family appears to be a very happy one!" said the count, as if speaking to himself.

"Oh, yes, I assure you, they want nothing than can render them happy; they are young and cheerful, they are tenderly attached to each other, and with twenty-five thousand francs a year they fancy themselves as rich as Rothschild."

"Five-and-twenty thousand francs is not a large sum, however," replied Monte-Cristo, with a tone so sweet and gentle, that it went to Maximilian's heart like the voice of a father; "but they will not be content with that: your brother-in-law is a barrister? or doctor?"

"He was a merchant, and had succeeded to the business of my poor father. M. Morrel, at his death, left 500,000 francs which were divided between my sister and myself, for we were his only children. Her husband, who, when he married her, had no other patrimony than his noble probity, his first-rate ability, and his spotless reputation, wished to possess as much as his wife. He labored and toiled until he had amassed 250,000 francs; six years sufficed to achieve this object. Oh, I assure you, it was a touching spectacle to see these young creatures, destined by their talents for higher stations, toiling together, and, unwilling to change any of the customs of their paternal house, taking six years to accomplish that which innovators would have effected in two or three. Marseilles resounded with their well-earned praises."

Maximilian had scarcely finished his story, during which the count's heart had seemed ready to burst, when Emmanuel entered, fully dressed. He saluted the count with the air of a man aware of the rank of his guest; then, after having led Monte-Cristo round the little garden, he returned to the house. A large vase of Japan porcelain, filled with flowers, stood in the parlor. Julie, suitably dressed, and her hair arranged (she had accomplished this feat in less than ten minutes), received the count on his entrance. Everything in this charming retreat, from the warble of the birds to the smile of the mistress, breathed tranquillity and repose.—"Madame," said the count at length. "I pray you to excuse my emotion, which must astonish you, accustomed to the happiness I meet here; but satisfaction is so new a sight to me, that I could never be weary of looking at yourself and your husband."

"We are very happy, monsieur," replied Julie; "but we have also known unhappiness, and few have ever undergone more bitter sufferings than ourselves." The count's features displayed an expression of the most intense curiosity.

"Our magnificence makes you smile, Count," said Maximilian, who had followed him with his eyes. "No, no," returned Monte-Cristo, pale as death, pressing one hand on his heart to still its throbbings, whilst with the other he pointed to a glass shade, beneath which a silken purse lay on a black velvet cushion. "I was wondering what could be the use of this purse, which contains a paper at one end and at the other a large diamond."—"Count," replied Maximilian, with an air of gravity, "those are our most precious family treasures."

"The stone seems very brilliant," answered the count.

"Oh, my brother does not allude to its value, although it has been estimated at 100,000 francs; he means, that the articles contained in this purse are the relics of the angel I spoke of just now."

"This I do not comprehend; and yet I may not ask for an explanation, madame," replied Monte-Cristo, bowing. "Pardon me, I had no intention of committing an indiscretion."

"Sir," returned Maximilian, raising the glass cover, and respectfully kissing the silken purse, "this has touched the hand of a man who saved my father from suicide, us from ruin, and our name from shame and disgrace,—a man by whose matchless benevolence we, poor children, doomed to want and wretchedness, can at present hear every one envying our happy lot. This letter" (as he spoke, Maximilian drew a letter from the purse and gave it to the count)—"this letter was written by him the day that my father had taken a desperate resolution, and this diamond was given by the generous unknown to my sister as her dowry." Monte-Cristo opened the letter, and read it with an indescribable feeling of delight. It was the letter written (as our readers know) to Julie, and signed "Sinbad the Sailor." "Unknown you say, is the man who rendered you this service—unknown to you?"

"Yes; we have never had the happiness of pressing his hand," continued Maximilian. "We have supplicated heaven in vain to grant us this favor, but all the affair has had a mysterious direction we cannot comprehend—all has been guided by a hand invisible, but powerful as that of an enchanter."

"Oh!" cried Julie, "I have not lost all hope of some day kissing that hand, as I now kiss the purse which he has touched. Four years ago, Penelon, the old sailor you saw in the garden, and who has become gardener—Penelon, when he was at Trieste, saw on the quay an Englishman, who was on the point of embarking on board a yacht, and he recognized him as the person who called on my father the 5th of June, 1829, and who wrote me this letter on the 5th of September. He felt convinced of his identity, but he did not venture to address him."

"An Englishman!" said Monte-Cristo, who grew uneasy at the attention with which Julie looked at him. "An Englishman, you say?"

"Yes," replied Maximilian, "an Englishman, who represented himself as the confidential clerk of the house of Thomson and French, at Rome. It was this that made me start when you said the other day, at M. de Morcerf's that Messrs. Thomson and French were your bankers. That happened, as I told you, in 1829. Tell me, did you know this Englishman?"

"But you tell me, also, that the house of Thomson and French have constantly denied having rendered you this service?"——"Yes."

"Then it is not probable that this Englishman may be some one who, grateful for a kindness your father had shown him, and which he himself had forgotten, has taken this method of requiting the obligation?"

"Everything is possible on such an occasion, even a miracle."

"What was his name?" asked Monte-Cristo.

"He gave no other name," answered Julie, looking earnestly at the count, "than that at the end of his letter—'Sinbad the Sailor.'"

"Which is evidently not his real name, but a fictitious one."

Then, noticing that Julie was struck with the sound of his voice,—
"Tell me," continued he, "was he not about my height, perhaps a little taller, his chin imprisoned, to use the word, in a high cravat; his coat closely buttoned up, and constantly taking out his pencil?"

"Oh, do you then know him?" cried Julie, whose eyes sparkled with joy.

"No," returned Monte-Cristo, "I only guessed. I knew a Lord Wilmore, who was constantly doing actions of this kind."

"Without revealing himself?"

"He was an eccentric being. If Lord Wilmore was your unknown benefactor, I fear you will never again see him. I parted from him, two years ago, at Palermo, and he was then on the point of setting out for the most remote regions; so that I fear he will never return."

"And he told you nothing?"

"Not a word."

"And yet you instantly named him."

"Ah, in such a case one supposes——"

"Sister, sister," said Maximilian, coming to the count's aid, "the count is quite right. Recollect what our excellent father so often told us, 'It was no Englishman that thus saved us.'" Monte-Cristo started "What did your father tell you, M. Morrel?" said he, eagerly.

"My father thought that this action had been miraculously performed—he believed that a benefactor had arisen from the grave to save us. Oh, it was a touching superstition, monsieur, and although I did not myself believe it, I would not for the world have destroyed my father's faith in it. How often did he muse over it and pronounce the name of a dear friend—a friend lost to him forever; and on his death-bed, when the near approach of eternity seemed to have illumined his mind with supernatural light, this thought, which had until then been but a doubt, became a conviction, and his last words were, 'Maximilian, it was Edmond Dantès!'"

At these words the count's paleness, which had for sometime been increasing, became alarming; he could not speak; he looked at his watch like a man who has forgotten the time; said a few hurried words to Mdme. Herbault, and pressing the hands of Emmanuel and Maximilian, —"Madame," said he, "I trust you will allow me to visit you from time to time; I value your friendship, and feel grateful to you for your welcome, for this is the first time for many years that I have thus yielded to my feelings;" and he hastily quitted the apartment.

"This Count Monte-Cristo is a singular man," said Emmanuel.

"Yes," answered Maximilian, "but I feel sure he has an excellent heart, and that he likes us."

"His voice went to my heart," observed Julie; "and two or three times I fancied I had heard it before."

CHAPTER XXXIV.

PYRAMUS AND THISBE.

ABOUT the centre of the Saint Honoré ward, and at the back of one of the most distinguished-looking mansions in this rich neighborhood, extended a large garden. This noble resort had fallen into utter disuse, from the period when the proprietors (and many years had elapsed since then) had confined themselves to the possession of the mansion with its thickly-planted court-yard, opening into the Faubourg Saint-Honoré, and the garden shut in by this gate, which formerly communicated with a fine kitchen-garden of about an acre in extent, let temporarily to some market-gardeners.

Horticulture seemed, however, to have been abandoned in the deserted kitchen-garden; and where the most choice and delicate of fruits and vegetables once reared their heads, a scanty crop of alfalfa alone bore evidence of its being deemed worthy of cultivation. A small, low door gave egress from the walled space we have been describing into the projected street, the ground having been abandoned as unproductive by its various renters, and had now fallen so completely in general estimation as to return not even a fraction of the poor rent it had originally paid. Towards the house chestnut trees rose high above the wall, without in any way affecting the growth of other luxuriant shrubs and flowers that eagerly pressed forward to fill up the vacant spaces, as though asserting their right to enjoy the boon of light and air also. At one corner, where the foliage became so thick as almost to shut out day, a large stone bench and sundry rustic seats indicated that this sheltered spot was either in general favor or particular use by some inhabitant of the hotel, which was faintly discernible through the dense mass of verdure that partially concealed it, though situated but a hundred paces off.

On the evening of one of the warmest spring days, might be seen, negligently thrown upon the stone bench, a book, a parasol, and a work-basket, from which hung a partly-embroidered cambric handkerchief, while, at a little distance from these articles was a girl standing close to the iron gate, endeavoring to discern something on the other side by means of the openings in the planks, whilst the earnestness of her attitude, and the fixed gaze with which she seemed to seek the object of her wishes, proved how much her feelings were interested in the matter. At that instant the little side-door, leading from the waste ground to the street, was noiselessly opened, and a tall powerful young man, dressed in a common grey blouse and velvet cap, but whose carefully-arranged hair, beard, and moustaches, all of the richest and glossiest black, but ill accorded with his plebeian attire, after casting a rapid glance around him, in order to assure himself he was unobserved, entered by this door, and carefully closing and securing it after him, proceeded with a hurried step towards the iron gate.

At sight of him she expected, though probably not under such a costume, the female we have before mentioned started in terror, and was about to make a hasty retreat. But the eye of love had already seen, even through the narrow chinks of the wooden palisades, the movement of the white robe, and observed the fluttering of the blue sash fastened around the slender waist of his fair neighbor. Pressing his lips close to the envious planks that prevented his further progress, he exclaimed, "Fear nothing, Valentine—it is I!" Again the timid girl found courage to return to the gate, saying, as she did so, "And wherefore come you so late to-day? It is almost the dinner-hour, and I have been compelled to exercise my utmost skill to get rid of the incessant watchfulness of my stepmother, as well as the espionage of my maid, who, no doubt, is employed to report all I do and say. Nor has it cost me a little trouble to free myself from the troublesome society of my brother, under pretence of coming hither to work undisturbed at my embroidery, which, by the way, I am in no hurry to finish. So pray excuse yourself as well as you can for having made me wait, and after that, tell me why I see you in so singular a dress, that at first I did not recognize you."

"Dearest Valentine!" said the young man, "let me tell you I have chosen a trade. Tired out with ranging fields and scaling walls, and seriously alarmed at the idea suggested by yourself, that if caught hovering about here your father would very likely have me sent to prison as a thief, a sort of thing not very desirable for an officer in the French army, whose continual presence in a place where no warlike projects could be supposed to account for it might well create surprise; so from a captain of Spahis I have become a gardener, and, consequently, adopted the costume of my calling."

"I beseech of you, Maximilian, to cease trifling, and tell me what you really mean."

"Simply, that having ascertained that the piece of ground on which I stand was to let, I made application for it, was readily accepted by the proprietor, and am now master of this fine crop of alfalfa! Think of that, Valentine! Henceforth we have nothing to fear. I am on my own ground, and have an undoubted right to place a ladder against the wall, and to look over when I please, without having any apprehensions of being taken off by the police as a suspicious character. I may also enjoy the precious privilege of assuring you of my fond, faithful, and unalterable affection, whenever you visit your favorite bower, unless, indeed, it offends your pride to listen to professions of love from the lips of a poor working man." A faint cry of mingled pleasure and surprise

escaped from the lips of Valentine, who almost instantly said, in a sad-
dened tone, as though some envious cloud darkened the joy which
illumined her heart, "Alas! no, Maximilian, this must not be, for many
reasons! We should presume too much on our own strength, and, like
others, perhaps, be led astray by our blind confidence in each other's
prudence."

"How can you for an instant entertain so unworthy a thought, dear
Valentine? Have I not, from the first blessed hour of our acquaintance,
schooled all my words and actions to your sentiments and ideas? And
you have, I am sure, the fullest confidence in my honor. You told me,
my dear Valentine, that you were engaged to M. d'Epinay, and that your
father was resolved upon completing the match, and that from his will
there was no appeal, as M. de Villefort was never known to change a
determination once formed. I kept in the background, as you wished.
You have permitted me to converse with you from time to time, Valentine, but forbidden my ever following you in your walks or elsewhere—
have I not obeyed?"

"It is indeed most true," said Valentine, as she passed the end of her
slender fingers through a small opening in the planks, thus permitting
her lover to press his lips to the taper finger that almost instantly disappeared, "and you are a true and faithful friend; a brother. I, who
have no friend but yourself upon earth, neglected and forgotten by my
father, harassed and persecuted by my stepmother, and left to the
sole companionship of a paralyzed and speechless old man, whose withered hand can no longer press mine, and whose eye alone converses
with me, while, doubtless, however fixed, chilled his frame, there still
lingers in his heart the warmest tenderness for his poor grandchild. Oh,
how bitter a fate is mine, to serve either as a victim or an enemy to all
who are stronger than myself, while my only friend and supporter is
but a living corpse! Indeed, indeed, Maximilian, I am very miserable,
and you are right to love me for myself alone."

"Dear Valentine," replied the young man, deeply affected, M. Franz
is not expected to return home for a year to come, I am told; in that
time many favorable and unforeseen chances may befriend us. Let us,
then, hope for the best: hope is so sweet a comforter."

"Maximilian," answered she; "do you not see what a poor, helpless
being I am, almost a stranger and an outcast in my father's house, where
even he is seldom seen; whose will has been thwarted, and spirits broken,
from the age of ten years, beneath the iron rod so sternly exercised over
me; oppressed, mortified, and persecuted, day by day, hour by hour,
minute by minute; no person has cared for, even observed my sufferings, nor have I ever breathed one word on the subject save to yourself.
My father abandons me from utter indifference, while my stepmother
detests me with a hatred so much the more terrible as it is veiled
beneath a continual smile."

"Hate you, sweet Valentine!" exclaimed the young man; "how is it possible for any one to do that?"

"Alas!" replied the weeping girl, "I am obliged to own that my stepmother's aversion to me arises from a very natural source—her overweening love for her own child, my brother Edward."

"But why should it?"——"And I much fear she envies me the fortune I already enjoy in right of my mother, and which will be more than doubled at the death of St.-Mérans, whose sole heiress I am. Mdme. de Villefort has nothing of her own, and hates me for being so richly endowed. Alas! how gladly would I exchange the half of this wealth for the happiness of at least sharing my father's love! God knows, I would prefer sacrificing the whole, so that it would obtain me a happy and affectionate home."

"Poor Valentine!"

"I seem to myself as though living a life of bondage, yet at the same time am so conscious of my own weakness that I fear to break the restraint in which I am held, lest I fall utterly powerless and helpless. Then, too, my father is not a person whose orders may be infringed with impunity; protected as he is by his high position and firmly-established reputation for talent and unswerving integrity, no one could oppose him; he is all-powerful with even his king; you he would crush at a word, and myself he would cause to expire of terror at his feet. Dear Maximilian, believe me when I assure you that I attempt not to resist my father's commands more on your account than my own; for, though I could willingly sacrifice myself, I would not peril your safety."

"How is that?" inquired the young man, perceiving that Valentine hesitated.

"Tell me truly, Maximilian, whether in former days, when our fathers dwelt at Marseilles, there ever existed any misunderstanding between them?"

"Not that I am at all aware of," replied the young man, "unless, indeed, any ill-feeling might have arisen from their being of opposite parties—your father being, as you know, a zealous partisan of the Bourbons, while mine was wholly devoted to the emperor; there could not possibly be any other difference between them. But now that I have answered your questions to the best of my power and knowledge, tell me, dearest, why you ask?"

"I will," replied his fair companion, "for it is but right you should know all. Then I must begin by referring to the day when your being made an officer of the Legion of Honor was publicly announced in the papers. We were all sitting in the apartments of my grandfather, M. Noirtier; M. Danglars was there also—you recollect M. Danglars, do you not, Maximilian, the banker, whose horses ran away with my stepmother and little brother, and very nearly killed them? While the rest of the company were discussing the approaching marriage of Mademoiselle Danglars, I was occupied in reading the paper aloud to my grandfather; but when I came to the paragraph concerning you, although I had done nothing else but read it over to myself all the morning (you know you had told me all about it the previous evening), I felt so happy, and yet so nervous, at the idea of pronouncing your beloved name aloud, and before so many people, that I really think I should have passed it over, but for the fear that my so doing might create suspicions as to the cause of my silence; so I summoned up all my courage, and read it as firmly and steadily as I could."

"Dear Valentine!"

"Well, would you believe it? directly my father caught the sound of your name he turned round quite hastily, and, like a poor silly thing, I was so persuaded that every one must be as much affected as myself by the utterance of your name, that I was not surprised to see my father start, and almost tremble; but I even thought (though that surely must have been a mistake) that M. Danglars underwent a similar emotion. He almost immediately rose and took his leave; then, for the first time, I observed the agitation of my grandfather, and I must tell you, Maximilian, that I am the only person capable of discerning emotion in the paralyzed frame of my poor afflicted relative. And I suspected that the emotion in his presence (for no one ever cares to refrain from saying and doing what they like before the dear old man, without the smallest regard to his feelings) had made a strong impression on his mind; for, naturally enough, it must have pained him to hear the emperor he so devotedly loved and served spoken of in that depreciating manner."

"The name of M. Noirtier," interposed Maximilian, "is celebrated throughout Europe; he was a statesman of high standing; and I know not whether you are aware, Valentine, that he took a leading part in every Bonapartean conspiracy set on foot during the restoration of the Bourbons."

"Oh, I have often heard whispers of things that seem to me most strange—the father a Bonapartist, the son a Royalist; what can have been the reason of so singular a difference in parties and politics? But to resume my story; I turned towards my grandfather, as though to question him as to the cause of his emotion; he looked expressively at the newspaper I had been reading. 'What is the matter, dear grandfather?' said I, 'are you pleased?' He gave me a sign in the affirmative. 'Oh, then, you were glad to hear that M. Morrel (I dared not pronounce the dear name of Maximilian) had been made an officer of the Legion of Honor; was that it, dear grandpapa?' He signified assent in a way that convinced me he was more than glad—that he was delighted; only think of the poor old man's being so pleased to think that you, who were a perfect stranger to him, had been made an officer of the Legion of Honor! Perhaps, though, it was a mere whim on his part, for he is almost falling into a second childhood! but, for all that, I love him dearly, and pray that he may long be spared to me."

"How singular," murmured Maximilian.

"Hush!" cried Valentine, suddenly, "conceal yourself!—Go, go! Some one comes!" Maximilian leaped at one bound into his crop of lucerne, which he commenced pulling up in the most pitiless manner, under the pretext of being occupied in weeding it.

"Mademoiselle! mademoiselle!" exclaimed a voice from behind the trees. "Madame is searching for you everywhere; there are visitors in the drawing-room."

"Who is it!" inquired Valentine, much agitated, "are they ladies?"

"Oh, no, mademoiselle! I believe it is some grand prince, or a duke, or a king, perhaps; stay, now I remember, they said he was the Count of Monte-Cristo, and that he wished particularly to see you."

"I will come directly," said Valentine aloud. The name caused an electric shock to the individual on the other side of the iron gate, on whose ear the *"I will come!"* of Valentine sounded the usual parting knell of all their interviews. "Now, then," said Maximilian, as, tired with his unusual employment, he stopped to rest himself, by leaning on the handle of a spade he had taken care to furnish himself with, "would I give much to know how it comes about that the Count of Monte-Cristo is acquainted with M. de Villefort."

CHAPTER XXXV.

TOXICOLOGY.

IT was really the Count of Monte-Cristo who had just arrived at Mdme. de Villefort's for the purpose of returning her husband's visit, and at this name, as may be easily imagined, the whole house was in confusion. Mdme. de Villefort, who was alone in her drawing-room when the count was announced, desired that her son might be brought thither instantly to renew his thanks to the count; and Edward, who heard nothing and nobody talked of for two whole days but this great personage, made all possible haste to come to him, not from obedience to his mother, not from any feeling of gratitude to the count, but from sheer curiosity, and that he might make some remark, by help of which he might find an opportunity for saying one of those saucy quips which made his mother say,—"Oh, that sad child! but pray excuse him, he is really *so* acute."

After the first and usual civilities, the count inquired after M. de Villefort. "My husband dines with the chancellor," replied the young lady; "he has just gone, and I am sure he'll be exceedingly sorry not to have had the pleasure of seeing you before he went." Two visitors who were there when the count arrived, having gazed at him with all their eyes, retired after that reasonable delay which politeness admits and curiosity requires. "Ah! what is your sister Valentine doing?" inquired Mdme. de Villefort of Edward; "tell some one to bid her come here, that I may have the honor of introducing her to the count."

"You have a daughter, then, madame?" inquired the count; "very young, I presume?"

"The daughter of M. de Villefort," replied the young wife, "by his first marriage, a fine well-grown girl."

"But glum," interrupted Master Edward, snatching the feathers out of the tail of a splendid parroquet that was screaming on its gilded perch, in order to make a plume for his hat. Mdme. de Villefort merely cried,—"Silence, Edward!" She then added,—"This young madcap is, however, very nearly right, and merely re-echoes what he has heard me say with pain a hundred times; for Mademoiselle de Villefort is, in spite of all we can do to rouse her, of a melancholy disposition and taciturn habit, which frequently injure the effect of her beauty. But what detains her? go, Edward, and see."

"Because they are looking for her where she is not to be found."

"And where are they looking for her?"

"With grandpapa Noirtier."

"And do you think she is not there?"

"She is under the great chestnut-tree," replied the spoiled brat, as he gave, in spite of his mother's cries, live flies to the parrot. Mdme. de Villefort stretched out her hand to ring, intending to direct her waiting-maid to the spot where she would find Valentine, when the young lady herself entered the apartment. She appeared much dejected; and any person who considered her attentively might have observed the traces of recent tears in her eyes.

Valentine was a tall and graceful girl of nineteen years of age, with bright chestnut hair, deep blue eyes, and that languishing air so full of distinction which characterized her mother. Her white and slender fingers, her pearly neck, her cheeks tinted with varying hues, gave her at the first view the aspect of one of those lovely Englishwomen who have been so poetically compared in their manner to a swan admiring itself. She entered the apartment, and seeing near her stepmother the stranger of whom she had already heard so much, saluted him without any girlish awkwardness, or even lowering her eyes, and with an elegance that redoubled the count's attention. He rose to return the salutation. "Mdlle. de Villefort, my daughter-in-law," said Mdme. de Villefort to Monte-Cristo, leaning back on her sofa and motioning toward Valentine with her hand.

"And Lord Monte-Cristo, king of China, emperor of Cochin-China," said the young imp, looking slyly towards his sister.

Mdme. de Villefort at this really did turn pale, and was very nearly angry with this household plague, who answered to the name of Edward; but the count, on the contrary, smiled, and appeared to look at the boy complacently, which caused the maternal heart to bound again with joy and enthusiasm.

"But, madame," replied the count, continuing the conversation, and looking by turns at Mdme. de Villefort and Valentine, "have I not already had the honor of meeting you before? I could not help thinking so just now; the idea came over my mind, and as the young lady entered the sight of her was an additional ray of light thrown on a confused remembrance; excuse me the remark."——"I do not think it likely, sir; Mdlle. de Villefort is not very fond of society, and we very seldom go out," said the young lady.

"Then it was not in society that I met with you or madame, or this charming little merry boy. Besides, the Parisian world is entirely unknown to me, for, as I believe I told you, I have been in Paris but very few days. No,—but, perhaps you will permit me to call to mind—stay!" The count placed his hand on his brow as if to collect his thoughts. "No —it was somewhere—away from here—it was at Perusa on a holiday, when chance brought us together; you, Mdme. de Villefort, and your son; I now remember having had the honor of meeting you."

I perfectly well remember Perusa sir, and the hotel, and the feast to which you allude," said Mdme. de Villefort, "but in vain do I tax my memory, of whose treachery I am ashamed, for I really do not recall to mind that I ever had the pleasure of seeing you before."

"I will assist your memory, madame," continued the count; "the day had been burning hot; you were waiting for horses, which were delayed in consequence of the festival. This lady was walking in the shade of the garden, and your son disappeared in pursuit of a bird."

"And I caught it, mamma, don't you remember?" interrupted Edward, "and I pulled three such beautiful feathers out his tail."

"You, madame, remained under the arbor formed by the vine; do you not remember, that whilst you were seated on a stone bench, and whilst as I told you, Mdlle. de Villefort and your young son were absent, you conversed for a considerable time with somebody?"

"Yes, in truth, yes," answered the young lady, turning very red, "I do remember conversing with an individual wrapped in a long woollen mantle; he was a medical man, I think."——"Precisely so, madame; this man was myself; for a fortnight I had been at that hotel, during which period I had cured my valet-de-chambre of a fever, and my landlord of the jaundice, so that I really acquired a reputation as a skilful physician. We discoursed a long time, madame, on different subjects; of Perugino, of Raffaelle, of manners, customs, of the famous *aquatofana,* of which they had told you, I think you said, that individuals in Perusa had preserved the secret."

"Yes, true," replied Madame de Villefort, with a kind of uneasiness, "I remember now."

"I do not recollect now all the various subjects of which we discoursed, madame," continued the count, with perfect calmness; "but I perfectly remember that, falling into the error which others had entertained respecting me, you consulted me as to the health of Mdlle. de Villefort."——"Yes, really, sir, you were in fact a medical man," said Mdme. de Villefort, "since you had cured the sick."

"A wit would reply to you, madame, that it was precisely because I was not, that I had cured my patients; for myself, I am content to say to you that I have studied chemistry and the natural sciences somewhat deeply, but still only as an amateur, you understand."——At this moment the clock struck six. "It is six o'clock," said Mdme. de Villefort, evidently agitated. "Valentine, will you not go and see if your grandpapa will have his dinner?" Valentine rose, and saluting the count, left the apartment without replying a single word.

"Oh, madame!" said the count, when Valentine had left the room, "was it on my account that you sent Mdlle. de Villefort away?"

"By no means," replied the lady quickly; "but this is the hour when we give to M. Noirtier the repast which supports his sad existence. You are aware, sir, of the deplorable condition of my husband's father?"

"Yes, madame, M. de Villefort spoke of it to me—paralysis, I think."

"Alas, yes! there is an entire want of movement in the frame of the poor old gentleman; the mind alone is still active in this human machine, and that is faint and flickering, like the light of a lamp about to expire. But excuse me, sir, for talking of our domestic misfortunes; I interrupted you at the moment when you were telling me that you were a skilful chemist."

"No, madame, I did not say so much as that," replied the count, with a smile; "quite the contrary. I have studied chemistry because, having determined to live in eastern climates, I have been desirous of following the example of King Mithridates."

"*Mithridates, rex Ponticus,*" said the young scamp, as he tore some beautiful portraits out of a splendid album, "the individual who breakfasted every morning with a cup of poison."

"Edward, you naughty boy!" exclaimed Mdme. de Villefort, snatching the mutilated book from the urchin's grasp; "you are positively past bearing; you really disturb the conversation: go, leave us, and join your sister Valentine in dear grandpapa Noirtier's room."

"The album," said Edward, sulkily.

"How dare you tear out the drawings?"

"Oh, it amuses me."——"Go—go directly."

"I won't go unless you give me the album," said the boy, seating himself doggedly in an arm-chair, according to his habit of never giving way.——"Take it, then, and pray disturb us no longer," said Mdme. de

Villefort, giving the album to Edward, who then went toward the door, led by his mother. The count followed her with his eyes.

"Let us see if she shuts the door after him," he muttered. Mdme. de Villefort closed the door carefully after the child, the count appearing not to notice her; then casting a scrutinizing glance around the chamber; the young wife returned to her chair, in which she seated herself. "Allow me to observe, madame," said the count, with that kind tone he could assume so well, "you are really very severe with that dear clever child."——"Oh, sometimes severity is quite necessary," replied Mdme. de Villefort, with all a mother's real firmness.

"It was his Cornelius Nepos that Master Edward was repeating when he referred to King Mithridates," continued the count, "and you interrupted him in a quotation which proves that his tutor has by no means neglected him, for your son is really advanced for his years."

"The fact is," answered the mother, agreeably flattered, "he has great aptitude, and learns all that is set before him. He has but one fault, he is somewhat wilful; but really, on referring for the moment to what he said, do you truly believe that Mithridates used these precautions, and that these precautions were efficacious?"

"I think so, madame, because I—I, who now address you, have made use of them, that I might not be poisoned at Naples, at Palermo, and at Smyrna—that is to say, on three several occasions of my life, when, but for these precautions, I must have lost my life."

"Yes, I remember now your mentioning to me at Perusa something of this sort."

"Indeed! did I?" said the count, with an air of surprise, remarkably well counterfeited. "I really did not remember it."——"I inquired of you if poisons acted equally, and with the same effect, on men of the North as on men of the South; and you answered me that the cold and sluggish habits of the North did not present the same aptitude as the rich and energetic temperaments of the natives of the South."

"And that is the case," observed Monte-Cristo, "but I perceive I have not much to teach you. Allow me to compliment you on your knowledge; such learning is very rare amongst ladies."

"Oh, I am aware of that," said Mdme. de Villefort; "but I have a passion for the occult sciences, which speak to the imagination like poetry; the two favorite studies of my youth were botany and mineralogy; and subsequently, when I learned that the use of simples frequetnly explained the whole history of a people, and the entire life of individuals in the East, as flowers betoken and symbolize a love affair, I have regretted I was not a man, that I might have been a Flamel, a Fontana, or a Cabanis."

"And the more, madame," said Monte-Cristo, "as the Orientals do not confine themselves, as did Mithridates, to make a cuirass of his poisons, but they also make them a dagger. Science becomes, in their hands, not only a defensive weapon, but still more frequently an offensive one; the one serves against all their physical sufferings, the other against all their enemies; with opium, with belladonna, with brucæd, snake-wood, the cherry-laurel, they put to sleep all those who would arouse them."

"Then," remarked Mdme. de Villefort, "they have discovered the secret of the famous *aquatofana* at Perusa."

"Eh, indeed, does mankind ever lose anything? The arts are removed, and make a tour of the world;—things change their names, and the vulgar do not follow them—that is all; but there is always the same result. Poison acts particularly on one organ or the other—one on the stomach, another on the brain, another on the intestines. Well, the poison brings on a cough, the cough an inflammation of the lungs, or some other complaint catalogued in the book of science, which, however, by no means precludes it from being mortal; and if it were not, would be sure to become so, thanks to the remedies applied by foolish doctors, who are generally bad chemists, and which will act in favor of or against the malady, as you please; and then there is a human being killed according to all the rules of art and skill, and of whom justice learns nothing, as was said by a terrible chemist of my acquaintance, the worthy Abbé Adelmonte of Taormine, in Sicily, who has studied these national phenomena very profoundly."

"It is quite frightful, but deeply interesting," said the young lady, motionless with attention. "I thought, I must confess, that these tales were inventions of the middle ages."——"Yes, no doubt, but improved upon by ours. What is the use of time, encouragements, medals, crosses, Monthyon prizes, &c., &c., if they do not lead society toward more complete perfection? Yet man will never be perfect until he learns to create and destroy: he does know how to destroy, and that is half way on the road."

"So," added Mdme. de Villefort, constantly returning to her object, "the poisons of the Borgias."

"Were objects of art, madame, and nothing more," replied the count. "Do you suppose that the real *savant* addresses himself stupidly to the mere individual? By no means. Science loves eccentricities, leaps and bounds, trials of strength, fancies, if I may be allowed so to term them."

"But," said she, "however skilfully it is prepared, crime is always crime; and if it avoid human scrutiny, it does not escape the eye of God. The Orientals are stronger than we are in cases of conscience, and, very prudently, have no hell—that is the point."

"Really, madame, this is a scruple which naturally must occur to a pure mind like yours, but which would easily yield before sound reasoning. The bad side of human thought will always be defined by the paradox of Rousseau, you know, the mandarin who is killed at 500 leagues distance by raising the tip of the finger. Man's whole life passes in doing these things, and his intellect is exhausted by reflecting on them. You will find very few persons who will go and brutally thrust a knife in the heart of a fellow-creature, or will administer to him, in order to remove him from the surface of the globe on which we move with life and animation, that quantity of arsenic of which we just now talked. Such a thing is really out of rule—eccentric or stupid. But if instead of committing an ignoble assassination, if you merely and simply remove from your path the individual who is in your way, and that without shock or violence; if there be no blood, no groans, no convulsions, and, above all, that horrid and compromising moment of accomplishing the act, then one escapes the clutch of the human law, which says to you, 'Do not disturb society!' This is the mode in which they manage these things, and succeed in eastern climes, where there are grave and phlegmatic persons who care very little for the questions of time in conjunctures of importance."

"Yet conscience remains?" remarked Mdme. de Villefort, in an agitated voice, and with a stifled sigh.

"Yes," answered Monte-Cristo, "happily, yes, conscience does remain; and if it did not, how wretched we should be! After every action requiring exertion, it is conscience that saves us, for it supplies us with a thousand good excuses, of which we alone are judges; and these reasons, how excellent soever in producing sleep, would avail us but very little before a tribunal, when we were tried for our lives.

"Thus was Lady Macbeth served by her conscience, when she sought to give her son, and not her husband (whatever Shakespeare may say), a throne. Ah, maternal love is a great virtue, a powerful motive—so powerful that it excuses a multitude of things, even if, after Duncan's death, Lady Macbeth had been at all pricked by her conscience."

Mdme. de Villefort listened with avidity to these appalling maxims and horrible paradoxes, delivered by the count with that ironical simplicity peculiar to him. After a moment's silence, the lady inquired, "Do you know," she said, "that you are a very terrible reasoner, and that you look at the world through a somewhat distempered medium? Have you really measured the world by scrutinies, or through alembics and crucibles? For, truth to say, you are a great chemist, and the elixir you administered to my son, which recalled him to life almost instantaneously——"

"Oh, do not place any reliance on that, madame; *one* drop of that elixir sufficed to recall life to a dying child, but three drops would have impelled the blood into his lungs in such a way as to have produced most violent palpitation; six would have suspended his respiration, and caused cyncope more serious than that in which he was; ten would have destroyed him. You know, madame, how suddenly I snatched him from those phials which he so imprudently touched?"

"Is it, then, so terrible a poison?"

"Oh, no! In the first place, let us agree that the word poison does not exist, because in medicine use is made of the most violent poisons, which become, according as they are made use of, most salutary remedies."

"What, then, is it?"

"A skilful preparation of my friend's the worthy Abbé Adelmonte, who taught me the use of it."

"As for me, so nervous, and so subject to fainting-fits, I should require a Doctor Adelmonte to invent for me some means of breathing freely and tranquillizing my mind, in the fear I have of dying some fine day of suffocation. In the meanwhile, as the thing is difficult to find in France, and your abbé is not probably disposed to make a journey to Paris on my account, I must continue to use the anti-spasmodics of M. Planché; and mint and Hoffman's drops are amongst my favorite remedies."

"But I," said Monte-Cristo, rising as he spoke—"I am gallant enough to offer it you."

"Oh, sir!"

"Only remember one thing—a small dose is a remedy, a large one is poison. One drop will restore life, as you have witnessed; five or six will inevitably kill, and in a way the more terrible inasmuch as, poured into a glass of wine, it would not in the slightest degree affect its flavor. But I say no more, madame; it is really as if I were advising you." The clock struck half-past six, and a lady was announced, a friend of Mdme. de Villefort who came to dine with her.——"If I had the honor of seeing you for the third or fourth time, instead of only for the second," said Mdme. de Villefort; "if your friend, instead of only yours under an obligation I should insist on detaining you to dinner, and not allow myself to be daunted by a first refusal."

"A thousand thanks, madame," replied Monte-Cristo, "but I have an engagement which I cannot break: I have promised to escort to the Académie a Greek princess of my acquaintance who has never seen your grand opera, and who relies on me to conduct her thither."

"Adieu, then, sir, and do not forget my recipe."

"Ah, in truth, madame, to do that I must forget the hour's conversation I have had with you, which is indeed impossible." Monte-Cristo bowed and left the house. Mdme. de Villefort remained immersed in thought. "He is a very strange man," she said, "and in my opinion is himself the Adelmonte he talks about." As to Monte-Cristo, the result had surpassed his utmost expectations. "Good!" said he, as he went away; "this is a fruitful soil, and I feel certain that the seed sown will not be cast on barren ground." Next morning, faithful to his promise, he sent the prescription requested.

CHAPTER XXXVI.

THE OPERA.

THE pretext of an opera engagement was so much the more feasible, as there chanced to be on that very night a more than ordinary attraction at the opera.

The curtain rose, as usual, to an almost empty house, it being one of the absurdities of Parisian fashion never to appear at the opera until after the commencement of the performances. Finally, the door of the state box opened, and Mdme. Danglars, accompanied by her daughter, entered, escorted by Lucien Debray, who assiduously conducted them to their seats.

"Ha, ha!" said Château-Renaud, "here come some friends of yours, Viscount! What are you looking at there? don't you see they are trying to catch your eye?" Albert turned round, just in time to receive a gracious wave of the fan from the baroness; as for Mdlle. Eugénie, she scarcely vouchsafed to waste the glances of her black eyes even upon the business of the stage. "I tell you what, my dear fellow," said Château-Renaud, "I cannot imagine what objection you can possibly have to Mdlle. Danglars—that is, setting aside her want of ancestry and somewhat inferior rank, which, by the way, I don't think you care very much about. Now, barring all that, I mean to say she is a deuced fine girl!"

"Handsome, certainly," replied Albert, "but not to my taste, which I confess, inclines to a softer, gentler, and more feminine style than that possessed by the young lady in question."

"Bless my heart!" exclaimed Château-Renaud, who, because he had seen his thirtieth summer, fancied himself duly warranted in assuming a sort of paternal air with his more youthful friend, "you young people are never satisfied: why, what would you have more? your parents have chosen you a bride who might serve as the living model of Diana, and yet you are not content."

"No, for that very resemblance affrights me; I should have liked something more in the manner of the Venus of Milo or Capua; but this Diana, continually surrounded by her nymphs, gives me a sort of alarm, lest she should some day entail on me the fate of Actæon."

And, indeed, it required but one glance of Mdlle. Danglars to comprehend the justness, as well as nature, of Morcerf's remark—"she was certainly handsome," but her beauty was of too marked and decided a character to please a fastidious taste. But that which completed the almost masculine look Morcerf found so little to his taste, was a dark mole, of much larger dimensions than these freaks of nature generally are, placed just at the corner of her mouth; and the effect tended to increase the expression of unbending resolution and self-dependence that formed the characteristics of her countenance. The rest of Eugénie's person was in perfect keeping with the head just described; she, indeed, reminded you of Diana, as Château-Renaud observed, but with a more haughty and resolute air. As regarded her attainments, the only fault to be found with them was the same that a fastidious connoisseur might have found with her beauty, that they were somewhat too erudite and masculine for so young a person.

The curtain fell almost immediately after the entrance of Mdme. Danglars into her box, the band quitted the orchestra for the accustomed half-hour's interval allowed between the acts, and the audience were left at liberty to promenade or pay and receive visits in their respective boxes. Morcerf and Château-Renaud were amongst the first to avail themselves of this permission. For an instant the idea struck Mdme. Danglars that this eagerness on the part of the young viscount arose from his impatience to join her party, and she whispered her expectations to her daughter, that Albert was hurrying to pay his respects to them. Eugénie, however, merely returned a dissenting movement of the head, while, with a cold smile, she directed the attention of her mother to an opposite box, situated on the first circle, in which sat the Countess Guiccioli, and where Morcerf had just made his appearance. "So we meet again, my traveling friend, do we?" cried the countess, extending her hand to him with all the warmth and cordiality of an old acquaintance; "it was really very good of you to recognize me so quickly, and still more so to bestow your first visit on me."

"Be assured," replied Albert, "that if I had been aware of your arrival in Paris, and had known your address, I should have paid my respects to you long ere this. Allow me to introduce my friend, Baron de Château-Renaud, one of the rare specimens of real gentlemen now to be found in France, and from whom I have just learned that you were a spectator of the races in the Champ-de-Mars, yesterday."

"Well, then," pursued Madame G——, with considerable animation, "you can probably tell me to whom belonged the winner of the Jockey-Club stakes?"

"I am sorry to say I cannot," replied the baron; "and I was just asking the same question of my friend Albert."

"You must know I felt so interested for the splendid roan horse, with his elegant little rider, so tastefully dressed in a pink satin jacket and cap, that I could not help praying for their success with as much earnestness as though the half of my fortune were at stake; and when I saw them outstrip all the others, and come to the winning-post in such a gallant style, I actually clapped my hands with joy. Imagine my surprise, when, upon returning home, the first object I met on the staircase was the identical jockey in the pink jacket! I concluded that, by some singular chance, the owner of the winning horse must live in the same hotel as myself; but, lo! as I entered my apartments I beheld the very gold cup awarded as a prize to the unknown horse and rider. Inside the cup was a small piece of paper, on which were written these words— 'From Lord Ruthven to Countess Guiccioli.' ''

"Precisely; I was sure of it," said Morcerf, "the owner of the horse was Lord Ruthven, our Lord Ruthven—the Vampire of the Argentino!"

"Mercy upon me!" exclaimed the countess; "but what makes you so convinced of his being the winner of the Jockey-Club prize?"

"Was not the winning horse entered by the name of Vampa, the name of the celebrated bandit by whom I was made prisoner? Now I argue from the horse and bandit bearing the same singular name, that the count was the person to whom the unknown horse belonged."

"But what could have been his motive for sending the cup to me?"

"In the first place, because I had spoken much of you to him, as you may believe; and in the second, because he delighted to see his country-woman take so lively an interest in his success."

"I trust and hope you never repeated to the count all the foolish remarks we used to make about him?"

"I should not like to affirm upon oath that I have not. Besides, his presenting you the cup under the name of Lord Ruthven proves his knowledge of the comparison instituted between himself and that individual."

"And so this singular being is in Paris? and what effect does he produce?"

"Why," said Albert, "certainly, during the first week of his arrival here, he was the great lion of the day; nothing else was thought of or talked about but the wonderful Count of Monte-Cristo and his extraordinary actions; then the coronation of the Queen of England took place, followed almost immediately afterwards by the robbery of Mdlle. Mars' diamonds; and two such interesting events turned public attention into other channels."

"My good fellow," said Château-Renaud, "the count happens to be so great a favorite of yours, that you treat him as carefully and delicately as though he were your best and most intimate friend. Do not believe what Albert is telling you, madame; so far from the sensation excited in the Parisian circles by the appearance of the Count of Monte-Cristo having abated, I take upon myself to declare that it is as strong as ever. His first astounding act upon coming amongst us was to present a pair of horses, worth 32,000 francs, to Mdme. Danglars; his second, the almost miraculous preservation of Mdme. de Villefort's life; now it seems that he has carried off the prize awarded by the Jockey Club! I therefore assert and maintain, in despite of whatever Morcerf may advance, that not only is the count the object of universal remark, interest, and curiosity, at this present moment, but also that he will continue to be so while he pleases to exhibit an eccentricity of conduct and action which, after all, may be his ordinary mode of amusing himself as well as the world."

At this moment the bell rang to announce the drawing up of the curtain for the second act.

The young men bowed, and quitted the box. Upon reaching their stalls, they found the whole of the audience standing up and directing their gaze towards the box formerly possessed by the ambassador of Russia. Following the universal example, the friends perceived that a gentleman in deep black, had just entered, accompanied by a female dressed after the Eastern style; the lady was young and surpassingly beautiful, while the rich magnificence of her attire drew all eyes upon her. "By heavens!" said Albert, "it is Monte-Cristo himself, with his fair Greek!"

The strangers were, indeed, no other than the count and Haydée. The sensation excited by the beauty and dazzling appearance of the latter soon communicated itself to every part of the theatre, and even ladies leaned forward from the boxes to admire the superb diamonds worn by the young Greek as they played and glittered among the cut-glass lustres. The second act passed away during one continued buzz of voices—one deep whisper—intimating that some great and universally-interesting event had occurred; all eyes—all thoughts were occupied with the young and beautiful female, whose gorgeous apparel and splendid jewels threw an air of insignificance upon all the fair visitants of the theatre; the stage was utterly neglected—all seemed to consider the contemplation of so much loveliness far more deserving attention. Upon this occasion an unmistakable sign from Mdme. Danglars intimated her desire to see Albert in her box directly the curtain fell on the second act, and neither the politeness nor good taste of Morcerf would permit his neglecting an invitation so unequivocally given. At the close of the act he therefore proceeded to the baroness's box. Having bowed to the two ladies, he extended his hand to Debray. By the baroness he was most graciously welcomed, while Eugénie received him with her accustomed coldness.

"My dear fellow!" said Debray, "you have just come in the very nick of time to help a fellow-creature regularly beaten and at a standstill. There is madame overwhelming me with questions respecting the count; she insists upon it that I can tell her his birth, education, and parentage, where he came from, and whither he is going. Being no conjuror, I was wholly unable to do this; so, by way of getting out of the scrape, I said, 'Ask Morcerf; he has got the whole history of his beloved Monte-Cristo at his fingers' ends;' whereupon the baroness made you a sign to come hither, and now I leave the solution of her questions in your hands; for my own part, I care nothing about the count or his mysterious doings."

"I am very sure no nabob of our time would have sent me a pair of horses worth 32,000 francs, wearing on their heads four diamonds at 5,000 francs each."

"He seems to have a mania for diamonds," said Morcerf, smiling; "and I verily believe that, like Potemkin, he keeps his pockets filled, for the sake of strewing them along the road, as Hop o' my Thumb did his pebbles."

"Perhaps he has discovered some mine," said Mdme. Danglars. "I suppose you know he has an order for unlimited credit on the baron's banking establishment?"

"I was not aware of it," replied Albert, "but I can readily believe it."

"And, further, that he stated to M. Danglars his intention of only staying a year in Paris, during which time he proposed to spend six millions. He must be the Shah of Persia, traveling *incog.*"

"Have you remarked the extreme beauty of that young female by whom he is accompanied, M. Lucien?" inquired Eugénie.

"Who is this young person, M. Morcerf?" inquired Eugénie; "does anybody know?"

"Allow me to state," said Albert, "that I can give you very tolerable information on that subject, as well as on most points relative to the singular person of whom we are now conversing—the young female is a Greek. I know one thing more, namely, that she is a musician, for one day that I chanced to be breakfasting with the count, I heard the sound of a guzla—it is impossible it could have been touched by any other finger than her own."

"I must try and persuade M. Danglars to invite him to a ball or dinner, or something of the sort, that he may be compelled to ask us in return."——"What!" said Debray, laughing; "do you know this mysterious count is a bachelor?"

"You have ample proof to the contrary, if you look opposite," said the baroness, as she laughingly pointed to the beautiful Greek.

"No, no!" exclaimed Debray; "that is not his wife, he told us himself she was his slave; do you not recollect, Morcerf, his telling us so at your breakfast?"

"Well, then," said the baroness, "if slave she be, she has all the air and manner of a princess."

"Of the Arabian Nights?"

"If you like; but tell me, my good Lucien, what is it that constitutes a princess? gold, silver, and jewels? and our Greek beauty there is one blaze of diamonds; I doubt if any queen's could equal them."

"To me she seems overloaded," observed Eugénie; "she would look far better if she wore fewer, and we should then be able to see her finely-formed throat and wrists."

"See, how the artist peeps out!" exclaimed Mdme. Danglars; "My poor Eugénie, you must conceal your passion for the fine arts."

"I admire all that is beautiful in art or nature," returned the young lady.

"What do you think of the count?" inquired Debray; "he is not much amiss, according to my ideas of good looks."

"The count?" repeated Eugénie, as though it had not occurred to her to observe him sooner; "the count? oh!—he is so dreadfully pale."

"I quite agree with you," said Morcerf; "and it is in that very paleness that consists the secret we want to find out. The Countess Guiccioli insists upon it he is a vampire."

"Is that she, mamma?" asked Eugénie; "almost opposite to us with that profusion of beautiful light hair?"

"Yes, yes, there she is!" cried Mdme. Danglers; "you should go and bring your Count of Monte-Cristo to us."——"What for?" asked Eugénie.

"Strange girl!" murmured the baroness.

"Adieu! I sacrifice myself, remember that," said Albert, as he made his parting bow. Just as he was passing the count's box, the door opened, and Monte-Cristo came forth. After giving some directions to Ali, who stood in the lobby, the count observed Albert, and, taking his arm, walked onwards with him. Carefully closing the box-door, Ali placed himself before it, while a crowd of wondering spectators assembled round the unconscious Nubian.

"Upon my word, you are at this moment the most celebrated and fashionable person in Paris."

"Really? and what has procured me so flattering a distinction?"

"What? why, yourself, to be sure! You give away horses worth thousands; you save the lives of ladies of high rank and beauty; you send thoroughbreds to contest the prize of the Jockey Club, the horses being rode by boys not larger than marmots; then, when you have carried off the golden trophy of victory, instead of setting any value on it, you give it to the first handsome woman you think of!"

"And who has filled your head with all this nonsense?"

"Why, in the first place, I heard it from Mdme. Danglars, who, by the by, is dying to see you in her box, or to have you seen there by others; secondly, I learned it from Beauchamp's journal; and thirdly, from my own imagination. Why, if you sought concealment, did you call your horse Vampa?"——"That was an oversight, certainly," replied the count; "but tell me, does the Count de Morcerf never visit the Opera? I have been looking for him, but without success."

"He will be here to-night."——"In what part of the house?"——"In the baroness's box, I believe."——"Is the charming young female with her—her daughter?"——"Yes."——"Indeed! then I congratulate you." Morcerf smiled. "We will discuss that subject at length some future time," said he. "But what think you of the music?"

"Your orchestra is rather too noisy."

"Let me recommend you, my dear Viscount, to come and sup with me whenever you wish to be regaled with music really worth listening to."——"I have already enjoyed that treat when breakfasting with you," said Morcerf.

"Ah, then, I suppose you heard Haydée's guzla; the poor exile frequently beguiles a weary hour in playing over to me the airs of her native land." Morcerf did not pursue the subject, and Monte-Cristo himself fell into a silent reverie. The bell rang at this moment for the rising of the curtain.

The third act had now commenced; and during its progress the Count de Morcerf made his appearance in the box of Mdme. Danglars. Morcerf was not one of those persons whose aspect would create either interest or curiosity in a place of public amusement; his presence, therefore, was wholly unnoticed, save by the occupants of the box in which he had just seated himself. The quick eye of Monte-Cristo, however, marked his coming; and a slight though meaning smile passed over his lips as he did so. Haydée, whose soul seemed centred in the business of the stage, like all unsophisticated natures, delighted in whatever addressed itself to the eye or ear.

The third act passed off as usual, after which the curtain again fell, and the spectators poured forth from the theatre into the lobbies and salon. The count also, quitting his, proceeded at once to the box of Mdme. Danglars, who could scarcely restrain a cry of mingled pleasure and surprise. "Welcome, Count," exclaimed she, as he entered. "I have been most anxious to see you, that I might repeat verbally those thanks writing can so ill express."

"Surely so trifling a circumstance cannot deserve a place in your remembrance. Believe me, madame, I had entirely forgotten it!"

"But it is not so easy to forget, my lord, that the very day following the one in which you kindly prevented my disappointment respecting the horses, you saved the life of my dear friend, Mdme. de Villefort, which I had placed in danger by lending her the very animals your generosity restored to me."

"This time, at least, I cannot accept of your flattering acknowledgments. In the latter affair you owe me nothing. Ali, my Nubian slave, was the fortunate individual who enjoyed the privilege of rendering to your friend the trifling assistance you allude to."

"Was it Ali," asked Morcerf, "who rescued my son from the hands of bandits?"

"No, my lord," replied Monte-Cristo, pressing with friendly warmth the hand held out to him by the general; "in this instance I may fairly and freely accept your thanks; but you have already tendered them, and fully discharged your debt—if, indeed, there existed one—and I feel almost mortified to find you still revert to the trifling aid I was able to render your son.——May I beg of you, Baroness, to honor me with an introduction to your charming daughter?"

"Oh! you are no stranger—at least not by name," replied Mdme. Danglars, "and the last two or three days we have really talked of nothing else but yourself. Eugénie," continued the baroness, turning toward her daughter, "Count Monte-Cristo." The count bowed, while Mdlle. Danglars returned a slight bow. "You have a charming young person with you to-night, Count," said Eugénie. "Your daughter, I presume?"

"No, indeed," said Monte-Cristo, astonished at the coolness and freedom. "The female you allude to is a poor unfortunate Greek left under my care."

"And what is her name?"

"Haydée," replied Monte-Cristo.

"A Greek?" murmured Morcerf.

"Yes, indeed, Count," said Mdme. Danglars; "and tell me, did you ever see at the court of Ali Tebelin, whom you so gloriously and valiantly served, a more exquisite beauty or richer costume than is displayed in the fair Greek before us?"

"Did I hear rightly, my lord," said Monte-Cristo, "that you served at Janina?"——"I was inspector-general of the pasha's troops," replied Morcerf; "and I seek not to conceal that I owe my fortune, such as it is, to the liberality of the illustrious Albanese chief."

"But look! pray look," exclaimed Mdme. Danglars.

"Where?" stammered out Morcerf.

"There, there!" said Monte-Cristo, as, wrapping his arm around the count, he leaned with him over the front of the box, just as Haydée, whose eyes were occupied in examining the theatre in search of the count, perceived his pale marble features close to the countenance of Morcerf, whom he was holding. This sight produced on the astonished girl an effect similar to that of the head of Medusa. She bent forward as though to assure herself of the reality of what she beheld, then uttering a faint cry, threw herself back in her seat. The scream that burst from the agitated Greek quickly reached the ear of the watchful Ali, who instantly opened the box-door to ascertain the cause. "Bless me!" exclaimed Eugénie, "what has happened to your ward, Count? she seems taken suddenly ill!"

"Very probably!" answered the count. "But do not be alarmed on her account! Haydée's nervous system is delicately organized, and she is peculiarly susceptible of the odors even of flowers—nay, there are some which cause her to faint if brought into her presence. However," continued Monte-Cristo, drawing a small phial from his pocket, "I have an infallible remedy for such attacks." So saying, he bowed to the baroness and her daughter, exchanged a parting shake of the hand with Debray and the count, and quitted for the box. Upon his return to Haydée, he found her extremely pale and much agitated. Directly she saw him she seized his hand, while the icy coldness of her own made Monte-Cristo start.

"With whom was my lord conversing a few minutes since?" asked she, in a trembling voice.

"With the Count of Morcerf," answered Monte-Cristo. "He tells me he served your illustrious father, to whom he owes his fortune!"

"Base, cowardly traitor that he is!" exclaimed Haydée, her eyes flashing with rage; "he it was who sold my beloved parent to the Turks, and the fortune he boasts of was the price of his treachery! Knowest thou not that, my dear lord?"

"Something of this I heard in Epirus," said Monte-Cristo; "but the particulars are still unknown to me. You shall relate them to me, my child. They are, no doubt, both curious and interesting."

"Yes, yes! but let us go hence, I beseech you. I feel as though it would kill me to remain longer near that dreadful man." So saying, Haydée arose, and wrapping herself in her white cashmere opera-cloak embroidered with pearls and coral, she hastily quitted the box at the moment when the curtain was rising upon the fourth act.

"Do you observe," said the countess to Albert, who had returned to her side, "that man does nothing like other people; he listens most devoutly to the third act of *Robert,* and when the fourth begins, makes a precipitate retreat."

CHAPTER XXXVII.

THE RISE AND FALL OF THE STOCKS.

SOME days after this meeting, Albert visited Monte-Cristo at his house, which had already assumed the palace-like appearance which the count's princely fortune enabled him to give even to his most temporary residences. He came to renew the thanks of Mdme. Danglars which had been already conveyed to the count through the medium of a letter. Albert was accompanied by Lucien Debray, who, joining in his friend's conversation, added some passing compliments, the source of which the count's talent easily enabled him to guess. He was convinced that Lucien's visit to him was to be attributed to a double feeling of curiosity, the larger half of which sentiment emanated from the Rue de la Chaussée d'Antin. In short, Mdme. Danglars, not being able personally to examine in detail the domestic economy and household arrangements of a man who gave away horses worth 30,000 francs, and who went to the opera with a Greek slave wearing diamonds to the amount of a million of money, had deputed those eyes, by which she was accustomed to see, to give her a faithful account of the mode of life of this incomprehensible individual. But the count did not appear to suspect there could be the slightest connection between Lucien's visit and the baronne's curiosity.

"You are in constant communication, then, with the Baron Danglars?" inquired the count of Albert de Morcerf.

"Yes, Count, you know what I told you?"

"All remains the same, then, in that quarter?"——"It is more than ever a settled thing," said Lucien: and, considering this remark was all that he was at that time called upon to make, he adjusted the glass to his eye, and biting the top of his gold-headed cane, began to make the tour of the apartment, examining the arms and the pictures.

"Ah!" said Monte-Cristo, "I did not expect the affair would have been so promptly concluded."

"Oh, things take their course without our assistance. My father and Danglars served together in Spain, my father in the army and Danglars in the commissariat department. It was there that my father, ruined by the revolution, and M. Danglars, who never had possessed any patrimony, both laid the foundations of their different fortunes."——"Mdlle. Danglars is too rich for me," replied Morcerf, "and that frightens me."

"Bah!" exclaimed Monte-Cristo, "everything does not depend on wealth, and it is a fine thing to have a good name, and to occupy a high station in society. Your name is celebrated, your position magnificent; and then the Count of Morcerf is a soldier, and it is pleasing to see the integrity of a Bayard united to the poverty of a Duguesclin: disinterestedness is the brightest ray in which a noble sword can shine. As for me, I consider the union a most suitable one; she will enrich you, and you will ennoble her." Albert shook his head, and looked thoughtful. "There is still something else," said he.

"My mother's is the dissenting voice; she has a clear and penetrating judgment, and does not smile on the proposed union. I cannot account for it, but she seems to entertain some prejudice against the Danglars."

"Then do not marry her," said the count.

"Well, I shall see. I will try and think over what is the best thing to be done; you will give me your advice, will you not? and if possible extricate me from my unpleasant position? I think, rather than give pain to my excellent mother, I would run the risk of offending the count." Monte-Cristo turned away; he seemed moved by this last re-mark. "Ah!" said he to Debray, who had thrown himself into an easy-chair at the farthest extremity of the salon, and who held a pencil in his right hand and an account book in his left, "what are you doing there? making a sketch?"

"No, no! I am doing something of a very opposite nature to paint-ing. I am calculating—by the way, Morcerf, this indirectly concerns you—I am calculating what the house of Danglars must have gained by the last rise in Haïti stock; from 206 they have risen to 409 in three days, and the prudent banker had purchased at 206, therefore he must have made 300,000 francs."

"That is not his best stroke of policy," said Morcerf; "did he not gain a million from the Spaniards this last year?"

"My dear fellow," said Lucien, "M. Danglars sold yesterday at 405, and pockets 300,000 francs. Had he but waited till today, the stocks would have fallen to 205, and instead of gaining 300,000 francs, he would have lost 20 or 25,000."

"And what has caused the sudden fall from 409 to 206?" asked Monte-Cristo. "I am profoundly ignorant of all these stock-jobbing intrigues."——"Because," said Albert, laughing, "one piece of news follows another, and there is often great dissimilarity between them."

"Ah," said the count, "I see that M. Danglars is accustomed to play at gaining or losing 300,000 francs in a day; he must be enormously rich?"——"It is not he who plays," exclaimed Lucien, "it is Mdme. Danglars: she is indeed daring."

"But you who are a reasonable being, Lucien, and who know how little dependence is to be placed on the news, since you are at the foun-tain-head, surely you ought to prevent it," said Morcerf, with a smile. "Your position as secretary to the ministry renders your authority great on the subject of political news; you never open your mouth but the stockbrokers immediately stenograph your words. Cause her to lose 2 or 300,000 francs in a short space of time, and that would teach her prudence."

Lucien half smiled. Monte-Cristo, although apparently indifferent, had not lost one word of this conversation, and his penetrating eye had even read a hidden secret in the embarrassed manner of the secretary. This embarrassment had completely escaped Albert, but it caused Lucien to shorten his visit; he was evidently ill at ease. The count, in taking leave of him, said something in a low voice, to which he answered, "Willingly, Count; I accept your proposal." The count returned to young Morcerf.

"Do you not think, on reflection," said he to him, "that you have done wrong in thus speaking of your mother-in-law in the presence of M. Debray?"——"Count," said Morcerf, "I beg of you not to apply that title so prematurely."

"Now, speaking without any exaggeration, is your mother really so very much averse to this marriage?"——"So much so that the baronne very rarely comes to the house, and my mother has not, I think, visited Mdme. Danglars twice in her whole life."

"Then," said the count, "I am emboldened to speak openly to you. I have thought of inviting the Danglars, and Villeforts to my country-house at Auteuil. If I were to invite you and the Count and Countess of Morcerf to this dinner, it would give it the air of a matrimonial rendezvous, or at least Mdme. de Morcerf would look upon the affair in that light, especially if Baron Danglars did me the honor to bring his daughter. In that case your mother would hold me in aversion, and I do not at all wish that; on the contrary, I desire to occupy a prominent place in her esteem."

"Indeed, Count," said Morcerf, "I will immediately call on M. Danglars, and tell him that my mother and myself leave Paris to-morrow. I have not seen you, consequently I know nothing of your dinner."

"How foolish you are! Have you forgotten that M. Debray has just seen you at my house?"

"Ah, true!"

"On the contrary, I have seen you, and invited you without any ceremony, when you instantly answered that it would be impossible for you to be amongst the number of my guests, as you were going to Tréport."——"Well, then, that is settled; but you will come and call on my mother before to-morrow?"

"Before to-morrow?—that will be a difficult matter to arrange; besides, I shall just be in the way of all the preparations for departure."

"You were only a charming man before, but, if you accede to my proposal, you will be adorable."

"What must I do to attain such a height?"——"You are to-day free as air—come and dine with me; we shall be a small party—only yourself, my mother and I. You have scarcely seen my mother, you shall have an opportunity of observing her more closely. She is a remarkable woman, and I only regret that there does not exist another who resembles her about twenty years younger; in that case, I assure you, there would very soon be a Countess and Viscountess de Morcerf. As to my father, you will not see him; he is officially engaged, and dines with M. le Grand Référendaire. We will talk over our travels; and you, who have seen the whole world, will relate your adventures—you shall tell us the history of the beautiful Greek who was with you the other night at the opera, and whom you call your slave, and yet treat like a princess. We will talk Italian and Spanish. Come, accept my invitation, and my mother will thank you."

"A thousand thanks," said the count, "your invitation is most gracious, and I regret exceedingly that it is not in my power to accept it.

I am not so much at liberty as you suppose; on the contrary, I have a most important engagement."

"Humph!" said Morcerf, "this is the second time you have refused to dine with my mother; it is evident you wish to avoid her." Monte-Cristo started. "Oh, you do not mean that," said he; "besides, here comes the confirmation of my assertion."

"Baptistin, what did I tell you this morning when I called you?" ——"To close the door against visitors as soon as the clock struck five," replied the valet. "Then to admit no one except Major Bartolomeo Cavalcanti and his son."

"You hear; Major Bartolomeo Cavalcanti; a man who ranks amongst the most ancient nobility of Italy. Then there is his son, a charming young man, about your own age, Viscount, bearing the same title as yourself, and who is making his *entrée* into Parisian society, aided by his father's millions. The major will bring his son with him this evening; he confides him to my care. He is a perfect nobleman, very polite, modest, and agreeable, such as may be found constantly in Italy, descendants of very ancient families. I have met him several times, and he has now communicated to me the fact of his arrival. The acquaintances one makes in traveling have a claim: they everywhere expect to receive the same attention which you once paid them by chance. Our good Major Cavalcanti comes to take a second view of Paris, which he only saw in passing through in the time of the Empire, when he was on his way to Moscow. I shall give him a good dinner: he will confide his son to my care; I will promise to watch over him; let him follow whatever path his folly may lead him, and then I shall have done my part."

"Certainly; I see you are a precious Mentor," said Albert. "Goodbye, we shall return on Sunday."

CHAPTER XXXVIII.

THE TWO CAVALCANTIS.

BOTH the count and Baptistin had told the truth when they announced to Morcerf the proposed visit of the major, which had served Monte-Cristo as a pretext for declining the invitation which he had received from Albert. Seven o'clock had just struck, and Bertuccio, according to the command which had been given him, had two hours before he left for Auteuil, when a hack stopped at the door, and after depositing its occupant, immediately hurried away, as if ashamed of its employment. The individual who alighted from the vehicle was about fifty-two years of age and dressed in a picturesque costume. He rang at the gate and demanded if it was not where the Count of Monte-Cristo inhabited, and being answered by the porter in the affirmative, entered, closed the gate after him, and began to ascend the steps of the house.

The small and angular head of the individual in question, his white hair and thick grey moustache, caused him to be easily recognized by Baptistin, who had received an exact description, and was awaiting him in the hall. Therefore, scarcely had the stranger time to pronounce his name when the count was apprised of his arrival. He was ushered into a simple and elegant room, and the count rose to meet him with a smiling air.

"Ah, my dear sir, you are most welcome; I was told that I should see you to-day at seven o'clock."

"Ah, so much the better; I feared this little precaution might have been forgotten, of informing you beforehand of my coming."

"I will prove it to you beyond a doubt."

"Oh, no, never mind that," said the Italian; "it is not worth the trouble."

"Let me see," said the count; "are you not the Marquis Bartolomeo Cavalcanti, ex-major in the Austrian service?"

"Was I a major?" timidly asked the old soldier.——"Yes," said Monte-Cristo, "you were a major; that is the title the French give to the post which you filled in Italy. Your visit here to-day is not of your own suggestion, is it?" said Monte-Cristo. "You were sent by the excellent Abbé Busoni?"

"Exactly so," said the delighted major, "whose letter I have."

"Give it me then;" and Monte-Cristo took the letter, which he opened and read. The major looked at the count with large staring eyes, and then took a survey of the apartment, but his gaze almost immediately reverted to the proprietor. "Yes, yes, I see. 'Major Cavalcanti, a worthy patrician of Lucca, a descendant of the Cavalcanti, of Florence,'" continued Monte-Cristo, reading aloud, "'possessing an income of half a million.'" Monte-Cristo raised his eyes from the paper, and bowed. "Half a million," said he, "magnificent! it must be so, for the abbé knows correctly the amount of all the largest fortunes in Europe."

"Be it half a million, then; but on my word of honor, I had no idea that it was so much."——"Because you are robbed by your steward. You must make some reformation in that quarter."

"You have opened my eyes," said the Italian, gravely; "I will show the gentleman the door."

Monte-Cristo resumed the perusal of the letter:—"'And who only needs one thing more to make him happy; to recover a lost and adored son, stolen in his infancy, either by an enemy of his noble family or by the gipsies.' "

"At the age of five!" said the major with a deep sigh, and raising his eyes to heaven.

"Unhappy father!" said Monte-Cristo, continuing:

" 'I have given him renewed life and hope, in the assurance that you have the power of restoring the son whom he has vainly sought for fifteen years.' " The major looked at the count with an indescribable expression of anxiety. "I have the power of so doing," said Monte-Cristo.

The major recovered his self-possession. "Ah! ah!" said he, "the letter was true then to the end?"

"Ah! true!" said Monte-Cristo, "there is a postscript."

" 'In order to save Major Cavalcanti the trouble of drawing on his banker, I send him a draft for 2,000 francs to defray his traveling expenses, and credit on you for the further sum of 48,000, which you still owe me.' " The major awaited the conclusion of the postscript, apparently with great anxiety.

"Then the postscript is as favorably received by you as the rest of the letter?"

"Certainly; the Abbé Busoni and myself have a small account open between us. I do not remember if it is exactly 48,000 francs, which I am still owing him; but I dare say we shall not dispute the difference. You attached great importance, then, to this postscript, my dear M. Cavalcanti?"

"I must explain to you," said the major, "that, fully confiding in the signature of Father Busoni, I had not provided myself with any other funds; so that if this resource had failed me, I should have found myself very unpleasantly situated."

"Is it possible that a man of your stamp should be embarrassed anywhere?" said Monte-Cristo.

"Why, really I know no one," said the major.

"But then you yourself are known to others?"

"Yes, I am known; but you will remit to me these 48,000 francs?"

"Certainly, at your first request." The major's eyes dilated with pleasing astonishment. "But sit down," said Monte-Cristo. The major drew an arm-chair toward him, and proceeded to seat himself.

"Now," said the count, "what will you take—a glass of port, sherry, or Alicant?"

"Alicant, if you please; it is my favorite wine."

Monte-Cristo rang; Baptistin appeared. The count advanced to meet him. "Well?" said he, in a low voice.

"The young man is here," said the valet, in the same tone. "In the blue drawing-room, according to your excellency's orders."

"That's right; now bring Alicant and wine wafers."

Baptistin left the room, and re-entered with glasses, wine, and crackers. The count filled one glass, but in the other he only poured a few drops of the ruby-colored liquid. The bottle was covered with webs, and all the other signs which indicate the age of wine more truly than do wrinkles on a man. The major made a wise choice; he took the full glass and a wafer.

"So, sir, you inhabited Lucca, did you? You were rich, noble, held in great esteem—had all that could render a man happy?"

"All," said the major, hastily swallowing, "positively all."

"And yet there was one thing wanting in order to complete your happiness? your lost child!"

"Ay," said the major, taking a second biscuit, "that consummation of my happiness was indeed wanting." The worthy major raised his eyes to heaven and sighed.

"Let me hear, then," said the count, "who this deeply-regretted son was; for I always understood you were a bachelor. A youthful indiscretion, I suppose, which you were anxious to conceal from the world at large?"

The major recovered himself, and resumed his usual calm manner, at the same time casting his eyes down, either to give himself time to compose his countenance, or to assist his imagination, all the while giving an under-look at the count, the protracted smile on whose lips still announced the same polite curiosity. "Yes," said the major, "I did wish this fault to be hidden from every eye."

"Not on your own account, surely," replied Monte-Cristo; "for a man is above all these things?"

"Oh, no, certainly not on my own account," said the major, with a smile and a shake of the head.

"But for the sake of the mother?" said the count.

"Yes, for the mother's sake—his poor mother!" cried the major, trying to moisten his eye with a tear.

"She belonged to one of the first families in Italy, I think, did she not?"

"She was of a noble family of Fiesole."

"And her name was Oliva Corsinari, was it not? A marchioness, whom you married at last, notwithstanding the opposition of her family?"

"Yes, I did so."

"And you have doubtless brought all your papers with you?" said Monte-Cristo. "The certificate of your marriage with Oliva Corsinari, and the register of your child's birth, that is of Andrea Cavalcanti— your son; is not his name Andrea?"

"I believe so," said the major. "I dare not positively assert it, as he has been lost for so long a time."

"Still," said Monte-Cristo, "you have all the documents with you?"

"I regret to say that, not knowing it was necessary to come provided with these papers, I neglected to bring them with me."

"That is unfortunate," returned Monte-Cristo. "They were indispensable. Supposing there were to be doubts raised as to the validity of your marriage or the legitimacy of your child? It would be fatal to his interests."

"It might cause him to fail in some desirable matrimonial speculation."

"*O peccato!*"

"You must know that in France they are very particular on these points; it is not sufficient, as in Italy, to go to the priest and say, 'We love each other, and want you to marry us.' Marriage is a civil affair in France, and in order to marry in an orthodox manner you must have papers which undeniably establish your identity."

"That is the misfortune! I have not these necessary papers."

"Fortunately, I have them, though," said Monte-Cristo.

"Ah, indeed!" said the major, who, seeing the object of his journey frustrated by the absence of the papers, feared also that his forgetfulness might give rise to some difficulty concerning the cash,—"that is a fortunate circumstance; really lucky, for it never occurred to me to bring them."

"I do not at all wonder at it—one cannot think of everything; but, happily, the Abbé Busoni thought for you."

"He is an admirable man," said the major; "and sent them to you?"

"Here they are."

The major clasped his hands in token of admiration. "You married Oliva Corsinari in the church of San Paolo del Monte-Cattini; here is the priest's certificate."

"Yes, indeed, there it is truly," said the Italian, looking on with astonishment.

"And here is Andrea Cavalcanti's baptismal register, given by the curé of Saravezza. Take these documents, then; they do not concern me. You will give them to your son, who will, of course, take great care of them."

"I should think so, indeed!"

"I am very glad you understand the value of these papers."

"I regard them as invaluable."

"Now," said Monte-Cristo, "as to the mother of the young man, has she not been dead these ten years?"

"I am still mourning her loss!" exclaimed the major, drawing from his pocket a checked handkerchief, and alternately wiping first the right and then the left eye.

"What would you?" said Monte-Cristo; "we are all mortal. Now, you understand, my dear M. Cavalcanti, that it is useless for you to tell people in France that you have been separated from your son for fifteen years. Stories of gipsies, who steal children, are not at all in vogue in this part, and would not be believed. You sent him for his education to a college in the provinces, and now you wish him to complete his education in the Parisian world. That induced you to leave Via Reggio, where you have lived since the death of your wife. If they should hear of the separation——"

"Ah, yes; what could I say?"

"That an unfaithful tutor, bought over by the enemies of your family——"

"By the Corsinari?"

"Precisely. Had stolen this child, in order that your name might become extinct."

"That will do well, since he is an only son."

"Well, now that all is arranged, do not let these newly-awakened remembrances be forgotten. You have, doubtless, already guessed that I was preparing a surprise for you?"——"An agreeable one?" asked the Italian.

"Ah, I see the eye of a father is no more to be deceived than his heart."

"Hum!" said the major.

"Some one has told you the secret; or, perhaps, you guessed that he was here."

"That who was here?"

"Your child—your son—your Andrea!"——"I did guess it," replied the major, with the greatest coolness possible. "Then he is here?"

"He is," said Monte-Cristo; "when the valet came in just now, he told me of his arrival. I understand all your emotion; you must have time to recover yourself. I will, in the meantime, go and prepare the young man for this much-desired interview, for I presume that he is not less impatient for it than yourself."

"I should quite imagine that to be the case," said Cavalcanti.

"Your interview will be private. But do not be uneasy; even if the powerful voice of nature should be silent, you cannot well mistake him; he will enter by this door. He is a fine young man, of fair complexion —a little too fair, perhaps—pleasing manners; but you will see and judge for yourself."

"By the way," said the major, "you know I have only the 2,000 francs which Abbé Busoni sent me; this sum I have expended upon traveling expenses, and——"

"And you want money; that is a matter of course, my dear M. Cavalcanti. Well, here are 8,000 francs on account."

The major's eyes sparkled brilliantly.

"It is 40,000 francs which I now owe you," said Monte-Cristo.

"Does your excellency wish for a receipt?" said the major, at the same time slipping the money into the inner pocket of his coat. "To show the Abbé Busoni."

"Well, when you receive the remaining 40,000 you can give me a receipt in full. Between gentlemen such excessive precaution is, I think, quite unnecessary."

"Yes, so it is, between noblemen."

"You will permit me to make one remark: I should advise you to leave off wearing that flashy dress."

"Indeed!" said the major, regarding himself with an air of complete satisfaction.

"Yes. It may be worn at Via Reggio; but that costume, however elegant in itself, has long been out of fashion in Paris."

"But what shall I wear?"

"What you find in your trunks."

"In my trunks? I have but one portmanteau."

"I dare say you have nothing else with you. What is the use of boring one's self with so many things? Besides, an old soldier always likes to march with as little baggage as possible."

"That is just the case—precisely so!"

"But you are a man of foresight and prudence, therefore you sent your luggage on before you. It has arrived at the Princes Hotel, Richelieu Street, where you are to take up your quarters."

"Then, in these trunks——"

"I presume you have given orders to your valet-de-chambre to put in all you are likely to need,—your plain clothes and your uniform. On grand occasions you must wear your uniform; that will look very well. Do not forget your crosses. They still laugh at them in France, and yet always wear them, for all that."

"Very well! very well!" said the major, who was in ecstasy at the attention paid him by the count.

"Now," said Monte-Cristo, "that you have fortified yourself against all painful excitement, prepare yourself, my dear M. Cavalcanti, to meet your lost Andrea." Saying which Monte-Cristo bowed, and disappeared behind the tapestry, leaving the major fascinated beyond expression with the delightful reception. Monte-Cristo entered the blue drawing-room, and found there a young man, of graceful demeanor and elegant appearance, who had arrived about half an hour previously. He was certainly the tall young man with light hair, red beard, black eyes, and brilliant complexion, whom his master had so particularly described to him.

When the count entered the room the young man was carelessly stretched on a sofa, tapping his boot with the gold-headed cane which he held in his hand. On perceiving the count he rose quickly. "The Count of Monte-Cristo, I believe?" said he.

"Yes, sir, and I think I have the honor of addressing M. le Comte Andrea Cavalcanti!"

"Count Andrea Cavalcanti," repeated the young man, accompanying his words with a bow.

"You are charged with a letter of introduction addressed to me, are you not?" said the count.

"I did not mention that, because the signature seemed to me so strange."

"The letter signed 'Sinbad the Sailor,' is it not?"

"Exactly so. Now, as I have never known any Sinbad, with the exception of the one celebrated in the 'Arabian Nights'——"

"Well? it is one of his descendants, a great friend of mine; he is a very rich Englishman, eccentric almost to insanity; and his real name is Lord Wilmore."

"Ah! indeed! then that explains everything," said Andrea, "that is extraordinary. He is, then, the same Englishman whom I met—at—yes, very well! I am at your lordship's service."

"If what you say be true," replied the count, smiling, "perhaps you will be kind enough to give me some account of yourself and your family?"——"Certainly, I will do so," said the young man, with a quickness which gave proof of his ready invention. "I am (as you have said) Count Andrea Cavalcanti, son of Major Bartolomeo Cavalcanti, a descendant of the Cavalcanti whose names are inscribed in the Golden Book at Florence. Our family, although still rich (for my father's income amounts to half a million), has experienced many misfortunes, and I myself was, at the age of five years, taken away by the treachery of my tutor, so that for fifteen years I have not seen the author of my existence. Since I have arrived at years of discretion and become my own master, I have been constantly seeking him, but all in vain. At length I received this letter from your friend, which states that my father is in Paris, and authorizes me to apply myself to you for information respecting him."

"Really, all you have related to me is exceedingly interesting," said Monte-Cristo, observing the young man with gloomy satisfaction; "and you have done well to conform in everything to the wishes of my friend Sinbad; for your father is indeed here, and is seeking you."

The count, from the moment of his first entering the drawing-room had not once lost sight of the expression of the young man's countenance; he had admired the assurance of his look and the firmness of his voice; but at these words, so natural in themselves, "Your father is indeed here, and is seeking you," young Andrea started, and exclaimed, "My father! is my father here?"

"Most undoubtedly," replied Monte-Cristo; "your father, Major Bartolomeo Cavalcanti." The expression of terror which, for the moment, had overspread the features of the young man, had now disappeared. "Ah! yes, that is the name, certainly. Major Bartolomeo Cavalcanti. And you really mean to say, that my dear father is here?"

"Yes; and I can even add that I have only just left his company. The story which he related to me of his lost son touched me to the quick; indeed, his griefs, hopes, and fears, on that subject might furnish material for a most pathetic poem. At length, he one day received a letter, stating that the parties who had deprived him of his son, now offered to restore him, or at least to give notice where he might be found, on condition of receiving a large sum of money, by way of ransom. Your father did not hesitate an instant, and the sum was sent to the frontier of Piedmont, with a passport signed for Italy. You were in the south of France, I think?"

"Yes," replied Andrea, with an embarrassed air, "I was in the south of France."

"Your father ought to have met with you on the road, for he took exactly the same route, and that is how we have been able to trace your journey to this place."

"But," said Andrea, "if my father had met me, I doubt if he would have recognized me; I must be somewhat altered since he last saw me."

"Oh! the voice of nature," said Monte-Cristo.

"True," interrupted the young man, "I had not looked upon it in that point of view."

"Now," replied Monte-Cristo, "there is only one source of uneasiness left in your father's mind, which is this—he is anxious to know how you have been employed during your long absence from him; how treated by your persecutors; and if they have conducted themselves toward you with all the deference due to your rank. Finally, he is anxious to see if you have been fortunate enough to escape the bad moral influence to which you have been exposed, infinitely more to be dreaded than any physical suffering; he wishes to discover if the fine abilities with which nature had endowed you have been weakened by want of culture; and, in short, whether you consider yourself capable of resuming and retaining in the world the high position to which your rank entitles you."

"Sir," returned the young man, with a reassurance of manner, "make your mind easy on this score. Those who took me from my father, and who always intended, sooner or later, to sell me again to my original proprietor, as they have now done, calculated that, in order to make the most of their bargain, it would be politic to leave me in possession of all my personal and hereditary worth, and even to increase the value, if possible. I have, therefore, received a very good education, and have been treated by these kidnappers very much as the slaves were treated in Asia Minor, whose masters made them grammarians, doctors, and philosophers, in order that they might fetch a higher price in the Roman market."

Monte-Cristo smiled with satisfaction; it appeared as if he had not expected so much from M. Andrea Cavalcanti.

"Besides," continued the young man, "if there did appear some defect in education, or offence against the established forms of etiquette, I suppose they would be excused, in consideration of the misfortunes which accompanied my birth, and followed me through my youth."

"Well," said Monte-Cristo, in an indifferent tone, "you will do as you please, Count, for you are the master of your own actions, and the person most concerned in the matter; but if I were you, I would not divulge a word of these adventures. You might excite a little curiosity, but it is not every one who likes to be made the centre of observation and the subject of unpleasant remark."——"I agree with your lordship," said the young adventurer, turning pale, and in spite of himself, trembling beneath the scrutinizing look of his companion, "such consequences would be extremely unpleasant."

"Nevertheless, you must not exaggerate the evil," said Monte-Cristo, "or by endeavoring to avoid one fault you will fall into another. You must resolve upon one simple and single line of conduct; and for a man of your intelligence, this plan is as easy as it is necessary; you must form honorable friendships, and by that means counteract the prejudice which may attach to the obscurity of your former life." Andrea visibly changed countenance. "I would offer myself as your surety and friendly adviser," said Monte-Cristo, "did I not possess a moral distrust of my best friends, and inclination to lead others to doubt them too; therefore, in departing from this rule, I should (as the actors say) be playing a part quite out of my line, and should, therefore, run the risk of being hissed, which would be an act of folly."

"However," said Andrea, "in consideration of Lord Wilmore, by whom I was recommended to you——"

"Yes, certainly," interrupted Monte-Cristo; "but Lord Wilmore did not omit to inform me, my dear Signor Andrea, that the season of your youth was rather a stormy one. Ah!" said the count, watching Andrea's countenance, "I do not demand any confession from you; it is precisely to avoid that necessity that your father was sent for from Lucca. You shall soon see him; he is a little stiff and pompous in his manner, and he is disfigured by his uniform; but when it becomes known that he is in the Austrian service, all that will be pardoned. In short, you will find your father a very presentable person, I assure you."

"Ah, sir, you have given me confidence; it is so long since we were separated, that I have not the least remembrance of him; and, besides, you know that in the eyes of the world a large fortune covers all defects."

"He is a millionaire—his income is 500,000 francs."

"Then," said the young man, with anxiety, "I shall be sure to be placed in an agreeable position."

"One of the most agreeable possible, my dear sir; he will allow you an income of 50,000 livres per annum during the whole time of your stay in Paris."

"Then in that case I shall always choose to remain there."

"You cannot control circumstances, my dear sir; 'man proposes, and God disposes.'" Andrea sighed. "But," said he, "so long as I do remain in Paris, and nothing forces me to quit it, do you mean to tell me that I may rely on receiving the sum you just now mentioned to me?"

"Yes, you will receive it from your father personally, but Lord Wilmore will be security for the money. He has, at the request of your father, opened an account of 5,000 francs a month at Danglars', one of the safest banks in Paris."

"And does my father mean to remain long in Paris?" asked Andrea.

"Only a few days," replied Monte-Cristo. "His service does not allow him to absent himself more than two or three weeks together."

"Ah! my dear father!" exclaimed Andrea, evidently charmed with the idea of his speedy departure.

"Therefore," said Monte-Cristo, feigning to mistake his meaning— "therefore I will not, for another instant, retard the pleasure of your meeting."

"Go, then, into the drawing-room, my young friend, where you will find your father awaiting you."

Andrea made a low bow to the count, and entered the adjoining room. Monte-Cristo watched him till he disappeared, and then touched a spring made to look like a picture, which, in sliding partially from the frame, discovered to view a small interstice, which was so cleverly contrived that it revealed all that was passing in the drawing-room now occupied by Cavalcanti and Andrea. The young man closed the door behind him, and advanced toward the major, who had risen when he heard steps approaching him. "Ah! my dear father!" said Andrea in a loud voice, in order that the count might hear him in the next room, "is it really you?"

"How do you do, my dear son?" said the major gravely.

"After so many years of painful separation," said Andrea, in the same tone, and glancing toward the door, "what a happiness it is to meet again!"——"Indeed it is, after so long a separation."

"Then we are once more reunited?" said Andrea.

"Once more!" replied the major.

"Never more to be separated?"

"Why, as to that—I think, my dear son, you must be by this time so accustomed to France as to look upon it almost as a second country."

"The fact is," said the young man, "that I should be exceedingly grieved to leave it."

"As for me, you must know I cannot possibly live out of Lucca; therefore I shall return to Italy as soon as I can."

"But before you leave France, my dear father, I hope you will put me in possession of the documents necessary to prove my descent."

"Certainly, I am come expressly on that account; it has cost me much trouble to find you, but I had resolved on giving them into your hands; and if I had to recommence my search, it would occupy all the few remaining years of my life."

Andrea seized the certificate of his father's marriage and his own baptismal register, and after having opened them with all the eagerness which might be expected under the circumstances, he read them with a facility which proved that he was accustomed to similar documents, and with an expression which plainly denoted an unusual interest. When he had perused the documents, an indefinable expression of pleasure lighted up his countenance, and looking at the major with a most peculiar smile, he said, in very excellent Tuscan,—"Then there is no longer any such thing in Italy as being condemned to the galleys?"

The major drew himself up to his full height.

"Why?—what do you mean by that question?"

"I mean that if there were, it would be impossible to draw up with impunity two such deeds as these. In France, my dear sir, half such a piece of effrontery as that would cause you to be quickly despatched to Toulon prison for five years, for change of air."

"Will you be good enough to explain your meaning?" said the major, endeavoring as much as possible to assume an air of the greatest majesty.

"My dear M. Cavalcanti," said Andrea, taking the major by the arm in a confidential manner, "how much are you paid for being my father?" The major was about to speak, when Andrea continued, in a low voice,—"Nonsense! I am going to set you an example of confidence; they give me 50,000 francs a year to be your son; consequently, you can understand that it is not at all likely I shall ever deny my parent." The major looked anxiously around him. "Make yourself easy, we are quite alone," said Andrea; "besides, we are conversing in Italian."

"Well, then," replied the major, "they paid me 50,000 francs down. I have proofs." The major drew from his pocket a handful of gold. "Most palpable," said he, "as you may perceive."

"You think, then, that I may rely on the count's promises?"

"To the letter; but at the same time, remember, we must continue to play our respective parts. I, as a tender father——"

"And I as a dutiful son, as they choose that I shall be descended from you."

"Who do you mean by they?"

"I can hardly tell, but I was alluding to those who wrote the letter; you received one, did you not?"

"From Abbé Busoni."

"Have you any knowledge of him?"

"No, I have never seen him."

"What did he say in the letter?"

The major placed a letter into the young man's hand. Andrea read in a low voice:—

"You are poor; a miserable old age awaits you. Would you like to become rich, or at least independent? Set out immediately for Paris, and ask of the Count of Monte-Cristo, Avenue des Champs Elysées, No. 30, the son whom you had by the *Marchesa* Corsinari, and who was taken from you at five years of age. This son is named Andrea Cavalcanti. In order that you may not doubt the kind intention of the writer of this letter, you will find enclosed an order for 2,400 francs, payable in Florence, at Gozzi's; also a letter of introduction to the Count of Monte-Cristo, on whom I give you a draft of 48,000 francs. Remember to go to the count on the 26th May at seven o'clock in the evening.

(Signed)   "ABBÉ BUSONI."

"I received a letter almost to the same effect."

"From Busoni?"——"No; from an English Lord, Wilmore, who takes the name of Sinbad the Sailor."

"And of whom you have no more knowledge than I of the Abbé Busoni?"

"You are mistaken; there I am in advance of you."

"You have seen him, then?"

"Yes, once."

"Where?"

"Ah! that is just what I cannot tell you; if I did, I should make you as wise as myself, which it is not my intention to do."

"And what did the letter contain?"

"Read it."

"'You are poor, and your future prospects are dark and gloomy. Do you wish for a name? should you like to be rich, and your own master?'"

"*Per Baccho!*" said the young man; "was it possible there could be two answers to such a question?"

"'Take the post-chaise which you will find waiting at the Porte de Gênes, as you enter Nice; pass through Turin, Chambéry, and Pont-de-Beauvoisin. Go to the Count of Monte-Cristo, Avenue des Champs-Elysées, on the 26th of May, at seven o'clock in the evening, and demand of him your father. You are the son of the Cavalcanti and the Marchesa Oliva Corsinari. The marquis will give you some papers which will certify this fact, and authorize you to appear under that title. An annual income of 50,000 livres will enable you to support it admirably. I enclose a draft for 5,000 livres, payable on Signor Ferrea, banker at Nice, and also a letter of introduction to the Count of Monte-Cristo, whom I have directed to supply all your wants.

"'SINBAD THE SAILOR.'"

"Humph!" said the major; "very good! Do you understand it?"

"Not in the least."

"There is a dupe somewhere."

"At all events, it is neither you nor I."

"It does not much concern us; do you think it does?"

"No! I agree with you there; we must play the game to the end, and consent to be blindfold."

Monte-Cristo chose this moment for re-entering the drawing-room. On hearing the sound of his footsteps, the two men threw themselves in each other's arms; and, in the midst of this embrace, the count entered.

"Well, Marquis," said Monte-Cristo, "you appear to be in no way disappointed in the son whom your good fortune has restored to you.——" "Ah! Count, I am overwhelmed with delight."

"And what are your feelings?" said Monte-Cristo, turning to the young man.

"My heart is overflowing with happiness."

"Happy father! happy son!" said the count.

"There is only one thing which grieves me," observed the major, "and that is the necessity there is for my leaving Paris so soon."

"Ah! my dear M. Cavalcanti, I trust you will not leave before I have had the honor of presenting you to some of my friends."

"I am at your service, sir," replied the major.

"Now, sir," said Monte-Cristo, addressing Andrea, "tell M. Cavalcanti something of the state of your finances."

"You have touched upon a tender cord."

"Your son says he requires money."

"Well! what would you have me do?" said the major.

"You should furnish him with some, of course," replied Monte-Cristo, at the same time advancing toward Andrea, and slipping a packet of bank-notes into the young man's hand.

"From your father."

"From my father?"

"Yes; did you not tell him just now that you wanted money? Well, then, he deputes me to give you this, for the first expenses of your settling in Paris."

"Ah! how good my dear father is!"

"Silence!" said Monte-Cristo; "he does not wish you to know that it comes from him."

"I fully appreciate his delicacy," said Andrea, cramming the notes hastily into his pocket.

"And now, gentlemen, I wish you good morning," said Monte-Cristo.

"And when shall we have the honor of seeing you again, lordship?" asked Cavalcanti.

"Ah!" said Andrea, "when may we hope for that pleasure?"

"On Saturday, if you will—yes.—Let me see—Saturday—I am to dine at my country-house, at Auteuil. Several persons are invited, and amongst others, M. Danglars, your banker. I will introduce you to him; for it will be necessary he should know you, as he is to pay your money."

"Full dress?" said the major, half aloud.

"Oh! yes, certainly," said the count; "uniform, cross, medals, and so on."

"And how shall I be dressed?" demanded Andrea.

"Oh! very simply. Go to Blin or Veronique for your suit. Baptistin will tell you where. The less pretension in your dress, the better will be the effect, as you are a rich man. If you mean to buy any horses, get them of Devedeux; and if a phaeton, go to Baptiste for it."

"At what hour shall we come?" asked the young man.

"About half-past six."

"We will be with you at that time," said the major. The two Cavalcanti bowed to the count, and left the house. Monte-Cristo went to the window, and saw them crossing the street, arm in arm. "There go two rascals!" said he. "It is a pity they are not really related!" then, after an instant of gloomy reflection said he: "Come, I will go to see the Morrels! I think that disgust is even more sickening than hatred."

CHAPTER XXXIX.

THE TRYSTING PLACE.

IN the enclosure surrounding Villefort's house, Maximilian was the first to arrive. He was intently watching for a shadow to appear amongst the trees, and awaiting with anxiety the sound of a light step on the gravel walk. At length, the long-desired sound was heard, and instead of one figure, as he had expected, he perceived that two were approaching him. The delay had been occasioned by a visit from Madame Danglars and Eugénie, which had been prolonged beyond the time at which Valentine was expected. In the space of about half an hour the ladies retired, and Maximilian understood that the Danglars' visit had at last come to a conclusion. In a few minutes Valentine re-entered the garden alone. For fear that any one should be observing her return, she walked slowly; and instead of immediately directing her steps toward the gate, she seated herself on a bank, and, carefully casting her eyes around, to convince herself that she was not watched, she presently rose, and proceeded quickly to join Maximilian.

"Good evening, Valentine," said a well-known voice.

"Good evening, Maximilian; I know I have kept you waiting, but you saw the cause of my delay."

"Yes, I recognized Mdlle. Danglars. I was not aware that you were so intimate with her."

"We were having a confidential conversation," returned Valentine; "she was telling to me her repugnance to marriage with M. de Morcerf; and I, on the other hand, was confessing to her how wretched it made me to think of marrying M. d'Epinay."

"Dear Valentine!"

"That will account to you for the unreserved manner which you observed between me and Eugénie; as in speaking of the man whom I could not love, my thoughts involuntarily reverted to him on whom my affections were fixed."

"Ah, how good you are to say so, Valentine! Does Mdlle. Danglars object to this marriage with Morcerf on account of loving another?"

"She told me that she loved no one," said Valentine; "disliked the idea of being married; would infinitely prefer leading an independent and unfettered life; and almost wished her father might lose his fortune, that she might become an artiste like her friend, Louise d'Armilly."

"Must you leave me soon?"

"Mdme. de Villefort sent to request my presence, as she had a communication to make on which a part of my fortune depended. Let them take my fortune, I am already too rich; and, perhaps, when they have taken it, they will leave me in peace and quietness. You would love me as much if I were poor, would you not, Maximilian?"

"Oh! I shall always love you. What should I care for either riches or poverty, if my Valentine was near me, and I felt certain that no one could deprive me of her? But do you not fear that this communication may relate to your marriage?"——"I do not think that is the case."

"But I was going to tell you that I met M. de Morcerf the other day. He has received a letter from his friend Franz, announcing his immediate return." Valentine turned pale, and leaned against the gate for support.

"Can it really be true, and is that why Mdme. de Villefort has sent for me? No, that cannot be the case, for the communication would not be likely to come through her instrumentality. It has appeared as if she secretly objected to the marriage, although she did not choose openly to oppose it."——"Is it so? Then I feel as if I could adore Mdme. de Villefort."

"Do not be in such a hurry to do that," said Valentine, with a sad smile.

"If she objects to your marrying M. d'Epinay, she would be all the more likely to listen to any other proposition."——"No, Maximilian, it is not suitors to which Mdme. de Villefort objects, it is marriage itself."

"Tell me what interest Mdme. de Villefort can have in your remaining unmarried?"

"Did I not tell you just now that I was rich, Maximilian—too rich? I possess nearly 50,000 livres in right of my mother; my grandfather and my grandmother, the Marquis and Marchioness St.-Méran, will leave me as much more: and M. Noirtier evidently intends making me his heiress. My brother Edward, who inherits nothing from his mother, will, therefore, be poor in comparison with me. Now, if I had taken the veil, all this fortune would have descended to my father, and, in reversion, to his son."

"Ah! how strange it seems that such a young and beautiful woman should be so avaricious."

"It is not for herself that she is so, but for her son; and what you regard as a vice becomes almost a virtue when looked at in the light of maternal love."

"But could you not compromise matters, and give up a portion of your fortune to her son?"

"How could I make such a proposition, especially to a woman who always professes to be entirely disinterested?"

"Valentine, I have always regarded our love in the light of something sacred; consequently, I have covered it with the veil of respect, and hid it in the inmost recesses of my soul; no human being, not even my sister, is aware of its existence. Valentine, will you permit me to make a confidant of a friend, and reveal to him the love I bear you?"

Valentine started. "A friend, Maximilian; and who is this friend? I tremble to give my permission."

"Listen, Valentine. Have you never experienced for any one that sudden and irresistible sympathy which made you feel as if the object of it had been your old and familiar friend, though, in reality, it was the first time you had ever met?"

"You have known him for some time, then?"

"Scarcely longer than eight or ten days."

"And do you call a man your friend whom you have only known for eight or ten days? Ah, Maximilian, I had hoped you set a higher value on the title of friend."

"Your logic is most powerful, Valentine; but say what you will, I can never renounce the sentiment which has instinctively taken possession of my mind. I feel as if it were ordained that this man should be associated with all the good which the future may have in store for me, and sometimes it really seems as if his eye was able to see what was to come, and his hand endowed with the power of directing events according to his own will."

"He must be a prophet, then," said Valentine; "do let me see this man, Maximilian; he may tell me whether I shall ever be loved sufficiently to make amends for all I have suffered."

"My poor girl! you know him already. He saved the life of your step-mother and her son."

"The Count of Monte-Cristo?"——"The same."

"Ah!" cried Valentine, "he is too much the friend of Mdme. de Villefort ever to be mine."

"The friend of Mdme. de Villefort! It cannot be; surely, Valentine, you are mistaken?"

"No, indeed, I am not; for I assure you, his power over our household is almost unlimited. He appears to exert a mysterious and almost uncontrollable influence over all the members of our family."

"If such be the case, my dear Valentine, you must yourself have felt, or at all events will soon feel, the effects of his presence. He meets Albert de Morcerf in Italy—it is to rescue him from banditti; he introduces himself to Mdme. Danglars—to give her a royal present; your step-mother and her son pass before his door—his Nubian saves them from destruction. This man evidently possesses the power of influencing events, both as regards men and things. I never saw more simple tastes united to greater magnificence. His smile is so sweet when he addresses me, that I forget it can ever be bitter to others. Ah! Valentine, tell me, if he ever looked on you with one of those sweet smiles? if so, depend on it, you will be happy."

"Me!" said the girl, "he never even glances at me; on the contrary, if I accidentally cross his path, he appears rather to avoid me. Ah, he is not generous, neither does he possess that supernatural penetration which you attribute to him; for if he had, he would have perceived that I was unhappy; and if he had been generous, seeing me sad and solitary, he would have used his influence to my advantage; and since, as you say, he resembles the sun, he would have warmed my heart with one of his life-giving rays. You say he loves you, Maximilian; how do you know that he does? All would pay deference to an officer like you, with a fierce moustache and a long sabre; but they think they may crush a poor weeping girl with impunity."

"Ah, Valentine! I assure you you are mistaken."

"If it were otherwise—if he treated me diplomatically—that is to say, like a man who wishes, by some means or other, to obtain a footing in the house, so that he may ultimately gain the power of dictating to its occupants—he would, if it had been but once, have honored me with the smile which you extol so loudly; but no, he saw that I was unhappy; he understood that I could be of no use to him, and therefore paid me no regard whatever. Ah! forgive me," said Valentine, perceiving the effect which her words were producing on Maximilian; "I do not deny the influence of which you speak, or that I have not myself experienced it; but with me it has been productive of evil rather than good."

"Well, Valentine," said Morrel, with a sigh, "we will not discuss the matter further. I will not make a confidant of him."

"Alas!" said Valentine, "I see that I have given you pain. I can only say how sincerely I ask pardon for having grieved you. But, indeed, I am not prejudiced beyond the power of conviction. Tell me what this count of Monte-Cristo has done for you?"

"I own that your question embarrasses me, Valentine, for I cannot say that the count has rendered me any ostensible service. Still, a secret voice seems to whisper to me that there must be something more than chance in this unexpected reciprocity of friendship. In his most simple actions, as well as in his most secret thoughts, I find a relation to my own. You will perhaps smile at me when I tell you that, ever since I have known this man, I have involuntarily entertained the idea that all the good fortune which has befallen me originated from him. However, I have managed to live thirty years without this protection, you will say; but I will endeavor a little to illustrate my meaning. He invited me to dine with him on Saturday, which was a very natural thing for him to do. Well, what have I learned since? That your mother and M. de Villefort are both coming to this dinner. I shall meet them there, and who knows what future advantages may result from the interview? This may appear to you to be no unusual combination of circumstances; nevertheless, I perceive some hidden plot in the arrangement—something, in fact, more than is apparent on a casual view of the subject."

"If you have no stronger proof to give me——"

"I have another," replied Maximilian; "but I fear you will deem it even more absurd than the first. Look through this opening, and you will see the beautiful new horse which I rode here."

"Ah! what a beautiful creature!" cried Valentine: "why did you not bring it close to the gate, that I might talk to it and pat it?"

"It is, as you say, a very valuable animal," said Maximilian. "You know that my means are limited, and that I am what would be designated a man of moderate pretensions. Well, I went to a horse-dealer's, where I saw this magnificent horse, which I have named Medea. I asked the price of it; they told me it was 4,500 francs. I was, therefore, obliged to give it up, as you may imagine; but I own I went away with rather a heavy heart, for I was altogether fascinated with it. The same evening some friends of mine visited me. I never play, for I am not rich enough to afford to lose, nor sufficiently poor to desire to gain. But I was at my own house, you understand, so there was nothing to be done but to send for cards, which I did. Just as they were sitting down to table, Monte-Cristo arrived. He took his seat amongst them; they played, and I won. I am almost ashamed to say that my gains amounted to 5,000 francs. We separated at midnight. I could not defer my pleasure, so I took a cabriolet and drove to the horse-dealer's. Feverish and excited, I rang at the door. The person who opened it must have taken me for a madman, for I rushed at once to the stable. Medea was standing at the rack, eating her hay. I immediately put on the saddle and bridle, to which operation she lent herself with the best grace possible; then, putting the 4,500 francs into the hands of the astonished dealer, I proceeded to fulfil my intention of passing the night in riding in the Champs Elysées. As I rode by the count's house I perceived a light in one of the windows, and fancied I saw the shadow of his figure moving behind the curtain. Now, Valentine, I firmly believe that he knew of my wish to possess this horse, and that he lost expressly to give me the means of procuring it."

"My dear Maximilian, you are really too fanciful; you will not love even me long. A man who accustoms himself to live in such a world of poetry and imagination must find far too little excitement in a common, every-day sort of attachment such as ours. But they are calling me. Do you hear?"——"Ah, Valentine! give me but one finger through this opening in the grating, that I may have the happiness of kissing it."

Valentine mounted the bank, and passed not only her finger but her whole hand through the opening. Maximilian uttered a cry of delight, and, springing forward, seized the hand extended toward him, and imprinted on it a fervent and impassioned kiss. The little hand was then immediately withdrawn, and the young man saw Valentine hurrying toward the house, as though she were almost terrified at her own sensations.

CHAPTER XL.

THE PARALYTIC.

WE will now relate what was passing in the house after the departure of Mdme. Danglars and her daughter, and during the conversation between Maximilian and Valentine, just detailed. Villefort entered his father's room, followed by his wife. Both of the visitors, after saluting the old man and speaking to Barrois, a faithul servant, twenty-five years in his service, took their places on either side of the paralytic.

M. Noirtier was sitting in an arm-chair, which moved upon casters, in which he was wheeled into the room in the morning, and in the same way drawn out again at night. He was placed before a large glass, which reflected the whole apartment, and permitted him to see, without any attempt to move, which would have been impossible, all who entered the room, and everything which was going on around him. M. Noirtier, although almost as immovable and helpless as a corpse, looked at the new-comers with a quick and intelligent expression, perceiving at once, by their ceremonious courtesy, that they were come on business of an unexpected and official character. Sight and hearing were the only senses remaining, and they appeared left, like two solitary sparks, to animate the miserable body which seemed fit for nothing but the grave. The speaking eye sufficed for all. He commanded with it; it was the medium through which his thanks were conveyed. Three persons only could understand this language of the poor paralytic; these were Villefort, Valentine, and the old servant of whom we have already spoken. But as Villefort saw his father but seldom, and then only when absolutely obliged, and as he never took any pains to please or gratify him when he was there, all the old man's happiness was centered in his granddaughter; Valentine, by means of her love, her patience, and her devotion, had learned to read in Noirtier's look all the varied feelings which were passing his mind. Villefort did not need the help of either Valentine or the domestic in order to carry on with his father the strange conversation which he was about to begin. As we have said, he perfectly understood the old man's vocabulary; and if he did not use it more often, it was only indifference and listlessness which prevented him from so doing; he therefore allowed Valentine to go into the garden, sent away Barrois, and after having taken a place on the right hand of his father, while Mdme. de Villefort seated herself on the left, he addressed him thus:—

"I trust you will not be displeased, sir, that Valentine has not come with us, or that I dismissed Barrois, for our conference will be one which could not with propriety be carried on in the presence of either; Mdme. Villefort and I have a communication to make to you."

Noirtier's face remained perfectly passive during this long preamble; whilst, on the contrary, the eye of Villefort was endeavoring to penetrate into the inmost recesses of the old man's heart.

"Sir," resumed Villefort, "we are thinking of marrying off Valentine." Had the old man's face been moulded in wax, it could not have shown less emotion at this news than was now to be traced there. "The marriage will take place in less than three months," said Villefort. Noirtier's eyes still retained their inanimate expression.

Mdme. de Villefort now took her part in the conversation, and added,—"We thought this news would possess an interest for you, sir, who have always entertained a great affection for Valentine; it therefore only now remains for us to tell you the name of the young man for whom she is destined. It is M. Franz de Quesnel, Baron Epinay."

During the time that his wife was speaking, Villefort had narrowly watched the countenance of the old man.

Noirtier's look was furious; it was very evident that something desperate was passing in the old man's mind, for the cry of anger and grief rose to his throat, and not being able to find vent in utterance, appeared almost to choke him, for his face and lips turned quite purple with the struggle. Villefort quietly opened a window, saying, "It is very warm and the heat affects M. Noirtier." He then returned to his place, but did not sit down. "This marriage," added Mdme. de Villefort, "is quite agreeable to the wishes of M. d'Epinay and his family; besides, he had no relations nearer than an uncle and aunt, his mother having died at his birth, and his father having been assassinated in 1815, that is to say, when he was but two years old; it naturally followed that the child was permitted to choose his own pursuits, and he has, therefore, seldom acknowledged any other authority but that of his own will."

"That assassination was a mysterious affair," said Villefort, "and the perpetrators have hitherto escaped detection; although suspicion has fallen on the head of more than one person." Noirtier made such an effort that his lips expanded into a smile.

"Now," continued Villefort, "those to whom the guilt really belongs, by whom the crime was committed, on whose heads the justice of man may probably descend here, and the certain judgment of God hereafter, would rejoice in the opportunity thus afforded of bestowing such a peace-offering as Valentine on the son of him whose life they so ruthlessly destroyed." Noirtier had succeeded in mastering his emotion more than could have been deemed possible with such an enfeebled and shattered frame. "Yes, I understand," was the reply contained in his look; and this look expressed a feeling of strong indignation, mixed with profound contempt. Villefort fully understood his father's meaning, and answered by a slight shrug of his shoulders. He then motioned to his wife to take leave. They bowed and left the room, giving orders that Valentine should be summoned to her grandfather's presence, and feeling sure that she would have much to do to restore calmness to the perturbed spirit. Valentine, with a color still heightened by emotion, entered the room just after her parents had left it. One look was sufficient to tell her that her grandfather was suffering, and that there was much on his mind which he was wishing to communicate to her.

"Dear grandpapa," cried she, "what has happened? They have vexed you, and you are angry?" The paralytic closed his eyes in assent. "Who has displeased you? Is it my father?"

"No."——"Mdme. de Villefort?"——"No."

"I?" The former sign was repeated. "Are you displeased with me?" cried Valentine in astonishment. M. Noirtier again closed his eyes. "And what have I done, dear grandpapa, that you should be angry with me?" cried Valentine.

There was no answer; and she continued, "I have not seen you all day. Has any one been speaking to you against me?"——"Yes," said the old man's look, with eagerness.

"Let me think a moment. I do assure you, grandpapa—Ah! M. and Mdme. de Villefort have just left this room, have they not?"

"Yes."

"Ah! I know," said she, lowering her voice and going close to the old man, "they have been speaking of my marriage,—have they not?"

"Yes," replied the angry look.

"I understand; you are afraid I shall be unhappy?"

"Yes."

"You do not like M. Franz?"

The eyes repeated several times, "No, no, no."

"Then you are vexed with the engagement?"——"Yes."

"Well, listen," said Valentine, throwing herself on her knees, and putting her arm round her grandfather's neck. "I am vexed, too, for I do not love M. Franz d'Epinay." An expression of intense joy illuminated the old man's eyes. "When I wished to retire into a convent, you remember how angry you were with me?" A tear trembled in the eye of the invalid. "Well," continued Valentine, "the reason of my proposing it was that I might escape this hateful marriage, which drives me to despair." Noirtier's breathing became thick and short. "Then the idea of this marriage really grieves you too? Ah, if you could but help me—if we could both together defeat their plan! But you are unable to oppose them; you, whose mind is so quick, and whose will is so firm, are, nevertheless, as weak and unequal to the contest as I am myself. Alas, you, who would have been such a powerful protector to me in the days of your health and strength, can now only sympathize in my joys and sorrows, without being able to take any active part in them. However, this is much, and calls for gratitude; and Heaven has not taken away all my blessings when it leaves me your sympathy and kindness."

At these words there appeared in Noirtier's eye an expression of such deep meaning that the girl thought she could read these words there, "You are mistaken; I can still do much for you."

"Do you think you can help me, dear grandpapa?" said Valentine.

"Yes." Noirtier raised his eyes; it was the sign agreed on between him and Valentine when he wanted anything.

"What is it you want, dear grandpapa?" said Valentine, and she endeavored to recall to mind all the things which he would be likely to need; and as the ideas presented themselves to her mind, she repeated them aloud; but finding that all her efforts elicited nothing but a constant *"No,"* "Come," said she, "since this plan does not answer, I will have recourse to another." She then recited all the letters of the alphabet from A down to N. When she arrived at that letter, the paralytic made her understand that was the initial letter of the thing which he wanted. "Ah," said Valentine, "the thing you desire begins with the letter N; it is with N that we have to do, then. Well, let me see, what can you want which begins with N? Na— Ne— Ni— No—"

"Yes, yes, yes," said the old man's eye.

"Ah, it is No, then?"——"Yes." Valentine fetched a dictionary, which she placed on a desk before Noirtier; she opened it, and, seeing that the old man's eye was thoroughly fixed on its pages, she ran her finger quickly up and down the columns. During the six years which had passed since Noirtier first fell into this sad state, Valentine's powers of invention had been too often put to the test not to render her expert in devising expedients for gaining a knowledge of his wishes; and the constant practice had so perfected her in the art, that she guessed the old man's meaning as quickly as if he himself had been able to seek for what he wanted. At the word *Notary,* Noirtier made a sign to her to stop. Valentine rang the bell, and ordered the servant to tell M. or Mdme. de Villefort that they were requested to come to M. Noirtier's room. M. de Villefort entered, followed by Barrois.

"Sir," said Valentine, "my grandfather wishes for a notary."

"What do you want with a notary?" asked Villefort. The invalid's eye remained fixed, by which expression he intended to intimate that his resolution was unalterable. "Is it to do us some ill turn? Do you think it is worth while?" said Villefort.

"Still," said Barrois, with the freedom and fidelity of an old servant, "if M. Noirtier asks for a notary, I suppose he really wishes for a notary; therefore I shall go at once and fetch one."

Three-quarters of an hour after, Barrois returned, bringing the notary with him.

"Sir," said Villefort, after the first salutations were over, "you were sent for by M. Noirtier, whom you see here. All his limbs have become completely paralyzed, he has lost his voice also, and we ourselves find much trouble in endeavoring to catch some fragments of his meaning." Noirtier cast an appealing look on Valentine, which look was at once so earnest and imperative, that she answered immediately. "Sir," said she, "I perfectly understand my grandfather's meaning at all times."

"That is quite true," said Barrois; "and that is what I told the gentleman as we walked along."——"Permit me," said the notary, turning first to Villefort and then to Valentine—"In order to render an act valid, I must be certain of the approbation or disapprobation of my client. Illness of the body would not affect the validity of the deed; but sanity of mind is absolutely requisite."

"Well, sir, by the help of two signs, with which I will acquaint you presently, you may ascertain with perfect certainty that my grandfather is still in the full possession of all his mental faculties. M. Noirtier, being deprived of voice and motion, is accustomed to convey his meaning by closing his eyes when he wishes to signify 'yes,' and to wink when he means 'no.' You now know quite enough to enable you to converse with M. Noirtier; try." Noirtier gave Valentine such a look of tenderness and gratitude that it was comprehended even by the notary himself.

"You have heard and understood what your granddaughter has been saying, sir, have you?" asked the notary. Noirtier closed his eyes. "And you approve of what she said—that is to say, you declare that the signs which she mentioned are really those by means of which you are accustomed to convey your thoughts?"

"Yes."

"Let us try what we can do, then," said the notary. "You accept this young lady as your interpreter, M. Noirtier?"

"Yes."

"Well, sir, what do you require of me, and what document is it that you wish to be drawn up?" Valentine named all the letters of the alphabet until she came to W. At this letter the eloquent eye of Noirtier gave her notice that she was to stop.

"It is very evident that it is the letter W which M. Noirtier wants," said the notary.

"Wait," said Valentine; and, turning to her grandfather, she repeated, "Wa—We—Wi—" The old man stopped her at the last syllable. Valentine then took the dictionary, and the notary watched her whilst she turned over the pages. She passed her finger slowly down the columns, and when she came to the word "Will," M. Noirtier's eye bade her stop.

"Will!" cried the notary; "it is very evident that M. Noirtier is desirous of making his will."——"Yes, yes, yes!" motioned the invalid.

"Really, sir, you must allow that this is most extraordinary," said the astonished notary, turning to M. de Villefort. "Yes," said the procureur, "and I think the will promises to be yet more extraordinary; for I cannot see how it is to be drawn up without the intervention of Valentine, and she may, perhaps, be considered as too much interested in its contents to allow of her being a suitable interpreter of the obscure and ill-defined wishes of her grandfather."

"No, no, no!" replied the eye of the paralytic.

"What!" said Villefort, "do you mean to say that Valentine is not interested in your will?"

"No."

"Sir," said the notary, whose interest had been greatly excited, and who had resolved on publishing far and wide the account of this extraordinary and picturesque scene, "what appeared so impossible to me an hour ago, has now become quite easy and practicable; and this may be a perfectly valid will, provided it be read in the presence of seven witnesses, approved by the testator, and sealed by the notary in the presence of the witnesses. As to the time, it will certainly occupy rather more than the generality of wills. There are certain forms necessary to be gone through, and which are always the same. As to the details, the greater part will be furnished afterwards, by the state in which we find the affairs of the testator, and by yourself, who, having had the management of them, can, doubtless, give full information on the subject. But besides all this, in order that the instrument may not be contested, I am anxious to give it the greatest possible authenticity; therefore, one of my colleagues will help me, and, contrary to custom, will assist in the dictation of the testament. Are you satisfied, sir?" continued the notary, addressing the old man.

"Yes," looked the invalid, his eye beaming with delight at his meaning being so well understood.

"What is he going to do?" thought Villefort, whose position demanded so much reserve, but who was longing to know what were the intentions of his father. He left the room to give orders for another notary to be sent, but Barrois, who had heard all that passed, had guessed his master's public wishes, and had already gone to fetch one. The public prosecutor then told his wife to come up. In the course of a quarter of an hour every one had assembled in the chamber of the paralytic; the second notary had also arrived. A few words sufficed for a mutual understanding between the two officers of the law.

In the strange yet clear mode of Noirtier he signified that he had nearly a hundred thousand francs of securities which would have been inherited by Valentine but should she marry Epinay, he revoked his intentions and would bestow it in charity.

The prosecutor pretended to be resigned, but quitted the room hastily with his wife.

CHAPTER XLI.

THE TELEGRAPH.

THE Villeforts found on their return that the Count of Monte-Cristo, come in their absence, had been ushered into the drawing-room, and was still awaiting them there. Mdme. de Villefort, not yet sufficiently recovered from her late emotion to allow of her entertaining visitors so immediately, retired to her bed-room, whilst her husband who could better depend upon himself, proceeded at once to the drawing-room. Although Villefort flattered himself that, to all outward view, he had completely masked the feelings which were passing in his mind, he did not know that the cloud was still lowering on his brow, so much so that the count immediately remarked his sombre and thoughtful air. "Faith!" said Monte-Cristo, after the first compliments were over, "what is the matter with you, M. de Villefort? Have I arrived at the moment that you were drawing up some case of capital indictment?" Villefort tried to smile. "No, Count," replied M. de Villefort, "I am the only victim in this case. It is I who lose my cause; and it is ill-luck, obstinacy, and folly which have caused it to be decided against me."

"To what do you allude?" said Monte-Cristo, with well-feigned interest. "Have you really met with some great misfortune?"

"Oh!" said Villefort, with a bitter smile, "it is only a loss of money which I have sustained, though, after all, 900,000 francs are worth regretting; but I am the more annoyed with this fate, chance, or whatever you please to call the power which has destroyed my hopes and my fortune, and may blast the prospects of my child also, as it is all occasioned by an old man relapsed into second childhood."

"What do you say?" said the count; "900,000 francs! it is indeed a sum which might be regretted even by a philosopher. And who is the cause of all this annoyance?"

"My father, as I told you."

"M. Noirtier! but I thought you told me he had become entirely paralyzed, and that all his faculties were completely destroyed?"

"Yes, his bodily faculties, for he can neither move nor speak, nevertheless, he thinks, acts, and wills in the manner I have described. I left him about five minutes ago, and he is now occupied in dictating his will to two notaries."——"But to do this he must have spoken?"

"He has done better than that—he has made himself understood."

"How was such a thing possible?"

"By the help of his eyes, which are still full of life, and, as you perceive, possess the power of inflicting mortal injury."

"My dear," said Mdme. de Villefort, who had just entered the room, "perhaps you exaggerate the evil."

"Good morning, madame!" said the count, bowing. Mdme. de Villefort acknowledged the salutation with one of her most gracious smiles. "What is this that M. de Villefort has been telling me?" demanded Monte-Cristo, "and what incomprehensible misfortune——"

"Incomprehensible is not the word!" interrupted the lawyer, shrugging his shoulders. "It is an old man's caprice."

"And is there no means of making him revoke his decision?"

"Yes," said Mdme. de Villefort; "and it is still entirely in the power of my husband to cause the will, which is now in prejudice of Valentine, to be altered in her favor." The count, who perceived that the Villeforts were beginning to speak in parables, appeared to pay no attention to the conversation, and feigned to be busily engaged in watching Edward, mischievously pouring ink into the bird's water-glass.

"My dear," said Villefort, in answer to his wife, "you know I have never been accustomed to play the patriarch in my family, nor have I ever considered that the fate of a universe was to be decided by my nod. Nevertheless, it is necessary that my will should be respected in my family, and that the folly of an old man and the caprice of a child should not be allowed to overturn a project which I have entertained for so many years. The Baron d'Epinay was my friend, as you know, and an alliance with his son is the most suitable thing that could possibly be arranged."

"What!" said the count, the approbation of whose eye Villefort had frequently solicited during the speech. "What! do you say that M. Noirtier disinherits Mdlle. Villefort because she is going to marry Baron Epinay?"——"Yes, sir, that is the reason," said Villefort, shrugging his shoulders.

"I believe I know M. Franz d'Epinay," said the count; is he not the son of General Quesnel, who was created Baron d'Epinay by Charles X.?"

"The same," said Villefort.

"Although General d'Epinay served under Napoleon, did he not still retain royalist sentiments? And was he not the person murdered one evening on leaving a Bonapartist meeting to which he had been invited on the supposition of his favoring the cause of the emperor?" Villefort looked at the count almost with terror.

"The facts were precisely what you have stated," said Mdme. de Villefort; "and it was to prevent the renewal of old feuds that M. de Villefort formed the idea of uniting in the bonds of affection the two children of these inveterate enemies."

"It was a sublime and charitable thought," said Monte-Cristo, "and the whole world should applaud it. It would be noble to see Mdlle. Noirtier de Villefort assuming the title of Mdme. d'Epinay." Villefort shuddered and looked at Monte-Cristo as if he wished to read in his countenance the real feelings which had dictated the words he had just pronounced. But the count completely baffled the lawyer's penetration, and prevented him from discovering anything beneath the never-varying smile he was so constantly in the habit of assuming.

"Although," said De Villefort, "it will be a serious thing for Valentine to lose the fortune of her grandfather, I do not think the marriage will be prevented on that account, nor do I believe that M. d'Epinay will be frightened at this pecuniary loss; he will, perhaps, hold me in greater esteem than the money itself, seeing that I sacrifice everything in order to keep my word with him; besides, he knows that Valentine is rich in right of her mother, and that she will, in all probability, inherit the fortune of Saint-Mérans, her mother's parents, who both love her tenderly."

"And who are fully as well worth loving and tending as M. de Noirtier," said Mdme. de Villefort; "besides, they are to come to Paris in about a month, and Valentine, after the affront she has received, need not consider it necessary to continue to bury herself alive by being shut up with M. Noirtier."

The count listened with satisfaction to this tale of wounded self-love and defeated ambition. "But it seems to me," said Monte-Cristo, "and I must begin by asking your pardon for what I am about to say, that if M. Noirtier disinherits Mdlle. de Villefort on account of her marrying a man whose father he detested, he cannot have the same cause of complaint against our dear Edward."

"True," said Mdme. de Villefort, with an intonation of voice which it is impossible to describe; "is it not unjust—shamefully unjust? Poor Edward is as much M. Noirtier's grandchild as Valentine, and yet, if she had not been going to marry M. Franz, M. Noirtier would have left her all his money; and supposing Valentine to be disinherited by her grandfather, she will still be three times richer than he." The count listened and said no more.

"However," said Mdme. de Villefort, returning to the one idea which incessantly occupied her mind, "perhaps it would be better to represent this unlucky affair to M. d'Epinay, in order to give him the opportunity of himself renouncing his claim to the hand of Mdlle. de Villefort."

"Undoubtedly," said Villefort, moderating his voice; "a marriage, once concerted and then broken off, throws a sort of discredit on a young lady; then, again, the old reports, which I was so anxious to put an end to, will instantly gain ground,—no, it will all go well; M. d'Epinay, if he is an honorable man, will consider himself more than ever pledged to Mdlle. de Villefort; unless he were actuated by a decided feeling of avarice; but that is impossible."

"I agree with M. de Villefort," said Monte-Cristo, fixing his eyes on Mdme. de Villefort; "and if I were sufficiently intimate with him to allow of giving my advice, I would persuade him, since I have been told M. d'Epinay is coming back, to settle this affair at once beyond all possibility of revocation. I will answer for the success of a project which will reflect so much honor on M. de Villefort." The proctor rose, delighted with the proposition, but his wife slightly changed color. "Well, that is all that I wanted, and I will be guided by a counsellor such as you are," said he, extending his hand to Monte-Cristo. "Therefore let everyone here look upon what has passed to-day as if it had not happened, and as though we had never thought of such a thing as a change in our original plans."

"Sir," said the count, "the world, unjust as it is, will be pleased with your resolution; your friends will be proud of you, and M. d'Epinay, even if he took Mdlle. de Villefort without any dowry, which he will not do, would be delighted with the idea of entering a family which could make such sacrifices in order to keep a promise and fulfil a duty." At the conclusion of these words, the count rose to depart. "Are you going to leave us, Count?" said Mdme. de Villefort.

"I am sorry to say I must do so, madame; I only came to remind you of your promise for Saturday."

"Ah!" said Villefort, "is it at your house in the Champs-Elysées that you receive your visitors?"

"No," said Monte-Cristo, "which is precisely the reason which renders your kindness more meritorious,—it is in the country, only a mile out—at Auteuil."

"At Auteuil?" said Villefort; "true, Mdme. de Villefort told me you lived at Auteuil, since it was to your house that she was taken. And in what part do you reside?"

"Fontaine street."

"Fontaine street!" exclaimed Villefort, in an agitated tone; at what number?"

"No. 28."

"Then," cried Villefort, "was it you who bought the Saint-Méran house?"

"Did it belong to Saint-Méran?" demanded Monte-Cristo.

"Yes," replied Mdme. de Villefort: "and, would you believe it, my husband would never live in it."

"Indeed!" returned Monte-Cristo; "that is a prejudice on your part, M. de Villefort, for which I am quite at a loss to account."

"I do not like Auteuil, sir," said the lawyer, making an evident effort to appear calm.

"But I hope you will not carry your antipathy so far as to deprive me of the pleasure of your company, sir!" said Monte-Cristo.

"No,—I hope—I assure you I will do all I can," stammered Villefort.

"Oh," said Monte-Cristo, "I allow of no excuse. On Saturday, at six o'clock, I shall be expecting you, and if you fail to come, I shall think—for how do I know to the contrary?—that this house, which has remained uninhabited for twenty years, must have some gloomy tradition or dreadful legend connected with it."

"I will come,—I will be sure to come," said Villefort, eagerly.

"Thank you," said Monte-Cristo; "now you must permit me to take my leave of you."

"You said before you were obliged to leave us, M. le Comte," said Mdme. de Villefort, "and you were about to tell us the nature of the engagement which was to deprive us of the pleasure of your society, when your attention was called to some other subject."

"Indeed, madame!" said Monte-Cristo; "I scarcely know if I dare tell you where I am going."——"Bah!"

"Well, then, it is to see a thing on which I have sometimes mused for hours together. A telegraph. So now I have told my secret."

"A telegraph!" repeated Mdme. de Villefort.

"Yes, a semaphore telegraph! I had often seen one placed at the end of a road on a hillock, and in the light of the sun its black arms always reminded one of the claws of an immense beetle; and I assure you it was never without emotion that I gazed on it, for I could not help thinking how wonderful it was that these odd signs should be sent by one man sitting at a table to another standing at a desk, and I should like to be the master spirit who dictates this mystic language."

"Shall I give you a letter to see an office in full work?"

"Never mind, they would not work naturally under inspection of the bearer of a government permit. What line is most interesting?"

"The Spanish one is most busy."

"Thanks!"

CHAPTER XLII.

THE PHANTOM.

AT first sight the exterior of the house at Auteuil presented nothing one would expect from the destined residence of the magnificent Count of Monte-Cristo; but this simplicity was but according to the will of its master; who positively ordered nothing to be altered outside; this was seen by examining the interior. The scene changed. M. Bertuccio had outdone himself in the taste displayed in furnishing, and in the rapidity with which it was executed. In three days had been planted an entirely bare court with poplars, large spreading sycamores shading the different parts of the house, before which, instead of the usual paving-stones, half hidden by the grass, there extended a turf lawn but that morning laid down, and upon which the water was yet glistening. Thus the house had become unrecognizable, and Bertuccio himself declared he scarcely knew it, encircled as it was by trees. The overseer would not have objected, while he was about it, to have made some improvements in the garden, but the count had positively forbidden it to be touched. Bertuccio made amends, however, by loading the antechambers, staircases, and chimneys with flowers. That which, above all, manifested the shrewdness of the steward, and the profound science of the master, the one in carrying out the ideas of the other, was, that this house, which appeared only the night before so sad and gloomy, impregnated with that sickly smell of time, had, in one day, acquired the aspect of life, was scented with its master's favorite perfumes, and had the very light regulated according to his wish. When the count arrived, he had under his touch his books and arms, his eyes rested upon his favorite pictures; his dogs, whose caresses he loved, welcomed him in the antechamber; the birds, whose songs delighted him, cheered him with their music; and the house, awakened from its long sleep, like the sleeping beauty in the wood, lived, sang, and bloomed like the houses we have long cherished, and in which, when we are forced to leave them, we leave a part of our souls. The servants passed gayly along the fine court-yard, some, belonging to the kitchens, gliding down the stairs, restored but the previous day, as if they had always inhabited the house; others filling the coach-houses, where the equipages appeared to have been installed for the last fifty years; and in the stables the horses replied by neighing to the grooms, who spoke to them with much more respect than many servants pay their masters.

On the other side of the house, to match with the library, was the conservatory, ornamented with rare flowers, blossoming in china jars; and in the midst of the greenhouse, marvellous alike to sight and smell, was a billiard-table, apparently abandoned during the last hour by the players, who had left the balls on the cloth. One chamber alone had been respected by Bertuccio. Before this room, to which you could ascend by the grand, and go out by the back staircase, the servants passed with curiosity, and Bertuccio with terror. At five o'clock precisely, the count arrived before the house followed by Ali. Bertuccio was awaiting this arrival with impatience, mingled with uneasiness; he hoped for some compliments, while, at the same time, he feared to have frowns. Monte-Cristo descended into the court-yard, walked all over the house, without giving any sign of approbation or displeasure, until he entered his bed-room, situated on the opposite side of the closed room; when he approached a little piece of furniture, made of rosewood, which we remember to have noticed on a previous occasion. "That will at least serve to put my gloves in," he said.

"Will your Excellency deign to open it?" said the delighted Bertuccio, "and you will find gloves in it." In all the rest of the furniture the count found everything he required—smell-bottles, cigars, trinkets, odds and ends.

"Good!" he said; and M. Bertuccio left enraptured, so great, so powerful, and real was the influence exercised by this man over all who surrounded him.

At precisely six o'clock the clatter of horses' hoofs was heard at the entrance door; it was our captain of Spahis, who had arrived on Medea. "I am sure I am the first," cried Morrel; "I did it on purpose to have you a minute to myself, before every one came. Julie and Emmanuel have a thousand things to tell you. Ah! really this is magnificent! But tell me, count, will your people take care of my horse?"

"Do not alarm yourself, my dear Maximilian—they understand."

"I mean, because she wants petting. If you had seen at what a pace she came, like the wind!"——"I should think so,—a horse that cost 5,000 francs!" said Monte-Cristo, in the tone which a father would use toward a son.

"Do you regret them?" asked Morrel, with his open laugh.

"I? Certainly not!" replied the count. "No; I should only regret if the horse had not proved good."——"It is so good, that I have distanced M. de Château-Renaud, one of the best riders in France, and M. Debray who both mount the minister's Arabians; and close at their heels are the horses of Mdme. Danglars, who always go at six leagues an hour."

"Then they follow you?" asked Monte-Cristo.

"See, they are here!" And at the same minute a carriage with smoking horses, accompanied by two mounted gentlemen, arrived at the gate, which opened before them. The carriage drove round, and stopped at the steps, followed by the horsemen. The instant Debray had touched the ground, he was at the carriage door. He offered his hand to the baroness, who, descending, took it with a peculiarity imperceptible to everyone but Monte-Cristo. But nothing escaped the count's notice; and he observed a little note, slipped with an indescribable ease, bespeaking frequent practice, from the lady's hand to that of the minister's secretary. After his wife the banker descended, pale, as though he had issued from his tomb, instead of his carriage. Mdme. Danglars threw a rapid and inquiring glance around, which could only be interpreted by Monte-Cristo, embracing the court-yard, and the front of the house; then, repressing slight emotion, which must have been seen on her countenance if she had permitted her face to become pale, she ascended the steps, saying to Morrel, "Sir, if you were a friend of mine, I should ask you if you would sell your horse?"

Morrel smiled with an expression very like a grimace, and then turned round to Monte-Cristo, as if to ask him to extricate him from his embarrassment. The count understood him. "Ah, madame!" he said, "I am witness that M. Morrel cannot give up his horse, his honor being engaged in keeping it. He laid a wager he would tame Medea in the space of six months. You understand now that if he were to get rid of it before the time named, he would not only lose his bet, but people would say he was afraid of it; and a brave captain of Spahis cannot risk this, even to gratify a pretty woman, which is, in my opinion, one of the most sacred obligations in the world."

"You see my position, madame," said Morrel, bestowing a grateful smile on Monte-Cristo.

"It seems to me," said Danglars, in his coarse tone, ill-concealed by a forced smile, "that you have already got horses enough." Mdme. Danglars seldom allowed remarks of this kind to pass unnoticed; but, to the surprise of the young people, she pretended not to hear it, and said nothing. Monte-Cristo smiled at her unusual humility, and showed her two immense porcelain jars, covered with marine plants, of a size and delicacy that could alone emanate from nature. The baroness was astonished. "Why," said she, "you could plant one of the chestnut-trees in the Tuileries inside! How can such enormous jars have been manufactured;"——"Ah, madame!" replied Monte-Cristo, "you must not ask of us, the manufacturers, such a question. It is the work of another age, constructed by the genii of earth and water."

"How so?—at what period can that have been?"

"I do not know; I have only heard that an emperor of China had an oven built expressly, and that in this oven twelve jars like this were successively baked. Two broke, from the heat of the fire; the other ten were sunk three hundred fathoms deep into the sea. The sea, knowing what was required of her, threw over them her weeds, encircled them with coral, and encrusted them with shells; the whole was cemented by two hundred years beneath these almost impervious depths, for a revolution carried away the emperor who wished to make the trial, and only left the documents proving the manufacture of the jars and their descent into the sea. At the end of two hundred years the documents were found, and they thought of bringing up the jars. Divers descended in machines, made expressly on the discovery, into the bay where they were thrown; but of ten three only remained, the rest having been broken by the waves. I am fond of these jars, upon which, perhaps, misshapen, frightful monsters have fixed their cold, dull eyes, and in which myriads of small fish have slept, seeking a refuge from the pursuit of their enemies." Meanwhile, Danglars, who had cared little for curiosities, was mechanically tearing off the blossoms of a splendid orange-tree, one after another. When he had finished with the orange-tree he began at the cactus; but this, not being so easily plucked as the orange-tree, pricked him dreadfully. He shuddered, and rubbed his eyes as though awaking from a dream.

"Sir," said Monte-Cristo to him, "I do not recommend my pictures to you, who possess such splendid paintings; but, nevertheless, here are several worth looking at."

"Stay!" said Debray; "I recognize this Hobbema."

"Ah, indeed!"——"Yes; it was offered to the Museum."

"Which, I believe, does not contain one?" said Monte-Cristo.

"No; and yet they refused to buy it."

"Why?" said Château-Renaud.

"You pretend not to know,—because the government was not rich enough."

"Major Bartolomeo Cavalcanti and Count Andrea Cavalcanti!" announced Baptistin. A black satin stock, fresh from the maker's hands, grey moustaches, a bold eye, a major's uniform, ornamented with three medals and five crosses—in fact, the thorough bearing of an old soldier —such was the appearance of Major Bartolomeo Cavalcanti, that affectionate father. Close to him, dressed in entirely new clothes, advanced smilingly Count Andrea Cavalcanti, the dutiful son, whom we also know. The three were talking together. On the entrance of the new-comers, their eyes glanced from father to son, and then, naturally enough, rested on the latter, whom they began criticizing.

"Cavalcanti!" said Debray.

"A fine name," said Morrel.

"Yes," said Château-Renaud, "these Italians are well named and badly dressed."

"You are fastidious, Château-Renaud," replied Debray, "those clothes are well cut and quite new."

"That is just what I find fault with. That gentleman appears to be well dressed for the first time in his life."

"Who are those gentlemen?" asked Danglars of Monte-Cristo.

"Ah! true. You do not know the Italian nobility; the Cavalcanti are all descended from princes."

"Have they any means?"

"Enormous!"

"What do they do?"

"Try to spend it all. They have some business with you, I think, from what they told me the day before yesterday. I, indeed, invited them here to-day on your account. I will introduce you to them."

"But they appear to speak French with a very pure accent," said Danglars.

"The son has been educated in a college in the South; I believe near Marseilles. You will find him quite enthusiastic."

"Upon what subject?" asked Mdme. Danglars.

"The French ladies, madame. He has made up his mind to take a wife from Paris."

"A fine idea that of his!" said Danglars, shrugging his shoulders. Mdme. Danglars looked at her husband with an expression which, at any other time, would have indicated a storm, but she controlled herself.

"The baron appears thoughtful to-day," said Monte-Cristo to her; "are they going to put him in the ministry?"

"Not yet, I think. More likely he has been speculating on the Bourse, and has lost money."

"M. and Mdme. de Villefort!" cried Baptistin. They entered. M. de Villefort, notwithstanding his self-control, was visibly affected; and when Monte-Cristo touched his hand, he felt it tremble. "Certainly, women alone know how to dissimulate," said Monte-Cristo to himself, glancing at Mdme. Danglars, who was smiling on the proctor and embracing his wife. After a short time, the count saw Bertuccio, who, until then, had been occupied on the other side of the house, glide into an adjoining room. He went to him. "What do you want, M. Bertuccio?" said he.

"Your excellency has not stated the number of guests."

"Count for yourself."

Bertuccio glanced through the door, which was ajar. The count watched him.

"Good heavens!" he exclaimed.

"What is the matter?" said the count.

"That lady in a white dress and so many diamonds—the fair one."

"Mdme. Danglars?"

"I do not know her name; but it is she, sir, it is she! the woman of this garden!—a mother—who was walking while she waited for——"

Bertuccio stood at the open door, with his eyes starting and his hair on end.

"Waiting for whom?" Bertuccio, without answering, pointed to Villefort with something of the gesture Macbeth uses to point out Banquo. "Oh, oh!" he at length muttered, "do you see him?"

"Him!—M. de Villefort, the Attorney General? Certainly I see him."

"Then I did not kill him!"

"No; you see plainly he is not dead. Instead of striking between the sixth and seventh left rib, as your countrymen do, you must have struck higher or lower; and life is very tenacious in these lawyers, or rather there is no truth in anything you have told me—it was a flight of the imagination, a dream of your fancy. You went to sleep full of thoughts of vengeance; they weighed heavily upon your stomach; you had the nightmare—that's all. Come, calm yourself, and reckon: the Villeforts, two; the Danglars, four; the Château-Renaud, Debray, Morrel, seven; Major Cavalcanti, eight."

"Eight!" repeated Bertuccio.

"Stop! You are in a shocking hurry to be off—you forget one of my guests. Lean a little to the left. Stay! look at M. Andrea Cavalcanti, that young man in a black coat, looking at Murillo's Madonna; now he is turning." This time Bertuccio would have uttered an exclamation, had not a look from Monte-Cristo silenced him.

"Benedetto?" he muttered; "fatality!"

"Half-past six o'clock has just struck, M. Bertuccio," said the count, severely; "I ordered dinner at that hour, and I do not like to wait;" and he returned to his guests, while Bertuccio, leaning against the wall, succeeded in reaching the dining-room. Five minutes afterwards the doors of the drawing-room were thrown open, and Bertuccio appearing said, with a violent effort, "The dinner is served."

The Count of Monte-Cristo offered his arm to Madame de Villefort. "M. de Villefort," he said, "will you conduct Baroness Danglars?"

Villefort complied, and they passed on to the dining-room.

It was evident that one sentiment pervaded the whole of the guests on entering the dining-room. Each one asked himself what strange influence had conducted them to this house; and yet astonished, even uneasy though they were, they still felt they would not like to be absent. Stimulated by an invincible curiosity, there were none present, even including Cavalcanti and his son, notwithstanding the stiffness of the one and the carelessness of the other, who were not thoughtful, on finding themselves assembled at the house of this incomprehensible man."

The repast was sumptuous; Monte-Cristo had endeavored completely to overturn Parisian ideas, and to feed the curiosity as much as the appetite of his guests. An Oriental feast passed in review before the eyes of the astonished Parisians, who understood that it was possible to expend thousands upon a dinner for ten, but only on the condition of eating pearls, like Cleopatra, or drinking potable gold, like Lorenzo de' Medici. Monte-Cristo noticed the general astonishment, and began laughing and joking about it. "Gentlemen," he said, "you will admit that, when arrived at a certain degree of fortune, the superfluities of life are all that can be desired; and the ladies will allow that, after having risen to a certain eminence of position, the ideal alone can be more exalted. Now, to follow out this reasoning, what is the marvellous?—that which we do not understand. What is it that we really desire?—that which we cannot obtain. Now, to see things which I cannot understand, to procure impossibilities, these are the study of my life. I gratify my wishes by two means—my will and my money.

"What would be the use of living 1800 years after Lucullus, if we can do no better than he could?"

The two Cavalcanti opened their eyes, but had the good sense not to say anything.

"All this is very extraordinary," said Château-Renaud; "still, what I admire the most, I confess, is the marvellous promptitude with which your orders are executed. Is it not true that you only bought this house five or six days ago?"

"Certainly not longer."

"Well, I am sure it is quite transformed since last week. If I remember rightly, it had another entrance, and the courtyard was paved and empty; while to-day we have a splendid lawn, bordered by trees which appear to be a hundred years old."

"Why not? I am fond of grass and shade," said Monte-Cristo.

"Yes," said Mdme. de Villefort, "the door was toward the road before; and on the day of my miraculous escape you brought me into the house from the road, I remember."

"Yes, madame," replied Monte-Cristo; "but I preferred having an entrance which would allow me to see the Bois de Boulogne over my gate."

"In four days!" said Morrel; "it is extraordinary!"

"Indeed,'" said Château-Renaud, "it seems quite miraculous to make a new house out of an old one; for it was very old, and dull too. I recollect coming for my mother to look at it when Saint-Méran advertised it for sale two or three years ago."——"Saint-Méran!" said Mdme. de Villefort; "then this house belonged to Saint-Méran before you bought it!"

"It appears so," replied Monte-Cristo.

"How? do you not know of whom you purchased it?"

"No, indeed; my steward transacts all this business for me."

"It is certainly ten years since the house had been occupied," said

Château-Renaud, "and it was quite melancholy to look at it, with the blinds closed, the doors locked, and the weeds in the court. Really, if the house had not belonged to the father-in-law of the Royal Prosecutor, one might have thought it some accursed place where a horrible crime had been committed."

Villefort, who had hitherto not tasted the three or four glasses of rare wine before him, here took one, and drank it off.

Monte-Cristo allowed a short time to elapse, and then said, "It is singular, baron, but the same idea came across me the first time I entered it; it looked so gloomy I should never have bought it if my steward had not acted for me. Perhaps the fellow had been bribed by the agent."

"It is probable," stammered out De Villefort; "but, believe me, I have nothing to do with this corruption. This house is part of the marriage-portion of Valentine, and Saint-Méran wished to sell it; for, if it had remained another year or two uninhabited, it would have fallen to ruin. It was Morrel's turn to become pale.

"There was, above all, one room," continued Monte-Cristo, "very plain in appearance, hung with red damask, which, I know not why, appeared to me quite dramatic."

"Why so?" said Danglars; "why dramatic?"

"Can we account for instinct?" said Monte-Cristo. "Are there not some places where we seem to breathe sadness?—why, we cannot tell. It is a chain of recollections—an idea which carries you back to other times, to other places—which, very likely, have no connection with the present time and place. And there is something in this room which reminds me forcibly of Desdemona's Stay. Since we have finished dinner, I will show it to you, and then we will take coffee in the garden. After dinner, the play." Monte-Cristo looked inquiringly at his guests. Mdme. de Villefort rose, the host did the same, and the rest followed their example. Villefort and Mdme. Danglars remained for a moment, as if rooted to their seats; they interrogated each other with cold glazed eyes.

"Did you hear?" said Mdme. Danglars.

"We must go," replied Villefort, offering his arm.

Every one else was already scattered in different parts of the house urged by curiosity; for they thought the visit would not be limited to the one room, and that, at the same time, they would obtain a view of the rest of the building, of which Monte-Cristo had created a palace Each one went out by the open doors. Monte-Cristo waited for the two who remained; then, when they had passed, he closed the march with a smile, which, if they could have understood it, would have alarmed them much more than a visit to the room they were about to enter They therefore began by walking through the apartments, many of which were fitted up in the Eastern style, with cushions and divans instead o beds, and pipes instead of furniture. The drawing-rooms were decorated with the rarest pictures, by the old masters; the boudoirs hung with draperies from China, of fanciful colors, fantastic design, and wonderful texture. At length they arrived at the famous room. There was nothing particular about it, excepting that, although daylight had disappeared it was not lighted, and everything in it remained antique, while the rest of the rooms had been re-decorated. These two causes were enough to give it a gloomy tinge.

"Oh!" cried Mdme. de Villefort, "it is really frightful."

Mdme. Danglars tried to utter a few words, but was not heard. Many observations were made, the result of which was the unanimous opinion that there was a sinister appearance in the room. "Is it not so?" asked Monte-Cristo. "Look at that large clumsy bed, hung with such gloomy, blood-colored drapery! And those two crayon portraits, that have faded, from the damp; do they not seem to say, with their pale lips and staring eyes, "Oh, we have seen!"

Villefort became livid; Mdme. Danglars fell into a long seat placed near the chimney.

"Oh!" said Mdme. de Villefort, smiling, "are you courageous enough to sit down upon the very seat perhaps upon which the crime was committed?

Mdme. Danglars rose suddenly.

"And then," said Monte-Cristo, opening a door concealed by the drapery. "Look at it, and tell me what you think of it."

"What a wicked-looking, crooked staircase," said Château-Renaud, smiling.

"I do not know whether the wine of Chios produces melancholy, but certainly everything appears to me black in this house," said Debray.

"Can you imagine," said Monte-Cristo, "some Othello, on a stormy, dark night, descending these stairs step by step, carrying a load, which he wishes to hide from the sight of man, if not from God?" Mdme. Danglars fainted on the arm of Villefort, who was obliged to support himself against the wall.

"Ah, Madame," cried Debray, "what is the matter with you? how pale you look!"

"What is the matter with her?" said Mdme. de Villefort; "it is very simple: M. de Monte-Cristo is relating horrible stories to us, doubtless intending to frighten us to death."

"Yes," said Villefort, "really, count, you frighten the ladies."

"What is the matter?" asked Debray, in a whisper, of Mdme. Danglars.——"Nothing," she replied, with a violent effort. "I want air! that is all."——"Will you come into the garden?" said Debray, advancing towards the back staircase.

"No, no!" she answered, "I would rather remain here."

"Are you really frightened Madame?" said Monte-Cristo.

"Oh, no, sir," said Mdme. Danglars; "but you suppose scenes in a manner which gives them the appearance of reality."

"As, yes!" said Monte-Cristo smiling; "it is all a matter of the imagination. Why should we not imagine this the apartment of an honest matron? And this bed with red hangings, a bed visited by the goddess Lucina? And that mysterious staircase, the passage through which, not to disturb their sleep, the doctor and nurse pass, or even the father carrying the sleeping child?" Here Mdme. Danglars, instead of being calmed by the soft picture, uttered a groan and fainted.

"Mdme. Danglars is ill," said Villefort; "it would be better to take her to her carriage."

"Oh! and I have forgotten my smelling-bottle!" said Monte-Cristo.

"I have mine," said Mdme. de Villefort: and she passed over to Monte-Cristo a bottle full of the red liquid whose good properties the count had tested on Edward.

"Ah!" said Monte-Cristo, taking it from her hand.

"Yes," she said, "at your advice I have tried."

"And have you succeeded?"

"I think so."

Mdme. Danglars was carried into the adjoining room; Monte-Cristo dropped a very small portion of the red liquid upon her lips; she returned to consciousness.

"Ah!" she cried, "what a frightful dream!"

Villefort pressed her hand to let her know it was not a dream. Danglars was sought, but, little interested in poetical ideas, he had gone into the garden, and was talking with Major Cavalcanti on the projected railway from Leghorn to Florence. Monte-Cristo seemed in despair. He took the arm of Mdme. Danglars, and conducted her into the garden, where they found Danglars taking coffee between the Cavalcanti. "Really, madame," he said, "did I alarm you much?"

"Oh no, sir," she answered, "but you know, things impress us differently, according to the mood of our minds." Villefort forced a laugh. "And then, you know," he said, "an idea, a supposition, is sufficient."

——"Well," said Monte-Cristo, "you may believe me if you like, but it is my belief that a crime has been committed in this house."

"Take care!" said Mdme. de Villefort, "the prosecutor is here."

"Ah," replied Monte-Cristo, "since that is the case, I will take advantage of his presence to make my declaration."

"Oh, this is very interesting," said Debray; "if there really has been a crime, we will investigate it."

"There has been a crime!" said Monte-Cristo. "Come this way, gentlemen; come, M. Villefort, for a declaration to be available, should be made before the competent authorities." He then took Villefort's arm, and, at the same time, holding that of Mdme. Danglars under his own, he dragged the lawyer to the tree, where the shade was thickest. All the other guests followed. "Stay," said Monte-Cristo, "here, in this very spot," (and he stamped upon the ground), "I had the earth dug up and fresh mould put in, to refresh these old trees; well, my man, digging, found a box, or rather the iron-work of a box, in the midst of which was the skeleton of a newly-born infant." Monte-Cristo felt the arm of Mdme. Danglars stiffen, while that of Villefort trembled. "A newly-born infant!" repeated Debray; "this affair becomes serious!"

"Who said it was a crime?" asked Villefort, with a last effort.

"How? is it not a crime to bury a living child in a garden?" cried Monte-Cristo. "And pray what do you call such an action?"

"But who said it was buried alive?"

"Why bury it there if it were dead? This garden has never been a cemetery."

"What is done to infanticides in this country?" asked Major Cavalcanti, innocently.

"Oh, their heads are soon cut off," said Danglars.

"Ah! indeed!" said Cavalcanti.

"I think so: am I not right, M. de Villefort?" asked Monte-Cristo.

"Yes, count," replied De Villefort, in a voice now scarcely human.

Monte-Cristo saw that the two persons for whom he had prepared this scheme could scarcely bear it, so, not wishing to carry it too far, he said, "Come, gentlemen, some coffee, we seem to have forgotten it;" and he conducted the guests back to the table on the lawn.

The lawyer had found time to whisper to Mdme. Danglars, "I must speak to you to-morrow, at my office, or in the courts, if you like, that is the surest place."

"I will go."

At this moment Mdme. de Villefort approached. "Thanks, my dear friend," said Mdme. Danglars, trying to smile; "it is over now, and I am much better."

CHAPTER XLIII.

THE BEGGAR.

M. DE VILLEFORT was the first to give the signal of departure. He offered a seat in his landau to Mdme. Danglars, that she might be under the care of his wife. Danglars, more and more delighted with Major Cavalcanti, had offered him a seat in his carriage. Andrea Cavalcanti found his tilbury waiting at the door; the tiger was standing on tiptoes to hold a large iron-grey horse. Andrea had spoken very little during dinner; he was an intelligent lad, and he feared to utter some absurdity before so many grand people, amongst whom he saw with dilating eyes the proctor. Then he had been seized upon by Danglars, who, taking a rapid glance at the stiff-necked old major and his modest son, and taking into consideration the hospitality of the count, made up his mind that he was in the society of some nabob come to Paris to finish the worldly education of his only son. He contemplated with unspeakable delight the large diamond which shone on the major's little finger; for the major, like a prudent man, in case of any accident happening to his bank-notes, had immediately converted them into valuables. Then, after dinner, on the pretext of business, he questioned the father and son upon their mode of living; and the father and son, previously informed that it was through Danglars the one was to receive his 48,000 francs and the other 50,000 livres annually, they were so full of affability, that they would have shaken hands even with the banker's servants, so much did their gratitude need an object to expend itself upon. Thus it was with much politeness that he heard Cavalcanti pronounce these words, "Tomorrow, sir, I shall have the honor of waiting upon you on business."

"And I, sir," said Danglars, "shall be most happy to receive you." Upon which he offered to take Cavalcanti in his carriage, if it would not be depriving him of the company of his son. To this Cavalcanti replied, by saying, that for some time past his son had lived independently of him; that he had his own horses and carriages, and that not having come together, it would not be difficult for them to leave separately. The major seated himself, therefore, by the side of Danglars, more and more charmed with the ideas of order and economy which ruled this man, and yet who, being able to allow his son 50,000 francs a year, might be supposed to possess a fortune of 500,000 or 600,000 livres.

As for Andrea, he began, by way of showing off, to scold his groom, who, instead of bringing the tilbury to the steps of the house, had taken it to the outer door, thus giving him the trouble of walking thirty steps to reach it. The groom heard him with humility, took the bit of the impatient animal with his left hand, and with the right held out the reins to Andrea, who, taking them from him, rested his polished boot lightly on the step. At that moment a hand touched his shoulder. The young man turned round, thinking that Danglars or Monte-Cristo had forgotten something they wished to tell him, and had returned just as they were starting. But instead of either of these, he saw nothing but a strange face, sunburnt, and encircled by a beard, with eyes brilliant as carbuncles, and a smile upon the mouth which displayed a perfect set of white teeth, pointed and sharp as the wolf's or jackal's. A red handkerchief encircled his grey head; torn and filthy garments covered his large bony limbs, which seemed as though, like those of a skeleton, they would rattle as he walked; and the hand with which he leaned upon the young man's shoulder, and which was the first thing Andrea saw, seemed of a gigantic size. Did the young man recognize that face by the light of the lantern in his tilbury, or was he merely struck with the horrible appearance of his interrogator? We cannot say; but only relate the fact that he shuddered and stepped back suddenly. "What do you want of me?" he asked.

"Pardon me, my friend, if I disturb you," said the man with the red handkerchief, "but I wish you to spare me the walk back to Paris. I am very tired, and not having eaten so good a dinner as you, I can scarcely support myself." The young man shuddered at this gross familiarity. "Tell me," he said—"tell me what you want?"

"Well, then, I want you to take me up in your fine carriage, and carry me back." Andrea turned pale, but said nothing.

"Yes!" said the man, thrusting his hands into his pockets, and looking impudently at the youth; "I have taken the whim into my head; do you understand, Master Benedetto?"

At this name, no doubt, the young man reflected a little, for he went toward his groom, saying,—"This man is right; I did indeed charge him with a commission, the result of which he must tell me; walk to the barrier, there take a cab, that you may not be too late." The surprised groom retired.

"Let me at least reach a shady spot," said Andrea.

"Oh, as for that, I'll conduct you to a splendid spot," said the man with the handkerchief; and, taking the horse's bit, he led the tilbury to a place where it was certainly impossible for any one to witness the honor that Andrea conferred upon him.

"Don't think I want the honor of riding in your fine carriage," said he; "oh, no, it's only because I am tired, and also because I have a little business to talk over with you."

"Come, step in," said the young man. It was a pity this scene had not occurred in daylight, for it was curious to see this rascal throwing himself heavily down on the cushion beside the young and elegant driver of the tilbury. Andrea drove past the last house in the village without saying a word to his companion, who smiled complacently, as though well pleased to find himself traveling in so comfortable a vehicle. Once out of Auteuil, Andrea looked around, in order to assure himself that he could neither be seen nor heard; and then, stopping the horse and crossing his arms before the man, he asked,—"Now, tell me why you come to disturb my tranquillity?"—"Let me ask you why you deceived me? When we parted, you told me you were going to travel through Piedmont and Tuscany; but instead of that, you come to Paris."

"How does that annoy you?"

"It does not; on the contrary, I think it will answer my purpose."

"So," said Andrea, "you are speculating upon me?"

"What fine words he uses! Well, well, don't be angry, my boy; you know well enough what it is to be unfortunate; and misfortunes make us jealous. I thought you were earning a living in Tuscany or Piedmont by acting as light porter or *cicerone;* and I pitied you sincerely, as I would a child of my own. You know I always did call you my boy!"

"Come, come, what then?"

"Patience! patience!"

"I am patient, but go on."

"All at once I see you pass through the barrier, with a groom, a tilbury, and fine new clothes. You must have discovered a mine, or else become a stockbroker."

"So that, as you acknowledge, you are jealous?"—"No, I am pleased —so pleased that I wished to congratulate you; but as I am not quite properly dressed, I chose my opportunity, that I might not compromise you."

"Yes, and a fine opportunity you have chosen!" exclaimed Andrea; "you speak to me before my servant."

"How can I help that, my boy? I speak to you when I can catch you. You have a quick horse, a light tilbury, you are naturally as slippery as an eel; if I had missed you to-night, I might not have had another chance."

"You see, I do not conceal myself."

"You are lucky; I wish I could say as much; I do conceal myself; and then I was afraid you would not recognize me, but you did," added Caderousse, with his unpleasant smile. "It was very polite of you."

"Come," said Andrea, "what do you want?"—"You do not speak affectionately to me, Benedetto, my old friend; that is not right; take care, or I may become troublesome." This menace smothered the young man's passion. He trotted his horse on. "You should not speak so to an old friend like me, Caderousse, as you said just now; you are a native of Marseilles, I am—"

"Do you know then now what you are?"

"No, but I was brought up in Corsica; you are old and obstinate, I am young and wilful. Between folks like us threats are out of place, everything should be amicably arranged. Is it my fault if Fortune, which has frowned on you, has been kind to me?"

"Fortune has been kind to you, then? Your tilbury, your groom, your clothes, are then not hired? Good, so much the better," said Caderousse, his eyes sparkling with avarice.

"Oh! you knew that well enough before speaking to me," said Andrea, becoming more and more excited. "If I had been wearing a handkerchief like yours on my head, rags on my back, and worn-out shoes on my feet, you would not have hailed me."

"You wrong me, my boy; now I have found you, nothing prevents my being as well-dressed as any one, knowing, as I do, the goodness of your heart. If you have two coats you will give me one of them. I used to divide my soup and beans with you when you were hungry."

"True," said Andrea.

"How did you come to be dining with that prince whose house you have just left?"

"He is not a prince; simply a count."

"A count, and a rich one too, eh?"

"Yes; but you had better not have anything to say to him, for he is not a very good-tempered gentleman."

"Oh! be satisfied! I have no design upon your count, and you shall have him all to yourself. But," said Caderousse, again smiling with the disagreeable expression he had before assumed, "you must pay for it— you understand?"——"Well, what do you want?"

"I think that with a hundred—a hundred and fifty francs a month I should be quite happy."

"Here are two hundred," said Andrea; and he placed ten gold pieces in the hand of Caderousse.

"Good!" said Caderousse.

"Apply to the steward on the first day of every month, and you will receive the same sum."

"Come, come; I always said you were a fine fellow, and it is a blessing when good fortune happens to such as you. But tell me all about it?"

"The fact is, I have found my father."

"What! a real father?"

"Yes, so long as he pays me—"

"You'll honor and believe him—that's right. What is his name?"

"Major Cavalcanti?"

"And who found this father for you?"

"The Count of Monte-Cristo."

"The man whose house you have just left?"

"Yes."

"I wish you would try and find me a situation with him as grandfather, since he holds the money-chest!"

"Well, I will mention you to him. Meanwhile, since you interest your-self in my affairs, I think it is now my turn to ask you some questions."

"Ah, true! Well; I shall rent a room in some respectable house, wear a decent coat, shave every day, and go and read the papers in a saloon. Then, in the evening, I will go to the theatre; I shall look like some retired baker. This is my wish."

"Come, if you will only put this scheme into execution, and be steady, nothing could be better."

"Do you think so? And you—what will you become? A peer of France?"

"Ah!" said Andrea, "who knows?"

"Major Cavalcanti is already one, perhaps; but then, hereditary rank is abolished."

"No politics, Caderousse! And now that you have all you want, and that we understand each other, jump down from the tilbury and dis-appear."

"Not at all, my good friend."

"How! not at all?"

"Why, I should certainly be arrested at the barriers! Then, to justify myself, I should say that you gave me the money; this would cause inquiries; it would be found that I left Toulon without giving due notice, and I should then be reconducted to the shores of the Mediterranean. Then I should become simply No. 106, and good-bye to my dream of resembling the retired baker! No, no, my boy; I prefer remaining hon-orably in the capital." Andrea scowled. Certainly, the reputed son of Major Cavalcanti was a hasty fellow. He drew up for a minute, threw a rapid glance around him; and, after doing so, his hand fell instantly into his pocket, where it began playing with a pistol. But, meanwhile, Cade-rousse, who had never taken his eyes off his companion, passed his hand behind his back, and unclasped a long Spanish knife, which he always carried with him, to be ready in case of need. The two friends, as we see, were worthy of and understood one another. Andrea's hand left his pocket inoffensively, and was carried up to the red moustachio, which it played with for some time. "Good Caderousse," he said, "how happy you will be!"

"I will do my best," said the innkeeper, reclasping his knife.

"Well, then, we will go into Paris. But how will you pass through the barrier without exciting suspicion? It seems to me that you are in more danger riding than on foot."

"Wait," said Caderousse, "we shall see." He then took the great-coat with the large collar, which the groom had left behind in the tilbury, and put it on his back; then he took off Cavalcanti's hat, which he placed upon his own head; and finally assumed the careless attitude of a servant whose master drives himself.

"But, tell me," said Andrea, "am I to remain bareheaded?"

"Pooh!" said Caderousse; "it is so windy that your hat can easily appear to have blown off."

"Come, come; enough of this," said Cavalcanti.

"What are you waiting for?" said Caderousse. "I hope I am not the cause."

"Hush!" exclaimed Andrea. They passed the barrier without accident. At the first cross street Andrea stopped his horse, and Caderousse leaped out.

"Well!" said Andrea, "my servant's coat and my hat?"

"Ah!" said Caderousse, "you would not like me to risk taking cold?"

"But what am I to do?"

"You! oh, you are young, whilst I am beginning to get old. We shall meet again, Benedetto;" and running into a court, he disappeared. "Alas!" said Andrea, sighing, "one cannot be completely happy in this world!"

CHAPTER XLIV

PLANS OF MARRIAGE.

It was not often that Danglars looked into his wife's own apartments, but the fancy took him. He waddled in, flopped himself down on the sofa and as a pet dog resented his intrusion, he seized him by the neck, and threw him to the other side of the room upon a couch. The animal uttered a yelp during the transit, but, arrived at its destination, it crouched behind the cushions, and, stupefied at such unusual treatment, remained silent and motionless.

"Do you know, sir," asked the baroness, "that you are improving? Generally you are only rude, but to-night you are brutal."

"It is because I am in a worse humor than usual," replied Danglars. Hermine looked at the banker with supreme disdain. These glances frequently exasperated the pride of Danglars, but this evening he took no notice of them.

"And what have I to do with your ill-humor?" said the baroness, irritated at the impassability of her husband; "do these things concern me? Keep your ill-humor at home in your chests: or, since you have clerks whom you pay, vent it upon them."

"Not so," replied Danglars; "your advice is wrong, so I shall not follow it. My chests are my Pactolus, as, I think, M. Demoustier says, and I will not retard its course, or disturb its calm. My clerks are honest

men, who earn my fortune, whom I pay much below their deserts, if
I may value them according to what they bring in; therefore I shall not
get into a passion with them; those with whom I will be in a passion
are those who eat my dinners, mount my horses, and exhaust my fortune."

"And pray who are the persons who exhaust your fortune? Explain
yourself more clearly, I beg, sir."

"Oh, make yourself easy!—I am not speaking riddles, and you will
soon know what I mean. The people who exhaust my fortune are those
who draw out 700,000 francs in the course of an hour."

"I do not understand you, sir," said the baroness, trying to disguise
the agitation of her voice and the flush of her face. "You understand
me perfectly, on the contrary," said Danglars: "but, if you will persist, I
will tell you that I have just lost 700,000 francs upon the Spanish loan."

"And pray," asked the baroness, "am I responsible for this loss?"

"Why not?"——"Is it my fault you have lost 700,000 francs?"

"Certainly it is not mine."——"Once for all, sir," replied the baroness,
sharply, "I tell you I will not hear cash named; it is a style of language
I never heard in the house of my parents or my first husband."

"Oh! I can well believe that, for neither of them was worth a penny."

"The better reason for my not being conversant with the slang of the
bank, which is here dinning in my ears from morning to night; that noise
of crowns jingling, which are constantly being counted and re-counted, is
odious to me. I only know one thing I dislike more, which is the sound
of your voice."

"Really!" said Danglars. "Well, this surprises me, for I thought
you took the liveliest interest in my affairs! Last February you were the
first who told me of the Haytian funds. You had dreamt that a ship had
entered the harbor at Havre, and brought news that a payment France
had looked upon as lost was going to be made. I know how clear-sighted
your dreams are; I therefore purchased immediately as many shares as
I could of the Haytian debt, and I gained 400,000 francs by it, of which
100,000 have been honestly paid to you. You spent it as you pleased, that
was your business. In March there was a question about a grant to a
railway. Three companies presented themselves, each offering equal
securities. You told me that your instinct,—and although you pretend
to know nothing about speculations, I think, on the contrary, that your
comprehension is very clear upon certain affairs,—well, you told me that
your instinct led you to believe the grant would be given to the company
called the Southern. I bought two-thirds of the shares of that company;
as you had foreseen, the shares became of triple value, and I picked up
a million, from which 250,000 francs were paid to you for pin-money.
How have you spent this 250,000 francs?—it is no business of mine."

"When are you coming to the point?" cried the baroness, shivering
with anger and impatience. "Patience, madame, I am coming to it."

"That's fortunate!"

"In April you went to dine at the minister's. You heard a private conversation respecting the affairs of Spain—on the expulsion of Don Carlos. I bought some Spanish shares. The expulsion took place and I pocketed 600,000 francs the day Charles V. repassed the Bidassoa. Of these 600,000 francs you took 50,000 crowns. They were yours, you disposed of them according to your fancy, and I asked no questions; but it is not the less true that you have this year received 500,000 livres."

"Well, sir, and what then?"

"Ah, yes, it was just after this that you spoiled everything!"

"Really, your manner of speaking—"

"It expresses my meaning, and that is all I want. Well, three days after that you talked politics with M. Debray, and you fancied from his words that Don Carlos had returned to Spain. Well, I sold my shares, the news was spread, and I no longer sold but gave them; next day I find the telegraph had been tampered with, madame! as if in order to spite me! for by this accident or intention, I lost 700,000 on the false news."

"Well?"

"Well! since I gave you a fourth of my gains, I think you owe me a fourth of my losses: the fourth of 700,000 francs is 175,000 francs."

"What you say is absurd, and I cannot see why M. Debray's name is mixed up in this affair."

"Because if you do not possess the 175,000 francs I reclaim, you must have lent them to your friends, and M. Debray is one of your friends."

"For shame!" exclaimed the baroness.

"Oh! let us have no gestures, no screams, no modern drama, or you will oblige me to tell you that I see Debray leave here, pocketing nearly the whole of the 500,000 livres you have handed over to him this year; while he smiles to himself, saying, that he has found that which the most skilful players have never discovered—that is, a game, where he wins without playing, and is no loser when he loses." The baroness became enraged. "Wretch!" she cried, "will you dare to tell me you did not know what you now reproach me with?"

"I do not say that I did know it, and I do not say that I did not know it. I have never interfered in your affairs, excepting for your good; treat me in the same way. You say you have nothing to do with my cash-box. Be it so. Do as you like with your own, but do not fill or empty mine. Besides, how do I know that this was not a political trick; that the minister, enraged at seeing me in the opposition, and jealous of the popular sympathy I excite, has not concerted with M. Debray to ruin me? Who ever heard of such an occurrence as this?—A false telegraphic despatch—it is almost impossible for signals to have been made different from those of the two last telegrams. It was done on purpose for me, I am sure of it."

"Sir," said the baroness, humbly, "are you not aware that the man employed there was dismissed, that they talked of prosecuting him, that orders were issued to arrest him, and that this order would have been put into execution if he had not escaped their researches by a flight which proves either his madness or his guilt? It was a mistake."

"Yes, which made fools laugh, which caused the minister to have a sleepless night, and his secretaries to stain several sheets of paper, but which has cost me 700,000 francs."

"But, sir," said Hermine, suddenly, "if all this is, as you say, caused by M. Debray, why, instead of going direct to him, do you come and tell me of it? Why to accuse the man do you address the woman?"

"Do I know M. Debray?—do I wish to know him?—do I wish to know that he gives advice?—do I wish to follow it?—do I speculate? No; you do all this, not I."

"Still it seems to me that, as you profit by it—"

Danglars shrugged his shoulders. "Foolish creature," he exclaimed. "Women fancy they have talent because they have managed two or three intrigues without being the talk of Paris! But know that I see, and always have seen, during the last sixteen years. What has been the result?— that, thanks to my pretended ignorance, there are none of your friends, from Villefort to Debray, who have not trembled before me, the master of the house,—the only title I desire with respect to you. I will allow you to make me hateful; but I will prevent your rendering me ridiculous, and, above all, I forbid you to ruin me."

The baroness had been tolerably composed until the name of Villefort had been pronounced; but then she became pale, and, rising, as if touched by a spring, she stretched out her hands as though conjuring an apparition; she then took two or three steps toward her husband, as though to tear the secret from him, of which he was ignorant, or which he withheld from some odious calculation, as all his calculations were. "Villefort!— What do you mean?"

"I mean that Nargonne, your first husband, being neither a philosopher nor a banker, or perhaps being both, and seeing there was nothing to be got out of a lawyer, died of grief or anger at finding, after an absence of nine months, that you had been in a delicate state, sick. I am brutal,— I not only allow it, but boast of it; it is one of the reasons of my success in commercial business. Why did he kill himself instead of you? Because he had no cash to save. My life belongs to my cash. M. Debray has made me lose 700,000 francs; let him bear his share of the loss, and we will go on as before; if not, let him become bankrupt for the 250,000 livres, and do as all bankrupts do—disappear. He is a charming fellow, I allow, when his news is correct; but when it is not, there are fifty others in the world who would do better than he."

Madame Danglars was rooted to the spot; she made a violent effort to reply to this last attack; but she fell upon a chair, thinking of Villefort, of the dinner scene, of the strange series of misfortunes which had taken place in her house during the last few days, and changed the usual calm of her establishment to a scene of scandalous debate.

The day following this scene, at the hour the banker usually chose to pay a visit to Mdme. Danglars, on his way to his office, his *coupé* did not appear in the yard. At this time, that is, about half-past twelve, Mdme. Danglars ordered her carriage, and went out. Danglars, placed behind a curtain, watched the departure he had been waiting for. He gave orders that he should be informed directly Mdme. Danglars appeared; but at two o'clock she had not returned. He then called for his horses, drove to the Chamber, and inscribed his name to speak against the budget. From twelve to two o'clock Danglars had remained in his study, unsealing his despatches, and becoming more and more sad every minute, heaping figure upon figure, and receiving, among other visits, one from Major Cavalcanti, who, as stiff and as exact as ever, presented himself precisely at the hour named the night before, to terminate his business with the banker. On leaving the Chamber, Danglars, who had shown violent marks of agitation during the sitting, and been more bitter than ever against the ministry, re-entered his carriage, and told the coachman to drive to the Avenue Champs-Elysées.

Monte-Cristo was at home; only he was engaged with some one, and begged Danglars to wait for a moment in the drawing-room. While the banker was waiting, the door opened, and a man dressed as a priest entered, who, doubtless more familiar with the house than he was, instead of waiting, merely bowed and, passing on to the further apartments, disappeared. A minute after the door by which the priest had entered re-opened, and Monte-Cristo appeared. "Pardon me," said he, "my dear baron, but one of my friends, the Abbé Busoni, whom you perhaps saw pass by, has just arrived in Paris; not having seen him for a long time, I could not make up my mind to leave him sooner, so I hope this will be sufficient reason for my having made you wait."

"Nay," said Danglars, "it is my fault; I have chosen my visit at a wrong time, and will retire."

"Not at all; on the contrary, be seated; but what is the matter with you? You look careworn; have you had another fall at the Bourse?"——
"No; I am safe for a few days at least. I am only annoyed about a bankrupt of Trieste."

"Really! Does it happen to be Jacopo Manfredi?"

"Exactly so. Imagine a man who has transacted business with me for I do not know how long, to the amount of a million francs during the year. Never a mistake or delay: a fellow who paid like a prince. Well, I was a million in advance with him, and now my fine Manfredi suspends payment!"

"This, with my Spanish blunder, made a pretty end to the month."
——"Then you really lost by that affair in Spain?"

"Yes; only 700,000 francs!—nothing more!"

"But making a million and a half in this month! six more such months and you will be at the end of the purse!"

"Not at all, Count! I am embarked on nothing but sure affairs now," replied Danglars, with the air of a mountebank trumpeting his own praises; "to involve me, three governments must crumble to dust."

"So much the better, I congratulate you, my dear M. Danglars," said Monte-Cristo; "I see I was deceived, and that you belong to the class next to first-rate fortunes."

"I think I may aspire to that honor," said Danglars with a smile, which reminded Monte-Cristo of one of those sickly moons which bad artists are so fond of daubing into their pictures of rains; "but, while we are speaking of business," he added, pleased to find an opportunity of changing the subject, "tell me what I am to do for M. Cavalcanti."

"Give him money, if he is recommended to you, and the recommendation seems good."

"Excellent! he presented himself this morning with a bond of 40,000 francs, payable at sight, on you, signed by Busoni, and returned by you to me, with your indorsement; of course, I immediately counted him over the forty bank-notes."

Monte-Cristo nodded his head in token of assent. "But that is not all," continued Danglars; "he has opened an account with my house for his son."

"May I ask how much he allows the young man?"

"Five thousand francs per month."

"Sixty thousand francs per year. I thought I was right in believing that Cavalcanti to be a stingy fellow. How can a young man live upon 5,000 francs a month?"

"But you understand that if the young man should want a few thousand more—"

"Do not advance it; the father will never repay it; you do not know these ultramontane millionaires; they are regular misers. And by whom were they recommended to you?"

"Oh, by the house of Fenzi, one of the best in Florence."

"I do not mean to say you will lose, but, nevertheless, mind you hold to the terms of the agreement."

"Would you not trust the Cavalcanti!"

"I? oh, I would advance six millions on his signature. I was only speaking in reference to the second-rate fortunes we were mentioning just now."

"And with all this, how plain he is! I should never have taken him for anything more than a mere major."

"And you would have flattered him, for certainly, as you say, he has no manners. The first time I saw him he appeared to me like an old lieutenant grown mouldy under the epaulet. But all the Italians are the same; they are like old Jews when they are not glittering in Oriental splendor."

"The young man is better," said Danglars. "Ah, I believe noblemen marry amongst themselves, do they not?" asked Danglars, carelessly; "they like to unite their fortunes."

"It is usual, certainly; but Cavalcanti is an original who does nothing like other people. I cannot help thinking he has brought his son to France to choose a wife."

"And you have heard his fortune mentioned?"——"Nothing else was talked of; only some said he was worth millions, and others that he did not possess a sou."

"And what is your opinion?"—"That all these old lieutenant-governors, and ancient free-lances for the Cavalcanti have commanded armies and governed provinces,—have buried their millions in nooks, the secret of which they have only transmitted to their eldest sons, who have done the same from generation to generation, and the proof of this is seen in their yellow and dry appearance, like the florins of the Italian republics, which, from being constantly gazed upon, have become reflected in them."

"Certainly," said Danglars, "and this is further supported by the fact of their not possessing an inch of land."

"Very little, at least; I know of none which Cavalcanti possesses, excepting his palace in Lucca."

"Ah? he has a palace?" said Danglars, laughing: "come, that is something."

"Yes; and more than that, he lets it to the Minister of Finances while he lives in a rented house. Oh! as I told you before, I think the good man very close!"

"Come, you do not flatter him."

"I scarcely know him; I think I have seen him three times in my life; all I know relating to him is through Busoni and himself; he was telling me this morning that, tired of letting his property lie dormant in Italy, a dead nation, he wished to find a method, either in France or England, of multiplying his millions; but remember, that though I place great confidence in Busoni, I am not responsible for this."

"Never mind; accept my thanks for the client you have sent me: it is a fine name to inscribe on my lips, and my cashier was quite proud of it when I explained to him who the Cavalcanti were. By the way, this is merely a simple question, when these kind of people marry off their sons, must they give them any fortune?"

"Oh, that depends upon circumstances. I know an Italian prince, rich as a gold mine, one of the noblest families in Tuscany, who, when his sons married according to his wish, gave them millions; and when they married against his consent merely allowed them thirty crowns a month. Should Andrea marry according to his father's views, he will, perhaps, give him one, two, or three millions. For example, supposing it were the daughter of a banker, he might take an interest in the house of the father-in-law of his son; then again, if he disliked his choice, the major takes the key, double-locks his coffer, and Master Andrea would be obliged to live like the younger son of an English peer, by shuffling cards or rattling dice."

"Ah! that boy will find out some Bavarian or Peruvian princess; he will want a crown and an immense fortune."

"No; these grand lords on the other side of the Alps frequently marry into plain families; like Jupiter, they like to cross the race. But do you wish to marry off Andrea, my dear M. Danglars, that you are asking so many questions?"

"Faith!" said Danglars, "it would not be a bad speculation, I fancy, and you know I am a speculator."

"You are not thinking of Mdlle. Danglars, I hope; you would not like poor Andrea to have his throat cut by Albert?"

"Albert!" repeated Danglars, shrugging his shoulders; "ah, yes; he would care very little about it, I think."

"But he is betrothed to your daughter, I believe, whose fortune will be great, no doubt, especially if the telegraph should not make any more mistakes."

"Oh! I do not mean her fortune only; but tell me, why did you not invite the Morcerfs to your dinner?"

"I did so, but the count excused himself on account of Mdme. de Morcerf being obliged to go to Dieppe for the benefit of sea air."

"Yes, yes," said Danglars, laughing, "it would do her a great deal of good."

"Why so?"

"Because it is the air she always breathed in her youth."

Monte-Cristo took no notice of this ill-natured remark.

"But still, if Albert be not so rich as Mdlle. Danglars," said the count, "you must allow that he has a fine name?"

"Look, at my coat-of-arms, it is worth more than Morcerf's."

"Why so?"

"Because, though I am not a baron by birth, my real name is, at least, Danglars, while his name is not Morcerf. I have been made a baron, so that I actually am one; he made himself a count, so that he is not one at all."

"Impossible!" "Listen, my dear count; Morcerf has been my friend, or rather my acquaintance, during the last thirty years. You know I have made the most of my arms, though I never forgot my origin."

"A proof of great humility or great pride," said Monte-Cristo.

"Well, when I was a clerk, Morcerf was a mere fisherman, one Johnny Newcomes, Fernand Mondego. I have bought enough fish of him to know his name."

"Then, why did you think of giving your daughter to him?"

"Because Fernand and Danglars, being about, both having become noble, both rich, are both equal in worth, excepting that there have been things mentioned of him never said of me."

"Ah, yes! what you tell me recalls to mind something about the name of Mondego. I have heard that name in Greece."

"In conjunction with the affairs of Ali Pacha?"

"Exactly so."——"This is the mystery," said Danglars, "I acknowledge I would have given anything to find it out."

"Probably you have some correspondent in Greece?"

"I should think so."

"Well, write to your correspondent, and ask him what part was played by a Frenchman named Fernand Mondego in the catastrophe of Ali Tobelen."

"You are right," exclaimed Danglars, rising quickly, "I will write to-day."

"And if you should hear of anything very scandalous—"

"I will communicate it to you."

"You will oblige me." Danglars rushed out of the room, and made but one leap into his carriage.

CHAPTER XLV.

THE OFFICE OF THE PROSECUTOR GENERAL.

LET us leave the banker driving his horses at their fullest speed, and follow Mdme. Danglars in her morning excursion to the Palace of Justice.

There was a great press of people in M. de Villefort's ante-chamber; but Mdme. Danglars had no occasion even to pronounce her name; the instant she appeared the doorkeeper conducted her by a private passage to Villefort's office. The magistrate was seated in an arm-chair, writing, with his back toward the door; he heard it open, and the door-keeper pronounce the words, "Walk in, madame," and then re-close it, without moving; but no sooner had the man's footsteps ceased, than he started up, drew the bolts, closed the curtains, and examined every corner of the room. Then, when he had assured himself that he could neither

be seen nor heard, and was consequently relieved of doubts, he said,—
"Thanks, madame,—thanks for your punctuality;" and he offered a chair
to Mdme. Danglars, which she accepted, for her heart beat so violently
that she felt nearly suffocated.

"It is a long time, madame," said the proctor, describing a half-
circle with his chair, so as to place himself exactly opposite to Madame
Danglars,—"since I had the pleasure of speaking alone with you; and
I regret that we have now met only to enter upon a painful conversation."

"Nevertheless, sir, you see I have answered your first appeal; although certainly, the conversation must be much more painful for me
than for you." Villefort smiled bitterly.

"Sir," said Mdme. Danglars, "you can feel for my emotion, can you
not? Spare me then, I beseech you. When I look at this room, whence
so many guilty creatures have departed trembling and ashamed—when
I look at that chair before which I now sit trembling and ashamed, oh!
it requires all my reason to convince me that I am not a very guilty woman
and you a menacing judge."

Villefort dropped his head, and sighed. "And I," he said, "I feel
that my place is not in the judge's seat, but in the prisoner's."

"I think, sir, you exaggerate your situation," said Mdme. Danglars,
whose beautiful eyes sparkled for a moment. "The paths of which you
were just speaking have been traced by all young men of ardent imagina-
tions. Besides the pleasure there is always remorse, from the indulgence
of our passions; and, after all, what have you men to fear from all this;
the world excuses, and notoriety ennobles you?"

"Madame," replied Villefort, "you know that I am no hypocrite, or,
at least, that I never deceive without a reason. If my brow be severe, it
is because many misfortunes have clouded it; if my heart be petrified,
it is that it might sustain the blows it has received. Women, on the contrary, are rarely tormented with remorse; for the decision does not come
from you; your misfortunes are generally imposed upon you, and your
faults the result of others' crimes."

"In any case, sir, you will allow," replied Mdme. Danglars, "that,
even if the fault were alone mine, I last night received a severe punishment for it."

"Poor thing!" said Villefort pressing her hand, "it was too severe for
your strength, for you were twice overwhelmed, and yet collect all your
courage, for you have not heard all!"

"Ah!" exclaimed Mdme. Danglars, alarmed, "what is there more to
hear?"

"You only look back to the past; and it is, indeed, bad enough. Well,
picture to yourself a future more gloomy still—certainly frightful, perhaps
sanguinary!" The baroness knew how calm Villefort naturally was, and

his present excitement frightened her so much that she opened her mouth to scream, but the sound died in her throat. "How has this terrible past been recalled?" cried Villefort.

"Alas!" said Hermine, "doubtless it is chance! Was it not by chance the Count of Monte-Cristo bought this house? Caused the earth to be dug? The unfortunate child disinterred under the trees? That poor innocent offspring of mine, which I never even kissed, but for whom I wept many, many tears. Ah, my heart flew to the count when he mentioned the dear spoil found beneath the flowers."

"Well, no, madame!—this is the terrible news I have to tell you," said Villefort, in a hollow voice—"no, nothing was found beneath the flowers; there was no child disinterred—no! You must not weep, no, you must not groan, you must tremble!"

"What can you mean?" asked Mdme. Danglars, shuddering.

"I mean that Monte-Cristo, digging underneath these trees, found neither skeleton nor chest, because neither of them was there!"

"Then you did not bury the poor child there, sir? Why did you deceive me? Where did you place it? tell me—where?"

"There! But listen to me! You recollect that sad night, when you were half expiring on that bed in the red damask room, while I, scarcely less agitated than you, awaited your delivery. The child was born, was given to me—without movement, without breath, without voice, we thought it dead." Mdme. Danglars moved rapidly, as though she would spring from her chair; but Villefort stopped, and clasped his hands as if to implore her attention. "We thought it dead," he repeated; "I placed it in the chest, which was to take the place of a coffin; I descended to the garden, I dug a hole, and then flung it down in haste. Scarcely had I covered it with mold, when the arm of the Corsican was stretched toward me; I saw the shadow rise, and, at the same time, a flash of light. I felt pain; I wished to cry out, but an icy shiver ran through my veins and stifled my voice; I fell lifeless and fancied myself killed. Never shall I forget your sublime courage, when, having returned to consciousness, I dragged myself to the foot of the stairs, where, expiring yourself, you came to meet me. We were obliged to keep silent upon the dreadful catastrophe. You had the fortitude to regain the house assisted by your nurse. A duel was the pretext for my wound. Though we scarcely expected it, our secret remained in our own keeping alone. I was taken to Versailles; for three months I struggled with death; at last, as I seemed to cling to life, I was ordered to the South. Four men carried me from Paris to Chalons, walking six leagues a day. Mdme. de Villefort followed the litter in her carriage. At Marseilles, my recovery lasted six months. I never heard you mentioned, and I did not dare inquire for you. When I returned to Paris, I learned that, widow of M. de Nargonne, you had married M. Danglars.

What had been the subject of my thoughts ever since consciousness had returned to me? Always the same—always the child's corpse, which, every night in my dreams, rising from the earth, fixed itself above the grave with a menacing look and gesture. I inquired immediately on my return to Paris: the house had not been inhabited since we left it, but it had just been let for nine years. I found the tenant. I pretended that I disliked the idea of a house belonging to my wife's father and mother passing into the hands of strangers. I had money with me; I made the tenant sign a cancelling deed, and I galloped to Auteuil. No one had entered the house since I had left it. It was five o'clock in the afternoon; I ascended in the red room, and waited for night. It was necessary, before everything else, and at all risks, that I should cause all traces of the past to disappear—destroy every material vestige: too much reality would always remain in my recollection. At length, one by one, all the noises in the neighboring country ceased. I understood that I had nothing to fear, that I should neither be seen nor heard, so I decided upon descending to the garden.

"I recollected that I was stabbed just as I was trampling the ground to fill up the hole; while doing so, I had leaned against a tree; behind me was an artificial rock, intended to serve as a resting-place for persons walking in the garden; in falling, my hand, relaxing its hold of the tree, felt the coldness of this stone. On my right I saw the tree, behind me the rock. I stood in the same attitude, and threw myself down. I rose, and again began digging and enlarging the hole; still I found nothing, nothing —the chest was no longer there!"

"Oh," cried Mdme. Danglars, "it was enough to drive you mad!"

"I hoped for a moment that it might," said Villefort; "but that happiness was denied me. However, recovering my strength and my ideas, 'Why,' said I, 'should that man have carried away the corpse?'"

"But you said," replied Mdme. Danglars, "he would require it as a proof?"

"Ah, no, madame, that could not be. Dead bodies are not kept a year; they are shown to a magistrate, and the evidence is taken. Now, nothing of the kind has happened."

"What then?" asked Hermine trembling violently.

"Something more terrible, more fatal, more alarming for us!—the child was, perhaps, alive, and the assassin may have saved it!"

Mdme. Danglars uttered a piercing cry, and, seizing Villefort's hands, exclaimed. "My child was alive! you buried my child alive, sir! You were not certain my child was dead, and you buried it. Ah———"

Mdme. Danglars had arisen, and stood before the proctor whose hands she wrung in her feeble grasp. "You understand, then, that if that were so," said he, rising in his turn, and approaching the baroness, to speak to her in a lower tone, "we are lost. This child lives, and some one knows it lives—some one is in possession of our secret; and since Monte-Cristo speaks before us of a child disinterred, when that child could not be found, it is he who is in possession of our secret."

"Just God, avenging God!" murmured Mdme. Danglars.

Villefort's only answer was a species of groan.

"But the child—the child, sir?" repeated the agitated mother.

"That Corsican had put it in the foundling hospital. I learned that the same night—the 20th of September—a child had been brought there, wrapped in part of a fine linen napkin, purposely torn in half. This portion of the napkin was marked with half a baron's crown, and the letter H."

"Truly, truly," said Mdme. Danglars, "all my linen is marked thus: Nargonne was a baronet, and my name is Hermine. Thank God! my boy was not then dead."

"Where is the child?"

Villefort shrugged his shoulders. "Do I know?" said he; "and do you believe that if I knew I would relate to you all its trials and all its adventures as would a novelist? Alas! no. I know not. A woman, about six months after, came to claim it with the other half of the napkin. This woman gave all the requisite particulars, and it was intrusted to her."

"But you should have inquired for the woman; you should have traced her."——"And what do you think I did? I feigned a criminal, and employed all the most acute bloodhounds and skilful agents in search of her. They traced her to Châlons, and there they lost her."

"They lost her?"

"Yes, for ever."

"But now I will begin with more perseverance and fury than ever, since fear urges me, not my conscience."

"But," replied Mdme. Danglars, "the Count of Monte-Cristo can know nothing, or he would not seek our society as he does."

"Oh, the wickedness of man is very great," said Villefort, "since it surpasses the goodness of God. In less than one week from this time I will ascertain who this Monte-Cristo is, whence he comes, where he goes, and why he speaks in our presence of children which have been disinterred in a garden." Villefort pronounced these words with an accent which would have made the count shudder had he heard him. Then he pressed the hand the baroness reluctantly gave him, and led her respectfully back to the door. Mdme. Danglars returned in another hackneycoach to the passage, on the other end of which she found her carriage, and her coachman sleeping peacefully on his box while waiting for her.

The royal prosecutor was of the opinion that no one is so well served as the man who acts for himself. So he disguised himself as a detective of his own force and proceeded with inquiries about the mysterious Sicilian noble. From Boville he learnt that the count was well known to a priest named Busoni and an English nobleman named Lord Wilmore. The latter was now and then in Paris, and the father also came to consult books in the royal library as he was an Orientalist of repute.

The police-card which Villefort carried gained him an audience of Father Busoni. The latter freely said that he knew the count from before he bought a title in Italy and the Islet of Monte-Cristo, as he had to have land to enjoy the count-ship. He was one Zaccone, son of a wealthy Genoese ship-builder. He knew, said the abbé, that the count was supposed to have him as his confessor, but it was not so: Monte-Cristo, he was sorry to say, was not a Catholic. Still he was a philanthropist on whom the Pope looked favorably—a sort of Quaker who did not wear the drab.

Busoni added that he believed Monte-Cristo had never before been in Paris, and as he was not sure of coming himself, he had entreated him to look after the Cavalcantis or at least the father.

He concluded by saying that his friend had bought the Auteuil house to turn it into a lunatic asylum for foreigners, demented in the French capital.

Lord Wilmore happened also to be in town. Villefort found him accessible enough, in stylish lodgings. He was not eager to air his French but the caller knew English. He was more communicative than the priest for he had no good feelings toward the Count of Monte-Cristo. He had fought against him in India, during wars between the pretty princess, and had met again while the Greeks were struggling for their independence. In this rebellion, Zaccone discovered a silver mine in Thessaly where he had disinterred his fortune, a million or two of francs, precariously obtained and continued.

He thought that the count was fooling away his time and money in the Auteuil speculation as he believed that he would strike mineral springs there.

"I hope that he will be ruined by that speculation and the others he is entangled with."

The cause of this feud was Monte-Cristo's seducing a wife of a friend of his, and they had fought three duels. He showed that the wound received in the latest encounter was not yet healed. He was now practicing shooting with a fashionable teacher and hoped to kill him next time.

In consequence Villefort returned home in so pleasant a mood that he slept that night soundly for the first time since the dinner-party.

CHAPTER XLVI.

THE BALL.

IT was during the warmest days of July, when the Saturday arrived upon which the ball of M. de Morcerf was to take place.

At the time the Countess de Morcerf returned to the rooms, after giving her orders, many guests were arriving, more attracted by the charming hospitality of the countess than by the distinguished position of the count; for, owing to a good taste of Mercédès, one was sure of finding some arrangements worthy of relating, or even copying in case of need. Mdme. Danglars came, not only beautiful in person, but radiant with splendor; she entered by one door at the same time Mercédès appeared at the other. The countess took Albert to meet Mdme. Danglars. He approached, paid her some well-merited compliments on her toilet, and offered his arm to conduct her to a seat. Albert looked around him. "You are looking for my daughter?" said the baroness, smiling.

"I confess it," replied Albert. "Could you have been so cruel as not to bring her?"

"Calm yourself. She has met Mdlle. de Villefort, and has taken her arm; see, they are following us, both in white dresses, one with a bouquet of camellias, the other with one of myosotis. But tell me—"—"Well, what do you wish to know?"

"Will not the Count of Monte-Cristo be here to-night?"

"Seventeen!" replied Albert. "What do you mean?"

"I only mean that the count seems the rage," replied the viscount, smiling, "and that you are the seventeenth person that asked me the same question. The count is in fashion; I congratulate him upon it."

"And have you replied to every one as you have to me?"

"Ah! to be sure, I have not answered you; be satisfied, we shall have this 'lion;' we are among the privileged ones."

Albert bowed to Mdme. Danglars, and advanced towards Mdme. de Villefort, whose lips opened as he approached. "I wager anything," said Albert, interrupting her, "that I know that you were going to ask me if the Count of Monte-Cristo were arrived, or expected."

"Not at all. It is not of him that I am now thinking. I was going to ask you if you had received any news of Franz?"

"He was leaving for home at the same time as his letter."

"Well, now then, the count?"

"The count will come, be satisfied."

"You know that he has another name beside Monte-Cristo? That is the name of an island, and he has a family name."

"Well! I'm sure," said Morcerf; "that is indeed news! Am I allowed to repeat it?"—"Yes, but cautiously; tell one thing at a time, and do not say I told you."

"Why so?"——"Because it is a secret just discovered."

"By whom?"——"The police."

"Then the news originated——"

"At the prefect's last night. Paris, you can understand, is astonished at the sight of such unusual splendor, and the police have made inquiries."——"Good! nothing more is wanting than to arrest the count as a vagabond, on the pretext of his being too rich."

"Indeed, this would doubtless have happened if his credentials had not been so favorable."——"Poor count! And is he aware of the danger he has been in?"

"I think not."——"Then it will be but charitable to inform him. When he arrives, I will not fail to do so."

Just then, a handsome young man, with bright eyes, black hair, and glossy moustache, respectfully bowed to Mdme. de Villefort. Albert extended him his hand. "Madame," said Albert, "allow me to present to you M. Maximilian Morrel, captain of Spahis, one of our best, and, above all, of our bravest officers."

"I have already had the pleasure of meeting this gentleman at Auteuil, at Monte-Cristo House," replied Mdme. de Villefort, turning away with marked coldness of manner. This answer, and, above all, the tone in which it was uttered, chilled the heart of poor Morrel. But a recompense was in store for him: turning round, he saw near the door a beautiful fair face, whose large blue eyes were, without any marked expression, fixed upon him, while the bouquet of myosotis was gently raised to her lips. The Count of Monte-Cristo had just entered. We have already said that there was something in the count which attracted universal attention wherever he appeared. Yet the Parisian world is so strange, that even this might not have won attention, had there not been, besides this, a mysterious story gilded by an immense fortune.

Meanwhile he advanced through the crowd of curious glances and exchange of salutations towards Mdme. de Morcerf, who, standing before a mantelpiece ornamented with flowers, had seen his entrance in a looking-glass placed opposite the door, and was prepared to receive him. She turned towards him with a serene smile just at the moment he was bowing to her. No doubt she fancied the count would speak to her, while on his side the count thought she was about to address him; but both remained silent, and after a mere bow, Monte-Cristo directed his steps to Albert, who received him cordially. Just then the count felt his arm jogged. He turned round; it was Danglars.

"Ah, is it you, Baron?" said he.

"Why do you call me baron?" said Danglars; "you know that I care nothing for my title. I am not like you, Viscount; you like your title, do you not?"

"Certainly," replied Albert, "seeing that without my title I should be nothing; while you, sacrificing the baron, would still remain the millionaire."

"Which seems to me the finest title under the royalty," replied Danglars.

"Unfortunately," said Monte-Cristo, "one's title to a millionaire does not last for life, like that of baron, peer of France or academician; for example, the millionaires Frank Poulmann, of Frankfort, just became bankrupts.

"Indeed!" said Danglars, becoming pale.

"Yes; I received the news this evening by courier. I had about a million in their hands, but, warned in time, I withdrew it a month ago."

"Ah," exclaimed Danglars, "they have drawn on me for 200,000 francs!"

"Whew!" said Monte-Cristo "here are 200,000 francs gone after—"

"Hush! do not mention business!" said Danglars; then, approaching Monte-Cristo, he added, "especially before young Cavalcanti!" after which he smiled, and turned toward the young man in question. Albert had left the count to speak to his mother, Danglars to converse with young Cavalcanti; Monte-Cristo was for an instant alone. Meanwhile the heat became excessive. The footmen were hastening through the rooms with waiters loaded with ices. Monte-Cristo wiped the perspiration from his forehead, but drew back when the waiter was presented to him; he took no refreshment. Mdme. de Morcerf lost not sight of Monte-Cristo; she saw that he took nothing, and even noticed the movement with which he withdrew from it.

"Albert," she asked, "did you notice that?"——"What, mother?"

"That the count will never accept an invitation to dine with us."

"Yes; but then he breakfasted with me—indeed, he made his first appearance in the world on that occasion."

"But your house is not M. de Morcerf's," murmured Mercédès; "and since he has been here I have watched him."

"Well?"——"Well, he has taken nothing yet."

"The count is very temperate." Mercédès smiled sadly. "Approach him," said she, "and the next waiter that passes, insist upon his taking something."

"It is a way of assuring me that his absence was intended."

A minute afterwards the blinds were thrown open, and through the jessamine and clematis that overhung the window might be seen the garden ornamented with lanterns, and the supper laid under the tent.

Dancers, players, talkers, all uttered an exclamation of joy—every one inhaled with delight the breeze that floated in. At the same time, Mercédès reappeared, paler than before, but with that immovable expression of countenance which she sometimes wore. She went straight to the group of which her husband formed the centre. "Do not detain these gentlemen here, Count," she said; "they would prefer, I should think, to breathe in the garden rather than suffocate here, since they are not playing."—— "Ah," said a gallant old general, "we will not go alone to the garden."

"Then," said Mercédès, "I will lead the way." Turning toward Monte-Cristo, she added, "Count, will you oblige me with your arm?" The count almost staggered at these simple words: then he fixed his eyes on Mercédès. It was but the glance of a moment, but it seemed to the countess to have lasted for a century, so much was expressed in that one look. He offered his arm to the countess; she leaned upon it, or rather just touched it with her little hand, and they together descended the steps, hedged with rhododendrons and camellias. Behind them, by another outlet, twenty persons rushed into the garden with loud exclamations of delight.

Mdme. de Morcerf entered an archway of trees with her companion. The count looked at Mercédès as if to interrogate her, but she continued walking in silence; on his side, Monte-Cristo also said nothing. They reached a building, ornamented with magnificent fruits, which ripened in the artificial temperature. The countess left the arm of Monte-Cristo, and gathered a bunch of Muscatel grapes. "See, Count," she said, with a smile, so sad in its expression that one could almost see the tears on her eyelids—"see, our French grapes are not to be compared, I know, with yours of Sicily and Cyprus, but you will make allowance for our northern sun." The count bowed, but stepped back. "Do you refuse?" said Mercédès, in a tremulous voice. "Pray excuse me, madame," replied Monte-Cristo, "but I never eat Muscatel grapes."

"Count," added Mercédès, with a supplicating glance, "there is a beautiful Arabian custom, which makes eternal friends of those who have together eaten bread and salt beneath the same roof."——"I know it, madame," replied the count; "but we are in France, and not in Arabia; and in France eternal friendships are as rare as the custom of dividing bread and salt with one another."

"But," said the countess, breathlessly, with her eyes fixed on Monte-Cristo, whose arm she convulsively pressed with both hands, "we are friends, are we not?" The count became pale as death, the blood rushed to his heart, and then again rising, dyed his cheeks with crimson; his eyes swam like those of a man suddenly dazzled. "Certainly, we are friends," he replied; "why should we not be such?" The answer was so little like the one Mercédès desired, that she turned away to give vent to a sigh, which sounded more like a groan. "Thank you," she said. And they recommenced walking. They went the whole length of the garden without uttering a word. "Sir," suddenly exclaimed the countess, after their walk had continued ten minutes in silence, "is it true that you have seen so much, traveled so far, and suffered so deeply?"

"My present happiness equals my past misery," said the count.

"Are you not married?" asked the countess. "I, married!" exclaimed Monte-Cristo, shuddering; "who could have told you so?"

"No one told me you were: but you have frequently been seen at the Opera with a young and lovely person."——"She is a slave whom I bought at Constantinople, madame, the daughter of a prince. I have adopted her as my daughter, having no one else to love in the world."

"How can you exist thus, without any one to attach you to life?"

"It is not my fault, madame. At Malta, I loved a young girl, was on the point of marrying her, when war came and carried me away. I thought she loved me well enough to wait for me, and even to remain faithful to my grave. When I returned she was married. This is the story of most men who have passed twenty. Perhaps my heart was weaker than those of the generality and I suffered more than they would have done in my place; you know all." The countess stopped for a moment, as if gasping for breath. "Yes," she said, "and you have still preserved this love in your heart—one can only love once—and have you forgiven her for all she has made you suffer?"

"Yes, I have pardoned *her*."

"But only her; do you, then, still hate those who separated you?"

"I hate them? not at all; why should I?" The countess placed herself before Monte-Cristo, still holding in her hand a portion of the grapes. "Take some," she said. "Madame, I never eat Muscatel grapes," replied Monte-Cristo, as if the subject had not been mentioned before. The countess dashed the grapes into the nearest thicket, with a gesture of despair. "Inflexible man!" she murmured. Monte-Cristo remained as unmoved as if the reproach had not been addressed to him. Albert at this moment ran in. "Oh, mother!" he exclaimed, "such a misfortune!"

"M. de Villefort comes to fetch his wife and daughter."

"Mdme. de Saint-Méran is just arrived in Paris, bringing the news of her husband's death which took place on the first stage after he left Marseilles. Mdme. de Villefort, who was in very good spirits, would neither believe nor think of the misfortune; but Mdlle. Valentine, at the first words, guessed the whole truth, notwithstanding all the precautions of her father; the blow struck her like a thunderbolt, and she fell senseless. He was her grandfather on the mother's side. He was coming here to hasten her marriage with Franz."

"Ah, indeed!"

She took two or three steps forward. Monte-Cristo watched her with an air so thoughtful, and so full of affectionate admiration, that she returned, taking his hand; at the same time she grasped her son's, and joined them together.

"We are friends; are we not?" she asked.

"Oh, madame, I do not presume to call myself your friend, but at times I am your most respectful servant." The countess left with an indescribable pang in her heart, and before she had taken ten steps the count saw her raise her handkerchief to her eyes. "Do not my mother and you agree?" asked Albert, astonished.

"On the contrary," replied the count, "did you not hear her declare that we were friends?" They re-entered the drawing-room, which Valentine and Madame de Villefort had just left. Monte-Cristo departed almost at the same time.

CHAPTER XLVII.

JOY AND SORROW.

A GLOOMY scene had indeed just passed at Villefort's. After the ladies had departed for the ball, the functionary had, as usual, shut himself up in his study, with a heap of papers calculated to alarm any one else, but which generally scarcely satisfied his inordinate desires. But this time the papers were a mere matter of form. Villefort had secluded himself, to study notes, precious documents, amongst which he had carefully arranged, in cipher only known to himself, the names of all those become his enemies. Their number was formidable, now that he had begun to fear, and yet these names, powerful though they were, had often caused him to smile with the same kind of satisfaction experienced by a traveler, who, from the summit of a mountain, beholds at his feet the sharp peaks, the almost impassable paths, and the ridges over which he has so perilously climbed. When he had run over all these names in his memory, again read and studied them, commenting meanwhile upon his lists, he shook his head.

"No!" he murmured, "none of my enemies would have waited so patiently and laboriously for so long a space of time, that they might now come and crush me with this secret. Sometimes, as Hamlet says—

"Deeds will rise,
Tho' all the earth o'erwhelm them, to men's eyes;"

but, like a phosphoric light, they rise but to mislead. The story has been told by the Corsican to some priest, who, in his turn, has also repeated it. M. de Monte-Cristo may have heard it, and to enlighten himself—but why should he wish to enlighten himself upon the subject?" asked Villefort, after a moment's reflection, "what interest can this Monte-Cristo, or Zaccone, son of a ship-owner of Malta, discoverer of a mine in Thessaly, now visiting Paris for the first time—take in discovering a gloomy, mysterious, and useless fact like this? However, amidst all the incoherent details given to me by Abbé Busoni and by Lord Wilmore, by his friend and his enemy, one thing appears certain and clear in my opinion: that in no period, in no case, in no circumstance, could there have been any contact between him and me."

But Villefort uttered words which even he himself did not believe. While he was endeavoring to calm his fears, imagining a future limited to the enjoyments of home, fearing to awaken the enemy that had so long slept, the noise of a carriage sounded in the yard, then he heard the steps of an aged person ascending the stairs, followed by tears and lamentations, such as servants always assume when they wish to appear interested in their masters' grief. He drew back the bolt of his door, almost directly an old lady entered, unannounced, carrying her shawl on her arm, and her bonnet in her hand. The white hair was thrown back from her yellow forehead, and her eyes, already sunken by the furrows of age, now almost disappeared beneath the eyelids so swollen with grief. "Oh, sir," she said; "oh, sir, what a misfortune! I shall die of it; oh! yes, I shall certainly die of it!"

And then, falling upon the chair nearest the door, she burst into a paroxysm of sobs. The servants, standing in the doorway, not daring to approach nearer, were looking at Noirtier's old servant, who, having heard a noise in his master's room, had run there also, and remained behind the others. Villefort rose, and ran toward his mother-in-law, for it was she.

"Saint-Méran is dead!" answered the old marchioness, without preface, without expression; she appeared stupefied. Villefort drew back, and clasping his hands together, exclaimed—"Dead! so suddenly?"

"A week ago," continued Mdme. de Saint-Méran, "we went out together in the carriage after dinner. M. de Saint-Méran had been unwell for some days; still, the idea of seeing our dear Valentine again inspired him with courage; and, notwithstanding his illness, he would leave; when, at six leagues from Marseilles, after having eaten some of the lozenges he is accustomed to take, he fell into such a deep sleep, that it appeared to me unnatural; still I hesitated to wake him, when I fancied his face became red, and that the veins in his temples throbbed more violently than usual. However, as it became dark, and I could no longer see, I fell asleep; I was soon awakened by a piercing shriek, as from a person suffering in his dreams, and he suddenly threw his head back. I stopped the postilion, I called M. de Saint-Méran, I applied my smelling-salts; but all was over, and I arrived at Aix by the side of a corpse."

Villefort stood with his mouth half open, quite stupefied. "It appears to have been an apoplectic stroke."

"And what did you do then?"

"I had him put into a leaden coffin, and I am preceding him by a few days.

"Where is Valentine, sir? It is on her account I am here; I wish to see Valentine." Villefort thought it would be terrible to reply that Valentine was at a ball: so he only said that she had gone out with her step-mother, and that she should be fetched. "This instant, sir—this instant, I beseech you!" said the old lady. Villefort conducted her to his apartment.

Villefort left her to the care of the women, while old Barrois ran, half-scared, to his master; for nothing frightens old men so much as when death relaxes its vigilance over them for a moment in order to strike some other old man. Then, while Mdme. de Saint-Méran, still on her knees, remained praying fervently, Villefort sent for a coach and went himself to fetch his wife and daughter from Morcerf's. He was so pale when he appeared at the door of the ball-room, that Valentine ran to him, saying—

"Oh, father! some misfortune has happened!"

"Your grandmamma has just arrived, Valentine," said M. de Villefort.

"And grandpapa!" inquired the girl, trembling with apprehension. M. de Villefort only replied by offering his arm to his daughter. It was just in time, for Valentine's head swam, and she staggered; Mdme. de Villefort instantly hastened to her assistance, and aided her husband in dragging her to the carriage, saying—"What a singular event! Who could have thought it? Ah, yes, it is indeed strange!" And the wretched family departed, leaving a cloud of sadness hanging over the rest of the evening. At the foot of the stairs, Valentine found Barrois awaiting her.

"M. Noirtier wishes to see you to-night," he said, in an undertone.

"Tell him I will come when I leave my dear grandmamma," she replied, feeling, with true delicacy, that the person to whom she could be of the most service just then was the widow.

At last she came up to Noirtier, on leaving Mdme. de Saint-Méran, who, in the midst of her grief, had at last yielded to fatigue, and fallen into a feverish sleep. Within reach of her hand they placed a small table, upon which stood a bottle of orangeade, her usual beverage, and a glass. Then, as we have said, the young girl left the bedside to see M. Noirtier. Valentine kissed the old man, who looked at her with such tenderness that her eyes again filled with tears, whose sources he thought must be exhausted. The old gentleman continued to dwell upon her with the same expression. "Yes, yes," said Valentine, "you mean that I have yet a kind grandfather left, do you not?" The old man intimated that such was his meaning. "Alas! happily I have," replied Valentine. "Within that, what would become of me?"

It was one o'clock in the morning. Barrois, who wished to go to bed himself, observed, that after such sad events, every one stood in need of rest. Noirtier would not say that the only rest he needed was to see his child, but wished her good-night, for grief and fatigue had made her appear quite ill. The next morning she found her grandmother in bed; the fever had not abated; on the contrary, her eyes glistened, and she appeared to be suffering from violent nervous irritability. "Oh, dear grandmamma! are you worse?" exclaimed Valentine, perceiving all these signs of agitation.

"No, my child, no!" said Mdme. de Saint-Méran, "but I was impatiently waiting for you and your father."

An instant afterwards Villefort entered. "Sir," said Mdme. de Saint-Méran, without using any circumlocution, and, as if fearing she had no time to lose, "you wrote to me concerning the marriage of this child to Franz d'Epinay? I must hasten the marriage, for I have but a short time to live."

"You, madame?"

"You, dear mamma?" exclaimed M. de Villefort and Valentine at the same time.

"I know what I am saying," continued the marchioness; "I must hurry you, so that, having no mother, she may at least have a grandmother to bless her marriage. I am all that is left to her belonging to my poor Renée, whom you have so soon forgotten, sir."——"Ah, madame," said Villefort, "you forget that I was obliged to give a mother to my child."

"A stepmother is never a mother, sir. But this is not to the purpose, our business concerns Valentine; let us leave the dead in peace."

All this was said with such exceeding rapidity, that there was something in the conversation that seemed like delirium.

"It shall be as you wish, madame," said Villefort; "more especially since your wishes coincide with mine; and as soon as M. d'Epinay arrives in Paris——"

"My dear mother," interrupted Valentine, "consider decorum—the recent death. You would not have me marry under such sad auspices?"

"My child," exclaimed the old lady, sharply, "let us hear none of those conventional objections that deter weak minds from forming their fortunes. I also was married at the death-bed of my mother, and certainly I have not been less happy on that account. This night I have had a fearful sleep. It seemed as though my soul were already hovering over my body; my eyes, which I tried to open, closed against my will: and what will appear impossible above all to you, sir, I saw, with my eyes shut, in the spot where you are now standing, issuing from that corner where there is a door leading into Mdme. Villefort's dressing-room—I saw, I tell you, silently enter, a white figure. It was the spirit of my husband!—Well, if my husband's soul can come to me, why should not my soul reappear to guard my granddaughter? the tie is even more direct, it seems to me."——"Oh! madame," said Villefort, deeply affected, in spite of himself, "do not yield to those gloomy thoughts; you will long live with us, happy, loved, and honored, and we will make you forget—"

"Never, never, never!" said the marchioness. "When does M. d'Epinay return?"

"We expect him every moment."

"It is well. As soon as he arrives inform me. We must be expeditious. And then I also wish to see a notary, that I may be assured that all our property returns to Valentine."——"Ah, my mother!" murmured Valentine, pressing her lips on the burning brow of her grandmother, "do you wish to kill me? Oh, how feverish you are! we must not send for a notary, but for a doctor!"

"A doctor!" said she, shrugging her shoulders, "I am not ill; I am thirsty—that is all."

"What are you drinking, dear mamma?"

"The same as usual, my dear, my glass is there on the table—give it me, Valentine." Valentine poured the orangeade into a glass, and gave it to her grandmother with a certain degree of dread, for it was the same glass, she fancied, that had been touched by the spectre. The marchioness drained the glass at a single draught, and then turned on her pillow, repeating,—"The notary! the notary!"

M. de Villefort left the room, and Valentine seated herself at the bedside of her grandmother. Two hours passed thus; Mdme. de Saint-Méran was in a feverish sleep, and the notary had arrived. Though announced in a very low tone, Mdme. de Saint-Méran arose from her pillow. "The notary!" she exclaimed, "let him come in."

The notary, who was at the door, immediately entered. "Go, Valentine," said Mdme. de Saint-Méran, "and leave me with this gentleman."

The girl kissed her grandmother, and left with her handkerchief to her eyes; at the door she found the footman, who told her the doctor was waiting in the dining-room. Valentine instantly ran down. The doctor was a friend of the family, and at the same time, one of the leading men of the day, and very fond of Valentine, whose birth he had witnessed. He had himself a daughter about her age; but whose life was one continued source of anxiety and fear to him from her mother having been consumptive.

"Oh," said Valentine, "we have been waiting for you with such impatience, dear M. d'Avrigny. It is for my poor grandmother; you know the calamity that has happened to us, do you not? My grandfather is dead from an apoplectic stroke."

"An apoplectic stroke?" repeated the doctor.

"Yes! and my poor grandmother fancies that her husband, whom she never left, has called her, and that she must go and join him."

"It is singular," said the doctor; "I was not aware that Mdme. de Saint-Méran was subject to such hallucinations."——"It is the first time I ever saw her thus," said Valentine, "and this morning she· frightened me so, that I thought her mad; and my father, a strong-minded man, himself appeared deeply impressed."

"We will go and see," said the doctor; "what you tell me seems very strange." The notary here descended, and Valentine was informed her grandmother was alone. "Go up-stairs," she said to the doctor.

"And you?"——"Oh, I dare not—she forbade my sending for you; and, as you say, I am myself agitated, feverish, and unwell. I will go and take a turn in the garden to recover myself." The doctor pressed Valentine's hand, and while he visited her grandmother, she descended the steps. We need not say which portion of the garden was her favorite walk. After remaining for a short time in the parterre surrounding the house, and gathering a rose to place in her waist or hair, she turned into the dark avenue which led to the bank; then from the bank she went to the gate. As usual, Valentine strolled for a short time among her flowers but without gathering them. The mourning in her heart forbade her assuming this simple ornament, though she had not yet had time to put on the outward semblance of woe. She then turned toward the avenue. As she advanced she fancied she heard a voice pronounce her name. She stopped astonished, then the voice reached her ear more distinctly, and she recognized Maximilian's.

"You here at this hour?" said she. "Yes, my poor girl," replied Morrel; "I come to bring and to hear bad tidings."

"This is, indeed, a house of mourning!" said Valentine; "speak, Maximilian; although the cup of sorrow seems already full."——"Dear Valentine," said Morrel, endeavoring to conceal his own emotion, "listen, I entreat you: what I am about to say is solemn. *Tomorrow* you will be engaged to M. d'Epinay, for he came this morning to Paris."

"You must advise me what to do."

"I am free," replied Maximilian, "and rich enough to support you. I swear to make you my lawful wife before my lips even shall have approached your forehead."

"My God," said Valentine, raising both her hands to heaven with a sublime expression, "I have done my utmost to remain a submissive daughter; I have begged, entreated, implored; he has regarded neither my prayers, my entreaties, nor my tears. It is done," cried she, wiping away her tears, and resuming her firmness, "I am resolved not to die of remorse, but rather of shame. Yes, you are right; Maximilian, I will follow you. I will leave the paternal home, I will give up all. Oh! ungrateful girl that I am," cried Valentine, sobbing, "I will give up all, even my dear old grandfather, whom I had nearly forgotten."

"No," said Maximilian, "you shall not leave him. M. Noirtier has evinced, you say, a kind feeling toward me. Well! before you leave, tell him all; his consent would be your justification in God's sight. As soon as we are married, he shall come and live with us; instead of one child, he shall have two. You have told me how you talk to him, and how he answers you; I shall very soon learn that language by signs, Valentine; and I promise you solemnly, that instead of despair, it is happiness that awaits us."

"Now listen to me, Maximilian; if by artifice, by entreaty, by accident—in short, if by any means I can delay this marriage, will you wait?"

"We will wait," said Morrel. "Instead of signing——"

"I will join you, and we will fly; but from this moment until then, let us not tempt Providence, Morrel; let us not see each other; it is a miracle, it is a providence that we have not been discovered; if we were surprised, if it were known that we met thus, we should have no further resource."

"You are right, Valentine; but how shall I ascertain?"

"From the notary, M. Deschamps."

"I know him."

"And for myself—I will write to you, depend on me. I dread this marriage, Maximilian, as much as you."

"Thank you, my adored Valentine, thank you."

It was on the following day, at about ten o'clock in the morning, as he was starting to call on Deschamps, the notary, that he received from the mail deliverer a small note, which he knew to be from Valentine, although he had not before seen her writing. It was to this effect:—

"Tears, entreaties, prayers, have availed me nothing. Yesterday, for two hours, I was at the church of Saint Philip, and for two hours I prayed most fervently. Heaven is as inflexible as man, and the signature of the contract is fixed for this evening at nine o'clock. I have but one promise and but one heart to give; that promise is pledged to you, that heart is also yours. This evening, then, at a quarter past nine, at the gate.

"Your betrothed,
"VALENTINE DE VILLEFORT."

"P. S.—My poor grandmother gets worse and worse; yesterday her fever amounted to delirium; to-day her delirium is almost madness. You will be very kind to me, will you not, Morrel, to make me forget my sorrow in leaving her thus? I think it is kept a secret from grandpapa Noirtier, that the contract is to be signed this evening."

Morrel was punctual.

No one came, and tired of waiting, Maximilian determined on the rash step of entering the house. But, passing through the garden, he was stopped by hearing a voice at a distance.

He stepped back and concealed himself completely, remaining perfectly motionless. He had formed his resolution; if it was Valentine alone, he would speak as she passed; if she was accompanied, and he could not speak, still he should see her, and know that she was safe; if they were strangers, he would listen to their conversation, and might understand something of this hitherto incomprehensible mystery. The moon had just then escaped from behind the cloud which had concealed it, and Morrel saw Villefort come out upon the steps, followed by a gentleman in black. They descended, and advanced toward the clump of trees, and Morrel soon recognized the other gentleman as Doctor d'Avrigny.

"Ah, my dear doctor," said the attorney, "Heaven declares itself against my house! what a blow! she is dead!" A cold dampness covered the young man's brow, and his teeth chattered. Who could be dead in that house, which Villefort himself had called accursed? "My dear M. de Villefort," replied the doctor, with a tone which redoubled the terror of the young man. "I have not led you here to console you; on the contrary, I have a terrible secret to communicate to you," said the doctor. "Let us sit down."

Villefort fell, rather than seated himself. The doctor stood before him, with one hand placed on his shoulder. Morrel, horrified, supported his head with one hand, and with the other pressed his heart, lest its beatings should be heard. "Dead! dead!" repeated he within himself; and he felt as if he were also dying.

"Speak, doctor—I am listening," said Villefort; "strike—I am prepared for everything!"

"Mdme. de Saint-Méran was, doubtless, advancing in years, but she enjoyed excellent health." Morrel began again to breathe freely, which he had not done the last ten minutes.

"Grief has consumed her," said Villefort—"yes, grief, doctor! After living forty years with the marquis——"

"It is not grief, my dear Villefort," said the doctor; "grief may kill, although it rarely does, and never in a day, never in an hour, never in ten minutes."

"Mdme. de Saint-Méran had three successive attacks, and at the third she expired."

"At the end of the first attack, I discovered symptoms of tetanus; you confirmed my opinion."

"Yes, before others," replied the doctor; "but now we are alone——"

"What are you going to say? Oh, spare me!"

"Mdme. de Saint-Méran has sunk under a violent dose of brucine or strychnine, which by some mistake, perhaps, has been given to her." Villefort seized the doctor's hand. "Oh, it is impossible!" said he; "I must be dreaming! It is frightful to hear such things from such a man as you! Tell me, I entreat you, my dear doctor, that you may be deceived."

"Has any one besides me seen Mdme. de Saint-Méran?"——"No."

"Has anything been sent for from a druggist's that I have not examined?"

"Nothing."

"Had Mdme. de Saint-Méran any enemies?"

"Not to my knowledge."

"Would her death affect any one's interest?"

"It could not indeed; my daughter is her only heiress—Valentine alone. Oh, if such a thought could present itself, I would stab myself to punish my heart for having for one instant harbored it."

"May not Barrois, the old servant, have made a mistake, and have given Mdme. de Saint-Méran a dose prepared for his master?"

"But how could a dose prepared for M. Noirtier poison Mdme. de Saint-Méran?"

"Nothing is more simple. You know poisons become remedies in certain diseases, of which paralysis is one. For instance, having tried every other remedy to restore movement and speech to M. Noirtier, I resolved to try one last means, and for three months I have been giving him brucine; so that in the last dose I ordered for him there were six grains. This quantity, which it is perfectly safe to administer to the paralyzed frame of M. Noirtier, which has become gradually accustomed to it, would be sufficient to kill another person."

"What do you propose to me, D'Avrigny?" said Villefort in despair, "so soon as another is admitted into our secret, an inquest will become necessary; and an inquest in my house—impossible! Still," continued the lawyer, looking at the doctor with uneasiness, "if you wish it—if you demand it, it shall be done. But, doctor, you see me already so grieved —how can I introduce into my house so much scandal, after so much sorrow? My wife and my daughter would die of it! And I, doctor— you know a man does not arrive at the post I occupy—one has not been public prosecutor twenty-five years without having amassed a tolerable number of enemies; mine are numerous. Let this affair be talked of, it will be a triumph for them, which will make them rejoice, and cover me with shame. Pardon me, doctor, these worldly ideas;

were you a priest I should not dare tell you that; but you are a man, and you know mankind. Doctor, pray recall your words; you have said nothing, have you?"

"My dear M. de Villefort," replied the doctor, "my first duty is humanity. I would have saved Mdme. de Saint-Méran, if science could have done it; but she is dead, my duty regards the living. Let us bury this terrible secret in the deepest recesses of our hearts."

"I thank you, doctor," said Villefort, with indescribable joy; "I never had a better friend than you." And, as if he feared Avrigny would recall his promise, he hurried him toward the house.

When they were gone, Morrel ventured out from under the trees, and the moon shone upon his face, which was so pale it might have been taken for a phantom. "I am manifestly protected in a most wonderful, but most terrible manner," said he; "but, Valentine, poor girl! how will she bear so much sorrow?"

As he thought thus, he looked alternately at the window with red curtains and the three windows with white curtains. The light had almost disappeared from the former: doubtless Mdme. de Villefort had just put out her lamp, and the night-lamp alone reflected its dull light on the window. At the extremity of the building, on the contrary, he saw one of the three windows open. A wax-light placed on the mantelpiece threw some of its pale rays without, and a shadow was seen for one moment on the balcony. Morrel shuddered, he thought he heard a sob.

It cannot be wondered at that his mind, generally so courageous, but now disturbed by the two strongest human passions, love and fear, was weakened even to the indulgence of superstitious thoughts. Although it was impossible Valentine could see him, hidden as he was, he thought he heard the shadow at the window call him; his disturbed mind told him so. This double error became an irresistible reality, and by one of those incomprehensible transports of youth, he bounded from his hiding-place, and with two strides, at the risk of being seen, at the risk of alarming Valentine, at the risk of being discovered by some exclamation which might escape the girl, he crossed the flower-garden, which, by the light of the moon, resembled a large white lake, and, having passed the rows of orange-trees which extended in front of the house, he reached the step, ran quickly up, and pushed the door, which opened without offering any resistance.

Morrel was mad. Happily he did not meet any one. Now, especially, did he find the description Valentine had given of the interior of the house useful to him; he arrived safely at the top of the staircase, and while feeling his way, a sob indicated the direction he was to take; he turned back: a door partly open enabled him to see his road, and to hear the sorrowing voice. He pushed it open and entered. At the other end of the room, under a white sheet which covered it, lay the corpse, still more alarming to Morrel since the account he had so unexpectedly overheard. By the side, on her knees, and her head buried in the cushion of an easy chair, was Valentine, trembling and sobbing, her hands extended above her head, clasped and stiff. He sighed, and whispered a name. Valentine, as her only apology for not having met him, pointed to the corpse under the sheet, and began to sob again. Neither dared for some time to speak in that room. They hesitated to break the silence which death seemed to impose; at length Valentine ventured.

"My friend," said she, "how came you here? Alas, I would say you are welcome, had not death opened the way for you into this house."

"Valentine," said Morrel, with a trembling voice, "your servants," said he, "were repeating the sorrowful story; from them I learned it all. But what has become of M. d'Epinay?"

"M. Franz arrived to sign the contract just as my dear grandmother was dying."

"Alas!" said Morrel, with a feeling of selfish joy; for he thought this death would cause the wedding to be postponed indefinitely. "But what redoubles my sorrow," continued the girl, as if the feeling was to receive its immediate punishment, "is that the poor old lady, on her death-bed, requested the marriage might take place as soon as possible; she also, thinking to protect me, was acting against me."

"Hark!" said Morrel. They both listened; steps were distinctly heard in the corridor and on the stairs.——"It is my father, who has just left his cabinet."

"To accompany the doctor to the door," added Morrel.

"How do you know it is the doctor?" asked Valentine, astonished.

"I imagine it must be," said Morrel. Valentine looked at the young man; they heard the street-door close; then M. de Villefort locked the garden-door, and returned up-stairs. He stopped a moment in the ante-room, as if hesitating whether to turn to his own apartment or into Mdme. de Saint-Méran's; Morrel concealed himself behind a door; Valentine remained motionless, grief seemed to deprive her of all fear. M. de Villefort passed on to his own room. "Now," said Valentine, "you can neither go out by the front-door nor by the garden." Morrel looked at her with astonishment. "There is but one way left you that is safe," said she; "it is through my grandfather's room."

She led the way down a narrow staircase to M. Noirtier's room; Morrel followed her on tiptoe; at the door they found the old servant. "Barrois," said Valentine, "shut the door, and let no one come in." She passed first. Noirtier, seated in his chair, and listening to every sound, was watching the door: he saw Valentine, and his eyes brightened. There was something grave and solemn in the approach of the girl which struck the old man, and immediately his bright eye began to interrogate. "Dear grandfather," said she hurriedly, "you know poor grandmamma died an hour ago, and now I have no friend in the world but you." His expressive eyes evinced the greatest tenderness. "To you alone, then, may I confide my sorrows and my hopes?" The paralytic motioned "Yes." Valentine took Maximilian's hand. The old man fixed his scrutinizing gaze with slight astonishment on Morrel. "This is M. Maximilian Morrel," said she; "the son of that good merchant of Marseilles, whom you doubtless recollect."

"Yes," said the old man.

"He brings an irreproachable name, which Maximilian is likely to render glorious, since at thirty years of age he is a captain, an officer of the Legion of Honor." The old man signified that he recollected him. "Well, grandpapa," said Valentine, kneeling before him, and pointing to Maximilian, "I love him, and will be only his; were I compelled to marry another, I would destroy myself."

The eyes of the paralytic expressed a multitude of tumultuous thoughts.

"And you will protect us, who are your children, against the will of my father?"

Noirtier cast an intelligent glance at Morrel, as if to say, "Perhaps I may." Maximilian understood him.

"Mademoiselle," said he, "you have a sacred duty to fulfil in your deceased grandmother's room, will you allow me the honor of a few minutes' conversation with M. Noirtier?"——"That is it," said the old man's eye.

Valentine rose, placed a chair for Morrel, requested Barrois not to admit any one, and having tenderly embraced her grandpapa, and sorrowfully taken leave of Morrel, she went away. To prove to Noirtier that he was in Valentine's confidence and knew all their secrets, Morrel took the dictionary, a pen, and some paper, and placed them all on a table where there was a light.

He related the manner in which he had become acquainted with Valentine, and how he loved her; and that Valentine, in her solitude and her misfortune, had accepted the offer of his devotion. He told him his birth, position, fortune; and more than once, when he consulted the look of the paralytic, that look answered, "That is good, proceed."

"And now," said Morrel, when he had finished the first part of his recital, "now I have told you of my love and my hopes, may I inform you of my intentions?"——"Yes," signified the old man.

"This was our resolution: a cab was in waiting at the gate, in which I intended to carry off Valentine to my sister's house, to marry her, and to wait respectfully M. de Villefort's pardon."

"No," said Noirtier.

"There is another way," said Morrel. The old man's interrogative eye said, "Which?"

"I will go," continued Maximilian, "I will seek M. Franz d'Epinay —I am happy to be able to mention this in Mdlle. de Villefort's absence—and will conduct myself toward him so as to compel him to challenge me."

When Morrel had finished, Noirtier shut his eyes several times, which was his manner of saying "No."

"Whence then will come the help we need—from chance?" resumed Morrel. "No."——"From you?"——"Yes."

There was so much firmness in the look which gave this answer, no one could, at any rate, doubt his will, if they did his power. "Oh, thank you a thousand times! But how, unless a miracle should restore your speech, your gesture, your movement, how can you, chained to that arm-chair, dumb and motionless, oppose this marriage?" A smile lit up the old man's face, a strange smile of the eyes on a paralyzed face. "Then I must wait?" asked the young man.

"Yes."——"But the contract?" The same smile returned. "Will you assure me it shall not be signed?"——"Yes," said Noirtier.

"Now," said Morrel, "do you wish me to retire?"——"Yes."

"Without seeing Valentine?"——"Yes."

Morrel then bowed and retired. He found the old servant outside the door, to whom Valentine had given directions; he conducted Morrel along a dark passage, which led to a little door opening on the garden. Morrel soon found the spot where he had entered; with the assistance of the shrubs he gained the top of the wall, and by his ladder was, in an instant, in the clover-field, where his cab was still waiting for him. He got in it, and thoroughly wearied by so many emotions, he arrived about midnight in the Rue Meslay, threw himself on his bed, and slept soundly.

CHAPTER XLVIII.

THE ESTOPPED ENGAGEMENT.

Two days after, a considerable crowd was assembled, toward ten o'clock in the morning, round the door of M. de Villefort's house, and a long file of mourning-coaches and private carriages extended along the street. Among them was one of a very singular form, come from a distance, a covered wagon, painted black. It was ascertained that, by a strange coincidence, this carriage contained the corpse of the Marquis Saint-Méran, and that those who had come, thinking to attend one funeral, would follow two. The two bodies were to be interred in the cemetery of Père-la-Chaise, where M. de Villefort had long since had a tomb prepared for the reception of his family. The remains of poor Renée were already deposited there, whom, after ten years of separation, her father and mother were now going to rejoin.

These two sudden deaths, so quickly following each other, astonished every one; but no one suspected the terrible secret which M. d'Avrigny had communicated, in his nocturnal walk, to M. de Villefort. They arrived in about an hour at the cemetery; the weather was mild, but dull, and in harmony with the funeral ceremony. Among the groups which flocked towards the family vault, Château-Renaud recognized Morrel, who had come alone in a cabriolet, and walked silently along the path bordered with yew-trees. "You here!" said Château-Renaud, passing his arms through the young captain's; "are you a friend of Villefort's? How is it I have never met you at his house?"——"I am no acquaintance of M. de Villefort's," answered Morrel, "but I was of Mdme. de Saint-Méran." Albert came up to them at this moment with Franz.

"The time and place are but ill-suited for an introduction," said Albert; "but we are not superstitious. M. Morrel, allow me to present to you M. Franz d'Epinay, a delightful traveling companion, with whom I made the tour of Italy. My dear Franz, M. Maximilian Morrel, an excellent friend I have acquired in your absence, and whose name you will hear me mention every time I make any allusion to affection, wit, or amiability." Morrel hesitated for a moment: he feared it would be hypocritical to accost in a friendly manner the man whom he was tacitly opposing, but his oath and the gravity of the circumstances recurred to his memory; he struggled to conceal his emotion, and bowed to Franz. "Mdlle. de Villefort is in deep sorrow, is she not?" said Debray to Franz.

"Extremely," replied he: "she looked so pale this morning, I scarcely knew her." These apparently simple words pierced Morrel to the heart. This man had then seen Valentine, and spoken to her! The young and high-spirited officer required all his strength of mind to resist breaking his oath.

Epinay was treated like one of the family, being passed into the vault, and he went home with the mourning father.

Scarcely had they entered his house then Villefort sent to tell Valentine to be ready in the drawing-room in half an hour, as he expected the notary and M. d'Epinay and his witnesses. The news caused a great sensation; Mdme. de Villefort would not believe it, and Valentine was thunderstruck. She looked round for help, and would have gone down to her grandfather's room, but meeting Villefort on the stairs, he took her arm, and led her into the drawing-room. In the ante-room, Valentine met Barrois, and looked despairingly at the old servant. One moment after, Mdme. de Villefort entered the drawing-room with little Edward. It was evident that she had shared the grief of the family, for she was pale and looked fatigued. She sat down, took Edward on her knees, and, from time to time, pressed almost convulsively to her bosom this child, on whom her affections appeared centered. Two carriages were soon heard to enter the courtyard. One was the notary's; the other, that of Franz's friends. In a moment the whole party was assembled. Valentine was so pale, one might trace the blue veins from her temples, round her eyes and down her cheeks. Franz was deeply affected. Château-Renaud and Albert looked at each other with amazement; the ceremony which was just concluded had not appeared more sorrowful than did that which was commencing. Mdme. de Villefort had placed herself in the shade behind a velvet curtain; and as she constantly bent over her child, it was difficult to read the expression of her face. M. de Villefort was, as usual, unmoved.

The notary, after having, according to the customary method, arranged the papers on the table, taken his place in an arm-chair, and raised his spectacles, turned towards Franz:—"Are you M. Franz de Quesnel, baron d'Epinay?" asked he, although he knew it perfectly.

"Yes, sir," replied Franz. The notary bowed. "I have, then, to inform you, sir, at the request of M. de Villefort, that your projected marriage with Mdlle. de Villefort has changed the feeling of M. Noirtier toward his grandchild; and that he disinherits her entirely of the fortune he would have left her. Let me hasten to add," continued he, "that the testator, having only the right to alienate a part of his fortune, and having alienated it all, the will will not bear scrutiny, and is declared null and void."

"Yes," said Villefort; "but I warn M. d'Epinay, that during my lifetime my father's will shall never be scrutinized, my position forbidding any doubt to be entertained."

M. de Villefort had scarcely said this when the door opened, and Barrois appeared.

"Gentlemen," said he, in a tone strangely firm for a servant speaking to his masters under such solemn circumstances,—"gentlemen, M. Noirtier de Villefort wishes to speak immediately to M. Franz de Quesnel baron d'Epinay:" he, as well as the notary, that there might be no mistake in the person, gave all his titles to the bridegroom elect.

Villefort started, Mdme. de Villefort let her son slip from her knees, Valentine rose, pale and dumb as a statue. Albert and Château-Renaud exchanged a second look, more of amazement than the first. The notary looked at Villefort.

"Pray go, Valentine," said M. de Villefort, "and see what this new fancy of your grandfather's is." Valentine rose quickly, and was hastening joyfully towards the door, when M. de Villefort altered his intention.

"Stop!" said he; "I will go with you."

"Excuse me, sir," said Franz, "since M. Noirtier sent for me, I am ready to attend to his wish; besides, I shall be happy to pay my respects to him, not having yet had the honor of doing so."

Noirtier was prepared to receive them, dressed in black, and installed in his arm-chair. When the three persons he expected had entered, he looked at the door, which his valet immediately closed.

"Listen," whispered Villefort to Valentine, who could not conceal her joy; "if M. Noirtier wishes to communicate anything which would delay your marriage, I forbid you to understand him." Valentine blushed, but did not answer. Villefort, approaching Noirtier—"Here is M. Franz d'Epinay," said he; "you requested to see him. We have all wished for this interview, and I trust it will convince you how ill-formed are your objections to Valentine's marriage."

Noirtier answered only by a look which made Villefort's blood run cold. He motioned to Valentine to approach, and by his usual method had her call Barrois to open a secret drawer in an old desk. A paper taken from this receptacle was to be given to Epinay. The young man was surprised to find it a "Report of the Meeting, 5th Feb., 1815, held in Our Hall, St. Jacques Street, by the Bonapartist Club." It detailed that Gen. Flavien Quesnel, made baron by Louis XVIII., was still believed faithful to Napoleon I. On challenging his creed, he declared that he was for the deposed monarch and against the Emperor. The committee took his word of honor that he would be silent on what he had heard and seen and he was conducted away blindfolded as he had been led in.

Unfortunately, his language had been taken as an insult by the chairman of the meeting who, when his eyes were unveiled, on the riverside, suggested that they should settle the dispute by arms. He was armed with a sword cane, the general with a sword, but in spite of this inequality the Bonapartist slew the royalist. The witnesses of the meeting and the duel appended their names: L. J. Beaurepaire, lieut.-col. of artillery, Brig.-gen. E. Duchampy and Claude Lecharpe I, Lord High Forester.

When Franz had finished reading this account, so dreadful for a son—when Valentine, pale with emotion, had wiped away a tear,— when Villefort, trembling, and crouched in a corner, had endeavored to lessen the storm by supplicating glances at the implacable old man,—he said to Noirtier: "Since you are well acquainted with all these details, attested by honorable signatures,—and appear to take some interest in me, although you have only manifested it hitherto by causing me sorrow, refuse me not one final satisfaction—tell me the name of the president of the club, that I may at least know who killed my father." Villefort mechanically felt for the handle of the door; Valentine, who understood sooner than anyone her grandfather's answer, and who had often seen two scars upon his right arm, drew back a few steps.

"Sir! sir!" cried Franz, turning to Noirtier, "do what you can!— make me understand in some way!"——"Yes," replied Noirtier.

Noirtier looked at the dictionary. Franz took it with a nervous trembling, and repeated the letters of the alphabet successively, until he came to M. At that letter the old man signified "Yes."——The young man's finger glided over the words, but at each one Noirtier answered by a negative sign. Valentine hid her head between her hands. At length, Franz arrived at the word MYSELF.——"Yes!"

"You!" cried Franz, whose hair stood on end; "you, M. Noirtier!— you killed my father?"

"Yes?" replied Noirtier, fixing a majestic look on the young man. Franz fell powerless on a chair; Villefort opened the door and escaped, for the idea had entered his mind to stifle the little remaining life in the old man's heart.

CHAPTER XLIX.

PROGRESS OF CAVALCANTI JUNIOR.

MEANWHILE M. Cavalcanti the elder had returned to his service, not in the army of Austria, but at the gambling-table of Lucca, of which he was one of the most assiduous courtiers. He had spent every penny that had been allowed for his journey as a reward for the majestic and solemn manner in which he had maintained his assumed character of father. M. Andrea at his departure inherited all the papers which proved that he had indeed the honor of being the son of the Marquis Bartolomeo and Oliva Corsinari. He was now fairly launched in that Parisian society which gives such ready access to foreigners, and treats them, not as what they really are, but as what they wish to be considered. Besides, what is required of a young man in Paris? To speak its language tolerably, to make a good appearance, to be a good gamester, and pay in cash. They are certainly less particular with a foreigner than with a Frenchman. Andrea had, then, in a fortnight, attained a very fair position. He was entitled Count, he was said to possess 50,000 livres per annum; and his father's immense riches, buried in the quarries of Saravezza, were a constant theme. A learned man, before whom the last circumstance was mentioned as a fact, declared he had seen the quarries in question, which gave great weight to assertions hitherto somewhat doubtful, but which now assumed the garb of reality.

Such was the state of society in Paris at the period we bring before our readers, when Monte-Cristo went one evening to pay M. Danglars a visit. M. Danglars was out, but the count was asked to go and see the baroness, and he accepted the invitation. It was never without a nervous shudder, since the dinner at Auteuil, and the events which followed it, that Mdme. Danglars heard Monte-Cristo's name announced. If he did not come, the painful sensation become most intense; if, on the contrary, he appeared, his noble countenance, brilliant eyes, amiability, and polite attention even toward Mdme. Danglars, soon dispelled every impression of fear. It appeared impossible to the baroness that a man of such delightfully pleasing manners should entertain evil designs against her; besides, the most corrupt minds only suspect evil when it would answer some interested end—useless injury is repugnant to every mind. When Monte-Cristo entered the boudoir, where the baroness was examining some drawings, which her daughter passed to her after having looked at them with M. Cavalcanti, his presence soon produced its usual effect; and it was with smiles that the baroness received the count, although she had been a little disconcerted at the announcement of his name. The latter embraced the whole scene at a glance.

The baroness was partially reclining, Eugénie sat near her, and Cavalcanti was standing. Cavalcanti, dressed in black, like one of Goethe's heroes, with japanned shoes and open white silk stockings, passed a white and tolerably nice-looking hand through his light hair, in the midst of which sparkled a diamond, which, in spite of Monte-Cristo's advice, the vain young man had been unable to resist putting on his little finger. This movement was accompanied by killing glances at Mdlle. Danglars, and sighs addressed to the same party. Mdlle. Danglars was still the same—cold, beautiful, and satirical. Not one of these glances, nor one sigh, was lost on her; they might have been said to fall on the shield of Minerva, which some philosophers assert protected sometimes the breast of Sappho. Eugénie bowed coldly to the count, and availed herself of the first moment when the conversation became earnest to escape to her study, whence very soon two cheerful and noisy voices being heard, in connection with some notes of the piano, assured Monte-Cristo that Mdlle. Danglars preferred to his society and Cavalcanti's, the company of Louise d'Armilly, her singing governess.

It was then, especially while conversing with Mdme. Danglars, and apparently absorbed by the charm of the conversation, that the count remarked M. Andrea Cavalcanti's solicitude, his manner of listening to the music at the door he dared not pass, and of manifesting his admiration. The banker soon returned. His first look was certainly directed toward Monte-Cristo, but the second was for Andrea. As for his wife, he bowed to her, as some husbands do to their wives, but which bachelors will never comprehend, until a very extensive code is published on conjugal life.

"Have not the ladies invited you to join them at the piano?" said

Danglars to Andrea. "Alas! no, sir," replied Andrea, with a sigh, still more remarkable than the former ones. Danglars immediately advanced toward the door and opened it.

The two young ladies were seated at the piano, accompanying themselves, each with one hand, a fancy to which they had accustomed themselves, and performed admirably. "Well!" said the banker to his daughter, "are we then all to be excluded?" He then led the young man into the study, and, either by chance or manœuvre, the door was partially closed after Andrea, so that from the place where they sat neither the count nor the baroness could see anything; but as the banker had accompanied Andrea, Mdme. Danglars appeared to take no notice of it.

The count soon heard Andrea's voice, singing a Corsican song, accompanied by the piano. While the count smiled at hearing this song, which made him lose sight of Andrea in the recollection of Benedetto, Mdme. Danglars was boasting to Monte-Cristo of her husband's strength of mind, who that very morning had lost three or four hundred thousand francs by a failure at Milan. The praise was well deserved, for had not the count heard it from the baroness, or by one of those means by which he knew everything, the baron's countenance would not have led him to suspect it. "Hem!" thought Monte-Cristo, "he begins to conceal his losses; a month ago he boasted of them." Then aloud,—"Oh! madame, M. Danglars is so skilful, he will soon regain at the Bourse what he loses elsewhere."

Danglars returned at this moment alone. "Well!" said the baroness, "do you leave M. Cavalcanti with your daughter?"——"And Mdlle. d'Armilly," said the banker; "do you consider her no one?" Then, turning to Monte-Cristo, he said, "Prince Cavalcanti is a charming young man, is he not? But is he really a prince?"

"I will not answer for it," said Monte-Cristo. "His father was introduced to me as a marquis, so he ought to be a count; but I do not think he has much claim to that title."

"Why?" said the banker. "If he is a prince, he is wrong not to maintain his rank; I do not like any one to deny his origin."

"Oh! you are a pure democrat," said Monte-Cristo, smiling.

"But do you see to what you are exposing yourself? If, perchance, M. de Morcerf came, he would find M. Cavalcanti in that room, where he, the bethrothed of Eugénie, has never been admitted."

"You may well say, perchance," replied the banker; "for he comes so seldom, it would seem only chance that brings him."

"But should he come, and find that young man with your daughter, he might be displeased."

"He! you are mistaken; M. Albert would not do us the honor to be jealous; he does not like Eugénie sufficiently. Besides, I care not for his displeasure."

"Still, situated as we are——"

"Yes, do you know how we are situated? At his mother's ball he danced once with Eugénie, and M. Cavalcanti three times, and he took no notice of it." The valet announced Albert de Morcerf. The baroness rose hastily, and was going into the study, when Danglars stopped her. "Stay!" said he. She looked at him in amazement. Monte-Cristo appeared to be unconscious of what passed. Albert entered, looking very handsome and in high spirits. He bowed politely to the baroness, familiarly to Danglars, and affectionately to Monte-Cristo. Then turning to the baroness: "May I ask how Mdlle. Danglars is?" said he.

"She is quite well," replied Danglars, quickly; "she is at the piano with M. Cavalcanti." Albert preserved his calm and indifferent manner; he might feel, perhaps annoyed, but he knew Monte-Cristo's eye was on him. "M. Cavalcanti has a fine tenor voice," said he, "and Mdlle. Eugénie a splendid soprano; and then she plays on the piano like Thalberg. The concert must be a delightful one."

"They suit each other remarkably well," said Danglars. Albert appeared not to notice this remark, which was, however, so rude that Mdme. Danglars blushed.

"I, too," said the young man, "am a musician—at least, my masters used to tell me so; but it is strange that my voice never would suit any other, and a soprano less than any." Danglars smiled, and seemed to say: It is of no consequence. Then, hoping, doubtless, to effect his purpose, he said,—"The prince and my daughter were universally admired yesterday. You were not of the party, M. de Morcerf?"

"What prince?" asked Albert. "Prince Cavalcanti," said Danglars, who persisted in giving the young man that title.

"Pardon me," said Albert, "I was not aware he was a prince. And Prince Cavalcanti sang with Mdlle. Eugénie yesterday? It must have been charming, indeed. I regret not having heard them. But I was unable to accept your invitation, having promised to accompany my mother to a German concert given by the countess of Château-Renaud."

Danglars was quite annoyed by the young man's indifference. He took Monte-Cristo aside. "What do you think of our lover?" said he.

"He appears cool! But, then, your word is given."——"Yes, doubtless, I have promised to give my daughter to a man who loves her, but not to one who does not. Even if Albert had Cavalcanti's fortune, he is so proud, I would not care to see him marry her."

"Oh!" said Monte-Cristo, "my fondness may blind me, but, I assure you, I consider Morcerf far preferable; and his father's position is good."

"Hem!" said Danglars. "Why do you doubt?"

"The past—that obscurity on the past."——"But that does not affect the son. Besides you cannot break it off thus; the Morcerfs are depending on this union."

"Then let them explain themselves; you should give the father a hint, you are so intimate with the family."

"I?—where the devil did you find out that?"

"At their ball; it was apparent enough. Why, did not the countess, the proud Mercédès, the disdainful Catalan, who will scarcely open her lips to her oldest acquaintances, take your arm, lead you into the garden, into the private walks, and remain there for half an hour?—But will you undertake to speak to the father?"——"Willingly, if you wish it." ——"But let it be done explicitly and positively. If he demands my daughter, let him fix the day—declare his conditions: in short, let us either understand each other, or quarrel. You understand—no more delay."——"Yes, sir, I will give my attention to the subject."——"I do not say I expect him with pleasure, but I do expect him. A banker must, you know, be a slave to his promise." And Danglars sighed as M. Cavalcanti had done half an hour before.

"Bravo!" cried Morcerf, as the scene closed. Danglars began to look suspiciously at Morcerf, when some one came and whispered a few words to him. "I shall soon return," said the banker to Monte-Cristo; "wait for me. I shall, perhaps, have something to say to you."

When Danglars entered, he was visibly agitated. Monte-Cristo observed it particularly and, by a look, asked the banker for an explanation. "I have just received my mail from Greece," said Danglars.

"How is King Otho?" asked Albert, in the most sprightly tone. Danglars cast another suspicious look toward him without answering, and Monte-Cristo turned away to conceal the expression of pity which passed over his features, but which was gone in a moment. "We shall go together, shall we not?" said Albert to the count.

"If you like," replied the latter.

Albert advanced toward Eugénie, smiling. Meanwhile, Danglars, stooping to Monte-Cristo's ear, said: "Your advice was excellent, there is a whole history connected with the names Fernand and Janina."

"Indeed!" said Monte-Cristo. "Yes, I will tell you all; but take away the young man; I cannot endure his presence."

"He is going with me. Shall I send the father to you?"

"Immediately."

"Very well." The count made a sign to Albert; they bowed to the ladies, and took their leave; Albert perfectly indifferent to Mdlle. Danglars' contempt, Monte-Cristo reiterating his advice to Mdme. Danglars on the prudence a banker's wife should exercise in providing for the future. M. Cavalcanti remained master of the field.

CHAPTER L.

HAYDEE'S STORY.

SCARCELY had the count's horses cleared the angle of the boulevard, when Albert, turning towards the count, burst into a loud fit of laughter—much too loud, in fact, not to give the idea of its being rather forced and unnatural. "Well!" said he, "I will ask you the same question which Charles IX. put to Catharine de Medicis, after the massacre of Saint Bartholomew. 'How have I played my little part?'"——"To what do you allude?" asked Monte-Cristo.

"To the installation of my rival at M. Danglars'!"

"What! do you think Cavalcanti is paying his addresses?"

"I am certain of it; his languishing looks and modulated tones fully proclaim his intentions. He aspires to the hand of the proud Eugénie."——"What does that signify, so long as they favor your suit?"

"But it is not the case, my dear Count; on the contrary I am repulsed on all sides."

"But the father has the greatest regard possible for you," said Monte-Cristo.

"He? oh, no! he has plunged a thousand daggers into my heart; tragedy-weapons, I own, which, instead of wounding, sheath their points in their own handles, but daggers which he nevertheless believed to be real and deadly. I will engage that before a week is past the door will be closed against me."

"You are mistaken, my dear Viscount, I am charged with the commission of endeavoring to induce your father to make some definite arrangement with the baron."——"By whom?"

"By the baron himself."——"Oh!" said Albert, with all the cajolery of which he was capable. "You surely will not do that, my dear Count?"

"Certainly I shall, Albert, as I have promised to do it."——"Well!" said Albert, with a sigh, "it seems you are determined to marry me off."

"I am determined to try and be on good terms with everybody, at all events," said Monte-Cristo.

They both went into the house; the drawing-room was lighted up; they entered it. "Tea, Baptistin," said the count. Baptistin left the room without waiting to answer, and in two seconds reappeared, bringing on a salver all that his master had ordered, ready prepared, and appearing to have sprung from the ground, like the repasts in fairy tales. "Really, my dear Count," said Morcerf, "what I admire in you is, not so much your riches, for perhaps there are people even wealthier than yourself, nor is it only your wit,—but it is your manner of being served, without any questions, in a moment, in a second; it is as if they guessed what you wanted by your manner of ringing, and made a point of keeping everything you can possibly desire in constant readiness."——"What you say is perhaps true: they know my habits."

"Ah! but what do I hear!" and Morcerf inclined his head toward the door, through which sounds seemed to issue resembling those of a guitar.

"My dear Viscount, you are fated to hear music this evening; you have only escaped from the piano of Mademoiselle Danglars to be attacked by the guzla of Haydée."——" Haydée! what an adorable name! Are there, then, really women who bear the name of Haydée anywhere but in Byron's poems?"

"Certainly there are. Haydée is a very uncommon name in France, but it is common enough in Albania and Epirus; it is as if you said, for example, Chastity, Modesty, Innocence,—it is a kind of baptismal name, as you Parisians call it."——"Oh, that is charming!" said Albert; "are there any more slaves to be had who bear this beautiful name?"

"Undoubtedly."——"Really, count, you do nothing, and have nothing like other people. The slave of Monte-Cristo! why, it is a rank of itself in France: and from the way in which you lavish money, it is a place that must be worth a hundred thousand francs a-year."

"A hundred thousand francs! the poor girl originally possessed much more than that; she was born to treasures, in comparison with which those recorded would seem but poverty."

"She must be a princess, then?"

"You are right; and she is one of the greatest in her country, too!"

"I thought so. But how did it happen that such a great princess became a slave?"

"How was it that Dionysius the Tyrant became a schoolmaster? The fortune of war, my dear Viscount,—the caprice of fortune; that is the way in which these things are to be accounted for."

"And is her name a secret?"——"As regards the generality of mankind it is; but not for you, my dear Viscount. You know the history of the pacha of Janina, do you not?"

"Of Ali Tebelen! oh! yes! it was in his service that my father made his fortune."

"True, I had forgotten that."

"Well! what is Haydée to Ali Tebelen?"——"Merely his daughter."

"What? the daughter of Ali Pacha?"

"Of Ali Pacha and the beautiful Vasiliki."

"And your slave?"——"Yes."

"But how did she become so?"

"Why, simply from the circumstance of my having bought her

one day, as I was passing through the slave market at Constantinople."

"Wonderful! really, my dear Count, you seem to throw a sort of magic influence over all in which you are concerned; when listening to you, existence no longer seems reality, but a waking dream. Now, I am perhaps going to make an imprudent and thoughtless request, but I may venture to ask you this favor: present me to your princess."

"I will do so; but on two conditions."

"I accept them at once."

"The first is, that you will never tell any one that I have granted the interview."

"Very well," said Albert, extending his hand; "I swear I will not."

"The second is, that you will not tell her that your father ever served hers."

"I give you my word that I will not."

"Enough, Viscount; I know you to be a man of honor." The count again struck the gong. Ali reappeared. "Tell Haydée," said he, "that I will take coffee with her, and give her to understand that I desire permission to present one of my friends to her." Ali bowed and left the room. "Now, understand me," said the count, "no direct questions, my dear Morcerf; if you wish to know anything, tell me, and I will ask her."——"Agreed." Ali reappeared for the third time, and drew back the tapestried hanging which concealed the door, to signify to his master and Albert that they were at liberty to pass on. "Let us go in," said Monte-Cristo.

Albert passed his hand through his hair, and twisted his moustache, then, satisfied as to his personal appearance, followed the count into the room, the latter having previously resumed his hat and gloves. Ali was stationed as a kind of advanced guard, and the door was kept by three French maids, commanded by Myrtho. Haydée was awaiting her visitors in the first room of her apartments, the drawing-room. Her large eyes were dilated with surprise and expectation, for it was the first time that any man, except Monte-Cristo, had been accorded an entrance into her presence. She was sitting on a sofa placed in an angle of the room, with her legs crossed under her in the Eastern fashion, in a nest in the rich Indian silks which enveloped her. Near was the instrument on which she had just been playing; it was elegantly fashioned, and worthy of its mistress. On perceiving Monte-Cristo, she rose and welcomed him with a kind of smile peculiar to herself, expressive at once of the most implicit obedience and also of the deepest love. Monte-Cristo advanced toward her and extended his hand, which she, as usual, raised to her lips.

Albert had proceeded no farther than the door, where he remained rooted to the spot, being completely fascinated by the sight of such surpassing beauty, beheld, as it was, for the first time, and of which an inhabitant of more northern climes could form no adequate idea.

"Whom do you bring?" asked the girl, in Romaic, of Monte-Cristo; "is it a friend, a brother, a simple acquaintance or an enemy."

"A friend," said Monte-Cristo, in the same language.

"What is his name?"

"Count Albert; it is the same man whom I rescued from the hands of the banditti at Rome."

"In what language would you like me to converse with him?"

"You will speak in Italian," said he. Then, turning towards Albert, —"It is a pity you do not understand either ancient or modern Greek, both of which Haydée speaks so fluently; the poor child will be obliged to talk to you in Italian, which will give you but a very false idea of her powers of conversation." The count made a sign to Haydée to address his visitor. "Sir," said she to Morcerf, "you are most welcome as the friend of my lord and master." This was said in excellent Tuscan, and with that soft Roman accent which makes the language of Dante as sonorous as Homer's. Then, turning to Ali, she directed him to bring coffee and pipes; and when he had left the room to execute the orders of his young mistress, she beckoned Albert to approach nearer to her. Monte-Cristo and Morcerf drew their seats toward a small table, on which were arranged music, drawings, and vases of flowers. Ali then entered, bringing coffee and chibooques; as to Baptistin, this portion of the building was prohibited to him. Albert refused the pipe which the Nubian offered him. "Oh, take it—take it," said the count: "Haydée is almost as civilized as a Parisian: the smell of a Havanna is disagreeable to her, but the tobacco of the East is a most delicious perfume, you know."

Ali left the room. The cups of coffee were all prepared, with the addition of a sugar-glass, which had been brought for Albert. Monte-Cristo and Haydée took the liquor in the original Arabian manner, that is to say, without sugar. Haydée took the porcelain cup in her little slender fingers, and conveyed it to her mouth with all the innocent _naïveté_ of a child when eating or drinking something which it likes. At this moment two women entered, bringing salvers filled with ices and sherbet, which they placed on two small tables appropriated to that purpose.

"On what subject shall I converse with her?" said Albert, in a low tone to Monte-Cristo.

"Just what you please; you may speak of her country and of her youthful reminiscences; or, if you like it better, you can talk of Rome, Naples, or Florence."

"Oh!" said Albert, "it is of no use to be in the company of a Greek if one converses as with a Parisian; let me speak to her of the East. At what age did you leave Greece, signora?" asked he.——"I left it when I was but five years old," replied Haydée.

"And how far back into the past do your recollections extend?"

"I could scarcely walk when my mother, who was called Basiliki, which means royal," said the girl, proudly, "took me by the hand, and after putting in our purse all the money we possessed, we went out, both covered with veils, to solicit alms for the prisoners, saying, 'He who giveth to the poor lendeth to the Lord.' Then, when our purse was full, we returned to the palace, and without saying a word to my father, we sent it to the convent, where it was divided amongst the prisoners."

"Count," said Albert, in a low tone to Monte-Cristo, "allow the signora to tell me something of her history. You prohibited my mentioning my father's name to her, but perhaps she will allude to him of her own accord in the course of the recital, and you have no idea how delighted I should be to hear our name pronounced by such beautiful lips." Monte-Cristo turned to Haydée, and with an expression which commanded her to pay the most implicit attention to his words, he said in Greek:—"Tell us the fate of your father; but neither the name of the traitor nor the treason." Haydée sighed deeply, and a shade of sadness clouded her beautiful brow.

"Oh! then I remember as if it were but yesterday sitting under the sycamore-trees, on the borders of a lake. Under the oldest and thickest of these trees, reclining on cushions, sat my father; my mother was at his feet, and I, childlike, amused myself by playing with his long white beard, which descended to his girdle, or with the diamond-hilt of the scimitar attached to his girdle. Then from time to time there came to him an Albanian, who said something, to which I paid no attention, but which he always answered in the same tone of voice, either 'Kill,' or 'Pardon.'"

"So young," said Albert, forgetting at the moment the count's command that he should ask no questions of the slave herself, "is it possible that you can have known what suffering is except by name?"

Haydée answered his remark with a melancholy smile. "You wish me, then, to relate the history of my past sorrows?" said she.

"I beg you to do so," replied Albert.

"Well! I was but four years old, when one night I was suddenly awakened by my mother. We were in the palace of Janina; she snatched me from the cushions on which I was sleeping, and on opening my eyes I saw hers were filled with tears. She took me away without speaking. When I saw her weeping I began to cry too. "Silence, child!" said she. At other times, in spite of maternal endearments or threats, I had, with a child's caprice, been accustomed to indulge my feelings of sorrow or anger by crying as much as I felt inclined; but on this occasion there was an intonation of such extreme terror in my mother's voice when she enjoined me to silence, that I ceased crying as soon as her command was given. She bore me rapidly away. I saw then that we were descending a large staircase; around us were all my mother's servants carrying trunks, bags, ornaments, jewels, purses of gold, with which they were hurrying away in the greatest distraction. Behind the women came a guard of twenty men, armed with long guns and pistols, and dressed in the costume which the Greeks have assumed since they have again become a nation. You may imagine there was something startling and ominous," said Haydée, shaking her head, and turning pale at the mere remembrance of the scene, "in this long file of slaves and women only half-aroused from sleep, or at least, so they appeared to me, who was myself scarcely awake. Here and there, on the walls of the staircase, were reflected gigantic shadows, which trembled in the flickering light of the pine-torches, till they seemed to reach to the vaulted roof above.

" 'Quick!' said a voice at the end of the gallery. This voice made every one bow before it, resembling in its effect the wind passing over a field of corn, by its superior strength forcing every ear to yield obeisance. As for me, it made me tremble. This voice was my father's. He marched the last, clothed in his splendid robes, and holding in his hand the rifle with which your emperor presented him. He was leaning on the shoulder of his favorite Selim, and he drove us all before him, as a shepherd would his straggling flock. My father," said Haydée, raising her head, "was that illustrious man known in Europe under the name of Ali Tebelen, pacha of Janina, and before whom Turkey trembled."

Albert, without knowing why, started on hearing these words pronounced with such a haughty and dignified accent; it appeared to him as if there was something supernaturally gloomy and terrible in the expression which gleamed from the brilliant eyes of Haydée at this moment; she appeared like a Pythoness evoking a spectre, as she recalled to his mind the remembrance of the fearful death of this man, to the news of which all Europe had listened with horror. "Soon," said Haydée, "we halted on our march, and found ourselves on the borders of a lake. My mother pressed me to her throbbing heart, and, at the distance of a few paces, I saw my father, who was glancing anxiously around. Four marble steps led down to the water's edge, and below them was a boat floating on the tide. From where we stood I could see, in the middle of the lake, a large black mass; it was the kiosk to which we were going. This kiosk appeared to me to be at a considerable distance, perhaps on account of the darkness of the night, which prevented any object from being more than partially discerned. We stepped into the boat. I remember well that the oars made no noise whatever in striking the water, and when I leaned over to ascertain the cause, I saw they were muffled with the sashes of our Palikares. Besides the rowers, the boat contained only the women, my father, mother, Selim, and myself. The Palikares had remained on the shore of the lake, ready to cover our retreat; they were kneeling on the lowest of the marble steps, and in that manner intended making a rampart of the three others, in case of pursuit. Our bark flew before the wind. 'Why does the boat go so fast?' asked I of my mother."

"'Silence, child! Hush! we are fleeing.' I did not understand. Why should my father flee?—he, the all-powerful—before whom others were accustomed to flee—who had taken for his device—

"'They hate me, then they fear me!'

"It was, indeed, a flight which my father was trying to effect. I have been told since, that the garrison of the castle of Janina, fatigued with long service had treated with the Seraskier Kourchid, sent by the sultan to gain possession of the person of my father; it was then that Ali Tebelen took the resolution of retiring (after having sent to the sultan a French officer in whom he reposed great confidence) to the asylum which he had long before prepared for himself, and which he called *kataphygion,* or the refuge."

"And this officer," asked Albert, "do you remember his name, signora?" Monte-Cristo exchanged a rapid glance with the girl, which was quite unperceived by Albert. "No," said she, "I do not remember it just at this moment; but if it should occur to me presently, I will tell you." Albert was on the point of pronouncing his father's name, when Monte-Cristo gently held up his finger in token of reproach; the young man recollected his vow, and was silent.

"It was towards this kiosk that we were rowing. A ground-floor, ornamented with arabesques, bathing its terraces in the water, and another floor, overlooking the lake, was all that was visible to the eye. But beneath the ground-floor, stretching out into the island, was a large subterraneous cavern, to which my mother, myself, and the women were conducted. In this place were together 60,000 purses and 200 barrels; the purses contained 25,000,000 of money in gold, and the barrels were filled with 30,000 pounds of gunpowder.

"Near these barrels stood Selim, my father's favorite, whom I mentioned to you just now. It was his duty to watch, day and night, a lighted fuse, and he had orders to blow up all—kiosk, guards, women, gold, and Ali Tebelen himself, at the first signal given by my father. I remember well that the slaves, convinced of the precarious tenure on which they held their lives, passed whole days and nights in praying, crying, and groaning. As for me, I can never forget the pale complexion and black eyes of the young soldier; and whenever the angel of death summons me to another world, I am quite sure I shall recognize Selim. I cannot tell you how long we remained in this state; at that period I did not even know what time meant; sometimes, but very rarely, my father summoned me and my mother to the terrace of the palace; these were my hours of recreation; I, who never saw anything in the dismal cavern but the gloomy countenances of the slaves and the lintstock of Selim. My father was endeavoring to pierce with his eager looks the remotest verge of the horizon, examining attentively every black speck which appeared on the lake, whilst my mother, reclining by his side, rested her head on his shoulder, and I played at his feet, admiring everything I saw with that unsophisticated innocence of childhood which throws a charm around objects insignificant in themselves, but which in its eyes are invested with the greatest importance. The heights of Pindus towered above us; the castle of Janina rose white and angular from the blue waters of the lake, and the immense masses of black vegetation which, viewed in the distance, gave the idea of lichens clinging to the rocks, were, in reality, gigantic fir-trees and myrtles.

"One morning my father sent for us; my mother had been crying all the night, and was very wretched; we found the pacha calm, but paler than usual. 'Basiliki,' said he to my mother, trembling perceptibly, 'the instant approaches which will decide everything. In the space of half-an-hour we shall know the emperor's answer. Go into the cavern with Haydée.'——'I will not quit you,' said Basiliki; 'if you die, my lord, I will die with you.'——'Go to Selim!' cried my father. 'Adieu! my lord,' murmured my mother, determining quietly to await the approach of death. 'Take away Basiliki!' said my father to his Palikares.

"As for me, I had been forgotten in the general confusion; I ran towards Ali Tebelen; he saw me hold out my arms to him and he stooped down and pressed his lips upon my forehead. Oh! how distinctly I remember that kiss! it was the last he ever gave me, and I feel as if it were still warm on my forehead. On descending, we distinguished through the lattice-work several boats which were gradually becoming more distinct to our view. At first they appeared like black specks, and now they looked like birds skimming the surface of the waves. During this time, in the kiosk, at the feet of my father, were seated twenty Palikares, concealed from view by an angle of the wall, and watching with eager eyes the arrival of the boats; they were armed with their long guns inlaid with mother-of-pearl and silver, and cartridges, in great numbers, were lying scattered on the floor; my father looked at his watch, and paced up and down with a countenance expressive of the greatest anguish. This was the scene which presented itself to my view when I left my father after that last kiss. My mother and I traversed the gloomy passage leading to the cavern. Selim was still at his post, and smiled sadly on us as we entered. We fetched our cushions from the other end of the cavern, and sat down by Selim. In great dangers the devoted ones cling to each other; and, young as I was, I quite understood that some imminent danger was hanging over our heads.

It was about four o'clock in the afternoon; and although the day was brilliant out of doors, we were enveloped in the gloomy darkness of the cavern. One single solitary light was burning there, and it appeared like a star set in a heaven of blackness; it was Selim's flaming lance. My mother was a Christian, and she prayed. Selim repeated from time to time these sacred words:—'God is great!' However, my mother had still some hope. As she was coming down, she thought she recognized the French officer sent to Constantinople, and in whom my father placed so much confidence, for he knew that all the soldiers of the French emperor were naturally noble and generous. She advanced some steps towards the staircase, and listened: 'They are approaching,' said she; 'perhaps they bring us peace and liberty!'——'What do you fear, Basiliki?' said Selim, in a voice at once so gentle and yet so proud; 'if they do not bring us peace we will give them war; if they do not bring life we will give them death.'

"'My child,' said Basiliki, 'may God preserve you from ever wishing for that death which to-day you so much dread!' Then, whispering to Selim, she asked what were his master's orders. 'If he send me his poniard, it will signify that the emperor's intentions are not favorable, and I am to set fire to the powder; if, on the contrary, he send me his ring, it will be a sign that the emperor pardons him and I will extinguish the match and leave the magazine untouched.'

"'My friend,' said my mother, 'when your master's order arrives, if it is the poniard which he sends, instead of despatching us by that horrible death which we both so much dread, you will mercifully kill us with this same poniard, will you not?'——'Yes, Basiliki,' replied Selim, tranquilly.

"Suddenly we heard loud cries; we listened: they were cries of joy; the name of the French officer who had been sent to Constantinople resounded on all sides amongst our Palikares; it was evident that he brought the answer of the emperor, and that it was favorable. Soon a figure appeared in the gray twilight at the entrance of the cave. 'Who are you?' cried Selim. 'But whoever you may be, I charge you not to advance another step.'—'Long live the emperor!' said the figure. 'He grants a full pardon to the Vizier Ali; and not only gives him his life, but restores to him his fortune and his possessions.' My mother uttered a cry of joy, and clasped me to her bosom. 'Stop!' said Selim, 'if you come from Ali himself, you know what you were charged to remit to me?'——'Yes,' said the messenger, 'and I bring you his ring.' Place the object which I desire to see in the ray of light which shines there, and retire whilst I examine it.'——'Be it so,' said the envoy, and he retired, after having first deposited the token agreed on in the place pointed out to him by Selim.

"Selim, still holding in his hand the lighted match, walked toward the opening, and aided by the faint light which streamed in, picked up the token.

"'It is well!' said he, kissing it; 'it is my master's ring!' And throwing the match on the ground, he trampled on it and extinguished it. The messenger uttered a cry of joy, and clapped his hands. At this signal four soldiers of the Seraskier Kourchid suddenly appeared, and Selim fell pierced by five blows. Each man had stabbed him separately; and, intoxicated by their crime, though still pale with fear, they sought all over the cavern to discover if there was any fear of fire, after which they amused themselves by rolling on the bags of gold. At this moment my mother seized me in her arms, and bounding lightly along numerous turnings and windings, known only to ourselves, she arrived at a private staircase of the kiosk, where was a scene of frightful tumult and confusion. The lower rooms were entirely filled with our enemies. Just as my mother was on the point of pushing open a small door, we heard the voice of the pacha sounding in a loud and threatening tone. My mother applied her eye to the crack between the boards; I luckily found a small opening, which afforded me a view of the apartment and what was passing within. 'What do you want?' said my father to some people who were holding a paper inscribed with characters of gold. 'What we want,' replied one of them, 'is to communicate to you the will of his highness. Do you see this firman?'——'I do,' said my father. 'Well, read it; he demands your head.'

"My father answered with a loud laugh, which was more frightful than even threats would have been, and he had not ceased when two reports of a pistol were heard; he had fired them himself, and had killed two men. The Palikares, prostrated at my father's feet, now sprang up and fired; and the room was filled with fire and smoke. At the same instant the firing began on the other side, and the balls penetrated the boards all round us. Oh! how noble did the grand vizier, my father, look at that moment, in the midst of the balls, his scimitar in his hand, and his face blackened with the powder of his enemies! and how he terrified them, even then, and made them fly before him! 'Selim! Selim! cried he, 'guardian of the fire, do your duty!'

"'Selim is dead!' replied a voice which seemed to come from the depths of the earth, 'and you are lost, Ali!' At the same moment an explosion was heard, and the whole flooring suddenly gave way; my father fell on one knee, and at the same moment twenty hands were thrust forth, armed with sabres, pistols, and poniards—twenty blows were instantaneously directed against one man, and my father disappeared in a whirlwind of fire and smoke kindled by these demons, and which seemed like hell itself opening beneath his feet. I felt myself fall to the ground; it was my mother who had fainted."

Haydée's arms fell by her side, and she uttered a deep groan, at the same time looking toward the count, as if to ask if he were satisfied with her obedience to his commands. Monte-Cristo rose and approached her;

he took her hand, and said to her in Romaic, "Calm yourself, my dear child, and take courage in remembering that there is a God who will punish traitors."

"It is a frightful story, count," said Albert, terrified at the paleness of Haydée's countenance, "and I reproach myself now, for having been so cruel and thoughtless in my request."

"Oh, it is nothing!" said Monte-Cristo. Then, patting the girl on the head, he continued,—"Haydée is very courageous; and she sometimes even finds consolation in the recital of her misfortunes."

"Because, my lord," said Haydée, eagerly, "my miseries recall to me the remembrance of your goodness."

Albert looked at her with curiosity, for she had not yet related what be most desired to know, namely, how she had become the slave of the count. Haydée saw at a glance the same expression pervading the countenances of her two auditors; she exclaimed,—"When my mother recovered her senses we were before the seraskier. 'Kill me,' said she, 'but spare the honor of the widow of Ali.'——'It is not I to whom you must address yourself,' said Kourchid.

" 'To whom, then?'——'To your new master.'

" 'Who and where is he?'——'He is here.'

"And Kourchid pointed out one who had more than any contributed to the death of my father," said Haydée, in a tone of chastened anger. "Then," said Albert, "you became the property of this man?" ——"No," replied Haydée, "he did not dare to keep us, so we were sold to some slave-merchants who were going to Constantinople. We traversed Greece, and arrived, half dead, at the imperial gates. They were surrounded by a crowd of people, who opened a way for us to pass, when, suddenly, my mother, having directed her eye to the object which was attracting their attention, uttered a piercing cry and fell to the ground, pointing, as she did so, to a head which was placed over the gates, and beneath which were inscribed these words,—

'THIS IS THE HEAD OF ALI TEBELEN, PACHA OF JANINA.'

"I cried bitterly, and tried to raise my mother from the earth, but she was dead! I was taken to the slave-market, and was purchased by a rich Armenian. He caused me to be instructed, gave me masters, and when I was thirteen years of age he sold me to the Sultan Mahmoud."

"Of whom I bought her," said Monte-Cristo, "as I told you, Albert, with the emerald which formed a match to the one I had made into a box for the purpose of holding my hasheesh."

"Oh; you are good! you are great! my lord!" said Haydée, kissing the count's hand, "and I am very fortunate in belonging to such a master." Albert remained quite bewildered with all that he had seen and heard. "Come! finish your cup of coffee," said Monte-Cristo; "the story is ended."

CHAPTER LI.

"WE HEAR FROM JANINA."

VILLEFORT retired to his study, where he received about two hours afterwards the following letter from Epinay:

"After all the disclosures made this morning, M. Noirtier de Villefort must see the utter impossibility of any alliance being formed between his family and that of Epinay. M. d'Epinay must say that he is shocked and astonished that M. de Villefort, who appeared aware of all the circumstances, should not have anticipated him in this announcement."

This harsh letter, coming as it did from a man generally so polite and respectful, struck a mortal blow at the pride of Villefort. Hardly had he read the letter when his wife entered.

M. de Villefort's communications on the subject were very limited and concise, he told her, in fact, that an explanation had taken place between M. Noirtier, M. d'Epinay, and himself, and that the marriage of Valentine and Franz would consequently be broken off. This was an awkward and unpleasant thing to have to report to those who were awaiting her return in the chamber of her father-in-law. She therefore contended herself with saying that M. Noirtier having, at the commencement of the discussion, been attacked by a sort of apoplectic fit, the affair would necessarily be deferred for some days longer. The next day M. Noirtier sent for the notary; the first will was torn up and a second made, in which he left the whole of his fortune to Valentine, on condition that she should never be separated from him. It was then generally reported that Mdlle. Villefort, the heiress of the marquis and marchioness de Saint-Méran, had regained the good graces of her grandfather, and that she would ultimately be in possession of an income of 300,000 livres. Whilst all the proceedings relative to the dissolution of the marriage-contract were being carried on at the house of Villefort, Monte-Cristo had paid his visit to Morcerf, who, in order to lose no time in responding to M. Danglars' wishes, and at the same time to pay all due deference to his position in society, donned his uniform of lieutenant-general, which he ornamented with all his crosses, and, thus attired, ordered his finest horses and drove to Danglars'. He was balancing his monthly accounts, and it was, perhaps, not the most favorable moment for finding him in his best humor.

"Well, Baron," said he, "here I am at last; some time has elapsed since our plans were formed, and they are not yet executed." Morcerf paused at these words, quietly waiting till the cloud should have dispersed which had gathered on the brow of Danglars, and which he attributed to his silence; but, on the contrary, to his great surprise, it grew darker and darker.

Morcerf, with a forced smile, rose, and, making a low bow to M. Danglars, said: "M. le Baron, I have the honor of asking you the hand of Mdlle. Eugénie Danglars for my son, Viscount Albert de Morcerf."

But Danglars, instead of receiving this address in the favorable manner which Morcerf had expected, knit his brow, and without inviting the count, who was still standing, to take a seat, he said: "Count, it will be necessary to reflect before I give you an answer."

"What do you mean?"——"I mean, that I have a good reason, but that it is difficult to explain."

"You must be aware, at all events, that it is impossible for me to understand motives before they are explained to me; but one thing at least is clear, which is, that you decline allying yourself with my family."

"No sir," said Danglars; "I merely suspended my decision, that is all."

"My dear Danglars," said Morcerf, "we have been acquainted for many years, and consequently we ought to make some allowance for each other's failings. You owe me an explanation, and really it is but fair that I should know what circumstance has occurred to deprive my son of your favor."

"It is from no personal ill-feeling toward the viscount, that is all I can say, sir," replied Danglars, who resumed his insolent manner as soon as he perceived that Morcerf was a little softened and calmed down. "And toward whom do you bear this personal ill-feeling, then?" said Morcerf, turning pale with anger. The expression of the count's face had not remained unperceived by the banker: he fixed on him a look of greater assurance than before, and said: "You may, perhaps, be better satisfied that I should not go farther into particulars."

A trembling, caused by suppressed rage, shook the whole frame of the count, and making a violent effort over himself, he said: "I have a right to insist on your giving me an explanation. Is it Mdme. de Morcerf who has displeased you? is it my fortune which you find insufficient? is it because my opinions differ from yours?"

"Nothing of the kind, sir," replied Danglars: there is no hurry. My daughter is only seventeen years old, and your son twenty-one. Whilst we wait, time will be progressing, events will succeed each other; things which in the evening look dark and obscure, appear but too clearly in the light of morning, and sometimes the utterance of one word, or the lapse of a single day, will reveal the most cruel calumnies."

"Calumnies, did you say, sir?" cried Morcerf, turning livid with rage. "Does any one dare to slander me?"

"Enough, sir," said Morcerf, "we will speak no more on the subject." And clenching his gloves with passion, he left the apartment.

The next morning, directly he awoke, Danglars asked for the newspapers; they were brought to him; he laid aside three or four, and at last fixed on the *Impartial,* the paper of which Beauchamp was editor. He hastily tore off the cover, opened the journal with nervous precipitation; arriving at the miscellaneous intelligence, he stopped, with a malicious smile, at a paragraph headed "JANINA." "Very good!" observed Danglars, after having read the paragraph; "here is a little article on Colonel Fernand, which, if I am not mistaken, would render the explanation which the count de Morcerf required of me perfectly unnecessary."

At the same moment, nine o'clock in the morning, Albert de Morcerf dressed in a black coat buttoned up to his chin, might have been seen walking with a quick and agitated step in the direction of Monte-Cristo's house in the Champs Elysées. When he presented himself at the gate the porter informed him that the count had gone out about half an hour previously.

Albert left, intending to take a turn on foot. As he was passing, he thought he saw the count's horses standing at Gossett's shooting-gallery; he approached, and soon recognized the coachman. "Is your master shooting in the gallery?" said Morcerf.

"Yes, sir," replied the coachman. Whilst he was speaking, Albert had heard the report of two or three pistol-shots. He entered, and on his way met the waiter. "Excuse me, M. le Vicomte," said the lad; "but will you have the kindness to wait a moment?"

"What for, Philip?" asked Albert, who, being a constant visitor there, did not understand this opposition to his entrance.

"Because the person who is now in the gallery prefers being alone, and never practises in the presence of any one."

"Not even before you, Philip? Then who loads his pistols?"

"His servant, a black."

"It is he, then."

"Do you know this gentleman?"

"Yes, and I am come to look for him; he is a friend of mine."

"Oh! that is quite another thing, then. I will go immediately and inform him of your arrival." And Philip, urged by his own curiosity, entered the gallery; a second afterward, Monte-Cristo appeared on the threshold. "I ask your pardon, my dear Count," said Albert, "for following you here; and I must first tell you that it was not the fault of your servants that I did so, I alone am to blame for the indiscretion. I went to your house, and they told me you were out, but that they expected you home at ten o'clock to breakfast. I was walking about in order to pass away the time till ten o'clock, when I caught sight of your carriage and horses."——"What you have just said induces me to hope that you intend breakfasting with me."

"No, thank you, I am thinking of other things besides breakfast, just now; perhaps we may take that meal at a later hour and in worse company."——"What on earth are you talking of?"

"I am to fight to-day."

"Yes, I understand that, but what is the quarrel? People fight for all sorts of reasons, you know."

"I fight in the cause of honor."

"Ah! that is something serious."

"So serious, that I come to beg you to render me a service: be my second."

"That is a serious matter, and we will not discuss it here; let us speak of nothing till we get home. Ali, bring me some water." The count turned up his sleeves, and passed into the little vestibule where the gentlemen were accustomed to wash their hands after shooting. "Come in, M. le Vicomte," said Philip in a low tone, "and I will show you something droll." Morcerf entered, and instead of the usual mark, he perceived some playing-cards fixed against the wall. At a distance Albert thought it was a complete suit, for he counted from the ace to the ten. "Ah! ah!" said Albert, "I see you were preparing for a game of cards."——"No," said the count, "I was making a suit of cards. Those are really aces and twos which you see, but my balls have turned them into threes, fives, sevens, eights, nines, and tens." Albert approached. In fact, the balls had actually pierced the cards in the exact places which the painted pips would otherwise have occupied, the lines and distances being as regularly kept as if they had been ruled with pencil. "The deuce!" said Morcerf.

"What would you, my dear Viscount?" said Monte-Cristo, wiping his hands on the towel which Ali had brought him; "I must occupy my leisure moments in some way or other. But come, I am waiting for you." Both then entered Monte-Cristo's carriage, which in the course of a few minutes deposited them safely at No. 30. Monte-Cristo took Albert into his study, and pointing to a seat, placed another for himself. "Now let us talk the matter over quietly," said the count. "With whom are you going to fight!"——"With Beauchamp."

"There appeared in his journal last night——but wait, and read for yourself." And Albert handed over the paper to the count, who read as follows:—

"A correspondent at Janina informs us of a fact of which until now we had remained in ignorance. The castle which formed the protection of the town was sold to the Turks by a French officer named Fernand, in whom the Grand Vizier, Ali Tebelen, had reposed the greatest confidence."

"Well!" said Monte-Cristo, "what does it signify to you if the castle of Janina was given up by a French officer?"

"It points to my father, the Count of Morcerf, whose Christian name is Fernand. He fought for the independence of the Greeks, and hence arises the calumny."

"Now, just tell me who the devil should know in France that the officer Fernand and the Count de Morcerf are one and the same person, and who cares now about Janina, which was taken as long ago as the year 1822 or 1823?"

"That just proves the blackness of the perfidy; they have allowed all this time to elapse, and then, all of a sudden, rake up events which have been forgotten, to furnish materials for scandal, in order to tarnish the lustre of our high position. I inherit my father's name, and I do not choose that the shadow of disgrace should darken it. I am going to Beauchamp, in whose journal this paragraph appears, and I shall insist on his retracting the assertion before two witnesses."

"Then let me offer one word of advice."

"Do so, then, but let it be the last."

"Do not take any witnesses with you when you go to Beauchamp— then the affair will rest between you and Beauchamp."

"I believe you are right, I will go alone."

"Go; but you would do better still by not going at all."

"But if, in spite of all my precautions, I am at last obliged to fight, will you not be my second?"

"My dear Viscount," said Monte-Cristo, gravely, "you must have seen before to-day that at all times and in all places I have been at your disposal, but the service which you have just demanded of me is one which it is out of my power to render you."

"We will say no more about it, then. Good-bye, Count." Morcerf took his hat, and left the room. He found his chariot at the door, and doing his utmost to restrain his anger, he drove at once to Beauchamp's house. Beauchamp was in his office. It was one of those gloomy, dusty-looking apartments, such as journalists' offices have always been from time immemorial. The servant announced M. Albert de Morcerf. Beauchamp repeated the name to himself, as though he could scarcely believe that he had heard right, and then gave orders for him to be admitted. Albert entered. Beauchamp uttered an exclamation of surprise on seeing his friend leap over and trample under foot all the newspapers which were strewed about the room. "Here! here! my dear Albert!" said he, holding out his hand to the young man. "Are you out of your senses, or do you come peaceably to take breakfast with me? Try and find a seat—there is one by that geranium, which is the only thing in the room to remind me that there are other leaves in the world besides leaves of paper."

"Beauchamp," said Albert, "it is of your journal that I come to speak."

"Indeed! what do you wish to say about it?"

"I desire that a statement contained in it should be rectified, in an article headed 'Janina.'"

"Is the officer alluded to a relation of yours, then?" demanded the journalist.

"He is my father," said Albert—"M. Fernand Mondego, Count de Morcerf, an old soldier, who has fought in twenty battles, and whose honorable scars they would denounce as badges of disgrace."

"Is it your father?" said Beauchamp; "that is quite another thing. Then I can well understand your indignation, my dear Albert. I will reperuse;" and he read the paragraph for the third time, laying a stress on each word as he proceeded. "But the paper nowhere indentifies this Fernand with your father."

"No; but the connection will be seen by others and therefore I will have the article contradicted." At the word *I will,* Beauchamp steadily raised his eyes to Albert's countenance, and then as gradually lowering them, he remained thoughtful for a few moments.

"The matter is worth looking into, and I will take pains to investigate the matter thoroughly."

"But what is there to investigate, sir?" said Albert, enraged beyond measure at Beauchamp's last remark. "If you do not believe that it is my father, say so immediately; and if, on the contrary, you believe it to be him, state your reasons for doing so."

"Wait a moment—no threats, if you please, M. Fernand Mondego, Vicomte de Morcerf; I never allow them from my enemies, and therefore shall not put up with them from my friends. The article was not inserted by me—I was not even aware of it; but you have, by the step you have taken, called my attention to the paragraph in question, and it will remain until it shall be either contradicted or confirmed by some one who has a right to do so."

"Sir," said Albert, rising, "I will do myself the honor of sending my seconds to you."

"Now, I am going to put a question to you, and one very much to the point, too. Do you insist on this retraction so far as to kill me if I do not make it, although I have affirmed on my honor, that I was ignorant of the thing with which you charge me, and although I still declare that it is impossible for any one but you to recognize the Count de Morcerf under the name of Fernand?"

"I maintain my original resolution."——"Very well, my dear sir; I require three weeks' preparation; at the end of that time I shall come and say to you, 'The assertion is false, and I retract it,' or, 'The assertion is true,' when I shall immediately draw the sword from its sheath, or the pistols from the case, whichever you please."

"Three weeks!" cried Albert; "they will pass as slowly as three centuries when I am all the time suffering dishonor."

"To-day is the 29th of August; the 21st of September will, therefore, be the conclusion of the term agreed on, and till that time arrives —and it is the advice of a gentleman which I am about to give you— till then we will refrain from growling and barking like two dogs chained within sight of each other."

CHAPTER LII.

THE LEMONADE.

Morrel was very happy. M. Noirtier had just sent for him and he was in such haste to know the reason of his doing so that he had not stopped to take a hack, placing infinitely more dependence on his own two legs than on the four legs of a cab-horse. On arriving at the house, Morrel was not even out of breath, for love lends wings to our desires.

The old servant introduced Morrel by a private entrance, closed the door of the study, and soon the rustling of a dress announced the arrival of Valentine. She looked marvellously beautiful in her deep mourning dress, and Morrel experienced such intense delight in gazing upon her that he felt as if he could almost have dispensed with the conversation of her grandfather. But the easy chair of the old man was heard rolling along the floor, and he soon made his appearance in the room.

"M. Morrel," said Valentine to the young man, who was regarding her with the most intense interest, "my grandfather, M. Noirtier, intends leaving this house, and Barrois is looking for suitable apartments for him in another. I shall not leave my grandfather, that is a thing understood between us. My apartment will be close to his. Now, M. de Villefort must either give his consent to this plan or his refusal; in the first case, I shall leave directly; and in the second, I shall await my majority, which will be completed in about ten months. Then I shall be free, I shall have an independent fortune, and——"

"And what?" demanded Morrel.

"And with my grandfather's consent I shall fulfil the promise which I have made you." Valentine pronounced these few last words in such a low tone, that nothing but Morrel's intense interest in what she was saying could have enabled him to hear them. "Once under my grand-father's roof, M. Morrel can visit me in the presence of my good and worthy protector, if we still feel that the union we contemplated will be likely to insure our future comfort and happiness; in that case I shall expect M. Morrel to come and claim me at my own hands. But, alas! I have heard it said that hearts inflamed by obstacles to their desire grow cold in time of security; I trust we shall never find it so in our ex-perience!"

"Oh!" cried Morrel, almost tempted to throw himself on his knees before Noirtier and Valentine, and to adore them as two superior beings, "what have I ever done in my life to merit such unbounded happiness?" ——"Until that time," continued the girl, in a calm and self-possessed tone of voice, "we will conform to circumstances, and be guided by the wishes of our friends, so long as those wishes do not tend finally to separate us; in one word, and I repeat it, because it expresses all I wish to convey,—we will wait."

Noirtier regarded the lovers with a look of ineffable tenderness, whilst Barrois, who had remained in the room in the character of a man privileged to know everything that passed, smiled on the youthful couple as he wiped the perspiration from his bald forehead. "How hot you look, my good Barrois!" said Valentine.

"Ah! I have been running very fast, mademoiselle; but I must do M. Morrel the justice to say that he ran still faster." Noirtier directed their attention to a waiter, on which was placed a decanter containing lemonade and a glass. The decanter was nearly full, with the exception of a little already drunk by M. Noirtier.

"Come, Barrois," said the girl, "take some of this lemonade; I see you are coveting a good draught of it."——"The fact is," said Barrois, "I am dying with thirst, and since you are so kind as to offer it me, I cannot say I should at all object to drinking your health in a glass of it."——"Take some, then, and come back immediately." Barrois took away the waiter, and hardly was he outside the door, which, in his haste, he forgot to shut, when they saw him throw back his head and empty to the very dregs the glass which Valentine had filled. Valentine and Morrel were exchanging their adieux in the presence of Noirtier when a ring was heard at the door-bell. It was the signal of a visit. Valentine looked at her watch.

"It is past noon," said she, "I dare say it is the doctor, grandpapa. Barrois!" cried Valentine, "Barrois!"

"I am coming, mademoiselle," replied he. "Barrois will open the door for you," said Valentine, addressing Morrel. "And now remember one thing, Mr. Officer, that my grandfather commands you not to take any rash or ill-advised steps which would be likely to compromise our hap-piness."

"I promise him to wait," replied Morrel; "and I will wait."

At this moment Barrois entered. "Who rang?" asked Valetine.

"Doctor d'Avrigny," said Barrois, staggering as if he would fall.

"What is the matter, Barrois?" said Valentine. The old man did not answer, but looked at his master with wild staring eyes.

At this moment M. de Villefort, attracted by the noise, appeared on the threshold. Morrel relaxed his hold of Valentine, and retreating to a distant corner of the room, he remained half hidden behind a curtain. Pale as if he had been gazing on a serpent, he fixed his terrified eyes on the agonized sufferer.

Noirtier, burning with impatience and terror, was in despair at his utter inability to help his old domestic, whom he regarded more in the light of a friend than a servant.

Villefort seemed stupefied with astonishment, and remained gazing intently on the scene before him without uttering a word. He had not seen Morrel. After a moment of dumb contemplation, during which his face became pale, and his hair seemed to stand on end, he sprang towards the door, crying out, "Doctor! doctor! come instantly; pray come!"

"Madame!" cried Valentine, calling her stepmother, and running up-stairs to meet her; "come quick, quick! and bring your bottle of smelling-salts with you."

"What is the matter?" said Mdme. de Villefort, in a harsh and constrained tone.

"Oh! come! come!"—Mdme. de Villefort now deliberately descended the staircase. In one hand she held her handkerchief, with which she appeared to be wiping her face, and in the other a bottle of smelling-salts. Her first look on entering the room was at Noirtier, whose face, independent of the emotion which such a scene could not fail of producing, proclaimed him to be in possession of his usual health; her second glance was at the dying man. She turned pale, and her eyes passed quickly from the servant, and rested on the master.

"In the name of heaven, madame," said Villefort, "where is the doctor? He was with you just now. You see this is a fit of apoplexy, and he might be saved if he could but be bled!"

"Grandpapa's bottle of lemonade was standing just by his side; poor Barrois was very thirsty, and was thankful to drink anything he could find." Mdme. de Villefort started. Noirtier looked at her with a glance of the most profound scrutiny. "He has such a short neck," said she. "Madame," said de Villefort, "I ask where is M. d'Avrigny? In God's name answer me!"——"He is with Edward, who is not quite well," replied Mdme. de Villefort, no longer able to avoid answering.

Villefort rushed up-stairs to fetch him himself. "Take this," said Mdme. de Villefort, giving her smelling-bottle to Valentine. "They will, no doubt, bleed him; therefore I will retire, for I cannot endure the sight of blood;" and she followed her husband up-stairs. Morrel now emerged from his hiding-place, where he had remained quite unperceived, so great had been the general confusion. "Go away as quick as you can, Maximilian," said Valentine, "and stay till I send for you. Go."

Morrel looked towards Noirtier for permission to retire. The old man, who had preserved all his usual coolness, made a sign to him to do so. The young man pressed Valentine's hand to his lips, and then left the house by a back staircase. At the same moment that he quitted the room, Villefort and the doctor entered by an opposite entrance. Barrois was now showing signs of returning consciousness; the crisis seemed past; a low moaning was heard, and he raised himself on one knee. D'Avrigny and Villefort laid him on a couch.

Spasm after spasm coursed through him, but ended suddenly. None of the remedies had even eased him.

"Dead?" cried Villefort, "and so soon?"

"Yes," said the doctor, looking at the corpse before him; "but that ought not to astonish you; the Saint-Mérans died as soon. People die very suddenly in your house, M. de Villefort."

"What!" cried the magistrate, with an accent of horror and consternation, "are you still harping on that terrible idea?"

"Still, sir; and I shall always do so," replied D'Avrigny, "for it has never for one instant ceased to retain possession of my mind: and that you may be quite sure I am not mistaken this time, listen well to what I am going to say, M. de Villefort." The magistrate trembled convulsively. "There is a poison which destroys life almost without leaving any perceptible traces. I know it well; I have studied it in all its qualities and in the effects which it produces. I recognized the presence of this poison in the case of Mdme. de Saint-Méran. As for this unfortunate Barrois, he has been poisoned," said D'Avrigny, "and I will maintain this assertion before God and man." Villefort said nothing, but he clasped his hands, opened his haggard eyes, and, overcome with his emotion, sank into a chair.

"In my house!" murmured he, "in my house!"

"Come, magistrate," said M. d'Avrigny, "show yourself a man; as an interpreter of the law, do honor to your profession by sacrificing your selfish interests to it."

"Do you then suspect any one?"

"Well, sir, you have in your establishment, or in your family perhaps, one of those frightful phenomena of which each century produces only one. Locuste and Agrippina, living at the same time, are an exception, and prove the determination of Providence to effect the entire ruin of the Roman empire, sullied by so many crimes. All these women had been, or were, beautiful. The same flower of innocence had flourished, or was still, flourishing on their brow, that is seen on the brow of the culprit in your house." Villefort shrieked, clasped his hands, and looked at the doctor with a supplicating air. But the latter pursued without pity.

" 'Seek whom the crime will profit,' says an axiom of jurisprudence."

"Have mercy on my child, sir!" murmured Villefort.

"You see it is yourself who have first named her—you, her father.——"Have pity on Valentine! Listen! it is impossible. I would as willingly accuse myself! Valentine, whose heart is pure as a diamond or a lily."

"No pity; the crime is flagrant. She herself packed all the medicines sent to Saint-Méran; and Saint-Méran is dead. Mdlle. de Villefort prepared all the cooling draughts which Madame de Saint-Méran took, and she is dead. Mdlle. de Villefort took from the hands of Barrois the lemonade which M. Noirtier has every morning, and he has escaped only by a miracle. She is the culprit!—the poisoner! Prosecutor, I denounce Mdlle. de Villefort; do your duty."

Villefort fell on his knees.

"Listen!" cried he; "pity me,—help me! No, my daughter is not guilty. I will not drag my daughter before a tribunal, and give her up to the executioner! The bare idea would kill me,—would drive me like a madman to dig my heart out with my fingernails! And if you were mistaken, doctor!—if it were not my daughter!—If I should come one day, pale as a spectre, and say to you, "Assassin! you have killed my child! Hold! if that should happen, although I am a Christian, M. d'Avrigny, I should kill myself."

"Well," said the doctor, after a moment's silence; "I will wait." Villefort looked at him as if he had doubted his words. "Only," continued M. d'Avrigny, with a slow and solemn tone, "if any one falls ill in your house, if you feel yourself attacked, do not send for me, for I will come no more. I will consent to share this dreadful secret with you; but I will not allow shame and remorse to grow and increase in my conscience, as crime and misery will in your house."

"Then you abandon me, doctor?"——"Yes, for I can follow you no farther; and I only stop at the foot of the scaffold. Some further discovery will be made, which will bring this dreadful tragedy to a close. Adieu!"

The doctor, without shaking hands with Villefort, or adding a word to what he had said, went out amid the tears and lamentations of the whole household. The same evening all Villefort's servants, who had assembled in the kitchen, and had a long consultation, came to tell Mdme. de Villefort they wished to leave. No entreaty, no proposition of increased wages, could induce them to remain; to every argument they

had struck me." Andrea shuddered; he always did so at Caderousse's ideas. "It is miserable—do you see?—always to wait till the end of the month."——"Oh!" said Andrea, philosophically, determined to watch his companion narrowly, "does not life pass in waiting? Do I, for instance, fare better? Well, I wait patiently, do I not?"

"If I were in your place——"

"Well."

"I would realize——"

"How would you realize?"

"I would ask for six months' in advance, under pretence of being able to purchase a farm, then with my six months' I would decamp."

"Well, well," said Andrea, "that is no bad thought."

"My dear friend," said Caderousse, "I have formed a plan." Caderousse's plans alarmed Andrea still more than his ideas; ideas were but the germ, the plan was reality. "Let me see your plan; I dare say it is a pretty one."

"Why not? Who formed the plan by which we left the stone cage of Melm! eh? was it not I? and it was no bad one I believe, since here we are."

"I do not say," replied Andrea, "that you never make a good one; but let us see your plan."

"Well," pursued Caderousse, "can you without expending one sou, put me in the way of getting fifteen thousand francs? No, fifteen thousand are not enough, I cannot again become an honest man with less than thirty thousand francs."

"No," replied Andrea, drily, "no, I cannot; though you shall have your five hundred francs," said Andrea; "but it is very hard for me, my poor Caderousse—you take advantage——"

"Bah!" said Caderousse, "when you have access to countless stores." One would have said Andrea anticipated his companion's words, so did his eye flash like lightning, but it was but for a moment. "True," he replied, "and my protector is very kind. I—I—I think——" Andrea stopped and looked around. "You think? Do not fear; *pardieu,* we are alone."——"I think I have discovered my father."

"Not old Cavalcanti?"

"No! Caderousse, it is Monte-Cristo."——"Bah!"

"Yes, you understand, that explains all. He cannot acknowledge me openly, it appears, but he does it through M. Cavalcanti, and gives him fifty thousand francs for it."

"Fifty thousand francs for being your father! I would have done it for half that, for twenty thousand, for fifteen thousand; why did you not think of me, ungrateful man?"

"Did I know anything about it, when it was all done when I was out there?"

"Ah! truly?"

"By his will, he leaves me five hundred thousand livres."

"Are you sure of it?"——"He showed it me; but that is not all—there is a codicil, in which he acknowledges me."

"Oh! the good father! the honest father!" said Caderousse, twirling a plate in the air between his two hands. "And your princely father, is he rich, very rich?"

"The other day a banker's clerk brought him fifty thousand francs in a portfolio about the size of your plate; yesterday his banker brought him a hundred thousand francs in gold." Caderousse was filled with wonder; the young man's words sounded to him like metal; and he thought he could hear the rushing of cascades of louis.

"How I should like to see all that!" cried he; "how beautiful it must be?"

"It is, in fact, magnificent," said Andrea.

"And does he not live in the Champs-Elysées?"

"Yes, a fine house standing alone, between a court-yard and a garden, you must know it."——"Possibly; but it is not the exterior I care for, it is the interior: what beautiful furniture there must be in it! It must be worth one's while to stoop, Andrea, when our good Monte-Cristo lets fall his purse."

"It is not worth while to wait for that," said Andrea; "money is as plentiful in that house as fruit in an orchard."

"Try to give me an idea of what it is."

"Faith, I should require pen, ink, and paper to make a plan."

"They are all here," said Caderousse, briskly. He fetched from an old bureau a sheet of white paper, and pen and ink. "Here," said Caderousse, "trace me all that on the paper, my boy." Andrea took the pen with an imperceptible smile, and began. "The house, as I said, is between the court and the garden; in this way, do you see?" Andrea traced the garden, the court, and the house.

"And where do the servants sleep?"——"Oh! they have a house to themselves."

"And he is not robbed?"

"No; his servants are all devoted to him."

"There ought to be some money in his desk?"

"There may be. No one knows what there is."

"And where is it?"

"On the first floor."

"Sketch me the plan of that floor, as you have done of the ground-floor, my boy."

Caderousse became thoughtful.

"Does he often go to Auteuil?" added he.

"Two or three times a-week. To-morrow, for instance, he is going to spend the day and night there. He has invited me to dine there."

Caderousse looked at the young man, as if to get at the truth from the bottom of his heart. But Andrea drew a cigar-case from his pocket, took a Havannah, quietly lit it, and began smoking.

"When do you want your five hundred francs?" said he to Caderousse.

"Now, if you have them." Andrea took five and twenty louis from his pocket.

"Yellow boys?" said Caderousse; "no, I thank you."

"You can change them, idiot; gold is at a premium."

"Exactly; and he who changes them will follow friend Caderousse, lay hands on him, and demand what farmers pay him their rent in gold. No nonsense, my good fellow; silver simply, round coins with the head of some monarch or other on them. Anybody may possess a five-franc piece."

"But do you suppose I carry five hundred francs about with me? I should want a porter."

"Well, leave them with your porter; he is to be trusted: I will call for them to-morrow; I shall not have time to-day."

"Well, to-morrow, I will leave them when I go to Auteuil."

"How sprightly you are!" said Caderousse; "one would say you were already in possession of your property."

"No, unfortunately; but when I do obtain it——"

"Well?"

"I shall remember old friends, I only tell you that."

"Yes, since you have such a good memory."

"What do you want? I thought you had ransomed me."

"I? What an idea! I was going to give you another piece of good advice."

"To leave behind you the diamond you have on your finger. We shall both get in trouble. You disguise yourself as a servant, and yet keep a diamond on your finger worth four or five thousand francs."

"Have you finished now?" said Andrea.—"do you want anything more?—will you have my waistcoat or my certificate? Make free now you have begun."

"No; you are, after all, a true pal; I will not detain you, and will try to cure myself of my ambition."

"But take care the same thing does not happen to you in selling the diamond you feared with the gold."

"I shall not sell it—do not fear it."

"Not at least till the day after to-morrow," thought the young man.

"Happy rogue!" said Caderousse; "you are going to find your servants, horses, carriage, and betrothed!"

"Yes," said Andrea.

"Well, I hope you will make a handsome wedding-present the day you marry Mdlle. Danglars."

"Sure," said Andrea; "I will let you know a week beforehand." They parted. Caderousse remained on the landing until he had not only seen Andrea go down the three stories, but also cross the court. Then he returned hastily, shut his door carefully, and began to study, like a clever architect, the plan Andrea had left him.

"Dear Benedetto," said he, "I think he will not be sorry to inherit his fortune, and he who hastens the day when he can touch his five hundred thousand will not be his worst friend."

CHAPTER LIV.

BURGLARY AND MURDER.

THE day following, Monte-Cristo set out for Auteuil, accompanied by Ali and several attendants, and also taking with him some horses whose qualities he was desirous of ascertaining. He was induced to undertake this journey, of which the day before he had not even thought, and which had not either occurred to Andrea, by the return of Bertuccio from Normandy, with intelligence respecting his house and yacht. The house was ready, and the sloop, which had arrived a week before, lay at anchor in a small creek, with her crew of six men, who, after having observed all the requisite formalities, were ready again to put to sea. The count praised Bertuccio's zeal, and ordered him to prepare for a speedy departure, as his stay in France would not be prolonged more than a month. As Bertuccio was leaving the room to give the requisite orders, Baptistin opened the door: he held a letter on a silver waiter.——"What do you do here?" asked the count, seeing him covered with dust; "I did not send for you, I think?"

Baptistin, without answering, approached the count, and presented the letter. "Important and urgent," said he. The count opened the letter, and read:—

"The Count de Monte-Cristo is notified that this night a man will enter his house in the Champs-Elysées with the intention of carrying off some papers supposed to be in the dressing-room. The count's well-known courage will render unnecessary the aid of the police, whose interference might seriously affect him who sends this advice. The count will be able to defend his property himself. Many attendants or apparent precautions would prevent the villain from the attempt, and the Count of Monte-Cristo would lose the opportunity of discovering an enemy whom chance has revealed to him who now sends this warning, one he might not be able to send another time, if this first attempt should fail and another be made."

"They do not want my papers," said Monte-Cristo; "they want to kill me; they are not robbers, but assassins. I will not allow the Police to interfere with my private affairs. I am rich enough, forsooth, to dispute authority on this occasion." The count recalled Baptistin, who had left the room after delivering the letter. "Return to Paris," said he; "assemble the servants who remain there. I want all my household at Auteuil."——"But will no one remain in the house, my lord?" asked Baptistin.——"Yes, the janitor; let everything remain as usual, only close the shutters of the ground-floor."

"And those of the first-floor?"

"You know they are never closed. Go!"

The count signified his intention of dining alone, and that no one but Ali should attend him. Having dined with his usual tranquillity and moderation, the count, making a signal to Ali to follow him, went out by the side-gate, and, on reaching the Bois de Boulogne, turned, apparently without design, towards Paris, and at twilight found himself opposite his house in the Champs-Elysées. All was dark; one solitary, feeble light was burning in the porter's lodge, about forty paces distant from the house, as Baptistin had said. Monte-Cristo leaned against a tree, and, with that eye which was so rarely deceived, searched the double avenue, examined the passers-by, and carefully looked down the neighboring streets, to see that no one was concealed. Ten minutes passed thus, and he was convinced no one was watching him. He hastened to the side-door with Ali, entered precipitately, and by the servants' staircase, of which he had the key, gained his bedroom without opening or disarranging a single curtain, without even the porter having the slightest suspicion that the house, which he supposed empty, contained its chief occupant.

Arrived in his bedroom, the count motioned to Ali to stop; then he passed into the dressing-room, which he examined: all was as usual—the precious secretary in its place, and the key in. He doubly locked it, took the key, returned to the bedroom-door, removed the double staple of the bolt, and went in. Meanwhile Ali had procured the arms the count required—namely, a short carbine and a pair of double-barrelled pistols. Thus armed, the count held the lives of five men in his hands.

It was about half-past nine. Two hours passed thus. It was intensely dark. It would be his bedroom they would attack, and they must reach it by the back staircase, or by the window in the dressing-room. The clock struck a quarter to twelve; the west wind bore on its moistened gusts the doleful vibration of the three strokes. As the last stroke died away, the count thought he heard a slight noise in the dressing-room; this first sound, or rather this first scratching, was followed by a second, then a third; at the fourth, the count knew what to expect. A firm and well-practised hand was engaged in cutting out a pane of glass with a diamond. The count felt his heart beat more rapidly. Inured as men may be to danger, forewarned as they may be of peril, they understand, by the fluttering of the heart and the shuddering of the frame, the enormous difference between dream and reality, between project and execution. However, Monte-Cristo only made a sign to apprise Ali, who, understanding that danger was approaching from the other side, drew nearer to his master. Monte-Cristo was eager to ascertain the strength and number of his enemies.

The window whence the noise proceeded was opposite the opening by which the count could see into the dressing-room. He fixed his eyes on that window—he distinguished a shadow in the darkness; then one of the panes became quite opaque, as if a sheet of paper were stuck on the outside, then the square cracked without falling. Through the opening an arm was passed to find the fastening, then a second; the window turned on its hinges, and a man entered. He was alone.

"That's a daring rascal!" whispered the count.

At that moment Ali touched him slightly on the shoulder. He turned; Ali pointed to the window of the room in which they were, facing the street. "Good!" said he, "there are two of them; one acts while the other watches." He made a sign to Ali not to lose sight of the man in the street, and returned to the one in the dressing-room.

The glass-cutter had entered, and was feeling his way, his arms stretched out before him. At last he appeared to have made himself familiar with all parts. There were two doors; he bolted them both.

When he drew near to that of the bedroom, Monte-Cristo expected he was coming in, and raised one of his pistols; but he simply heard the sound of the bolts sliding in their brass rings. It was only a precaution. The nocturnal visitor, ignorant of the count's having removed the staples, might now think himself at home, and pursue his purpose with full security. Alone and uncontrolled, the man then drew from his pocket something which the count could not discern, placed it on a stand, then went straight to the secretary, felt the lock, and, contrary to his expectation, found that the key was missing. But the glass-cutter was a prudent man, who had provided for all emergencies. The count soon heard the rattling of a bunch of shapeless keys, such as the locksmith brings when called to force a lock, and which thieves call lockpicks. "Ah, ah!" whispered Monte-Cristo, with a smile of disappointment, "he is only a thief!"

But the man in the dark could not find the right key. He reached the instrument he had placed on the stand, touched a spring, and immediately a pale light, just bright enough to render objects distinct, was reflected on the hands and countenance of the man. "Hold!" exclaimed Monte-Cristo starting back, "it is—"

Ali raised his hatchet. "Don't stir," whispered Monte-Cristo, "and put down your ax; we shall require no arms." Then he added some words in a low tone, for the exclamation which surprise had drawn from the count, weak as it had been, had startled the man, who remained in the position of the old grinder. It was an order the count had just given, for immediately Ali went noiselessly, and returned, bearing a black gown and a three-cornered hat. Meanwhile Monte-Cristo had rapidly taken off his greatcoat, waistcoat, and shirt, and one might distinguish by the glimmering through the open panel that he wore a shirt of mail. This soon disappeared under a long cassock, as did his hair under a priest's wig; the three-cornered hat over this effectually transformed the count into a priest.

The man, hearing nothing more, had again raised himself, and, while Monte-Cristo was completing his disguise, had advanced straight to the secretary, whose lock was beginning to crack under his tool.

"Well done!" whispered the count, who depended on the secret spring, which was unknown to the picklock, clever as he might be—"well done! you have a few minutes' work there." And he advanced to the window. The man whom he had seen seated on a fence had got down, and was still pacing the street; but, strange as it appeared, he cared not for those who might pass; his attention was engrossed with what was passing at the count's, and his only aim appeared to be to discern every movement in the dressing-room.

Monte-Cristo suddenly struck his finger on his forehead, and a smile passed over his lips; then drawing near to Ali, he whispered:

"Remain here, concealed in the dark, and whatever noise you hear, whatever passes, only come in or show yourself if I call you." Ali bowed in token of strict obedience. Monte-Cristo then drew a lighted taper from a closet, and when the thief was deeply engaged with his lock, silently opened the door, taking care that the light should shine directly on his face. The door opened so quietly that the thief heard no sound; but, to his astonishment, the room was in a moment light. He turned.

"Good evening, dear M. Caderousse!" said Monte-Cristo; "what are you doing here at such an hour?"

"The Abbé Busoni!" exclaimed Caderousse; and, not knowing how this strange apparition could have entered when he had bolted the doors, he let drop his bunch of keys, and remained motionless and stupefied. The count placed himself between Caderousse and the window, thus cutting off from the thief his only chance of retreat. "Busoni!" repeated Caderousse, fixing his haggard gaze on the count.

"Yes, doubtless, Abbé Busoni himself!" replied Monte-Cristo. "And I am very glad you recognize me, dear M. Caderousse; it proves you have a good memory, for it must be about ten years since we last met." This calmness of Busoni, combined with his irony and boldness, staggered Caderousse.

"So you would rob the Count of Monte-Cristo?" continued the mock priest. "Come, come, I see you are still the same—an assassin."—— "Since you know everything, you know it was not I—it was La Carconte; that was proved at the trial, since I was only condemned to the galleys."

"Is your time, then, expired, since I find you in a fair way to return there?"

"No, I was liberated by some one."

"That some one has done society a great kindness."

"Ah," said Caderousse, "I had promised——"

"A bad relapse, that will lead you, if I mistake not, to Execution Place. So much the worse, so much the worse—*diavolo!* as they say in my country."

"Poverty——"

"Pshaw!" said Busoni, disdainfully; "poverty may make a man beg, steal a loaf of bread at a baker's door, but not cause him to open a secretary in a house supposed to be uninhabited. And when the jeweler Johannes had just paid you 45,000 francs for the diamond I had given you, and you killed him to get the diamond and the money both, was that also poverty?"

"Pardon!" said Caderousse; "you have saved my life once, save me again!"

"That is but poor encouragement."

"Are you alone, or have you there soldiers ready to seize me?"

"I am alone," said the abbé, "and I will again have pity on you and will let you escape, at the risk of the fresh miseries my weakness may lead to, if you tell me the truth."

"Ah," cried Caderousse, clasping his hands, and drawing nearer to Monte-Cristo, "I may indeed say you are my deliverer!"

"You mean to say you have been freed from confinement?"

"Yes, in truth."

"Who was your liberator?"

"An Englishman, Lord Wilmore."——"I know him; I shall know if you lie. Was this Englishman protecting you?"

"No, not me, but a young Corsican, my companion."

"What was this Corsican's name?"

"Benedetto. He had no other; he was a foundling."

"Then this young man escaped with you?"——"He did."

"And what is become of this Benedetto?"

"No, in truth; we parted at Hyères." And to give more weight to his protestation, Caderousse advanced another step towards the abbé, who remained motionless in his place, as calm as ever, and pursuing his interrogation. "You lie!" said Busoni, with a tone of irresistible authority. "You lie! This man is still your friend, and you, perhaps, make use of him as your accomplice."

"Oh, father!"——"Since you left Toulon what have you lived on? Answer me!"——"On what I could get."

"You have lived on the money he has given you."

"True!" said Caderousse: "Benedetto has become the son of a great lord, a natural son. The Count of Monte-Cristo's the very same in whose house we are."

"Benedetto the count's son!" replied Monte-Cristo, who began to understand; "and what name does the young man bear meanwhile?"

"Andrea Cavalcanti."

"Is it, then, that young man whom my friend the Count of Monte-Cristo has received into his house, and who is going to marry Mademoiselle Danglars?"

"Exactly."

"And you suffer that, you wretch!—you, who know his life and his crime?"

"Why should I stand in a partner's way?" said Caderousse.

"You are right; it is not you who should apprise M. Danglars, it is I."

"Do not do so, because you would bring us to ruin."

"And you think that to save such villains as you I will become an abettor of their plot—an accomplice in their crimes?"

"Father," said Caderousse, drawing still nearer.

"I will expose all to M. Danglars."

"By Heaven!" cried Caderousse, drawing from his waistcoat an open knife, and striking the count in the breast, "you shall disclose nothing!" To Caderousse's great astonishment, the knife, instead of piercing the count's breast, flew back blunted. At the same moment the count seized with his left hand the assassin's wrist, and wrung it with such strength that the knife fell from his stiffened fingers, and Caderousse uttered a cry of pain. But the count, disregarding his cry, continued to wring the bandit's wrist, until, his arm being dislocated, he fell first on his knees, then flat on the floor. The count then placed his foot on his head, saying: "I know not what restrains me from crushing thy skull, rascal!"

"Ah, mercy—mercy!" cried Caderousse. The count withdrew his foot. "Rise!" said he. Caderousse rose.

"What a wrist you have, father!" said Caderousse, stroking his arm, all bruised by the fleshy pincers which had held it.

"Silence! God gives me strength to overcome a wild beast like you; in the name of that God I act—remember that, wretch!—and to spare thee at this moment is still serving Him."

"Oh!" said Caderousse, groaning with pain.

"Take this pen and paper, and write what I dictate."

"I don't know how to write."

"You lie! Take this pen, and write!"

Caderousse, awed by the superior power of the abbé, sat down and wrote:

"SIR,— The man whom you are receiving at your house, and to whom you intend to marry your daughter, is a felon who escaped with me from confinement at Toulon. He was No. 59, and I No. 58. He was called Benedetto; but he is ignorant of his real name, having never known his parents."

"Sign it!" continued the count.

Caderousse signed it. "The address, 'Baron Danglars, banker, Chaussée d'Antin.'" Caderousse wrote the address. The abbé took the note. "Now," said he, "that suffices—be gone!"

"You wish me to get out at that window?"

"You got in very well."

"But swear that you will not strike me as I go down."

"Cowardly fool!"

"Father," said Caderousse, "make one more trial—try me once more!"

"I will," said the count. "If you reach your home safely, leave Paris, leave France; and wherever you may be, so long as you conduct yourself well, I will send you a small annuity; for, if you return home safely, then——"

"Then?" asked Caderousse, shuddering.

"Then I shall believe God has forgiven you, and I will forgive you too."

"As true as I am a Christian," stammered Caderousse, "you will make me die of fright!"

He then descended, but it was only when he felt his foot touch the ground that he was satisfied he was safe.

Monte-Cristo returned to his bedroom, and glancing rapidly from the garden to the street, he saw first Caderousse, who, after walking to the end of the garden, fixed his ladder against the wall at a different part from where he came in. The count then, looking over into the street, saw the man who appeared to be waiting run in the same direction, and place himself against the angle of the wall where Caderousse would come over. Caderousse climbed the ladder slowly, and looked over the coping to see if the street was quiet. No one could be seen or heard. The clock of the Invalides struck one. Then Caderousse sat astride the coping, and, drawing up his ladder, passed it over the wall; then began to descend, or rather to slide down by the two stanchions, which he did with an ease which proved how accustomed he was to the exercise. But, once started, he could not stop. In vain did he see a man start from the shade when he was half-way down—in vain did he see an arm raised as he touched the ground. Before he could defend himself that arm struck him so violently in the back that he let go the ladder, crying, "Help!" A second stab struck him almost immediately in the side, and he fell, calling, "Murder!" Then, as he rolled on the ground, his adversary seized him by the hair, and struck him a third blow in the chest. This time Caderousse endeavored to call again, but he could only utter a groan, and he shuddered as the blood flowed from his three wounds. The assassin, finding he no longer cried, lifted his head up by the hair; his eyes were closed, and mouth distorted. The murderer, supposing him dead, let fall his head and disappeared. Then Caderousse, feeling that he was leaving him, raised himself on his elbow, and, with a dying voice, cried, with great effort, "Murder! I am dying! Help, father—help!"

This mournful appeal pierced the darkness. The door of the back-staircase opened, then the side-gate of the garden, and Ali and his master were on the spot with lights.

"What is the matter?" asked Monte-Cristo.

"Help!" cried Caderousse; "I am murdered!"

"We are here;—take courage!"

"Ah, it's all over! You are come too late;—you are come to see me die. What blows! what blood!" He fainted. Ali and his master conveyed the wounded man into a room. Monte-Cristo motioned to Ali to undress him, and he then examined his dreadful wounds. "My God!" he exclaimed, "Thy vengeance is sometimes delayed, but only that it may fall the more effectually." Ali looked at his master for further instructions. "Conduct here immediately the Royal Prosecutor Villefort, who lives in the Faubourg St. Honoré. As you pass the lodge, wake the porter, and send him for a surgeon." Ali obeyed, leaving the abbé alone with Caderousse, who had not yet revived.

When the wretched man again opened his eyes, the count looked at him with a mournful expression of pity, and his lips moved as if in prayer. "A surgeon, M. l'Abbé—a surgeon!" said Caderousse.

"I have sent for one," replied the abbé.

"I know we cannot save my life, but he may strengthen me to give my evidence against my murderer Benedetto."

"Your comrade?"

"Yes. After giving me the plan of this house, doubtless hoping I should kill the count and he thus become his heir, or that the count would kill me and I should be out of his way, he waylaid me and has murdered me."

"Oh, send for some one to whom I can denounce the wretch!"

"Shall I write your deposition? You can sign it."

"Yes, yes," said Caderousse; and his eyes glistened at the thought of this posthumous revenge. Monte-Cristo wrote:

"I die murdered by the Corsican Benedetto, my chain-companion in the galleys at Toulon, No. 59."

"Quick, quick!" said Caderousse, "or I shall be unable to sign it."

Monte-Cristo gave the pen to Caderousse, who collected all his strength, signed it, and fell back on the bed, saying: "You will relate all the rest, M. l'Abbé; you will say he calls himself Andrea Cavalcanti. He lodges at the Hôtel des Princes. Oh, I am dying!" He again fainted. The abbé made him smell the contents of the phial, and he again opened his eyes. His desire for revenge had not forsaken him.

"He will be guillotined, will he not?" said Caderousse. "Promise me that, and I will die with that hope."

"Remember my words: 'If you return home safely, I shall believe God has forgiven you, and I will forgive you also.'"

"And you did not warn me!" cried Caderousse, raising himself on his elbows. "You knew I should be killed on leaving this house, you should have prevented Benedetto from killing me."

"I?" said the count, with a smile which petrified the dying man, "when you had just broken your knife against the coat of mail which protected my breast! Yet, perhaps, if I had found you humble and penitent, I might have prevented Benedetto from killing you; but I found you proud and blood-thirsty, and I left you in the hands of God."

"I do not believe there is a God!" howled Caderousse; "you do not believe it: you lie—you lie!"

"There is a Providence, there is a God," said Monte-Cristo, "of which you are a striking proof, as you lie in utter despair, denying Him; while I stand before you, rich, happy, safe, and entreating that God in whom you endeavor not to believe, while in your heart you still believe in Him."——"But who are you, then?" asked Caderousse, fixing his dying eyes on the count. "Look well at me!" said Monte-Cristo, putting the light near his face. "Well! Abbé Busoni." Monte-Cristo took off the wig which disfigured him, and let fall his black hair, which added so much to the beauty of his pallid features. "Oh!" said Caderousse, thunderstruck, "but for that black hair, I should say you were the Englishman, Lord Wilmore."

"I am neither Abbé Busoni, nor Lord Wilmore," said Monte-Cristo: "think again, do you not recollect me?" There was a magic effect in the count's words, which once more revived the exhausted powers of the miserable man.

"Yes, indeed," said he, "I think I have seen you and known you formerly."

"Yes, Caderousse, you have seen me, you knew me once."

"Who then are you? and why, if you knew me, do you let me die?"

"Because nothing can save you, your wounds are mortal."

The count had watched the approach of death. He knew this was the last struggle, he approached the dying man, and leaning over him with a calm and melancholy look, he whispered,—"I am—I am——" And his almost closed lips uttered a name so low that the count himself appeared afraid to hear it. Caderousse, who had raised himself on his knees, and stretched out his arm, tried to draw back, then clasping his hands, and raising them with a desperate effort, moaned:—"Oh! my God! my God! pardon me for having denied Thee; Thou dost exist: Thou art, indeed, man's father in heaven, and his Judge on earth. My God, my Lord, I have long despised Thee! Pardon me, my God; receive me, O my Lord!" Caderousse sighed deeply, and fell back with a groan. The blood no longer flowed from his wounds. He was dead.

"*One!*" said the count, mysteriously, his eyes fixed on the corpse, disfigured by so awful a death. Ten minutes afterwards the surgeon and the procureur du roi arrived; the one accompanied by the porter, the other by Ali, and were received by the Abbé Busoni, praying by the side of the corpse.

CHAPTER LV.

MORCERF ON THE DEFENCE.

THE daring attempt to rob the count was the topic of conversation throughout Paris for the next fortnight: the dying man had signed a deposition declaring Benedetto to be the assassin. The police had orders to make the strictest search for the murderer. Caderousse's knife, dark lantern, bunch of keys, and clothing, excepting the waistcoat, which could not be found, were deposited at the registry; the corpse was conveyed to the Morgue. The count told every one this adventure had happened during his absence at Auteuil, and that he only knew what was related by the Abbé Busoni, who that evening, by mere chance, had requested to pass the night in his house to examine some valuable books in his library. Bertuccio alone turned pale whenever Benedetto's name was mentioned in his presence: but there was no reason why any one should notice his doing so. Villefort, being called on to prove the crime was preparing the case with the same ardor as he was accustomed to exercise when called on.

But three weeks had already passed, and the most diligent search had been unsuccessful; the attempted robbery and the murder of the robber by his comrade were almost forgotten in anticipation of the approaching marriage of Mdlle. Danglars to the Count Andrea Cavalcanti. It was expected this wedding would shortly take place, as the young man was received at the banker's as the betrothed. Letters had been despatched to M. Cavalcanti, as the count's father, who highly approved of the union, regretted his inability to leave Parma at that time, and promised a wedding gift of a hundred and fifty thousand livres. It was agreed that the three millions should be intrusted to Danglars to improve; some persons had warned the young man of the circumstances of his future father-in-law, who had of late sustained repeated losses, but with sublime disinterestedness and confidence the young man refused to listen, or to express a single doubt to the baron. The baron adored Count Andrea Cavalcanti; not so Mdlle. Eugénie Danglars. With an instinctive hatred of matrimony, she suffered Andrea's attentions in order to get rid of Morcerf; but when Andrea urged his suit, she betrayed an entire dislike to him. The baron might possibly have perceived it, but attributing it to caprice, feigned ignorance.

The delay demanded by Beauchamp had nearly expired. Morcerf appreciated the advice of Monte-Cristo to let things die away of their own accord; no one had taken up the remark about the general, and no one had recognized in the officer who betrayed the Castle of Janina the noble count in the House of Lords. One morning Albert was awakened by his valet, who announced Beauchamp. Albert rubbed his eyes, ordered his servant to introduce him into the small smoking-room on the ground-floor, dressed himself quickly, and went down. He found Beauchamp pacing the room: on perceiving him Beauchamp stopped.

"Albert," said Beauchamp, with a look of sorrow which stupefied the young man, "let us first sit down and talk."

"Rather, sir, before we sit down, I must demand your answer."

"Albert," said the journalist, "I have just returned from Janina."

"Impossible!"

"Here is my passport; examine the *visas*—Geneva, Milan, Venice, Trieste, Janina. Will you believe the government of a republic, a kingdom, and an empire?" Albert cast his eyes on the passport, then raised them in astonishment to Beauchamp. "You have been to Janina?" said he.

"The paragraph was correct, my friend."

"What! that French officer——"

"Yes."——"The traitor who surrendered the castle of the man in whose service he was——"

"Pardon me, my friend, that man was your father!" Albert advanced furiously towards Beauchamp, but the latter restrained him more by a mild look than by his extended hand. "My friend," said he, "here is a proof of it."

Albert opened the paper; it was an attestation of four notable inhabitants of Janina, proving that Colonel Fernand Mondego, in the service of Ali Tebelen, had surrendered the castle for two million crowns. The signatures were perfectly legal. Albert tottered and fell overpowered in a chair. It could no longer be doubted: the family name was fully given.

"I hastened to you," continued Beauchamp, "to tell you, Albert, in this changing age, the faults of a father cannot revert upon his children. Now I have these proofs, Albert, and I am in your confidence, no human power can force me to a duel which your own conscience would reproach you with as criminal, but I come to offer you what you can no longer demand of me. Do you wish these proofs, these attestations, which I alone possess, to be destroyed? Do you wish this frightful secret to remain with us? Confided to me, it shall never escape my lips; say, Albert, my friend, do you wish it?"

Albert threw himself on Beauchamp's neck. "Ah! noble fellow!" cried he.

"Take these," said Beauchamp, presenting the papers to Albert.

Albert seized them with a convulsive hand, tore them in pieces; and, trembling lest the least vestige should escape, and one day appear to confront him, he approached the waxlight, always kept burning for cigars, and consumed every fragment. "Dear, excellent friend!" murmured Albert, still burning the papers.

"Let all be forgotten as a sorrowful dream," said Beauchamp.

"I am broken-hearted," said Albert. "Listen, Beauchamp! I cannot thus, in a moment, relinquish the respect, the confidence, and pride with which a father's untarnished name inspires a son. Oh! Beauchamp, Beauchamp! how shall I now approach mine? Shall I draw back my forehead from his embrace, or withhold my hand from his? I am the most wretched of men. Ah! my mother, my poor mother!" said Albert, gazing through his tears at his mother's portrait; "if you know this, how much must you suffer?"

"Come," said Beauchamp, taking both his hands, "take courage, my friend."

"What?" said Albert, seeing Beauchamp hesitated.

"Are you going to marry Mdlle. Danglars."

"Why do you ask me now?"——"Because the rupture of fulfilment of this engagement is connected with the purveyor of that paragraph."

——"How?" said Albert, whose brow reddened: "you think, M. Danglars

—— Well, the engagement is broken off."——"Well!" said Beauchamp. Then, seeing the young man was about to relapse into melancholy, "Let us go out, Albert," said he; "a ride in the wood in the phaeton, or on horseback, will refresh you; we will then return to breakfast, and you shall attend to your affairs, and I to mine."

But two days after, in the government organ, appeared this paragraph:

"The French officer in the service of Ali, Pacha of Janina, alluded to three weeks since in the 'Impartial,' who not only surrendered the castle of Janina, but sold his benefactor to the Turks, styled himself truly at that time Fernand, as our honorable brother states; but he has since added to his Christian name a title of nobility and a family name. He now calls himself the Count of Morcerf, and ranks among the peers."

Thus this terrible secret, which Beauchamp had so generously destroyed, appeared again as an armed phantom.

The same day, a great agitation was manifest in the House of Peers among the usually calm groups of the noble assembly. Every one had arrived almost before the usual hour, and was conversing on the melancholy event which was to attract the attention of the public towards one of their most illustrious members. Some were perusing the article, others making comments and recalling circumstances which substantiated the charges still more. The count was no favorite with his colleagues. Like all upstarts, he had had recourse to a great deal of haughtiness to maintain his position. The true nobility laughed at him, the talented repelled him and the honorable instinctively despised him. Such were the extremities to which the count was driven: the finger of God once pointed at him, every one was prepared to raise the hue and cry after him.

The Count of Morcerf alone was ignorant of the news. He did not take in the paper containing the defamatory news, and entered the house without observing the hesitation of the door-keepers or the coolness of his colleagues. Business had already commenced half-an-hour when he entered. At length an honorable peer, Morcerf's acknowledged enemy, ascended the tribune with that solemnity which announced the expected moment had arrived. There was an imposing silence; Morcerf alone knew not why such profound attention was given to an orator who was not always listened to with so much complacency. The count did not notice the introduction, in which the speaker announced that his communication would be of that vital importance that it demanded the undivided attention of the House; but, at the names Janina and Colonel Fernand, he turned so awfully pale that every member shuddered and fixed his eyes upon him. Moral wounds have this peculiarity, they conceal themselves but never close; always painful, always ready to bleed when touched, they remain fresh and open in the heart.

Morcerf was so completely overwhelmed by this enormous and unexpected calamity that he could scarcely stammer a few words as he looked round on the assembly. The president put it to the vote, and it was decided the examination should take place. The count was asked what time he required to prepare his defence. Morcerf's courage had revived when he found himself alive after this horrible blow. "My lords," answered he, "it is not by time I could repel the attack made on me by enemies unknown to me, and, doubtless, hidden in obscurity; it is immediately!"

A committee of twelve members were chosen to examine the proofs brought forward by Morcerf. The examination would commence at eight o'clock that evening in the committee-room, and, if it were necessary to postpone it, it would be resumed each evening at the same hour. Morcerf asked leave to retire; he had to collect the documents he had long been preparing against this storm, which his sagacity had foreseen.

At eight o'clock all were in their places, and M. de Morcerf entered at the last stroke. He produced documents, proving that the Vizier of Janina had, to the last moment, honored him with his entire confidence, since he had entrusted him with a negotiation of life and death with the emperor. He produced the ring, his mark of authority, with which Ali Pacha generally sealed his letters, and which the latter had given him that he might, on his return at any hour of the day or night, or even in his harem, gain access to him. Unfortunately, the negotiation failed, and when he returned to defend his benefactor, he was dead. "But," said the count, "so great was Ali Pacha's confidence, that, on his death-bed, he resigned his favorite mistress and her daughter to my care."

Meanwhile, the president carelessly opened a letter which had been brought to him; but the first lines aroused his attention: he read them again and again, and fixing his eyes on M. de Morcerf, asked, "you say the Vizier confided his wife and daughter to your care?"

"Yes, sir," replied Morcerf, "but in that, like all the rest, misfortune pursued me; on my return, Basiliki and her daughter Haydée had disappeared."

"Have you any idea what has become of them?"

"Yes, sir; I heard they had fallen victims to their sorrow, and, perhaps, to their poverty. I was not rich; my life was in constant danger; I could not seek them, to my great regret." The president frowned imperceptibly. "Gentlemen," said he, "you have heard the defence. Can you, my lord, produce any witnesses to the truth of what you have asserted?"—— "Alas! no, sir," replied the count, "all those who surrounded the Vizier, or who knew me at his court, are either dead or scattered; alone, I believe, of all my countrymen, I survived that dreadful war: I have only the letters of Ali Tebelen, which I have placed before you; the ring, a token of his good-will, which is here; and, lastly, the most convincing proof I can offer, namely, after an anonymous attack, the absence of all witness against my veracity and the purity of my military life." A murmur of approbation ran through the assembly. It only remained to put it to the vote, when the president resumed: "Gentlemen, and you, my lord, you will not be displeased, I presume, to listen to one who calls himself a very important witness, and who has just presented himself. He is, doubtless, come to prove the perfect innocence of our colleague. Here is a letter I have just received on the subject; shall it be read, or shall it be passed over? and shall we not regard this incident?" M. de Morcerf turned pale, and clenched his hands on the papers he held. The committee decided to hear the letter; the count was thoughtful and silent.

The door-keeper was called. "Is there any one in the lobby?" said the president.

"A female, accompanied by a servant." Every one looked at his neighbor. "Introduce the female," said the president. Five minutes after, the door-keeper again appeared: all eyes were fixed on the door. Behind the door-keeper walked a female enveloped in a large veil, which completely concealed her. It was evident, from her figure and the perfumes she had about her, that this was a young and elegant woman, but that was all. The president requested her to throw aside her veil, and it was then seen she was dressed in the Grecian costume, and was remarkably beautiful.

The president himself advanced to place a seat for the young lady; but she declined availing herself of it. As for the count, he had fallen on his chair; it was evident his legs refused to support him.

"Madame," said the president, "you have engaged to furnish the committee with some important particulars respecting the affair at Janina, and you have stated that you were an eye-witness of the events."——"I was, indeed!" said the stranger, with a tone of sweet melancholy, and with the sonorous voice peculiar to the East.

"I am Haydée, the daughter of Ali Tebelen, Pacha of Janina, and of Basiliki, his beloved wife."

The blush of mingled pride and modesty which suddenly suffused the cheeks of the young female, the brilliancy of her eyes, and her highly important communication, produced an inexpressible effect on the assembly. As for the count, he could not have been more overwhelmed if a thunderbolt had fallen at his feet and opened before him an immense gulf.

Haydée, still calm, but whose calmness was more dreadful than the anger of another would have been, handed to the president the record of her sale, registered in Arabic. It had been supposed some of these papers might be in the Arabic, Romaic, or Turkish language, and the interpreter of the House was in attendance. One of the noble peers, who was familiar with the Arabian language, having studied it during an Egyptian campaign, followed with his eyes as the translator read it aloud.

A dreadful silence succeeded the reading of this paper.

The count had not uttered one word the whole of this time. His colleagues looked at him, and doubtless pitied his blighted prospects, which sank under the perfumed breath of a woman. His misery was depicted by sinister lines on his countenance. "M. de Morcerf," said the president, "do you recognize this lady as the daughter of Ali Tebelen, Pacha of Janina?"——"No," said Morcerf, attempting to rise; "it is a base plot, contrived by my enemies." Haydée, whose eyes had been fixed upon the door, as if expecting some one, turned hastily, and, seeing the count, shrieked, "You do not know me?" said she. "Well, I fortunately recognize you! You are Fernand Mondego, the French officer, who led the troops of my noble father! you surrendered the Castle of Janina! you were sent by him to Constantinople, to treat with the emperor for the life or death of your benefactor, brought back a false mandate granting full pardon! you with that, obtained the pacha's ring, which gave you authority over Selim, the firekeeper! it was you who stabbed Selim! you sold us, my mother and me, to the slave merchant, El-Kobbir! Assassin! you have still on your brow your master's blood! Look, gentlemen, all!"

These words had been pronounced with such enthusiasm and evident truth that they completely changed the opinion of the assembly respecting the accused nobleman.

The count looked around him with an expression which might have softened tigers, but which could not disarm his judges. Then he raised his eyes toward the ceiling, but withdrew them immediately, as if he feared the roof would open and reveal to his distressed view that second tribunal called heaven, and that other judge named God. Then, was a hasty movement, he tore open his coat, which seemed to stifle him, and flew from the room like a madman; his footstep was heard one moment in the corridor, then the rattling of his carriage-wheels as he was driven rapidly away. "Gentlemen," said the president, when silence was restored, "is the Count of Morcerf convicted of felony, treason, and outrage?" ——"Yes," replied all the members of the committee of inquiry with a unanimous voice.

CHAPTER LVI.

THE PUBLIC INSULT.

ON hearing this affair, Albert did not wait to consult with his father but flew to challenge Danglars, who, he learned, had supplied the information to the press. As may readily be believed, there was no disposition in the banker to go out on the field; he hastened to cover himself with the declaration that Monte-Cristo has put him on the course to write to Janina.

Albert, accompanied by Beauchamp, proceeded to the latter's residence.

Beauchamp wished to go in alone; but Albert observed, as this was an unusual circumstance, he might be allowed to deviate from the etiquette of duels. The cause which the young man espoused was one so sacred, that Beauchamp had only to comply with all his wishes; he yielded, and contented himself with following Morcerf. Albert bounded from the porter's lodge to the steps. He was received by Baptistin. The count had, indeed, just arrived, but he was bathing, and had forbidden that any one should be admitted. "But after his bath?" asked Morcerf.

"He is going to the opera."

"Very good," replied Albert; "that is all I wished to know." Then, turning back toward Beauchamp, "if you have anything to attend to, Beauchamp, do it directly. If you have any appointment for this evening, defer it till to-morrow. I depend on you to accompany me to the opera; and, if you can, bring Château-Renaud with you."

Beauchamp availed himself of Albert's permission, and left him, promising to call for him at a quarter before eight. On his return home, Albert expressed his wish to Franz, Debray, and Morrel, to see them at the opera that evening. Then he went to see his mother, who, since the events of the day before, had refused to see any one, and had kept her room. He found her in bed, overwhelmed with grief at this public humiliation. The sight of Albert produced the effect which might naturally be expected on Mercédès, she pressed her son's hand, and sobbed aloud; but her tears relieved her. Albert stood one moment speechless by the side of his mother's bed. It was evident, from his pale face and knit brows, that his resolution to revenge himself was growing weaker. "My dear mother," said he, "do you know if M. de Morcerf has any enemy?" Mercédès started; she noticed that the young man did not say "my father." "My son," she said, "persons in the count's situation have many secret enemies. Those who are known are not the most dangerous. You noticed, on the evening of the ball we gave, M. de Monte-Cristo would eat nothing in our house." Mercédès raised herself on her feverish arm. "M. de Monte-Cristo!" she exclaimed; "and how is he connected with the question you asked me?"

"You know, my mother, M. de Monte-Cristo is almost an Oriental, and it is customary with them to secure full liberty of revenge by not eating or drinking in the house of their enemies."

"Do you say M. de Monte-Cristo is our enemy?" replied Mercédès, becoming paler than the sheet which covered her. "Who told you so? Why, you are mad, Albert! M. de Monte-Cristo has only shown us kindness. M. de Monte-Cristo saved your life; you, yourself, presented him to us. Oh! I entreat you, my son, if you had entertained such an idea, dispel it; and my counsel to you—even more, my prayer, is, retain this friendship."

An ironical smile passed over Albert's lips. Mercédès saw it, and, with her double instinct of a woman and a mother, she guessed all, but, prudent and strong-minded, she concealed both her sorrows and her fears. Albert was silent; an instant after, the countess resumed: "You came to inquire after my health; I will candidly acknowledge I am not well. You should install yourself here and share my solitude. I do not wish to be left alone."

"Mother," said the young man, "you know how gladly I would obey your wish; but an urgent and important affair obliges me to leave you the whole evening."

"Well!" replied Mercédès, sighing; "go, Albert, I will not make you a slave to your filial piety." Albert pretended he did not hear, bowed to his mother, and went to his room, and dressed with unusual care. At ten minutes to eight Beauchamp arrived; he had seen Château-Renaud, who had promised to be in the orchestra before the curtain was raised.

Albert wandered about the theatre until the curtain was drawn. He hoped to meet with Monte-Cristo either in the lobby or on the stairs. The bell summoned him to his seat, and he entered the orchestra with Château-Renaud and Beauchamp. But his eyes scarcely quitted the box between the columns, which remained obstinately closed during the whole of the first act. At last, as Albert was looking at his watch, about the hundredth time, at the commencement of the second act the door opened, and Monte-Cristo, dressed in black, entered, and leaning over the front of the box, looked round the pit. Morrel followed him, and looked also for his sister and brother-in-law; he soon discovered them in another box, and kissed his hand to them.

The count, in his survey of the pit, encountered a pale face and threatening eyes, which evidently sought to gain his attention. He recognized Albert, but thought it better not to notice him, as he looked so angry and discomposed. Without communicating his thoughts to his companion, he sat down, drew out his opera-glass, and looked another way. Although apparently not noticing Albert, he did not, however, lose sight of him; and when the curtain fell at the end of the second act, he saw him leave the orchestra with his two friends. Then his head was seen passing at the back of the boxes, and the count knew the approaching storm was intended to fall on him. He was at the moment conversing cheerfully with Morrel, but he was well prepared for what might happen. The door opened, and Monte-Cristo, turning round, saw Albert, pale and trembling, followed by Beauchamp and Château-Renaud.

"Well," cried he, with that benevolent politeness which distinguished his salutation from the common civilities of the world, "my cavalier has attained his object. Good evening, M. de Morcerf." The countenance of this man, who possessed such extraordinary control over his feelings, expressed the most perfect cordiality. Morrel only then recollected the letter he had received from the viscount, in which, without assigning any reason, he begged him to go to the opera, but he understood that something terrible was brooding.

"We are not come here, sir, to exchange hypocritical expressions of politeness, or false professions of friendship," said Albert, "but to demand an explanation, Count." The trembling voice of the young man was scarcely audible. "An explanation at the opera?" said the count, with that calm tone and penetrating eye which characterizes the man who knows his cause is good. "Little acquainted as I am with the habits of Parisians, I should not have thought this the place for such a demand."——"Still, if people will shut themselves up," said Albert, "and cannot be seen because they are bathing, dining, or asleep, we must avail ourselves of the opportunity whenever they are to be seen."

"I am not difficult of access, sir." These words were heard by those in the adjoining boxes and in the lobby. Thus the attention of many was attracted by this altercation. "Where are you come from, sir? You do not appear to be in the possession of your senses."

"Provided I understand your perfidy, sir, and succeed in making you understand that I will be revenged, I shall be sane enough," said Albert, furiously.

"I do not understand you, sir," replied Monte-Cristo; "and if I did, your tone is too high. I am at home here, and I alone have a right to raise my voice above another's. Leave the box, sir!" Monte-Cristo pointed toward the door with the most commanding dignity. "Ah! I shall know how to make you leave your home!" replied Albert, clasping in his convulsed grasp the glove, which Monte-Cristo did not lose sight of.—— "Well, well!" said Monte-Cristo, quietly, "I see you wish to quarrel with me; but I would give you one counsel, and do not forget it: it is a bad habit to make a display of a challenge. Public display is not becoming to every one, M. de Morcerf." At this name a murmur of astonishment passed round the group of spectators of this scene. They had talked of no one but Morcerf the whole day. Albert understood the allusion in a moment, and was about to throw his glove at the count, when Morrel seized his hand, while Beauchamp and Château-Renaud, fearing the scene would surpass the limits of a challenge, held him back. But Monte-Cristo, without rising, and leaning forward in his chair, merely extended his hand, and taking the damp, crushed glove from the clenched hand of the young man,—"Sir," said he, in a solemn tone, "I consider your glove thrown, and will return it to you round a bullet. Now, leave me, or I will summon my servants to throw you out of the door."

Wild, almost unconscious, and with eyes inflamed, Albert stepped back, and Morrel closed the door. Monte-Cristo took up his glass again as if nothing had happened; he certainly must have had a heart of brass and face of marble. Morrel whispered, "What have you done to him?"

"The Count de Morcerf's downfall exasperates the young man."

"Have you anything to do with it?"

"It was by Haydée the house was informed of his father's treason."

"Indeed!" said Morrel. "I had been told, but would not credit it, that the Greek slave I have seen with you here in this very box was the daughter of Ali Pacha."

"It is, notwithstanding, true."

"Then," said Morrel, "I understand it all, and this scene was premeditated."——"How so?"

"Yes. Albert wrote to request me to come to the opera, doubtless that I might be a witness to the insult he meant to offer you."

"Probably," said Monte-Cristo, with his imperturbable tranquillity.

"But what will you do with him?"

"As certainly, Maximilian, as I now press your hand, I will kill him before ten o'clock to-morrow morning."

Morrel, in his turn, took Monte-Cristo's hand in both of his, and he shuddered to feel how cold and steady it was. He saw it was useless to say more, and refrained. The curtain, which had been drawn during the scene with Albert, again fell, and a rap was heard at the door.

"Come in!" said Monte-Cristo, without his voice betraying the least emotion; and immediately Beauchamp appeared.

"I have come only to make arrangements for the duel," said Beauchamp.

"It is quite immaterial to me," said Monte-Cristo, "and it was very unnecessary to disturb me at the opera for such a trifle. Tell your client that, although I am the insulted party, in order to carry out my eccentricity, I leave him the choice of arms, and will accept without discussion, without dispute, anything, even combat by drawing lots, which is always stupid, but with me different from other people, as I am sure to gain. I shall kill him—I cannot help it. Only by a single line this evening at my house, let me know the arms and the hour; I do not like to be kept waiting."——"Pistols, then, at eight o'clock, in the Bois de Vincennes," said Beauchamp, quite disconcerted, not knowing if he was dealing with an arrogant braggadocio or a supernatural being.

"Very well, sir," said Monte-Cristo. "Now all that is settled, do let me see the performance, and tell your friend Albert not to come any more this evening; he will hurt himself with all his ill-chosen barbarisms: let him go home and go to sleep." Beauchamp left the box, perfectly amazed.

M. de Monte-Cristo waited, according to his usual custom, until the tenor had sung his famous "Suivez-moi;" then he rose, and went out. Morrel took leave of him at the door, to be with him the next morning at seven o'clock, and to bring Emmanuel with him, as second. Then he stepped into his *coupé,* calm and smiling, and was at home in five minutes. No one who knew the count could mistake his expression, when, on entering, he said, "Ali, bring me my pistols with an ivory butt."

Ali brought the box to his master, who examined his arms with a solicitude very natural to a man who is about to intrust his life to a little powder and shot. These were salon pistols. A cap was sufficient to drive out the ball, and from the adjoining room no one would have suspected the count was keeping his hand in. He was just taking one in his hand, and looking for the point to aim at, on a little iron plate, which served him as a target, when his cabinet-door opened, and Baptistin entered. Before he had spoken a word the count perceived in the next room a female, veiled, who had followed closely after Baptistin, and now seeing the count with a pistol in his hand and swords on the table, rushed in. Baptistin looked at his master, who made a sign to him, and he went out, closing the door after him.

The stranger cast one look around her, to be certain they were quite alone, then bending, as if she would have knelt, and joining her hands, she said, with an accent of despair,—"Edmond, you will not kill my son?" The count retreated a step, uttered a slight exclamation, and let fall the pistol he held.

"What name did you pronounce then, Mdme. de Morcerf?" said he.

"Yours!" cried she, throwing back her veil,—"yours, which I alone, perhaps, have not forgotten. Edmond, it is not Mdme. Morcerf who is come to you, it is Mercédès."—"Mercédès is dead, madame," said Monte-Cristo; "I know no one now of that name."

"Mercédès lives, sir, and she remembers, for she alone recognized you when she saw you, and even before she saw you, by your voice, Edmond, —by the mere sound of your voice, and from that moment she has followed your steps, watched you, feared you, and she needs not to inquire what hand has dealt the blow which now strikes M. de Morcerf."

"Fernand, do you mean?" replied Monte-Cristo, with bitter irony; "since we are recalling names, let us remember them all."

Monte-Cristo had pronounced the name of Fernand with such an expression of hatred, that Mercédès felt a thrill of horror run through every vein.

"You see, Edmond, I am not mistaken, and have cause to say, 'Spare my son!'"

"Madame, it is not I who strike M. de Morcerf; it is Providence which punishes him."

"And why do you represent Providence?" cried Mercédès. "Why do you remember, when it forgets? What are Janina and its vizier to you, Edmond? What injury has Fernand Mondego done you in betraying Ali Tebelen?"

"And, madame," replied Monte-Cristo, "all this is an affair between the French captain and the daughter of Basiliki. It does not concern me, you are right; and if I have sworn to revenge myself, it is not on the French captain, nor on the Count de Morcerf, but on the fisherman Fernand, the husband of the Catalan Mercédès."

"Ah! sir," cried the countess, "how terrible a vengeance for a fault which fatality made me commit! for I am the only culprit, Edmond; and if you owe revenge to any one, it is to me, who had not fortitude to bear your absence and my solitude."

"But," exclaimed Monte-Cristo, "why was I absent? And why were you alone?"

"Because you had been arrested, Edmond, and were a prisoner."

"And why was I arrested? Why was I a prisoner?"

"I do not know," said Mercédès.

"You do not, madame; at least, I hope not. But I will tell you. I was arrested and became a prisoner, because in the arbor of La Réserve, the day before I was to marry you, a man named Danglars wrote this letter which the fisherman Fernand himself posted." Monte-Cristo went to a secretary, opened a drawer by a spring, from which he took a paper which had lost its original color, and the ink of which had become a rusty hue; this he placed in the hands of Mercédès. It was Danglars' letter to the prosecutor, which Monte-Cristo, disguised as a clerk from the house of Thomson and French, had taken from the bundle of Edmond Dantès, on the day he had paid the two hundred thousand francs to M. de Boville. Mercédès read with terror the fatal lines.

"How dreadful!" said Mercédès, passing her hand across her brow, moist with perspiration; "and that letter——"

"I bought it for two hundred thousand francs, madame," said Monte-Cristo; "but that is a trifle, since it enables me to justify myself to you."

"And the result of that letter——"

"You well know, madame, was my arrest; but you do not know how long that arrest lasted. You do not know that I remained for fourteen years within a quarter of a league of you, in a dungeon in the Château d'If. You do not know that each day of those fourteen years I renewed the vow of vengeance which I had made the first day; and yet I knew not you had married Fernand, my libellor, and that my father had died of hunger!"

"Can it be?" cried Mercédès, shuddering.

"That is what I heard on leaving my prison, fourteen years after I had entered it, and that is why, on account of the living Mercédès and my deceased father, I have sworn to revenge myself on Fernand, and—I have revenged myself."

"And you are sure the unhappy Fernand did that?"

"I am satisfied, madame, he did what I have told you; besides, that is not much more shameful than a Frenchman, by adoption, having passed over to the English; a Spaniard, by birth, having fought against the Spaniards; a stipendiary of Ali having betrayed and murdered Ali. Compared with such things, what is the letter you have just read? A lover's deception, which the woman who has married that man ought certainly to forgive, but not so the lover who was to have married her. Well! the French did not avenge themselves on the traitor; the Spaniards did not shoot the traitor; Ali, in his grave, left the traitor unpunished; but I, betrayed, sacrificed, buried, have risen from my grave, by the grace of God, to punish that man. He sends me for that purpose, and here I am." The poor woman's head and arms fell; and she fell on her knees. "Forgive, Edmond, forgive for my sake, who love you still!"

The dignity of the wife stopped the enthusiasm of the lover and the mother. Her forehead almost touched the carpet, when the count sprang forward and raised her.

The count, fearing to yield to the entreaties of her he had so ardently loved, recalled his sufferings to the assistance of his hatred.

"Revenge yourself then, Edmond," cried the poor mother; "but let your vengeance fall on the culprits; on him, on me, but not on my son!" Monte-Cristo groaned, and seized his beautiful hair with both hands.

"Edmond," groaned Mercédès, with her arms extended toward the count, "since I first knew you, I have adored your name, have respected your memory. Edmond, my friend, do not compel me to tarnish that noble and fine image reflected incessantly on the mirror of my heart. Edmond, if you knew all the prayers I have addressed to God for you while I thought you were living and since I have thought you must be dead! Yes, dead, alas! And I, too, Edmond—oh! believe me—guilty as I was—oh! yes, I too, have suffered much!"

"Have you guessed that your father died in your absence?" cried Monte-Cristo, again thrusting his hands in his hair; "have you seen the woman you loved giving her hand to your rival while you were perishing at the bottom of a dungeon?"

"No," interrupted Mercédès, "but I have seen him whom I loved on the point of murdering my son." Mercédès pronounced these words with such deep anguish, with an accent of such intense despair, that Monte-Cristo could not restrain a sob. The lion was daunted; the avenger was conquered. "What do you ask of me?" said he,—"your son's life? Well! he shall live!"

Mercédès uttered a cry which made the tears start from Monte-Cristo's eyes; but these tears disappeared almost instantaneously, for, doubtless, God had sent some angel to collect them; far more precious were they in his eyes than the richest pearls of Guzeral and of Ophir.

"Oh!" said she, seizing the count's hand, and raising it to her lips: "oh! thank you, thank you, Edmond! now you are exactly what I dreamt you were, such as I always loved you. Oh! now I may say so."

"So much the better," replied Monte-Cristo; "as that poor Edmond will not have long to be loved by you. Death is about to return to the tomb, the phantom to retire in darkness. You do not suppose, that publicly outraged in the face of a whole theatre, in the presence of your friends and those of your son—challenged by a boy, who will glory in my pardon as in a victory—you do not suppose I can for one moment wish to live. What I most loved after you, Mercédès, was myself, my dignity, and that strength which rendered me superior to other men; that strength was my life. With one word you have crushed it, and I die."

"But the duel will not take place, Edmond, since you forgive?"

"It will take place," said Monte-Cristo, in a most solemn tone, "but instead of your son's blood which will stain the ground, mine will flow."

"Edmond," said Mercédès, "I have but one word more to say to you, though you will see my face is pale, my eyes dull, my beauty gone; Mercédès, in short, no longer resembles her former self, though her heart is still the same. Adieu, then, Edmond; I have nothing more to ask of heaven—I have seen you again—and have found you as noble and as great as formerly you were. Adieu, Edmond, adieu, and thank you."

The clock struck one when the carriage which conveyed Mdme. de Morcerf away rolled on the pavement and made Monte-Cristo raise his head. "What a fool I was," said he, "not to tear my heart out on the day when I resolved to avenge myself!"

CHAPTER LVII.

THE ENCOUNTER.

AFTER Mercédès had left Monte-Cristo, a gloomy shadow seemed to overshadow everything. Around him and within him the flight of thought appeared stopped; his energetic mind slumbered, as does the body after extreme fatigue. "What," said he to himself, while the lamp and the wax lights were nearly burnt out, and the servants were waiting impatiently in the ante-room; "what! this edifice which I have been so long preparing—which I have reared with so much care and toil, is to be crumbled by a single touch, a word, even a slight breath! Yes, this creature of whom I thought so much, I was so proud, after appearing so worthless in the dungeons of the Château d'If, and whom I had succeeded in making so great, will be but a lump of clay to-morrow. Alas! it is not the death of the body I regret; but the ruin of projects, so slowly carried out, so laboriously framed. Providence is now opposed to them, when I most thought it would be propitious. It is not God's will they should be accomplished. This burden, almost as heavy as a world, which I had raised, and I had thought to bear to the end, was too great for my strength, and I was compelled to lay it down in the middle of my career. And all this—all this, because my heart, which I thought dead, was only sleeping; because it has awoke and has beaten again; because I have yielded to the pain of the emotion excited in my breast by a woman's voice.

"Folly! to carry generosity so far as to place myself as a mark for that young man to aim at. He will never believe my death was a suicide; and yet it is important for the honor of my memory,—and this, surely, is, not vanity, but a justifiable pride,—it is important the world should know that I have consented, by my free will, to stop my arm, already raised to strike, and that with that arm, so powerful against others, I have struck myself. It must be, it shall be." Seizing a pen, he drew a paper from a secret drawer in his bureau, and traced at the bottom of that paper, which was no other than his will, drawn since his arrival in Paris, a codicil, clearly explaining the nature of his death. "I do this, O my God!" said he, with his eyes raised to heaven, "as much for Thy honor as for mine. I have during ten years considered myself the agent of Thy vengeance; and other wretches, like a Morcerf, a Danglars, a Villefort, even that Morcerf himself, must not imagine that chance has freed them from their enemy. Let them know, on the contrary, that their punishment, which had been decreed by Providence, is only delayed by my present determination; and although they escape it in this world, it awaits them in another, and that they are only exchanging time for eternity."

While he was thus agitated by these gloomy uncertainties, these wretched waking dreams of grief, the first rays of twilight pierced his windows, and shone upon the pale blue paper on which he had just traced his justification of Providence. It was just five o'clock in the morning, when a slight noise reached his ear, which appeared like a stifled sigh; he turned his head, looked around him, and saw no one; but the sound was repeated distinctly enough to convince him of its reality. He arose, and quietly opening the door of the drawing-room, saw Haydée, who had fallen on a chair with her arms hanging down, and her beautiful head thrown back. She had been standing at the door to prevent his going out without seeing her, until sleep, which the young cannot resist, had overpowered her frame, wearied as she was with watching so long. The noise of the door did not awaken her, and Monte-Cristo gazed at her with affectionate regret. "She remembered she had a son," said he; "and I forgot I had a daughter." Then, shaking his head sorrowfully, "Poor Haydée!" said he; "she wished to see me to speak to me, she has feared or guessed something. Oh! I cannot go without taking leave of her; I cannot die without confiding her to some one." He quietly regained his seat, and wrote under the other lines,—

"I bequeath to Maximilian Morrel, captain, and son of my former patron, Pierre Morrel, shipowner at Marseilles, the sum of twenty millions, a part of which may be offered to his sister Julia and brother-in-law Emmanuel, if he does not fear this increase of fortune may mar their happiness. These twenty millions are concealed in my cave at Monte-Cristo, of which Bertuccio knows the secret. If his heart is free, and he will marry Haydée, the daughter of Ali, pacha of Janina, whom I have brought up with the love of a father, and who has shown the love and tenderness of a daughter for me, he will thus accomplish my last wish. This will has already constituted Haydée heiress of the rest of my fortune; which, without the twenty millions, and the legacies to my servants, may still amount to sixty millions."

He was finishing the last line when a cry behind him made him start, and the pen fell from his hand. "Haydée," said he, "did you read it?"

"Oh! my lord," said she, "why are you writing thus at such an hour? why are you bequeathing all your fortune to me? Are you going to leave me?"

"I am going on a journey, dear child," said Monte-Cristo, with an expression of infinite tenderness and melancholy; "and if any misfortune should happen to me——" The count stopped.

"Well! if you die," said she, "bequeath your fortune to others; for, if you die I shall require nothing;" and, taking the paper, she tore it in pieces and threw it into the middle of the room. Then, the effort having exhausted her strength, she fell, not asleep this time, but fainting on the floor.

"Alas!" murmured he, with intense suffering; "I might then have been happy yet." Then he carried Haydée to her room, resigned her to the care of her attendants, and returning to his cabinet, which he shut quickly this time, he again copied the destroyed will. As he was finishing, the sound of a cab entering the yard was heard. Monte-Cristo approached the window, and saw Maximilian and Emmanuel alight. "Good!" said he; "it was time," and he sealed his will. One moment afterwards he heard a noise in the drawing-room, and went to open the door himself. Morrel was there, he had come twenty minutes before the time appointed. "I am, perhaps, come too soon, Count," said he, "but I frankly acknowledge, I have not closed my eyes all night, nor any one in my house. I required to see you strong in your courageous assurance, to recover myself." Monte-Cristo could not resist this proof of affection, he not only extended his hand to the young man, but flew to him with open arms. "Morrel," said he, "it is a happy day for me, to feel I am beloved by such a man as you. Good morning, Emmanuel; you will come with me then, Maximilian?"

"Did you doubt it?" said the young captain.

"But if I were wrong——"

"I watched you during the whole scene of that challenge yesterday; I have been thinking of your firmness all this night, and I said, 'Justice must be on your side, or man's countenance is no longer to be relied on."

Then ringing the bell once, "Look," said the count to Ali, who came immediately, "take that to my lawyer's. It is my will, Morrel. When I am dead, you will go and examine it."

"What!" said Morrel, "you dead?"

"Yes: must I not be prepared for everything, dear friend?"

"I hoped to get an exchange of arms, to substitute the sword for the pistol, the pistol is blind."——"Have you succeeded?" asked Monte-Cristo, quickly, with an imperceptible gleam of hope.

"They positively refused."——"Morrel," said the count, "have you ever seen me fire a pistol?"——"Never."

"Well, we have time; look." Monte-Cristo took the pistols he held in his hand when Mercédès entered, and fixing an ace of clubs against the iron plate, with four shots he successively shot off the four stems of the club. At each shot Morrel turned pale. He examined the balls with which Monte-Cristo performed this dexterous feat, and saw that they were no larger than deer-shot. "It is astonishing!" said he; "look, Emmanuel." Then turning towards Monte-Cristo: "Count," said he, "in the name of all that is dear to you, I entreat you not to kill Albert! the unhappy youth has a mother, wound him—but do not kill him."

"I will tell you, Morrel," said the count, "that I do not need entreating to spare the life of M. de Morcerf; he shall be so well spared, that he will return quietly with his two friends, while Morcerf will kill me." Morrel looked at him in utter unconsciousness. "But what has happened, then, since last evening, count?"——"The same thing which happened to Brutus the night before the battle of Philippi; I have seen a phantom."——"And that phantom——"

"Told me, Morrel, I had lived long enough." Maximilian and Emmanuel looked at each other. Monte-Cristo drew out his watch. "Let us go," said he; "it is five minutes past seven, and the appointment was for eight o'clock." A carriage was in readiness at the door. Monte-Cristo stepped into it with his two friends. As the clock struck eight, they drove up to the place of meeting.

Morrel walked over to Beauchamp and Château-Renaud, who came to meet them. They saluted affably or at least courteously.

Meanwhile Albert had arrived within ten paces of the group formed by the five young men. He jumped from his horse, threw the bridle on his servant's arms, and joined them. He was pale, and his eyes were red and swollen; it was evident that he had not slept. A shade of melancholy gravity overspread his countenance, which was not natural to him. "I thank you, gentlemen," said he, "for having complied with my request; I feel extremely grateful for this mark of friendship."

"M. Morrel," said Château-Renaud, "will you notify the Count of Monte-Cristo that M. de Morcerf is arrived, and we are at his command?" Morrel was preparing to fulfil his commission. Beauchamp had meanwhile drawn the pistol-case from the carriage. "Stop, gentlemen!" said Albert; "I have two words to say to the Count of Monte-Cristo."

"In private?" asked Morrel.

"No, sir; before all who are here."

"What does he want with me?" said Monte-Cristo.

"Approach, gentlemen," said Albert; "I wish you not to lose one word of what I am about to have the honor of saying to the Count of Monte-Cristo; for it must be repeated by you to all who will listen to it, strange as it may appear to you."

"Proceed, sir," said the count.

"Sir," said Albert, at first with a tremulous voice, but which gradually became firmer; "I reproached you with exposing the conduct of M. de Morcerf in Epirus, for, guilty as I knew he was, I thought you had no right to punish him; but I have since learned you have that right. It is not Fernand Mondego's treachery towards Ali Pacha which induces me so readily to excuse you, but the treachery of the fisherman Fernand toward you, and the almost unheard-of miseries which were its consequences; and I say, and proclaim it publicly, that you were justified in revenging yourself on my father; and I, his son, thank you for not using greater severity." Had a thunderbolt fallen in the midst of the spectators of this unexpected scene, it would not have surprised them more than did Albert's declaration. As for Monte-Cristo, his eyes slowly rose toward heaven with infinite gratitude. He could not understand how Albert's bravery, of which he had seen so much among the Roman bandits, had suddenly stooped to this humiliation. He recognized the influence of Mercédès, and saw why her noble heart had not opposed the sacrifice she knew beforehand would be useless. "Now, sir," said Albert, "if you think my apology sufficient, pray give me your hand. Next to the merit of infallibility which you appear to possess, I rank that of candidly acknowledging a fault. But this confession concerns me only. I acted well as a man, but you have acted better than man. An angel alone could have saved one of us from death—that angel came from heaven, if not to make us friends (which, alas! fatality renders impossible), at least to make us esteem each other."

Monte-Cristo, with moistened eye, heaving breast, and lips half open, extended to Albert a hand, which the latter pressed with a sentiment resembling respectful fear.

"Providence still!" murmured the departing count; "now only am I fully convinced of being the emissary of God!"

In a quarter of an hour Albert was entering the mansion. As he alighted, he thought he saw behind the curtain of the count's bedroom his father's pale face. Albert turned away his head with a sigh, and went to his own apartments.

His servant, notwithstanding his prohibition, came to his room. "What do you want?" asked he, with a more sorrowful than angry tone. "Pardon me, sir," replied the valet; "you had forbidden me to disturb you, but the Count of Morcerf had called me. Since he has sent, it is doubtless to question me on what happened. What must I answer?"

"You will say I apologized to the Count of Monte-Cristo. Go."

The valet bowed and retired, and Albert returned to his inventory. As he was finishing this work, the sound of horses prancing in the yard, and the wheels of a carriage shaking his window, attracted his attention. He approached the window, and saw his father get into it, and it drove away. The door was scarcely closed when Albert bent his steps to his mother's room; and no one being there to announce him, he advanced to her bedroom, and, distressed by what he saw and guessed, stopped for one moment at the door. As if the same soul had animated these two beings, Mercédès was doing the same in her apartments as he had had just done.

"Oh, my mother!" exclaimed Albert, so overcome he could scarcely speak, "it is not the same with you and me—you cannot have made the same resolution I have, for I am come to warn you that I bid adieu to your house, and—and to you!"

"I also," replied Mercédès, "am going, and I acknowledge I had depended on your accompanying me; have I deceived myself?"

"My mother," said Albert, with firmness, "I cannot make you share the fate I have planned for myself. I must live henceforth without rank and fortune, and to begin this hard apprenticeship I must borrow from a friend the loaf I shall eat until I have earned one. So, my dear mother, I am going at once to ask Franz to lend me the small sum I shall require to supply my present wants."

"Albert, my child," said Mercédès, "if I had a stronger heart, that is the counsel I would have given you; your conscience has spoken when my voice became too weak; listen to its dictates. Do not despair; you have life before you, my dear Albert, for you are yet scarcely twenty-two years old; and as a pure heart like yours wants a spotless name, take my father's—it was Herrera. I am sure, my Albert, whatever may be your career, you will soon render that name illustrious. Then, my friend, return to the world still more brilliant from the reflection of your former sorrows; and if am wrong, still let me cherish these hopes, for I have no future to look forward to: for me the grave opens when I pass the threshold of this house."

"I will fulfil all your wishes, my dear mother," said the young man. "Yes, I share your hopes; the anger of heaven will not pursue us—you so pure, and me so innocent. But since our resolution is formed, let us act promptly. M. de Morcerf went out about half an hour since; the opportunity is favorable to avoid an explanation."

"I am ready, my son," said Mercédès. Albert ran to fetch a hack; he recollected where his mother would find a humble but decent lodging, and thither he intended conducting her. As the hackney-coach stopped at the door, and Albert was alighting, a man approached, and gave him a letter. Albert recognized the bearer. "From the count," said Bertuccio. Albert took the letter, opened it, and read it; then looked round for Bertuccio, but he was gone. He returned to Mercédès, with tears in his eyes and heaving breast, and, without uttering a word, he gave her the letter. Mercédès read:

ALBERT,—While showing you that I have discovered your plans, I hope also to convince you of my delicacy. You are free, you leave the count's hotel, and you take your mother to your home; but reflect, Albert,

you owe her more than your poor noble heart can pay her. Keep the struggle for yourself, bear all the suffering, but spare her the trial of poverty
which must accompany your first efforts; for she deserves not even the
shadow of the misfortune which has this day fallen on her, and Providence wills not the innocent should suffer for the guilty. I know you
are going to leave the Rue du Helder without taking anything with you;
do not seek to know how I discovered it; I know it—that is sufficient.
Now, listen, Albert. Twenty-four years ago I returned, proud and joyful, to my country. I had a betrothed, Albert, a lovely girl, whom I
adored, and I was bringing to my betrothed a hundred and fifty louis,
painfully amassed by ceaseless toil. This money was for her; and, knowing the treachery of the sea, I buried our treasure in the little garden of
the house my father lived in at Marseilles. Your mother, Albert, knows
that poor house well. It was under a beautiful fig-tree my father had
planted the day I was born, which overshadowed the spot. Well, Albert,
this money, which was formerly designed to promote the comfort and
tranquillity of the woman I adored, may now, from a strange and painful circumstance, be devoted to the same purpose. Oh, feel for me, who
could offer millions to that poor woman, but who returns her only the
piece of bread, forgotten under my poor roof since the day I was torn
from her I loved. You are a generous man, Albert, but perhaps you may
be blinded by pride or resentment; if you refuse me, if you ask another
for what I have a right to offer you, I will say it is ungenerous of you
to refuse the life of your mother at the hands of a man whose father
was allowed to die in all the horrors of poverty and despair by your
father."

Albert stood pale and motionless to hear what his mother would decide after she had finished reading this letter. Mercédès turned her eyes
with an ineffable look toward heaven. "I accept it," said she; "he has a
right to pay the dowery, which I shall take with me to some convent!"
Putting the letter in her corsage, she took her son's arm, and, with a
firmer step than even she herself expected, she went down-stairs.

CHAPTER LVIII.

THE SUICIDE.

MEANWHILE Monte-Cristo had also returned home. Every transport of a daughter finding a father, all the delight of a mistress seeing an adored lover, were felt by Haydée during the first moments of this meeting, which she had so eagerly expected. Doubtless, although less evident, Monte-Cristo's joy was not less intense; joy to hearts which have suffered long is like the dew on the ground after a long drought; both the heart and the ground absorb that beneficent moisture falling on them, and nothing is outwardly apparent.

Monte-Cristo was beginning to think, what he had not for a long time dared to believe, that there were two Mercédès in the world, and he might yet be happy. His eyes elated with happiness, were reading eagerly the moistened gaze of Haydée, when suddenly the door opened. The count knit his brow. "M. de Morcerf!" said Baptistin, as if that name sufficed for his excuse. In fact, the count's face brightened. "Ask M. de Morcerf into the drawing-room," said he to Baptistin, while he led the beautiful Greek girl to a private staircase.

The general was pacing the room the third time, when, in turning, he perceived Monte-Cristo at the door.

"Why! it is M. de Morcerf," said Monte-Cristo quietly; "I thought I had heard wrong."

"Yes, it is I," said the count, whom a frightful contraction of the lips prevented from articulating freely.

"May I know the cause which procures me the pleasure of seeing M. de Morcerf so early?"

"Had you not a meeting with my son this morning?" asked the general.

"I had," replied the count.

"And I know my son had good reasons to wish to fight with you, and to endeavor to kill you. Doubtless you made, then, some apology or explanation?"

"I explained nothing, and it is he who apologized to me, a result I expected."

"You expected my son would be a coward!" cried the count.

"M. Albert de Morcerf is no coward!" said Monte-Cristo.

"A man who holds a sword in his hand, and sees a mortal enemy within reach of that sword, and does not fight, is a coward! Why is he not here, that I may tell him so?"

"Sir," replied Monte-Cristo, coldly, "I did not expect you had come here to relate to me your little family affairs. Go and tell M. Albert that, and he may know what to answer you."

"Oh, no, no!" said the general, smiling faintly, "I did not come for that purpose; you are right! I came to tell you that I also look upon you as my enemy! I came to tell you that I hate you instinctively? That it seems as if I had always known you, and always hated you; and, in short, since the young men of the present day will not fight, it remains for us to do so till one of us is dead!" said the general, whose teeth were clenched with rage.

"Until one of us dies," repeated Monte-Cristo, moving his head slightly up and down.

"Let us start, then; we need no witnesses."

"Truly," said Monte-Cristo, "it is unnecessary, we know each other so well!"

"On the contrary," said the count, "we know so little of each other."

"Indeed!" said Monte-Cristo, with the same indomitable coolness; "let us see. Are you not the soldier Fernand who deserted on the eve of the battle of Waterloo? Are you not the Lieutenant Fernand who served as guide and spy to the French army in Spain? Are you not the Captain Fernand who betrayed, sold, and murdered his benefactor, Ali? And have not all these Fernands, united, made the Lieutenant-General de Morcerf, peer of France?"

"Oh!" cried the general, as if branded with a hot iron, "wretch! to reproach me with my shame, when about, perhaps, to kill me. No, I did not say I was a stranger to you; I know well, demon, that you have penetrated into the darkness of the past, and that you have read, by the light of what torch I know not, every page of my life; but, perhaps, I may be more honorable in my shame than you under your pompous coverings. No—no, I am aware you know me; but I know you not, adventurer, sewn up in gold and jewelry. You have called yourself, in Paris, the Count of Monte-Cristo; in Italy, Sinbad the Sailor; in Malta, I forget what. But it is your real name I want to know, in the midst of your hundred names, that I may pronounce it when we meet to fight, at the moment when I plunge my sword through your heart."

The Count of Monte-Cristo turned dreadfully pale, his eye seemed to burn with a devouring fire; he bounded toward a dressing-room near his bedroom, and, in less than a moment, tearing off his cravat, his coat and waistcoat, he put on a sailor's jacket and hat, from beneath which rolled his long black hair. He returned thus, formidable and implacable, advancing with his arms folded, toward the general, who could not understand why he had disappeared: but who on seeing him again, and feeling his teeth chatter and his legs sink under him, drew back, and only stopped when he found a table to support his clenched hand.

"Fernand," cried he, "of my hundred names I need only tell you one, to overwhelm you! But you guess it now; do you not?—or, rather, you remember it? For, notwithstanding all my sorrows and my tortures, I show you to-day a face which the happiness of revenge makes young again—a face you must often have seen in your dreams since your marriage with Mercédès, my betrothed!"

The general, with his head thrown back, hands extended, gaze fixed, looked silently at this dreadful apparition; then seeking the wall to support him, he glided along close to it until he reached the door, through which he went out backwards, uttering this single, mournful, lamentable, distressing cry,—"Edmond Dantès?"

Then, with sighs which were unlike any human sound, he dragged himself to the door, reeled across the courtyard, and falling into the arms of his valet, he said, in a voice scarcely intelligible,—"Home! home!" Two persons were coming down the stairs: he had only time to creep into a cabinet to avoid them. It was Mercédès leaning on her son's arm and leaving the hotel. They passed close by the unhappy being, who, concealed behind the damask door, almost felt Mercédès' dress brush past him, and his son's warm breath pronouncing these words,—"Courage, my mother! Come, this is no longer our home!"

The words died away, the steps were lost in the distance. The general drew himself up, clinging to the door; he uttered the most dreadful sob which ever escaped from the bosom of a father abandoned at the same time by his wife and son. He soon heard the clatter of the iron step of the hackney-coach, then the coachman's voice, and then the rolling of the heavy vehicle shook the windows. He darted to his bedroom to see once more all he had loved in the world; but the hackney-coach drove on without the head of either Mercédès or her son appearing at the window to take a last look at the house or the deserted father or husband. And at the very moment when the wheels of that coach crossed the gateway a report was heard, and a thick smoke escaped through one of the panes of the window, which was broken by the explosion.

CHAPTER LIX.

VALENTINE.

On leaving Monte-Cristo, Morrel walked slowly toward Villefort's. Noirtier and Valentine had given him leave to go twice a week, and he was now availing himself of that permission. He arrived; Valentine was expecting him. Uneasy and almost wandering, she seized his hand and led him to her grandfather. This uneasiness, amounting almost to wildness, arose from the report Morcerf's adventure had made in the world; the affair of the opera was generally known. Morrel could read an indescribable joy in the eyes of his beloved, when she knew that the termination of this affair was as happy as it was unexpected.

"Now," said Valentine, motioning to Morrel to sit down near her grandfather, while she took her seat on his footstool, "now let us talk about our own affairs. You know, Maximilian, grandpapa once thought of leaving this house, and taking an apartment away from M. de Villefort's. He asserts the air here is not good for me."

"Indeed!" said Morrel; "in that M. Noirtier may be right; your health has not appeared good the last fortnight."——"Not very," said Valentine. "And grandpapa is becoming my physician; and I have the greatest confidence in him, because he knows everything."

"Do you then really suffer?" asked Morrel, quickly.

"Oh, it must not be called suffering; I feel a general depression, that is all. I have lost my appetite." Noirtier did not lose a word of what Valentine said. "And what treatment do you adopt for this singular complaint?"——"A very simple one," said Valentine. "I swallow every morning a spoonful of the mixture prepared for my grandfather. When I say one spoonful, I began by one—now I take four. Grandpapa says it is a panacea." Valentine smiled, but it was evident she suffered.

Maximilian, in his devotedness, gazed silently at her. She was very beautiful, but her usual paleness had increased; her eyes were more brilliant than ever, and her hands, which were generally white like mother-of-pearl, now more resembled wax, to which time was adding a yellowish hue.

"But," said Morrel, "I thought this mixture, of which you now take four spoonfuls, was especially prepared for M. Noirtier?"

"I know it is very bitter," said Valentine; "so bitter, that all I drink afterwards appears to have the same taste." Noirtier looked inquiringly at his granddaughter. "Yes; grandpapa," said Valentine; "it is so. Just now, before I came down to you, I drank a glass of sugar and water;

I left half, because it seemed so bitter." Noirtier turned pale, and made a sign that he wished to speak. Valentine rose to fetch the dictionary. Noirtier watched her with evident anguish. The blood was rushing to the girl's head: her cheeks were becoming red. "Oh!" cried she, without losing any of her cheerfulness, "this is singular! A dimness! Did the sun shine in my eyes." And she leaned against the window.

"The sun is not shining," said Morrel, more alarmed by Noirtier's expression than by Valentine's indisposition. He ran towards her. The girl smiled. "Comfort yourself!" said she to Noirtier. "Do not be alarmed, Maximilian; it is nothing, and has already passed away. But listen! Do I not hear a carriage in the courtyard?" She opened Noirtier's door, ran to a window in the passage, and returned hastily. "Yes," said she, "it is Mdme. Danglars and her daughter, come to call on us. Goodbye! I must run away, for they would send here for me; or, rather, farewell till I see you again. Stay with grandpapa, Maximilian; I promise you not to persuade them to stay."

Morrel watched her as she left the room; he heard her ascend the little staircase which led both to Mdme. de Villefort's apartments and to hers. As soon as she was gone, Noirtier made a sign to Morrel to take the dictionary. Morrel obeyed; guided by Valentine, he had learned how to understand the old man quickly. Accustomed, however, as he was, and having to repeat most of the letters of the alphabet, and to find every word in the dictionary, it was ten minutes before the thought of the old man was translated by these words, "Fetch the glass of water and the decanter from Valentine's room." Morrel rang immediately for the servant who had taken Barrois' situation, and in Noirtier's name gave that order. The servant soon returned. The decanter and the glass were completely empty. Noirtier made a sign that he wished to speak. "Why are the glass and decanter empty?" asked he; "Valentine said she only drank half the glassful." The translation of this new question occupied another five minutes. "I do not know," said the servant, "but the housemaid is in Mdlle. Valentine's room; perhaps she has emptied them."—— "Ask her," said Morrel, translating Noirtier's thought this time by his look. The servant went out, but returned almost immediately. "Mdlle. Valentine passed through the room to go to Mdme. de Villefort's," said he; "and in passing, as she was thirsty, she drank what remained in the glass; as for the decanter, M. Edward had emptied that to make a pond for his ducks." Noirtier raised his eyes to heaven, as a gambler does who stakes his all on one stroke. From that moment the old man's eyes were fixed on the door, and did not quit it.

It was indeed Mdme. Danglars and her daughter whom Valentine had seen; they had been ushered into Mdme. de Villefort's room. "My dear friend," said the baroness, while the two young people were shaking hands, "we come to be the first to announce to you the approaching marriage of my daughter with Prince Cavalcanti." Danglars kept up the title of prince. The popular banker found it answered better than count. "Allow me to present you my sincere congratulations," replied Mdme. de Villefort. "Prince Cavalcanti appears a young man of rare qualities."

"And," said Mdme. de Villefort, "I need not ask you if you share this liking?"

"I!" replied Eugénie, with her usual candor. "Oh, not the least in the world, madame! But, since I am to be married whether I will or not, I ought to be thankful to Providence for having released me from my engagement with M. Albert de Morcerf, or I should this day have been the wife of a dishonored man."——"It is true," said the baroness. "We have had a narrow escape."

Deeply engaged in inward contemplation, Valentine had ceased for a moment to join in the conversation. She would, indeed, have found it impossible to repeat what had been said the last few minutes, when suddenly Mdlle. Danglars' hand, pressed on her arm, aroused her from her lethargy.

"What is it?" said Eugénie, "you are very pale!"

"Oh, do not be alarmed! I have been so for some days."

Artless as she was, the maiden knew this was an opportunity to leave, besides, Mdme. de Villefort came to her assistance. "Retire, Valentine," said she; "you are really suffering, and these ladies will excuse you; drink a glass of water, it will restore you." Valentine kissed Eugénie, bowed to Mdme. Danglars, who had already risen to take her leave, and went out. "The poor child," said Mdme. de Villefort, when Valentine was gone, "she makes me very uneasy, and I should not be astonished if she had some serious illness."

Meanwhile, Valentine, in excitement which she could not quite understand, had crossed Edward's room without noticing some trick of the imp, and through her own rooms had reached the little staircase. She was at the bottom excepting three steps; she already heard Morrel's voice, when suddenly a cloud passed over her eyes, her stiffened foot missed the step, her hands had no power to hold the baluster, and, falling against the wall, she rolled down these three steps rather than walked. Morrel bounded to the door, opened it, and found Valentine extended on the floor. Rapid as lightning, he raised her in his arms and placed her in a chair. Valentine opened her eyes.

"Comfort yourself, dear grandpapa," said she, endeavoring to smile; "it is nothing—I was giddy, that is all."——"Another giddiness!" said Morrel, clasping his hands. "Oh, attend to it, Valentine, I entreat you." ——"But no," said Valentine,—"no, I tell you it is all past, and it was nothing. Oh! you are too timid for an officer, for a soldier who, they say, never knows fear. Ah!" She burst into a forced and melancholy laugh, her arms stiffened and twisted, her head fell back on her chair, and she remained motionless. The cry of terror which was stopped on Noirtier's lips, seemed to start from his eyes. Morrel understood it; he knew he must call assistance. The young man rang the bell violently; the housemaid, and the servant who had replaced Barrois, ran in at the same moment. Valentine was so pale, so cold, so inanimate, that, without listening to what was said to them, they were seized with the fear which pervaded that house, and they flew into the passage crying for help. Mdme. Danglars and Eugénie were going out at that moment; they heard the cause of the disturbance.

"I told you so!" cried Madame de Villefort. "Poor child!"

At the same moment M. de Villefort's voice was heard calling from his cabinet. "What is the matter?" Morrel consulted Noirtier's look, who had recovered his self-command, and with a glance indicated the closet where, once before, under somewhat similar circumstances, he had taken refuge. He had only time to get his hat, and throw himself breathless into the closet; the master's footstep was heard in the passage. Villefort sprang into the room, ran to Valentine, and took her in his arms. "A physician! a physician! M. d'Avrigny!" cried Villefort; "or rather I will go for him myself." He flew from the apartment, and Morrel, at the same moment, darted out at the other door. At the same time Monte-Cristo's voice seemed to resound in his ear, who had said, only two hours before, "Whatever you want, Morrel, come to me; I have some power."

Meanwhile M. de Villefort arrived in a hired cab at M. d'Avrigny's door. He rang so violently that the porter came alarmed. Villefort ran up-stairs without saying a word. The porter knew him, and let him pass, only calling to him, "In his cabinet." Villefort pushed, or rather forced, the door open. "Ah!" said the doctor, "have you another invalid?"

"Yes, doctor," cried Villefort, seizing, with a convulsive grasp, a handful of hair, "it is Valentine's turn!"

"Your daughter!" cried D'Avrigny, with grief and surprise.

"You see you were deceived," murmured the magistrate; "come and see her, and on her bed of agony entreat her pardon for having suspected her."

"Each time you have applied to me," said the doctor, "it has been too late: still I will go. But let us make haste, sir; with the enemies you have to do with there is no time to be lost."

"Oh! this time, doctor, you shall not have to reproach me with weakness. This time I will know the assassin, and will pursue him."

"Let us try first to save the victim before we think of revenging her," said D'Avrigny. "Come." The same cab which had brought Villefort took them back at full speed, at the same moment when Morrel rapped at Monte-Cristo's door. The count was reading, with an angry look, something which Bertuccio had brought in haste. Hearing Morrel announced, the count raised his head. He, as well as the count, had evidently been much tried during those two hours, for he had left him smiling, and returned with a disturbed air. The count rose, and sprang to meet him. "What is the matter, Maximilian?" asked he.

"I have just left a house where death has just entered, to run to you."
——"From M. de Morcerf's?" asked Monte-Cristo.

"No," said Morrel; "is some one dead in his house?"

"The general has just blown his brains out," replied Monte-Cristo, with great coolness.

"Oh! what a dreadful event!" cried Maximilian.

"Not for the countess, nor for Albert," said Monte-Cristo; "a dead father or husband is better than a dishonored one: blood washes out shame."

"Poor countess!" said Maximilian, "I pity her very much; she is so noble a woman."

"Pity Albert also, Maximilian; for, believe me, he is the worthy son of the countess. But let us return to yourself: you have hastened to me; can I have the happiness of being useful to you?"

"Yes, I need your help; that is, I thought, like a madman, you could lend me your assistance in a case where God alone can succor me."

"Tell me what it is," replied Monte-Cristo.

"One evening I was in a garden; a clump of trees concealed me; no one suspected I was there. Two persons passed near me—allow me to conceal their names for the present; they were speaking in an under-tone, and yet I was so interested in what they said, that I did not lose a single word."

"This is a gloomy introduction, if I may judge from your paleness and shuddering, Morrel."

"Oh! yes, very gloomy, my friend! Some one had just died in the house to which that garden belonged. One of those persons whose conversation I overheard was the master of the house, the other, the physician. The former was confiding to the latter his grief and fear; for it was the second time within a month that death had entered suddenly and unexpectedly that house, apparently destined to destruction by some exterminating angel, as an object of God's anger. "And what did the doctor answer?" asked Monte-Cristo.

"He replied—he replied, that the death was not a natural one, and must be attributed to poison."

"Indeed!" said Monte-Cristo, with a slight cough, which, in moments of extreme emotion, helped him to disguise a blush, or his paleness, or the intense interest with which he listened: "indeed, Maximilian, did you hear that?"——"Yes, my dear Count, I heard it; and the doctor added, that if another death occurred in a similar way, he must appeal to justice." Monte-Cristo listened, or appeared to do so, with the greatest calmness. "Well!" said Maximilian, "death came a third time, and neither the master of the house nor the doctor said a word. Death is now, perhaps, striking a fourth blow. Count, what am I bound to do, being in possession of this secret?"

"My dear friend," said Monte-Cristo, "you appear to be relating an adventure which we all know by heart. I know the house where you heard it, or one very similar to it. You were walking one evening in M. de Villefort's garden: from what you relate, I suppose it to have been the evening of Mdme. de Saint-Méran's death. You heard M. de Villefort talking to M. d'Avrigny about the death of M. de Saint-Méran, and that, no less surprising, of the countess. M. d'Avrigny said he believed they both proceeded from poison; and you, honest man, have ever since been asking your heart, and sounding your conscience, to know if you ought to expose or conceal this secret. It is a family of Atrides; God has condemned them, and they must submit to their punishment. They will all disappear like the fabrics children build with cards, and which fall, one by one, under the breath of their builder, even if there are two hundred of them. Three months since, it was M. de Saint-Méran; Mdme. de Saint-Méran two months since; the other day it was Barrois: to-day, old Noirtier, or young Valentine."

"You knew it?" cried Morrel, in such a paroxysm of terror that Monte-Cristo started; he whom the falling heavens would have found unmoved; "you knew it, and said nothing?"

"And what is it to me?" replied Monte-Cristo, shrugging his shoulders: "do I know those people? and must I lose the one to save the other? Faith, no, for between the culprit and the victim I have no choice."

"But I," cried Morrel, groaning with sorrow,—"I love her!"

"You love?—whom?" cried Monte-Cristo, starting on his feet, and seizing the two hands which Morrel was raising towards heaven.

"Valentine de Villefort, who is being murdered at this moment! Do you understand me? I love her; and I ask God and you how I can save her?"

Monte-Cristo uttered a cry which those only can conceive who have heard the roar of a wounded lion. "Unhappy man!" cried he, wringing his hands in his turn; "you love Valentine!—that daughter of an accursed race!" Never had Morrel witnessed such an expression—never had so terrible an eye flashed before his face—never had the genius of terror he had so often seen, either on the battle-field or in the murderous nights of Algeria, shaken around him more dreadful fire. He drew back terrified.

As for Monte-Cristo, after this ebullition, he closed his eyes, as if dazzled by internal light. In a moment he restrained himself so powerfully that the tempestuous heaving of his breast subsided, as turbulent and foaming waves yield to the sun's genial influence when the cloud has passed. This silence, self-control, and struggle lasted about twenty seconds, then the count raised his pallid face.

"I tell you to hope. Do you understand me?" cried Monte-Cristo. "Remember that I never uttered a falsehood and am never deceived. It is twelve o'clock, Maximilian: thank heaven that you came at noon rather than in the evening, or to-morrow morning. Listen, Morrel!—it is noon; if Valentine is not now dead, she will not die."

"Oh! Count, you overwhelm me with that coolness. Have you, then, power against death?—Are you superhuman?—Are you an angel?" And the young man, who had never shrunk from danger, shrank before Monte-Cristo with indescribable terror. But Monte-Cristo looked at him with so melancholy and sweet a smile, that Maximilian felt the tears filling his eyes.

"I can do much for you, my friend," replied the count. "Go; I must be alone." Morrel, subdued by the extraordinary ascendency Monte-Cristo exercised over everything around him, did not endeavor to resist it. He pressed the count's hand, and left.

Meanwhile, Villefort and D'Avrigny had made all possible haste, Valentine had not revived from her fainting fit on their arrival, and the doctor examined the invalid with all the care the circumstances demanded, and with an interest which the knowledge of the secret doubled. Villefort, closely watching his countenance and his lips, waited the result of the examination. Noirtier, paler than even the girl, more eager than Villefort for the decision, was watching also intently and affectionately. At last D'Avrigny slowly uttered these words:—"She is still alive!"

They carried Valentine away to her own rooms; she had revived, but could scarcely move or speak, so shaken was her frame by the attack. She had, however, just power to give her grandfather one parting look; who, in losing her, seemed to be resigning his very soul; D'Avrigny followed the invalid, wrote a prescription, ordered Villefort to take a cab, go in person to a chemist's to get the prescribed medicine, bring it himself, and wait for him in his daughter's room. Then, having renewed his injunction not to give Valentine anything, he went down again to Noirtier, shut the doors carefully, and after convincing himself no one was listening, said, "Do you know anything of this young lady's illness?"

"Yes," said the old man.

"We have no time to lose; I will question, and do you answer me." Noirtier made a sign that he was ready to answer. "Did you see poor

Barrois die?" Noirtier raised his eyes to heaven. "Do you know of what he died?" asked D'Avrigny, placing his hand on Noirtier's shoulder.——"Yes," replied the old man.——"Do you think he died a natural death?" A sort of smile was discernible on the motionless lips.

"Then you have thought Barrois was poisoned?"——"Yes."

"Do you think the poison he fell a victim to was intended for him?"

"No."——"Do you think the same hand which unintentionally struck Barrois has now attacked Valentine?"——"Yes."

"Then will she die, too?" asked D'Avrigny, fixing his penetrating gaze on Noirtier. He watched the effect of this question on the old man. "No!" replied he, with an air of triumph which would have puzzled the most clever diviner. "Then you hope?" said D'Avrigny, with surprise,—— "Yes."

"What do you hope? that the assassin will be tried?"——"No."—— "Then you hope the poison will take no effect on Valentine?"——"Yes."

"It is no news to you," added D'Avrigny, "to tell you an attempt has been made to poison her?" The old man made a sign that he entertained no doubt upon the subject. "Then how do you hope Valentine will escape?" Noirtier kept his eyes steadily fixed upon the same spot. D'Avrigny followed the direction, and saw they were fixed on a bottle containing the mixture which he took every morning. "Ah! ah!" said D'Avrigny, struck with a sudden thought, "has it occurred to you to prepare her system to resist poison?—And you have succeeded!" exclaimed D'Avrigny. "Without that precaution Valentine would have died before assistance could have been procured. The dose has been excessive, but she has only been shaken by it; and this time, at any rate, Valentine will not die." A superhuman joy expanded the old man's eyes, which were raised toward heaven with an expression of infinite gratitude. At this moment Villefort returned. "Here, doctor," said he, "is what you sent me for."

"Was this prepared in your presence?"

"Yes," replied the lawyer.

"Have you not let it go out of your hands?"——"No." D'Avrigny took the bottle, poured some drops of the mixture it contained in the hollow of his hand, and swallowed them. "Well," said he, "let us go to Valentine; I will give instructions to every one, and you, M. de Villefort, will yourself see that no one deviates from them."

At the moment when D'Avrigny was returning to Valentine's room, accompanied by Villefort, an Italian priest, of serious demeanor and calm and firm tone, hired for his use the house adjoining the hotel of M. de Villefort. No one knew why the three former tenants of that house left it. About two hours afterwards its foundation was reported to be unsafe; but the report did not prevent the new occupant establishing himself there with his modest furniture the same day at five o'clock. The lease was drawn up for three, six, or nine years by the new tenant, who, according to the rule of the proprietor, paid six months in advance. This new tenant was called Signor Giacomo Busoni. Workmen were immediately called in, and the same night the passers-by saw with surprise carpenters and masons occupied in repairing the lower part of the tottering house.

CHAPTER LX.

THE MARRIAGE CONTRACT.

TOWARD five o'clock in the afternoon of the day fixed for the signing of the contract between Mdlle. Danglars and Andrea Cavalcanti, as a fresh breeze shook the leaves in the little garden situated in front of the Count of Monte-Cristo's house, and the latter was preparing to go out while his horses were impatiently stamping the ground, held in by the coachman, who had been seated a quarter of an hour on his box, the elegant phaeton with which we are familiar, rapidly turned the angle of the entrance-gate, and threw, rather than set down, on the steps of the door, M. Andrea Cavalcanti, as much decked and as gay as if he, on his side, was going to marry a princess. He inquired after the count with his usual familiarity, and, bounding lightly to the first story, met him on the top of the stairs. The count stopped on seeing the young man. As for Andrea, he was launched, and when once launched nothing stopped him. "Ah! good morning, my dear Count," said he. "Ah, M. Andrea!" said the latter, with his half-jesting tone; "how do you do."

"Charmingly, as you see. I am come to talk to you about a thousand things."

The count returned to a small drawing-room on the first floor, sat down, and, crossing his legs, motioned to the young man to take a seat also. Andrea assumed his gayest manner. "You know, my dear Count," said he, "the ceremony is to take place this evening. At nine o'clock the contract is to be signed at my father-in-law's."——"Ah! indeed?" said Monte-Cristo, "you are fortunate, M. Cavalcanti! it is a most suitable alliance you are contracting, and Mdlle. Danglars is a pretty girl."

"Yes, indeed she is," replied Cavalcanti, with a very modest tone.

"Above all, she is very rich,—at least, I believe so," said Monte-Cristo: "it is said M. Danglars conceals at least half of his fortune."

"And he acknowledges fifteen or twenty millions," said Andrea, with a look sparkling with joy.

"Without reckoning," added Monte-Cristo, "that he is on the eve of entering into a railroad speculation by which it is generally believed he will gain ten millions."

"Ten millions! Do you think so? It is magnificent!" said Cavalcanti, quite confounded at the metallic sound.

"Without reckoning," replied Monte-Cristo, "that all his fortune will come to you, and justly too, since Mdlle. Danglars is an only daughter. Besides, your own fortune, as your father assured me, is almost equal to that of your betrothed. But, enough of money matters. Do you know, M. Andrea, I think you have managed this affair rather skilfully?"

"Not badly, by any means," said the young man; "I was born for a diplomatist. But I must not forget one grand point."——"Which?"

"That I have been singularly assisted by your lordship."

"By me? Not at all, Prince," said Monte-Cristo, laying a marked stress on the title; "what have I done for you? Are not your name, social position, and merit sufficient?"

"No," said Andrea,—"no; it is useless for you to say so, Count. I maintain that the position of a man like you has done more than my name, my social position, and my merit."

"You are completely mistaken, sir," said Monte-Cristo, coldly, who felt the perfidious manœuvre of the young man, and understood the bearing of his words; "you only acquired my protection after the influence and fortune of your father had been ascertained; "for, after all, who procured for me, who had never seen either you or your illustrious father, the pleasure of your acquaintance?—Two of my good friends, Lord Wilmore and Abbé Busoni. What encouraged me not to become your surety, but to patronize you?—It was your father's name so well known in Italy and so highly honored. Personally, I do not know you." This calm and perfect ease made Andrea feel he was, for the moment, restrained by a stronger hand than his own, and that the restraint could not be easily broken through.

"Oh! then my father has really a very large fortune, Count?"

"It appears so, sir," replied Monte-Cristo.

"Then, I come to ask a favor of you."——"Of me!"

"To take my father's part."

"Ah! my dear sir! What! after the numerous relations I have had the happiness to sustain toward you, you know me so little as to ask such a thing! Ask me to lend you half a million, and, although such a loan is somewhat rare, on my honor you would annoy me less! Know, then, what I thought I had already told you, that, in the moral participation particularly with this world's affairs, the Count of Monte-Cristo has never ceased to entertain the scruples and even the superstitions of the East. I, who keep a seraglio at Cairo, at Smyrna, and at Constantinople, preside at a wedding?—never!"——

"But what must be done?" said Andrea, disappointed.

"You said just now, you had a hundred friends."

"Agreed; but you introduced me at M. Danglars'."

"Not at all! let us recall the exact facts. You met him at a dinner party at my house, and you introduced yourself at his house; that is a totally different affair."

"But, at least you will be there?"

"Will all Paris be there?"

"Oh, certainly."

"Well, like all Paris, I shall be there too," said the count.

"And will you sign the contract?"

"I see no objection to that; my scruples do not go thus far."

"Well, since you will grant me no more, I must be content with what you give me.—All is well, excepting your refusal, which quite grieves me."

"You must attribute it only to natural scruples under similar circumstances."

"Well," said Andrea, "let it be as you wish: this evening, then, at nine o'clock."——"Adieu till then." Notwithstanding a slight resistance on the part of Monte-Cristo, whose lips turned pale, but who preserved his ceremonious smile, Andrea seized the count's hand, pressed it, and disappeared.

At half-past eight in the evening, Danglars' rooms were filled with a perfumed crowd, who sympathized but little, but participated in that love of being present wherever there is anything fresh to be seen, which attracts inconstant butterflies, famished bees, and buzzing drones.

Mdlle. Eugénie was dressed with elegant simplicity. Her eyes, however, betrayed that perfect confidence which contradicted the girlish simplicity of attire. The crowd moved to and fro in those rooms like an ebb and flow of turquoises, rubies, emeralds, opals, and diamonds. As usual, the oldest women were the most decorated, and the ugliest the most conspicuous.

At the moment when the hand of the massive time-piece pointed to nine on its golden face, and the hammer struck nine times, the name of Monte-Cristo resounded in its turn, and, as if by an electric shock, all the assembly turned toward the door. The count was dressed in black, and with his habitual simplicity. His only jewelry was a chain, so fine that the slender thread was scarcely perceptible on his white waistcoat. A circle was formed immediately round the door. The count perceived at one glance Mdme. Danglars at one end of the drawing-room, M. Danglars at the other, and Eugénie in front of him. He first advanced toward the baroness, who was chatting with Mdme. de Villefort, who had come alone, Valentine being still an invalid; and without turning aside, so clear was the road left for him, he passed from the baroness to Eugénie, whom he complimented in such rapid and measured terms, that the proud artist was quite struck. Near her was Louise d'Armilly, who thanked the count for the letters he had so kindly given her for Italy, of which she intended immediately to make use. On leaving these ladies he found himself with Danglars, who had advanced to meet him.

Having accomplished these three social duties, Monte-Cristo stopped, looking around him with that expression peculiar to a certain class, which seems to say, "I have done my duty, now let others do theirs." The lawyers arrived at this moment, and arranged their papers on the velvet cloth embroidered with gold which covered the table prepared for the signature. One of the notaries sat down, the other remained standing. They were about to proceed to the reading of the contract, which half Paris assembled was to sign.

The contract was read during a profound silence. But as soon as it was finished, the buzz was redoubled through all the drawing-rooms; the brilliant sums, the rolling millions which were to be at the command of the affianced, and which crowned the display which had been made in a room entirely appropriated for the purpose of the wedding presents and the young lady's diamonds, had resounded with all their delusion on the jealous assembly.

The baron was to sign first; then the representative of M. Cavalcanti, senior; then the baroness; afterwards the future couple, as they are styled on the ceremonious stamped papers. The baron took the pen and signed, then the representative. The baroness approached, leaning on Mdme. de Villefort's arm. "My dear," said she, as she took the pen, "is it not vexatious? An unexpected incident, in the affair of murder and theft at the Count of Monte-Cristo's, in which he nearly fell a victim, deprives us of the pleasure of seeing M. de Villefort."

"Indeed," said M. Danglars, in the same tone in which he would have said, "Faith, I care very little about it!"

"Indeed," said Monte-Cristo, approaching, "I am much afraid I am the involuntary cause of that absence. You remember," continued the count, during the most profound silence, "that the unhappy wretch who came to rob me, died at my house; it was supposed he was stabbed by his accomplice, on attempting to leave it."

"Yes," said Danglars.

"In order to examine his wounds, he was undressed, and his clothes were thrown into a corner, where officers of justice picked them up, with the exception of the waistcoat, which they overlooked." Andrea turned pale, and drew towards the door; he saw a cloud rising on the horizon, which appeared to forebode a coming storm.

"Well! this waistcoat was discovered to-day, covered with blood, and with a hole over the heart." The ladies screamed, and two or three prepared to faint. "It was brought to me. No one could guess what the dirty rag could be; I alone supposed it was the waistcoat of the victim. My valet, in examining this mournful relic, felt a paper in the pocket and drew it out; it was a letter addressed to you, baron."

"To me!" cried Danglars.

"But," asked Mdme. Danglars, looking at her husband with uneasiness, "how could that prevent M. de Villefort——"

"In this simple way, madame," replied Monte-Cristo; "the waistcoat and the letter were both, what is termed, convictive evidence: I therefore sent it all to the royal prosecutor. You understand, my dear baron, legal proceedings are the safest in criminal cases; it was, perhaps, some plot against you." Andrea looked steadily at Monte-Cristo, and disappeared in the second drawing-room.

"Possibly," said Danglars; "this murdered man was an old galley-slave?"

"Yes," replied the count; "a felon named Caderousse." Danglars turned slightly pale, Andrea reached the ante-room beyond the little drawing-room.

"But go on signing," said Monte-Cristo; "I perceive my story has caused a general emotion, and I beg to apologize to you, baroness, and to Mdlle. Danglars."

The baroness, who had signed, returned the pen to the notary. "Prince Cavalcanti!" said the latter; "Prince Cavalcanti, where are you?"—— "Andrea! Andrea!" repeated several young people, who were already on sufficiently intimate terms with him to call him by his Christian name. ——"Call the prince! inform him it is his turn to sign!" cried Danglars to one of the door-keepers.

But at the same instant the crowd of guests rushed, terrified, into the principal salon, as if some frightful monster had entered the apartments. There was, indeed, reason to retreat. An officer was placing two soldiers at the door of each drawing-room, and was advancing toward Danglars, preceded by a police justice girded with his scarf. Mdme. Danglars uttered a scream and fainted. Danglars, who thought himself threatened (certain consciences are never calm),—Danglars appeared before his guests with a terrified countenance.

"Which of you gentlemen," asked the magistrate, "answers to the name of Andrea Cavalcanti?" A cry of stupor was heard from all parts of the room. They searched; they questioned. "But who then is Andrea Cavalcanti?" asked Danglars, in amazement.

"A galley-slave, escaped from confinement at Toulon."

"And what crime has he committed?"

"He is accused," said the commissary, with his inflexible voice, "of having assassinated a man named Caderousse, his former companion in prison, at the moment he was making his escape from the house of the Count of Monte-Cristo." Monte-Cristo cast a rapid glance around him. Andrea was gone.

CHAPTER LXI

JUDICIAL STERNNESS.

WE will leave the banker contemplating the enormous columns of his debt before the phantom of bankruptcy, and follow the baroness, who, after remaining for a moment as if crushed under the weight of the blow which had struck her, had gone to seek her usual adviser, Lucien Debray. The baroness had looked forward to this marriage as a means of ridding herself of a guardianship which, over a girl of Eugénie's character, could not fail to be rather a troublesome undertaking. She very much regretted that the marriage of Eugénie had not taken place, not only because the match was good, and likely to ensure the happiness of her child, but because it would also set her at liberty. She ran therefore to Debray's, but he was absent and tired of waiting she returned home. The baroness ran lightly up-stairs, and with an aching heart entered her apartment, contiguous to Eugénie's. She was fearful of exciting any remark, and listened at Eugénie's door, then, hearing no sound, she tried to enter, but the bolts were drawn. Mdme. Danglars fancied that, fatigued with the terrible excitement of the evening, she had retired to her bed and slept. She called her lady's maid and questioned her.

"Mdlle. Eugénie," she said, "retired to her apartment with Mdlle. d'Armilly; they took tea together, after which they desired me to leave, saying they required me no longer." Since then the lady's maid had been below, and, like every one else, she thought the young ladies were in their own room; Mdme. Danglars, therefore, went to bed, and began to muse over the past events. In proportion as her ideas became clearer, so did occurrences at the scene of the contract increase in magnitude; it no longer appeared mere confusion; it was a tumult; it was no longer something distressing, but disgraceful.

How could she extricate herself from this labyrinth? To whom would she apply to help her out of this painful situation? Debray, to whom she had run, with the first instinct of a woman toward the man she loves, and who yet betrays her,—Debray could but give her advice; she must apply to some one more powerful than he. The baroness then thought of M. de Villefort. It was M. de Villefort who had caused Cavalcanti to be arrested; it was M. de Villefort who had remorselessly brought misfortune into her family, as though they had been strangers. The inflexibility of the prosecutor should stop there; she would see him the next day, and if she could not make him fail in his duties as a magistrate, she would, at least, obtain all the indulgence he could allow.

At nine o'clock next morning she rose, and without ringing for her maid, or giving the least sign of her existence, she dressed herself in the same simple style as on the previous night; then running down-stairs, she called a hack and drove to Villefort's house. For the last month this wretched house had presented the gloomy appearance of a lazaretto infected with the plague. Mdme. Danglars involuntarily shuddered at the aspect; she approached the door with trembling knees, and rang the bell. Three times did the bell ring with a dull, heavy sound, seeming to participate in general sadness, before the janitor appeared and peeped through the door, which he opened just wide enough to allow his words to be heard. He saw a lady, a fashionable, elegantly-dressed lady, and yet the door remained on the chain.

"Do you intend opening the door?" said the baroness.

"First, madame, who are you?"

"The Baroness Danglars: you have seen me twenty times."

"Possibly, madame. And now, what do you want!"

"Oh, how extraordinary! I shall complain to M. de Villefort of the impertinence of his servants."

"Madame, this is precaution, not impertinence; no one enters here without an order from Dr. d'Avrigny, or without speaking to my master.".

"Well! my business is with him."

"Is it pressing business?"

"You can imagine so, since I have not even used my carriage. But enough of this; here is my card; take it to your master."

The concierge closed the door, leaving Mdme. Danglars on the street. She had not long to wait; directly afterward the door was opened wide enough to admit her, and when she had passed through, it was again shut. Without losing sight of her for an instant, the man took a whistle from his pocket as soon as they entered the court, and sounded it. The footman appeared on the door-steps. "You will excuse this poor fellow, madame," he said, as he preceded the baroness; "but his orders are precise, and M. de Villefort begged me to tell you he could not act otherwise than he had done."

The baroness began by complaining. But Villefort, raising his head, bowed down by grief, looked up at her with so sad a smile that her complaints died upon her lips. "Forgive my servants," he said, "for a terror I cannot blame them for; from being suspected they have become suspicious."

Mdme. Danglars had often heard of the terror to which the magistrate alluded, but without the evidence of her own eyesight she could never have believed the sentiment had been carried so far. "You too, then, are unhappy?" she said. "Yes, madame," replied the magistrate.

"Then you pity me!"——"Sincerely, madame."——"And you understand what brings me here?"——"You wish to speak to me about the circumstance which has just happened?"——"Yes, sir, a fearful misfortune."——"When I hear misfortunes named, madame," he said, "I have within the last few months contracted the bad habit of thinking of my own, and then I cannot help drawing up an egotistical parallel in my mind. This is the reason that by the side of my misfortunes yours appear to me mere mischances; this is why my dreadful position makes yours appear enviable. But this annoys you; let us change the subject. You were saying, madame——"

"I came to ask you, my friend," said the baroness, "what will be done with this impostor?"

"Impostor!" repeated Villefort; certainly, madame, you appear to extenuate some cases, and exaggerate others. Impostor, indeed! M. Andrea Cavalcanti, or rather M. Benedetto, is nothing more or less than an assassin!"

"Sir, I do not deny the justice of your correction; but the more severely you arm yourself against that unfortunate, the more deeply will you strike our family. Come, forget him for a moment, and, instead of pursuing him, let him fly."

"You are too late, madame; the warrant is out."

"Well, should he be arrested—do you think they will arrest him?"

"I hope so."

"If they should arrest him (I know that sometimes prisons afford means of escape), will you leave him in prison?"——The other shook his head. "At least keep him there till my daughter be married."

"Impossible, madame; justice has its formalities."

"What! even for me?" said the baroness, half jesting, half in earnest. "For all, even for myself among the rest," replied Villefort.

"Ah!" exclaimed the baroness, without expressing the ideas which the exclamation betrayed. Villefort looked at her with that piercing glance which read the secrets of the heart. "Yes, I know what you mean," he said; "I will answer you." Villefort drew his arm-chair nearer to Mdme. Danglars; then, resting both hands upon his desk, he said, in a voice more hollow than usual:

"There are crimes which remain unpunished because the criminals are unknown, and we might strike the innocent instead of the guilty; but when the culprits are discovered (Villefort here extended his hand toward a large crucifix placed opposite to his desk)—I swear to you, by all I hold most sacred, that, whoever they may be, they shall die! Now, after the oath I have just taken, and which I will keep, madame, dare you ask for mercy for that wretch, escaped convict, then an assassin?"

"And who is this wretch?"——"His parents are unknown."

"But who was the man who brought him from Lucca?"

"Another rascal like himself, perhaps his accomplice."

The baroness clasped her hands. "Villefort!" she exclaimed, in her softest and most captivating manner, "this young man, though a murderer, is an orphan, abandoned by everybody."

"So much the worse, or rather, so much the better; it has been so ordained that he may have none to weep his fate."

"His dishonor reflects upon us."

"Is not death in my house?"

"Oh, sir," exclaimed the baroness, "you are without pity for others! Well, then, I tell you they will have no mercy on you!"

"Be it so!" said Villefort, raising his arms to heaven.

"But, sir, he has fled; let him escape—inaction is a pardonable offence."

"I tell you it is too late; early this morning the telegraph was employed, and at this very minute——"

"Sir," said the valet-de-chambre, entering the room, "a dragoon has brought this despatch from the Interior." Villefort seized the letter, and hastily unsealed it. Mdme. Danglars trembled with fear; Villefort started with joy. "Arrested!" he exclaimed; "he was taken at Compiègne, and all is over." Mdme. Danglars rose from her seat, pale and cold. "Adieu, sir!" she said.

"Adieu, madame!" replied the lawyer, as in an almost joyful manner he conducted her to the door. Then, turning to his desk, he said, striking the letter with his right hand, "Come, I had a forgery, three robberies, and two incendiaries; I only wanted a murder, and here it is. It will be a splendid session!"

In receiving the news of Andrea's capture, the whole was not in Villefort's hands.

The Italian adventurer had succeeded in reaching Compiègne, but he was badly hampered for lack of a passport, indispensable in those times. He stayed at the first hotel, pretending that he had put up there before.

He had refreshed his toilet, and moderated its festal appearance and seemed a gentleman on his excursions after a pretty girl outside of the capital.

He purposed disguising himself meanly on the morrow and traveling by night by side-paths to the frontier.

The sun awakened him at seven. He went to the window and was horrified to see that the hotel was surrounded by the rural constabulary. He jumped to the conclusion that they were after him. The worlar-arm telegraph had indeed been employed to notify the authorities in all directions of the flight of the murderer of Caderousse.

Benedetto was a lad of resources and he did not delay in fastening his door and climbing up the chimney. But the roof, he feared, would soon be searched, and he considered it wise to slip down another flue and reach thereby some room where he might exit unnoticed.

Two-thirds down, however, his foot slipped and down he slid upon a hearth. This fall was almost noiseless, and would not have mattered perhaps if the room had been unoccupied.

As bad luck would happen, the bed was tenanted by two young women, who sprang up in bed as the soot-befouled young man rolled into the apartment.

Mutual recognition was in the glances exchanged between the three equally surprised persons, Mdlle. Danglars, Mdlle. Armilly and Andrea.

Eugénie had fled in masculine attire with her inseparable friend. With a large sum in cash and jewels, they were making their way to the frontier, for refuge in some land where they could go upon the musical stage.

The first emotion over, they begged the assassin to return as he had come; but already the excitement had spread through the house, and a maid, previously piqued by the aspect of the girl in the gentleman's apparel, had applied her eye to the keyhole and seen the begrimed young man in the ladies' room.

It was no excuse that he would have been the husband of the banker's daughter: he had to yield and the delighted police captain hurried to send the telegram to the royal prosecutor, as stated.

Danglar's daughter and her companion proceeded in the opposite direction, to Brussels.

CHAPTER LXII.

THE SPIRIT OF DEATH.

VALENTINE had not yet recovered. Bowed down with fatigue, she was indeed confined to her bed, and it was in her own room, and from the lips of Mdme. de Villefort, that she heard of all the strange events we have related. But Valentine was so weak that this recital scarcely produced the same effect it would have done had she been in her usual health. During the daytime Valentine's perceptions remained tolerably clear, owing to the constant presence of M. Noirtier, who ordered himself to be carried to his granddaughter's room, and watched her with his paternal tenderness; Villefort also, on his return from the courts, frequently passed an hour or two with his father and child. At six o'clock Villefort retired to his study, at eight M. d'Avrigny arrived himself, bringing the night draught prepared for the girl, and then M. Noirtier was carried away. A nurse of the doctor's choice succeeded them, and never left till about ten or eleven o'clock, when Valentine was asleep. As she went down-stairs she gave the keys of Valentine's room to M. Villefort, so that no one could reach the sick-room excepting through Mdme. de Villefort's. Every morning Morrel called on Noirtier to receive news of Valentine, and, extraordinary as it seemed, each day found him less uneasy.

Eleven o'clock had struck. Ten minutes had elapsed since the nurse left. The night-lamp threw out countless rays, each resolving itself into some strange form to her disordered imagination, when suddenly, by its flickering light, Valentine thought she saw the door of her library, in the recess by the chimney, open slowly, though she in vain listened for the sound of the hinges on which it turned. At any other time Valentine would have seized the bell-pull, and summoned assistance, but nothing astonished her in her present situation. Behind the door a human figure appeared; but she was too familiar with such apparitions to be alarmed, and therefore only stared, hoping to recognize Morrel. The figure advanced toward the bed, and appeared to listen with profound attention. At this moment a ray of light glanced across the face of the midnight visitor.

"It is not he!" she murmured, and waited, in the assurance of its being but a dream, for the man to disappear or assume some other form. Still, she felt her pulse, and, finding it throb violently, she remembered that the best method of dispelling such illusions was to drink, for a draught of the beverage prepared by the doctor to allay her fever seemed to cause a reaction of the brain, and for a short time she suffered less. Valentine therefore reached toward the glass, but as soon as her trembling arm left the bed the ghost advanced more quickly toward her, and approached the young girl so closely that she fancied she heard his breath, and felt the pressure of his hand. This time the illusion, or rather the reality, surpassed anything Valentine had before experienced; she began to believe herself really alive and awake, and the belief that her reason was this time not deceived made her shudder. The pressure she felt was evidently to arrest her arm, and she slowly withdrew it. Then the figure, from whom she could not detach her eyes, and who appeared more protecting than menacing, took the glass, and, walking toward the night-light, held it up, as if to test its transparency. This did not seem sufficient; the phantom—for he trod so softly that no sound was heard—then poured out about a spoonful into the glass, and drank it. Valentine witnessed this scene with a sentiment of stupefaction. Every minute she had expected that it would vanish and give place to another vision; but the man, instead of dissolving like a shadow, again approached her, and said in an agitated voice, "Now you may drink."

Valentine shuddered. It was the first time one of these visions had ever addressed her in a living voice, and she was about to utter an exclamation. The man placed his finger on her lips. "The Count of Monte-Cristo!" she murmured.

It was easy to see that no doubt now remained in the girl's mind as to the reality of the scene; her eyes started with terror, her hands trembled, and she rapidly drew the bed clothes closer to her. Still, the presence of Monte-Cristo at such an hour, his mysterious, fanciful, and extraordinary entrance into her room, through the wall, might well seem impossibilities to her shattered reason. "Do not call any one—do not be alarmed," said the count; "do not let a shade of suspicion or uneasiness remain in your breast; the man standing before you, Valentine (for this time it is no phantom), is nothing more than the tenderest father and the most respectful friend you could dream of."

Valentine could not reply.

"Listen to me," he said, "or, rather, look upon me; look at my face, paler even than usual, and my eyes, red with weariness—for four days I have not closed them, for I have been constantly watching you, to protect and preserve you for Maximilian." The blood mounted rapidly to the cheeks of Valentine, for the name just pronounced by the count dispelled all the fear, with which his presence had inspired her. "Maximilian!" she exclaimed, and so sweet did the sound appear to her, that she repeated it—"Maximilian! has he then told all to you?"

"Everything. He told me your life was his, and I have promised him you shall live."

"Are you a doctor?"

"Yes, the best you could have at the present time, believe me."

"But you say you have watched," said Valentine, with an indignant expression of pride and modest fear : "Sir, I think you have been guilty of an unparralleled intrusion, and that which you call protection is more resembling an insult."

"Valentine," he answered, "during my long watch over you, all I have observed has been what people visited you, what nourishment was prepared, and what beverage was served ; then, when the latter appeared dangerous to me, I entered, as I have now done, and substituted, in the place of the poison, a healthy draught ; which, instead of producing the death intended, caused life to circulate in your veins."

"Poison ! Death !" exclaimed Valentine, half believing herself under the influence of some feverish hallucination ; "what are you saying, sir?"

——"Hush ! my child," said Monte-Cristo, again laying his finger upon her lips ; "I did say poison and death. But drink some of this ;" and the count took a bottle from his pocket, containing a red liquid, of which he poured a few drops into the glass. "Drink this, and then take nothing more to-night." Valentine stretched out her hand ; but scarcely had she touched the glass when she drew it back in fear. Monte-Cristo took the glass, and drank half its contents, and then presented it to Valentine, who smiled, and swallowed the rest. "Oh! yes," she exclaimed, "I recognize the flavor of my nocturnal beverage which refreshed me so much, and seemed to ease my aching brain. Thank you, sir, thank you!"

"This is how you have lived during the last four nights, Valentine," said the count. "But, oh! how I passed that time ! Oh! the wretched hours I have endured! the torture to which I have submitted when I saw the deadly poison poured into your glass, and how I trembled lest you would drink it before I could find time to pour it out!"

"Sir," said Valentine, at the height of her terror, "you say you endured tortures when you saw the deadly poison poured into my glass ; but if you saw this you must also have seen the person who poured it?"

"Yes."

"What you tell me is horrible, sir. What? attempt to murder me in my father's house—in my room—on my bed of sickness? Oh! leave me, sir ; you are tempting me ; you make me doubt the goodness of Providence ; it is impossible, it cannot be !"

"Are you the first that this hand has stricken? Have you not seen M. de Saint-Méran, Mdme. de Saint-Méran, Barrois, all fall? Would not M. Noirtier also have fallen a victim, had not the treatment he has been pursuing for the last three years neutralized the effects of the poison?"

"Oh, heaven!" said Valentine ; "is this the reason why grandpapa has made me share all his beverages during the last month?"

"Your grandfather knows, then, that a poisoner lives here ; perhaps, he even suspects the person. He has been fortifying you, his beloved

poured into the glass, and which Valentine had drunk; it was indeed the poison, which could not deceive M. d'Avrigny, now examining it so closely: it was doubtless a miracle from heaven, that, notwithstanding her precautions, there should be trace or proof remaining to denounce the crime. While Mdme. de Villefort remained rooted to the spot like a statue of terror, and Villefort, with his head hidden in the bed clothes, saw nothing around him, D'Avrigny approached the window, that he might the better examine the contents of the glass, and dipping the tip of his finger in, tasted it. "Ah!" he exclaimed, "it is no longer brucine that is used; let me see what it is!"

Then he ran to one of the cupboards in Valentine's room, which had been transformed into a medicine closet, and taking from its silver case a small bottle of nitric acid, dropped a little of it into the liquor, which immediately changed to a blood-red color. "Ah!" exclaimed D'Avrigny, in a voice in which the horror of a judge unveiling the truth was mixed with the delight of a student discovering a problem. Mdme. de Villefort was overpowered; her eyes first flashed and then swam; she staggered toward the door, and disappeared. Directly afterward the distant sound of a heavy body falling on the ground was heard, but no one paid any attention to it; the nurse was engaged in watching the chemical analysis, and Villefort was still absorbed in grief. M. d'Avrigny alone had followed Mdme. de Villefort with his eyes, and watched her precipitate retreat. He lifted up the drapery over the entrance to Edward's room, and his eye reaching as far as Mdme. de Villefort's apartment, he beheld her extended lifeless on the floor.

"Go to the assistance of Mdme. de Villefort," he said to the nurse. "Mdme. de Villefort is ill."

"But Mdlle. de Villefort——" stammered the nurse.

"No longer requires help," said D'Avrigny, "since she is dead."—— "Dead!—dead!" groaned forth Villefort, in a paroxysm of grief, which was the more terrible from the novelty of the sensation in the iron heart of that man.

"Dead!" repeated a third voice. "Who said Valentine was dead?"

The two men turned round, and saw Morrel standing at the door, pale and terror-stricken.

Noirtier had encouraged him to go.

Villefort rose, half ashamed of being surprised in such a paroxysm of grief. The terrible office he had held for twenty-five years had succeeded in making him more or less than man. His glance, at first wandering, fixed itself upon Morrel. "Who are you, sir," he asked, "that forget that this is not the manner to enter a house stricken with death? Go, sir, go!" But Morrel remained motionless; he could not detach his eyes from that disordered bed, and the pale corpse lying on it. "Go!—do you hear?" said Villefort, while D'Avrigny advanced to lead Morrel out. Maximilian stared for a moment at the corpse, gazed all round the room, then upon the two men; he opened his mouth to speak, but finding it impossible to give utterance to the innumerable ideas that occupied his brain, he went out, thrusting his hands through his hair in such a manner that Ville-fort and D'Avrigny, for a moment diverted from the engrossing topic, exchanged glances, which seemed to convey,—"He is mad!"

But, in less than five minutes, the staircase groaned beneath an extraordinary weight. Morrel was seen carrying, with superhuman strength, the arm-chair containing Noirtier up-stairs. When he reached the landing, he placed the arm-chair on the floor and rapidly rolled it into Valentine's room. This could only have been accomplished by means of unnatural strength supplied by powerful excitement. But the most fearful spectacle was Noirtier being pushed toward the bed, his face expressing all his meaning, and his eyes supplying the want of every other faculty. That pale face and flaming glance appeared to Villefort like a frightful apparition. Each time he had been brought into contact with his father, something terrible had happened. "See what they have done!" cried Morrel, with one hand leaning on the back of the chair, and the other extended toward Valentine. "See, father, see!"

Villefort drew back and looked with astonishment on the young man, who, almost a stranger to him, call Noirtier "father." At this moment the whole soul of the old man seemed centered in his eyes, which became bloodshot; the veins of the throat swelled; his cheeks and temples became purple, as though he was struck with epilepsy; nothing was wanting to complete this but the utterance of a cry. And the cry issued from his pores, if we may thus speak—a cry, frightful in its silence. D'Avrigny rushed toward the old man and made him inhale a powerful restorative.

"Sir!" cried Morrel, seizing the moist hand of the paralytic, "they ask me who I am, and what right I have to be here? Oh, you know it, tell them, tell them!" And the young man's voice was choked by sobs. As for the old man, his chest heaved with his panting respiration. One could have thought he was undergoing the agonies preceding death. At length, happier than the young man, who sobbed without weeping, tears glistened in the eyes of Noirtier. "Tell them," said Morrel, in a hoarse voice, "tell them I am her betrothed. Tell them she was my beloved, my noble girl, my only blessing in the world. Tell them—oh! tell them, that corpse belongs to me." The young man who presented the dreadful spectacle of a strong frame crushed, fell heavily on his knees before the bed, which his fingers grasped with convulsive energy. D'Avrigny, unable to bear the sight of this touching emotion, turned away; and Villefort, without seeking any further explanation, and attracted toward him by the irresistible magnetism which draws us toward those who have loved the people for whom we mourn, extended his hand toward the young man. But Morrel saw nothing; he had grasped the hand of Valentine, and, unable to weep, vented his agony in gnawing the sheets. For some time nothing was heard in that chamber but sobs, exclamations, and prayers. At length Villefort, the most composed of all, spoke: "Sir," said he to Maximilian, "you say you loved Valentine, and were betrothed to her. I knew nothing of this engagement, or love, yet I, her father, forgive you, for I see your grief is real and deep; and, besides, my own sorrow is too great for anger to find a place in my heart. But you see the angel whom you hoped for has left this earth—has nothing more to do with the adoration of men. Take a last farewell, sir, of her sad remains; take the hand you expected to possess once more within your own, and then separate yourself from her for ever. Valentine now alone requires the priest who will bless her."

"You are mistaken, sir," exclaimed Morrel, raising himself on one knee, his heart pierced by a more acute pang than any he had yet felt— "you are mistaken; Valentine, dying as she has, not only requires a priest, but an avenger. *You,* M. de Villefort, send for the priest; *I* will be the avenger."——"What do you mean, sir?" asked Villefort, trembling at the new idea inspired by the delirium of Morrel.

"I tell you, sir, that two persons exist in you; the father has mourned sufficiently, now let the Attorney General fulfil his office."

The eyes of Noirtier glistened, and D'Avrigny approached.

"Gentlemen," said Morrel. "I denounce the crime; it is your place to seek the assassin." The young man's implacable eyes interrogated Villefort, who, on his side, glanced from Noirtier to D'Avrigny. But instead of finding sympathy in the eyes of the doctor and his father, he only saw an expression as inflexible as Maximilian's. "Yes!" indicated the old man.——"Assuredly!" said D'Avrigny.

"Sir," said Villefort, striving to struggle against this triple force and his own emotion,—"sir, you are deceived, no one commits crimes here. I am stricken by fate. It is horrible, indeed, but no one assassinates."

The eyes of Noirtier lighted up with rage, and D'Avrigny prepared to speak. Morrel, however, extended his arm, and commanded silence. "And I say that murders *are* committed here," said Morrel, whose voice, though lower in tone, lost none of its terrible distinctness: "I tell you that is the fourth victim within the last four months. I tell you, Valentine's life was attempted by poison four days ago, though she escaped, owing to the precautions of M. Noirtier. I tell you that the dose has been doubled, the poison changed, and that this time it has succeeded. I tell you that you know these things as well as I do, since this gentleman has forewarned you, both as a doctor and a friend."

"Oh, you rave, sir!" exclaimed Villefort, in vain endeavoring to escape the net in which he was taken.

"I rave?" said Morrel; "well, then, I appeal to Dr. d'Avrigny himself. Ask him, sir, if he recollects some words he uttered in the garden of this hotel on the night of Mdme. de Saint-Méran's death. You thought yourselves alone, and talked about that tragical death, and the fatality you mentioned then is the same as caused the murder of Valentine." Ville-fort and D'Avrigny exchanged looks. "Yes, yes," continued Morrel; "re-call the scene, for the words you thought were only given to silence and solitude fell into my ears. Certainly, after witnessing the culpable in-dolence manifested by M. de Villefort towards his own relatives, I ought to have denounced him to the authorities; then I should not have been an accomplice to thy death, as I now am, sweet, beloved Valentine: but the accomplice shall become the avenger. This fourth murder is apparent to all, and if your father abandons you, Valentine, it is I, and I swear it, that will pursue the assassin." And this time, as though nature at least had taken compassion on the vigorous frame, nearly bursting with its own strength, the words of Morrel were stifled in his throat; his breast heaved; the tears, so long rebellious, gushed from his eyes; and he threw himself, weeping, on his knees, by the side of the bed.

Then D'Avrigny spoke. "And I, too," he exclaimed, in a low voice, "I unite with M. Morrel in demanding justice for crime; my blood boils at the idea of having encouraged a murderer by my cowardly concession." ——"Oh! merciful heavens!" murmured Villefort. Morrel raised his head, and reading the eyes of the old man, which gleamed with unnatural lustre,—"Stay," he said, "M. Noirtier wishes to speak."——"Yes," in-dicated Noirtier, with an expression the more terrible, from all his facul-ties being centered in his glance.

"Do you know the assassin?" asked Morrel.

"Yes," replied Noirtier.——"And will you direct us?" exclaimed the young man. "Listen, M. d'Avrigny! listen!" Noirtier looked upon Mor-rel with one of those melancholy smiles which had so often made Val-entine happy, and thus fixed his attention. Then, having riveted the eyes of his interlocutor on his own, he glanced toward the door.

"Do you wish me to leave?" said Morrel sadly.

"Yes," replied Noirtier.

"Must I leave alone?"——"No."

"Whom am I to take with me?—the prosecutor?"——"No."

"The doctor?"——"Yes."

"Oh!" said Villefort, inexpressibly delighted to think the inquiries were to be made privately,—"I can understand my father." D'Avrigny took the young man's arm, and led him out of the room. A more than deathlike silence then reigned in the house. At the end of a quarter of an hour a faltering footstep was heard, and Villefort appeared at the door of the apartment where D'Avrigny and Morrel had been standing, one ab-sorbed in meditation, the other with grief. "You can come," he said, and led them back to Noirtier. Morrel looked attentively on Villefort. His face was livid, large drops rolled down his face! and in his fingers he held the fragments of a pen which he had torn to atoms. "Gentlemen," he said, in a hoarse voice, "give me your word of honor that this horrible secret shall forever remain buried amongst ourselves!" The two men drew back.

"Justice will be done," said Villefort. "My father has revealed the culprit's name; my father thirsts for revenge as much as you do, yet even he conjures you as I do to keep this secret. Rest assured, gentlemen, that within three days, in a less time than justice would demand, the revenge I shall have taken for the murder of my child will be such as to make the boldest heart tremble;" and as he spoke these words he ground his teeth, and grasped the old man's senseless hand.

Morrel rushed to the bed, and, after having pressed the cold lips of Valentine with his own, hurriedly left, uttering a long, deep groan of despair and anguish. We have before stated that all the servants had fled. M. de Villefort was, therefore, obliged to request M. d'Avrigny to superintend all those arrangements consequent upon a death in a large city, more especially under such suspicious circumstances. It was something terrible to witness the silent agony, the mute despair of Noirtier, whose tears silently rolled down his cheeks. Villefort retired to his study, and D'Avrigny left to summon the coroner. M. Noirtier could not be persuaded to quit his grandchild. At the end of a quarter of an hour M. d'Avrigny returned with his associate; they found the outer gate closed, and not a servant remaining in the house; Villefort himself was obliged to open it. But he stopped on the landing; he had not the courage to revisit the room of death. The two doctors, therefore, entered the room alone. Noirtier was near the bed, pale, motionless, and silent as the corpse. The coroner approached with the indifference of a man accustomed to spend half his time amongst the dead; he then lifted the sheet which was placed over the face, and just unclosed the lips.

"Alas!" said D'Avrigny, "she is indeed dead, poor child! You can leave."——"Yes," answered the doctor laconically, dropping the sheet he had raised.

The doctor then laid his report on the corner of the table, and, having executed his office, was conducted out by D'Avrigny. Villefort met them at the door of his study; having in a few words thanked the coroner, he returned to D'Avrigny, and said,—

"And now the priest."

"Is there any particular priest you wish to pray with Valentine?" asked D'Avrigny.

"No," said Villefort; "fetch the nearest."

"The nearest," said the district doctor, "is a good Italian abbé, who lives next door to you. Shall I call on him as I pass?"

"D'Avrigny," said Villefort, "be so kind, I beseech you, as to accompany this gentleman. Here is the key to the door, so that you can go in and out as you please: you will bring the priest with you, and will oblige me by introducing him into my child's room."

As the doctors entered the street, they saw a man in a cassock standing on the threshold of the next door. "This is the abbé of whom I spoke," said the doctor to D'Avrigny. D'Avrigny accosted the priest. "Sir," he said, "are you disposed to confer a great obligation on an unhappy father who has just lost his daughter? I mean M. de Villefort, the royal prosecutor."

"Ah!" said the priest, with a marked Italian accent; "yes, I have heard that death is in that house."

"It is a girl."

"I know it, sir; the servants who fled from the house informed me. I also know that her name is Valentine, and I have already prayed for her."

"Thank you, sir," said D'Avrigny; "since you have commenced your sacred office, deign to continue it. Come and watch by the dead, and all the wretched family will be grateful to you."

"I am going, sir; and I do not hesitate to say that no prayers will be more fervent than mine."

D'Avrigny took the priest's hand, and without meeting Villefort, engaged in his study, they reached Valentine's room, which on the following night was to be occupied by the undertakers. On entering the room, Noirtier's eyes met the abbé's and no doubt he read some particular expression in them, for he remained in the room. D'Avrigny recommended the attention of the priest to the living as well as to the dead, and the abbé promised to devote his prayers to Valentine and his attentions to Noirtier. In order, doubtless, that he might not be disturbed while fulfilling his sacred mission, the priest, as soon as D'Avrigny departed, rose, and not only bolted the door through which the doctor had just left, but also that leading to Mdme. de Villefort's room.

CHAPTER LXIII.

DANGLARS' SIGNATURE.

THE next morning rose sad and cloudy. During the night the undertakers had executed their melancholy office. During the evening two men carried Noirtier from Valentine's room into his own, and, contrary to all expectation, there was no difficulty in withdrawing him from his child. Abbé Busoni had watched till daylight, and then left without calling any one. D'Avrigny returned about eight o'clock in the morning; he met Villefort on his way to Noirtier's room, and accompanied him to see how the old man had slept. They found him in the large arm-chair, which served him for a bed, enjoying a calm, nay, almost a smiling sleep.

"Grief has stunned him," replied D'Avrigny; and they both returned thoughtfully to the study.

"See, I have not slept," said Villefort, showing his undisturbed bed; "grief does not stun me. I have not been in bed for two nights; but then look at my desk; I have filled out those papers, and drawn the accusation against the assassin Benedetto. Oh, work! work! my passion, my joy, my delight! it is for you to alleviate my sorrows!" and he convulsively grasped the hand of D'Avrigny.

At twelve o'clock the mourning-coaches rolled into the paved court, and the street was filled with a crowd of idlers, equally pleased to witness the festivities or the mourning of the rich, and who rush with the same avidity to a funeral procession as to the marriage of a duchess. Gradually the reception-room filled, and some of our old friends made their appearance—we mean Debray, Château-Renaud, and Beauchamp, accompanied by all the leading men of the day at the bar, in literature, or the army, for M. de Villefort moved in the first Parisian circles, less owing to his social position than to his personal merit.

"Poor girl!" said Debray, like the rest, paying an involuntary tribute to the sad event,—"Poor girl! so young! so rich! so beautiful! Could you have imagined this scene, Château-Renaud, when we saw her, at the most three weeks ago, about to sign that contract?"

"Indeed, no!" said Château-Renaud. "But whom are you seeking, Debray?"

"I am seeking the Count of Monte-Cristo," said the young man.

"I met him on the Boulevard, on my road here," said Beauchamp. "I think he is about to leave Paris; he was going to his banker."

"His banker? Danglars is his banker, is he not?" asked Château-Renaud of Debray.

"I believe so," replied the secretary, with slight uneasiness.

Beauchamp told the truth when he said, that on his road to the funeral he had met Monte-Cristo, who was directing his steps toward Danglars'. The banker saw the carriage of the count enter the courtyard, and advanced to meet him with a sad, though affable smile. "Well!" said he, extending his hand to Monte-Cristo, "I suppose you have come to sympathize with me, for indeed misfortune has taken possession of my house."

"Still, Baron," said Monte-Cristo, "family griefs, or indeed any other affliction which would crush a man whose child was his only treasure, are endurable to a millionaire. Philosophers may well say, and practical men will always support the opinion, that money mitigates many trials; and if you admit the efficacy of this sovereign balm, you ought to be very easily consoled; you, the king of finance, who forms the intersecting point of all the powers of Europe, nay, the world!"

Danglars looked at him obliquely, as though to ascertain whether he spoke seriously. "Yes," he answered, "if a fortune brings consolation, I ought to be consoled; I am rich."——"So rich, dear sir, that your fortune resembles the pyramids: if you wished to demolish them you could not; if it were possible, you would not dare!" Danglars smiled at the good-natured pleasantry of the count. "That reminds me," he said, "that when you entered I was on the point of signing five little bonds; I have already signed two, will you allow me to do the same to the others?"——"Pray do so."

There was a moment's silence, during which the noise of the banker's pen was alone heard, while Monte-Cristo examined the gilt mouldings on the ceiling. "Are they Spanish, Haitian or Neapolitan bonds?" said Monte-Cristo. "Neither," said Danglars, smiling, "they are bonds on the bank of France, payable to bearer. Stay," he added, "Count, you, who may be called the emperor, if I claim the title of king of finance, have you many pieces of paper of this size, each worth a million?"

The count took the papers, which Danglars had so proudly presented to him, into his hands, and read:—

"To the Governor of the Bank. Please to pay to my order, from the fund deposited by me, the sum of a million.

"BARON DANGLARS."

"One, two, three, four, five," said Monte-Cristo; "five millions! It is a fine thing to have such credit; really, it is only in France these things are done. Five millions on five little scraps of paper!—it must be seen to be believed."

"You do not doubt it?"——"No!"

"You say so with a tone! stay, you shall be convinced; take my clerk to the bank, and you will see him leave it with an order on the Treasury for the same sum."

"No!" said Monte-Cristo, folding up the five notes, "most decidedly not; the thing is so curious, I will make the experiment myself. I am credited on you for six millions. I have drawn nine hundred thousand francs, you therefore still owe me five millions and a hundred thousand francs. I will take the five scraps of paper that I now hold as bonds, with your signature alone, and here is a receipt in full for the six millions between us. I had prepared it beforehand, for I am much in want of money to-day." And Monte-Cristo placed the bonds in his pocket with one hand, while with the other he held out the receipt to Danglars. If a thunderbolt had fallen at the banker's feet, he could not have experienced greater terror.

"Then I may keep this money?"——"Yes," said Danglars, while the perspiration started from the roots of his hair. "Yes, keep it—keep it."

Monte-Cristo replaced the notes in his pocket with that indescribable expression which seems to say, "Come, reflect; if you repent there is still time."

"No," said Danglars, "no, decidedly no; keep my signatures. But you know none are so formal as bankers in transacting business; I intended this money for the hospital, and I seemed to be robbing them if I did not pay them with these precise bonds. How absurd! as if one crown were not as good as another. Excuse me;" and he began to laugh loudly, but nervously.

"Certainly, I excuse you," said Monte-Cristo, graciously, "and pocket them." And he placed the bonds in his pocket-book.——"But," said Danglars, "there is still a sum of one hundred thousand francs?"

"Oh! a mere nothing," said Monte-Cristo. "The balance would come to about that sum; but keep it, and we shall be quits."

"Count," said Danglars, "are you speaking seriously?"

"I never joke with bankers," said Monte-Cristo in a freezing manner, which repelled impertinence; and he turned to the door, just as the footman announced,—"M. de Boville, receiver-general of the hospitals."

"Faith!" said Monte-Cristo; "I think I arrived just in time to obtain your signatures, or they would have been disputed with me."

Danglars again became pale, and hastened to conduct the count out. Monte-Cristo exchanged a ceremonious bow with M. de Boville, who was standing in the waiting-room, and who was introduced into Danglars' room as soon as the count had left. The count's sad face was illumined by a faint smile, as he noticed the portfolio which the receiver-general held in his hand. At the door he found his carriage, and was immediately driven to the bank. Meanwhile Danglars, repressing all emotion, advanced to meet the receiver-general. We need not say that a smile of condescension was stamped upon his lips. "Good morning, creditor," said he; "for I wager anything it is the creditor who visits me."——"You are right, Baron," answered M. de Boville; "I have brought my receipt."

"My dear M. Boville, your widows and orphans must oblige me by waiting twenty-four hours, since Monte-Cristo, whom you just saw leaving here—has just carried off their five millions."

"How so?"

"The count has an unlimited credit upon me; a credit opened by Thomson and French, of Rome; he came to demand five millions at once, which I paid him with the cheques on the bank; my funds are deposited there; and you can understand that if I draw out ten millions on the same day, it will appear rather strange to the governor. Two days will be a different thing," said Danglars, smiling.

"Come," said Boville, with a tone of entire incredulity, "five millions to that gentleman who just left, and who bowed to me as though he knew me!"——"Here is his receipt. Believe your own eyes," M. de Boville took the paper Danglars presented him, and read:—

"Received of Baron Danglars the sum of five millions one hundred thousand francs; which will be repaid when ever he pleases by the house of Thomson and French of Rome."

"It is really true," said De Boville.

"Do you know the house of Thomson and French?"——"Yes, I once had business to transact with it to the amount of 200,000 francs; but since then I have not heard it mentioned."——"It is one of the best houses in Europe," said Danglars, carelessly throwing down the receipt on his desk.

"And he had five millions in your hands alone! Why, this Count of Monte-Cristo must be a nabob!"

"Indeed I do not know what he is; he has three unlimited credits—one on me, one on the Rothschilds, one on Lafitte; and you see," he added, carelessly, "he has given me the preference, by leaving a balance of 100,000 francs." M. de Boville manifested signs of extraordinary admiration. "I must visit him," he said, "and obtain some pious grant from him."

"Oh! you may make sure of him; his charities alone amount to 20,000 francs per month."

"It is magnificent! I will set before him the example of Mdme. de Morcerf and her son. They gave all their fortune to the hospitals, because they would not spend money so guiltily acquired."——"And what are they to live upon?"

"The mother retires into the country, and the son enters the army."

"Well, I must confess, these are queer scruples."

"I registered their deed of gift yesterday."

"And how much did they possess?"

"Oh! not much! from twelve to thirteen hundred thousand francs. But to return to our millions."

"Certainly," said Danglars in the most natural tone in the world. "Are you, then, pressed for this money?"

"Yes; for the examination of our cash takes place to-morrow."

"To-morrow!—Why did you not tell me so before? Why, it is as good as a century! At what hour does the examination take place?"

"At two o'clock."

"Send at twelve," said Danglars, smiling.

"I will come myself."

"Better still, since it will afford me the pleasure of seeing you." They shook hands. "By the way," said M. de Boville, "are you not going to the funeral of poor Mdlle. de Villefort, which I met on my road here?"———"No," said the banker; "I have appeared rather ridiculous since that affair of Benedetto, so I remain in the background."

"Bah! you are wrong. How were you to blame in that affair! Everybody pities you, sir; and, above all, Mdlle. Danglars!"

"Poor Eugénie!" said Danglars; "do you know she is going to embrace a religious life? she decided on leaving Paris with a nun of her acquaintance; they are gone to seek a very strict convent in Italy or Spain."

"Oh! it is terrible!" and M. de Boville retired with this exclamation, after expressing acute sympathy with the father.

But he had scarcely left before Danglars exclaimed, "Fool!!!" Then, enclosing Monte-Cristo's receipt in a little pocket-book, he added: —"Yes, come at twelve o'clock; I shall then be far away." Then he double-locked his door; emptied all his drawers, collected about fifty thousand francs in bank-notes, burned several papers, left others exposed to view, and then commenced writing a letter to his wife.

"I will place it on her dressing-table myself to-night," he murmured. Then taking a passport from his drawer he said,—"Good, it is available for two months longer."

CHAPTER LXIV.

AFTER THE FUNERAL.

M. DE BOVILLE had indeed met the funeral procession which conducted Valentine to her last home on earth. The weather was dull and stormy, a cold wind shook the few remaining yellow leaves from the boughs of the trees, and scattered them amongst the crowd which filled the Boulevards. As they left Paris, an equipage with four horses, at full speed, was seen to draw up suddenly: it contained Monte-Cristo. The count left the carriage and mingled in the crowd who followed on foot. At length they arrived at the cemetery. The piercing eye of Monte-Cristo glanced through clusters of bushes and trees, and was soon relieved from all anxiety, for he saw a shadow glide between the yew-trees, and Monte-Cristo recognized him whom he sought. When the procession stopped, this shadow was recognized as Morrel; who, with his coat buttoned up to his throat, his face livid, and convulsively crushing his hat between his fingers, leaned against a tree, situated on an elevation commanding the mausoleum, so that none of the funeral details could escape his observation. Everything was conducted in the usual manner.

Monte-Cristo heard and saw nothing, or rather he only saw Morrel, whose calmness had a frightful effect on those who knew what was passing in his heart. The funeral over, the guests returned to Paris. Château-Renaud looked for a moment for Morrel; but while watching the departure of the count, Morrel had quitted his post, and Château-Renaud, failing in his search, joined Debray and Beauchamp.

Monte-Cristo concealed himself behind a large tomb, and waited the arrival of Morrel, who, by degrees, approached the tomb now abandoned by spectators and workmen. Morrel threw a glance around, but before it reached the spot occupied by Monte-Cristo, the latter had advanced yet nearer, still unperceived. The young man knelt down. The count, with outstretched neck, and glaring eyes, stood in an attitude ready to pounce upon Morrel upon the first occasion. Morrel bent his head till it touched the stone, then clutching the grating with both hands, he murmured,—"Oh! Valentine!" The count's heart was pierced by the utterance of these two words; he stepped forward, and touching the young man's shoulder, said,—"I was looking for you, my friend." Monte-Cristo expected a burst of passion, but he was deceived, for Morrel turning round, said with calmness,—

"You see I was praying." The scrutinizing glance of the count searched the young man from head to foot. He then seemed more easy.

"Shall I drive you back to Paris?" he asked.

"No, thank you."

"Do you wish anything?"

"Leave me to pray." The count withdrew without opposition, but it was only to place himself in a situation where he could watch every movement of Morrel, who at length rose, brushed the dust from his knees, and turned toward Paris, without once looking back.

"Ah, Count!" exclaimed Julie with the delight manifested by every member of the family whenever he visited.

"Maximilian has just returned, has he not, madame?" asked the count.

"Yes, I think I saw him pass; but pray, call Emmanuel."

"Excuse me, madame, but I must go up to Maximilian's room this instant," replied Monte-Cristo, "I have something of the greatest importance to tell him."

"Go, then," she said, with a charming smile, which accompanied him until he had disappeared. Monte-Cristo soon ran up the staircase conducting from the ground-floor to Maximilian's room; when he reached the landing he listened attentively, but all was still.

"What shall I do?" he uttered, and reflected a moment; "shall I ring? No, the sound of a bell, announcing a visitor, will but accelerate the resolution of one in Maximilian's situation, and then the bell would be followed by a louder noise." Monte-Cristo trembled from head to foot, and as if his determination had been taken with the rapidity of lightning, he struck one of the panes of glass with his elbow; the glass was shivered to atoms, then withdrawing the curtain, he saw Morrel, who had been writing at his desk, bound from his seat at the noise of the broken window.

"I beg a thousand pardons!" said the count, "there is nothing the matter, but I slipped down and broke one of your panes of glass with my elbow. Since it is open, I will take advantage of it to enter your room; do not disturb yourself—do not disturb yourself!" And passing his hand through the broken glass, the count opened the door. Morrel, evidently discomposed, came to meet Monte-Cristo, less with the intention of receiving him than to exclude his entry.

"Are you hurt, sir?" coldly asked he.

"I believe not. But what are you about there? you were writing."

"Ah, true, I was writing. I do sometimes, soldier though I am."

Monte-Cristo advanced into the room; Maximilian was obliged to let him pass, but he followed him.

The count looked around him. "Your pistols are beside your desk," said Monte-Cristo, pointing with his finger to the pistols on the table.

"I am on the point of starting on a journey," replied Morrel, disdainfully.——"My friend!" exclaimed Monte-Cristo, in a tone of exquisite sweetness.——"Sir?"——"My friend, my dear Maximilian, you are going to destroy yourself!"

"Indeed, Count!" said Morrel, shuddering; "what has put this into your head?"——"I tell you that you are about to destroy yourself," continued the count, "and here is the proof of what I say;" and, approaching the desk, he removed the sheet of paper which Morrel had placed over the letter he had begun, and took the latter in his hands.

Morrel rushed forward to tear it from him; but Monte-Cristo, perceiving his intention, seized his wrist with his iron grasp. "You wish to destroy yourself," said the count; "you have written it."

"Well!" said Morrel, changing his expression of calmness for one of violence—"well, and if I do intend to turn this pistol against myself, who shall prevent me—who will dare prevent me? You, who have deceived me with false hopes, who have cheered and soothed me with vain promises, when I might, if not have saved her, at least have seen her die in my arms! you, who pretend to understand everything, even the hidden sources of knowledge! you, who enact the part of a guardian angel upon earth, and could not even find an antidote to a poison administered to a girl! Ah, sir, since you have devised a new torture after I thought I had exhausted them all, then, Count of Monte-Cristo, my pretended benefactor—then, Count of Monte-Cristo, the universal guardian, be satisfied, you shall witness the death of your friend;" and Morrel, with a maniacal laugh, again rushed towards the pistols.

"And I again repeat, you shall not commit suicide."

"Prevent me, then!" replied Morrel, with another struggle, which, like the first, failed in releasing him from the count's iron grasp.

"I will prevent you."

"And who are you, then, that arrogate to yourself this tyrannical right over free and rational beings?"

"Who am I?" repeated Monte-Cristo. "He who saved your father's life when he wished to destroy himself, as you do to-day—because I am the man who sent the purse to your young sister. And the Pharaoh to Morrel—because I am the Edmond Dantès who dandled you, a child, on my knees." Morrel made another step back, staggering, breathless, crushed; then all his strength gave way, and he fell prostrate at the feet of Monte-Cristo. Then his admirable character underwent a complete and sudden revulsion; he rose, bounded out of the room, and rushed to the stairs, exclaiming energetically, "Julie, Julie! Emmanuel, Emmanuel!"

Monte-Cristo endeavored also to leave, but Maximilian would have died rather than relax his hold of the handle of the door, which he closed upon the count. Julie, Emmanuel, and some of the servants, ran up in alarm on hearing the cries of Maximilian. Morrel seized their hands, and, opening the door, exclaimed, in a voice choked with sobs, "On your knees! on your knees! he is our benefactor—the saviour of our father! He is——"

He would have added "Edmond Dantès," but the count seized his arm and prevented him. Julie threw herself into the arms of the count; Emmanuel embraced him as a guardian angel; Morrel again fell on his knees, and struck the ground with his forehead. Then the iron-hearted man felt his heart swell in his breast, a flame seemed to rush from his throat to his eyes; he bent his head. For a while, nothing was heard in the room but a succession of sobs, while the incense from their grateful hearts mounted to heaven. Julie had scarcely recovered from her deep emotion when she rushed out of the room, descended to the next floor, ran into the drawing-room with childlike joy, and raised the crystal globe, which covered the purse given by the stranger. Meanwhile, Emmanuel, in a broken voice, said to the count, "Oh, Count, how could you, hearing us so often speak of our unknown benefactor, seeing us pay such homage of gratitude and adoration to his memory, how could you continue so long without discovering yourself to us? Oh, it was cruel to us, and—dare I say it?—to you also."

"Listen, my friends," said the count—"I may call you so, since we have really been friends for the last eleven years: the discovery of this secret has been occasioned by a great event which you must never know. I wished to bury it during my whole life in my own bosom, but your brother Maximilian wrested it from me by a violence he repents of now, I am sure." Then turning round, and seeing that Morrel had thrown himself into an arm-chair, he added in a low voice, pressing Emmanuel's hand significantly: "My kind friends, leave me alone with Maximilian." Julie drew her husband to the door. "Let us leave them," she said.

The count was alone with Morrel, who remained motionless as a statue.

"Come," said Monte-Cristo, touching his shoulder with his finger, "are you a man again, Maximilian?"

"O, do not fear, my friend," said Morrel, raising his head, and smiling with a sweet expression; "I shall no longer attempt my life. My grief will kill me of itself."

"My friend," said Monte-Cristo, with an expression of melancholy equal to his own, "listen to me: one day, in a moment of despair like yours, since it led to a similar resolution, I, like you, wished to kill myself; one day your father, equally desperate, wished to kill himself too. If any one had said to your father, at the moment he raised the pistol to his head—if any one had told me, when in my prison I pushed back the food I had not tasted for three days—if any one had said to either of us then, 'Live! the day will come when you will be happy, and will bless life!'—no matter whose voice had spoken, we should have heard him with the smile of doubt, or the anguish of incredulity; and yet how many times has your father blessed life while embracing you! how often have I myself——"

"Ah," exclaimed Morrel, interrupting the count, "you had only lost your liberty, my father had only lost his fortune, but I have lost my love."

"Look at me," said Monte-Cristo, with that expression which sometimes made him so eloquent and persuasive—"I have told you to hope."

"Then have a care, I repeat, for you seek to persuade me, and if you succeed I should lose my reason, for I should hope that I could again behold Valentine." The count smiled.

"I tell you to hope, because I have a method of curing you."

"Count, you render me sadder than before, if it be possible. You think the result of this blow has been to produce an ordinary grief, and you would cure it by an ordinary remedy—change of scene." And Morrel dropped his head with disdainful incredulity. "What can I say more?" asked Monte-Cristo. "I have confidence in the remedy I propose, and only ask you to permit me to assure you of its efficacy."

"Count, you prolong my agony."

"I feel so much pity towards you, Maximilian, that—listen to me attentively—if I do not cure you in a month, to the day, to the very hour, mark my words, Morrel, I will place loaded pistols before you, and a cup full of the deadliest Italian poison—a poison more sure and prompt than that aimed at Valentine."

"In a month, then, on your honor, if I am not consoled, you will let me take my life into my own hands, and, whatever may happen, you will not call me ungrateful?"

"In a month you will find on the table, at which we shall then be sitting, good pistols and a delicious draught; but, on the other hand, you must promise me not to attempt your life before that time."

"Oh! I also swear it." Monte-Cristo drew the young man toward him, and pressed him for some time to his heart. "And now," he said, "after to-day, you will come and live with me; you can occupy Haydée's apartment, and my daughter will at least be replaced by my son."

CHAPTER LXV.

THE ASSIZES.

THE Benedetto Case, as it was called in the high court, and best resorts, in general, had produced a tremendous sensation. Every one, therefore, ran to the court: some to witness the sight, others to comment upon it.

It was one of those magnificent autumn days which make amends for a short summer. One of the softest and most brilliant days of September shone forth in all its splendor.

Beauchamp, one of the kings of the press, and therefore claiming the right of a throne everywhere, was looking round on every side. He perceived Château-Renaud, and Debray, who had just gained the good graces of an usher and persuaded the latter to let them stand before, instead of behind him. The worthy officer had recognized the minister's secretary and the millionaire, and, by way of paying extra attention to his noble neighbors, promised to keep their places while they paid a visit to Beauchamp.

"Well!" said Beauchamp, "we shall see our friend!"

"Yes, indeed!" replied Debray. "That worthy prince. Deuce take those Italian princes!"

"Bah!" said Beauchamp, "he played the prince very well."

"Yes, for you who detest those unhappy princes, Beauchamp, and are always delighted to find fault with them; but not for me, who discover a gentleman by instinct, and who scent out an aristocratic family like a very bloodhound of heraldry."

"Then you never believed in the principality?"

"Yes! in the principality, but not in the prince."

"Not so bad," said Beauchamp. "Stay, surely I am not deceived. They said she had left town?"

"Mdlle. Eugénie?" said Château-Renaud: "has she come here?"

"No! but her mother."

"Mdme. Danglars? Nonsense! Impossible!" said Château-Renaud; "only ten days after the flight of her daughter, and three days from the bankruptcy of her husband?"

Debray colored slightly, and followed with his eyes the direction of Beauchamp's glance.

"Come," he said, "it is only a veiled lady, some foreign princess; perhaps the mother of Cavalcanti. But how is it that Mdme. de Ville-fort is not here?"

"Poor, dear woman!" said Debray, "she is no doubt occupied in distilling balm for the hospitals, or in making cosmetics for herself or friends. Do you know she spends two or three thousand crowns a year in this amusement? But I wonder she is not here. I should have been pleased to see her, for I like her very much."

"And I hate her," said Château-Renaud. "But to return to what you were saying, Beauchamp."

"Well! do you know why people die so fast in M. de Villefort's house? No? Well, gentlemen, the reason people die so fast at M. de Villefort's, is, that there is an assassin in the house!"

The two young men shuddered, for the same idea had more than once occurred to them. "And who is the assassin?" they asked together.

"Little Edward!" A burst of laughter from the auditors did not in the least disconcert the speaker, who continued: "Yes, gentlemen; Edward, who is quite an adept in the art of killing."

"It is absurd," said Debray.

"Does his mother, then, keep poisons in her laboratory?"

"How can I tell? You are questioning me like a prosecutor! I only repeat what I have been told."

"It is incredible!"——"No, my dear fellow, it is not at all incredible! The generation who follow us are very precocious!"

"I do not see the Count of Monte-Cristo here!"

"He is worn out," said Debray; "besides, he could not well appear in public, since he has been the dupe of the Cavalcanti, who, it appears, presented themselves to him with false letters of credit, and cheated him out of 100,000 francs upon the hypothesis of this principality."——"Ah, now I think of it, the Count of Monte-Cristo cannot appear in the hall!" said Beauchamp.——"Why not?"

"Because he is an actor in the drama."

"Has he assassinated any one then?"——"No, on the contrary, they tried to assassinate him. You know that it was in leaving his house that Caderousse was murdered by his friend Benedetto. You know that the famous waistcoat was found in his house, containing the letter which stopped the signature of the marriage-contract. Do you see the waistcoat? There it is, all blood-stained, on the desk, as a testimony of the crime."

"Ah, very good."——"Hush, gentleman! here is the court: let us go back to our places."

The judges took their places in the midst of the most profound silence; the jury took their seats; M. de Villefort, the object of unusual attention, almost of general admiration, sat in the arm-chair, and cast a tranquil glance around him. Every person looked with astonishment on that grave and severe face, the calm expression of which personal griefs had been unable to disturb; and the aspect of a man who was a stranger to all human emotions, excited a kind of terror.

"Officers!" said the president, "lead in the accused."

At these words the public attention became more intense, and all eyes were turned towards the door through which Benedetto was to enter. The door soon opened, and the accused appeared. The same impression was experienced by all present; and no one was deceived by the expression of his countenance. His features bore no sign of that deep emotion which stops the beating of the heart and blanches the cheek. His hands, gracefully placed, one upon his hat, the other in the opening of his white waistcoat, were not at all tremulous; his eye was calm, and even brilliant. Scarcely had he entered the hall, when he glanced at the whole body of magistrates and assistants: his eye rested longer on the president, and still more so on the official accuser. By the side of Andrea was placed the lawyer who was to conduct his defence, chosen by the court; for Andrea disdained to pay any attention to those details. The lawyer was a young man whose face expressed a hundred times more emotion than that which characterized the prisoner.

The president called for the indictment, corrected, as we know, by the sharp and implacable pen of Villefort. During the reading of this, which was long, attention was continually drawn toward Andrea, who bore the burden with Spartan unconcern. Villefort had never been so concise and eloquent: the crime was represented under the liveliest colors; the former life of the prisoner, his transformation, a review of his life from the earliest period, were set forth with all the talent that a knowledge of human life could furnish to a mind like that of the procureur du roi. Benedetto was thus for ever ruined in public opinion before the sentence of the law could be pronounced. Andrea paid no attention to the successive charges which were brought against him. M. de Villefort, who examined him attentively, and who no doubt practised upon him all the psychological studies he was accustomed to use, in vain endeavored to make him lower his eyes, notwithstanding the depth and profundity of his gaze. At length the charge was read.

"Accused," said the president, "your name and surname?"

Andrea arose. "Excuse me, sir," he said, in a clear voice, "but I see you are going to adopt a course of questions through which I cannot follow you. I have an idea, which I will explain by-and-by of making an exception to the usual form of accusation. Allow me, then, if you please, to answer in different order, or I will not do so at all." The astonished president looked at the jury, who themselves looked upon the prosecutor. The whole assembly manifested great surprise; but Andrea appeared quite unmoved.

"Your age?" said the president: "will you answer that question?"

——"I will answer that question, as well as the rest, sir, but in its turn."

"Your age?" repeated the president.

"I am twenty-one years old; or, rather, I shall be in a few days, as I was born the night of the 27th of September, 1817." Villefort, who was busy taking down some notes, raised his head at the mention of this date.

"Where were you born?" continued the president.

"At Auteuil, near Paris." M. de Villefort a second time raised his head, looked at Benedetto, as if he had been gazing at the head of Medusa, and became livid. As for Benedetto, he gracefully wiped his lips with a fine cambric pocket-handkerchief.

"Your profession?"

"First I was a forger," answer Andrea, as calmly as possible; "then I became a thief; and, lately, have become a murderer." A murmur, or rather storm, of indignation burst from all parts of the assembly. The judges themselves appeared stupefied! and the jury manifested tokens of disgust for a stoicism so unexpected from a fashionable man. Villefort pressed his hand upon his brow, which, at first pale, had become red and burning; then he suddenly rose, and looked around as though he had lost his senses—he wanted air.

"Are you looking for anything, sir?" asked Benedetto, with his most pleasing smile. Villefort answered nothing, but sat, or rather threw himself down again upon his chair.

"And now, prisoner, will you consent to tell your name?" said the president. "The brutal affectation with which you have enumerated and classified your crimes calls for a severe reprimand on the part of the court, both in the name of morality, and for the respect due to humanity. You appear to consider this a point of honor, and it may be for this reason you have delayed acknowledging your name. You wished it to be preceded by all these titles."

"It is quite wonderful, sir, how fully you have read my thoughts," said Benedetto, in his softest voice and most polite manner. "This is, indeed, the reason I begged you to alter the order of the questions." The public astonishment had reached its height. There was no longer any deceit or bravado in the manner of the accused. The audience seemed to dread some thunder-cloud would burst over the gloomy scene.

"Well!" said the president; "your name?"

"I cannot tell you my name, since I do not know it; but I know my father's, and will utter it."

"Repeat your father's name," said the president. Not a whisper, not a breath was heard in that vast assembly; every one waited anxiously.

"My father is the Attorney General," replied Andrea, calmly.

"The Attorney General?" said the president, stupefied, and without noticing the agitation which spread over the face of M. de Villefort. ——"Yes; and if you wish to know his name, I will tell it,—it is Villefort."

The explosion, which had been so long restrained, from a feeling of respect to the court of justice, now burst forth like thunder from the breasts of all present; the court itself did not seek to restrain the movement. The exclamations, and insults addressed to Benedetto, who remained perfectly unconcerned, the energetic gestures, the stir of the gendarmes, the sneers of the scum of the crowd—always sure to rise to the surface in case of any disturbance—all this lasted five minutes, before the door-keepers and magistrates were able to restore silence. In the midst of this tumult the voice of the president was heard to exclaim,—"Are you playing with justice, prisoner, and do you dare set your fellow-citizens an example of disorder which even in these times has never been equaled?"

Order was re-established in the hall, with the exception of a few who still moved and whispered. A lady, it was said, had just fainted; supplied with a smelling-bottle, she had recovered. During the tumult, Andrea had kept his smiling face toward the assembly; then, leaning with one hand on the oaken rail of his bench, in the most graceful attitude possible, he said:—"Gentlemen, I assure you I had no idea of insulting the court, or of making a useless disturbance in the presence of this honorable assembly. You ask my age; I tell it. You ask where I was born; I answer. You ask my name; I cannot give it, since my parents abandoned me. But though I cannot give my own name, not possessing one, I can tell them my father's. Now I repeat, my father is named Villefort, and I am ready to prove it."

There was an energy, a conviction, and a sincerity in the manner of the young man, which silenced the tumult. All eyes were turned for a moment toward the procureur du roi, who sat as motionless as though a thunderbolt had changed him into a corpse. "Gentlemen!" said Andrea, commanding silence by his voice and manner. "Do you wish for details? I will give them. I was born in No. 28, Rue de la Fontaine, in a room hung with red damask: my father took me in his arms, telling my mother I was dead; wrapped me in a napkin marked with an H and an N; and carried me into a garden, where he buried me alive."

A shudder ran through the assembly when they saw that the confidence of the prisoner increased in proportion with the terror of M. de Villefort.

"A man who had sworn vengeance against my father, and had long watched his opportunity to kill him, introduced himself that night into the garden in which my father buried me. He was concealed in a thicket; he saw my father bury something in the ground, and stabbed him in the midst of the operation; then, thinking the deposit might contain some treasure, he turned up the ground, and found me still living. The man carried me to the Foundling Hospital, where I was entered under the number 37. Three months afterwards, a woman traveled from

Rogliano to Paris to fetch me, and having claimed me as her son, carried me away. Thus, you see, though born in Paris, I was brought up in Corsica."

There was a moment's silence, during which one could have fancied the hall empty, so profound was the stillness. "I might have lived happily amongst those good people, who adored me; but my perverse disposition prevailed over the virtues which my adopted mother endeavored to instil into my heart. I increased in wickedness till I committed crime. One day when I cursed Providence for making me so wicked, and ordaining me to such a fate, my adopted father said to me, 'Do not blaspheme, unhappy child! the crime is your father's not yours; who devoted you to death, or to a life of misery, in case, by a miracle, you should escape his doom.' Since then I ceased to blaspheme, but I cursed my father. This is why I have uttered the words for which you blame me; and filled this whole audience with horror. If I have committed an additional crime, punish me; but if you will allow that ever since the day of my birth my fate has been sad, bitter, and lamentable, then pity me."

"But your mother?" asked the president.

"My mother thought me dead; she is not guilty. I did not even wish to know her name, nor do I know it." Just then a piercing shriek ending in a sob, burst from the centre of the crowd, who encircled the lady who had before fainted, and who now fell in violent hysterics. She was carried out of the hall, and in doing so, the thick veil which concealed her face dropped off, and Mdme. Danglars was recognized. Notwithstanding his shattered nerves, the stunning sensation in his ears, and the madness which turned his brain, Villefort rose as he perceived her.

"The proofs! the proofs!" said the president; "remember this tissue of horrors must be supported by the clearest proofs."

"Look at M. de Villefort, and then ask me for proofs."

Every one turned toward the lawyer, who, unable to bear the universal gaze now riveted on him alone, advanced, staggering, into the midst of the court, with his hair dishevelled, and his face indented with the mark of his nails. The whole assembly uttered a long murmur of astonishment.

"Father!" said Benedetto, "I am asked for proofs, do you wish me to give them?"

"No, no, it is useless!" stammered M. de Villefort, in a hoarse voice; "no, it is useless!"

"How useless?" cried the president, "what do you mean?"

"I mean that I feel it impossible to struggle against this deadly weight which crushes me. Gentlemen, I know I am in the hands of an avenging God! We need no proofs; everything relating to this young man is true." A dull, gloomy silence, like that which precedes some awful phenomenon of nature, pervaded the assembly, who shuddered in dismay. "What! M. de Villefort," cried the president, "do you yield to a hallucination? What! are you no longer in possession of your senses? This strange, unexpected, terrible accusation has disordered your reason. Come, recover."

The public prosecutor dropped his head: his teeth chattered like a man under a violent attack of fever, and yet he was deadly pale.

"I am in possession of all my senses, sir," he said; "my body alone suffers, as you may suppose. I acknowledge myself guilty of all the young man has brought against me, and from this hour hold myself under the authority of my successor."

And as he spoke these words with a hoarse, choking voice, he staggered toward the door, mechanically opened by a door-keeper. The whole assembly were dumb with astonishment at the revelation and confession which had produced a catastrophe so different from that which had been expected during the last fortnight.

"The sitting is adjourned, gentlemen," said the president; "fresh inquiries will be made, and the case will be tried next session by another magistrate." As for Andrea, calm and more interesting than ever, he left the hall, escorted by gendarmes, who involuntarily paid him some attention. "Well, what do you think of this, my fine fellow?" asked Debray of the usher, slipping a louis into his hand. "They will find extenuating circumstances," he replied.

CHAPTER LXVI.

EXPIATION.

NOTWITHSTANDING the density of the crowd, M. de Villefort saw it open before him. Thus Villefort passed through the mass of spectators and officers of the Palais, and withdrew. Having staggered as far as his carriage, he awakened his sleeping coachman by opening the door himself, threw himself on the cushions, and the carriage drove on. One thought filled his mind; he saw the workings of a Divine hand in all that had happened. The carriage rolled rapidly. Villefort, while turning restlessly on the cushions, felt something press against him. He put out his hand to remove the object; it was a fan which Mdme. de Villefort had left in the carriage; this fan awakened a recollection which darted through his mind like lightning. He thought of his wife.

"Oh!" he exclaimed, as though a red-hot iron were piercing his heart. During the last hour his own crime had alone been presented to his mind; now another object, not less terrible, suddenly presented itself.

His wife!

Before he left home to fulfil a public duty, he had carried out what he esteemed his family charge: he called his wife to him and revealed that the authoress of the poisonings in his household was no longer unknown to him. He uttered in his coldest tone his sentence of death upon her and asked if she had not reserved some of the poison to save him from having her despatched on the scaffold?

He had left her crushed with the discovery. Recovered from the shock, might she not even now be preparing to carry out this doom upon herself?

Villefort again groaned with anguish and despair. "Ah!" he exclaimed, "that woman became criminal only from associating with me! I carried the infection of crime with me, and she has caught it as she would the typhus-fever, the cholera, the plague! And yet I have punished her—*I* have dared to tell her—*I* have—'Repent and die!' But no! she must not die, she shall live and follow me. We will flee from Paris, and go far as the earth reaches. I told her of the scaffold; oh, heavens! I forgot that it awaits me also! How could I pronounce that word? Yes, we will fly: I will confess all to her,—I will tell her daily that I also have committed a crime!—Oh! what an alliance with the tiger and the serpent! worthy wife of such as I am! She *must* live that my infamy may diminish hers." And Villefort dashed open the window in front of the carriage. "Faster! faster!" he cried, in a tone which electrified the coachman. The horses, impelled by fear, flew toward the house.

The carriage stopped at the door of the hotel. Villefort leaped out of the carriage, and saw his servants, surprised at his early return: he could read no other expression on their features. Neither of them spoke to him; they merely stood aside to let him pass by, as usual, nothing more. As he passed by M. Noirtier's room, he perceived, through the half-open door, two figures; but he experienced no curiosity to know who was visiting his father; anxiety carried him on further.

"Come," he said, as he ascended the stairs leading to his wife's room, "nothing is changed here." He rushed toward the door; it was bolted; he stopped, shuddering. "Heloïse!" he cried. He fancied he heard the sound of a piece of furniture being removed. "Heloïse!" he repeated.

"Who is there?" answered the voice of her he sought. He thought that voice more feeble than usual.

"Open the door!" cried Villefort; "open, it is I." But notwithstanding this request, notwithstanding the tone of anguish in which it was uttered, the door remained closed. Villefort burst it open with a violent blow. At the entrance of the room which led to her boudoir, Mdme.

de Villefort was standing erect, pale, her features contracted, and her eyes glaring horribly. "Heloïse! Heloïse!" he said, "what is the matter? Speak!" The young woman extended her stiff white hand toward him. "It is done, sir!" she said, with a rattling which seemed to tear her throat. "What more do you want?" and she fell on the floor. Villefort ran to her and seized her hand, which convulsively clasped a crystal bottle with a golden stopper. Mdme. de Villefort was dead. Villefort, maddened with horror, stepped back to the threshold of the door, fixing his eyes on the corpse: "My son!" he exclaimed suddenly, "where is my son?—Edward, Edward!" The corpse was stretched across the doorway leading to the room in which Edward must be; those glaring eyes seemed to watch over the threshold, and the lips expressed a terrible and mysterious irony. Through the open door a portion of the boudoir was visible, containing an upright piano, and a blue satin couch. Villefort stepped forward two or three paces, and beheld his child lying —no doubt asleep on the sofa. The unhappy man uttered an exclamation of joy; a ray of light seemed to penetrate the abyss of despair and darkness. He had only to step over the corpse, enter the boudoir, take the child in his arms, and flee, far away.

He took the child in his arms, pressed him, shook him, called him, but the child replied not. He was dead. A folded paper fell from Edward's breast. Villefort, thunderstruck, fell upon his knees; the child dropped from his arms, and rolled on the floor by the side of its mother. He picked up the paper, and, recognizing his wife's writing, ran his eyes rapidly over its contents: they were as follows:

"You know that I was a good mother, since it was for my son's sake I became criminal. A good mother cannot depart without her son."

Villefort could not believe his eyes,—he could not believe his reason; he dragged himself toward the child's corpse, and examined it as a lioness contemplates its dead cub. Then a piercing cry escaped from his breast, and he cried, "Still the hand of God." The two victims alarmed him; he could not bear the solitude only shared by two corpses. He descended the little stairs with which we are acquainted, and entered Noirtier's room. The old man appeared to be listening attentively and as affectionately as his infirmities would allow to the Abbé Busoni, who looked cold and calm, as usual. Villefort, perceiving the abbé, passed his hand across his brow. He recollected the call he had made upon him after the dinner at Auteuil, and then the visit the abbé had himself paid to his house on the day of Valentine's death. "You here, sir!" he exclaimed; "do you, then, never appear but to act as an escort to death?"

Busoni turned round, and perceiving the excitement depicted on the magistrate's face, the savage lustre of his eyes, he understood that the scene at the assizes had been accomplished; but beyond this he was ignorant. "I came to pray over the body of your daughter."

"And, now, why are you here?"

"I come to tell you that you have sufficiently repaid your debt, and that from this moment I will pray to God to forgive you as I do."

"Good heavens!" exclaimed Villefort, stepping back fearfully, "surely that is not the voice of the Abbé Busoni!"

"No!" the abbé threw off his false tonsure, shook his head, and his hair, no longer confined, fell in black masses around his manly face.

"It is the face of the Count of Monte-Cristo!" exclaimed the lawyer, with a haggard expression.

"You are not exactly right, sir; you must go farther back."

"That. voice! that voice!—where did I first hear it?"

"You heard it for the first time at Marseilles, twenty-three years ago, the day of your marriage with Mdlle. de Saint-Méran. Refer to your papers."

"You are not Busoni?—you are not Monte-Cristo? Oh, heavens! you are, then, some concealed, implacable, and mortal enemy! I must have wronged you in some way at Marseilles. Oh! woe to me! what have I done to you? Tell me, then! Speak!"

"You condemned me to a horrible, tedious death,—you killed my father—you deprived me of liberty, of love, and happiness."

"Who are you, then? Who are you?"

"I am the ghost of a wretch you buried in the dungeons of Castle If. The form of the Count of Monte-Cristo was given to that spectre when he at length issued from his tomb, enriched with gold and diamonds, to reconduct him to you!"

"Ah! I recognize you!" exclaimed the Attorney General, "you are——"

"I am Edmond Dantès?"

"You are Edmond Dantès!" cried Villefort, seizing the count by the wrist, "then come here!" And he dragged Monte-Cristo up the stairs; who, ignorant of what had happened, followed him in astonishment, presaging some new catastrophe. "Hold, Edmond Dantès!" he said, pointing to the bodies of his wife and child. "See! are you well avenged?" Monte-Cristo became pale at this horrible sight; he felt he had passed beyond the bounds of vengeance, and that he could no longer say, "God is for and with me." "My child!" cried Villefort, then, uttering a burst of laughter, he rushed down the stairs.

The servant, instead of answering, pointed to the garden. Monte-Cristo ran after, and, in the garden, beheld Villefort, encircled by his servants, with a spade in his hand, and digging the earth with fury. "It is not here!" he cried. "Oh, I *will* find it!" he cried; "you may pretend he is not here, but I *will* find him, though I dig for ever!"

Monte-Cristo drew back in horror. "Oh!" he said, "he is mad!" And as though he feared that the walls of the accursed house would crumble around him, he rushed into the street, for the first time doubting whether he had the right to do as he had done. "Oh! enough of this,—enough of this," he cried, "let me save the last." On entering his house, he met Morrel, who wandered about like a ghost. "Prepare yourself Maximilian," he said, with a smile; "we leave Paris to-morrow."

"Have you nothing more to do here?" asked Morrel.

"No," replied Monte-Cristo; "God grant I may not have done too much already."

The next day they indeed left, accompanied alone by Baptistin, Haydée had taken away Ali, and Bertuccio remained with Noirtier.

CHAPTER LXVII.

MARSEILLES AGAIN.

THE journey of Maximilian and the count was performed with that marvellous rapidity which the unlimited power of the count ever commanded, towns fled from them like shadows on their path, and trees shaken by the first winds of autumn seemed like giants madly rushing on to meet them, and retreating as rapidly when once reached. Ere long Marseilles presented herself to view. Powerful memories were stirred within them by the sight. They stopped on the Cannebière. A vessel was setting sail for Algiers, on board of which the bustle usually attending departure prevailed. The passengers and their relations crowded on the deck, friends taking a tender, but sorrowful leave of each other, some weeping, others noisy in their grief, formed a spectacle, exciting even to those who witnessed similar ones daily, but which had not the power to disturb the current of thought that had taken possession of the mind of Maximilian from the moment he had set foot on the broad pavement of the quay.

"Here," said he, leaning heavily on the arm of Monte-Cristo,— "here is the spot where my father stopped, when the Pharaoh entered the port; it was here that the good old man whom you saved from death and dishonor, threw himself into my arms. I yet feel his warm tears on my face, and his were not the only tears shed, for many who witnessed our meeting wept also." Monte-Cristo gently smiled and said,— "I was there;" at the same time pointing to the corner of a street. As he spoke, and in the very direction he indicated, a groan, expressive of bitter grief, was heard; and a woman was seen waving her hand to a passenger on board the vessel about to sail. Monte-Cristo looked at her with an emotion that must have been remarked by Morrel had not his eyes been fixed on the vessel.

"Oh! heavens!" exclaimed Morrel, "I do not deceive myself—that young man who is waving his hat, that youth in the uniform of a lieutenant, is Albert de Morcerf!"

"Yes," said Monte-Cristo, "I recognized him."——"How so?—you were looking the other way." The count smiled, as he was in the habit of doing when he did not want to make any reply, and he again turned his looks toward the veiled female, who soon disappeared at the corner of the street. Turning to his friend,—"Dear Maximilian," said the count, "have you nothing to do in this land?"——"I have to weep over the grave of my father," replied Morrel, in a broken voice.

"Well, then, go,—wait for me there, and I will soon join you."

"You leave me, then?"——"Yes; I also have a pious visit to pay."

In the Meillan Alley house given to his old love, Monte-Cristo found her seated under an arbor of Virginian creeper, with her head bowed, weeping bitterly. She had raised her veil, and with her face hidden by her hands, was giving free scope to those sighs and tears which had been so long restrained by the presence of her son. Monte-Cristo advanced a few paces, which were heard on the gravel. Mercédès raised her head, and uttered a cry of terror on beholding a man before her.

"Madame," said the count, "it is no longer in my power to restore you to happiness, but I offer you consolation; will you deign to accept it as coming from a friend?"——"I am, indeed, most wretched," replied Mercédès. "Alone in the world, I had but my son, and he has left me!"

"He possesses a noble heart, madame," replied the count, "and he has acted rightly. Leave him to build up the future for you, and I venture to say you will confide it to safe hands."

"Oh!" replied the wretched woman, mournfully shaking her head, "the prosperity of which you speak, and which, from the bottom of my heart, I pray God in His mercy to grant him, I can never enjoy. The bitter cup of adversity has been drained by me to the very dregs, and I feel that the grave is not far distant. You have acted kindly, Count, in bringing me back to the place where I have enjoyed so much bliss. You have spared me, yet of all those who have fallen under your vengeance I was the most guilty. They were influenced by hatred, by avarice, and by self-love; but I was base, and, for want of courage, acted against my judgment. Nay, do not press my hand, Edmond; you are thinking of some kind expression, I am sure, to console me, but do not bestow it on me, for I am no longer worthy of kindness. See (and she exposed her face completely to view)—see, misfortune has silvered my hair, my eyes have shed so many tears that they are encircled by a rim of purple, and my brow is wrinkled. You, Edmond, on the contrary, you are still young, handsome, dignified; it is because you have never doubted the mercy of God, and He has supported and strengthened you in all your trials."

As Mercédès spoke, the tears chased each other down her wan cheeks; the unhappy woman's heart was breaking, as memory recalled the changeful events of her life. Monte-Cristo, however, took her hand and imprinted a kiss on it; but she herself felt that it was with no greater warmth than he would have respectfully bestowed one on the hand of some marble statue of a saint.

"No, Mercédès," said Monte-Cristo, "no; you judge yourself with too much severity. You are a noble-minded woman, and it was your grief that disarmed me. Still, I was but an agent, led on by an invisible and offended Deity, who chose not to withhold the fatal blow that I was destined to hurl. I take that God to witness, at whose feet I have prostrated myself daily for the last ten years, that I would have sacrificed my life to you, and, with my life, the projects that were indissolubly linked with it. But—and I say it with some pride, Mercédès—God required me, and I lived. Examine the past and the present, and endeavor to dive into futurity, and then say whether I am not a Divine instrument. The most dreadful misfortunes, the most frightful sufferings, the abandonment of all those who loved me, the persecution of those who did not know me, formed the trials of my youth; when suddenly, from captivity, solitude, misery, I was restored to light and liberty, and became the possessor of a fortune so brilliant, so unbounded, so unheard-of, that I must have been blind not to be conscious that God had endowed me with it to work out His own great designs. From that time I viewed this fortune as confided to me for a particular purpose. Not a thought was given to a life which you once, Mercédès, had the power to render blissful; not one hour of peaceful calm was mine, but I felt myself driven on like an exterminating angel. From good-natured, confiding, and forgiving, I became revengeful, cunning, and wicked, or rather, immovable as fate. Then I launched out into the path that was opened to me: I overcame every obstacle, and reached the goal; but woe to those who met me in my career!"

"Enough!" said Mercédès, "enough, Edmond!"——"Before I leave you, Mercédès, have you no request to make?" said the count.

"I desire but one thing in this world, Edmond—the happiness of my son."

"But have you no request to make for yourself, Mercédès?"

"For myself I want nothing. I live, as it were, between two graves. The one that of Edmond Dantès, lost to me long, long since. He had my love! That word ill becomes my faded lip now, but it is a memory dear to my heart, and one that I would not lose for all that the world contains. The other grave is that of the man who met his death from the hand of Edmond Dantès. I approve of the deed, but I must pray for the dead."

"Yes, your son shall be happy, Mercedes," repeated the count.

"Then I shall enjoy as much happiness as this world can possibly confer."

"But what are your intentions?"

"To say that I shall live here, like the Mercédès of other times, gaining my bread by labor, would not be true, nor would you believe me. I have no longer the strength to do anything but to spend my days in prayer. However, I shall have no occasion to work, for the little sum of money buried by you, and which I found in the place you mentioned, will be sufficient to maintain me. Rumor will probably be busy respecting me, my occupations, my manner of living—that will signify but little." Monte-Cristo dropped his head and shrank from the vehemence of her grief.

"Will you not even say you would see me again?" he asked.

"Nay, we shall meet again!" said she, pointing solemnly to heaven, "I say this that you may know that I hope."

He departed, sad because he expected never to see her more.

Burying his head in his cloak, he murmured the name of a woman. The victory was complete; he had overcome his doubts. The name he pronounced, in a voice of tenderness, amounting almost to love, was Haydée's.

On landing, the count turned towards the cemetery, where he felt sure of finding Morrel. He, too, ten years ago, had piously sought out a tomb, and sought it vainly. He, who returned to France with millions, had been unable to find the grave of his father, who had perished from hunger. Morrel had, indeed, placed a cross over the spot, but it had fallen down, and the grave-digger had burnt it, as he did all the old wood in the churchyard. The worthy merchant had been more fortunate. Dying in the arms of his children, he had been by them laid by the side of his wife, who had preceded him in eternity by two years. Two large slabs of marble, on which were inscribed their names, were placed on either side of a little enclosure, railed in, and shaded by four cypress-trees. Morrel was leaning against one of these, mechanically fixing his eyes on the graves. His grief was so profound, he was nearly unconscious.

"Maximilian," said the count, "you should not look on the graves, but there;" and he pointed upwards.

"The dead are everywhere," said Morrel; "did you not yourself tell me so as we left Paris? have pity upon me. I am so unhappy."

"I have known a man much more unfortunate than you, Morrel."

"Impossible!"

"Alas!" said Monte-Cristo, "it is the infirmity of our nature always to believe ourselves much more unhappy than those who groan by our sides!"

"What can be more wretched than the man who has lost all he loved and desired in the world?"

"Listen, Morrel, and pay attention to what I am about to tell you, I knew a man who like you had fixed all his hopes of happiness upon a woman. He was young, he had an old father whom he loved, a betrothed bride whom he adored. He was about to marry her, when one of those caprices of fate,—which would almost make us doubt the goodness of Providence, if that Providence did not afterwards reveal itself by proving that all is but a means of conducting to an end,—one of those caprices deprived him of his mistress, of the future of which he had dreamed (for in his blindness he forgot he could only read the present), and plunged him into a dungeon."

"Ah!" said Morrel, "one quits a dungeon in a week, a month, or a year."

"He remained there fourteen years, Morrel," said the count, placing his hand on the young man's shoulder. Maximilian shuddered.

"During that time he had many moments of despair. He also, Morrel, like you, considered himself the unhappiest of men."

"Well?" asked Morrel.——"Well! at the height of his despair God assisted him through human means. At first, perhaps, he did not recognize the infinite mercy of the Lord, but at last he took patience and waited. One day he miraculously left the prison, transformed, rich, powerful. His first cry was for his father; but that father was dead."

"My father, too, is dead," said Morrel.

"Yes; but your father died in your arms, happy, respected, rich, and full of years; his father died poor, despairing, almost doubtful of Providence; and when his son sought his grave ten years afterwards, his tomb had disappeared, and no one could say, 'There sleeps the father you so well loved.'"

"Oh!" exclaimed Morrel.

He was, therefore, a more unhappy son than you, Morrel, for he could not even find his father's grave!"

"But then he had the woman he loved still remaining?"

"You are deceived, Morrel, that woman——"

"She was dead?"

"Worse than that: she was faithless, and had married one of the persecutors of her betrothed. You see, then, Morrel, that he was a more unhappy lover than you."

"And has he found consolation?"

"He has found calmness, at least."

"And does he ever expect to be happy?"

"He hopes so, Maximilian." The young man's head fell on his breast.

"You have my promise," he said after a minute's pause, extending his hand to Monte-Cristo. "Only remember——"

"On the 5th of October, Morrel, I shall expect you at the island of Monte-Cristo. On the 4th a yacht will wait for you in the port of Bastia, called the *Eurus*. You will give your name to the captain, who will bring you to me. It is understood—is it not?"

"But, Count, do you remember that the 5th of October——"

"Child!" replied the count, "not to know the value of a man's word! I have told you twenty times that if you wish to die on that day, I will assist you. Morrel, farewell!"——"Do you leave me?"

Morrel accompanied the count to the harbor. The white steam was ascending like a plume of feathers from the black chimney. The steamer soon disappeared, and in an hour afterward, was scarcely distinguishable in the horizon amid the fog.

CHAPTER LXVIII.

PEPPINO.

AT the same time that the steamer disappeared behind Cape Morgiou, a man, traveling post on the road from Florence to Rome, had just passed the little town of Aquapendente. He was traveling fast enough to make a great deal of ground without becoming altogether suspicious. This man, dressed in an overcoat, a little the worse for the journey, but which exhibited the riband of the Légion d'Honneur still fresh and brilliant, a decoration which also ornamented the under coat, might be recognized, not only by these signs, but also from the accent with which he spoke to the postilion, to be a Frenchman.

The carriage entered by the Porto del Popolo, turned to the left, and stopped at the Hotel d'Espagne. Pastrini, our old acquaintance, received the traveler at the door, hat in hand. The traveler alighted, ordered a good dinner, and inquired the address of the house of Thomson and French, which was immediately given to him, as it was one of the most celebrated in Rome.

The Frenchman came back to the hotel radiant, and went to sleep, with his wallet under his pillow.

The next morning Danglars, for it was the banker, awoke late, though he went to bed so early; he had not slept well for five or six nights, even if he had slept at all. He breakfasted heartily; and caring little, as he said, for the beauties of the Eternal City, ordered post-horses at noon. But Danglars had not reckoned upon the formalities of the police and the idleness of the posting-master. The horses only arrived at two o'clock, and the cicerone did not bring the passport till three.

"Which road?" asked the postilion in Italian. "The Ancona road," replied the baron. Pastrini interpreted the question and answer, and the horses galloped off. Danglars intended traveling to Venice, where he would receive one part of his fortune, and then proceeding to Vienna, where he would find the rest, he meant to take up his residence in the latter town, which he had been told was a city of pleasure.

He had scarcely advanced three leagues out of Rome when daylight began to disappear. Danglars had not intended starting so late, or he would have remained; he put his head out and asked the postilion how long it would be before they reached the next town. *"Non capisco,"* was the reply. Danglars bent his head, which he meant to imply, "Very well." The carriage again moved on. "I will stop at the first posting-house," said Danglars to himself.

He still felt the same self-satisfaction which he had experienced the previous evening, and which had procured him so good a night's rest. He was luxuriously stretched in a good English coach, with double springs; he was drawn by four good horses, at full gallop; he knew the relay to be at a distance of seven leagues. What subject of meditation could present itself to the banker, so fortunately become bankrupt?

Danglars thought for ten minutes upon his wife in Paris; another ten minutes upon his daughter traveling about with Mdlle. d'Armilly; the same period was given to his creditors, and the manner in which he intended spending their money; and then, having no subject left for contemplation, he shut his eyes, and fell asleep.

The carriage stopped. Danglars fancied they had reached the long-desired point; he opened his eyes, looked through the window, expecting to find himself in the midst of some town, or at least village; but he saw nothing but a kind of ruin, where three or four men went and came like shadows. Danglars waited for a moment, expecting the postilion to come and demand payment, having finished his stage. He intended taking advantage of the opportunity to make fresh inquiries of the new conductor; but the horses were unharnessed, and others put in their places, without any one claiming money from the traveler. Danglars, astonished, opened the door; but a strong hand pushed him back, and the carriage rolled on. The baron was completely roused. "Eh!" he said to the postilion, "eh, *mio caro?*"

This was another little piece of Italian the baron had learnt from hearing his daughter sing Italian duets with Cavalcanti. But *mio caro* replied not. Danglars then opened the window.

"Come, my friend," he said, thrusting his hand through the opening, "where are we going?"——"*Dentro la testa!*" answered a solemn and imperious voice, accompanied by a menacing gesture. Danglars thought *dentro la testa* meant "Put in your head!" Danglars observed a man in a cloak galloping at the right hand of the carriage.

"Some patrol!" he exclaimed. "Can I have been signalled by the French telegraphs to the pontifical authorities?" He resolved to end his anxiety. "Where are you leading me?" he asked. *"Dentro la testa,"* replied the same voice, with the same menacing accent.

Danglars turned to the left; another man on horseback was galloping on that side. "Decidedly!" said Danglars, with the perspiration on his forehead, "I am arrested." And he threw himself back not this time to sleep, but to think. Directly afterwards the moon rose. He then saw a dark mass, against which it seemed the carriage must dash; but it turned round, leaving behind it the mass, which was no other than one of the ramparts encircling Rome.

"Oh! oh!" cried Danglars, "we are not returning to Rome; then it is not justice which is pursuing me! Gracious heavens! another idea presents itself; what if they should be——"

His hair stood on end. He remembered those interesting stories, so little believed in Paris, respecting Roman bandits; he remembered the adventures that Morcerf had related when it was intended he should marry Mdlle. Eugénie. "They are robbers, perhaps!" he muttered. Just then the carriage rolled on something harder than the gravelled road. Danglars hazarded a look on both sides of the road, and perceived monuments of a singular form; and his mind now recalled all the details Morcerf had related and comparing them with his own situation, he felt sure he must be on the Appian Way. On the left, in a sort of valley, he perceived a circular excavation. It was Caracalla's circle. On a word from the man who rode at the side of the carriage, it stopped. At the same time the door was opened. *"Scendi!"* exclaimed a commanding voice. Danglars instantly descended; though he did not yet speak Italian, he understood it very well. More dead than alive, he looked around him. Four men surrounded him, besides the postilion.

Pushing Danglars whenever he happened to stop, they arrived by a gentle declivity at the centre of a cross-road of sinister appearance. Indeed; the walls, hollowed out in sepulchres, placed one above the other, seemed, in contrast with the white stones, to open their large dark eyes, like those which we see on the faces of the dead. A sentinel slapped his rifle-butt with his left hand. "Who goes there?" he cried.

"Peppino! but where is the captain?"

"There!" said the sentinel, pointing over his shoulder to a sort of large hall, hollowed out of the rock, the lights from which shone into the passage through the large arched openings. "Fine spoil! captain, fine spoil!" said Peppino, in Italian, and taking Danglars by the collar of his coat, he dragged him to an opening resembling a door, through which they entered the hall, of which the captain appeared to have made his dwelling-place.

"Is this man?" asked the captain, who was attentively reading Plutarch's "Life of Alexander."

"Himself, captain—himself."

"Very well, show him to me." At this rather impertinent order, Peppino raised his torch to Danglars' face, who hastily withdrew, that he might not have his eyelashes burnt. His agitated features presented the appearance of pale and hideous terror. "The man is tired," said the captain, "conduct him to his bed."

"Oh!" murmured Danglars, "that bed is probably one of the coffins hollowed in the wall, and the sleep I shall enjoy will be death from one of the poniards I see glistening in the shade."

From the depths of the hall were now seen to rise from their beds of dried leaves or cowhide the companions of the man who had been found by Albert de Morcerf reading "Cæsar's Commentaries," and by Danglars studying the "Life of Alexander." The banker uttered a groan and followed his guide; he neither supplicated nor exclaimed. He no longer possessed strength, will power, or feeling; he followed where they led him. At length, he found himself at the foot of a staircase, and he mechanically lifted his foot five or six times. Then a low door was opened before him, and bending his head to avoid striking his forehead, he entered a small room cut out of the rock. The cell was clean, though naked; and dry, though situated at a distance under the earth. Danglars, on beholding it, brightened, fancying it a type of safety. "Oh, God be praised!" he said; "it is a rebel bed!"

"*Ecco!*" said the guide, and pushing Danglars into the cell, he closed the door upon him.

A bolt grated; Danglars was a prisoner; besides, had there been no bolt, it would have been impossible for him to pass through the midst of the garrison who held the Catacombs of St. Sebastian, encamped round a master whom our readers must have recognized as the famous Luigi Vampa. Danglars, too, had recognized the bandit, whose existence he would not believe when Albert de Morcerf mentioned him in Paris; and not only did he recognize him, but also the cell in which Albert had been confined, and which was probably kept for the accommodation of strangers. These recollections were dwelt upon with some pleasure by Danglars, and restored him to some degree of tranquillity. Since the bandits had not despatched him at once, he felt that they would not kill him at all. They had arrested him for the purpose of robbery, and as he had only a few louis about him, he doubted not he would be ransomed. He remembered that Morcerf had been taxed at 4,000 crowns; and as he considered himself of much greater importance than Morcerf, he fixed his own price at 8,000 crowns: 8,000 crowns amounted to 48,000 francs, he would then have about 5,050,000 francs. With this sum he could manage to keep out of difficulties. Therefore, tolerably secure in being able to extricate himself from his position, provided he were not rated at the unreasonable sum of 5,050,000 francs, he stretched himself on his bed, and, after turning round two or three times, fell asleep with the tranquillity of the hero whose life Luigi Vampa was studying.

CHAPTER LXIX.

LUIGI VAMPA'S BILL OF FARE.

WE awake from every sleep except the one dreaded by Danglars. He awoke. In such a situation a single moment suffices to change the strongest doubt into certainty. "Yes, yes," he murmured, "I am in the hands of the brigands of whom Albert de Morcerf spoke." His first idea was to breathe, that he might know whether he was wounded. He borrowed this from "Don Quixote," the only book he had ever read, but which he still slightly remembered.

"No," he cried, "they have not wounded, but perhaps they have robbed me!" and he thrust his hands into his pockets. They were untouched; the hundred louis he had reserved for his journey from Rome to Venice were in his trousers pocket, and in that of his great-coat he found the little note-case containing his letter of credit for 5,050,000 francs. "Singular bandits!" he exclaimed; "they have left me my purse and pocket-book. As I was saying last night, they intend me to be ransomed. Hollo! here is my watch! Let me see what time it is." Danglars' repeater, which he had carefully wound up on the previous night, struck half-past five. Without this, Danglars would have been quite ignorant of the time, for daylight did not reach his cell. Should he demand an explanation from the bandits, or should he wait patiently for them to propose it. The last alternative seemed the most prudent, so he waited until twelve o'clock. During all this time a sentinel, relieved at eight o'clock, had been watching his door. Danglars suddenly felt a strong inclination to see the person who kept watch over him. He had remarked that a few rays, not of daylight but from a lamp, penetrated through the ill-joined planks of the door; he approached it just as the brigand was refreshing himself with a mouthful of brandy, which, owing to the leathern bottle containing it, sent forth an odor which was extremely unpleasant to Danglars. "Faugh!" he exclaimed, retreating to the extreme corner of his cell.

At twelve, this man was replaced by another, and Danglars, wishing to catch sight of his new guardian, approached the door again. He was an athletic, gigantic bandit, with large eyes, thick lips, and a flat nose; his red hair fell in disheveled masses like snakes around his shoulders. "Ah! ah!" cried Danglars, "this fellow is more like an ogre than anything else; however, I am rather too old and tough to be very good eating!" We see that Danglars was quite collected enough to jest; at the same time, as though to disprove the ogreish propensities, the man took some black bread, cheese, and onions from his wallet, which he began devouring voraciously. "May I be hanged," said Danglars, glancing at the bandit's dinner through the crevices of the door,—"may I be hanged if I can understand how people can eat such filth!" and he withdrew to seat himself upon his goatskin, which recalled to him the smell of the brandy.

But the secrets of nature are incomprehensible, and there are certain invitations contained in even the coarsest food which appeal very irresistibly to a fasting stomach. Danglars felt his own not to be very well supplied just then; and gradually the man appeared less ugly, the bread less black, and the cheese more fresh, while those dreadful vulgar onions recalled to his mind sauces and side-dishes, which his cook prepared in a very superior manner whenever he said, "M. Deniseau, let me have a nice little fricassée to-day." He rose and knocked at the door; the bandit raised his head. Danglars knew that he was heard, so he redoubled his blows. *"Che cosa?"* asked the bandit. "Come, come," said Danglars, tapping his fingers against the door, "I think it is quite time to think of giving me something to eat!" But whether he did not understand him, or whether he had received no orders respecting the nourishment of Danglars, the giant, without answering, recommenced his dinner. Danglars felt his pride hurt, and not wishing to commit himself with the brute, threw himself down again on his goatskin and did not breathe another word.

Four hours passed by, the giant was replaced by another bandit. Danglars, who began to experience gnawings at the stomach, rose softly, again applied his eye to the crack of the door, and recognized the intelligent countenance of his guide. It was, indeed, Peppino who was preparing to mount guard as comfortably as possible by seating himself opposite to the door, and placing between his legs an earthern pan, containing chick-pease stewed with bacon. Near the pan he also placed a pretty little basket of grapes and a bottle of Orvieto. Peppino was decidedly an epicure. While witnessing these preparations Danglars' mouth watered. "Come," he said to himself, "let me try if he will be more tractable than the other!" and he tapped gently at the door. "Coming!" exclaimed Peppino, who, from frequenting the house of Pastrini, understood French perfectly.

Danglars immediately recognized him as the man who had called out in such a furious manner, "Put in your head!" But this was not the time for recrimination, so he assumed his most agreeable manner and said with a gracious smile,—"Excuse me, sir, but are they not going to give me any dinner?"

"Does your excellency happen to be hungry?"

"Happen to be hungry! that's excellent, when I have not eaten for twenty-four hours!" muttered Danglars. Then he added aloud, "Yes, sir, I am hungry—very hungry!"——"What would your excellency like?" and Peppino placed his pan on the ground, so that the steam rose directly under the nostrils of Danglars.—"Give your orders!"

"Have you kitchens here?"

"Kitchens?—of course! complete ones."

"And cooks?"

"Excellent!"

"Well! a fowl, fish, game, it signifies little, so that I eat."

"As your excellency pleases! You mentioned a fowl, I think?"

"Yes, a fowl." Peppino, turning round, shouted, "A fowl for his excellency!" His voice yet echoed in the archway when a young man, handsome, graceful, and half-naked, appeared, bearing a fowl in a silver dish on his head, without the assistance of his hands. "I could almost believe myself at a Paris restaurant!" murmured Danglars.

"Here, your excellency!" said Peppino, taking the fowl from the young bandit and placing it on the worm-eaten table, which, with a stool and the goatskin bed, formed the entire furniture of the cell. Danglars asked for a knife and fork. "Here, excellency," said Peppino, offering him a little blunt knife and a boxwood fork. Danglars took the knife in one hand and the fork in the other, and was about to cut up the fowl. "Pardon me, excellency," said Peppino, placing his hand on the banker's shoulder; "people pay here before they eat. They might not be satisfied, and——"

"Ah! ah!" thought Danglars, "this is no longer like Paris, without reckoning that I shall probably be fleeced! Never mind, I will carry it off well! I have always heard how cheap poultry is in Italy; I should think a fowl is worth about twelve sous at Rome.——There," he said, throwing a louis down. Peppino picked up the louis, and Danglars again prepared to carve the fowl. "Stay a moment, your excellency," said Peppino, rising; "you still owe me something."——"I said they would fleece me," thought Danglars; but resolving to resist the extortion, he said, "Come, how much do I owe you for this fowl?"

"Your excellency has given me a louis on account."

"A louis on account for a fowl!"——"Certainly; and your excellency now owes me 4,999 louis!" Danglars opened his enormous eyes on hearing this gigantic joke. "Come, come, this is very droll—very amusing—I allow; but, as I am very hungry, pray allow me to eat. Stay, here is another louis for you."——"Then, that will make only 4,998 louis," said Peppino, with the same indifference. "I shall get them all in time."

"Oh! as for that," said Danglars, angry in his perseverance in the jest, —"as for that you will never succeed. Go to the devil! You do not know with whom you have to deal!" Peppino made a sign, and the youth hastily removed the fowl. Danglars threw himself upon his goatskin, and Peppino, re-closing the door, again began eating his peas and bacon. Though Danglars could not see Peppino, the noise of his teeth allowed no doubt as to his occupation. He was certainly eating, and noisily too, like an ill-bred man. "Brute!" said Danglars. Peppino pretended not to hear him, and, without even turning his head, continued to eat slowly. Danglars' stomach felt so empty, it seemed as though it would be impossible ever to fill it again; still he had patience for another half-hour, which appeared to him like a century. He again rose and went to the door. "Come, sir, do not keep me starving here any longer, but tell me what they want." ——"Nay your excellency, it is you should tell us what you want. Give your orders, and we will execute them."

"Then open the door directly." Peppino obeyed. "I want something to eat! To eat—do you hear?"

"Are you hungry?"

"Come, you understand me."

"What would your excellency like to eat?"

"A piece of dry bread, since the fowls are beyond all price in this accursed place."——"Bread! very well. Hello, there! some bread!" he exclaimed. The youth brought a small loaf. "How much?" asked Danglars.

"Four thousand nine hundred and ninety-eight louis," said Peppino; "you have paid the two louis in advance."

"What! 100,000 francs for a loaf?"

"One hundred thousand francs!" repeated Peppino.

"But you only asked 100,000 francs for a fowl!"

"We have a fixed price for all our meats. It signifies nothing whether you eat much or little—whether you have ten dishes or one—it is always the same price."

"What! still keeping up this silly jest? My dear fellow, it is perfectly ridiculous—stupid! You had better tell me at once that you intend starving me to death."

"Oh dear, no, your excellency, unless you intend to commit suicide. Pay and eat."

"And what am I to pay with, brute?" said Danglars, enraged. "Do you suppose I carry 100,000 francs in my pocket?"

"Your excellency has 5,050,000 francs in your pocket; that will be fifty fowls at 100,000 francs a-piece, and half a fowl for the 50,000."

Danglars shuddered. The bandage fell from his eyes, and he understood the joke, which he did not think quite so dull as he had done just before. "Come," he said, "if I pay the 100,000 francs will you be satisfied and allow me to eat at my ease?"

"Certainly," said Peppino.

"But how can I pay them?"

"Oh, nothing easier: you have an account opened with Messrs. Thomson and French, Via dei Banchi, Rome; give me a bill for 4,998 louis on these gentlemen and our banker shall take it." Danglars thought it as well to comply with a good grace; so he took the pen, ink, and paper Peppino offered him, wrote the bill, and signed it. "Here," he said, "here is a bill at sight."

"And here is your fowl." Danglars sighed while he carved the fowl; it appeared very thin for the price it had cost. As for Peppino, he read the paper attentively, put it into his pocket, and continued munching his peas.

The next day Danglars was again hungry; certainly the air of that dungeon was very appetizing. The prisoner expected that he would be at no expense that day, for, like an economical man, he had concealed half of his fowl and a piece of the bread in the corner of his cell. But he had no sooner eaten than he felt thirsty; he had forgotten that. He struggled against his thirst till his tongue clave to the roof of his mouth; then, no longer able to resist, he called out. The sentinel opened the door; it was a new face. He thought it would be better to transact business with his old acquaintance, so he sent for Peppino. "Here I am, your excellency," said Peppino, with an eagerness which Danglars thought favorable to him. "What do you want?"

"Something to drink."

"Your excellency knows that wine is beyond all price outside Rome."

"Then give me water," cried Danglars, endeavoring to parry the blow.

"Oh, water is even more scarce than wine, your excellency; there has been a drought."

"Come," thought Danglars, "we are going to repeat the old story." And, while he smiled as he attempted to regard the affair as a joke, he felt his temples moist with perspiration.

"Come, my friend," said Danglars, seeing he made no impression on Peppino, "you will not refuse me a glass of wine?"

"I have already told you that we do not sell retail."

"Well, then, let me have a bottle of the least expensive."

"They are all the same price."

"And what is that?"

"Twenty-five thousand francs per bottle."

"Tell me," cried Danglars, in a voice of extreme bitterness—"tell me that you wish to despoil me of all; it will be sooner over than devouring me piecemeal."

"It is possible such may be the master's intention."

"The master!—who is he?"

"The person to whom you were conducted yesterday."

"Let me see him."——"Certainly." And the next morning Luigi Vampa appeared before Danglars.

"You sent for me?" he said to the prisoner.

"Are you, sir, the chief of the people who brought me here?"

"Yes, your excellency. What then?"

"How much do you require for my ransom?"——"Merely the 5,000,000 you have about you." Danglars felt a dreadful spasm dart through his heart. "But this is all I have left in the world," said he, "out of an immense fortune. If you deprive me of that, take away my life also."

"We are forbidden to shed your blood."

"And by whom are you forbidden?"

"By him we obey."

"You do, then, obey some one?"

"Yes, a chief."

"I thought you said you were the chief?"

"So I am of these men; but there is another over me."

"And did your superior tell you to treat me thus?"

"Yes."

"But my purse will be exhausted."

"Probably."

"Come," said Danglars, "will you take a million?"

"No."

"Two millions?—three?—four? Come, four? I will give them to you on condition that you let me go."

"Why do you offer me 4,000,000 for what is worth 5,000,000? This is a kind of usury, banker, I do not understand."

"Take all then—take all, I tell you, and kill me!"

"Come, come, calm yourself. You will heat your blood, and that would produce an appetite it would require a million a day to satisfy. Be more economical."

"But when I have no more money left to pay you?" asked the infuriated Danglars.

"Then you must suffer hunger."

"Suffer hunger?" said Danglars becoming pale.

"Most likely," replied Vampa coolly.

"But you say you do not wish to kill me?"

"No."

"And yet you will let me perish with hunger?"

"Ah, that is a different thing."

"Well, then, wretches!" cried Danglars, "I will defy your infamous calculations!—I would rather die at once! You may torture, torment, kill me, but you shall not have my signature again!"

"As your excellency pleases," said Vampa, as he left the cell. Danglars, raving, threw himself on the goatskin.

His resolution not to sign lasted two days, after which he offered a million for some food. They sent him a magnificent supper, and took his million.

From this time the prisoner resolved to suffer no longer, but to yield. At the end of twelve days, after having had a splendid dinner, he reckoned his accounts, and found he had only 50,000 francs left. Then a strange reaction took place: he who had just abandoned 5,000,000 endeavored to save the 50,000 francs he had left; and, sooner than give them up, he resolved to enter again upon his life of privation—he yielded to rays of hope resembling madness. He, who for so long a time had forgotten God, began to think that miracles were possible: that the accursed cave might be discovered by the officers of the Papal States, who would release him; that then he would have 50,000 remaining, which would be sufficient to save him from starvation; and, finally, he prayed that this sum might be preserved to him, and as he prayed he wept. Three days passed thus, during which his prayers were frequent, if not heartfelt. Sometimes he was delirious, and fancied he saw old Dantès stretched on a pallet; he, also was dying of hunger.

On the fourth, he was no longer a man, but a living corpse. He had picked up every crumb that had been left from his former meals, and was beginning to eat the matting which covered the floor of his cell. Then he entreated Peppino, as he would a guardian angel, to give him food; he offered him 1,000 francs for a mouthful of bread. But Peppino did not answer. On the fifth day he dragged himself to the door of the cell.

"Are you not a Christian?" he said, falling on his knees. "Do you wish to assassinate a man who, in the eyes of heaven, is a brother? Oh, my former friends, my former friends!" he murmured, and fell with his face to the ground. Then rising with a species of despair he exclaimed. "The chief! the chief!"

"Here I am," said Vampa, instantly appearing; "what do you want?"

"Take my last gold," muttered Danglars, holding out his pocketbook, "and let me live here; I ask no more for liberty—I only ask to live!"

"Then you suffer a great deal?"——"Oh, yes, yes, cruelly!"

"Still, there have been men who suffered more than you."

"I do not think so."

"Yes; those who have died of hunger."

Danglars thought of the old man whom, in his hours of delirium, he had seen groaning on his bed. He struck his forehead on the ground and groaned. "Yes," he said, "there have been some who have suffered more than I have, but then they must have been martyrs at least."

"Do you repent?" asked a deep, solemn voice, which caused Danglars' hair to stand on end. His feeble eyes endeavored to distinguish objects, and behind the bandit he saw a man in a cloak, half lost in the shadow of a stone column.

"Of what must I repent?" stammered Danglars.

"Of the evil you have done," said the voice.

"Oh, yes! oh, yes! I do indeed repent." And he struck his breast with his emaciated fist.

"Then I forgive you," said the man, dropping his cloak, and advancing to the light.

"The Count of Monte-Cristo!" said Danglars, more pale from terror than he had been just before from hunger and misery.

"You are mistaken—I am not the Count of Monte-Cristo!"

"Then who are you?"

"I am he whom you sold and dishonored—I am he whose betrothed you prostituted—he upon whom you trampled that you might raise yourself to fortune—he whose father you condemned to die of hunger—he whom you also condemned to starvation, and who yet forgives you, because he hopes to be forgiven—I am Edmond Dantès!" Danglars uttered a scream, and fell prostrate. "Rise," said the count, "your life is safe; the same good fortune has not happened to your accomplices—one is mad, the other dead. Keep the 50,000 francs you have left—I give them to you. The 5,000,000 you robbed from the hospitals has been restored to them by an unknown hand. And now eat and drink; I will entertain you tonight. Vampa, when this man is satisfied, let him be free." Danglars remained prostrate while the count withdrew; when he raised his head he saw nothing more than a kind of shadow disappearing in the passage, before which the bandits bowed. According to the count's directions, Danglars was waited on by Vampa, who brought him the best wine and fruits; then, having conducted him to the road, and pointed to his post-chaise, he left him leaning against a tree. He remained there all night, not knowing where he was. When daylight dawned, he saw that he was near a stream; he was thirsty, and dragged himself toward it. As he stooped down to drink, he perceived that his hair had become quite white.

CHAPTER LXX.

THE FIFTH OF OCTOBER.

IT was about six o'clock in the evening; an opal-colored light, through which an autumnal sun shed its golden rays, descended on the blue sea.

A light yacht, chaste and elegant in its form, was gliding amidst the first dews of night over the immense lake. Standing on the prow was a tall man, of a dark complexion, who saw with dilating eyes that they were approaching a dark mass of land in the shape of a cone, rising from the midst of the waves. "Is that Monte-Cristo?" asked the traveler, to whose orders the yacht was for the time submitted, in a melancholy voice.

"Yes, your excellency," said the captain, "we have reached it!"

Ten minutes afterwards, the sails were brailed, and they cast anchor about one hundred paces from the little harbor. The canoe was already in the sea, loaded with four rowers and the pilot.

After they landed, the young man looked round for some one to show him his road, for it was quite dark. Just as he turned, a hand rested on his shoulder and a voice, which made him shudder, exclaimed,— "Good evening, Maximilian! you are punctual, thank you!"

"Ah! is it you, Count?" said the young man, in an almost joyful accent, pressing Monte-Cristo's hand with both his own.

Morrel looked at the count with surprise. "Count," he said, "you are not the same here as in Paris." The count's brow became clouded. "You are right to recall me to myself, Maximilian," he said; "I was delighted to see you again, and forgot for the moment that all happiness is fleeting. You cannot take me for a commonplace man, a mere rattle, emitting a vague and senseless noise. When I ask you if you are consoled, I speak to you as a man for whom the human heart has no secrets. Have you still that devouring thirst, which can only be appeased in the grave?"

"Yes: I did wait;—yes; I did hope, Count, but, Count I shall sleep calmly, deliciously in the arms of death!" Morrel pronounced these words with an energy which made the count shudder. "My friend," continued Morrel, "you named the fifth of October as the term of the delay you asked,—to-day is the fifth of October," he took out his watch; "it is now nine o'clock,—I have yet three hours to live."

"Be it so?" said the count, "come."

Morrel mechanically followed the count, and they had entered the grotto before he perceived it. He felt a carpet under his feet, a door opened, perfumes surrounded him, and a brilliant light dazzled his eyes. Morrel hesitated to advance, he dreaded the enervating effect of all that he saw. Monte-Cristo drew him in gently. "Why should we not spend the last three hours remaining to us of life, like those ancient Romans, who, when condemned by Nero, their emperor and heir, sat down at a table covered with flowers, and gently glided into death, through the perfume of heliotropes and roses?"

"Now I understand," he said, "why you had me brought here to this desolate spot, in the midst of the ocean, to this subterranean palace; it was because you loved me, was it not, Count? It was because you loved me well enough to give me one of those sweet means of death of which we were speaking; a death without agony, a death which allows me to fade away while pronouncing Valentine's name and pressing your hand."

"Yes; you have guessed rightly, Morrel," said the count, "that is what I intended."

"It is well," said Monte-Cristo, whose countenance brightened at these words, "you wish it; you are inflexible; yes, as you said, you are indeed wretched, and a miracle alone can cure you; sit down, Morrel, and wait."

Morrel obeyed; the count rose, and unlocking a closet with a key suspended from his gold chain, took from it a silver casket. He placed the casket on the table; then opening it, took out a little golden box, the top of which flew open when touched by a secret spring. This box contained an unctuous substance partly solid, of which it was impossible to discover the color, owing to the reflection of the polished gold, sapphires, rubies, emeralds, which ornamented the box. It was a mixed mass of blue, red, and gold. The count took out a small quantity of this with a gilt spoon, and offered it to Morrel, fixing a long, steadfast glance upon him. It was then observable that the substance was greenish.

"This is what you asked for," he said, "and what I promised to give you."

"I thank you from the depths of my heart," said the young man, taking the spoon from the hands of Monte-Cristo. The count took another spoon, and again dipped it into the golden box.

"Stay!" said the young man. "You who love, and are beloved; you, who have faith and hope,—oh! do not follow my example; in your case it would be a crime. Adieu, my noble and generous friend, adieu; I will go and tell Valentine what you have done for me." And slowly, though without any hesitation, only waiting to press the count's hand fervently, he swallowed the mysterious substance offered by Monte-Cristo. Then they were both silent. An overpowering sadness took possession of the young man; his hands relaxed their hold; the objects in the room gradually lost their form and color; and his disturbed vision seemed to perceive doors and curtains open in the wall.

"Friend," he cried, "I feel that I am dying; thanks!" He made a last effort to extend his hand, but it fell powerless beside him. Then it appeared to him that Monte-Cristo smiled, not with the strange and fearful expression which had sometimes revealed to him the secrets of his heart, but with the benevolent kindness of a father for a son. Morrel, overpowered, turned round in the arm-chair; a delicious torpor was insinuated into every vein; a change of ideas presented itself to his brain, like a new design on the kaleidoscope; enervated, prostrate, and breathless, he became unconscious of outward objects, he seemed to be entering that vague delirium preceding death. He wished once again to press the count's hand; but his own was unmovable; he wished to articulate a last farewell, but his tongue lay motionless and heavy in his throat, like a stone at the mouth of a sepulchre.

The count had just opened a door. Immediately a brilliant light from the next room, or rather from the palace adjoining, shone upon the room in which he was gently gliding into his last sleep. Then he saw a woman of marvellous beauty appear on the threshold of the door separating the two rooms. Pale, and sweetly smiling, she looked like an angel of mercy conjuring the angel of vengeance. "Is it heaven that opens before me?" thought the dying man; "that angel resembles the one I have lost." Monte-Cristo pointed out Morrel to the young woman, who advanced toward him with clasped hands and a smile upon her lips.

"Valentine! Valentine!" he mentally ejaculated; but his lips uttered no sound; and, as though all his strength was centered in that eternal emotion, he sighed and closed his eyes. Valentine rushed toward him; his lips again moved.

"He is calling you," said the count; "he to whom you have confided your destiny—he from whom death would have separated you, calls you to him. Happily, I vanquished death. Henceforth, Valentine, you will never again be separated on earth; since he has rushed into death to find you. Without me, you would both have died. May God accept my atonement of these two existences!"

Valentine seized the count's hand, and, in her irresistible impulse of joy, carried it to her lips.

"Oh! thank me again!" said the count; "tell me till you are weary, that I have restored you to happiness; you do not know how much I require this assurance."

"Oh! yes, yes, I thank you with all my heart," said Valentine; "and if you doubt the sincerity of my gratitude, oh, then, ask Haydée! ask my beloved sister Haydée, who, ever since our departure from France, has caused me to wait patiently for this happy day, while talking to me of you."

"You then love Haydée?" asked Monte-Cristo, with an emotion he in vain endeavored to dissimulate. "Well, then! I have a favor to ask of you."

"Of me! Oh, am I not happy enough without that pleasure?"

"Yes; you have called Haydée your sister; let her become so indeed, Valentine; render her all the gratitude you fancy you owe me; protect her, for (the count's voice was thick with emotion) henceforth she will be alone in the world."

"Alone in the world!" repeated a voice behind the count, "and why?"

Monte-Cristo turned round; Haydée was standing pale, motionless, looking at the count with an expression of fearful amazement.

"Oh, heavens!" exclaimed Monte-Cristo, "can my suspicions be correct? Haydée would it please you not to leave me?"

"I am young," gently replied Haydée; "I love the life you have made so sweet to me, and should regret to die."

"You mean then that if I leave you, Haydée——"

"I should die; yes, my lord."

"Do you then love me?"

"Oh, Valentine! he asks if I love him. Valentine, tell him if you love Maximilian." The count felt his heart dilate and throb; he opened his arms, and Haydée, uttering a cry, sprang into them. "Oh, yes!" she cried, "I do love you! I love you as one loves a father, brother, husband! I love you as my life, for you are the best, the noblest of created beings!"

"Let it be then, as you wish, sweet angel; God has sustained me in my struggle with my enemies, and has given me this victory; He will not let me end my triumph with this penance; I wished to punish myself, but He has pardoned me! Love me then, Haydée! Who knows? perhaps your love will make me forget all I wish not to remember."

"What do you mean, my lord?"——"I mean that one word from you has enlightened me more than twenty years of slow experience; I have but you in the world, Haydée. Come, Haydée, come!" and throwing his arm around the girl's waist, he pressed the hand of Valentine, and disappeared.

An hour had nearly passed during which Valentine, breathless and motionless, watched steadfastly over Morrel. At length she felt his heart beat, a faint breath played upon his lips, a slight shudder announcing the return of life, passed through the young man's frame. At length, his eyes opened, but they were at first fixed and expressionless; then sight returned, and, with it, feeling and grief. "Oh!" he cried, in an accent of despair, "the count has deceived me; I am yet living;" and extending his hand toward the table he seized a knife.

"Dearest!" exclaimed Valentine, with her adorable smile, "awake, and look on me!" Morrel uttered a loud exclamation, and frantic, doubt-ful, dazzled as though by a celestial vision, he fell upon his knees.

* * * * * *

The next morning, at daybreak, Valentine and Morrel were walking arm-in-arm on the sea-shore, Valentine relating how Monte-Cristo had appeared in her room; how he had told her of everything; how he had revealed the crime; and, finally, how he had saved her life by allowing her to seem dead. They had found the door of the grotto opened, and went forth, the few remaining stars yet pressing through the morning light. Morrel soon perceived a man standing amidst the group of rocks, who was awaiting a sign from them to advance; he pointed him out to Valentine. "Ah! it is Jacopo," she said, "the captain of the yacht," and she beckoned him toward them.

"Do you wish to speak to us?" asked Morrel.

"I have a letter to give you from the count."

"From the count!" murmured the two young people.

"Yes; read it." Morrel opened the letter and read:

"MY DEAR MAXIMILIAN,

"There is a felucca for you at anchor. Jacopo will conduct you to Leghorn, where M. Noirtier awaits his granddaughter, whom he wishes to bless before you lead her to the altar. All that is in this cave, my friend, my house in the Champs Elysées, and my Château at Tréport, are the marriage gifts bestowed by Edmond Dantès upon the son of his old master, Morrel. Mdlle. de Villefort will share them with you; for I entreat her to give to the poor the immense fortune reverting to her from her father, now a madman, and her brother, who died last September with his mother. Tell the angel who will watch over your future destiny, Morrel, to pray sometimes for a man, who, like Satan, thought himself, for an instant, equal to God; but who now acknowl-edges, with Christian humility, that God alone possesses supreme power and infinite wisdom. Perhaps those prayers may soften the re-morse he feels in his heart. As for you, Morrel, this is the secret of my conduct toward you. There is neither happiness nor misery in the world; there is only the comparison of one state with another, nothing more. He who has felt the deepest grief is best able to experience su-preme happiness. We must have felt what it is to die, Morrel, that we may appreciate the enjoyments of life.

"Live, then, and be happy, beloved children of my heart! and never forget, that until the day when God will deign to reveal the future to man, all human wisdom is contained in these two words,—'*Wait and hope.*'

"Your friend,
"EDMOND DANTÈS, Count of Monte-Cristo."

During the perusal of this letter, which informed Valentine, for the first time, of the madness of her father and the death of her brother, she became pale, a heavy sigh escaped from her bosom, and tears, not the less painful because they were silent, ran down her cheeks; her happiness cost her very dear. Morrel looked round uneasy. "But," he said, "the count's generosity is too overwhelming; Valentine will be satisfied with my humble fortune. Where is the count, friend? Lead me to him." Jacopo pointed toward the horizon.

The eyes of both were fixed upon the spot indicated by the sailor, and on the blue line separating the sky from the Mediterranean Sea, they perceived a large white sail. "Gone!" said Morrel: "Gone!—Adieu, my friend!—adieu, my father!"

"Gone!" murmured Valentine: "Adieu, my friend!—adieu my sister!"

"Who can say whether we shall ever see them again?" said Morrel, with tearful eyes.

"My friend," replied Valentine, "has not the count just told us, that all human wisdom was contained in these two words.—*'Wait and hope?'*"

THE END